The Hoomar
Box Set 01

including the works of
C. C. Brower, S. H. Marpel,
J. R. Kruze, and R. L. Saunders.

THE HOOMAN SAGA LIBRARY 01

First edition. November 24, 2019.

Copyright © 2019 C. C. Brower et al..

ISBN: 978-1393281122

Written by C. C. Brower et al..

Table of Contents

To all our many devoted and loyal fans -

We write and publish these stories <u>only</u> for you.

(Be sure to get your bonuses at the end of the story...)

Preface

WHILE YOU DON'T FORESEE any one story or series growing large enough to need its own Box Set, any popular series – or a set of prolific co-authors – can create that need out of necessity.

The Hooman Saga started with the story of a single girl who somehow escaped her human slavery of a moon colony and returned to earth. Surviving that crash landing, she was then immediately surprised to find herself rescued by a sentient wolf talking to her inside her mind.

Together, they escaped the organized feral wild canine breeds that hunted them.

And then she had to undergo their psychic testing, which no human had ever survived before.

But all she wanted was to free her family in that moon colony. Only 248,000 miles away - with no working technology to lift anyone from this planet.

As these stories were written by C. C. Brower, other authors came forward to explore the earlier stories that had to explain how most of the major cities had lifted off this planet and left those few human remaining to a new Dark Age, with virulent diseases that eradicated most of the highly populated areas.

The few humans remaining were in isolated encampments and lived in fear of any other human contact.

And meanwhile, were eking out a living under conditions that hadn't been seen since the first settlers arrived in that wilderness.

How these cities developed their technology, and what their own conditions were – all these questions were asked by other authors. And they provided their inspired answers.

Then S. H. Marpel brought his own characters in as cross-overs from his "Ghost Hunters" series – along with J. R. Kruze addition of key elements that explained how Brower's story was a possible progression from our current reality. R. L. Saunders biting satire then filled in the cracks with his brand of humor.

Between these four, we now know how everything got started, how it went from here to there, and left us wondering what's next.

Of course, at this writing, there are rumors of Books Three, Four, and Five all in the works. But we'll have to leave those for the next Box Set, won't we?

Editor's Notes:

BOOK II, PART 1 WAS originally written as a novella in its own right. Those chapters do not have their own titles. Book I and Book II, Part 2 were both written as a series of short stories and then compiled into their own larger anthologies.

At the end of Book II, Part 2, there is a "Character List" which tells where the S. H. Marpel (and J. R. Kruze) characters had their origin stories. This short list then explains the crossovers for your own "extra-curricular studies". All so you can enjoy, and perhaps better understand, their motivations and decisions (as well as where they got their unusual abilities.)

Good Hunting!

• • • •

ROBERT C. WORSTELL
    Chief Editor, Living Sensical Press

The Hooman Saga - Book I

BY C. C. BROWER, J. R. Kruze, R. L. Saunders, S. H. Marpel

Book One Introduction

IT CAME TO ME ONE DAY that I and my co-authors had been writing the Hooman Saga Book One all along. In our short stories. And remarkably, they didn't overlap or contradict – too much.

So instead of working for months to piece together and write a new history, I would be better invested in editing these into shape so you could see what happened before Sue came back to Earth and met Tig and his pack in Book Two.

It's really all here.

You get the biting satire of R. L. Saunders and the common-sense insight of J. R. Kruze, the fascinating supernatural characters of S. H. Marpel - along with the fantasy and science fiction world I created. Between the four of us, we tell a not-too-unlikely possible future based on our current news and trends.

That's if you sincerely believe in what passes for "news" these days.

If not, then this is just another anthology of what used to be called "speculative fiction."

Regardless, it was all a lot of fun to write and collaborate on.

I've included some notes at the start of these stories to help tie the history of these together, to bridge any gaps.

And none of us are prohibited from coming up with additional stories to fill in those gaps. There are a lot of people and characters in these pages that I, for one, would not mind hearing from again.

I hope we've written these well enough so you do, too.

(You can then expect this book to be updated, perhaps.)

Please enjoy.

• • • •

C. C. BROWER

Mind Timing

BY R. L. SAUNDERS

• • • •

From another time and space, we've often been visited by unknown people and creatures. Not often do we hear of someone being brought back from an alternate future to our current one. This one actually sets the stage for what happens to our cities, starting with what is happening now...

• • • •

I

WHEN THE LAST OF THE long-languishing news media died, it was with barely a whimper. No bang. Not even a sullen pop. And eyes were dry all around. No one mourned, few even noticed.

Two glasses clinked at the Club in celebration. And that was all the wake they deserved.

I and my visitor-turned-conspirator were the only witnesses.

To the end of a global catastrophe that now never happened.

• • • •

HE HAD ENTERED UNINVITED and unwelcome that first day, long ago. It's not that women couldn't have male visitors at the Club. As long as they were properly chaperoned or in the very public areas. But in those days, and by that time, no one expected that a white male presented any challenge or hazard.

Women ran politics, they ran business, they ran the world. Women scientists explored the known universe and profited from their discoveries.

"Mari, a *man* is here to see you." The female maître d' at my elbow quietly announced.

This interrupted my news scanning, but was cautiously done. Alarmed Club members could get a bit defensive. And in these days, that could be dangerous to other Club patrons.

I sensed this as something unique, something out of the usual, the humdrum. It was actually a change I had been praying for.

So when that lone white male called at the all-female Club and asked for me by name, I accepted. He was shown to the middle of the main lounge, where two overstuffed chairs sat separated by a small side table. A distance surrounding them for room to move in case anything untoward developed.

While such a visit took time away from my scheduled daily poker game. I was tired of the usual bitching banter that accompanied each hand as we all knew the other's tells and bluffs.

It was time for new blood. Or a new game.

He entered wearing a very impeccable three-piece wool-blend suit, the shade of a fast quarter-horse out of the gate. Close behind him was our maitre d', who was a black belt in more martial disciplines than I could name on the fingers of both hands. She was our security. Not that we needed it. Because we were all qualified in many such disciplines. Hours in our basement gym was both socially demanded, and required. Because men had run the society into the ground, and after they lost their hold, most often became the last of the criminal class.

Women ran things, but because they had to fight their way to the top.

This male "suit" was accepted into our midst, in front of me, because it was more he was entering the lionesses den. One that was hidden behind the curtains, lace, and ruffles. Like the barred and electrified windows the Club maintained between themselves and the street. Like the concealed pistols, stiletto blades, and reinforced plexi-carbon fingernails most of us sported. For self-defense, of course.

No, I had no physical fear of any man who showed up in front of me.

But his attitude, like the quaint brown felt bowler he passed off to our maitre d', was precise and a statement of its own. Old-fashioned. Of a time before the sexes were at war. Before women had won.

"...and this civilization became just that, ma'am, an unending civil war." the stranger finished my thought.

"Intriguing, sir. I don't know your name and already you are inside my head, the ultimate hack to privacy," I replied, showing a hint of outrage.

"And you have every reason to be upset, Marigold. My name is Peter. And I am at your service." At that he extended a well-manicured hand, in the quaint, nearly extinct custom of hand-shaking.

I rose and took his hand more out of curiosity, knowing that my thin layer of dermal plasticine protected me from any direct poison, nano-biotic, or bacterial infection. Beside pheronomic door sensors had already passed him while x-ray scanning him against any weapons.

"Welcome, Peter. Call me Mari. You are just the mystery I've been seeking to relieve the tedium around here." I replied. He had a firm grip, one calculated to show respect, as that of an equal, not dominant or afraid. The skin was not calloused, but not soft. Unscarred. No missing digits.

"Thank you for seeing me without notice." Peter said.

I indicated the other matching overstuffed chair, the two separated by the ornate marble-topped side table between us. And we each sat, crossed our legs and studied the other for a few moments

"How you understand my thoughts is some parlor trick?" I asked.

"More like being able to recall conversations in retrospect. But you'll realize that soon enough. We've met before," Peter replied.

"Not like Merlin, you are living your life backwards?" I asked.

"More like the vast majority of us are. Like the old phrase, 'those who refuse to study their own history..."

"...are condemned to repeat it.'" I finished.

"And life in these days and times is nothing more than a series of mental calculations to determine what could happen and what did. So most conversations have already occurred, most actions are taken by result of causes that have long ago ceased to be more than a continuing habit."

Peter accepted an iced tea from our waitress, as did I. She left with a studied grace, her high-grade stainless steel tray balanced in her hand, and at the ready to become shield or weapon as needed.

We both sipped, while I studied this puzzle before me.

"An interesting challenge to our culture. I've heard of no paper that has been submitted to the Academy for review..." I started.

"...because any review would not uphold it or even understand the principles it posits," He answered. "Our modern culture is no better than the one it replaced, which was no better than the one which brought us out of the caves or led us up from flea-scratching apes..."

"And as it is running circular to itself, then it is no better than any before it," I finished. "Meaning that all thought and action then continues in infinite loops until entropy finally collapses the universe on our very heads."

"Not exactly, but that is the accepted apparency," Peter said.

"You are then implying that there is an existence outside this time and space which doesn't follow the paths we and our forebears have traveled before," I said.

"Actually, your existence is more the fiction than fact. The universe I come from has 'asked' me to come and interview you with the idea that this endless cycle might be interrupted long before the quaint concept of 'entropy' might have its way," Peter said.

Shocked to my core, and the very challenge I was looking for. I sipped again, delighted with the hint of lemon in our green tea.

"The next question you would then ask yourself is whether you are up to that challenge," Peter said.

"And again, that nasty habit of mind-reading you've been displaying," I replied.

"I'll give you a few seconds to study what you just said." Peter now spoke in terse terms. "Your reply will determine if I leave or stay. I have other appointments with several similarly qualified women of power and station."

I mused on this. He had uncrossed his legs, and his straightened back showed him prepared to stand and depart, all depending on my answer.

"Nasty. The key term was 'nasty.' That showed my habitual thoughts, which then led you to suspect that my mental habits might not be open to change. I apologize. And ask your patience."

At that Peter relaxed, again sitting back against the tufted cushion of his chair, his eyes reading my face as an open book. I had met with the challenge I had asked for. The game was afoot, as I liked to paraphrase. Obvious to him, my apology was sincere. But even in these seconds of thought, he was well ahead of me. And I needed to act.

"Where and when are you from?" I asked.

He smiled. "As if that would make a difference. And perhaps it may. But we are 'wasting time' as you would say, working through these loops again. The question is: do you accept?" Peter asked.

"When do we leave?" I replied.

"Now." Peter set his drink on the side-table, stood and again extended his hand. All in one very smooth, singular motion.

I rose as well, calling the attention of our maître d' with a subtle half-raised hand that she was expecting. She started to return in our direction with his bowler.

"And may I ask where we are going?"

Peter replied, "Not so much where as when..."

At that, the room shimmered around us, placing us temporarily in physical limbo.

II

WHEN THE SHIMMERING stopped, we were back in what seemed the 20-teens. Standing outside a vacant lot in Los Angeles. About where the Club would be built some great time later. The polluted air stank of car exhaust, only matched by the tar-smell of the road next to us. We stood on cracked concrete sidewalk, ringed on both sides by dry grasses and gravel. Screaming sirens in the distance accented the noisy roar of traffic that passed us, with clumsy buses buffering blasts of air about us as we stood in the sultry heat. The sun was overhead, a dim light in that haze called sky. Everything had a yellowish cast as a result.

What was called "normal" for that day and age.

Peter spoke in a pitch to be heard above the traffic. "Let's go to that chain restaurant you can see from here. It will be quiet and cool enough to think clearly as I explain these principles to you that you'll need for this challenge."

He talked as we walked down the mostly vacant sidewalk. That old phrase and song was correct, nobody walked in L.A. So he was able to explain most of the basics to me in simple terms, uninterrupted except where we had to cross intersections and wait our turn for car traffic.

While he kept a good pace, I was able to keep up as sensible flats had long replaced high-heels (King Louie's invention) as well as slacks replacing skirts (except in Scotland, where women preferred the freedom as did their men. But those customs in that locale had always been a bit frisky.)

Peter also matched his longer pace to mine, a bit of courtesy, but also as he needed to see my reaction, which he couldn't do if he was forging ahead.

By the time we reached the restaurant front door, we were both well cooked and wearing a sheen of moisture. For some reason the old phrase, "Men sweat, women glow." came to mind. Not the first anachronism I would encounter in this alternate time.

The air-conditioned interior of the orange-and-brown outfitted restaurant was welcome. It tended to make that "glow" turn to drops that dove down my neck and below the white starched collar of my blouse.

When we were shown to our booth, I quickly pulled a paper napkin from below the stainless "silverware" to mop the worst of it off my face and neck. Peter pulled some extras from the container on the table for us to use, as he similarly cleared the running drops off his own angular jaw. I could only imagine how that wool suit was heating him up.

"Actually, wool tends to wick the moisture away, an old Arab trick from the desert. The trick is to wear only cotton or silk underneath. And yes, as you were thinking, boxers." Peter said.

My mouth was hanging open, and so I shut it, focusing on breathing to avoid the reddish tinge creeping up from my chest. It had been a long time since a man had given me a reaction like that. Not unpleasant, but that found me off-guard. I never liked being caught off guard. Especially by my own thoughts.

"Most of that is the time we are in. It's the contagion of mental habit. And why L.A. is key to the entire challenge. You'd might think New York would be first, but the simpler and easier route runs through here." Peter said.

I replied, "You know that mind-reading stuff would be fascinating if it weren't so..."

"...invasive of your privacy. Sorry. Different space/time culture. Once I get you up to real telepathy instead of simple empathy, it will get easier for you," Peter said.

At that the waitress came over. Peter ordered, "We'll have your special, with two large iced teas, sweet. And apple pie ala mode. Thanks." The waitress was surprised to receive such a succinct statement, as she wrote it down. And as she picked up the unopened menus, she gave him more than one curious glance. Tucking a errant wisp of hair behind an ear with her free hand, she moved quickly away, with a little more flounce than she arrived with.

I sat to digest this without speaking. The teas returned soon, along with the waitress picking up our spent paper napkins to get a few more up-close glances at Peter.

But these were the days when women courted openly, something that would seem anachronistic in our own time.

"Or maybe just suppressed," Peter said. "Oh, sorry again, but not sorry. There is some elements of human nature which get out of hand every now and then, but rapidly balanced out. Your particular time is out of balance. And we are here as a challenge to see if we can fix that."

"Suppressed? An interesting concept. Of course our history said the reverse. That women were suppressed by the males until they rose up as equals and eventually became the superior sex," I said.

"Superior implies inferior. Let's say co-equal is more ideal. But the problem isn't history, it's again the point of whether it's interpreted or ignored." Peter said.

"And who is this challenge directed against?" I asked.

"Not an individual, but a thought-habit that was started some time ago. And we've traced it back to a off-wordly, out-of-time experiment," Peter replied.

At that precise point, the waitress returned with the plates of their diner special, a true American spread, served 24 hours a day in true American binge fashion. A stack of pancakes with sausage and two over-easy eggs. Matched by a slab of something called "hash browns." All the sugar, salt, and partially-hydrogenated oils, plus added trans-fats you could stuff into your unsuspecting and soon obese self.

All an historical footnote. Until this current, present. Where now I was just about to give my body the shock of its life. Welcome to this new millennium, not even a quarter of the way into it. A time when lifespan is shortened by diet, and humankind nearly extinguished itself over the next century. If it weren't for the handful of survivors in rural enclaves called "farms" there would have been no genetic material to re-start humankind.

"Dig in. You'll never know what you've been missing with all your pure diets and wholesomeness," Peter smiled as he cut a portion of those golden-brown flap jacks covered with artificial butter whipped and scooped up into a tiny ball. Covered with corn-derived sweetener that itself would add to heart disease. Grown with corn that was laced with a nutrition-inhibitor called glysophate, genetically modified to be immune to it - while the human body was not.

I watched him stuff the five layers of pancake into his mouth and catching the dripping fake butter and fake syrup with his tongue, while quickly bringing his paper napkin to dab off any he missed. Taking a swig of reconstituted orange juice, which was pretty much devoid of any natural sugars, he then smiled at me.

"Go ahead. You only live once. And cocaine doesn't even taste this good."

I cut a tiny bite with my fork and tentatively tasted it. The thrill raced through my tongue and brought sensations to my mouth and brain that I had never experienced. Chewing thoughtfully brought a massive flood of hormones into play which had laid dormant through all the specified diets and training our own culture had carefully maintained for several centuries after the Collapse.

"Damn! You're right. This stuff is amazing!"

And for the next 5 minutes, we stuffed our faces with this poisonous mass-produced 21st century diet, downing it all with our artificially flavored and sweetened tea.

As we finished our plates, right down to the unhygienic idea of licking them clean, the observant waitress came over with our apple pie (also questionably raised, sliced and cooked between dough of similar poisons as our stack of pancakes. It had been heated with ultra-short wavelength microwaves to give those molecules excitement enough to re-radiate lower-length heat. Enough to begin melting the scoop of artificial ice cream, allowing it to run in streams across the pie. Another beautiful golden and off-white sight to the eyes.

"Now, this is the coup-de-gras," Peter said with all sincerity, slicing off a forkful with a slice of the ice cream and pushing the whole wad into his mouth. Closing his eyes with delight as he savored the addictive artificial ingredients that were making his brain and glands work overtime. A true rush.

After a small taste, I also had to shut my eyes to experience the exotic flavor and affect it was having on my body.

. . . .

SOON WE WERE COMPLETELY full and sitting back against our plastic-covered foam seats. Delighted as only an addict can be.

"Just to top all that off, let's get some of their world-famous coffee." Signaling with his hand, the waitress brought over two thick mugs, and filled them both with black Java-bean coffee. Leaving us each a plastic container that at least honestly said it was all artificial, Peter showed me how to open it and pour the white liquid into the mug, stirring it to make the contents more light brown.

Peter sipped his lightly. "Like piping-hot tea. Careful you don't burn yourself."

I gingerly tried it and the caffeine brought a new rush to replace the sugar high which had been dissipating. "So the creamer is to cool it off. Amazing concept. Incredibly addictive. No wonder these people nearly wiped themselves off. Eliminate war in a single lifetime, only to kill everyone off with abundant and addictive instant gratification."

Peter nodded. And smiled with an addicts glee. "Yes, it's true. Destined for doom. Only saved by the discovery of fusion drives and a misguided attempt at salvation by flying their largest cities off as spaceships to other planets."

"Oh?" I asked. "That part wasn't in the history I was taught."

"Well, it's actually one of those alternate facts that historians managed to ignore. The timeline existed like that, but their view is that farmers again saved the cities and the women took over at that point to sort things out. The cities were never heard from again, at least not officially. UFO's and what not have always been around." Peter explained.

By that point, we had both finished our coffees and the waitress had removed our plates, then returned with the bill. Peter pulled out a piece of plastic and she took it to return soon with a couple of candies and the receipt.

"More coffee?" She asked.

We both shook our heads no. She smiled and picked up our cups, lingering over a look at Peter's profile a little longer before mincing off. I noticed she had written a series of numbers separated by hyphens on that paper.

"Code?" I asked.

"Mating ritual." Peter replied. He did stuff the receipt along with the plastic card into it's faux leather folding container, which he kept securely in his suit's inner breast pocket, I noticed.

My senses were still filled with the sensations of all the sugars, fats, and salt.

"Me, too." Peter said. "I had to bring you here to experience this first hand. This culture is routinely drugging itself. Obesity is a side effect. But we have to change their mental habits that make meals like this profitable – or at least try. Come, I'll call us a cab and we can ride to our final stop."

As we rose, he allowed me to go first, and put a hand behind my back without touching me. As if to steady me in case the after-effects were too much.

Making our way to the door, Peter pulled a plastic and metal device from his pocket, touched the front screen of it several times and put it to his ear. A short conversation later, a yellow vehicle soon drove right in front of where we were standing.

We got in back and were soon being jounced around by the driver jockeying for position with other "freeway" vehicles. When we weren't zooming along, we were stuck at a crawl where the driver still continued to try to get us into a faster lane. Obviously paid by the mile of transport, not the minute.

Shortly, we had left the freeway and were traveling on double-lane surface streets, finally turning up to a single lane, bi-directional paved surface in what seemed a residential area. The pace was slower now, other traffic rare.

We had no reason to talk, and our metabolism was not motivating us to further conversation. While I had a thousand questions, I had no energy to ask even one. Just keeping my head from nodding and eyelids open was effort enough.

Eventually, the driver pulled to the side. Getting out on the passenger side, Peter paid with that plastic chip again, but also handed some paper slips to the smiling driver through that opened side window before he drove off with another rush.

All very strange to me, as I touched my credit-chip implant in my right arm near the wrist. All of this could be much simpler...

"But we'll leave that conversation for another time," Peter said. "No, I didn't want to interrupt your view of this world as it is, even though you may describe it as through a drug-induced euphoria."

I smiled at that as we walked the short walkway to the front entrance. Too true. My current state could easily be described as drugged. While I had only met Peter hours before, something in him inspired trust. This was no date-rape scenario he had concocted. But we would know shortly. If so, I would bet my reflexes and weapons against his height and strength.

III

HE OPENED THE LARGE white door and allowed me to enter before him.

Cool air bathed my face. I felt tired after that meal, very strange.

"That room to your left is yours. You'll find a nice bed, and sanitary facilities. Rest as long as you like. There is a manual lock on the door, but you won't be disturbed," Peter briefed me, with a gesture toward a mahogany-tinted door to my left, down a short hallway.

Then he smiled that winning smile of his and turned right to travel down a similar hallway to a near identical door opposite, again with its own hallway..

While I could see a larger living area ahead of us, and had more questions, I was wrung out from the artificial everything I'd just consumed, plus the change in time. I turned and walked carefully to the door, the opened it.

Locking it behind me wasn't difficult. The question was whether he had a key.

I turned and took in the room. It was simple in furnishing. A huge bed in the center of the room that looked so soft, covered in a padded comforter. A single padded chair. Two matching side tables framing the bed, both with lamps, both secured to the wall on either side.

I kicked off my shoes, shucked out of my own jacket to leave it folded, laying on the side of that bed.

Before I relaxed, I moved the heavy chair over to the door, then opened one of my sturdier locking clasp knives, jamming it into the carpet directly in front of the front chair leg in line with the door handle.

Now I could relax. The noise would alert me if anyone tried to enter.

I intended to sit down on the bed and let my head clear.

But soon, I laid back and closed my eyes. Just for a second...

• • • •

AND I WOKE UP WITH the room dark, alert. Scanning the room, I found nothing had changed. I was still fully dressed, the jacket as I had left it. The light that had come in the windows was gone. Evidently the earth had rotated out of the sunshine. How long we had been in shadow or how long we would be, I could not tell. For I didn't know what time it was here.

The darkness didn't wake me. It was my own reflexes. Something had made a subtle sound. Or something else had wakened me.

Calling for lights didn't affect their status. I quickly scanned the room and felt my clothes and jackets for weapons. All present. Nothing had changed while I dozed.

Standing up failed to turn the lights on, waving my arms had no effect.

A sudden realization came to me. This was a mechanical age where they had actual hard-wired switches to turn things on and off. Just as they needed a human driver to operate that taxi.

It would be logical to have a switch by the door. My night vision gave me dim shapes, plus my memory helped me retrace my steps. Also, it should be about elbow height or slightly higher. Stepping to avoid the chair, I ran my hand along the wall and upward, finding a peg sticking out of a wall plate. Turning this upward made the lights blaze and my eyes flinch in their drug-influenced daze.

Now I could explore the room. Probably should find and use those sanitary facilities, as I felt a need to eliminate.

There was the door. One twist and a quick pull showed nothing of note. Another wall switch turned on the lights.

An interesting seat with a hinged cover must be were one did their "duty."

• • • •

AND MINE I DID SIMPLY enough. Although it was fascinating to work out how the water was plumbed with various knobs and levers. I tried them all to see how they worked. Most fascinating was the puzzle of how to get the overhead sprinkler nozzle working. Two levers had to be operated in sequence to make the water flow into the nozzle overhead instead of the over-large white basin below.

And a flimsy curtain to channel the water into that huge basin. No vacuum jets to pull the moisture into filters for recycling.

Truly primitive times. I wondered how long before our more efficient fog-mist cleansers would take to be invented. Just remove your clothes, walk in and through, then a drying wind would remove the moisture in the time it took to walk through it. Often built in a curved arrangement, where you would then return to your closet where you started, to select fresh clothing.

While I felt a bit soiled in these clothes from the sweat and heat of yesterday, I didn't know how I was to replace these with clean versions, so I continued to explore.

Just then, I heard a tapping on some surface in the larger room. Alert to someone trying to break in, I pulled a stiletto blade from a side pocket while I made my way over to my jacket on the bed where I could get my large-caliber pistol to hand. It was a choice between that and the smaller caliber derringer, but better overpowered than under.

The tapping was coming from the door.

And I heard Peter's muffled voice from the other side, "How are you doing? I heard you up and about. Is everything OK?"

"Just fine, thank you." I sheathed the stiletto and pocketed my pistol in the jacket as I shrugged it on.

Walking to the door, I pulled the knife out of the floor and kept it in hand, concealed. The other hand moved the chair and then shifted the mechanical lock back.

Opening the door, just a crack wide enough to peer through, I saw it was only Peter, I let the tenseness of my shoulders, stomach, and thighs release. There was no danger. Only a single man. A defenseless white male.

Peter was dressed in a pale violet shirt and light gray slacks, wearing only dark gray socks against the tan carpeted floor. Hardly the danger I had prepared for.

"I didn't want to intrude, but when I heard the water running and saw the light on, I knew you were up and around. So I came to do my hostly duties of showing you around." Peter said. "While we are here, please let me show you your wardrobe." He didn't step forward, but waited for me to allow him entrance.

It was that thin line of manners which separated the barbarism we were currently in and the culture of my own time. Men knew their place there - or would be quickly reminded of it. The blade concealed in my hand would have been my first reminder.

As I stepped back and he passed by me into the room, I was able to pick out his particular scent. Something along the line of charcoal, and a light earthy smell.

"I've been out gardening," Peter explained. "Hope that doesn't bother you. It helps me clear my mind."

No, of course I didn't mind, even though he was again reading my mind without asking. For some reason I found that scent exciting. And for a strange reason didn't care if he picked up that thought.

"Over here is a selection that should fit you." Peter walked to two matching wide panels in the wall with recessed handles colored the same as the paint. These panels he slid open silently and they continued on their tracks to almost disappear into the walls. His extended arms showed that the walk-in closet was at least 8 feet wide, just in its opening.

Inside were hanging garments overhead and a long set of drawers below. A rack for shoes resting on the drawer section top was filled in every opening, and extended the length of the drawers. It only stopped for a section of hanging dresses and gowns.

"I'll leave you to explore at your convenience. I think you'll find a wide variety of clothing and undergarments that are sized to be comfortable." Peter turned and walked over to a console that contained a large flat screen. A narrow shelf held a plastic control unit that he picked up. The flat screen came to life with light and low sound.

"These numbered buttons will allow you to find the various programs and catch up on these social nuances they currently call entertainment. There are also some fashion programs that will show you how the various clothing is arranged and worn." Peter was rapidly flicking through the remote buttons. As he mentioned a program, he was able to show it on the screen.

Finally, he turned the screen off and returned the remote.

"You've found the bathroom and probably figured out all you need. Other than the bed, that is about all there is to this room." Peter continued. "I'll leave you to change or you can come and I'll show you a 'hair of the dog' mixture that will help wash away that all-day breakfast we had this afternoon. Your choice, of course."

"Of course. And thank you," I replied. "While my body would like something a bit fresher to wear, my mind is telling me that this fog around my head should leave."

Peter smiled. "Wise choice. We aren't going anywhere tonight, but the questions you have can wait until both your head and body are comfortable again. Will you come this way, please?"

A perfect gentleman, I thought as I followed him. And managed to quietly unlock and stow the clasp knife as I walked behind him.

He led through a great central room that contained a large ring of couches in front of a massive screen over an unlit fireplace. To the side of them was a large, long hardwood table with seats enough to fit all those spaces on the couch. Evidently for eating, although a board conference would also be appropriate. In that case, the large screen might serve for presentations, though I saw no projector.

Finally, he lead to a bar that connected the cooking and preps area to the eating area. On its top, centered, there was a tall, clear carafe of cooling pinkish drink, sitting in an ice bath.

"'Hair of the dog' is a phrase which refers to an old remedy for rabies, which was to consume the hair of the dog that bit you. In this age, it mostly referred to having a small amount of alcohol the morning after having over-consumed such the night before," Peter explained as he poured out a large portion into a tall glass tumbler. "This is known as a protein-drink, but is fruit and plant-based. It has some natural sugars in it as well as protein to help you wash those various chemicals we consumed earlier out of your system." He placed the tumbler in front of me.

I tasted it lightly, and found it quite good. A larger sample encouraged me to take an even larger draught.

Peter looked on with amusement. "Good, isn't it? I'm working on my second large tumbler already."

I nodded as I kept drinking. It was as if my body craved this drink like water to a dehydrated man at a desert oasis. One with a fruit bar.

Empty, I put glass down on the bar top. Peter smiled and handed me a cloth napkin.

I dabbed at sides of my mouth where the pink drink still remained. And smiled back.

"Thanks. Truly refreshing," I said. "The most delightful dog-hair I've ever drank."

"You are almost ready for the challenge. As you already suspect, this is one of the most important and risky you've ever faced."

IV

PETER'S EYES WERE FIRM, his brow set as well as the corners of his mouth. He was serious.

"You brought me all the way here just to tell me that?" I asked. "I've allowed myself to be drugged, perhaps just then again, and moved to a time and location that I do not know. So risk is something I was prepared for. Tell me something I don't know."

"Or tell you something that you are not aware of," Peter continued. "You were practically bored to tears when I entered your Club several hundred years from now. And came with me armed to the teeth with multiple weapons from a 'more enlightened' time. Where the local laws currently don't even have permits for most of those now-unknown weapons, but they would be confiscated were you ever arrested. Just for carrying them."

He had moved through the doorway, standing now behind the counter in the kitchen it was part of.

He took the carafe and snapped on a plastic lid, turning away from the counter to place it in a tall cabinet behind him, one I presumed was for refrigeration and preservation. Then he returned, picking up my glass and rinsing it in what had to be a narrow bar sink on his side of that counter. The sound of a clink told that he had placed it upside down to drain. Not the most sanitary, perhaps, but a simple expedient.

Placing both hands on the counter, to show he meant no harm to me, his next statement might be alarming. I shifted my stance slightly to the balls of my feet, prepared.

"I find your heightened awareness amusing," he smiled. "And you know I don't have any weapons on me while I can make out at least a dozen on you. But that is logical, since I am the one who needs to earn your trust. In your time it was the male, particularly the white male, who was the most dangerous and unpredictable. Here, in this time, you are a queen to almost everyone you meet, because of your advanced mental and physical training.

"And there is also the error you've been raised with. Also why I had to bring you here. In your time, you were to have an unfortunate accident of your own Club a couple of hours after we left. Ultimately, you would have died. Because you sought relief from your own boredom.

"It was your own advanced training that killed you. In that time. Not now."

Peter moved his hands down and turned to leave the kitchen back into the long main room. He turned off the kitchen lights as he passed through that doorway.

I shifted my position slightly and moved back to appear as normal as possible, turning to walk down the side of the conference table.

He walked along the side of the long table I'd put between us, both seeming to sense my high preparedness and to ease it.

"This is the problem of that time. Both sexes are in such a high state of conflict that it is too close to an actual war between them. One that would be the end of the human race. And this is why artificial intelligence failed where artificial insemination succeeded. To preserve the human race. Although your genomic work proved that it's better for Nature to decide the sex of the child. Not humans, before or after it is born.

"That much of the history of this time was preserved. For Nature has ways of equalizing the balance when it shifts too far off course." Peter was talking he walked.

And now we had reached the end of the table. He stopped on his side, at the corner.

"That is what our challenge consists of. You need to interact with this culture in order to revert a certain mental habit that has crept in," Peter looked at me with his steel-blue eyes.

Those eyes were simple truth. His brows weren't elevated or narrowed. He was simply gauging my reaction and staying neutral so I could react without his influence.

I appreciated that. Again, this man was intuitive beyond bounds. It fit his tale of being from another time-line.

"The principles of this challenge we went over on our way here. This is another nexus where the decision is yours. We can continue, or the challenge is over and you will return to the time you left, the instant following." Peter waited for my response.

I knew the correct response had to be physical. "Obviously, I need to refresh myself and get into something more comfortable and less aggressive. I won't need any weapons with you..."

"...as you are safer with me here and now than you could be in any time and space. The combat we seek isn't between us, but rather before us," Peter finished.

I smiled at this. He had a quaint way of talking, of explaining things. They matched my scientific outlook. Maybe a little too closely. "Well then, I'll get cleaned up and find something more appropriate for our next conversation," I said.

A small smile started at the corners of his mouth. "And that next conversation should be rewarding. We have so much still to cover..."

V

SHOWERED (I BELIEVE the phrase is) and dutifully clean, I dressed and walked back into the main room (called the "living area") barefoot on the soft, deep carpeting. I was wearing a matching gray set of yoga pants, a crop top, and a comfortable cotton fleece top called a "sweatshirt" (probably due to its absorptive properties.) I had not a single weapon on me, even having removed my fingernail add-ons. Because I needed to earn Peter's trust to get him to tell me what I had to know.

Peter rose from the center of the couch set as I entered, another courtesy from a long-lost time. I crossed in front of him to sit in the corner farthest from the door. A position that denoted I was willing to trust him with my life. Or was a damned fool. As I passed, I again caught that earthy fragrance he wore and realized that it wasn't gardening or an added scent. This was his own particular scent. And I found it intriguing.

Peter sat as I did. He was also barefoot, and wore a simple light blue cotton t-shirt that fit his broad shoulders as if tailored, but not tight. He had no need to show off his physique to me. I could tell by his walk and gait that he was used to a lot of daily exercise.

He smiled at me. "And I'll be 'staying out of your head' as the saying goes. You can finish your own sentences. Because in my own time-space, it makes our communication faster, but here it sets you on edge. Mental privacy matters more here, as you have reminded me."

"Thank you for that, Peter." I noticed he had been reading from a set of documents in front of him off a narrow mahogany-colored tea table. While more inside, there were a few loose sheets of paper on top of their gray card stock folder. "But I have some questions before we continue. How is it that I'm able to know the local names for rooms and fabrics? I haven't had time to study the programs on that screen, er, TV set."

"Mental habits," Peter answered. "They are like the global winds that move around every planet and every bit as penetrating. What people think are private thoughts actually spread from one to the other with impunity. This is the reason for mob action, and for both the elevation and degradation of cultures. Why the rural areas are more peaceful and the cities are more violent. And why half of all scientific studies are wrong - inside the same study itself. We covered this earlier, but it had to sink in by experiencing it. We become what we think about. And it is a definite 'we' that is the cause and effect."

"Then how is it that we just don't all become a great mental "melting pot" residue?" I asked.

"Because we are individuals first, and work as a team or herd or pack secondarily. No two people consider the same, just as they don't observe the same accident 'facts.' There are as many slightly different accounts as their are witnesses. Prosecutors and defense attorneys wanting to determine the 'truth' will emphasize one version over the others, and so accomplish the legal result they want," Peter explained.

"Yet we still have choice over what we think, and can so choose our own results," I said.

"Yes, as long as one is aware that as you become what you think about, and so the world is what you think it as," Peter added.

"That then brings us to why we are here?" I asked.

"Indirectly, yes." Peter pulled one of the paper-clipped sets of papers and handed it to me. "You'll have to wade through some of the scientific academia-ese on the back papers, but the summary sheet pretty much lays it out."

I looked over the front sheet carefully, and then scanned through the rest. Peter had selected this data as key and knew my background. I got excited.

"This is amazing stuff. It was – or will be - only theoretical in my time," I said with wide eyes.

"It's actually little known here and now. Those that might know this to be true aren't listened to in these days." Peter said. "It's because of the viral mental habit that created what they call 'news' in this era."

I frowned. We didn't even have that term.

Peter noticed the frown. "You don't have the term, but you have been effect of the result. That news reader you were scanning when we met is part of the 'news media' in this time. Mostly those are owned by conglomerate corporations who also own televised broadcast media, and even a temporal fad called 'social media' at this time. But there lies the problem and the solution. Our job is to simply leverage certain factors which have been pointed out as crucial to tipping the scales."

He handed me another paper which I scanned quickly.

Then I stood to move over to reach the papers on the table myself sitting closer to him in the process.

Peter relaxed and watched me work, one arm hanging over the couch back, which turned him slightly toward me. A perfect angle for him to observe.

I was so intrigued with the rest of the papers, I hardly noticed until I finished.

He was smiling as I put down the last paper. "Want some more of that protein shake?"

I nodded and sat back. Watching him walk the distance to the bar.

Putting my hands down to each side, one wound up feeling the warmth Peter had left on rising. This again raised my pulse in a not-unwelcome manner. And his scent rose again from the couch fabric, which compounded the effect.

Peter soon returned with two tall glasses, along with a white cloth napkin for each. I took the glass and napkin from one of his hands, while he sat calmly in his earlier position.

We both sipped in quiet.

"You know, this is darned good," I said.

"Yes. All natural and invigorating," he said.

I set my glass on the tea table, on top of its own cloth napkin. And then just relaxed on that couch next to Peter, considering what we had covered. The heat from him came over to me, although we weren't touching. This made thinking a bit difficult for some reason. But a welcome distraction.

Soon my thoughts were only about Peter.

I didn't really understand how this could be. Perhaps it was the "mental habits" floating around this city, or those of Peter himself. Either way, it didn't matter. I liked the sensations, much different from those sugar/salt/fat laced pancakes and caffeine-powered coffee.

What was different is that the society I came from treated men as something to be wary of, that sex was a personal thing, not related to having children directly. Now I saw the direct connection on an intimate level.

It was intoxicating to experience.

"You know, this is getting hard to concentrate," I said.

"Is it alarming to you? We can move to the table," Peter said.

"No, it's a unique experience, one I think I want more of," I replied.

"In answer to your question, this isn't a mindset habit of this culture, rather the result of your moving away from the mass mindset of your own culture," Peter said.

I looked up to his face as he turned to look back at me. His angular jaw and hard lines somehow seemed softened to me, as if I were looking through a filtered lens.

"And I won't 'try anything' on you without your permission, meaning that it's up to you what you want to explore as part of this experience," he said.

I sent my hand up to the back of his head and pulled his face close to mine. "I hope you don't mind that I'm not experienced in this sort of thing," I said softly.

He whispered back to me, as our faces were nearly touching. "I'm yours to teach you whatever you want."

Our lips touched, and the time for talking was over...

VI

AT FIRST LIGHT, I FOUND myself alone in my own bed, a smile on my lips.

Touching them, I remembered what I had experienced and learned that night. Which made my smile broaden. Parts of me were feeling differently this morning. Not sore or abused, but rather - "sensual" I think the term is.

Flipping off the single sheet, I rose and made my way to the bathroom and used its namesake. Filling the tub with hot water, just warm enough to be soothing and relax, I found a cake of organic olive oil soap and a cotton washcloth to carefully clean myself. This sensation of a bath was so different. Again, "sensual" came to mind.

The growling of my stomach reminded me that with all that exercise requires refilling with food. So I rose, toweled off (yet another remarkable sensation) and left the tub to drain as I went to select something to wear.

In minutes, I was into a workout outfit that perhaps was a bit revealing to my curves, but I was in need of burning off those pancakes from yesterday and toning up in general. Unless this house had a workout room, there was probably room here on the floor for most of the exercises I needed.

But first, I went to see what proteins I could find in the kitchen.

Peter was already there, and the smells from his cooking were incredible. My stomach rumbled in appreciation when my nose and salivary glands went into operation.

As I reached the counter, Peter pushed a plate toward me, and set a tall glass of milk beside it. A fork and cloth napkin were already there, with two mahogany colored high chairs present.

"It's four range-free pullet eggs with natural cottage cheese in an omelet. Oh, I added some buckwheat and milk to it for some real weight. That's whole milk, not pasteurized or homogenized. They call it 'raw' for some reason. I thought you would want some substantial breakfast before you exercised. Oh, yes, we do have an exercise room, big enough for sparring with a weight machine to the side," Peter said.

Then he put his own plate and tall glass on the counter, turned off the range, and came around to sit beside me. He was also dressed for exercise in a sleeveless T and bike shorts. My outfit was modest compared to the lines his showed. I forced my eyes away from his well-defined arms back to my breakfast.

"Are these jellies or jams, and what is in them?" I asked, pointing to the small jars in front of the plates.

"I like the Amish-made jellies. They use turbinado sugar, and locally picked fruit. In front of you are blackberry and gooseberry jelly and wild plum jam," he answered. "Try a little of each. Their tastes are distinctive."

Once I started sampling each one with a fresh bit of buckwheat omelet, I was delighted with each mouthful, almost moaning with the new tastes, as my mouth was too full to talk. Mixing two of them together produced even more combinations of taste. And finally I used the last bit of omelet to clean the plate of any residual jelly and jam. The whole milk rinsed it all down nicely and gave me a contented feeling, as well as a definite reason to exercise this morning.

Peter had been watching me and his smile hardly quit as he was chewing. He finished about the time I sat back in my high chair, patting my tummy in contentment. He dabbed his lips with his cloth napkin and then gathered the plates and utensils, scooting them to the side and back of the counter.

"You go ahead. I'll clean up. It's that white door to your right, next to the fireplace. I'll be in soon." He rose and went around to the kitchen side of the counter. I heard water running and his humming a song as I left for the exercise room.

After all, there was nothing else for me to see or do since he was on that side of the counter. And I did need to work all that off, to get my mind clear for more studies...

VII

AFTER A THOROUGH ROUND of exercising (and thankfully he was in the corner on the exercise bike all the time, so I could simply face away to concentrate on kicks, punches, and tumbling) we met again at the table after we had both showered and dressed for studies.

I was in an off-white blouse, buttoned to the neck and long-sleeved, tucked into dark-gray, almost black slacks. Black comfortable pumps completed a business-like approach. He already had spread out some material, with a stack of more gray folders on the table to study. He was wearing a light blue, loose cotton faux turtle neck sweater, also in long sleeves but pushed up on from his forearms, black jeans and some moc-toed loafers over black socks. Both of us were comfortable, and ready for study.

He had made a place for me across a corner of the table, so we could have enough space to study and converse, without the distraction of proximity.

My pile of material was short, but I could see that he was simply reviewing, so that large stack to his left would soon be added to the pile on my left, between us.

I pulled up one of the dining chairs and began my studies.

• • • •

HOURS LATER, WE'D COMPLETED the reading. A pot of green tea had filled and refilled a pair of stout coffee cups repeatedly as we worked our way through it. An empty plate held only the crumbs of sinfully rich toll-house cookies with butterscotch chips. (Ensuring that I would be visiting the exercise room tomorrow and probably every day as long as Peter's cooking kept feeding me this way.)

"You have questions," Peter said. His mild, but direct style had grown on me. He was still reading me like an open book, but was careful to leave my sentence endings alone.

I began, "Let me state the obvious first. The core problem is religion. Or rather lack of it. Except for the bi-coastal megalopolises, no one is believing what passes for 'news' and both newspapers and news media are losing reader/viewership across the boards. They are going broke. Social media is failing and proving to be unworkable, even depressing. With the Internet becoming widespread, people no longer need or want to have centralized news broadcast to them."

"Correct," Peter said.

"Then why do we need to do anything? It's already collapsing and will wind up with small pockets of area with high crime and rampant sexual diseases, plus higher taxes and lower jobs as job creators leave for rural areas with lower cost of living, which includes taxes," I said.

"True again," Peter said. "The trick is to preserve the genetic pool when the cities ultimately discover fusion-powered flight and take off for the stars. The one thing we need to watch out for is the release of incurable diseases from these cities to remote 'treatment' facilities on their peripheries. And that solution is to raise the health of 'Flyover Country' peoples who will become isolated for a time when the cities do leave. And you've been tasting the preventatives for this, natural and low-processed foods, locally grown and distributed, needing no preservatives for long shelf-life and long transportation."

"The real solution is to encourage their 'clinging to guns and religion', which have kept them safe and prosperous up until the last decade or so," Peter said.

"Well, that might be, but what are you and I supposed to do about this?" I asked.

Peter opened up one last folder and slid it over to me. I began to read, and understand the simplicity of it...

VIII

AFTER THE PLAN TOOK hold, Peter returned me to my own time. Things were changed. The war between the sexes of my time never took hold. While the Club still existed, it was now devoted to the more feminine studies in addition to fitness and self-defense classes. Family were welcome to visit, and both Men's and Women's Clubs supported Family Centers where pregnancy and support functions were held, as well as chaperoned meeting areas for teenagers where they could enjoy dances and interaction.

Sabbath and religious holy days replaced 'holidays' on the calendars. Sex returned to a normalized relationship between consenting adults according to ancient texts (which sometimes gave additional advice to enhance that interaction.) The most popular degree in the private colleges that survived was "Comparative Religions". This replaced the failed MBA programs, as cross-studies of such scriptures were found to hold the key to outrageously prosperous businesses.

How did we do it?

It was mostly all found in the New Testament. Once we could point the proselytizing churches into providing unemployment counseling for fired news people, those reporters and execs learned how to use their content-creation and marketing skills to expose their former employers as anti-religion, anti-gun, and anti-sex. That led to boycotts and hastened the dissolution of most non-bi-coastal and non-metropolitan areas.

I did get used to the high heels and modest dresses for interviewing the church officials. Peter returned to three piece suits. Fortunately, it was only for a few months as we quickly recruited a large organization of replacements that fanned out across Flyover Country.

As those churches expanded their memberships, they shared these Scripture-based teachings with other churches and soon their private schools and colleges replaced the existing government-funded ones, who lost funds as they lost enrollments.

Cities, more isolated and failing than ever, soon "seceded" from the Federal government and built walls around themselves to stop the "contagion" of ideas from outlying areas. The rest of the state could no longer be taxed by them and quickly formed replacement governments to capture that revenue base.

The agreement was mutual, as neither really wanted the "contagions" of the other. While the cities attempted several times to form their own national union, these were unsuccessful, as there was little agreement between them. Being composed of numerous extreme minorities, they found it difficult to agree consistently to form a majority consensus. Also, their transportation had to start and end within those cities themselves, without connecting flights anywhere in Flyover Country.

Contagion avoidance, again.

The Flyover economies adjusted and boomed. Health quality improved remarkably, once the traditional scriptures were mined for diet tips. Local-oriented agriculture, manufacturing, and shipping helped life expectancies improve, as well as median income, so that while the population decreased naturally, so did the needs for lifestyle excesses. Humility and minimalism became more popular than decadent consumption.

And since hunting resumed as a national sport, all violent crime dropped with the nullification of gun laws. Guns were widely carried in the backs of truck windows, as well as on the hips of local citizens. Good guys with guns, as well as family counseling based on religious principles tended to discover and resolve personal problems before they created new ones for others. Prisoners were counseled with classic religious texts and recidivism dropped. (Yes, offenders who escaped from cities were returned to those cities with no exceptions, if they recovered from any defensive shooting.)

And healthy genetic material was preserved for rebuilding the human race.

We are now its proof.

• • • •

PETER AND I ARE EXPECTING our next child and enjoy each other's company more than ever. He's also taught me the advanced mathematics of retrospective analysis, so I can appear to "read minds" with the best of them.

Actually, he's teaching this class tonight. Yes, it makes sex incredible. No reason to blush. Just sign here. We'll see you at the matinée, then. Sure, you can bring your lover. Yes, you're right. Thank you and here's your receipt. Pick up your text at the door...

The Lazurai

BY J. R. KRUZE

• • • •

Initially, "The Lazurai" stood alone as a unique SF short story. But then it hit me that perhaps the legend of the Lazurai had an application to solving one of the plot holes in this anthology. Without giving out a spoiler, look for a clue below – where Kruze mentions the "Sentient Life Act"...

• • • •

I

AT THE OPEN DOOR TO the empty concrete dome, inside the long chain link fence, you can see those sheets of paper tacked to a bulletin board, each page protected by plastic against the weather.

You can read it from where you stand, if you focus your binoculars just right:

They call me Death.

But I gave you only love as my gift.

Blame it all on the terrorists. Or the scientists. Or the government.

Doesn't matter. I'm alive because I'm a freak. And I was made in the image of you.

Some say it was after they found viruses were sentient. And passed that Sentient Life Act. But people say a lot of things.

I can't die, you see. And so the government scientists gave me more life to give away in return. That life can cause death.

But I'm not a terrorist, I was a victim of terrorism.

I remember none of this, as I was just a babe laying in my bed in a maternity ward. A bomb went off nearby. Most everyone died in the hospital. It wasn't the explosion that mattered but what was in it.

More than half of the babies in that room with me lived. And kept living. While all around us were getting sick and dying, we kept gurgling and smiling when anyone in their hazmat suits came around. We only wanted to be fed, and cradled, and listen to the funny voices and faces they made for us behind their Plexiglas face-guards.

The few babies released to their families resulted in most of their family getting sick and dying. Any remaining lost their minds. The babies were then recovered and returned by people in hazmat suits.

So all of us who survived that day were taken in by the government, and research was begun to see how and why and what we had become.

Finally, they found a common virus in us, they called Lazarus.

It kept us alive, and killed most other humans around us, other than other babies. The youngest ones had the best chance of surviving any infection.

When we became older, we were moved to a sealed dome where we could grow older. And be watched.

Our ability to make people sick got worse after we became teenagers. No adult was with us very long. The Lazarus virus came out of our pores, and then made its way through any known fabric, plastic, or even metal.

One day, they gassed us all. And a few hours later, we were still alive. Made our eyes tear up, but that was about it. A few days later, they tried other chemicals. And then different illnesses they had stored up. Even tried to burn us, blow us up.

Didn't work.

No one else knew about this. Because they were all told that we had died. And our dome cemented over. A Chernobyl solution.

As you're reading my story today, you know that also failed.

You see, we absorbed the chemicals and antivirals and diseases they released among us. And in our system, we were able to then release them back through our pores. In strange and different combinations.

Without oxygen, our systems would change to live on other compounds. In a vacuum, our bodies would create air by digesting the materials we touched.

And that is how we had food and fluids after we were put in the concrete. We lived several years that way.

Until the day we ate our way through the concrete. And the fences, and learned to digest the metal slugs they shot us with. We got very good at healing ourselves.

All they could do is retreat. And retreat, and keep away from us.

Exactly what we didn't want.

All we wanted was to be loved. All we had was each other. The other Lazurai.

We went back to our concrete bunker. And made it into a home.

We built in skylights, and found enough clear plastic to waterproof the holes. If we needed building materials, we just went out to find them. Someone finally got smart enough to leave a walkie-talkie with enough spare batteries so we could put our requests out. Then whatever we needed was delivered to a neutral zone, usually through remote-controlled trucks, that would self-unload their contents and drive away, blowing themselves up shortly after leaving their cargo.

People didn't want us to get transportation.

One of those supply runs brought us our Internet access, and we found more about the world.

Eventually, one by one, we left. They couldn't stop us.

We left in search of love. Understanding. Humanity.

We each were walking Death.

Mostly.

II

THIS MORNING, CHUCK opened up the highway store again. Like he had most days for the last 20 years.

He sat on the faded wooden bench, under the faded metal awning out front and waited.

The morning was still cool, a slight breeze from the south that would mean another hot day. Not enough to raise the dust. In the shade, it was comfortable. The bench was wooden, but curved to support your back. And he had his step stool out there to keep his booted feet up off the ground.

Nearby, a tall thermos of lemonade spiked with vodka was busy perspiring. Ice cubes slowly melting, sometimes shifting with a light tinkle as they settled in.

Lately, he'd been putting that extra "juice" in it. Just to take the edge off.

Didn't expect much customers coming in today, if any. Like the last few weeks.

Once a Lazurai was rumored in the area, people left. And mostly didn't come back.

Chuck didn't have much of a choice. And didn't care anyway.

He stayed with his wife, Charlene. She had her good days and others. Mostly others, more recent.

He'd gotten an OK from the doctor to bring her home from the hospital, to those rooms in the back where they'd lived in for so long. She wasn't expected to live as long as she had, so every day seemed another blessing. But they both knew what was in her was eating her up. Day to day, they kept going.

Chuck had gotten used to being her nurse. For awhile, one of the professional nurses had come by once or twice a week to answer his questions and check in on him. But she hadn't been around in weeks. Not since the rumor got started.

He'd heard of entire cities emptied out just because of a traveling Lazurai rumor. And when the story didn't pan out, it didn't mean people would come back.

His store was stocked OK, everything except propane canisters, electrical generators, and gas cans. The crowd had bought these all out, on their way to somewhere else. There was still plenty of gas in the ground for the pumps out front. If the power lines went dead, he had his own generator hardwired in and bolted down so it couldn't "disappear." If need be, he could last for months just cannibalizing the fuel in the ground and what food he had on the shelves. As long as he didn't get tired of beer nuts and beef strips.

It might get lonely, though.

He stayed because Charlene stayed.

Charlene didn't want to leave for treatment, as she'd be too far from the baby's grave out back.

That seemed to be the turning point for her. She never seemed to recover after the baby had died.

Death was such a weighted term. But it was more accurate than anything else.

He remembered that day when they held the small ceremony out back. One of the few days he didn't open up the store. The local lay-pastor had come out to say a few words. And a friend with a backhoe had dug the hole in that dried, hard ground. Chuck had bought a concrete cross, but couldn't afford to have the baby's name carved into it.

Charlene was in a wheelchair that day, and never left it to walk again since. Only left it to lay down in their bed, which she had left less often as her illness got worse.

Chuck left a folding chair out there by the grave, where he could come and talk to their baby, to tell it all the things he had on his mind. Even read children's stories out loud. And sometimes Charlene would ask about what he had told the baby. Sometimes, she'd ask Chuck to sing a hymn for the baby, for her.

Chuck used to have a great voice for singing. They'd go every Sunday down the road to a little town that was big enough for a small congregation in one of the store fronts there. Chuck would sing the hymns along with everyone else, often leading them with his strong baritone.

Nowadays, he hardly could get through half the verses before he would break down and sob.

That was the reason for the chair. Sobbing things out helped him get through the next few days.

Otherwise, most of his day was dusting the shelves, sweeping dust from the floor out the front door, or sitting where he was. Waiting.

III

LATE MORNING THAT DAY, he saw someone walking. Miles off yet. Coming toward him, along the edge of the road and staying off the pavement. Chuck could tell because the highway was laser straight for miles in both directions.

You could hear anything coming when there was traffic. And then hear it going.

Walkers made no noise, and took a long time to get there. A long time to get gone.

"Well Mr. Lazurai, take your time. I'm in no hurry." Chuck said out loud to no one in particular.

He figured that this had to be a Lazurai as he was walking.

People told stories about them: they wouldn't always kill you right off. If they liked you, then you had a few days. The people that lived were cursed anyway, as anyone they knew would leave them alone after that. As what the Lazurai gave a person could also affect the other people around them. Big or small community, it didn't matter. Viruses spread.

Chuck didn't care. He would not leave Charlene and she would not leave her baby. So if this was the end, he was as ready as he would be.

By the time the walker was nearly in earshot, Chuck had finished off the rest of his lemonade and was ready for a refill. But he stayed on that bench in the shade and waited to meet this person.

His only real hope is that the end would be swift and painless. For everyone concerned.

The walker just kept coming. The dark hood of a jacket over its head. Dust covering its boots and lower half of its jeans. Hands in pockets. Like sunshine was bad for it. As cool as the day was, a dark jacket would make everything a lot hotter.

Chuck was in a gray t-shirt, faded jeans and his thick hunting boots. Denim cap on his head with a frayed visor finished the local look.

When the walker came up to the porch, a small breeze came up from the east. The smell of the venison in the slow cooker inside wafted out along with the barbecue sauce and the coffee Chuck had brewed that morning.

"Good morning. What can I do for you?" Chuck called out as carefully as he could, more out of habit than instinct.

The walker stopped before store's awning. Still standing in the sun. There was no reply.

Chuck simply waited. Watching. Nothing to do at this point.

After a voice-clearing cough, the walker at last said, "It is a good morning."

Chuck didn't reply, just smiled. Why he smiled was still probably out of habit.

"Why are you still here?" the walker asked.

"Nowhere to go."

"Most people just run off, even if they don't have anywhere to go."

"That's their choice, I guess."

"What made you choose to stay?"

"Wife's sick in back, and she won't leave her baby. So there's not any choice to it. I won't leave her."

The hooded head raised as the sound of the word baby. And a light face showed up at the edge of that hood.

"You have a baby?"

"Did. Buried out back."

"Sorry. For all of you."

Chuck paused at that. The sound of that 'sorry' was honest. "Not to seem rude, but why would a Lazurai be sorry about anything?"

"And you think I'm a Lazurai?"

"Well, I heard weeks ago that one was heading our way. And you're walking instead of driving. I could be wrong, but are you?"

"Some people call me that. The name I prefer is Rochelle."

"OK, Rochelle. That's a lot prettier. Won't you come in out of the sun?"

"Aren't you afraid of me?"

"Sure, but that's not going to make anything any easier. You might as well come up here and get out of that hot sun. It's a little cooler in the shade."

"Thanks." Rochelle came up on the concrete porch under the awning and sat in one of the chairs next to that bench.

She raised her hands to her hood and lowered it. That action revealed a startling beauty with dark green eyes and straight auburn hair pulled back into a ponytail. Her skin was light, but she had freckles across the bridge of her nose.

Rochelle looked at Chuck with unblinking eyes, but more in question than accusation. They both looked at each other, until Chuck looked away.

Rochelle then gazed out across the plain where the dried prairie grass was bent from the weather. She relaxed in her chair and extended her feet out in front, crossing them. "It always feels good to stretch your legs after so much walking."

"I imagine it does. Say, I'm about to get a refill. Did you want something to drink?"

Rochelle glanced at his face again and noticed the corners of his mouth were starting a smile. "Sure, some water would be nice."

"How about some lemonade? I've got a pitcher full back there."

"Sure."

As Chuck got up with his thermos glass, he rose with a practiced and unhurried ease like he would for any paying customer. Not that he would ask her for anything. Death doesn't have to pay.

Soon, he returned with a tall plastic sixteen-ounce tumbler, a plastic cap on it, and a paper-covered straw. Gaudy logos covered it, in contrast to the dark and dusty jacket Rochelle wore.

Handing the cup and straw to her, Chuck noticed her fingernails were clean and well-trimmed, silver rings on several fingers.

Rochelle smiled with straight teeth and a look that could melt any teenager's heart. "Thanks."

Rochelle took the straw and set it down by her leg on the chair. Then carefully she took the lid off the filled cup and drank deeply. She paused when she got about a third of it down, knowing she should take small sips to allow her body to adjust.

The silence returned again.

At last, Chuck spoke. "Have you been walking long?"

"All day so far, and most of the day before that."

"Heading somewhere in particular?"

"Not really. Just walking."

"I may be out of line here, but all that walking will end up take you somewhere. Most people know where they want to go when they start out..."

"Nope. Not for me. I'm just walking."

Another fresh breeze came through the store, and reminded Chuck of what he was cooking.

"Hey, are you hungry? It's a little early for lunch, but late for breakfast. Would you like to join me for some venison stew?"

Rochelle brightened at this, all the creases from her face erasing at the thought. "It's been months since I've had someone else's cooking. My breakfast was a trail bar."

"OK, you just sit there and I'll bring you out a plate of it. We don't have a table inside, and you don't need to be standing at a display counter after all those miles your dogs have covered. Be right back."

Rochelle smiled at her feet being called 'dogs' and the idea of some hot food.

Chuck returned soon with two plastic foam plates, and some corn bread. He had put a plastic fork and spoon on each plate. Rochelle thanked him as he handed her one.

They sat and ate in silence. The wind rustled the brown and gray grasses, while a skeleton tree with a small clump of shade provided a perch for a lone hawk out in the distance.

Rochelle loosened her jacket by unzipping it partly. That exposed a t-shirt that had some rock band logo on it. She had curled her feet under her chair while she ate, sat the tall drink by one chair leg. Once the plate was cleared, she sat it down on the bench seat and picked up the drink again, sipping it with pauses.

"Thanks, Chuck."

"How did you know my name?"

"Road sign. Figured that you must be the Chuck in 'Chuck's Place.'"

Chuck smiled. "Yea, that would be me."

Rochelle looked directly at him. "I don't know how many years its been since someone talked to me like you have."

"Like I have?"

"Nice-like. As if you cared."

"Well, what choice do I really have? People are people. It doesn't seem right to treat them nasty even when you're facing the end."

"Do you think I've bringing you your end?"

"Well, aren't you? Aren't you a Lazurai?"

"Not actually. Something like a third generation."

Rochelle then told the story of how she had come into contact with someone who had been in contact with one of the original Lazurai. By the time she had found out, she was already cursed by her own family and community. She'd been asked to leave and did. She'd never heard from them again, or even tried to call them.

"Most of the original Lazurai are gone. They literally faded into the earth or canyons, or even vacant concrete buildings. Loneliness does strange things to people. And they didn't have to be human anymore, especially if they weren't wanted. They'd lean up against a wall, all depressed, and then just melt into it. Or sit in a canyon until they just faded into the rocks they were sitting on. Some seemed to evaporate into the air. But those are all legends.

"There are isolated camps of people who were infected by them, and they've learned to master their situation. So much so that they can pass for normal, and move through cities entirely un-noticed and not make anyone sick.

"Others used to work for the military, at least until they were being experimented on too many times. Vengeance only goes so far as motivation. And trusting the government too much has never worked well, if you read your history. Corporations are no better, and usually worse.

"So a private and reflective life is the usual outcome. No one but our own kind understand what it's like. And when you get a group of them together, it usually winds up getting attacked one way or the other. Ends up badly for everyone."

Chuck closed his open mouth. "So you don't make people sick? Don't kill them?"

"I can if I want. Mostly I don't want. Why would I want to?"

"But isn't that what the originals did?"

"That was all they knew how to do. They didn't have control over it. And everyone who got close would die, so they quickly turned pretty sour, mostly."

"How did the next generation survive?"

"In their travels, they'd sometimes find babies. And babies are able to adapt easier than kids or adults. The ones that did then would inherit the genes from whoever had found them. Just through their physical touch. And the Lazurai took special care of those young ones, as babies didn't judge them and would give them love in return."

She looked up at Chuck again. "Tell me about why you're still here when everyone else left. Tell me about your life."

So Chuck in turn told her about the baby and Charlene. All the doctors and treatments. And finally Charlene's decision to simply go back home. To the only home the two of them had ever known together.

When he was done, they were both silent again.

The sun had climbed while they were talking and the porch's shade had shortened considerably.

Rochelle then asked, "Can I see her?"

Chuck rose without a word and took her plate with his to drop in the trashcan on the other side of the open door. He motioned to Rochelle. "I think Charlene's still asleep."

Rochelle rose out of her chair and they then went inside.

IV

CHARLENE WAS ASLEEP, eyes closed tightly into a pain-filled frown. She was gaunt, thin. Her brown hair was brittle and had streaks of gray in it. Her breath came in wheezes. While she was dressed in a comfortable cotton blouse, with a fan circulating the air overhead, it was obvious there was little comfort for her in that bed.

Rochelle sat in the chair by the bedside and took Chalene's hand. And looked at her. After a few moments, she looked back up at Chuck.

"She's in pain, but is still strong. It's her spirit that is keeping her here. And your love."

Chuck felt a tear come down one cheek. "You can tell that from just touching her?"

"That and more." Rochelle returned Charlene's hand to the bedcover and patted it. Charlene had quit frowning, her face relaxed. She looked at peace.

Rochelle rose to face Chuck. "Please take me to your baby."

Chuck led her out the screened back door out to the concrete cross in the ground a dozen yards away. There were children's toys tied with mono-filament fishing line to it.

Rochelle kneeled next to the cross and put her hand on the mound where a thin covering of gray grass lay. She touched the sun-faded toys and rearranged them so they were closer.

Chuck's voice was gravelly. "I tied them on so they wouldn't blow away in the wind storms..." He stopped at this, choked up.

Rochelle looked up to Chuck, and saw his eyes brimming with tears. "I think there is something I can do for all of you. But you're going to have to do something for me."

Chuck nodded as a tear fell onto the dusty ground.

V

YOU CAN STILL VISIT Chuck's Place. It's still there. Chuck is a lot older now. Charlene had a "miraculous" recovery and given a clean bill of health by her doctors. Never been sick a day since, other than when the wind whips the pollen around, but that's temporary. Doctor's claimed the bedrest and fresh air helped the healing and her excellent health since.

Chuck and Charlene just smile at each other and let people believe what they want.

They never mention their visitor to anyone. As far as they're concerned, it was just another empty rumor that had wrecked so many communities. Another conspiracy theory.

A few years after Charlene was up and around again, they had another child. Red-haired and hazel-eyed. They named her Rochelle. She grew up strong and healthy. You can catch her running the checkout stand most weekends. Usually surrounded by some of the local boys who hang on every word she says and watching for her heart-melting smile.

Rochelle doesn't mind, as long as they keep buying stuff she can ring up.

The grave out back has become a sort of tourist destination now. You can see piles of crutches left there, and old wheelchairs stacked nearby. People have found that there's some healing properties in that old concrete cross and the ground nearby. But that's just what they say.

If you ask Chuck, he'll nod and agree with whatever you say. If you press him, he'll say that we each have our road to walk in this life, and how we treat people is important.

If you ask Charlene or Rochelle, they just look off in the distance or at each other and smile.

The Lazurai Returns

BY C. C. BROWER AND J. R. Kruze

• • • •

The trick to the Lazurai is in how they evolve as a (super) species of humans...

• • • •

I

WHAT BROUGHT ME TO 'Cagga was a string of miracles. More of a hobby than an actual case. I was on a case following a cold trail of a Lazurai.

You might have heard about them on the news. But probably not. There was a terrorist bombing some years back that involved a hospital. Only the youngest babies survived. If you could call it that. The government hushed it up and eventually leaked it out that all of them had died.

The problem was, they didn't. Because they couldn't die and they couldn't be killed. The government tried. Because they were walking death to anyone else they touched or even got near. As bad things always get worse (like when the government is involved) they escaped. And a few of us were given the details of the case so we could track them down.

I'm a private investigator, sometimes bounty hunter. And I'm the last surviving tracker that was on the Lazurai case. Because the other trackers died and the original Lazurai just disappeared. A trail would lead into long forgotten wastelands, and just end. Sometimes, there might be a strange inscription in a rock. I remember seeing one that was the permanent outline of a human being. Life-size. Like he had been absorbed into the side of a cliff. They bored into the side of it and found his DNA actually inside those rocks.

But no foul play, just weird.

The last one I know of was what they call a third-generation infection. The original Lazurai found babies and turned them. They grew to become teen-agers and turned other babies. No record of the Lazurai giving birth, just their converting other's babies.

Into some sort of deadly superhuman. But these were the toughest to track. Because there wasn't a track of death following them in all cases. That was mostly the conventional way to find Lazurai - find a "serial killer" who was tracked by movement, not by a particular "MO" of type of death. You'd see a string of deaths and a viral outbreak that happened on a trail, usually a back highway.

Eventually, all the trails quit. And no one ever could figure out why. If you were very smart and very lucky, you'd find some sign where they seemed to melt into the landscape like that one I just told you about. (Dumb and unlucky often wound up as a dead tracker.)

We didn't even know how old the Lazurai lived. It was very possible that they were immortal, only ending this existence on their own, but not by natural or unnatural causes. The government had tried everything on them at first. They only adapted and became more lethal. But like I said, most of the original set had suicided.

The few babies they contacted were the next problem, but these mostly learned to control themselves as they grew through teenage years and not be virally infectious to everyone around them. (Probably helped having someone to raise them who didn't die off on contact or exposure.)

Very occasionally, those could be flushed out. Or their families and community would force them to leave. And again, enough shunning would result in their simply disappearing.

The third generation was the worst to track. They were only lethal by direct choice. Occasional deaths would happen, and it would track to someone of these who got real angry. The government got a few of these scooped up. But their original infection and DNA mutation always beat whatever drugs and treatment they tried to "cure" it. They've got a lab, way deep underground, where the "best" thing they came up with was to drive the person into apathy so they just walked into the wall and absorbed themselves into it. There are outlines all around the walls there, like painted discolorations.

Only it isn't paint. And they don't know that those Lazurai couldn't just "un-absorb" themselves one day. So no one ever goes down there, except their captured Lazurai.

But they ran out of available Lazurai to capture, and all the other leads dried up.

I don't know the last time I've had a paycheck for chasing one down. I went back to chasing regular human-type criminals down. A guy's gotta live, somehow. I'm good at figuring things out, finding things out. So the Lazurai went onto a back burner for me. Like I said, became a hobby.

This one was different. She left a string of miracles behind her. People healed when medicine couldn't. By her touch. And it's the hardest thing to get their "cures" to talk about it. Like you don't want to giveaway someone who just saved your life.

I get that. So I'm not tracking this girl to bring her in. I've got personal reasons now. And she's probably my only hope.

II

CHUCK'S OLD BEATER truck got me right outside the suburban borders of 'Cagga. Then I finally let it die. That truck I'd gotten started with a new crankcase of oil, new transmission fluid, and a full tank of gas. And I had to touch a few parts under the hood.

It literally became part of me. So it would start up only for me, and no one else could make it run. They'd try. I'd even leave the keys in it and watch them from a diner window sometimes. They'd see me drive in, see the windows down, look inside for the keys and nip in there as quick as they could. But the battery was always dead.

If they tried to tow it for scrap, it wouldn't come out of gear and the brakes would lock up solid. The funniest time was once was when I was watching them over a third cup of coffee and a second slice of pie. Like I had nothing to do that day. But I could feel them coming for it, so I just waited and smiled to the waitress who brought me re-fills, as I looked out their big front diner window.

The guys pulled up with a beater tow truck, of all things. And they couldn't get the rear end of my truck off the ground. Straps broke. Chains broke. And their hoist motor burned out. Smoke rose off it. Even tried to back into it to get it to break free. All they did was bend their own backend up. Like they had hit a battleship or a concrete bridge support.

I paid off the waitress in coin, then came out to have some fun with them.

They were really pissed and frustrated beyond belief. Just standing there. They knew the cops wouldn't mess with them, not in their own neighborhood.

So I just came up, this white girl with red hair. and put on an innocent look.

And got some of the most foul-mouthed nonsense coming back at me. But me, I was like that truck. I didn't ask to be hit on or abused. So anyone that tried to get near me got sicker and sicker they closer they came. When they moved away, they felt better the further away they got.

Funny, huh?

At last, I just walked up to the truck, opened the door and slid in. Turned the key, started up with a roar, then adjusted my mirrors (smiled to them through that reflection) and drove off in second gear like nothing had happened.

Just once did anyone try to come after me.

Their truck just stopped dead in the street. Engine dead. All wheels locked. I just drove on, under the posted speed limit, obeying all the local laws.

• • • •

ANYWAY, HERE I WAS in 'Cagga.

I stopped once I saw their fencing and gates. Turned down a side street in their empty suburbs so their guards wouldn't get alarmed.

In those days, they only had chain-link fence up. With razor wire on the top. That was to replace the troops after they seceded. Fed troops they didn't want.

No troops, but having to go through a checkpoint with no papers or ID, that would be a little difficult. Probably could make one up if I could see one and hold it in my hands, but not today.

And 'Cagga was calling me for some reason, to meet someone. That's my way these days. I get an idea someone needs me and then head that direction. I'll get what I need as I need it – along the way or when I get there. Always the way it's been, since as long as I knew.

So my next thing was to walk over through the suburban lots in between the empty houses until I was about half-way between this last check point and the next. Then I just walked up to the fence and cut it by touch. More like dissolved it, and absorbed what I touched.

Yea, that sounds weird, but you get used to the concept after awhile. The original Lazarai learned to breathe vacuum and eat concrete, along with every single disease the government had in its lock-boxes. I'd never had to do it, but I'd tried and tested about everything I touched and found out I could absorb about anything. Even drowning was impossible, as I could get along fine for hours at the bottom of a pool. Quiet down there.

The difference to my generation was that we knew we didn't have to. Besides, I really liked chocolate cake or pecan pie much more. Anything home-made. As well as a good Caesar's salad or some barbecued ribs. And craft beer. The finer things in life.

So I was through the fence and moving fast. I didn't sense any proximity alarms or motion detectors, but that didn't mean much. I had places to be and people to see.

Just didn't know where or who, not just yet. And the closer I got the more I knew.

III

I WAS LIVING ON BORROWED everything at this point. I was able to pick up an overdue bounty at the local Interpol office, but that exchange rate was pretty bad. Those funds would last just a few days in this overpriced city. One "fortunate" thing is that the city police had pulled back to just protecting the government facilities, as the finance area had rent-a-cops, as did any manufacturing and the posh neighborhoods. Restaurants and better stores mostly all moved into the ground floor or higher in one of the high-rises, so paid a percentage for their protection. (Like cities within cities, if you think about it.)

That left the wanted criminals hiding out in the rest of the city, scrabbling by with the gangs and the just-too-poor. And like the South Side, it was mostly shoot-or-get-shot. Most of the one-story buildings had been gutted, and the two story jobs and higher were armored up to that second floor.

I did the math on the rewards, and figured out I'd barely break even with the payoff's I'd have to make to the mob bosses and their lieutenants for information. I had one day to poke around and another day to get out of 'Cagga - or join one of the street gangs as an enforcer. I'd done some mean and nasty things to keep alive in my time, but sucking up to a bunch of punks just to keep from getting killed would be a new low. I'd rather take my chances in Ole-Mex and their cartels.

One day.

Her trail went to 'Cagga and she's probably here already.

One day to find her and - do what, exactly? I didn't know. Couldn't be killed. Only long stretches in isolation seemed to have any effect. One day of isolation, even if I had her in my hands now - that's just a joke.

More like the plan had to be getting a positive ID on her and then re-group with some more resources. But by then she could have moved on.

Sticking my hands in my pockets, I found my meds bottle. It rattled with the few doses I had left. A mental note to see if their free clinics would help a visiting law enforcement type. Maybe, maybe not.

Next to the wanted posters were some floor-to-ceiling bulletproof glass, tinted with reflection on the outside.

I was watching the two-bit hustlers operating right in front of what passed for police in this town.

One redhead caught my eye. Kinda strawberry blond in a faded jeans jacket - too large with rolled up sleeves. The three-card hustlers I could figure out. But she looked like she was handing out money to the little kids. Dimes and quarters.

They'd come up as a rag-tagged bunch, and bring her rocks. She'd put close her hand over their rock and then make a pass - the rock would be gone from her open hand. But then would close her palm and make another pass - and then hand them a coin. All depended on how big a rock they gave her. But I didn't see any half-dollars go anywhere.

Probably smart. The littlest kids would get rolled for it, and the big kids didn't deserve it.

Funny how only the smallest could approach her. Adults and teens kept a distance from her, making funny faces if they got too close. I could see how the coins for rocks gimmick could be slight-of-hand, but the perimeter trick was something that simply didn't make sense. Still, it kept her safe. Giving out money was something only politicians could do with any safety - and then never from the street, never in person.

At last, the mob of kids got their quarters or dimes and moved along. As well as the people who couldn't get into her perimeter.

Now she stood alone on the sidewalk, a light rain falling. Alone in a crowd of people,

But then she turned toward my glass. From her side she couldn't see me, but the way she was looking, she seemed to know I was standing there looking at her, looking at me.

I wondered what to do - she might be that girl I was looking for. Matched the description.

As I moved toward the door, some sidewalk people moved in between us. And by the time I was through their security and outside, she had vanished.

IV

OF COURSE, I KNEW HE knew. Because, like I said, the closer I get, the more certain I got. This was the town, that was the place I was supposed to be. There was the guy who I needed to meet.

I was across the street by the time he came out. And he looked almost frantic to find me.

So I gave him a knowing glimpse as I peeked over my shoulder and rounded a corner. Then I ducked into a little recess in the brickwork and faded into the brick itself, just like the early Lazurai did - but I didn't give up my consciousness. It was harder to see him, but other senses worked pretty well. I knew when he rushed by. Then I came out again when he was down the sidewalk a few dozen yards.

Trailing him was a cinch. He wasn't expecting it, and I didn't feel like anything most people recognized. Lazurai don't emit like regular humans. Until you've met one, and worked around one, you can't put your finger on what it feels like. Just different somehow. We could feel others of our kind even miles away. Like how I found this guy. The closer we get, the stronger the sense.

He was some sort of detective. But I could smell the sickness in him. The meds have their own scent, but the dying tissue inside him reeked of death. And death was something I was too familiar with.

We were nearly there, but I'd have to lead him the rest of the way. Otherwise, the gangs would make mince-meat of him. Literal minced meat on the sidewalk. Broad daylight or not.

He was slowing down, getting uncertain. I just kept up my pace.

Just before we were going to collide, I slipped my arm inside his and gave it a squeeze. "Keep walking," I told him, quiet-like. "Another couple of blocks and I'll treat you to lunch. Don't look around. Act normal."

"What...." he started to ask.

"Don't. Just let me show you the ropes. There are gangs on both sides of us. We don't want to get in between one of their shooting wars. But they both know me as harmless. You'll be my guest at the Don's place. Their form of organized welfare. Just smile and nod like a tourist."

The detective nodded and smiled and tried to relax. Our pace was a bit rushed but everyone on that street understood except him. He was my patsy, my dupe, and off-limits to any gang-banger that wanted to cross me. Just not worth it to them. I carried a "rep" they wanted no part of.

Soon we were at the door, I opened it and pushed him in ahead of me.

V

THE PLACE WAS AN OLD church. From the outside, it looked like someone had built a warehouse right onto the back of it. And we came in through the transept and found ourselves on a clear path right over to a long line of tables with a highway of day-old buns and bagels on plastic racks. These ended with two immense soup kettles bolted to the floor, steaming into the already humid air.

This blond pulled me right along and now shoved a bowl and large spoon into my hands, motioning me along down the line in front of her. I got a couple of dark brown buns and the wait staff ladled my bowl with some sort of ham and bean soup. As I paused by the end of the kettles, the blond came up to my side again, her own hands full.

"This way."

She led us to a single dining table with benches on each side, straight ahead of us. These sat well away from long rows of these type of tables and benches filling the old church nave instead of pews. It looked like this single eating area was where the staff took their own meals, or something.

We sat down at her motion, sliding to the farthest end by the wall.

She started almost inhaling that soup. Hungry, I guess. I took more of my time with mine. But gave her one of my buns once she'd finished hers and her soup.

"They make the best soup here. Bread's local and donated, but they make this great soup. You know the difference between edible food and great food? Love. It's the love they put into it." And she smiled.

Just a light, wistful smile. It completely changed her face. Made her look pretty. Innocent.

I didn't know what to expect with this. I was surprised. More than anything that had happened today, anything I'd ever seen, more than anything I'd ever been told about.

This one girl was still a human, no matter her powers or abilities or supposed danger to the rest of us. She didn't have to live on air or food. But she lived for love.

I quit eating, just looking at her. And she noticed.

"Yea, smiles are contagious. Worse than any disease anywhere. Can't be stopped, just held back. Some day, in some way, they come out again and start spreading. Even us Lazurai - the one's you've been hunting - have no control over a smile. Look - your own face. Oh no, you've been infected..."

She touched my face. I let her.

And smiled at her simple joke.

She smiled back and moved her hand to mine. We just sat there for awhile. Something had changed in me. I could feel it in my heart. This was the true legacy of the government testing and destruction - all those inhumane actions couldn't stop one little thing.

Love.

And it was spread by smiles.

VI

"I'M ROCHELLE. THE Lazurai you've been hunting." I still held his hand. "You're former detective Decker. Rick Decker."

He just nodded. "You read that from my skin?"

That made me smile. For all he knew, he was missing so much about me. "No, you had some APB's out on the 'Net for my body type with my name. Funny thing is, it wouldn't have worked if I didn't want to be found."

"Why's that?"

"You were watching me with that coin trick, weren't you?"

He just nodded.

"The real trick is to make your palms sweat. Turning concrete into silver alloy isn't that hard. You just have to turn your largest body organ into both sending and receiving mode. Most people only use it as another way to get rid of waste - sweat, smells, and so on. But the skin absorbs an incredible amount of material. That's why it can dry out, become brittle. Here, feel this."

I put the back of his hand to my face and held it up to my cheek. Then looked into his eyes.

A single tear came out of his. And rolled down his cheek to fall into his soup.

He turned his hand over to put his fingers on my face, and his palm. He moved it down the corner of my jawline and onto my neck.

I let him. In fact, I encouraged it. When he got his fingers over my pulse, he could feel my heart beating. It was a bit faster than normal.

Then he just took my hand in his and held it on the table for awhile. Looking into my eyes, not saying anything, but telling me his whole world.

Sure, he was sick inside. But he and I had one cure for each other. We had to learn to love, to trust, to simply co-exist and depend on each other.

VII

WE GOT BACK OUT THROUGH the checkpoint gate with no problem. I had official ID. So did she.

A few minutes earlier, I let her touch my Fed ID and look at how it was made. Then she took a Styrofoam cup, half full of cold coffee, and made it disappear into one hand. Didn't spill a drop.

She sat with her eyes shut for a few seconds, and then put her palms together. When she opened them, they held a laminated photo ID of herself with all the same type and seals, even the official hologram and magnetic stripe.

I took it from her and compared them side-by-side. They were both suitably worn from use. Basically identical marks on each. That was the only way you could tell one of them was fake. But if you come right down to it, every ID in the world is fake. Only the human love in each of us is individual, right down to the whorls on our fingertips.

And our ID's passed us through their checkpoints with no problem.

We walked over to her truck. Still there, and mostly in shade.

And it started right up, with her driving.

So we headed out. South.

There was a small town out there on the Midwest prairies, a little village between bigger towns, one where her kind - our kind - live quiet and normal existences. We held elections, had to deal with regulations from the state and Feds. And I fit right in. Got elected sheriff. As I had a background other police-type officials could check, and I knew how they reacted, what they thought they wanted. Not that we had any crime, really.

Sure, when you can make money come out of your hands, who had to steal – or even work?

But most of our people love to work with their hands and make things. Real craftsmanship.

And we hold a small festival every year, where people from out of town come in and buy our stuff. Wood carvings, jewelry, metal sculpture, they eat our home-made food, drink our craft beer.

Rochelle runs the "fortune telling" booth, And she teaches them how to read palms. Usually has a long line waiting, some even come back year after year, just to have her hold their hand and talk to them.

Sure, like she did me, she also gives them a little healing along with the palm reading.

But most important is that she leaves them all infected.

With her smile.

Our Second Civil War

BY R. L. SAUNDERS AND C. C. Brower

• • • •

Saunders' satire can get a bit biting. But one never tires of a heroine imprisoned against her will, waiting for a knight to come to her rescue – particularly in unique ways. And even if that "knight" usually wears all brown...

• • • •

I

I COULD HEAR HER SCREAM in my dreams. Every night. Who she was and how to find her was a mystery.

But I knew I had to try. Or the dreams would never let me sleep normal again.

Not that it was going to be easy. Ever since the Great Secession, it was nearly impossible to get people into (or out of) the big city areas. You could get news out of their jammed "acronym media networks" easier.

But 'Cagga was less impossible than most. And that was where my dreams told me to search first.

I was here to get those dreams out of my sleep.

I'd been called many times, for many things, but this was the most annoying one I'd ever had to live. Not that you'd call it living. Because sleep was one continuing nightmare for me. Not really a lot of sleep, just a lot of waking in a cold sweat, plus a lot of tossing and turning. I even had to get my own room because of all the yelling I'd do.

So going to 'Cagga was for my own survival, as well as anyone around me.

Lots of smiles got me through 'Cagga's gates. The guards didn't want to shake my hand, but waved me through behind the glass in their guard booth. Us "unclean" were only going to another slightly less unclean space - where the guards never went.

Just to find this woman or girl or whoever is keeping me awake at night.

She was in here somewhere. I hoped.

• • • •

LET ME BRING YOU UP to speed:

I'd been a foot-soldier in those civil wars, and had become a Brownie in self-defense. Because I wanted to help people. Got trained in first aid and counseling.

There had been decades of guerrilla warfare through the corporate media and their supporters in the East and West Megalopolises. That was also where the "social" networks had their headquarters - of course both the "media" and "socials" only allowed what they wanted spread.

Those lies caused violence, and someone was needed to patch them up. Or so I thought at the time.

The more people found out that they were being depressed and strung along, they quit social media and quit corporate news. Life became easier and simpler, more peaceful that way.

Which meant they were training everyone who saw through it to simply ignore them. Sad. Yuge fail.

People tend to move to where they find people who think like themselves. So it became that cities had higher densities of "victimized" minorities. While independent "cusses" grew their food and shipped their orders out of warehouses, and drove their trucks for "overnight" delivery. Those "independents" lived outside the cities, and for awhile were like the "pony express" of moving orders to "re-distribution" centers just outside them. But that only lasted for awhile, until the walls were built.

People also learned to stay out of cities where the protests were staged. That's where the violence was going to happen. It wasn't violence against the rest of the rural and suburban nation, but violences between the far left and extreme far left factions. Essentially, the cities were becoming even more violent, while the rest of the nation sympathized, but stayed away.

I'd finally given up working in cities after being attacked in one too many after-protest triage centers. The final straw was when they started protesting the "lack of diversity" in the doctors, nurses, and paramedics that were trying to stitch and bandage and medicate the wounded and dying they created.

It was easier helping people to find their own balance in life, some version of religion they could believe in, that worked for them. Even if it meant carrying a gun in self-defense, or letting others around them carry. Something you couldn't do inside their "tolerant" cities.

All that violence kept tourist dollars out out of cities. They should have learned from Russia's Crimean fiasco years ago - money likes peace. And their millionaires mostly left or entrenched themselves with walls and private security (as well as the usual well-placed "contribution" to various politicians, and buying up the media.) Because city resident's taxes went higher and higher, while more benefits were paid to people without a way to earn them. Unemployed violent protest-mobs were easy to stir into a riot, especially when they could be recorded easily and broadcast widely.

That set the stage for a settlement. The cities wanted to live their life (as it was) without "interference" while the rest of the country was tired of having to hear about their victimage lifestyle. Because what passed for "news" was simply their opinions about how the rest of the nation should act. Made up. Just for city residents.

While the rest of the nation yawned and turned to family viewing, like old specials recorded decades earlier. When people used to "live and let live" and welcomed Mr. Rogers into their homes.

They said the Second Civil War was over in minutes. Only took some high mucky-muck that long to sign a paper. Then the cities were allowed to go their own way, more or less. They didn't want anything to do with the "deplorable, intolerant bigots clinging to their religion and their guns" while the rest of the country was tired of their violence-inciting rhetoric, two-faced politicians, and fake news.

Of course, cities had already built their walls around themselves. To replace having to have National Guardsman with their "assault weapons" encircle their boundaries. People felt "triggered", they said. (Odd choice of words.) The rest of the nation didn't want the city violence spreading out into their quiet neighborhoods. "Good Riddance!" was a headline from the online alternative media.

For cities like 'Cagga, it just meant that their cost of raw materials was going up. Getting anything to their port on GLakes was now subject to U. S. Federal tariffs, as they controlled the waterways.

They could always fly anything in from N'Yack or L'angalez if they wanted, as long as they could land on water. But you could only carry so much. Fuel and parts weren't cheap. A different sort of tax. There was some talk about bringing back the Zeppelins, but it was just talk. No place big enough in those cities to build them and not enough raw materials.

Not to mention that there were tariff wars between Feds and Secessionist Cities that made getting anything in or out of urban areas nearly impossible.

And once they seceded, the media imprint only really reached their own populations, since they lost their broadcast licenses to anywhere else in the nation they had left. No one else tuned in, anyway. For awhile, some of the suburbs had jamming stations that would cross-broadcast across their signal.

Once the cities cut power and water, that pretty much made the suburbs into wilderness or desert. Useless for farming. Ghost towns only good for deconstruction into building materials for cities.

What really made the suburbanites move out was the plagues. They started in city hospitals when their antibiotics and medicines wouldn't work. And their solution was to put them in clinics outside their walls to protect everyone inside. Of course, this meant that their diseases would spread to all those "deplorables" who lived out there.

Being anywhere near a city became a death sentence. Eventually, the cities were forced to keep their own sick inside their walls. Of course the media never told the stories of what their "final solution" had become the "cure." But there were rumors.

Cagga joined the bi-coastal cities to form an ad-hoc nation of their own, but those cities were few - if well-populated. "Give them a few years, and then we'll have to clean up their mess, just like North Korea" went the phrase. So far, it's been a decade. Ten years of relative quiet outside their walls. Peace, prosperity, and mining the former suburbs outside for building materials while they were converted back into farmland, or at least treeless, featureless parks. Like yuge moats around castles in the old days.

Mostly (formerly suburban) farmers grew hay to begin with, until bored city guards started sniping them. Then they just sowed salt instead of fertilizer, using up-armored tractors with steel wheels. Deserts grew in self-defense. And trees beyond that, where trees grew to provide cover. And kids learned to use their ammunition for hunting and leave the pitied guards alone.

I had to remember that old movie where the one-eyed "Snake" got a high mucky-muck out of Nyack as the whole island had become a prison. Not too far off, now. But like I said, the rest of the country didn't much care. Cities were islands of themselves. As long as they kept to themselves, no one else cared.

· · · ·

AND IF THE REST OF the country was at peace and you could make a decent living without being hassled for how you acted or what you believed in, then why should you or I care?

Because I was being haunted by this continuing nightmare. Every night. Every time I closed my eyes. Not the living nightmare the cities had devolved into - the nightmare living behind my eyes when I closed them.

Me, I was a Brownie. Because outside of the cities, we mostly wore brown habits. Mine itched constantly. But the high-percentage wool blend was actually cooler in summer and warmer in winter than almost anything else. Inside the cities, where my calling told me to go, I wore what they wore - mostly torn and dirty cast-offs.

One reason was to be inoffensive, as the "Tolerance Edicts" were harsh on "hate" talk or "signals". The other reason was to avoid getting beaten up by the gang factions that ruled inside those walls. Being different was just another invitation.

Brownies didn't much get worked over, as they were just so damned pleasant all the time. That's me. Mr. Happy. Not that I am all that happy, but everyone else is so sad that it makes me look like a lit 100 watt bulb in a box of dead ones.

II

HE WAS COMING, I WAS certain. Because he kept showing up in my dreams. To save me, I hoped.

Otherwise, I'd die soon. Life inside cities was tough enough. Easier to give up and have an "accident."

I almost called him "Obi-Wan". Almost. But I didn't have an army of white-suited soldiers chasing me in some star ship. Nothing in Cagga was white. Or not very long. Gray, brown, dull black. Lots of darkness all around.

And the street lights at night were mostly gone, so everyone could do almost whatever they wanted. As long as it was what your gang approved of. And they had to get the Don's approval in turn.

That real power was in the Mob bosses. And you almost thanked 'Bama for them. "For 'Bama gave his only gay soul to reconcile the sins of the masses, as the great Trans gave her blessing to save us all from eternal damnation..." So the secular church preachers preached over and over. The hymn of Tolerance was well known to all children, as the Secular Progressive Church of the Righteous was the only government-approved religion.

Yes, there was no heaven or hell outside of what we were living here and now, so redemption was by paying taxes and voting for the church-sponsored candidate. If you weren't living in heaven, then you hadn't paid or voted enough. Amen.

Even the old 10 commandments devolved to just three - offending someone inside your own gang, tax avoidance, and killing someone in your own gang who didn't deserve it.

The Don was the pope, and his cardinals were the gang lords. Their territory kept you safe as long as you worked within their rules. And those rules said who you were tolerant of and who you weren't.

Not that complicated.

My problem is that I was pretty. Not my fault. The other problem was being born inside the K-gang, where the lighter color you were, the more prized you were. And so I didn't have much of a choice who I was going to wind up with. Unless I got scarred somehow. And then I'd be in hell, for sure.

I just didn't like where I was or what I was becoming.

If I'd been born in the territory of the Andro-non gang, then being distinctively male or female would count. Stacked or well-hung got you favors. In the LG-plus gang, it was being gay or lezzie was what counted. Straights didn't live long. You could be whatever you wanted, and could change what you said you were any minute of the day, but you had to queerify yourself, that was definite. There were other gangs like the Nazoids, Feministas, Antifa-fa's, pretty much any minority group except white straights had a gang.

Wherever you were born you were in that gang. Unless you got special pardon from the Don to move - and that took a lot of money. Of course, I didn't have any, so all I had was my good looks. My momma (bless her soul) used to pray that the Don would take me as one of his angels-in-waiting. Every gang was supposed to elevate (give up) one to the Don to use as he saw fit. So he usually had a dozen females around him to, well, fit him.

The problem was I didn't want this. I wanted just to live a simple life. I wanted a garden with a guy I could work with to make that garden better. And maybe have some children who would see the sunshine during the day and the star-shine at nights. Let the snakes take care of the mice and the toads take care of the flies and bugs, along with the birds. I didn't want to have to hunt with gangs looking for offenders. I sure didn't want my face and my legs to be my "ticket" anywhere. And there hadn't been any children born in the gangs for as long as I could remember.

Sometimes I had real heretical thoughts, like why did the Great 'Bama have to go and become a martyr? Why did the arch-angel Hill get booted from the hierarchy by the great Satan with orange hair? Why can't we just all get along?

None of those sinful thoughts get you anywhere, not even admitting them in a confession. Especially not admitting them in a confession. Because the preachers passed their notes on the sins confessed up the chain of command. Even kept spreadsheets and databases on debased thoughts and especially actions you took. The Don could call for these at any moment. But not coughing up something sinful at confession wasn't cool, either. Those preachers had to be recording something, or it looked like they were hiding something. And that could get them iced.

Sure, you're thinking - just get in good with the "cardinal" gang lord and you're safe. Not so fast. Because the 'lords had to go to confession, too. So the 'lords could be nixed by the preachers. Meaning the 'lords were always having the preachers spied on to see what they were doing. And their choirboys and gals were usually on the 'lord's payroll as informers. Because the 'lords also had the ear of the Don. There was checks and balances.

And the Don saw that it was good. And rested with his angels to wait on him as he saw fit.

Tony was our 'lord and he was hot on me. But I was cool on him. Because he was a jerk. Of course I couldn't tell him so, because he could ice me and make it look like an accident - like I accidentally lost my way into LG-plus gang territory as a straight chick. So I played along with him and strung him out as best I could.

Worse, one day the Don dropped in for a surprise inspection and found Tony trying to grope me like usual. And he says, 'Hey Antone - wass with this chicky-boom-boom you got? Howse come you haven't sent her up to Angeltown to help me out with my pains and anguishes?' Of course, Tony was all red-faced and made up a story on the spot that 'I wuz in training and learning the finer points' so that I 'didn't embarrass anybody by doin' somethin' stoopid.'

The Don saw through this at once, but smiled to Tony and says, 'Well thass fine, Antone. You juss send her up when yur dun with yur trainin' and my Chief Angel will check her out. But I tells you what - do you one better. I'll send the Chief over later today so she can find out what you've been trainin' her on and gives you some pointers. Mebbe she's ready already. Mebbe not.'

So the Don is fixing to leave, and then turns and says - 'Ohyea - Antone. Be sure she gets all confessed with that preacher of yours - and you, too. Okaydokay?'

I had to hold it all in at that point. Because I wasn't 'stoopid' like Tony thought I was.

But I was really stuck 'in-betwixt that rockin' hardplace' as the scriptures are told.

I was gonna be screwed one way or another. And I didn't like either choice.

III

STILL HAD NO CLUE HOW to find this gal, but my prayers got answered - I worked out to start helping at the one of the soup kitchens so could see all the gangs come through for that side of town. Only about three or four of these in this sector, so it wouldn't take long to survey all of them. And the kitchens were always short of help, especially people that were so cheery to everyone.

It was the first kitchen, the first day when I saw her come through. All sad-faced and so on. When I tried to cheer her up, she looked at me and something clicked into the 'on' position.

So I managed to touch her fingers when I filled up her bowl. And that shock of recognition startled both of us. That was her, OK. And she knew I was there to help her, somehow.

Of course, neither of us knew how or if I was even going to see her again. Or if I was going to be able to help her.

All I really knew is that she was the face of my nightmare.

• • • •

WHEN DOC CAME IN, I looked forward to the next break to pick his brain about that girl and her gang.

Doc was dressed head to toe in black, as usual. And nodded to me as I filled his bowl. "Hey, you're the new guy. Got a name?"

"Simon. Or Sam, as most call me."

"OK Sam, nice to meet you. " He saluted with the bun in his other hand and headed to the crew table by the transept exit.

As soon as we fed the gang's bouncers, who ate last to ensure everyone followed the rules, we kitchen staff were free for a few minutes until they left and the next gang came in. I grabbed my bowl and bun, then headed over to where Doc was almost finished. Good timing to get some info from him.

"Hey Sam. You're a Brownie, aren't you?" Doc asked.

"Yea, Doc. And you know we come only when called. Hate to be abrupt on this, but the person who called me is eating out there." I replied.

"That pretty one, the one who's cleaner than the rest." Doc said.

"Right. Do you know her scoop?" I asked.

"Home grown. Been in that gang since her mother died. Something new popped up yesterday. Seems the Don wants her has part of his angel-harem. He asked me to check her out for any diseases he could catch. So I'll see her this afternoon. But no, that's a solo gig. You can't come along." Doc was a man of short sentences.

Obviously read my face and mind like a book as he talked.

"But," he continued. "The local preacher is supposed to do a confessional on her - get the goods. And meanwhile, after I get done, the Chief Angel is going to do her own interview." Doc finished with the worst news.

Finishing the rest of his roll, he continued. "The opening for you is that the preacher is out in another gang, and too busy to get to her, so he'll take a substitute."

That brightened me up. "Doc, thanks. Owe you one for sure."

Doc just looked me over. "You Brownies have done more for me already than I could ever repay. Otherwise, you wouldn't have gotten the time of day from me." His eyes could get cold real fast, but then he smiled, a jagged crack in that ice. "Just kidding. Follow me out. Take the bun, leave the soup. You could use less of that," he glanced at my gut.

I got his point.

He rose, I rose. Followed him out as he said. We stopped by Stan and Dolly, who nodded that they could cover the next shift on their own. Dolly took my hand and held it for awhile, looking into my eyes with a smile.

"It's going to be alright," she said. "You'll do fine. Come back around if you get a chance. You're good help." And then the first members of the next gang started in single-file to get their bun-and-soup meal.

Doc led me out into the warehouse out back. He paused by a hanging rack of clothes and picked out a whitish-looking robe. "Not the cleanest, but preachers aren't saints. Here." He handed the robe to me and

I put it on over what I was wearing. A little long for my height, but better than too short.

We went out to the street from there, and met the same gang that had just fed.

On their territory. Not in the Don's neutral zone, the one he'd mandated for the soup kitchen.

I stood near the Doc, as my only protection against that gang of hundreds.

IV

TONY WAS STANDING THERE with me by his side. Doc was in front of us, with some new preacher face. Wait, that was the guy that touched my hand in the soup line. I could feel my face soften at this, and then put the hard lines back up.

Of course he saw me recognize him. So did Doc. Whatever they were planning better be good. I figured I had about 24 hours to live before hell took over.

"Hey Tony, how's things?" Doc asked.

"So-so." Said Tony. His typical wordy response. But he got and held his job by what he did with his hands, not his mouth. And he also knew I was supposed to go with the Doc for a checkup. But Tony kept me by his side as long as he could. Doc showing up didn't make Tony's day any better. So Tony's hands pushed me toward them.

I stumbled and moved over to stand between Doc and this new preacher guy. Not touching either.

Tony simply grunted, then nodded to his lieutenants. The gang moved off as a smooth action. Within minutes, they had melted into the forests of buildings and trash and grime.

Doc nodded and led us toward the Don's park. The preacher guy brought up the rear.

Once there, that preacher peeled off so Doc could sit on one of the benches and talk. This was the most beautiful part of the city, and none of us were ever allowed to visit, only see it from the top of the high rises or on the ABS media feeds.

The Don kept this neutral to everyone, and access very limited. The people who maintained this were under special protection of the Don, and under his watch. The Doc came here to check on their health. And came here to check on people where he needed quiet.

Which is why we were sitting on one of the benches among the close-cropped grass and the long reflective pool. Peaceful. The most peace I've ever known.

And Doc was looking, no - peering - into my eyes. Just a couple of feet away, but any closer would be intimate. He was holding onto my wrist with one hand, and my palm with his other.

"Any coughs or itching lately?" Doc asked.

"No, other than allergies," I replied.

Doc pulled out a stethoscope, putting it on my chest and into his ears. Moving it around for awhile in different spots around my heart. Then he told me to turn away from him, and listened to me breathe. Even coughed for him once.

Then he put his hand on my shoulder and turned me back around.. "Physically, you're fine. What do you think about becoming one of the Don's 'angels'?" He asked.

I looked down at my feet and put my hands together, rubbing my thumbs on each other. "Fine, I guess."

"Meaning, you don't want to disappoint the Don, but working directly for him wasn't your first choice." Doc summarized. "What is your first choice?"

"Freedom to make my own life. To live simpler. To have a family. To make my own choices." I replied.

"And your life hasn't had a lot of choices so far. Much less freedom." Doc was peering into my eyes again.

"No." A tear formed in my eye. Then they ran from both eyes down my cheeks.

Doc just sat there. He put one hand on both of mine, then his hand was replaced by another. I couldn't see, because my hands were blurry in my eyes. But this hand came from the other side than where Doc was sitting. And I knew this new touch. I'd felt it before.

V

TAKING ONE ARM, SHE brushed her face clean. Using the fingers of that hand, she wiped her eyes clear, then looked into my face.

"My name is Sam," I told her. And she had a face like an angel. Not one of the Don's helpers, but a real angel. I didn't know what to say next.

"Mine is Mary. I haven't seen you before. Have you been working with another gang?" Mary said.

"N-No, I came to see you." I stuttered.

"Me?" Mary asked.

"You were in my dreams, or actually, nightmares. So I had to come." I replied.

"Just in time." Mary smiled at me. And I melted all over again.

An awkward silence developed. Me sitting here with my mouth open and no words coming out. Her with her beautiful smile.

At last she looked away and I was able to think again. Never had I been so affected before. None of my counselor training prepared me for anything like this.

Looking off into the dingy skies, the words finally started up again. "I take it you wanted help getting your choice and freedom back."

Mary looked down and gripped her hands again. That struck a nerve. "Yes, you've been in my dreams as well. Of course, you looked much taller there."

"Yes, I get that a lot. I'm a bit taller and more muscular in all my dream sendings. Six-pack abs and one of those sultry looks." I joked.

Mary smiled at that. But at least this time I didn't melt.

"Now what am I going to do with you?" I asked.

"Hey, don't you have a plan?" She looked concerned.

"Well, so far, the plan was to find you. Doc helped me get this far. Now I guess it's time for new plans. Like how to get you out of this mess." I replied.

And it was her turn to be speechless - but not for long. "What were you thinking, just rolling in here and giving me a glad hand and howdy-do? No plan, nothing." Mary was frowning now.

Disappointment ruled.

. . . .

WE DIDN'T HAVE LONG to sit in our glum thoughts.

Across the park, a long-legged angel was walking toward us. How she managed those platform high-heel boots was a question for another day. At least it was a hot day. Her lack of clothes almost looked like they were painted on. All tight black leather and vinyl over spandex. Slit up to here and parted down to there. Nothing that would keep her warm otherwise. But the heat she was putting off would make any red-blooded citizen pant - or fume in intolerant jealousy.

She stalked up with a walk that would fit a runway queen. Long coal-black hair put up in a style that the Don must like. Made her look well over 6 feet tall. She had a long knife in a scabbard belted low on her hip, with a smaller blade handle peaking out of one boot top.

While her black hair waved in the light breeze, anything else that wasn't tight - jiggled.

I managed to keep my mouth shut this time. Probably out of courtesy to Mary, who became even more glum.

This was the Angel Chief that Mary was dreading. This was a preview of what she was expected to become. 'One sexy be-yatch' as Tony would say.

"Hi. I'm Goldie." The angel stalked up to us and stood with one cocked hip, with the hand on that side resting on it. The other traced an errant strand behind her ear as she looked Mary over. "Here, stand up so we can see what you got."

Mary stood, downcast and holding her hands in front of her.

Goldie looked her up and down, then came forward a step. She raised her hand to Mary's chin and pulled her head up to look into her eyes. "Doc says you're clean. So that's a plus. Let's see you walk. Go over to the pool edge and back here.

Mary did as she was told, coming back to the spot she started. Now she was looking into Goldie's eyes to see what trick she was expected to do next.

"Not bad. But Tony doesn't know squat about how you gotta 'slink' to tell your story. You walk like a trained she-panther, ready to run or pounce on command. Good for the streets. But the Don won't find it 'fits' with the rest of his angels. We can work on that." Goldie peered into her eyes and scanned the rest of her. "Good shape. A little spare. You need some more cushion in places, but the food we get will help you with that."

Goldie came forward and flipped up Mary's collar. Then tugged Mary's jacket so the top snap opened. Goldie peered down her front, then stated. "Light on top. Still, if you get the right outfit, we can push up what you got to make it look like more." Then Goldie stood back a pace. "So, what do you think about all this?"

Mary stumbled to find words after the livestock show and meat grading. "I - I guess I'm OK with it."

"With what? What do you think you're in for?" Goldie asked.

"Serving the Don, being a representative for my gang as part of his angel court." Mary replied.

"And you know good Anglish, too. That's a bonus. The Don might not talk straight, but he likes people that do - as long as you don't go trying to correct him." Goldie shifted back to her hand-on-cocked-hip pose. "But you know what? I think ABS is gonna love you. A little trim, a little makeup and you could be their new cover-girl angel. Most of these broads have mouths that would sour milk on the shelf, they know more ways to spit out an f-bomb than any comedian. You, though - you'd come off good in an interview. And it's time for their ratings sweep. Not like they have any competition, but it's still 'Always Broadcast Something' and the anchors are always trying to out-do each other to grab a better time slot. Yup, you're the one."

At that, Goldie stepped forward to grab Mary's arm and pulled her to her side as she turned and started walking back the direction she came from. Goldie glanced back at me. "Come on preacher-man, you're going to be her chaperon in all this. You're going to make sure none of these media-types does something they shouldn't. Because the Don would get tight if they tried. And they won't try to grope her or worse if there's a preacher watching. Me, I've got other stuff to do, but I'll take you both down to ABS for interviews."

There was no one else around in the Don's park. Doc had left, and all the people he was there to see were also gone. With Goldie's long steps, we were soon off grass and across a cement walkway toward a private staircase heading down.

Mary was being brave in all this, even though Goldie's grip looked like a vise from where I was following them. Of course I couldn't see Mary's face, but I could sense what was going through her head. She was out of that gang scene, but this new world she was heading into was the one she'd been dreading.

Walking out of the bright-lit garden into the darker stairwell below seemed to match Mary's mood.

VI

WHEN GOLDIE BROUGHT me and Sam into ABS headquarters, it was a completely different world. Lots of glass and plastic and aluminum everywhere. Like the whole place was a stage backdrop. Actually, I do remember some of these as shots I'd seen on the few TV's we had around. (Few because they were government-provided and not quickly replaced when some protest turned violent enough to break them. It was one of our 'rights' to watch the TV-media, but not yet a cardinal sin if we didn't.)

Goldie brought us up to the sparkling, neat and tidy reception desk, where a sparkling, neat and tidy gender-neutral receptionist was waiting.

"Hello Miss Goldie, and welcome to your visitors!" The receptionist sparkled to us.

"This is Mary and her preacher-chaperon." Goldie looked directly into the receptionist's eyes. "Mary is here for your tryout interview - the one you've been wanting the Don to provide for your sweeps. The preacher man is here to report to the Don about how you treat her."

The receptionist swallowed at this, a definite pause which showed Goldie her point was taken. Then everything was all smiles again. Turning to Mary, the receptionist looked her over. "Definitely interview-caliber. Give us a smile, darling."

Goldie poked Mary with her elbow. Mary weakly smiled toward the receptionist.

"You'll do just fine. After we're through prepping you, that smile will come as easy as breathing." She smiled one of her automatic number-6 smiles, then turned to Goldie like this was an interview. "And thank you Miss Goldie, we know how to contact you if we need anything else."

Goldie just shrugged. "That you do." To Mary: "You take care of yourself and make the Don look good." To me: "And you report everything to Don once she's done." We both nodded back. We had our orders.

Goldie pivoted on one of her heels and stalked out with her runway walk.

By the time Goldie reached the auto-opening double-glass doors, another gender-neutral assistant had glided up to where we stood and motioned us to follow.

Through a series of long and narrowing hallways, where many people were busy doing all sorts of things to guests with their hair and hands and clothing, just to get them ready for yet another three-minute talking head-shot interview. A massive assembly-line creating talent from sometimes very raw material.

At last we went through into a larger room with racks and racks of clothing hung on them. Different colors, different styles, enough to fit almost anyone with any suit or dress or in between.

The assistant finally stopped in a large blank area. Pointing to two large "X's" taped on the floor, Mary and I each took our respective position. Another assistant rolled a screen between us, and turned on a bright light behind Mary so that I could see her outline. "Preacher, this is so you can report to the Don that Mary was only treated with respect and courtesy." Then that assistant (he/she?) left.

Two more wordless assistants brought in several hangers worth of clothes and draped them over other chairs beyond the light. They then helped Mary (with respect and courtesy) out of her jacket, slacks, blouse, and shoes into the clothes they had brought. The whole process took minutes. The assistants tucked and pulled various cinches and bands to make the effect the one they wanted. Finally, they helped her back into her own street shoes that they had quickly cleaned, buffed, and shined. A few tweaks to the hems above those shoes and they both stood back to look her over. Mary turned once, twice, and I saw their shadows nod at each other. One left towing the screen away, the other to the opposite direction.

With the light still behind her, Mary did look like an angel. All in off-white, with a jacket coming down only to her waist, over a blouse and pants combination that looked street-savvy, but in a modern executive assistant mold.

The original assistant returned and looked at me, then snapped his/her(?) fingers once. The other two returned with a new pastoral frock for me, just about the same as the one I had, but clean. No shoe shining for me. Still the same ripped, torn, dirty street clothes underneath as I came in with. Obvious I was going to be background shot material, if I showed up on camera at all. But it was nice to have something that smelled somewhat clean - if only a fake "clean" smell, it was better than what I had before.

Mary was smiling, even with all the changes she'd been through. New clothes were nice. It took the edge off things. She came over to me and tweaked my robe a bit, tucking the torn edges of my shirt collar down. "At least they could have given you a better shirt."

"As long as I don't upstage you, that's the key part. Besides, I won't be on camera anyway." I replied.

She wrinkled her forehead. "I hope they don't ask me embarrassing questions, or stuff I can't answer."

As if on cue came some very female assistant with a pencil behind one ear and an ear-bud with microphone in the other. She was carrying a clipboard and talking to someone we couldn't hear or see as she walked. "Yes, I understand. No. You're right. OK - I'm here with the new Don's angel and have to get her ready. That's right. Bye." She touched her ear bud and sighed. "I'm Sue. Glad to meet you. Did they ever do a good job with your outfit. Hope they let you keep it. The Don would like to see you in that. Most of his girls are so, well - dark - in their outfits. You really do look like an angel." She touched Mary's hair gently. "Oh, where is makeup? Let's go this way and get you started."

Turning toward me, she glanced at her clipboard. "And you must be Sam the preacher-man, here to keep an eye on Mary, un-contrary. Yes, I love to make rhymes. Fills the odd parts of days. Please, come this way." And Sue led us off through the racks of clothes.

Mary took my arm and hugged it close to her. I enjoyed that, as I'm sure she did. It was reassuring.

We all went through some propped-open double doors into a room that had a row of chairs like an old-time barber shop. Sue gestured Mary into one of them and me into a folding chair over to the opposite side. Sue looked at me. "Not that you couldn't use a trim yourself, but she's the star and you're an extra. I like to think that is short for 'extra-special.'" And smiled she watched me sit, necessary before she could move off again.

Two more silent assistants came out, moving to Mary. One got busy with a comb and scissors, the other with a makeup brush and lip gloss. By the time they were finished - that seemed like seconds - she was ready for any sort of closeup they could throw at her. One of the assistants gave her a large mirror with a handle so she could see the result. Mary smiled wide at the change. She wasn't used to real mirrors, just her reflection in broken glass store fronts with dingy street lighting or harsh sunlight.

When they took the mirror away and helped her out of her chair, Mary didn't quit smiling. No one had done anything like this for a very long time, maybe since her mother was still alive. So I imagine it felt like Christmas.

Mary came over and pulled me up in order to hug me, and I patted her back as she did. She felt good inside and felt good to me. Of course, I was smiling wide, too. But that's normal for me.

Sue came back at that point. "Well look at you two - and how do you do? OK, we're off to our last stop. Where they coach you for the interview. She came around to scparate us by taking one in each arm. Then walked us briskly out of make up and down a wide hall where the body traffic was all in our direction. Even the arrows on the floor pointed in the direction we were being pulled. This was definitely an assembly-line operation.

What we were going to be turned into at the end of it was the next question.

VII

"WELCOME TO THE FRONT lines of our constant battle with ignorance and intolerance. My name is Bill, and I'll be your producer-director." The pudgy, broad man held his thick hand out for shaking - first to Mary and then to me.

Sue seemed to have evaporated silently at that point. With our attention on this balding, wide-set and suspendered man, she was nowhere to be seen.

Bill had his own clipboard and ear-bud mic. "Mary and Sam. Mary is our on-air talent and Sam is - emotional support, shall we say. So Mary is our talent for this shot." His attention focused directly on Mary at this point. "Here, Mary, you stand on this 'x', and I'll stand on this one."

By standing on that "X" Mary moved into some bright lights that made her eyes narrow. She soon learned not to look into them, but just at Bill, who had kept talking. Behind them was a wall of green.

Another genderless assistant came to show me into a folding chair off to the side where I could see and hear everything. By my side appeared a small table with a bowl of fresh strawberries and a small pile of napkins. I put a few into a napkin and started eating from these. To avoid appearing starved, I took each one and savored it before starting a new one. I took this as just another test of my patience.

Bill was talking to Mary and putting her at ease. Asking about her life growing up and letting her develop her own answers. He had about 20 questions that he didn't have to refer to the clipboard for. Apparently, this was a kind of "man on the street" interview with simple questions.

Then he started to go off script, asking her questions about what she thought of government, how the Second Civil War had turned out, and how her life had changed since then. As Mary had been born just before the walls were finished, she had perspective of growing up inside it. She had seen the changes, not all of them good.

But her answers were apparently what Bill had been looking for. Bill was getting more animated and smiling more as he got his answers. At one point, he tapped his ear bud to talk to someone. Holding his hand up in the air, he wanted Mary to be quiet and stand there while he talked. That hand went to a single finger, as if to say it would only be a minute.

I didn't catch what he said, exactly, lots of "she's the one", "yes, her answers are good", "a natural talent the Don will like", and a few more things. He was selling someone on the idea for something. At least it sounded good.

Bill finally took his finger down to take Mary by the arm and lead her over to me. I swallowed the strawberry I was working on, then folded the rest of them into the napkin and into a pocket of the robe I was wearing, with a mental note not to forget those berries when I had to turn in this robe later. I also grabbed a few more napkins to stuff into the pocket on the other side.

"She's a natural talent. Very good. Very. So we are changing the shot. We were just going to do a short interview with the Don's new angel - and wardrobe did a great job of making her look like one - and instead we're going to do an outdoor shot against a real background." He looked at Mary directly. "You are perfect for some talent we had that, well, is - unfortunately - unavailable. But the shot has taken months to set up and all those 'permissions' we needed were expensive to get, so we can use Mary here to do that shot." Bill was grinning ear to ear. Like he loved discovering talent.

Taking both our arms, he started walking us toward yet another set of double doors. While his legs were every bit as short as mine, he had no problem ushering us along as he talked at a similar clip. "...This is an external shot, and we are going to get Mary's reactions to the new suburbia reclamation project. 'New' being relative, but it looks the best out of all the possible sites we have, and the lighting will be right. Mary, the questions will be similar to those we've already been through, so that was just a rehearsal we just did."

Bill stopped us just before the doors. Above them was an Exit sign. "This is one of our newer vehicles you're going to ride in. For your safety and ours, please don't open the windows. It's fully air conditioned and comfortable. Just wait inside and someone will come for you when its your time." He then opened the double doors, and then another door with a special twist-lock handle opened away from us into a small room that was carpeted and padded just about everywhere. Ushering us in, he closed it behind us with a thump. There was no handle on the inside that we could see, just a set of buttons.

The room was mostly beiges and browns, with walls that rounded into the ceiling. Windows on the two sides were frosted so we couldn't see out and nothing could see us inside. A long couch went around the edges of the room, except for a couple of tall cabinets on each side of the single door into the room. The wall in front had a large logo of ABS plastered on it.

Just as we were taking all this in, the room began moving as a slow rumble started up somewhere below us. Mary and I quickly sat down on the couch to hold on. The swaying along with the changing lights and shadows told us we were really in some sort of portable "green room" for on-air talent - and we were going somewhere.

VIII

I'M JUST GLAD SAM WAS along. I scooted near him and held his hand. Both of us were fairly alarmed at being moved along Gawd-knows-where, but Sam was taking it all better than I was.

"Have you ever done anything like this before?" I asked.

"Not really, although being trucked around as a paramedic is a bit like it. Only you're riding with a bunch of medical supplies and equipment. Like then, you are going somewhere that you're needed, but nowhere you really know." Sam replied.

Sam reached into his pocket and pulled out a napkin with some strawberries in it. Somewhat squashed, but I hadn't had any in years. My mother used to grow them in pots on the window sill with her herbs. A tear came to my eye just thinking about it.

Sam noticed. "You're OK aren't you?"

I was careful not to get any of the pulpy fruit on my new outfit. "I'm fine. It's just that things remind me of my mom sometimes. Strawberries are one of them - but it's a good thing to be reminded now and then. Life was better back then, and can be better again."

Sam smiled at this. "You're going to do good on this interview. People need hope. You can't live on hope alone, but life is pretty poor without it."

I smiled back. "Sam, you're a real wonder." And I kissed him on his cheek. He went beet red at this. "Not girl-shy are you? Even as a paramedic, you've seen a lot worse, I bet."

"Worse, yes. More personal, no. I'm just happy to be with you and helping you. I don't particularly know where that blush comes from. Sure medically I know, but..." Sam trailed off.

"It's a heart thing, Sam. Not the blood pumping kind, but the real deep-down loving kind." He gave me a fresh napkin from his other pocket. I wiped my hands off and handed it back. Then I grabbed him into a big hug and held on for awhile.

When I let go, he wasn't blushing anymore. "Look Sam, you've felt it, too. I don't know what it means, but I know I like it. Like it was somehow meant to be." And then I kissed him on his lips, lightly.

He looked deep into my eyes. "Better save that lip gloss for the shot, although I know they probably have someone who will touch it up."

And our transport just kept rolling along and stopping and starting. But we held our arms around each other the rest of the way.

Until we finally stopped and the engine noise quit. Shadows on both sides meant we were parked in a row with other units like ours. Still, we had no real way to get out until they came for us.

Wherever we were now, anyway.

IX

THE WAIT WASN'T A LONG one. Cuddled like we were, it wasn't uncomfortable. So we didn't worry much.

Finally, we heard some clanking outside the door and the sound of a hiss as it was unsealed and then popped inward. At that, we sat apart, but just held hands.

Bill showed his broad face again. He was sweating and had a ball cap in his hand. "OK, kids. We're there now. Come this way and I'll tell you all about it. He disappeared and we took this as a cue to follow.

The clanking had made steps from the back of the truck to the ground. With a little railing on one side to hang onto. Our truck was one in a row of them, with more trucks in different places for the cameras and sound, plus the generators to run everything.

The city walls were about a mile away. Mary looked at my face in wonder. She had never been outside those walls since she was born.

The next few miles were flat and featureless, except for small piles of rubble here and there. Like everything had been scraped off the face of the earth and vanished out of existence. Our attention went to the noise where they were setting up the shot. Big reflectorized "sunny boards" were being positioned to put the light where it was needed. And some of the grips were being stand-ins for the interviewer and Mary, so they could get the lighting and sound set up.

All in front of a pastoral background with rolling prairie grasses waving in the slight breeze. Trees in the far distance and puffy clouds.

This was real life. And it smelled like freedom to both of us.

But if we ran, we'd be chased. Neither of us could out-run some of these longer-legged crew. Sure, there weren't any armed guards, but if we ran it would be the same thing as dead when we got back inside that city.

"Hey Mary." I said, real quiet.

"What?" She leaned her head to me.

"I've got an idea you're going to like." Then I whispered it in her ear. Her face was puzzled when I started, but grinning when I finished.

"Do you think it will work?" She asked.

"Worth a try." I replied.

Right then Bill trotted up, puffing at the exertion in this heat. "We're about ready to start. Let's get you in position and your face and hair touched up. Sam, you get to stand over there (he pointed) where you can hear and see everything that's happening."

Mary took her spot while a couple of genderless assistants tweaked her hair and face for the lighting they were going to use, as well as setting her hair so the wind wouldn't whip it around.

I stood between a couple of burly-looking guys who had arms the size of my thigh and shoulders were just over my head. Apparently moved heavy equipment for their living.

Our plan had better work, or we weren't going very far.

X

THE STAR BROADCASTER was last to come out of her trailer. She was pulling tissues out of her collar where the makeup had been touched up. An assistant was trailing her, with a binder in hand, a huge bag over one shoulder, and stooping to pick up the tissues every time the star dropped one. The star was prattling on about something or other, while the assistant agreed with everything she said.

The star was blond, tall, and wore perfect lips. A dark business blazer with the ABS logo on the right breast, over a light skirt just short enough or hitched up high enough to show off her legs, but not be suggestive. Well, not over-suggestive. She was built like a model and maybe used to be one. Wearing pink, spiked heels that were rough walking in this uneven sod and gravel, but high enough to make her calves and other features accentuate with every step. Still, they looked painful to wear out here.

She came up to me and held out a thin, limp hand. "I'm Peggy, the evening special report newscaster. Glad to meet you..." The assistant muttered my name. "...Mary. Glad to have you on our show. They certainly have cleaned you up well. But you'll be back to your old gang before you know it." With that, she pulled her hand quickly out of my grasp so the assistant could clean it with a pre-moistened sanitizing wipe.

She and the assistant reviewed her questions out of the binder while I stayed on my spot that was quickly becoming hotter with all the sunlight reflected on me.

The assistant was pointing out the teleprompter, which Peggy was squinting at. Then the assistant ran over to the prompter operator so he could make the text larger. He was shaking his head, but did it anyway. Then the assistant ran back and Peggy pasted a number-5 smile on and let it drop as quickly. Then held out her hand, palm up. She was waiting for the microphone, which shortly appeared there.

Both Peggy and I had our own lapel mic's installed, and these were tested. The wireless hand mic was for show, mostly, but was also back up and could record ambient noise to mix in later.

Too soon, Bill came over and told Peggy she was "live in 15." He scooted out of the camera range over to the teleprompter and counted down on his fingers from five to one and then pointed at Peggy.

At that Peggy smiled her number-1 smile and began her canned introduction. Then they waited for a prerecorded video to roll. Only Bill could see that and was holding up his hand again to start counting down.

At that point, Peggy would start my live interview.

I just hoped this worked.

XI

FROM WHERE I WAS STANDING, Mary and Peggy both looked great. They had three cameras rolling so they could do closeups on both Mary and Peggy, with a two-shot of the pair from over Peggy's shoulder.

Mary answered directly, and clearly, showing her home-schooling and her Mother's diction. Unseen from the camera, Bill was talking into Peggy's ear piece and suggesting follow-up questions. I could see from Mary's face where the questions started getting a lot more personal than anything asked in the practice interview.

But Mary relaxed when she noticed Bill was asking the questions. She started gesturing more broadly to the land around them and looking off into the distance. Mary was talking about hope. I could read it on her face.

Suddenly, she got a pained look and clutched her stomach. Doubling over, she started a deep, hacking cough. Peggy and anyone nearby started backing up.

I started to move toward her, but the guys on each side held me back. "I'm a paramedic!" I shouted at them. They both let go at that point and let me get to her side on the ground.

The cameras kept rolling as we crouched there. Peggy, Bill and the rest of the crew started backing away toward the trucks and drivers got in those cabs ready to start them up at a moment's notice.

With my hand on Mary's back, I pulled out a napkin so she could wipe her mouth. She also wiped off the sweat from her forehead. Then she looked straight into the camera.

And collapsed into my arms.

The trucks all started up at once. Peggy kicked off her pink heels and started running for her life, wrecking her stockings and hitching up her already short skirt to run faster. Only the cameramen took their shouldered equipment with them, the rest dropped everything to scamper into already-rolling trucks. Leaving in towering dust trails before their doors were even shut. Bill and Peggy fought to get into the last cab of that convoy and finally both squeezed in with the driver.

Somehow slamming shut the passenger side door as the truck lurched away with grinding gears.

All I could see after their huge cloud of dust blew away was a few sunny-board reflectors tipped on their side, a boom mic laying in the dust, and some water coolers. With scattered trash blowing in the breeze.

We were alone, abandoned.

XII

THEN WE LOOKED AT EACH other and started laughing. Hard.

So much I finally had to just lay down on the ground and enjoy it. Freedom is laughter.

Sam followed me to the ground with his own chuckling and laid next to me. We both watched the white clouds move their bright, slow sky-dance as our laughter and chuckles slowed.

Once I got my breath back, I rolled over and kissed him. Long and hard. He hugged me back and we kissed some more. Just forget the lip gloss.

"We did it." I told him, hardly believing it.

"Yes we did." Sam said as we both sat up, arm in arm. "Hey, I know it's cold, but that water cooler water will probably wash those strawberries off your face."

I smiled and nodded.

On the way over, we found Peggy's assistant had left her big bag in the rush. Other than a couple of sandwiches and an apple (as well as a cosmetic kit which I insisted we keep) we dumped the rest on the ground. Also on the ground we found a wide-brimmed hat that fit Sam, and an adjustable red ball cap for me.

"Yea, these guys don't know their plague symptoms from the common cold. If you'd really had their plague then you wouldn't be standing up there giving a long interview on TV." Sam said. "By the way, what was it that you were saying with all that arm waving?"

I just smiled. "I told them that all this reminded me that freedom was out in front of us, that you had to grab hold of hope and hold it close, to never let it go. Because miracles are possible if you keep believing."

Sam just nodded as he smiled his sweet smile and kept putting the leftover chilled water bottles into that big bag.

Miles to go before we got to any real civilization, but we were on our way.

Hand in hand.

A Sweet Fortune

R. L. SAUNDERS

....

There was a comment in one of these stories where all sorts of valuable goods were unavailable in warehouses to the people who lived in cities. Another Saunders satire tells just what it takes to get into and out of these cities – an up-armored semi-trailer rig. Of course, the driver is surprised by the bonus he receives...

....

I

THE DRIVE UP TO 'CAGGA was almost as bad as working down from upstate to N'Yack. Only you got to see more farms and less plantations.

I'd driven them both and didn't much like one or the other. But I somehow survived both trips, more than once, and so I kept getting hired to make them. Sure, they paid more, but that was the deal. You had to have a human driver to get across their borders and through their security. And you had to be a mean SOB to get out in one piece.

Of course, it didn't hurt that my rig was built from a pair of surplus MRAPs. Built to survive even IED's that these polite, "Tolerant" urbanites left around as their form of "free speech" to make their "statement" on the underside of one of the trucks that was bringing them their food and other vital supplies.

Food wasn't the same as raw material like sawdust. They didn't have no trees in there, so they didn't make anything out of actual wood. But they didn't mind we brought them leftover sawdust from the cutting some farmers did to make real furniture everyone else bought. In those cases (like our scrap metal salvage, plastic recovery, and gravel-rebar mix) they just had these big lots outside where trucks didn't have to go into the city proper and security was more devoted to keeping track of their own cranes as the tractors outside filled the bucket to unload somewheres inside.

But the land outside the city was owned by some individual with connections and they took the risk that someone would sneak out and sabotage their tractors. They'd tried importing containers of raw stuff, but those usually got a hole blown in them once they were left inside the city's high border walls and so wouldn't be worth anything when they came back across. So that owner had a crane that reached over the city walls and would drop down to pick up a load in its big claws, then hoist it into the city to dump for re-manufacturing.

I don't recall the last time anything got built inside one of those places. Things just got rebuilt.

And the people in there were mostly rebuilt, too. Hardly anyone come in or out these days, except us driving fools. But we were just crazy enough to try, and had enough sense to be able to count toes and fingers to make sure we came out with the same amount as when we went in.

Anyways, I like to talk, and so I'm getting far off the mark for this story.

You wanted to know how I got hitched and started a family all on the same day, the one where I almost lost my life a few times before I met her.

II

SO I WAS DRIVIN' UP to Cagga in my old MRAP 8x8. It was really two front ends stitched together with a special-built 18-foot trailer in between. A Cummings diesel in each end. Cab was on top, and she unloaded from either end. I could drive from either end, too. Only the back end had some overnighter quarters for me and my dog. And those had to be stripped down as they were 'spected coming and going. Since I was up front, I couldn't leave nothing that a 'Specter could make off with - even though I had cameras on everything. (One time, some damn fool tried to make off with my bunk. But then he found it was welded down. So he settled for trashing my cushions and blankets, cuttin' big holes in them. Said he was lookin' for Contraband. Dumass.)

Anyways, me and Fido (look, you name your dog whatever you want. I'd never seen nor heard of any dog actually named Fido, so that was his moniker.) Me and Fido was moving along pretty well. And of course, things got slower the closer we got in. Cause of all the potholes where people wouldn't fix them up no more. Out in the back of the State of L'Nois, they had toll roads that paid to get things fixed. But closer in, like N'Yack, there were more plantations than farms, and they took to maintaining their own gated and private routes into the city, plus paid off the guards to let them come and go with a simple pass and not get inspected and personally frisked every time they went in or out. (And I heard Cal-i-Forn was even worse. Never been there, no need or want.)

So nobody wanted to keep track of the main roads outside of the walls, since them plantation owners had their own private delivery services for stuff that come in on uni-rails above those private roads. What did they care about truckers and transport? Not like they did anything with the people who had to live inside except to pay them a little more than they were worth to keep them from quitting.

We was goin' pretty slow getting into Cagga and I was tryin' to miss the worst holes. My tires were armored and foam-filled, but that didn't mean they couldn't go bust. And I knew for dam sure that there weren't no replacements in those towns. They always kept the Federal military out and their own Police cruisers ran on flexi-steel made from reinforced carbon-stainless composite. Talk about bullet and bomb proof...

Yeah, almost oxy-mo-ironic. That place was a war zone but they didn't want the military anywhere near them. Go figure.

I was just thinkin' that when some dam fool lobbed a Molotov at me. I had the window down just a crack because of the heat, but was able to jimmy it up pretty quick. Right after I locked the steering to keep it goin' straight. No, nothin' happened except scorched some paint. Of course, the guy got run over right in the middle of his protest speech. But we were far enough out that the PC police wouldn't pay him any mind. Besides, it was Wednesday, which is "don't give a flying hump" day. As long as their Press weren't around the guvment guys didn't have to care for nothin'.

Next chance at near-death was someone with a fiberglass javelin with a stainless armor-piercing tip on it. He (or was it a she - can't much tell these days as they go so fluid back and forth) launched it from sling to give it enough power to go through my window. Almost got me. But his-ser aim was a bit low and I wore that thing right up to the city gates. Almost nobody figures I'm riding up high, 'specially when the front is painted to look like a regular big rig. He got it to stick where he thought I was driving from, but I was sittin' a couple of feet higher.

Now he was close enough that the local patrol come screaming out with their sirens pointed at him. Then he took off runnin' and hopped a nearby fence, leaving some of his clothes and jacket on the barbwire stretched of the top of it. Then they stopped chasing, as he was on someone's personal backyard. And their junkyard dog went after his butt. By then, I was way past him to care much.

You think I wood-uv got tired of this mess, but I was getting paid purty good to get these rare and tasty artifacts into the city proper. All pre-packaged and boxed up in their originals.

Rare, like I said. Like I was told. Because all those blank boxes had to arrive unopened. Every one of them. That was the deal. And they paid me a literal fortune to bring them in. Had to. No one else would. And they weren't coming to get them for the same reason. They'd rather pay for someone to get near killed to get them delivered.

Not to mention they hated Flyover Country with a passion.

Third attempt was an actual IED. And close in, as well. Musta not liked my crossed stars-and-bars custom license plates. (Of course, I just does that to tease em. If anyone tries to take them off, then the gennies kick in with a few thousand volts and that's probably the last time they grab onto anything, until they are over a couple of months or so of rehab.)

So this here IED had to be controlled somewhere close. Because they waited to blow it up in the middle of the rig. But the bottom of this deal was V-shaped armor plated and so it mostly just wiggled a bit as the suspension tightened up. But both sides of that road were missing that private fence and a few feet of private housing as well.

Me, I just kept rolling. I noted down the mile marker, as I'd have to avoid that hole on the way back.

But that wasn't as bad as what I went through after I got inside...

III

UP IN THE CAB, I HAD three bucket seats across. All with racing webbing that would auto-cinch up tight if anything really rocked my world. The middle one was for Fido. And he wore a special rig that was Kevlar with internal inflatable that allowed him to lounge most of the trip, but would make him into a tethered bouncing ball if anything happened.

I could drive from either side, but stuck to the left to make the guards happy. The right-hand seat was my dummy. Them numskull "Tolerance" protesters would often target him to get some "collateral damage." Of course, he was mostly armor inside, and full of spare parts in between those layers. Cause some fruit-loop guard would try to jab him every now and then to make sure I wasn't sneaking someone in or out. Then he'd get one of those several thousand volt shocks if he connected to anything metal.

Fruitlooped, like I said. Or he was after he tried that once.

So the guys that knew me spread the word and they only hauled out a ladder to my driving side and left my buddy alone.

We finally made it to their tall concrete security walls that ringed the city proper. Then we waited for them to let me into the airlock (not really, it was open to the weather but had automatic everything inside to check with cameras and x-rays and all sorts of stuff. I wore a lead vest, plus an apron over everything vital, and my buddy did too, because I had electronic replacement parts in that stomach of his that I didn't want fried.)

Sure, I could let loose a EMP if they tried anything funny - and they knew that from scanning it. Even put a label on the outside so they could read about it with their cameras. Only had to use it once. And after they paid me off enough to never come back again, and I didn't. (Because that left them blind on that side for weeks until they could rebuild it. Seems they'd hired too many fruit-loops instead of ex-military.)

The guard finally let me out of the airlock to stop forward of their inside gate.

That was when they had to bring out their 12 foot ladder to climb up to my window. Of course, I didn't roll it down. I had my own little airlock to pass papers back and forth. And it was definitely air-tight so nobody could put a gas grenade in there. Seen that happen to somebody I knew. Not nice.

Mostly, I just held up my papers against the bulletproof, lead-lined window glass. They'd have to come up with a bucket and squeegee to clean the grime off my glass so they could read them. Another reason they respected me when I came up. I cut them no slack. Not worth my time or my life.

And like I said, I already almost died three times just gettin' that far. Just that day, too.

Nothing was getting this cargo until it was secured in their unloading dock somewheres inside Cagga.

They were to pay me a near fortune. A quarter of it in advance. Figured if I could pull this off, I'd sell this rig after I bought my own land. I was lookin' at an old air force base that had a few underground silos...

Anyway, they finally waved me through - only after they were careful enough to get off the ladder and move it out of the way. Not that I would have. These guys were vets and knew I respected them, but also were smart enough to get everything out of the way when I started out again.

That got me into Cagga. And a few more threats on my life, but not right off.

Driving through Cagga went OK, up to the point my directions gave out.

IV

AS MUCH AS I GOT ALL the electronics I can use in this cab, they don't much help when you got lied to.

That location didn't have no warehouse. It didn't even have a building or garage with big steel garage door. That location was an empty lot.

I smelled a setup. So I put everything into lockdown mode, which included raising the armor siding on all the windows and putting the air flow on filter-recycle. Only then did I try to figure out where I really was and how to get where I needed to go.

But I wasn't having any luck. The area was being jimmy-jammed. Meaning the radio waves were all garbled from the microwaves down through AM-FM bands.

Then I noticed a recurring beat on my gravity wave locater. Like someone was using it to talk to me, or to someone.

Those waves are for earth quake warning. Like bombs going off. Very, very low. And unstoppable. So someone figured that it was good for talking on. Typical city-geek stuff. Too much time on their hands. Too much left-over welfare payments.

Anyway, I cross-connected my walkie to the output after I figured that out, and started hearing a voice. It sounded like a pre-recorded SOS. Female. Young-sounding.

And I was probably their next sucker. That's why the armor went up first. Rocket launcher with an anti-tank shell loaded, probably somewhere nearby.

But it was the weirdest SOS. She was actually teaching class. And was getting feedback with some different sounding beeps. This god-forsaken arm-pit of Cagga and she was teaching the neighborhood kids like they were all underground.

About that time, I saw a armor-reinforced black SUV start rolling slowly down the street toward me. And slower, the closer it came. That allowed me to get a good look and run my scanners. Like they were.

I knew they had four people in there by heat signature. They "knew" I had two people, maybe a little person or small kid, too. Or maybe just a bag of hamburger that looked like a person to their 'scope.

They almost stopped. But I hit a switch and two 50-cal's lumbered into position over the top of my cab with laser pinpoints on the driver and passenger side front windshield areas. At that, they floored it and cut a Huey leaving a small cloud of dust and spitting gravel as the roared out of Dodge.

The lessons had stopped. Some morse code was going on between them now. I could follow some of it, but a lot was either code or gibberish or something other than English.

Then it said something funny.

"You are the one we've been waiting for. Our only hope. Help us Obi-Wan."

I cued the mic to tap back, "We are not the droids you are looking for."

The answer came back, "I find your lack of faith disturbing."

I cued, "Your mind tricks don't work on me."

The reply, "I sense great fear in you, Skywalker."

I cued, "This ain't like dusting crops, farm boy."

The reply, "Do or do not, there is no try."

I grabbed the mic at that point and yelled into it, "Cut the crap, jack. Who are you and what do you want, Yoda?"

A young woman's voice came back, "A trip to Alduran, I mean, out of Cagga."

I answered, "But what would you have to trade to me? What do I get out of it?"

Her voice returned, "You were the chosen one. That's why you've got a fortune riding in that truck. You are where you should be. Got a belly hatch?"

"How did you know?" I asked.

She replied, "All those models had a maintenance bay. I'll cut the jammer and you can check your account. Half of the payment is there now."

The low static I'd been hearing in the background shut off and I started hearing Lim Rushbaugh's program, "...so first there was this bicoastal dad who did a single term, then a womanizer who did two terms, then the bi-coastal's son who figured he was a Texan, and that went nowhere. Then we got a closet-gay commie with his trannie, then finally an orange-haired populist, who..." I shut it off as I knew all that history. I could tell you that the cities shut themselves off from the rest of the world due to their own hate of anything that wasn't PC and minority-pandering. I probably listened to him too much. But once they started lying, it was a downhill slide to irrelevance. Media, Politico's bi-coastal suck-ups, the whole lot. It was a good thing when they seceded.

And why I had this huge discovery salvaged from a backwater Flyover town and their forgotten warehouse.

"Well, do you see it?" she asked.

"Sorry, I got distracted - yeah, it's there," I said.

"OK, then pull up and put your belly plate over that manhole in front of you." she replied.

"How do I know this isn't a trap? Couldn't you transfer that all out again?" I asked.

"Check your accounts again. Only you can do that. Because it's untraceable bitcoin," she answered. "Besides, look in front of you."

The man hole cover moved and a thin white arm pushed a satchel onto the pavement. Then turned it over. What looked like solid gold bars and silver coins were poured out.

Well that settled it. Leaving the armor up, I put it into granny-low and crept forward.

V

IT TOOK A COUPLE OF hours for them to maneuver the boxes through the belly plate and into the drainage tunnels.

Meanwhile, I manned the 50 cal's and looked for action. I did see somebody checking me out with a telescope as the sunlight glinted off it. But moving one of the guns in his direction with that laser gave him an eyeful and I wasn't bothered again.

Finally, I could feel the hatch shut. And someone tapped on the wall in between us.

I grabbed the mic, "What the hell? This ain't no school bus!"

"Do you want to get paid?" the woman returned, calm as ice.

"Not if I can't spend it. You know no one has left this city since they seceded," I replied, a bit hot. "They make the rules here and one of them is no one in or out, under penalty of death."

"You've already got half a fortune. We can leave your truck and you get leave of Cagga. I'll just keep what they already paid me to find you. If you want your other half, you do as I say," said the woman.

I paused to think this over. Fido was no help. The A/C was keeping him cool, but all he did was sit there and grin while he panted and looked at me like one of us was about to do something stupid.

The voice came again, "Look, just hear me out. I've got a plan that will work. Besides, I'm just middle-level on this. I've already paid the rest your fortune. Check your account again. But if you want me out of this truck of yours, then you'll give up another fortune just as large. What you got paid was half of what I got paid. And you can have that, too. Deal?"

She was telling the truth. The entire amount was there. So I transferred it somewhere else quickly. And a few hops after that. Felt better now. Took a deep breath.

"OK," I answered at last. "You got my attention."

"Good. There's an underpass ahead, about two blocks. And if you level out your 50-cal's they'll just fit underneath," she said. "The satellites have to be alerting their watchers by now. We need to move."

And she knew this truck, damn her. But she was earning my respect. She knew this city and the planning she was going to be telling me about should be pretty good.

VI

MOVING THIS ARMORED rig didn't start right away, but I got this bucket moving and saw the underpass up ahead. It was actually a double underpass. I could fit the whole rig under there and be off satellite eyeballs. Simple.

Meanwhile, she had reactivated the jamming, which was probably giving everything fits overhead. If they were trying to track us, they'd have a hard time. Because they were getting shadows of shadows.

Reaching the darkness under all that 'crete left the cab swathed in the eerie glows of the dash panel. But turning on a light in the cab would allow almost anyone to see in. Except, the armor was still up. I pulled down some roller shades over the front and sides and that allowed me privacy and turning on lights to see with. But I only turned on the red lights, so I could see in the dark she was coming in from.

"OK, unlock it and let's talk," she radioed.

Figuring that I would have been dead by now otherwise, I figured it was a risk worth taking. At least I'd die rich...

I unlocked my side and then she unlocked her side. But I let her open them both. Each swung into their own side, and the hinge was next to me on my side. Motioning Fido to the passenger floor pan, I shifted to put my foot next to that hinge and pulled my .45, pointed it and waited.

The door on my side swung slowly toward me until my foot stopped it.

Then I saw a mirror on a extension rod poke around the edge.

Her live voice came next, "OK, I see what you have. We've got a Mexican standoff until you trust me. I'm not going to throw anything in there. But I'll drop what we have."

Two snub-nosed .38 revolvers fell into the center seat. Both were empty of bullets.

It still would have been a standoff, except Fido started smiling and thumping his heavy tail against the floorboard.

He's a good judge of character, so I removed my foot and swung the door around with my free hand.

A freckled, blue-eyed blond, slimmed into a tight knit top with tighter curls all over her boy-cut hair grinned back at me.

"Well, hello handsome!" she said. "My name is Dora."

And just like that, I was in love.

VII

ONCE SHE WAS THROUGH the hatch, petted Fido and was sitting all sweet-smelling next to me, she turned around and looked back through the hatch.

"It's OK, you can come on, now," she said to someone.

Of course that startled me and I reached for that .45 again, but then I saw almost a mirror image of her poke her little sweet head through, with a smile that could melt the snow off a mountain.

I was in love all over again. Fatherly type of stuff. My heart "grew two sizes that day" sort of thing.

"Is that all?" I asked.

"Yes. She's all. She's everything." Dora hugged the kid like the most valuable thing in her world.

And then that kid did something that brought tears to my eyes. She stood on the seat and hugged me, two-day grizzle and sweat-smelling shirt, everything.

I was speechless and grinning ear to ear.

Dora settled the kid between us. I handed them both a cooled bottle of water. And we sat for a few minutes in quiet.

"Thanks for everything," she said.

"Well, I... guess it was worth it," I replied.

"This is Junie. She's what worth it," Dora said.

We all sat in that A/C'd cab, drank our water, and watched Junie make fast friends with Fido.

After awhile, Dora looked at me. "I should tell you our plan, then." And she rattled off a very detailed lineup of events that were inventive and precise. Like she had been working this out for a very long time.

• • • •

IT TOOK US A COUPLE of hours to rearrange things.

When we left that underpass with all the armor back down and the 50-cal's tucked away, we circled around and headed back out. Like we had all the time in the world.

I stopped at the checkpoint and got inspected again. (My camera showed that their flunkie fruit-loop tried taking the welded-down bed again, but only flipped the cushions around instead of anything stupid. Of course, I had my hand on the shock button if he tried anything.)

And not too surprisingly, they let us go. Me and Fido and the dummy.

Since we were leaving town, none of these "Tolerant" protesters wanted anything to do with us. Because Media didn't care, once you left the city walls for Flyover Country.

A couple dozen miles outside of Cagga, we quit driving by the plantations with their surveillance cameras. Then the dummy opened up the jacket to undo the lead vest and padding.

The kid climbed out, sheened in sweat, but smiling like that was the best adventure she'd had for a long time. Next she helped pull the hat and mask of the dummy, where Dora was soaked in sweat herself. Smiling from ear to ear.

And then Junie helped Dora push all that lead covering through the access doors into the storage area, where it fell to the floor with several thumps.

Once we got out of Cook County, going south on what used to be I-57, the roads smoothed out and we picked up speed.

Outside of a couple of fill-ups (where the two girls hid in back) we weren't interrupted straight through the upper part of Missouri into Kansas.

Along that trip, she told me how she had planned this for years. "In Cagga, we were mostly in an underground bunker all the time. Because if you weren't in the good side, then you were walled off where even the cops don't travel, except in bullet-proof SUV caravans.

"After my mom died, all I had left was little Junie here. And we didn't go out on the street. I taught myself learned to code and learned to hack. Junie's picking it up pretty good for her age. So I learned to deal and get stuff delivered. Anything we couldn't grow or build indoors or underground.

"Then I found out what people really wanted was the stuff that's sitting out there in Flyover warehouses that no one will deliver here.

"I found someone who had found a stash of stuff in a warehouse that his family owned. But they'd given up getting anything in there back into Cagga. He told me price was no problem, that he'd pay in advance if I could guarantee delivery. So I looked around and found you and this rolling war-wagon you use for deliveries."

Junie interrupted to ask if she and Fido could play catch in the empty storage area. I turned on the stowage lights for them while Dora found his favorite throwing ball under the seat - the one that squeaked. They went off to giggle and pant at each other, back and forth, with squeaks.

"The guy figured your one load of goods could keep him going for years on the black market. Because it was contraband in the PC-controlled ward he lived in. But people couldn't get enough of them, and they hadn't been manufactured for years. Meanwhile, his money wasn't buying him anything he really wanted. And the boxes of stuff you brought was more valuable than any drugs, although the delivery had to be made on the West side and trucked underground to make it over into where he lived by the lake shore.

"That was his guys who came to pick it up from us."

Dora was nodding off by that time, and rose up to peak at Junie, who had curled up next to Fido on some shipping blankets.

Dora stretched out across the two seats with her head on my thigh and the dummy's jacket over her.

And slept until I pulled into the old Air Force base outside of nowhere, Kansas.

I made a few calls, transferred some funds, and the caretaker got a special delivery the next day with papers to sign. He turned over the keys to me and drove out of the base, down the dusty road in front of it. I shut the big gate, then activated the alarms.

Dora, Junie, and me headed over to the old Commissary to use their grill to make some double cheeseburgers and enjoy some real milkshakes. Hand in hand. Family.

"By the way, Dora," I asked. "What was in those boxes?"

She looked up at me and smiled.

"Twinkies."

Becoming Michelle

BY R. L. SAUNDERS AND C. C. Brower

• • • •

Gang life in cities took over most of the areas other than the financial district or government centers. The emphasis of metro-politicians on "identity" gave quite an inspiration for this story – as well as pushing the development of how the cities are organized. We also find out more about "Doc" here...

• • • •

I

AFTER THE SECOND TIME I got beat up, I figured I needed to change my lifestyle.

It didn't matter if you were white, black, gay, straight, male, female - someone got offended at how you looked or acted. It didn't matter how much or who you paid for "protection." They couldn't be around all the time, and someone else was always wanting a piece of you.

The weird part was that I was expert in being anything anyone wanted.

I just couldn't change fast enough to suit everyone.

That was my job, and why I got hired. Why they kept keeping me on and kept giving me bonuses and pay raises. Because I could be anyone or any type of person they needed.

My family tree spread out like one of those Eastern Banyan trees. Wide, really wide. I had some of probably every race you can name somewhere in there.

And my upbringing was modern-progressive. I got to choose my sex and my name whenever I wanted, any time I wanted.

So I was born "Michelle" but called myself Mica or Mike or Michael - whatever a person wanted to hear when they came in the corporate front door. I was their receptionist. No, I was their host/hostess. And I was able to change to suit their preferences.

A chameleon.

I studied people, and could spot by the time they crossed that long lobby whether they wanted me to be male or female, colored or white or something else, gay/straight/bi- or anything they wanted.

Mostly, I got it right on the money. Which is why they paid me so well.

My job was to set the new customer at ease instantly and help them find whatever they wanted at the corporation.

If that meant I put up with being hit on, insulted, butt-slapped, or pinched, even groped - it was all in a day's work. Often several times in a day's work. Because I was paid to be submissive or dominant, alluring or indifferent. Often appearing to be several different things at once.

It was how you held yourself, how you acted, how you responded.

But no matter how good I was, it didn't matter out on the street. Someone would decide you offended them. Or you had "appropriated" something another culture had that didn't belong to you.

The worst days were when I would wear makeup that made me look definitely one way or another. Like they would have a group of female straight execs come in, so I would make myself male-looking with extra shadow above and below my eyebrows, and under my jawline to make it look like I had a jutting brows and a strong jaw - very masculine. My extra shoulder padding and solid heels gave that look, as well as my low range vocal made me sound masculine. Sometimes putting a roll of half-dollars in my front pocket completed the look they were wanting.

I could count how many times I'd get pinched riding up the elevator with them, always having to stand the front with the "guests" behind me...

Because I was someone else's employee. And couldn't cause a fuss or complain. They knew it.

Or I was very feminine to another set of female execs, coy and gossipy. All with a different outfit and mascara. Thinner brows, longer eyelashes.

To the average person, particularly in a crowd, not being anyone important, I'd be androgynous. Nobody in particular. And even the uni-sex crowd got offended by that.

Of course, I got pretty quick at avoiding the slaps and gropes and pinches. Except when I was with several of them in a group.

And that was always the way with the roaming gangs after work. Too many all at once.

Those started up after the "Tolerance Edicts." And the police got neutered as far as protecting anyone besides their own butts. Most of the city was "no-go" for them after that. They only traveled in bullet- and bomb-proof caravans, and only to protect city officials. Sure, they were being sued several times a week for imagined "discrimination" and that only made it worse. They even invested in 3D imaging so that their body cams showed every inch around them and were basically tamper-proof.

That didn't matter. They were neutered. Even dropped the "protect and serve" motto. Literally scraped it off their up-armored SUV's. They were bodyguards for the city executives and their lackey press. You couldn't pay them enough to do anything else, even when the law said they had to.

Because if they ever lost their job, they were probably dead within a week. Cop-hating became a hobby with people. More popular than sports on the 24-7-365 media feed.

The media were in on the scam. They were polite enough in person when a cop was around, but on the 'tube they could be downright vicious. Because they thought it made their ratings go up, and that affected how much advertisers could be forced to pay.

But all this thinking wasn't smart. Because now it was dark, I was trying to find my way home. The trick was to stay in the territories I had bought protection from. That was where all my pay raises and bonuses had gone. Because I was in the "donut hole" of having enough that should have bought a good living, but not enough to buy protection to ensure that it was. I couldn't afford even an armed guard to protect me between my work and my apartment.

That left me was traveling the long and gerrymandered route along the edge of where they would protect me until I could get close enough to sprint to the relative safety of my apartment complex and their snoring, dull paid "guards." The ones who would only protect you if you got through that armored front door in one piece, preferably not bleeding on their carpet.

And it wasn't my luck that night. Because the borders had shifted again, always without warning to their victims.

Soon I saw myself surrounded by a bunch of dark hoodie-wearing thugs. Male-female, it didn't matter. They were out to hunt.

Turning left and right, I saw only that the noose was tightening. Standing bodies with their faces in shadow. Weapons in their hands that I could see, and more weapons underneath their long sleeves I couldn't.

Part of that money had been spent in martial arts training, after the second time I was mugged. And that had occurred right outside the front door of my apartment. I could still see the shocked fear and remorse of those security guards as they kept themselves protected behind the armed glass.

Broward. That was my apartment. And still a block away. Not that it would matter in a few minutes.

I decided. Throwing my bag at the face of the biggest one, who was instantly swarmed by the smaller (females?) who were at his sides and behind them. They wanted my dress clothes.

Then I launched behind me at some smaller thugs, who still were taller than me by a head or so.

Unexpected, I was able to deck three of them and take off running through that gap. In the wrong direction to get to my apartment.

At least I was wearing my street running shoes. And I ran for my life.

But they knew the turf better, as they lived it. And no matter how many turns I took, how I dodged into and out of traffic, they boxed me in again.

The trick was to protect my face and my right arm. The rest I could heal. But heavy makeup and shades to cover eye bruises would only go so far. I needed my job to survive.

Feinting right and left, I worked to get an opening. But found none.

The ones carrying the long pipes came closer, where they could strike and still be safe. I was dodging them OK for now, but was being pushed back against the others who had knives.

Turning my back on any of them was the trick. Any wrong move would save or cost me my life.

One, a smallish one, jumped on my back. That one was simple enough to hurl.

But then I felt my right wrist seized. And I panicked, trying to desperately free it. My jacket was pulled and hood ripped from my head and down around my shoulders.

"An-dro! An-DRO! AN. DRO!!" The shout became a chant.

I still struggled to free myself.

Both arms were held now and I could only focus on my right wrist. And the knife near it.

Pulling suddenly to right and then left, I got the guy off balance and kicked him in the crotch with the same movement.

That got me a pipe across the back of my head.

And blackness...

II

I'D SEEN WHERE THE girl had been taken, down an alleyway where no one else would go.

Except me. Harmless old me.

Because that was my calling. To make the poor rich, to enable the blind to see.

First I had to save that life.

Using the echoes of the high walls, I started making sounds that sounded like a wild cat - or several - were loose in the alleys behind them. The dead-end alley would echo worse than a simple street. Or so I hoped.

Mixing wild screams with over-tipped trash cans and taking two lids to bang like cymbals against each other and the antique fire escapes, the result was like a pack of coyotes - rabid zombie dogs - were coming toward them.

I heard their own noises and chanting quiet. And they were scurrying for the openings that weren't there. Because the one thing they feared more than massively multi-organized SWAT teams was the wild animals that survived in these walled cities, that bred like rabbits and trained to survive from pups, to feed on the carrion left by the gangs. They had no fear of humans. And gave no mercy.

Meat was meat to them.

The gang massed and pushed down the alley in a mob, tightly bunched and as fast as they could without leaving anyone behind.

I ducked behind a dumpster and made myself small as they passed.

As they rounded a corner of the alley back out in the street, they separated to avoid the cameras.

And then I turned back to whoever they had attacked in order to save her if I could.

They had left her in a bundle on the ground. Her right wrist was exposed and seeping blood. At least they had left her hand attached.

I pulled out a thin wad of cloth and padding from inside my coat and tore it into strips. Winding them tight around her wrist and hoping they hadn't cut anything serious. I checked the rest of her for other injuries, and only found an ugly bump on the back of her head. Looks like they were only recruiting tonight...

Then I looked around and found an old shopping cart. A blessing. Mysterious Ways, I guess. I picked her light form up and set her as gently as possible inside it, keeping the legs elevated as well as her wrist. Shaking all the dirt I could from an old blanket, I covered the cart and the girl with it, then started moving back to the opening.

We had blocks to cover, if she could make it.

As I pulled my hood up to cover my head, I prayed to all the saints that we did. And my spirits raised with their instant response.

"And miles to go before I sleep..."

III

WHEN I CAME TO, AT least they had left my clothes on me. Torn, bloody, but mostly in one set of pieces.

And someone was standing over me, a respectful distance away, not looking like he wanted to give me more pain.

I sat up, or tried to. Gawd my head hurt. And I was actually loosely tied down to some sort of gurney, one of those rolling hospital beds.

The furthest I got was up on my left elbow, because my right arm was tied down with web strapping.

At least I was still alive.

But when I saw the bandages on my right wrist beyond the webbing, I knew that I was as good as dead already.

So I gingerly laid back on the gurney, so I didn't bump my head again. My eyes hurt and my sinuses burned. Worse than any hangover.

That put my head over to my left, where I saw this this smallish guy looking at me. Dressed in some sort of brown overall, with a brown jacket, and a brown cap.

A Brownie.

I thought they had been run out of the city years ago.

"Well, we were, but some of us came back anyway. Just not wearing brown," came the thought in my head.

"What—-?" I tried to speak.

"Shh-shh-shh. Stay calm," the graveled voice came through my ears this time. "You've been hurt bad, robbed. But you're alive. Been with us a couple of days now. Doc said you had a mild concussion. He'll be happy to know you're awake."

I looked at him. He came closer.

"Yes, I saved you and moved you here." The Brownie kept talking, trying to answer obvious questions and calm me down. "The reason you are tied is because you moved around in your sleep. Your wrist was cut, and we stitched it shut again. But it needs to be still to heel. Here, let me loosen these."

At that he untied the strap holding my arm down, with as much tenderness as he could. And untied the loose sash that was holding me down. Then he moved away with a surprising swiftness I didn't think possible.

The web strapping and sash stayed for me to remove.

I carefully sat up, and the gurney didn't move. It's wheels had been locked. Leaving my right wrist as it lay, I pulled the sash down across my waist, then carefully plucked at the webbing. My wrist was tender and had pain when I moved it. The bandages were tight around some sort of splint that kept it from moving.

"What did you do to my wrist?" I asked.

"My doctor friend had to stop the bleeding and put things back together again. He told me that it would heal in a few weeks, but not to move the bandages for a few days, to leave the splint on so the tissues would mend together," said the Brownie.

"So I have you to thank for saving my life," I said. "What should I call you?"

"Many call me Andrew, but Andy is fine," he answered.

"Did the doctor tell you if the chip was still there?" I asked.

Andy looked down, "No, the gang took it."

Tears started falling from my eyes and my breaths stuck in my chest, coming out as sobs. Each sob causing pain in on side of my chest. I put my splinted right wrist against my chest and covered it tightly with my left hand and arm. Then sobbed my heart out, regardless of how much it hurt me.

Because my life was gone. They had stolen my life. I was already a dead person walking.

IV

SHE WAS SITTING THERE, crying her eyes out, wracked with sobs. And I could do nothing. This was the worst I experience in these cases. The bottom of despair.

So I did what I always did, I prayed. To myself, not aloud. Because people seldom understand the words or the meaning behind them. And use these to fuel their fears instead.

I ask to be filled with your breath of life, as above and so below.

Let me understand true peace as I find it within and surrounding me.

As my thoughts are in me, they are in everyone.

Let me find completeness in all things, and give of myself wholly as I help others accept my giving.

Help me find my way in wholeness. To become, to act, to assist.

And so I confirm with our soul.

Her eyes were wide at this, the tears having left to run down her cheeks and absorb into her dirty and bloody clothing. She then recited as best she could remember:

"Our Father who art in Heaven, Hallowed be thy name. Thy Kingdom come, they Will be done, on Earth the same as Heaven. Give us this day our bread, and forgive us as we forgive others, For You are the wholeness and power and glory forever. Amen,"

Her smile seemed to light up the room. Without makeup of any kind, her short hair tousled, and the street dirt streaked down her face, this was a very honest smile.

I knew that Grace had found a home in her, that she understood something in her core.

"I remember that old saying from my childhood, well, as much as I can," she said. "And the people who come by our corporate reception each week to pass out their slips of paper. I've read these words. Only now do I seem to get a hint of their real meaning."

"There are many meanings. And the one you choose is the one best for you," I replied.

Her smile was contagious and I smiled back. I opened my arms wide with my palms facing her.

"Come," she said. And her arms were wide as well.

I came over to her and gently put my own arms around her.

She winced, but still kept her arms around my back. And I could feel her tears start again, as they fell to my own exposed neck.

At last she loosened her arms and I was able to move back.

"Cracked ribs, my doctor friend said. You will have to rest here for a few days while you decide what you want to do," I said.

She moved her left arm down her side under her shirt, and she felt the strapped ribs underneath. "So you've seen all of me?"

"We did have to unclothe you to check for broken bones and any cuts. There was a lot of blood. So we cleaned you up as best we could and then re-dressed you," I answered. "We didn't find any other clothing around the area where you were found, but they brought back some cleaner clothes about your size if you'd like to change into them."

Her face went downcast. And her breathing rough again, as if she were going to start sobbing. That wouldn't be good for her ribs.

"What should I call you?" I asked.

Her head down, something came out muffled, but I didn't get it. "Could you tell me again?" Another muffle.

I stepped closer and put a hand softly on her shoulder. She then looked into my eyes. A time passed where we simply looked at each other.

"Michael, er, Mica." and then paused. "Oh hell. Michelle is my birth-name," she said. Then looked away.

"Is that what you want to be called?" I asked.

"It doesn't much matter. You know my sex, you know more about me than anyone is allowed to know. And you know I'm unaltered," she spit out.

"All of us are part and parcel of the Greater One, so whatever you want to be is your choice. Andrew isn't the name I was given, either," I said. "My birth name was Farley, which means roughly, 'found in the bull pasture.'"

She smiled at this. "Were you raised on a farm?"

I smiled back, "Yes, but not in a pasture. And we didn't have cattle, mostly goats and sheep. They are easier to protect from wolves and coyotes."

"So why are you here, and why did you save me?" Michelle asked.

"That is my calling, what I hear to do. I just trusted my feet to take me into the direction I needed to go. And they led me to you just in time," I answered.

"How did you get into the city? They don't let Brownies in. 'Dissent and insurrection isn't tolerated,' as the Edict is wrote," she said.

"But they do need things fixed. I repaired the outer gate for them on my way in. And if you smile and nod enough, then they think you're harmless. They can always use some broken things fixed. Like that gate. They were afraid to go out that far and had just put up with it scraping and screeching for a long time it looked like. Anyway, it was an easy fix they didn't need to be afraid of. Old teachings tend to die slowly, though," I said.

"Meaning you fix people, too, and your feet said I needed fixing," Michelle said.

"Something like that," I answered. But you must be hungry by now. Let me help you down and I'll bring you some food. Sit over here and I'll be right back..."

V

THE FOOD WAS VERY GOOD. A thick soup, kinda like a thin stew. Made from what I didn't care. It tasted great and filled a gnawing hole in my stomach area.

Of course, I didn't say a word as I wolfed it down. But my smile said tons when I looked at Andrew again.

"I wondered if I would ever see your smile. It makes you look - better," he said.

"Better?" I asked. "Did you want to say something different?"

"Well, I don't mean to offend, but yes. I wanted to say your smile makes you look - pretty," Andy said, with worry lines on his forehead.

I smiled back, regardless. "That's something I haven't heard in years. Probably not since I left home. We weren't aloud to gendrify our compliments at school or anywhere else. Because it would offend someone, somehow."

"Yes, people seem to get offended so easily. And there are even more laws - edicts - protecting the offended than the rights of the innocent 'offender'," said Andy. His worry turned into a frown as he looked down into his own empty bowl. Without looking up, he asked, "Would you like some more?"

"Andy." I said, waiting until he looked at me again. "I am the least offensive person you have ever met. It was my job, until a few days ago to be completely inoffensive. And I was very good at it."

Andy smiled at this. And it made his face look - handsome.

"Well, that relieves me," he said. "My job is mostly to be the most unoffensive person around, and that is my protection as well, I guess. Other than prayer."

"If anyone was offended from our meeting, it should have been me. You saw me naked and knew my sex. Something I've had to hide all my life," I said.

Andrew's smile turned to a puzzled look, "How is that? The gangs don't hide their sex, other than those dark hoodies they wear. But it's pretty obvious."

"It was all started after the first Gay-In-Chief and his Trans wife were murdered a few years after he went out of office. Of course this is ancient history. But what I was taught in school is that the pivot point of the Great Tolerance Movement started there. Their advocates started with 'Cagga and N'Yack, and S'atl, then S'angels. There were resolutions by the DC 'Gress to allow states to do more of what they wanted, particularly the bigger cities among them. And then it wasn't long before the secessions started. That led to necessary protective Walls."

Andy relaxed his face. "Oh that's what they taught you. Here, our bowls need filling again before the soup-run starts. I'll be right back."

Soon he returned with our bowls filled, and I felt more inclined to take my time emptying it now.

"Andy, what's your version of what happened?" I asked.

"Well, it's something that is a bit murky. Because people don't like to talk about it. 'Live and let live' is more an operating motto than a trite saying out beyond the walls. The short answer is that they don't want what the cities have almost as much as the cities don't want to share - or receive *anything* from Flyover Country.

"Once N'Yack and Cagga seceded, they started building walls around their legal limits to keep everyone out. And the Fed's Army kept people from going in or out while they did. To avoid a Constitutional Crisis, they said, but it was obvious that they were already in one.

"And yes, it was the surprise death of both the Gay and his Trans that started it all. Because the leaked coroner results confirmed that it was suicide, they both were male and had some incurable disease that they shared. So they made the accident look like some conspiracy had done it to them.

"But the Press took off with the 'vast right wing conspiracy' again, and pushed for physical separation from the rest of the 'deplorable' country. The media kept the push up until the rest of the country was tired of it and let them go. Along with their tiring media.

"The cities built the walls at their own expense, and more cities joined the movement. S'atl was simple, but S'angels had riots as people didn't want to be part of that city. So they walled off most of the downtown city and fought to keep a harbor out of it. The riots were very messy.

"Feds kept their troops out of it. Cities didn't want them and their assault rifles. S'cramento state government moved down into L'angels for what good it did them, as they couldn't tax anything beyond their own walls. So the farmers and small business people moved in and started up a new government.

"Frisco kept their harbor, and so there was regular packet runs up and down the coast for years. S'Dego opened their border to Mexico, and so they have access to manufactured goods that they trade for electronics up coast. But those are the only four cities that have any real trade agreements. Like a country of their own, more or less."

Andy went back to eating, lost in thought as I was. Between us, we had a lot of differences to sort out, but at least we could share.

"Why did this gang go after me?" I asked. "'Andro', they called me. Does that now mean that they are offended by androgynous people?"

"I'm afraid you are exactly right. They are offended by the people trying to be the most inoffensive." Andy replied. "They just moved in a few days ago, forming a new coalition to run the streets. Meaning the section mob boss wanted higher profits, so knocked some heads together to get more cooperation."

"And my apartment was in the wrong location for the new territory," I sighed. "But the housing closer to my job cost more than I could get paid. Unless I wanted to sell my body to some exec there. And that wouldn't last long."

I sat back and remembered some of the dates I'd had. Some had ended violently, the worst being the female dates. Although the guys who wanted gay sex would leave me sore enough.

A large gong-sounding alarm went off. I jumped.

"Oh, that's just the noon bell. It actually is a bell. This warehouse was built into the back of an old church. The bell sounds off for the soup line," Andy rose and scooped up the two bowls and spoons. "Come, we could use your help."

I looked down at my clothes and felt my face.

"No, you're dressed and look just fine. You'll be seeing worse. Come on, this way." With that Andy moved off smoothly, like a dancer glides through a practiced move.

He opened a large door on the side of the room, and I followed...

VI

WE ENTERED WHAT USED to be a huge church, in one of the transepts, or side branches of the cross formed in a traditional Catholic church layout. This side held a long layout of tables, which had a huge cast-iron stove supporting two immense low kettles on it, steaming. The tables went off in a straight line down its center, almost to where it met the nave.

Behind the stove and long tables were rolling racks of various breads. Two people were putting some of these trays out on the tables as we entered.

They looked up at us when we entered. Andy introduced me, "Sam, Dolly, this is Michelle. She's going to be on the soup kettle today and I'll be assisting her. Could you two manage the breads OK?"

Dolly came right up and gave me a big hug, while Sam looked on with a smile.

Her curly blond hair seemed familiar to me.

"Michelle!" she stood back with her hands on both my shoulders. "It's been sooo long, I always wondered what became of you!"

I looked into her eyes above her wide smile and freckled nose. "Dolls - that's you isn't it?" And I hugged her as best I could with the splint on that right arm. "I was so worried when you disappeared."

Now she held my good left hand in her right. "I know, it was days before I could get around, and by then I couldn't prove who I was, so there was no severance pay to pick up." Dolly turned her right wrist over to show her scar. "At least I got all the motion back in it. I was lucky. Some people bleed out when they cut the whole hand off. But under the new boss, that's forbidden. He likes people who can work." She looked down at my splinted right hand. "Just recently arrived, I guess. Well, I'm sooo happy to see you again. Oh, I'd better get ready. This is a tough crowd to entertain."

Another brief hug and she was off down the road. She hugged Sam and whispered something in his ear.

Andy came up behind me and said my name quietly before putting a light hand on my shoulder, still making me jump. "Oh, I'm sorry. But we need to get over to the soup. You just ladle with your left hand and keep your right away from the hot soup and stove. I'll hold the bowls for you to fill. One scoop will do it. You'll do just fine."

When we got there, the line had started. I was too busy to notice much after that, since the line moved so quickly.

Andy kept up a steady patter as he kept filling bowls hand-after-hand. He would recognize people and try to talk with them, smiling all the time. While he got a lot of surly looks, most were responsive. Sam and Dolly were also handing out smiles with every piece of bread, so this also lightened almost everyone's mood. The bouncers came last. These were the biggest of the bunch, and had kept the crowd from just rolling in on their own and swamping us. They had kept everyone into a single-file line. Two smaller figures accompanied them, one was holding extra bread and the other a tray to hold four bowls - I figured the big guys got their second helpings in advance.

There was a break in the action at that point, so Andy brought over a tall 5-gallon pot of soup to refill the two low kettles. He nodded at me to get out of the way as he lifted the steaming pots to pour them. I was too happy to move away from that steam, as the sweat was running in streams down my face, and my bandaged arm was not very absorbent. I took that break to grab a cloth towel and do a proper mop of my face and neck.

"Here, let me help you." Dolly had come over after refilling the table. "We've got a bit of a break now." She pulled out a good-sized bandanna, held it by opposite corners, then flipped it into a simple headband. I held my head down a bit while she tied it into place. I was about a head taller than her, but she still reached up to tweak it into place for me..

Dolly then put her arm across my back and leaned her head on my shoulder. "Are they taking care of you? You were my favorite at the Corp."

I patted her hand with my good one. "Well, I'm still alive, but a bit worse for wear. And thanks for the vote of confidence. It was tough filling your shoes when you didn't come in that day. I'm glad to see things worked out for you."

"As best as things can when you're taken off the grid and become a nobody. I heard the Anti-Andro's got you. For me, it was the Feminista's. They thought they could recruit me after they cut out my chip and beat me up, but it wasn't a smart recruiting tool. Sam rescued me and I've been working here ever since."

"What is this place?" I asked. "It seems pretty organized."

"It actually is. The city provides the food and we cook it up. The mob boss makes sure that the gangs in this area cooperate with each other. This is a truce area. Everyone has to eat, so no one gets hurt here. No one is allowed to take offense or incite anything. And that goes out for about a block in all directions." Dolly rattled off, without taking her head off my shoulder.

Sam was still setting some trays out, quietly, looking our way occasionally, but with a quiet smile on his face.

Dolly saw me looking at him. "Isn't he just the cutest thing on two legs? I'm just so in love with him I could just spit. Waking up beside him every morning is the best day of my life, every day. Oh look, you've got to meet the Doc."

A tall, gaunt man came up, dressed as much in dark clothing as the rest, but somewhat more refined. He wore a regular suit jacket and dark shirt, but they were cleaner than most. Some plastic gloves stuck slightly out of one pocket and part of a stethoscope peeked out of the other.

He put his bread and soup bowl down on the table. "May I?" The Doc pointed to my splinted wrist.

I held it up for him and he felt it carefully. I noticed he was missing a couple of fingers off his own right hand.

"Looks like we got you plugged OK. Just keep that on and try not to itch it. I'll be around tomorrow to change that bandage and look for any infection. If it starts throbbing, let Andy know. He knows how to get in touch with me." Doc picked up his bread roll and soup along with a spoon and moved along, taking a seat at the far end of the transept, at a short table that sat next to the door that Andy and I came in.

As I looked after him, Dolly returned to my side again. "Doc had a rough one. He said something that ticked off some guv'ment official, who made sure that he not only lost his chip, but also any chance of being a surgeon again. So he works here and patches up the people that the gangs leave alive and in one piece. He also patches up people after the fights. But the new mob boss - the 'Don' - he mostly keeps people from getting two serious at each other. Bad for business, he says, (mocking a deep, gruff voice) 'We need people to do the jobs around here, not fill incinerators.'" Dolly smiled at her little joke.

All this background was a bit much for me. I turned and leaned against one of the tables.

"Oh, Michelle - this has got to be tiring for you. Here, I've got a roll for each of us, let's go see if we can talk to Doc. Andy's already there, so is Sam."

She took my good arm in hers and put a roll in my hand while she bit off a piece of the other for herself. She nudged me forwards and we soon sidled up on the benches by the table.

I wound up squeezing in next to Andy, who in turn squeezed Doc. Dolly pushed right up next to Sam, even though that left nearly half the bench empty. Dolly was always friendly. Sam took it in stride and put his arm around her. That left his soup hand free, and Dolly fed him pieces of bread she tore off her bun. Both were lost in their shared world.

Andy and I were nibbling on our own bun with one hand, while the Doc used his two arms. He liked the soup and it showed.

"Well, Doc, any news?" Andy asked.

"Finally got a decent night's sleep, first in months," Doc replied. "The new Don has enforced the new boundaries. And told them to lay off the corporate types. As long as they keep paying him, they'll have their safety on the streets. Michelle, you were the last straw. Seems someone liked you a lot, or you are too hard to replace. Since they basically have to raise their replacements nowadays, there aren't many people who are ready to fill your job."

I sat up straighter at that.

Andy smiled wistfully at that. "But unfortunately that doesn't mean you'll get your job back. Because they can't prove you exist. Your chip was spent and destroyed, so all your personal DNA data is gone. Anyone that looks remotely like you could apply."

I added, "But the Corp destroyed that chip as soon as they got the cops to track it down for them. Company policy. CYA, basically." Slumping down again, I had nowhere to go. I couldn't even go back to my old apartment to get my things - the gangs probably cleaned up someone to look like me and used my chip to get in and clean it all out. Moving day. I was broke and homeless.

Andy nudged me with his shoulder. "But you're here now and we can help you."

Dolly stopped feeding Sam and they both looked over. "Yea, Michelle, we get to help you sort everything out. And we needed some more help in our little kitchen anyway."

Another doleful gong sounded.

"That's our cue." Dolly stuffed the last piece of roll in Sam's mouth, then kissed him on the cheek. She took Sam's bowl and spoon and slid off the smooth bench, almost skipping back up to the food line.

"Another sitting coming in," Sam explained. He nodded to Doc, who grunted and went back to his eating.

I slid out and pocketed the rest of my roll in what I hoped was a fairly clean pocket on my left side. Andy followed, but stuffed his roll in his mouth to chew and swallow as he walked next to me.

Ahead, another pair of bouncers were keeping their particular gang in check. Some of the other members that weren't in line were cleaning up after the gang before. Doleful looks all around.

Sam whispered to me, standing on my left again by the soup kettles, "They are always a bit grumpy when they come in, but the medicine that cures all that is cheerfulness - and good smelling and good tasting food."

At that, the bouncers let the first in line come through, holding the next behind them back so that there was an orderly flow of people.

At the end, the bouncers came along with their little helpers.

Then the second bouncer stopped and looked at my face closely. "Don't I know you?"

The whole church got quiet quickly.

VII

"WE HAD SOME BUSINESS not too far from here last night. And someone got a bit personal with me. Kicked me where they shouldn't have. Still hurts."

The bouncer was looking at Michelle closely, and her splinted wrist.

"Why don't you go and take a pee in this and I'll see if you had any permanent damage," Doc held a plastic cup in front of his face, standing next to him by the kettle. "Or should I ask the Don if you should have some time off and a full checkup?"

The bouncer glared at Doc for what seemed like a full minute, then looked back at Michelle. "Nah, a little girl like you couldn't kick that hard. This was an Andro, anyway. It deserved what it got." The bouncer turned with his full soup bowl and two rolls in his other hand, then stalked out of the transept to join the rest of his gang in the nave.

"Thanks, Doc," I said. "This place is takes long enough to clean up as it is."

"Don't mention it, Andy," Doc replied. "The Don will hear about it anyway. That big meathead deserved far more than that, I'm sure." At that the Doc went back down the now empty line and picked up another roll to stuff in one of his pockets as he strode off through the other trancept. Another door on its far end let him out to the street.

Michelle relaxed and slumped. I put my hand on her shoulder. "The truce is older than the current Don, even though he enforces it better. Doc has some unofficial pull with his guv'ment connections. The work he does out here keeps their hospital clear of some of the less 'disciplined' gang members. And the hospitals can concentrate on the ulcers and plastic surgery of the more toady Corp execs that way."

I looked her in the eyes directly, "You're safe here. Know that."

Dolly came up and hugged her on the other side, while Sam was again refilling the bread trays down the long table-row.

"I've got to get these kettles filled up again. One more serving after this one. Then we'll be able to clean up everything and start cooking the next one."

Dolly squeezed her one last time and then stepped off to help Sam.

I let Michelle rest to the side while I loaded up the serving kettles one last time.

Soon the church bell gonged again, and the third gang came in. This was uneventful. We started cleaning up after the last of them were served. A few grabbed some leftover buns on their way out, but carefully. Any disrespectful actions would get reported to the Don and he hated to have to police such a small thing as table manners. As it was, the bouncers glared at those few the entire time, closing the door behind them.

Dolly went out to clear the tables and wipe them down with disinfectant. Sam was trundling the empty bread racks out to another room. I showed Michelle how we opened small petcocks in the bottom of the big kettles to drain the residual soup out. "Then they have a little hinge contraption that raises them on their sides for cleaning," I explained. The leftover soup and bread goes out to some homeless who aren't part of gangs and won't or can't come into the church."

I poured a bucket of hot water and disinfectant soap and another bucket of hot rinse water, handing the scrubbers to Michelle. "You don't have to do anything besides look pretty and hold these," I teased. Her face cracked into a smile. "You've been on your feet a lot today, when rest is what you need. Fortunately, this is a sit-down job."

I put down the two buckets and pulled a couple of chairs over. Michelle gratefully sat in one while I cleaned out the kettles by hand. While I normally whistled at this, I hummed a tune instead, just in case Michelle wanted to talk.

She was just as happy just to sit and do nothing. Certainly a change from her job at the Corp. And she had been through so many changes the last couple of days.

And miles to go before she slept. Well, before she slept peacefully, anyway.

At last the cleaning was done and we left the transept. The light switches were by the same door we'd come in earlier.

The room turned dark despite it being early afternoon.

VIII

LIFE HAD SETTLED DOWN into a bit of a pattern of running the soup kitchen and sleeping a lot to heal my cracked ribs and other strained body parts.

One day, Andy took me to another "Free Zone" where the gangs had to stay out of, where only the Don's and their guests could come. Doc went with us, or perhaps we were his guest. Guests of a guest. Something like that.

It was a beautiful day. Fleecy clouds in a deep blue sky. Sun shadowed us behind the tall high-rises. Walking on pristine concrete walks with cast-iron and shiny slatted wood benches which faced a long reflecting pool at intervals. I guess some architect thought city people needed reflection from time to time.

I certainly did.

The Doc left us to take another bench down a few hundred feet from us. We were all watching the pool cleaners at work, and the gardeners tend to grass clipping and bush trimming. This was the other reason we were here. We watched as the cleaners found a reason to come near Doc, one at a time, and have short conversations with him. They'd then leave to get back to their jobs.

Andy explained, "He has a bunch of regular patients. This is his regular rounds for them. If you watch closely, you can see him hand out little pill packages. When he holds their hand, he's taking their pulse. Some of these guys the Dons owe a favor to, others they want to keep on a short leash. So Doc keeps an eye on their physical and mental health and reports to their respective Don about how they are doing.

"Doc has found his own peace at this. No stress of the hospital rules. And he's always available for emergencies. Doesn't do dental work or eyesight stuff, but has some connections for that.

"It's all a system that allows everyone to live and let live." Andy was silent for awhile after that.

"Live and let live. You've said that before. I've just never seen it work," I said.

"Well, Michelle, you've led a sheltered life, even if you don't think so," said Andy.

My face scrunched up at that. "Sheltered?"

Andy smiled. "What I meant by that is that this city, any city, only allows a certain kind of thinking in it. Like that idea that you have to avoid offending anyone to survive. But actually, that is one of the most offensive things you can do."

"Like acting androgynous and getting beat up by the Anti-Andro gang?" I asked.

"Well, there's that. But the point I was making is when you are offending yourself." Andy replied. "That's far more dangerous than getting beat up."

I turned toward him. My right hand was now free of splint and bandages. And my hair was long enough to need tucking behind an ear. "What do you mean? I've never heard of this before."

"The idea is that your own individuality is important. By trying to get your security from outside you, to expect approval from others, to spend your whole life under someone else's control or working to escape from it - that is when you have threatened your own personal being. And so you find yourself afraid all the time. That fear will kill you off sooner or later," Andy said.

I thought about this carefully. Fear is all I had known my entire life. Even when I was a kid, my childhood was in two worlds. But fear was present in both. No place was truly safe. As I grew older, this city had become even more violent. Only when the Dons started coordinating between themselves did things even out.

"Are you sure?" I asked. "Is it that simple?"

"'Heaven is within you.' 'As you think in your heart, so are you.' All those old phrases add up to one point. You have to respect yourself to find yourself. Then you don't need anyone else's approval, only your own. You'll find that your security comes from within, as all you need is your own self-control. Then anything you are afraid of disappears." Andy said.

We were quiet for awhile at this.

"But where to I start? That is my whole life I've been living like this." I asked.

"Breathe." Andy said.

"Huh?" I asked

"Just take a deep breath, hold it for a second or two, and then let it out." Andy said. "Like this." And he showed me. "Now you try."

I took a deep breath and exhaled slowly like him.

"Feel the relaxation that happens when you do?" Andy asked.

I nodded.

"That's letting go. Whenever you feel tense or upset, develop the habit of taking a deep breath before you speak or act. Then whatever is triggering you will move off and you'll find a bit of peace in you. That peace is you, part of you. The more peace you can build inside of you is how you get more peace outside of you." Andy said.

That all made sense somehow. I didn't know how, but I knew this was a workable piece of truth.

We looked out at the reflective pool and the clouds above as reflected from above.

Too soon, the peacefulness was ended. Doc came over, walking easily. His hands in his pockets.

"Well, have you two love birds gotten everything sorted out?" He asked.

"I... I mean, Andy..." I stuttered.

"Oh you haven't seen this coming?" Doc asked. He tut-tutted. "I didn't think that head thump you'd gotten had affected your thinking."

My face turned red. I looked at Andy.

He just smiled back at me. "Doc sometimes sees things that other people don't. He surprises me all the time." Andy said. "But it is time to go, and we did have a good time today, didn't we?"

I nodded and stood.

Doc smiled and led away, while we followed.

I took Andy's hand as we walked along. It felt good, even if someone else had to point out the obvious.

And that's when I learned to accept and start becoming Michelle for real.

IX

SOME WEEKS LATER, AFTER the last gang of the day had left, one of them came back and handed Andy a note. He read it quickly and then stuffed it in his pocket with a frown. That day we cleaned the kettles in silence. Andy lightened up, but didn't whistle or hum as we cleaned.

We cleaned out the deep sinks after everything else, rinsing them with the last of the hot rinse water, now only lukewarm, and opening the double-sink hot-water tap to clean the last of that water as well. Sponges and scours went on a stainless shelf above the sink and we were done.

I followed Andy out of the transept, and he turned out the lights out of habit, but I grabbed the door and his hand before he could absent-mindedly shut me into that dark.

Out into the warehouse, I stopped him by grabbing his hand. "Andy, what is it?"

"I'm going to have to leave. Something has come up. I'll be leaving tonight." Andy replied.

"OK, I'm coming with you." I said.

"No, I..." and he looked in my eyes. The determination he saw there just made him shrug. "Well, I guess I know you well enough by now to know I can't talk you out of it." He smiled at me.

I leaned over and pecked a kiss on his cheek. "No, you're right, as usual."

"But it's going to be a bit tricky. Brownies can't come and go as they want. And you're not even a Brownie." Andy said.

"Where you go, I go." I said. And crossed my arms to make that point.

Andy just smiled. "OK, Michelle. You win. Get a small bag if you need one. You'll only be able to wear what you have on, so if you need a change of underwear or socks, put two sets on."

X

I FOUND MICHELLE AN old coat and a slouch hat. Then I taught her how to look at the ground and walk hunched over. With a little practice, she picked it right up. I had Dolly work over her hair and give it a different temporary color.

Walking on the borders we got to the main security exit just before twilight and traveled the long empty block between barbed wire and mesh fences. It was built originally as a double-wide highway, and it dwarfed us.

Michelle's shuffle made her look shorter than I was. And I also had her cough as she walked, every few steps.

By the time we finally shuffled up to the security booth, we had been scanned and re-scanned. Neither of us had chips, and our faces weren't in their systems.

One of the guards came up to us and grabbed off our hats. "Gotta see your faces. Rules." He thumbed up at a faded sign on the security booth outer wall.

When he pulled off Michelle's hat, he stared at her and dropped her hat on the ground, taking a step back. I looked over at her and had to work to keep my own calm.

Michelle then went into a paroxysm of coughing, and I lightly patted her back. Her hands were on both knees and she spit onto the pavement at her feet. I picked up her hat and handed it to her. She put it back on her head and then leaned on me for support, her head on my shoulder, an arm around my neck. The cap again covered her features.

The guard had started back-stepping once he saw her face, and almost fell through the guard shack door with it's raised step inside. Quickly sliding the door shut, he said something that was unintelligible and pointed out the gate.

He hit a switch inside with his fist and the gates started rolling out of our way. Not fast enough for him, he pounded the button again and again.

We started slowly toward the gate and made our way through it before it was all the way open, where it started closing again. The second and third gates were all open for us as well.

Once through the third gate (it nearly closed on us) we still had to keep up the charade for another mile until we could hit a bend in the road. The dark was closing in fast, which was a help.

Their microphones on each side, as well as cameras meant we still had to keep quiet. Well, except for Michelle's regular coughing.

Although the emergency sirens were wailing as their Haz-Mat team rolled up to clean up that area Michelle had spit on.

Finally out of their sight and hearing, we moved off the paved road and into some real dark.

I took off her hat and looked at her makeup job through the light from the few remaining street lamps.

"Where did you learn to do that?" I asked.

"I had to do a lot of makeup at my old job. And I also had to know the indicators of that plague they thought they'd eradicated. That coughing bit kept him from realizing that those lesions he thought he was seeing were just a layer of face paint." Michelle replied.

I took her in my arms and kissed her, face paint and all.

Then I showed her the note.

It was in my own handwriting: "It's time to go." That's all it said.

She punched me in the gut at that and then gave me a big hug.

We walked to the next town arm in arm as the stars started coming out in the moonlit sky.

The Case of the Forever Cure

BY C. C. BROWER AND J. R. Kruze

• • • •

As hinted earlier, here's where the Lazurai turn into a secret, hidden asset...

• • • •

I

IT'S HARD DETECTIVE work when you could only interview through thick glass while wearing a hazmat suit.

It's worse when you're trying to find out why someone is healing the terminally ill and being very successful at it.

Because since this one nurse took over, people had quit dying.

But the hospital wouldn't let them out of quarantine. Until my investigation was complete.

No pressure.

The second problem was how I was getting paid. All in cash, Random serial numbers, unmarked and used bills. Occasionally someone included a note, printed out by a laser printer on common paper stock. No fingerprints on anything. Completely anonymous.

And all I wanted was they stay off my back if they wanted to keep it that way.

Because this coin had two faces. Let me do my job finding what you asked me to, or I'd find out the flip side as well.

That was the message I sent the last time I got a note from them with advice on it. And no more notes since.

I told them three weeks. Period. I'd solve it or give them their money back. Minus expenses.

No notes since. And I had under a week left, with no leads. Yes, I was getting a bit nervous.

But I didn't have to deal with perfectly healthy people who weren't even allowed to talk to their family. Or me.

It all depended on this one head nurse named Cathy.

II

IT WASN'T ANY REAL surprise to me that these patients started getting better.

But my methods were unorthodox, and had been kept a secret for nearly half a century at this point. I was called in as a last resort by some very insistent, and very connected family of one of the patients.

And now he's fine, but neither I or him or anyone else can talk to anyone outside.

Well, I've got this detective fellow named Johnson who somehow wangled a way into my over-booked schedule. 30 minutes a day. Uninterrupted. And that's a miracle all on its own.

Typically, we are understaffed. And all volunteer. None of us were expected to ever return from the quarantine. But all their doctors and nurses had gotten ill as well, so they'd asked - no, begged for people to basically suicide in order to help these people live out their last days with some sort of dignity.

They got half the number they wanted, which was twice what they actually expected.

But they were city folks. Pretty cold and pessimistic. Hard to get a smile out of them.

And that was our secret weapon - infectious smiles. Works every time. Because you have to heal from the inside out, not just pile on more drugs and pills.

The main trouble was with the quarantine security equipment. The technicians to fix it were also sick. If that equipment failed before we got this outbreak under control, it would roll through all the population of this suburb and those beyond it like no plague before it. And the infected would spread it further, all within a few hours of contacting it. All innocent carriers.

What was worst, it left babies alone. The ones that needed help the most. That was why we were here, originally. To solve why the babies weren't getting sick - and feed them and change them and cuddle them meanwhile.

But when the last of the nurses collapsed, we had to break into the worst areas and sacrifice ourselves. Because the walls were all glass, and we could see the entire ward from the maternity section. Damned if we were just going to stand there and watch them all die...

III

IN BETWEEN OUR TALKS, I had access to all their electronic reports, and all the medical files on the patients. Mainly because I was authorized by the CDC to snoop anywhere I needed to. This meant their families and their family's lawyers were all purposely kept out of the loop. Privacy be damned if you knew you had a plague that could cripple civilization starting with everyone around you.

Of course, they made me sign huge stacks of non-disclosure agreements and bonds that would keep me in hock for the rest of my life, if not in prison.

The money was good, so I took it. All untraceable cash, but I told you that already. And I already made plans to disappear after this, since more than likely they'd make me disappear permanent-like, otherwise.

All those electronic reports didn't give me much besides headaches. I was going over them for the fourth time. It wasn't adding up.

Sure, you had the babies that didn't get sick. But only when these student nurses and their barely graduated head nurse broke quarantine to take over was when the patients started getting better.

All I knew is that whatever they were doing wasn't in these reports.

They were keeping something from me. But so were the people who hired me.

My daily half-hour was coming up. Just enough time to get into that damned hazmat suit again and go through decontamination just to get into the interview cubicle.

Maybe this time, I'd get something I could use. Like my gramma used to say, "Hope springs eternal."

Whatever.

IV

"HEY CATHY, HOW'S IT going?"

"Fine, Detective Johnson, how's the real world?"

"Call me Reg, OK?"

"OK, Reg-OK - how's the real world" She smiled at her own joke. Something that lightened her tired face.

I had to smile at that, which just made hers wider. "At least you've got some time for humor, even if sleep is tight."

"Sleep is always tight for nurses, but we make do."

"Well, over to questions, then. I've been over and over your reports and I just don't get it. How come you and your students don't get sick from what your patients have?"

"We've been over this ground before, Reg. It's our proprietary training and our faith in that training."

"But you don't seem to be doing anything different, other than you ignore safety protocols and do what seems to be normal nursing actions."

"And we didn't have time or the necessary suits available when we had to break quarantine to save the life of that nurse. After that, it's of little consequence. We are still alive and that again goes back to our faith."

That line of questioning was getting me nowhere, as usual. Science didn't account for faith more than a placebo effect. "Your student nurses and you all come from very small towns, and it looks like you were all adopted."

Her eyebrow raised. "That's of no concern to you. Our methods could be taught to anyone. It might be that our students have more personal moral values than those found in larger metropolitan areas. Or maybe it goes to the love of our families, which again goes back to that 'faith' point you find so disturbing."

I hadn't realized my face gave away so much. "I don't mean to question your faith..."

"Don't you? Are you quite certain? You've almost done nothing but. And if it weren't for those children, we wouldn't be here and we shouldn't be having these questions. And if whoever is paying you had an ounce of courage, they'd come right out and see this scene for themselves." Her frown deepened as she leaned toward the glass.

"I'm sorry to offend you and I don't..."

"Don't give me that 'sorry to offend' crap! Just like those insane 'Tolerance Edicts.' All they've done has been to harass a lot of innocent people who just want to live the life they were given. A small minority few don't have more rights than anyone else..."

"Cathy, Cathy, please. I'm sorry, OK? Sorry. You look much prettier when you aren't upset, and I'm sure your job goes easier as well. How 'Cagga and the Secessionists treat people should be none of our concern. How your nurses are actually curing your patients is all I want to find out."

She calmed at this, a little bit. "I'm sorry, too, Reg. I'd prefer to be smiling more. These long hours have us all a bit on edge."

"Is that singing something you do as part of your training?"

"Oh, well that singing is between us nurses. It's not part of nurse training, but are just some hymns from my local church that seem to help everyone keep their spirits up."

"I see from the video's that some of the patients are singing along now. Most of them were unconscious when you went in there."

She had to smile at this. "Yes, we're finding that they have some healthy lungs in there. Probably good exercise for their Cardiod-pulmonary. Mr. Smith has an amazing baritone, and Clara - she insists we call her that - has a contralto good enough to sing a church solo." She looked away. "I don't know if you can hear it from there, but they just hit that chorus on 'Little Brown Church in the Wild-wood.'" Cathy was nodding her head. "Singing helps everyone."

At that point, the buzzer went off. I had minutes to get into decontamination before the interview area would be showered from overhead nozzles. It happened once before. Made talking impossible.

Cathy stood with graceful ease. "See you tomorrow." She smiled and gave me a half-wave.

From that angle, I could see my own reflection and how impersonal and bureaucratic I looked.

I rose to leave, and she was already gone, her own door closing automatically behind her.

V

"SO – CATHY, DID HE ask anything different today?" A blond student asked.

"No, Sue, just more of the same."

"Mr. Smith wants to get out of bed today, insisting I let him or bring you to him so he can talk you into it."

I just smiled at her. "I'm sure he'd love to 'talk' with me. With his hands where they shouldn't go. Ever notice that I hold both of his hands when I'm near him?"

"More like I noticed that I need to start doing that myself. He's very personal with his touches. Must be feeling a lot better."

I shook my head, still smiling. "Give him a broom and have him start using his hands to clean up the store room. Just make sure those meds are locked up first. If he's still frisky after that, he can pull some hot water and start mopping. Just not around the other patients where we have to walk. Use some ammonia in it, and he'll be doing us all a favor with the smells in this place."

Sue nodded and moved off.

I picked up the charts and found we had seemed to turn the corner for all of them. I remembered how my teacher, Rochelle, cautioned against optimism that we would be able to save all our patients all the time. "Only faith works miracles..." was her phrase for it. The rest of it was "...and trust in God to fix what humans screw up." A bit sardonic for her, but it got the point across for us, especially now.

That reminded me to check the babies again. That's what really kept us going around here. Some of them would be trying to walk if they were kept here much longer. Already most were into higher-walled beds they couldn't climb over - yet.

Another reason to smile and hope.

Rochelle would be proud of us all - if we were ever allowed to call her...

VI

THAT NIGHT, ALARMS went off.

I jumped from my cot in the administration room and reached for a non-existent gun in a missing holster. Habit.

Lights were strobing and it took me minutes to figure out where the stupid off-switch was. I turned the lights to "On-Full" and saw the problem.

Our only remaining maintenance tech was out cold on the floor. I felt his head - fever. And foam coming out of his mouth.

Contagion.

So I did what I needed to do. I pulled him up in a fireman's carry and went right through all the double doors I needed to so we were both in with Cathy, the nurses, and the other quarantined patients.

Cathy looked up and rushed toward me. Sue was already motioning me to an empty bed near the doors I'd just barged in through.

They both went to work taking his vitals and hooking up the monitors. I found a chair that was out of their way and dropped into it.

About then, the situation sank in. I was one of the walking dead, now. Maybe minutes before I got infected myself and into the same state as Carlos, our last tech in this death trap.

Cathy turned around and saw me, then gave me a sad smile. "No, it's not that bad. Come with me." She bent down and grabbed my hand, pulling me upright to follow her. I'd have sworn I was being pulled by a half-back from the line of scrimmage. So much power in such a small package.

She took me into the same room with the babies and over to where one was crying. Picking up the curly-headed tyke, she pushed him into my arms, putting a towel over one of my shoulders. "Walk him up and down the floor until he goes back to sleep. Then take another one that your alarms woke up and repeat the process. Your job is to get all these kids back to sleep. No, they are perfectly safe in your hands, and as long as you keep holding one, they'll keep you from being infected any more than you already are."

She winked at me. "So? Get walking. That's your prescription." Then spun on her heel to see how the new patient was doing.

I walked and walked the rest of that night. I got them all to quit crying after awhile, but it didn't mean they didn't want to be walked. One or more of them would be standing up in their crib looking at me with hopeful, round eyes. I'd always smile and start again.

I guess that was the point. Smiling was something to do with their method. And I had to have faith in their method. Or I'd be dead in days.

VII

ONE OF THE OTHER STUDENT nurses came in after a few hours and took over. Reg put down the last one he was carrying, who was too content to just lay down and sleep.

The nurse nodded at him to go outside. I met him as he came through the double doors.

"Time for your own check up. It looks like the 'baby-cure' did it's job." I looked at the towel on his shoulder and saw the drool that had leaked through to his shirt. "Congratulations, you are officially inoculated."

He picked it up and folded the wet spot inside, then felt his shoulder. "That would be about right. Hey, how does that work? I should have come down like Carlos there hours ago."

"It wasn't their drool that inoculated you, it was touching them. We rotate all the nurses and myself through this duty once a day, and the rule is to not wear gloves, but only use bare hands. Kissing the occasional darling head is also permitted." I had to smile at this, they were all just too cute.

I took his hand and led him into one of the two chairs next to our maintenance tech's bed.

"How's Carlos doing? Will he make it?" Reg asked, concerned.

"He'll be OK, it will take a couple of days before he'll do much but sleep it off."

"What did you give him?"

"Just a simple saline solution. When he's up to swallowing, we'll get him onto something he'll like."

"Such as?"

"A home remedy of apple-cider vinegar and honey, plenty diluted. That will keep his electrolytes balanced until he gets over the hump of it. Good thing you got him here fast. Most of these patients were days or weeks with the wrong treatment, and is why they are taking so long to recover."

"Treatment? You haven't given him any pills or injections..."

"Because he won't need any. We treat him by what you might call 'laying on of hands.' That works best and is the core of the therapy."

"You're kidding."

"No, I'm not." And frowned at him. "About this time, your professional skepticism comes in and we quit having a conversation, then I tell you to lay down and get some rest."

"Sorry, I did read about what you've been doing to all these patients. It's just as you said. The only thing you've had to do is to slowly get them off the meds they were on. That's in all the reports. But I can see that none of your student nurses are wearing gloves at all. And not even face masks."

I gave him a wry, lop-sided smile. "The worse thing you could catch in here would be the common cold. Way too sterile for me. I'd bring some plants in here, maybe some non-allergic flowers if I could. A therapy dog would be a great addition. But my 'druthers' don't count for much. Maybe since our quarantine is gone, it might."

Reg frowned at this. "No, it's going to get worse. I've read up on the procedures. The next thing that is supposed to happen is to seal us all and gas us. Eventually pour cement over the entire building."

VIII

IT WAS CATHY WHO HAD to sit down at that point. She shook her head. "I was afraid of that. Something my great-grandfather had to survive."

"Your great-grandfather was encased in cement?"

Cathy looked up at me, and took my hand. "Sorry, I spoke out of turn. But I guess it's a good as time as any to tell you. Ever heard of the Lazurai Project?"

I shook my head no.

"How about that terrorist bombing of a Cook County civilian hospital about 50 years ago?"

"Dirty bomb with chem warfare agents. Killed everyone. Huge tragedy."

"Everyone except the babies. But they were changed by the chemicals and radiation. They became toxic to everyone they touched. And as they grew older, the chance of contagion grew, so that even being in a hazmat suit wouldn't protect you. Those kids were raised in isolation from any adults and only had each other. Somehow, the government got them shipped to a remote desert location and put them into a dome. Some damned fool in Washington finally gave the order to kill them all as a solution. But none of their chemicals worked, not even their most deadly pathogens. So they finally just cemented the dome over."

My mouth dropped open. Shocked was a slight description of what I was feeling.

"They'd been experimenting with them for years by then, and their families had already been told that they were dead. But puberty forced the government's hand, as they now were extremely hazardous to the rest of humankind. People were getting sick and dying just being downwind. And so, the concrete. Problem was, the Lazurai kids could dissolve and absorb almost anything just with their hands. Even bullets and explosions didn't stop them."

"So, what happened to them?"

"They all escaped. And learned to deal with trackers that found them. Towns and cities evacuated when they found out a Lazurai was headed their way. Most of them suicided eventually, as they could no longer approach any other human. Occasionally, they found babies alive after their families had died, and raised those babies on their own, in secret. One of those babies was my grandfather. He then grew to become a teen ager and started roaming on his own, but was able to control his infectious 'abilities' and get near people - until they eventually found out. Getting attacked by others only made the Lazurai infect as self-defense. And then the government would get involved and they 'd have to disappear again." A tear formed at the corner of Cathy's eye.

I truly felt sorry for those kids. And put my hand on Cathy's where it lay on her chair arm.

She turned her hand over and held onto mine, looking me in the eyes with her own blue ones. "The story does have a happy ending. Those kids adopted other babies, and those babies also grew up and adopted. In each generation, the control over their abilities was improved. What you're touching now is the hand of a fourth-generation Lazurai. As are all of these student-nurses, also."

IX

HE DIDN'T FLINCH AT that. Probably because we'd been talking for nearly three weeks by then, even though he had to wear that stupid, useless hazmat suit.

"So that all means that you and your students could dissolve concrete if you had to?"

I had to smile at this. "Well, yes. Of course, that would start an old hunt up all over again. And we'd all survive being gassed, even those kids in there. But a lot of these adults wouldn't. It takes a long time to help an adult to change. Too many habits they've built in."

Reg's mind was racing. He was one of those "adults" now. He was looking off into space and I could see his eyes move as he considered various options. "How soon before Carlos is awake? Can you speed it up - I need to talk to him."

"Now that you know, we can probably give him some advanced treatments and have him able to talk in maybe 15 minutes or so." I rose and patted his shoulder so he stayed there. Nodding to Sue and another nearby nurse I motioned them over to the maintenance tech's bed.

We put our hands on his exposed arms, closed our eyes and concentrated.

It didn't take that quarter of an hour. He woke and saw us, then smiled.

Reg had stood to watch us and came closer. He started talking to Carlos in a quiet voice, explaining what had happened and asking him questions about protocols and other details.

We nurses all had our own duties to take care of, which now meant accelerating our treatments on everyone. Just in case.

X

THE LAST ARMY TRUCK pulled out at dawn from the quarantine zone. The concrete pumpers and forms were already in place. A colonel signaled them to start. It took about two days to completely cover the building. The last dosage of gas had been given just hours before the concrete pumpers quit. By the time they cleaned out their equipment, it had been 48 hours.

A second chain link fence now surrounded the original and the buildings nearby were evacuated. Dozers and earth moving equipment were already in place to level all the nearby buildings for a block in all directions. Supplies for a third chain link fence to surround that perimeter were stacked on site, waiting for the demolition to complete. Typical government efficiency.

Cathy, Sue, Carlos and I were all on that last truck. Dressed in hazmat suits and accompanying the body bags, both small and large.

We were driven out to a large transport plane where another crew of haz-mat-suited government types carefully transferred the body bags and us into its open hatch. Two other cargo planes of the same type were nearby on that runway.

All the planes took off together. Not long after, a fourth identical plane rose up as ours started descending. It wasn't too long before we lost sight of those three planes in the clouds that formed overhead.

Soon our plane touched down with lurching bumps on a little-used airfield, just long enough to allow a landing for the big plane.

By then we had every one woken out of their trances and sitting belted-in on benches at each side of the plane's hold. They had dressed before they left the medical compound, in the street clothes they came in or others from what was available. The babies were shared between the adults, and formula bottles appeared from supplies (warmed by the hands of one of the Lazurai student-nurses to body temperature.)

The ramp was lowered and we were met by a small group of people who ushered us into waiting buses.

We drove to an upscale hotel on the suburbs of 'Cagga, well outside their city borders. The top two full floors had been rented in advance, sealed off from any access. The reason was to "debrief" the patients and tell them their options.

Most of the adults were going to have very long, healthy lives after this. They could return to their families if they wanted. Otherwise, officials would dutifully break the news of their death as delicately as possible.

Those who wanted to continue their treatment and training were allowed to select one of several small villages in various states for relocation.

The babies were returned to their parents with special private schooling awarded, up to and including college if they wanted it, all expenses paid. Orphans were accepted by the villages willingly.

Carlos returned to his own family, with the idea and promise of relocating them to one of the villages.

All were briefed that no one would believe their story about the existence of Lazurai. A more suitable explanation was that "some very experimental techniques were employed that fortunately had a 'miracle cure' result. But were too technical for laymen to understand or try to duplicate." A number was given them to a government phone which would only accept messages.

• • • •

CATHY AND I SAT IN an empty restaurant in the top of that hotel, enjoying a quiet dinner.

"I'd ask how this was all arranged, but I'm sure that I don't need to know."

"Well, I'll tell you something as unbelievable as it is true. First, the government is very happy to cooperate with us. Very. We are their worst enemy and best ally. Second, there is a guy named 'Peter' who knows something called 'advanced mathematics of retrospective analysis' which in short says that you can predict behavior and events if you understand history well enough. And he saw this particular problem coming. That infectious outbreak is common to secessionist cities and metro hospitals in general." She speared a small piece of steak and chewed thoughtfully before continuing.

"It was his idea and financing to set up these nursing colleges in the Lazurai villages years before any of this, then provide 'volunteer' teams into various hospital staffs at the appropriate time to stem off the worst contagion. A few of the larger cities in the Midwest already have been solved, although the best we can do for the coastal megalopolises is to convert it into a widespread 'Legionnaire Disease' outbreak. The result is that while it will still be a plague, the entire human race won't be wiped out."

I nearly dropped my fork at her casual explanation of a global epidemic. "You mean there is nothing we can do?"

Cathy shook her head and looked down at her plate.

I reached over and touched her hand with mine. The same hand that had saved countless lives, including mine.

She looked up again, bleary eyed, but smiling. "At least I got you out of this deal. I hear you decided to come to my village so we can continue our conversations."

I had to smile in return. "The deal was no hazmat suits and way more than 30 minutes per day."

She was grinning at that point. "You know, they have a wonderful view of the Illinois plains from here. Would you like to pick up your questions where we left off?"

We rose and walked to the balcony, through their glass doors, and held each other around our waists as we talked. For a very long time.

Coda

IN A DISTANT ABANDONED government facility, an elevator creaked to a sub-sub-level and flickering fluorescent lights turned on bank by bank. They exposed a huge empty room with concrete walls. Around the walls at varying intervals were discolored patches in the shapes of humans, as if someone had outlined around them and colored inside.

The elevator opened and a man wearing a three-piece wool-blend suit emerged, along with a woman in skin-tight black leather. They carried nothing in their hands. No weapons of any kind.

Because they knew what they were up against, the challenge ahead of them.

Walking into the center of the room, the man cleared his throat.

"It's time. You can come out now."

One by one, at varying timings, a shape emerged from the walls in front of each human outline.

They each were forms of one of the four elements - dust, fire, air, or water. All were in motion, but none were moving beyond their spot.

The man and woman in the center of the room were silent, thinking, communicating with all present on a level far beyond what any typical human can sense or understand. After a long time, the couple took each other's hand and bowed their heads.

At that, the elemental forms each shimmered, and disappeared.

When the last form had left, the couple turned back to the elevator and entered it, still holding hands as the doors closed. Distant rumblings took their elevator car back up to the surface.

Meanwhile the lights began turning out, one bank at a time. At last the room was dark as it had been for decades before.

The next phase in our planet's evolution had begun.

Ham & Chaz

BY C. C. BROWER & J. R. Kruze

• • • •

This story adds expands to the background of the Lazurai healers. It also introduces a few characters that have reappeared through several stories across multiple universes. Here we a young romance budding between young Lazurai who don't know their full capabilities...

• • • •

FINDING OUT YOU'RE immortal as a teenager can set your world on fire.

But finding out at the same time that getting angry could kill everyone around you can dampen that pretty quickly.

Who wants to live forever if you can't get close enough to someone that they can piss you off and live to see the next sunrise with you?

Meaning - it was time to take a road trip to sort things out.

When my uncle offered a summer gig cooking out of his food truck for a big-city contract, I jumped at it.

But when he stopped to pick up another helper down the road, I was bummed. *She was a looker, a great cook, but I didn't know if I could trust myself with her - in every way...*

I

"CHAZ? YOU READY?" UNCLE Jean was rustling around in his food truck, opening and closing cabinets, double-checking everything.

I swung my duffel up the steps into the truck. "Sure thing."

He looked at my bag, and the jacket I was wearing. "That's all you're bringing? We're going to be there all summer."

"Just packed light. Enough t-shirts for a fresh change every day, skivvies, socks, jeans. It's going to be hot, humid and maybe we'll get rained on every now and then. Didn't figure a raincoat would be worth it. I know every inch of this truck and know how little space there is to stow anything not vital to cooking or living."

Jean just smiled. "That's my nephew. Always practical."

There was a school bus bench seat that was bolted down just behind the driver's air-ride bucket. I stowed my duffel behind that bench seat and flopped down across it. "Ready when you are."

Jean moved around my legs and slid into the bucket, pulling the shoulder belt across his broad frame to click it in position. Then checked his mirrors. Turning on the ignition, the big van started smoothly. He checked the gages as it warmed up and turned into a throaty purr. "You've added another few inches to your length since last summer." Almost an after thought.

"Not so many that my favorite t shirts don't stay tucked in. There's not so many inches this year, and they tell me not so many more in my future."

"You can count on those nurses to give you the straight scoop. Handy having that nursing school in town. Free check-up for just about anything. Of course for you, the check ups go both ways."

"How do you figure? I'm no doctor and you wouldn't catch me being a male nurse."

I could see his face in the big bus mirror he'd installed above him to keep an eye on his cabinets and passengers. "Just as long as you can get your checkups at the beginning of each semester when the new student-nurses flock in."

I just smiled and looked out the window. Jean knew me better than I knew myself sometimes.

Uncle Jean checked the non-existent traffic on that street before he clicked the fine-tuned transmission in gear to roll and lurch out of the steep driveway onto graveled roadway in front of it. It would still be a few miles before we got to the nearest state road and actual pavement.

I was looking forward to getting to some real civilization as a break from these rural villages. My whole life had been spent in them, it seemed. Only long trips to state fairs brought any semblance of organized culture near me.

While I loved the quiet and peace that pastures and woods brought, I was itching to find what the rest of the world had available.

II

"IS THAT ALL YOU'RE taking?" Mom was hovering around me, trying not to appear anxious, but she and I both knew she was nervous about my trip.

"Mom, I'll be find. Uncle Jean will make sure I'm safe. And besides, all those classes you make me take in self-defense don't exactly make me a victim waiting to happen."

"I know, I know. And when you get back, you can work on getting your next belt. All I want you to know is that we wanted you to be able to defend yourself, not look for trouble." Her forehead frowned again.

"Mom. Look, it's that Zen stuff that I like in these classes. They help me control any situation. I know my limits. I know when to back away. OK?"

She smiled and moved off a bit, knowing her hovering wasn't going to do either of us any good. "Oh, I almost forgot..." A few quick steps into the kitchen and then she was back by the front door where I had my knapsack and book bag. In her hands were two rolled-over lunch bags.

I had to smile. Mom was always looking out for everyone.

"This is a snack for the road." She held up the smaller of two bags, a brown one. Then lifted the bigger white bag. "And these are your Uncle Jean's favorite treats. But I know you like them, too."

Just then we could both hear the down-shifting gears of a heavy truck outside on the graveled street. Through the front door window, I could see the big food van slow to a stop.

I kissed Mom on the cheek and grabbed the rucksack. She bent to pick up the book sack and put the two lunch bags inside it on top, holding out the long straps together so I could put them on my shoulder.

I opened the door, slipped the straps on my arm, then pushed through the screen door out onto the paving stone walk to our graveled street.

"Be careful..." She called from the doorway.

I smiled and waved.

Jean had the door open for me and was smiling as he moved down the van steps to greet me. Giving me a big hug in spite of the bags I was carrying, he then turned and went back ahead of me to his driver's seat.

I made my way up the steps and saw the young man in the bus bench seat. I had to pause. He wasn't the same boy I'd met every year at the summer festivals. Longer, and now some beard showing up on his chin. His eyes were darker, even moody now. And a frown crossed his forehead as he swung his long legs down and got up to give me the bench to sit on.

"Hi, Hami."

"Hi, Chaz. Been awhile."

"Missed the festival last year."

"Yea, things come up. You didn't miss much."

"There's space under the bench for your things, I'll ride shotgun for awhile."

Chaz meant the fold-down seat just inside the van's front door. Where the only place to put your legs was usually curled up underneath it. Not comfortable for a long trip.

I stowed my knapsack under the bench, but put the book bag on the bench seat. "Jean, Mom made something for you, but she only told me you'd like it." I pulled out the white bag and handed it to him.

Jean took the bag into his lap and opened the top, then closed his eyes with the smells making his face widen into a smile of contentment. "Macaroons. She knows the way to my heart."

He waved out the still-open door to Mom, who was standing in the doorway, holding the screen open to see us off. She smiled back. Jean closed the front side door to the van, and put it into gear.

Chaz flipped down the seat by the door and got his own seat belt on to match Jean's. Then stretched his long legs out to rest them on the dash. Putting those new inches of his to good use.

Jean handed him the bag of cookies, and Chaz held it open in return, so he could take a couple in his large hand. Chaz then turned to me to see if I wanted any.

I shook my head no and settled in to get my own seat belt on.

But I couldn't get that vision of Chaz' dark eyes out of my head. Moody, maybe, but I knew we were needing to have a talk about things – comparing notes, or something.

Soon we were onto that paved state road. There were still some miles ahead before we could get onto the Interstate and start feeling that freedom that travel brings.

III

WE DROVE PRETTY MUCH straight through. I don't know how Jean does all that driving. But I do understand why he invested in that up-scaled bucket seat with the air suspension. The other big investment was on the power steering, a smooth transmission, and what must be an endless supply of patience.

Hami had been busy in the back for the last hour, rearranging things, and setting up some dishes so she'd be ready to start cooking when we stopped. I tried to see what she was working on, but she wouldn't have it. Just shushed me out of the back and told me to find something else to do.

Like I had any choice. No matter how big this van was, it got cramped real quick. "Hey Hami, can I read one of your books?"

"As long as you don't start wagging your jaw at me about 'mushy' romance." And punctuated that with some clattering steel pans.

I found some thick novel, I think it was Gaskell's "North and South" - another dry classic, but when I stretched out on that hard cushion called a bus seat, I lost myself for the next hour or so. She was right about the mush in there. But I didn't see any Doc Savage or L'Amour in her bag, so this beggar couldn't be choosy. (Still, not even a Doyle-Holmes collection?)

Finally we got to a lot outside a one-story long hospice we were going to work outside of. It was getting dark, but I could see some yellow tapes strung around the place and white placards with red letting posted on poles. I think I read "Quarantine" somewhere in all that.

Once we pulled up, Jean let me be first out the door. And the exotic urban smells almost floored me. Exhaust fumes and hot asphalt, all mixed in a humid soup that made it hard to breathe.

Jean had a few words with Hami, then came outside himself. "I've got to go check in, or try to, anyway. Hami says her 'miracle' will be ready in 15 minutes or so. Why don't you get one of the folding tables out with a couple of chairs and pull out the awning?"

I nodded, he turned and left. I didn't feel like saying much, and that was fine with him. Moving around outside felt better than sitting and waiting. I knew where he stowed everything from working his truck last summer. Getting everything set up before Hami was ready to bring out her dishes was quick. I pulled out a checkered plastic table cover in lieu of scrubbing everything down in the darkening twilight. Although the outside lights gave enough to eat by, the anti-bug yellow glow made sure you identified all your food by smell.

And I didn't know if "miracle" was Jean's term or Hami's, but some breezes through the open windows of the van brought me smells that made me realize how long it was since I'd eaten.

Jean reappeared when Hami got the rest of the pots and hot pads down, taking several trips until I just told her to slide the screens aside and I'd help her. Her last trip was with a covered desert dish that was beading with condensation.

Jean had brought drinks for us. Three tall iced coffees from some local quick-stop convenience store.

We all sat, held hands, and bowed our heads for a moment. Then we dug in, coordinating taking a helping with being able to pass it to the next open hot pad. Hami took a few of the empty pans off, pushing them back through the van's windows and closing the screens behind them.

We were all tired, the food was great, and so the conversation didn't really start until we finished.

"Where did you learn to cook?" I asked.

Hami frowned. "I'm supposed to take that as a compliment, since you cleaned your plate." Statement of fact.

"Yea, I mean, sorry. I really wanted to find out if it was a book or lessons from your mother or grandmother or what. Like I wouldn't mind learning if I could." Of course all that came out of my mouth clumsy, backhanded.

Jean and Hami looked at each other. Jean just shrugged. She handed him the dessert dish.

"Well, see if you still think so after this last one."

And yes, I did, after having a little bit of heaven melt down my throat.

"I thought you had to bake cheesecake."

"Thoughts can be deceiving," Hami replied, with a wry smile.

I turned to Jean, "OK, now that you have your cook, what am I supposed to do this trip?"

Jean just smiled and looked at the two of us. "You're going to be the best summer cook team I've ever had. Hami is great, and that's no doubt, but you're the fastest short order grill cook I've ever seen. And believe it when I tell you that it's going to get fast around here. Almost all the local restaurants have closed due to the outbreak. So they are bringing in special volunteer teams."

"Outbreak?" Hami and I both spoke at once.

Jean just smiled broader. "Yes, it's just what you're thinking. No, we aren't at risk. When is the last time either of you even heard of any flu going around either of our little towns?"

We both sat back and started piecing it together.

IV

"LAZURAI EFFECT." UNCLE Jean said at last.

That term rang a bell somehow.

"That's also why you are both adopted. You've got special genes and can't get infected by the normal stuff. Hell, probably by anything. There is one catch, though."

Both Chaz and I leaned forward at this.

"You can't allow yourself to get pissed off by anyone or anything. Because the same stuff that keeps you healthy all the time can make anyone around you quite ill, and quite fast. I'm only telling you this because it's probably something your parents haven't bothered to tell you so far. And they let me do it, because - well..."

I nodded. The pieces were falling in place. My mom had left my summer schedule open, while I was usually piled higher and deeper with activities. She knew I wanted to get out of town and see the world, especially when my reading list was filled with exotic locations. And the video's I'd bring home or download were about traveling.

Chaz spoke first, though. "So all our training and studies, even the sports we took were to help us get to the point of taking our first road trip, but you're here to tell us the ground rules."

Jean smiled again, but then got serious and leaned forward. "Only because you two can handle it..."

"Rite of passage." I finished.

Jean nodded. "All that Zen and meditation and inner counting you've studied. Both of you. You're going to need it in the next few days and weeks. Because you can both be unsung heroes, keeping your secret and solving their little problems - or you can make everything much, much worse. Your choice."

Then he sat back and sipped his iced coffee. And waited for the next questions.

It took awhile.

I spoke first. "Why keep what we are and everything about us a secret?"

Jean answered, "Because while people say they want immortality, they also can't accept the responsibility of it. The original Lazurai learned that the hard way. And why you don't see many of them around. That you can recognize, anyway. It's been the children they raised who have learned to master the talents and abilities the first ones were given. Your parents, your grandparents, all back to the originals have been working to this point."

Chaz would wait no longer. "Wait, so our genetic make-up has something to do with this outbreak. Meaning we can heal somehow?"

Jean replied, "Ever notice how fast you recover from a scratch or cut? How about a bruise from some of your sports? Some of that is you, some is from the people around you that are your family or your fellow towns-people. But the thing you have to remember is that the original Lazurai had no control over this. And even people downwind got sick - and died."

That thought took over - a place neither Chaz nor I had wanted to go.

Jean smiled to lighten the mood. "Of course, both of you are great under pressure, both of you are great cooks. You'll do just fine. After I help you two set up in the morning, I'll leave you to it - I have to get some supplies lined up and attend to some other matters around town. But just remember this - I'll always be around if you need me."

Chaz and I nodded.

"OK, then. We're camping out. Hami, you've got the van, Chaz and I have the outdoors."

We all pitched in to clean up. Jean showed us where the sleeping rolls, pads, and ground tarps were. Parking lots and van floors weren't soft, but we'd make do. Just more adventure.

Of course, sleep didn't come easy that night.

V

THEY WERE WAITING FOR us before dawn.

Hungry people. Lots of them. Jean nudged my feet and I sat up, rubbing my eyes.

"No rest for the wicked."

I rolled up our sleeping gear and stowed it while Jean went inside to make sure Hami was up - she was. And he came back out with a wad of her sleeping bag and pad for me to roll up and stow. Jean then went around back to start the generator. I heard Hami firing up the grill and soon got all the smells of it. Meanwhile, I unfolded the chairs again and set out the small condiments table. Hami opened up the screen window and passed out the napkins, salt/pepper packages, and plastic-ware.

Everyone was pretty orderly and started forming into lines. I heard some coughing, some sneezing, but nothing really serious. Of course, in the dark, it was hard to tell much beyond the yellow glow under our awning. I did see some white nurse's and doctor's outfits in the line out there.

The guys in front of the line just smiled at me when I gave them any attention. And I smiled back. Our work was cut out for us, but they were honestly happy to see us.

Jean was inside, doing a final check to see everything was in place. I pulled up a trash can and put a liner in it, one of many I could see filling today.

Then I headed inside the van to get started.

• • • •

THE DAY ROLLED THROUGH with just enough breaks that we got our own meals in between. Jean showed up regularly, often riding up with someone's delivery truck with more supplies.

Both of us got frazzled from working in the humid heat. And I had to take my "quick-counts" for "centering" myself often – just keep going on an even keel. Hami seemed to deal better with it than me. But she got to smile at the customers and seeing them smile back. Of course, I was focused right on the hot grill, while my bandanna kept my brow sweat wicked to the side and out of my eyes.

All I could see most of the time was the next order and the last one going out.

And Hami's cute backside every now and then.

But mostly my mind had to stay on what I was cooking and my supply of hamburger and cheese. For our menu was simple. It had burgers and cheese in different combinations. And we never had any complaints.

By our long lines, we didn't have much competition, either. Jean had understated how much we were needed. We were on our feet for most of that day. Hot, sweaty work with few breaks.

Finally, after sunset, the lines quit. Before then, there was no shutting them down. People just kept coming. Some said it was the first meal they'd had in days. Most paid in cash, but we also accepted the local version of government welfare cards. Our truck had some sort wi-fi connection that was locked down within an inch of itself. It took care of their payments somehow.

All Hami and I needed to do was just keep everything moving.

What helped was the intermittent showers that cooled everything off. The hungriest stayed in line, but that line shortened to the few who could stand under our awning. Hami and I could take a break during those showers and clean up inside the van a bit. Then the rain would let up, the line would stretch out again and we'd get going on their requests.

• • • •

JEAN WAS BACK BY NIGHTFALL. He brought us both some ice cream in pints. We ate it as he walked us over to a nearby truck stop that had shower facilities. Hami went first, and I caught up Jean on how it went that day. I went next, then Jean was in for his.

I didn't have much to say to Hami, nor she to me. Tired, too tired to say anything.

But she looked over at me with her eyes. Those hazel eyes of hers set off against her deep red hair always got my attention, even when she was a little girl at the festivals. Not that she couldn't lead most of the boys around just by her looks alone.

While I was remembering our years of growing up, she just moved over and hugged me.

My surprise was evident. Not that I didn't like it, I just wasn't expecting it.

"That's for staying cool today. You really kept it together. All I had to watch out for was your elbows. Those patties were almost flying out of there on their own. Thanks."

I was speechless. "Well, you did good, too."

She just smiled and went back to leaning her shoulders and hips against the brick wall and combing out her long red hair.

"Boy, I hope the rest of the days aren't as bad." I said to no one in particular.

Jean surprised me by answering. "Some will be worse. But you both did real good today. I'm proud of you and your parents will be, too. We helped a lot of people today."

Jean smiled at both of us. "Ready?"

We walked back to the truck. It was dark and late. You could still hear the traffic, and occasional music blaring out of someone's open car or truck windows. Still humid, still gritty. Far from the open fields and graveled roads of home.

VI

THE NEXT COUPLE OF weeks went by too quickly.

Uncle Jean gave us lessons at night after our showers, when we felt more refreshed and awake again. He taught us to pull from within ourselves to change the world around us.

One night, a gang showed up. They drove by us as we were walking, and then came back, and parked ahead of us - on the wrong side of that street. About five of them, in one car. One stood on the sidewalk ahead of us, just waiting. The others fanned out for an ambush.

But the closer we came, the more agitated they got. And sicker. If they moved off, they felt better. But the last one, the leader, tried to stay the course right in front of us. He wanted something.

Sad for him, all he got was a bad case of up-chucks, right behind his own car. Lucky he missed it.

We just kept walking.

Jean told us, after we were out of their earshot. "All that martial arts training wasn't so you could get into fights and kick butts all over town. It was to learn your own self-control. What you saw back there was just an inkling of how you can affect the environment around you. And there's only one defense against something that powerful."

We walked on for a little bit. Finally the suspense was just too much. So I asked, "OK what is it?"

Uncle Jean just looked at me with a side-wise glance. "Hami, what's the secret to your cooking? There's some ingredient you use that only master chefs ever really learn. Usually something they can only get by cooking with their mother or grandmother..."

Chaz was hanging on this one.

I stopped walking and they both stopped with me while I figured it out. I knew that something, and knew what it was, but I never had to put it into words before. It was just "something". Like the look on my Mom's face when I got the recipe just right. Usually with a big hug, no matter what was on the front of our aprons.

Then it hit me. "Love?"

Jean smiled. Chaz lit up like a light bulb.

"Of course. Love!" I was dumbfounded not to think about it that way before. "Chaz, those kind were the best burgers you ever served at the festivals. The ones that went to your friends and family. Tasted the best, gave you the longest lasting full stomach and never an upset one. It's not on any recipe anywhere. And I've studied lots of them."

Jean put his arms around the two of us and we started walking again. I put mine around his shoulders and Chaz put his on top of mine.

Big smiles all around.

And sleep came easy that night.

Except for one dream.

VII

"HAMI, WAKE UP - WAKE up." Chaz was shaking me. Or I was shaking and he was trying to get it to stop.

I sat up from my place on the floorboards of the van and grabbed onto him with both arms, like I didn't want to let go.

He turned and sat beside me and held on as well.

"What was that all about? The whole truck was shaking. And we could feel it out there."

"You two OK?" Jean was in the doorway, looking in at us.

"Now we are," I told him. "Just a very bad dream." I stroked Hami's hair to help her calm down. She softened and leaned against me.

"Thanks." She looked up into my eyes. "I'm glad you are here, both of you - but especially you, Chaz."

Jean quietly left to inspect the outside of the truck and check things out.

"You know you're always welcome, Hami. Whatever you need, just ask."

She gave me a tight squeeze at that.

With her head on my shoulder, she was much calmer now. I could smell the fragrance of her hair and the soap she used. Not that I could tell you now exactly what scent it was. I was still concerned with her dream. Something powerful enough to shake a truck was nothing to take lightly.

"Chaz, I think there is something more we need to ask Jean." She started to get up, but waited for me, since only one of us could get up with enough grace out of that twisted position we were in. My legs were crossed on top of hers, so I had to move first.

Then I helped her up and we held each other as we squeezed down the narrow steps and out the front side door of the van.

Jean was there, waiting for us. Somehow, he had three iced coffees in his large hands. He'd turned on the awning bug light and set up the folding table and three chairs, like he knew we'd have questions. I moved my chair next to Hami's and also got my bedroll to put around her.

After I sat down and opened up my own drink, she snuggled back next to me, putting my arm around her shoulders again.

Jean was understanding, but wanted to know more. Still, he waited until Hami wanted to talk. We both did.

"It was one of those chases, some monster I couldn't see. And then I tripped and fell, but a long, long ways. Then I was caught by something - like a huge invisible spider's web. And no matter how I tried, I couldn't get out."

Jean quietly asked, "What were you feeling right then?"

"Fear. Pure fear."

"And what are you feeling right now?"

She looked at him with big eyes, and then looked into mine. "Love. Unconditional love."

"So that's what you have to remember at all times, in all situations. Let go of the Fear, the anger, all those negative emotions, and just find the love you always carry with you."

Hami frowned as she looked at him again. "But it was all so real."

"Regardless. That is the one lesson you have to keep with you. Lack of that is the only thing that can stop anything in its tracks. But love is also the universal solvent. Nothing can stand in its path." Jean looked away, into the darkness of the pre-dawn. "That is the one lesson that all the Lazurai had to learn and learned to pass on to everyone they meet. It's where anyyone draws their real power from."

He sipped his ice coffee. "Here's an example. Remember I told you that if you get angry, people could get sick and die? Well how come those gang-bangers, the ones that moved away got better? And do you remember after we walked away from that one heaving behind his car? What happened as we got away from him?"

Hami frowned. "I remember looking back. He stood up after that. Seemed fine."

"He was fine. If I wanted him hurt, he would have been. Seriously hurt. But that would do nothing, he would learn nothing. And that kid has a lot of lessons still to learn. He's got a lot of understandings to master. No matter how he gets treated, he has to decide what he's going to learn from every situation he gets himself into. Just as you two do. Just as all of us always have and always will."

Hami nodded and hugged me again.

Jean got up at that point. "Well, no real damage done to the truck or anything else around here." He picked up his own bedroll and pad. "It looks like we still have a couple of hours before dawn. I'll leave you two to talk it over." Then he turned and went around to the other side of the van.

We both just sat there and held each other. I pulled my bedroll across both our shoulders and in front of us to keep warm.

"Chaz, thanks. Again."

"Anytime, you know that."

"I do now, for certain." She looked out into the sky beyond the awning and the yellow bug-light. "Do you think someone knew more than we did - I mean about us?"

"Like we were going to get together sometime, or maybe that they wanted to see if they left us alone together..."

"Something like that, Chaz."

I just kissed the top of her head. "I don't know if we'll ever know for sure. Like it matters at all now."

And we held each other until it started lightening up in the eastern sky.

An overcast day after sleep interrupted by nightmares. Didn't seem like the best beginning to a day.

Other than watching a new sunrise in the arms of one you love, anyway.

VIII

THE LINES WERE SLOWER forming that day. Chaz rolled up all the bedrolls and Jean did a check of the supplies, like usual. I cleaned up the van and wiped down everything, turned the grill on low to warm up. Made sure I had enough order pads and backup pencils to take orders.

Jean took off to get our deliveries for the day, and I handed Chaz the condiments through the screen window. He then came in to scrape down the grill and put some buns on to warm.

The first in line stepped forward and the day started as usual.

Well, mostly usual. The lines were quieter, less jokes and talking. And fewer people in those lines. But it wasn't a Sunday or other holiday. After a few hours, I saw someone going backwards down the line talking to people. And most of the people he talked to left the line to move away. The bulk of them walked went over to the chain-link fence on the edge of the hospice parking lot. Some went further.

Then three cars came roaring in with a lurch through the entrance, then screeching to a halt. Two in front, and one in back.

Gang bangers. I recognized the face of that one who got sick the other night. He was still a sicko pasty-white, his skinny face sticking out of his dark hoodie and leather jacket. The rest crowded out and approached our van ahead of him, but he only came forward when he saw they weren't getting sick this time.

"Chaz." I nodded outside. A fast look and then he turned all the burners off and moved everything to the cooler back where it wouldn't start a fire from over-cooking.

Then took my hand in his.

"I'd like to place an order!" That was the sicko. "I'd like to order the two of you out of there so we can deal with you. Our way. This is our turf, and what we say goes!" He looked around to the rest of his guys, and they all nodded.

Yet their fear was tangible. We could feel it where we stood.

Chaz just held my hand tighter.

I leaned down to the window and opened up the screen. "So you're feeling better since last night? Listen, we only take orders for food. And we serve the best food you can get on this side of Kansas City - maybe in the whole of KC. So get in line and we'll help you get fed today. Have your cash or Welfare card ready and we'll get started."

Some of the gang bangers actually started moving behind that leader like they would rather be getting a burger than giving grief.

Sicko just glowered at them and pushed them back. "No. We don't want your food. We want to take some payment in kind out of you and your boyfriend. You've been serving up stuff without permission. You owe us! So you can start paying now, or we can make you pay a different way."

One of his goons started for the front van door. Chaz hit a big red button and all the doors and windows locked down. The awning rolled up on it's own.

The other goons moved in and started to bang their sticks on the Plexiglas. Then they picked up the edges of the van and started rocking it.

My eyes went wide, but Chaz just narrowed his. He turned to me and took both my hands.

"Remember this, Hami - I love you. No matter what. No matter why. I love you."

I nodded, with tears in my own eyes, not of fear or grief, but of understanding. "I love you, too. Forever and always. Now, let's get some real loving happening to those boys outside."

We both closed our eyes and saw the world from within. Emotions became colors. The darkest emotions also had the darkest colors. People had these colors surrounding them. Reds and oranges for some.

Ours were bluish. And we concentrated on pushing more love into each other and outward from there. I could see Chaz' face clearly, and I'm sure he could see mine as well. We were both smiling at this. Any yellow or tint of red was pushed back out away from us and we soon saw the familiar van insides as blue and whitish-blue outlines.

The rocking stopped. Without us opening our eyes, we saw them backing away their reds were going more yellow as their own fears started replacing their pent up anger. And they kept backing away.

We didn't open our eyes or let up. Chaz and I just kept pushing that love outward as fast as we could, as strong as we could. We saw them run back to their cars, but those were dead. By then our blue sphere was beyond their cars, and they piled out of them, holding onto their stomach and mouths, struggling to get away. Running or walking or crawling – just to get some distance from us.

We just kept moving the blue sphere outwards until they had all left the front gate on foot and were across the street. Many just kept running after that.

About then a huge thunderstorm let loose overhead and the entire area was pelted in thick rain, washing everything away.

IX

CHAZ AND I FELL INTO each other's arms and just held on to each other until the storm passed.

About then, Uncle Jean opened the van door and came up the steps. Somehow dry as a bone. "Well, I see you two love-birds don't need any help with gang-bangers." He was all smiles.

A patrol car came up with lights flashing. An officer in dripping rain gear came in behind Jean. "Is everything OK, anyone hurt?" Both Chaz and I shook our heads "no" and smiled. The officer smiled back. We could hear him shout to someone to "get those plates run", and saw a police tow truck enter and back up into position behind one of the gang-banger's cars.

The crowd came back from the fences and up to the van see how we were doing. They hadn't gotten wet at all, for some reason. But were very glad that we were all OK.

Soon, after they helped us get the tables and chairs back, along with the awning rolled back down and everything cleaned up, they were all in line again. And then we were back at serving hungry customers like always.

• • • •

A FEW DAYS LATER, JEAN came back with some guy wearing a lab coat. He shook all our hands and thanked us over and over for all our help. Apparently this was the guy who had contracted with the company that recruited Jean and us. The quarantine had been lifted, and he was bringing back in his own cafeteria cooks and serving staff again.

About then a patrol car came by (they had been making regular rounds to visit us daily since the 'banger incident) but today it was the Police Chief himself who wanted to inspect the scene. Somehow, he didn't know why, but there had been a remarkable drop in crime in this area. People were taking care of little incidents on their own, while various known and notorious gang-bangers had either turned themselves in or been escorted by "friends or family members" into the local station house.

Our little food cart was ground zero for a circle that went out for blocks. They didn't even have to give out traffic or parking tickets. And so their extra officers were being reassigned to other precincts. He just came by to tell us all that, and thank us for being there.

Chaz and I were busy serving customers and didn't catch the exact conversation, especially when they moved their talking out of the van. (But I kept an eye on their gestures and asked Jean later about the details.)

Jean thanked both the lab coat guy and the police chief, and told them the sad news that we were moving on that night. But he had heard of several restaurants that had opened up in the last week, and more were in the plans. It seems that they "happened to come by" our little hospice parking lot and saw the long lines that stretched out of it and down the sidewalk.

And Jean pointed right across the street from us to one that had just opened up with big blue awnings. They had a walk-up window for only burgers and cheese combinations, just like ours. And they already had a long line. Then we saw Jean point down the block where a fast-food place with a drive-through was being renovated.

Both of those gentlemen shook Jean's hand again. And thanked him over and over.

The last of our line didn't take long to serve, and we had cleaned up and put away everything just as the clearing clouds were beginning to tinge red.

Jean did a final check of the truck while Chaz and I took our last full trash bag liner out to the roll-off bin by the gate. Hand in hand as we came back, smiling and relieved.

Jean was waiting for us with both damp and dry towels to clean up with, plus a couple of iced coffees.

Following him into the van, Chaz and I settled into the cozy bench seat and belted in. The truck started smoothly and Jean slowly rolled us out of that lot. Soon we were back on the interstate.

Darkness had fallen by then, and I snuggled up next to Chaz. He'd kept one of the bedrolls out, and covered us with it. The last thing I remembered was his kissing my head.

X

WHEN DAYLIGHT BROKE the scenery had changed.

While we expected to see rolling pastures with oaks and hickories and elms, we saw scrub brush, cacti, and junipers.

"Uncle Jean, where are we?"

I could see his reflection in the mirror above his head, his face smiling. "Nearly there, Chaz. Specifically, close to the border of Nevada and California. Technically, close to the middle of nowhere."

We were rolling down a two-lane highway now, the patched holes and tarred cracks were making the van bump every now and then as we moved along. The sky was clear, no real wind or traffic. Soon we turned off onto an old state blacktop road with barely a stripe on it. That took us a few miles into more desert. We finally saw what looked like a ghost town coming up ahead.

All that stood was a couple of buildings on one side. The biggest one was a two-story wood-frame structure with a squared off false front and a painted steel awning beneath it.

"Great place, isn't it kids?" Jean was beaming at this scene.

He pulled the van over right in front and shut down the engine. We all unbuckled and got out, with Uncle Jean almost jumping down the steps.

"Well, how do you like it?"

We saw big glass windows, cleaned to be nearly invisible, with simple curtains across their insides. Dual screen doors and what looked like a long bar inside. Several benches and chairs were waiting under that porch shade for locals. But no one was around to enjoy them.

I looked at Hami and then back at Jean. "Well, it needs some work. And the location isn't great. But that porch is in permanent shade on the north, so that's a feature."

"Chaz, I think you're missing the bigger picture here. Think of it as a graduation present."

I looked at Hami under my arm, and she looked up at me. Her face changed and she put her other hand as a shade in front of her forehead so she could read something above that awning.

I did the same. My jaw dropped.

The sign on the building front said "Ham & Chaz - Sandwiches, Etc."

Uncle Jean had to laugh at our faces. "Of course I'll be around for awhile to help set you up and get things running. But there are some other people who live around here you will want to meet.

Beyond him we saw several cars and trucks coming toward us from every direction of the compass, using dirt roads or paved. Taking their time.

Hami and I had a new home, and a new town, and a new family.

Together.

Peace: The Forever War

BY C. C. BROWER

· · · ·

How the cities perfected their domes was through their connection to the military-industrial complex...

· · · ·

IT HAD BEEN A VERY fast, very brutal war.

Jerusalem now lay buried beneath waters. All sides had agreed to a permanent truce.

And the United States had agreed to be the caretaker of religious freedom over the grave of the oldest and most contested worshiping area on this planet.

Japan was the final say in the peace accords.

For now, we had time to bind our wounds, to care for our widows and orphans. To settle refugees in their new homes.

Out of the new budget that the United States committed, a dome was to be raised over the city to protect the religious artifacts, with the idea of creating a new open worship area for all faiths.

It was astonishing to find such an agreement once the entire area had sank and become useless to everyone.

And no one believed that for a second.

That's why General Marshall broached the idea to the president of creating an international religious freedom zone. But without any United Nations interference. It would strictly be the United States' responsibility to maintain it.

Of course, the detractors and their lackey press told of "Marshall's Folly." And the billions it would take to fund archaeological work for centuries.

In the military, we saw a different scene. The dome we would raise would not only preserve this area from the elements, but would also allow us to build and test defensive fields while preserving the peace.

Because that water, as filthy and irradiated as it was, was fresh, not saline. It meant that the desert could be made to bloom if its source were protected. The far-thinking strategists of Israel also saw this. They could not, on their own, defend that city and also rebuild it. For all the neighboring countries, it was just as well to have that area sunk such that no one could use it.

And the United States was a perfect patsy to pour their money into their ideals of religious and intellectual freedom as they wished. At least no one else could have that mess, either.

They all, then agreed that the United States could do what they wanted, as long as it would not become a part of any nation, but a protectorate. And unlike Puerto Rico and Guam, it had no remaining citizens. Voting and citizenship was no issue. As far as the world was concerned, they would never be. Like Atlantis.

The dome came in two stages while we built the third.

Its foundation was laid out in the founding documents as inclusive of Jerusalem proper, but able to take any land from Israel or as captured by other countries "in order to preserve the religious and archaeological treasures for all nations."

Meaning, we had free rein to build as we wished. Technically, they had just agreed to any contiguous formation of land we wanted to grab for this project. But engineering said we needed a perfect, circular formation. Larger domes are less expensive and more efficient the larger they get. Estimates by Buckminster Fuller pointed out that domes built over several miles would be self-supporting due to the hot air they contained. Domes that large over cities would tend to float above ground instead of resting on it.

The scientist Bartholomew Fisk who discovered the field effect, pointed out that a spherical field dome would have a similar effect. There would be more need for gravimetric anchors to hold the field to the earth as it would tend to become independent as a body and cause seismic effects around the area. In short, become a moon. Moored into the Earth instead of resting on its surface.

Once the initial area was laid out, we had a circular foundation to build. We started by taking old Roman concrete formulas to build it. This gave us the strongest possible base to build on. As well, it didn't require much water.

The geodesic dome itself was a new architectural wonder. No one had ever built on this magnitude. The idea was simple to pay for it. Build it, then charge low-fee admission to all who wanted access. Governments were encouraged to subsidize the worshippers as they journeyed on pilgrimages to the holy sites underneath. Or that's the PR plan they were told.

Meanwhile, Israel was a partner in the construction. They saw the potential for their own security.

At first, we used the water at the base to shower the ruins and remove the radioactivity. Because Iran and rogue terrorists they supported had planted their dirty bombs, these had weakened deep underground caves and forced the city to descend as the waters rose.

To handle the radiation in the water, pumping and filtering was built in place, recycling the water back into radiation-removing aerial sprays, while Deuterium itself was mined and secured. That "dirty" water was used to fuel low-output pre-fusion reactors that became the power supply for construction.

Israeli scientists first guessed how much potential output could ultimately be produced, but were silenced by their military-influenced leaders, paid for in the Deuterium and the new technology for those reactors by the U.S. Such reactors were safer from direct attack or terrorist sabotage than any other nuclear reactor. But the real point was that they made fusion reaction possible in their next generation. And so, unlimited energy and independence from fossil fuels. The intense output of even small fusion reactors required a high-energy manufacturing base to absorb it. Oddly, the Roman practice of burning lime for concrete was able to absorb that energy for a time.

Israeli companies were paid in energy to produce concrete to supply the dome. Afterwards, many concrete walls were built around and within their country, some reaching deep into the earth. Their battery-powered vehicles were recharged by fusion-electricity. Of course, pure energy weapons were secretly developed.

The key point was unknown to the broad masses for a long time. Fisk protective spheres were not only able to protect against the elements, but could be used to seal off an area completely against any intrusion. Meaning a complete and impenetrable defense against attack. Because the dome was weakened when you opened any part of it, firing weapons from within it wasn't technically feasible. Fisk had made his breakthrough in theory, years before it the Jerusalem dome became a reality. And had left copious notes. But not lived to see it.

Americans and Israelis worked in secret to make smaller versions of the reactors and domes, for remote use, bombs, and offensive weapons. All in the background.

As the water was purified, it became made available first for watering local agriculture as tests, then for animal and finally human consumption. Of course, these tests were rolled out slowly. The aquifers that were initially responsible for the city's sinking were carefully mapped. For both security and conservation, domes were raised over the growing areas so that the water would not simply evaporate. Long lines of insulated drip tubing were strung between trees so that as the roots would sink as deep as the tree was high, these trees would then collect water to them.

The additional effect was to produce more moisture into the air, which then formed a micro-climate in the area. Clouds and fog were seen in areas that only knew desert for centuries. Eventually, the area around Jerusalem became a sort of Eden due to these works.

Little of this was visible to the many intelligence satellites that other nations poised over the city. The dome itself was opaque to light and most electronic bandwidths. A small part of the fusion output was used to light the dome within, matching the natural sunlight cycles without. An artificial "sun" was created that would mimic the brightness above as the earth turned, such that the sun appeared to "move" through the skies, rising and setting as usual.

The city was stabilized and raised as needed. The remains of discovered war casualties were recovered and repatriated as they were identified. Those unable to be identified were preserved with DNA samples and the rest of their body cremated, those ashes stored in catacombs beneath the city.

Peace came to this area.

Once the major shrines had been excavated and partially restored, limited numbers of pilgrims were permitted to visit. They were carefully screened and researched for their background. It took years to get permission to visit at the beginning. Those allowed in were only the most supportive of the efforts, especially religious leaders and politicians.

Eventually, the Fisk energy dome was stably expanded beyond the physical dome over the city itself. This is where the story got interesting...

The War Bringeth

BY C. C. BROWER

. . . .

Before the cities lifted, they had to get their own internal jobs scene under control. Here's one project that kept a lot of people busy and productive. It also lays out the scene for what was happening outside those city walls in Flyover Country...

. . . .

I

WE WERE CALLED TO WAR. And all volunteers. Not for god or country but for our corporation.

The global one. The one we were all warned against. It came in the back door that had built into our culture. The China-Russia pact had founded it, and gradually its handouts and bribes co-opted all the governments until it was just the U.S. and a handful of holdouts that weren't on board. Until they were.

Our job was simple. We coded. All day, all night. Jacked in and plugged in with all the nutrients we needed to keep us going. All volunteer. Dopamine rushes on intervals for meeting quotas. Adrenaline when needed and appropriate.

And it was all good. We had all the pleasures we could want. Plenty of pay and bonuses. The trick, that the "Corp" as we called it, was that we were all losers until we were winners. In our pods, jacked in, we had access to about everything we could want. As long as we did what we were asked, then we could get anything we wanted. Anything. The only thing that didn't really work out was being unplugged. The horror stories we found out were very, very bad. Coders had come back after "vacations" and didn't want to talk about them. You could tell by reading their endocrine levels. They came back exhausted, in shock, and their production nowhere near what it should be to compete in the Games.

That was all there was. The Corp and the Games. All else was secondary. Our job was simply to do the coding, create the new world we wanted to see, everyone wanted to see. And let the old world rot because that was all it was good for.

No one in here wanted the "real world." It was only filled with horrors. All our friends and family were online, And the ones that worked outside had troubles. Sad. We were inside and happy.

Because the whole world was Corp. It controlled everything. Literally. All the power, all the food production, all the entertainment and news. Sure, people could say and do whatever they wanted. But if they wanted to talk to someone else, they had to go through the Corp. If they wanted a better job, they had to do through the Corp. More pay, better living, all Corp.

In the old days, it went by many names. And they eventually bought out each other, or had the principles on the boards of the others, and they all were jacked into each other's lives so much, it became obvious that they couldn't work without cooperating with the rest. And sooner or later, the Board ran everything. It wasn't a CEO here and a CEO there, it was a few people who made the top decisions, and the sub-boards they controlled would then get their marching orders, They then sent their marching orders downstream to other boards and everything got done.

If you didn't produce, you missed the pay raises, the bonuses, the promotions, the perks. We saw this every day. The Code shows everything. Our view is the "matrix" as it used to be called. We don't need our eyes or our bodies as everything is cared for.

The Game is to build a new world. Because the old one is rotting out from under us. The Enviro's got on board quickly. Particularly after they found their funding depended on tweaking their policies slightly, or protesting a different government agency instead of the one they'd picked out. And the leaders of these enviro groups got promoted into high board positions inside the Corp, up their own chain of leadership.

Politicians were able to keep playing their game of getting elected, getting kickbacks, staying in office indefinitely. Because all the votes were electronic. All the media was electronic. It was all in the Code. Media and votes got people re-elected. Simple. All Code. Everyone who was anyone was online. And everyone else had to plug in someway in order to get what they wanted. Surveys were online. Payments were online.

The only people who weren't into the Code were the "Preppers", the "Amish", and the "Luddites". And there were so few of them, no one really cared. No story the media needed to follow. They could all go ahead and deal in their "cash" and "gold" and so on. The real wealth was stored in the Code. The payment was by jacking in.

This was where we started having the One World Corp we all had dreamed of. It ended squabbles between governments over resources. If someone needed something, it would show up. As long as they were plugged into the Corp. There was no reason to emigrate anywhere unless it was to move closer to the cities that had pods they could plug into. India and China and other areas quickly found that they could plug in their citizens to pods and solve their pollution and employment problems. People didn't have to travel anywhere after they were plugged in. They could access all the entertainment they wanted through the Code. They didn't need to have children since their families were taken care of and they could "hook up" with virtually anyone and achieve the same release they would with actual sex.

No one had to do any physical work any more. AI Bots did the gardening and farming, created the electronics and metal and plastic extrusions on demand. There was next to no waste as everything was recycled back into the next needed products.

The Corp pods and the Code took care of everything a person could need.

Except until it didn't.

II

JOE SAW THE BIG DOMES rising from his patio on the mountainside. He still had his telescope. An old antique manual one with real lenses.

He was happier now than ever before. The farm on that mountainside gave him all he needed, and his greenhouse enabled him to grow almost anything year round. It had taken him years to work up his trees and permaculture garden to give him the best possible food. His land was steep and looked like something out of Machu Picchu. Lots of terraces, and water basins up and down slope. You could hardly see where his house was as it was surrounded by growing things. And goats.

He was happy almost all the time. And he'd been that way since he unplugged and dropped out. This very marginal land was perfect for him since the Corp had no use for it and would have none. Actually, they had already mined this area years back and taken everything they could. That was how he could find all the rocks to build his terraces. The mining had left heaps of these. His home was actually the entrance to one of their many tunnels. Another opening was his barn for sheltering his goats during the worst weather. And some hydroponics were there, which could replace winter hay they needed in the few times they got snowed in.

So he had pretty much everything he wanted. Anything he didn't have, he could go down into the local village to barter. Festival days were great for that, and they had their weekly auctions.

That was where he met Joan. And his other reason for visiting the village. He thought Joan was cute and smart. And she seemed to feel the same way about him, the way she smiled and put extra things in the boxes of supplies he got from her store.

Today, he was studying that big dome. He hated the domes. They showed up wherever there were Corp pod-cities. And enveloped them. Big translucent domes. You'd see where their exhaust came out a few hundred yards downwind. Of course, they simply tunneled over to where the existing stacks rose from the old power station. Then plugged in their excess heat and smoke through those stacks. Of course, since the government and the enviro's were all plugged in, there weren't any complaints about the emissions. Especially since it was all "sustainable" and didn't exhaust natural resources. Fusion. That was their breakthrough. No more pesky climate change "gases." And scrubbers supposedly pulled out the "dangerous" radioisotopes to recycle them back into the fusion process. This enabled more energy out of the process. Of course, the government investigations always gave them a clean bill of health. Meanwhile, the domes filtered the air, so the vast bulk of the population lived cleaner, healthier lives than ever before." So it was reported in the Corp media, which was all media.

Joe knew all this because he used to be plugged in, lived in a pod, swam in Code all day and night. At this thought, he rubbed the scar on the back of his neck where the jack used to be. They used to get those jacks installed in all the kids, particularly if they showed a talent for coding. Corp would give them and their parents "scholarships" to get the action done. And the government gave a payment disguised as a tax break for "child care" to the poor who couldn't afford it. Until there were no more kids. By that time, everyone was either plugged in or wasn't going to.

People like Joe who saw where it was going from the inside out. And unplugged on purpose.

Joe was tired of thinking about these things. He would rather farm, or read his books. And that was actually how he met Joan. She ran a lending library from the back of her craft shop. If she had several copies, you could swap for one of them to keep. But she would also take books in trade for other books. Like the old coffee shops who traded their Internet connections for selling scones and java.

There just wasn't much use for Internet out here anymore. Because they just wanted your data and wanted you to buy their stuff. To do that, you had to give your data. Their ideal was for you to become part of their Code. Of course, their ads sucked. Because they couldn't get data on people who refused to jack in. The people who didn't use their plastic chip-cards. People who would swap goods or services for money and money for goods or services. Or goods for services.

To be off-grid wasn't an enforceable crime. You just lost government services, Meaning the Corp didn't approve of you. Voting became a waste of time since you were giving your data so the Corp could approve the outcome. It was all in the Code. And to not think about the Code meant simply putting your attention on other things.

Joe took a second bandanna out of his pocket to wipe his face. He had a first bandanna folded up and tied around his forehead, under his wide-brimmed straw hat, but it didn't catch everything. Another hot day. But everything was watered now. And his basins were repaired and reinforced to catch the next rains. So he could get out of the sun and relax for a while. Once he cooled down, he'd get back to his books again. He was on the third or fourth time through most of them. But it calmed him down.

His view was the other thing in his life that calmed him. The opening to his home looked right off across the mountain side. He had a flat stone patio with a shade of living trees, shrubs, and vines overhead. The hardwood easy chair he had built held his weight and was tall enough to nap in if he wanted. A foot stool under his feet, and a small table with his books sat by one arm of the chair, and a solid block of a tree trunk sat on the other, big enough to hold a cool drink.

Life was good since he unplugged. The surgery to make it permanent had cost him plenty. And getting a scan to ensure he wasn't still chipped - another expense. He didn't trust the satellites. Because he understood the Code and knew what the Corp would do for any threat it found.

It took him years to arrange his pay so that it would result in precious metals and physical cash enough to make the shift. He had carefully arranged to miss out on the various promotions and bonuses. And Joe knew where the Code was missing data. The Code was as arrogant as it's coders. They called the people who dropped out "Luddites", "Amish", and "Preppers" like they were second-class citizens. The Code made sure that if they decided to drop out and unplug that they had no benefits for doing so. Their benefits were those that the some who were plugged in would want, but not what the unplugged wanted. So it was simple to be a "collector" of "antique" money items in exchange for giving someone else your dopamine Code credits. There were some old "banks" which were used by collectors for their "antiques." And these were all off-grid for that reason. No electronics allowed for any reason. Battery-powered LEDs, with very simple circuits were preferred over oil lamps or candles. These got recharged by simply sitting them on top of a wood stove, or plugged into an off-grid power source like that. Simple living. And most people had a stockpile of these lamps, for when their circuits quit working a decade from now.

III

POPULATION CONTROL, sustainable, jobs and food for everyone. The enviro's loved them. The politicians loved them. The people could get anything and everything they wanted just by plugging in. The Corp was everything, employed everyone. On paper, the governments still existed. But in reality, they just worked for the Corp. There wasn't any need for military since there wasn't any problem with land ownership. When drones and AI took over the fighting, as well as the media coverage, no one would have to be out there to risk their lives. Anyone out there in the field of battle was basically a combatant, so was simply a target. If they wanted to surrender, a big transport ship would land and take them away. All the reports said most of them were successfully jacked into the system, except for a few who were "infected" and died of "complications."

Anyone who didn't want to surrender got rid of their weapons and went underground. The thermal views from satellites showed where everyone was. And as long as they were simply tending their gardens, farming their crops, or herding their livestock, on one cared. Threat analysis = 0. And as in the days of the Samurai, when all weapons became illegal, the weapons became the tools in their hands and the hands that held them. You didn't ever want to be carrying a metal weapon, and the 3D-printed plastic ones didn't resemble any known weapon, but would be deadly in self-defense within a short range.

That was the whole scene that showed the Code's flaws. Everything inside the Corp was high-tech. Everything was monitored. You could speak to turn on your lights or music or videos. And everything you said or watched or listened to was scooped up by the Code and digested. And that's what you got recommended for you, based on what your friends had recommended to them. Everyone was monitored by the Code for the Corp. And were reminded that the Corp was all they needed to be happy. People who didn't subscribe to the Code were shunned as eccentric. Called things like "bomb-throwers" or "racist" or "sexist". Until no one knew what those terms meant any more. People chose their sex, chose their race, and changed them anytime they felt like it. Once you plugged into the Code, you were whatever avatar you chose. If you wanted sex, you paid for the type and kind you wanted. All the sensations came through your plugs. Your body waste was removed by your plugs, your food was delivered by your plugs. You didn't need to sleep because you were alway jacked into the Code. They had mastered your REM cycles and subconscious dreaming and put this to work well. Since people dreamed all the time, anyway, it was simple to just let people jack into the Code and let the Code sort it all out. Waking and dreaming became the same. You worked at code, you dreamed of code.

People worked with the data in the Code and organized it. They did their part that they were assigned, and what they did was studied and improved and perfected for the Code and became part of the Code. All so the Corp could take care of them and keep giving them their happiness through their plugs. The more you worked, the happier you were.

The Corp wanted you happy, and productive coders were happy coders.

So they invented the War Games.

• • • •

THESE WERE VIRTUAL, like everything. Deep inside our physical body code is the necessity for winning. Through history, it has been War that traditionally filled the outlet for this need. Sometimes it was perverted into controlling other's bodies, as slavery or harassment. But all those efforts were to amass resources so that they would win whatever war was running or coming. The violent tendencies in humankind could not be easily erased in the males of the species, just as seemingly illogical nurturing outlets were necessary in the females. Those two tendencies could not be subverted. And were not opposable. Nurturing people couldn't be made to oppose Violent people. Violence was really just an outlet for Providing. Winners had more resources, and they needed to "spend" these on the people who supported them. Nurturers wouldn't necessarily fight (unless you threatened their "child") but they would support someone who would win and provide for them. As the sexual orientations became fluid, these two urges became the dominant themes for living. The Code saw that this was needful and saw that it was good.

This developed teams of Providers and Nurturers, who could then be organized in larger teams, in "competitions" and "leagues" in order to "fight" and "win" against other teams. The whole point was to have larger-than-life heroes (as touted in the Corp entertainment media) who struggled against nearly insurmountable odds. The Code knew what people wanted and gave it to them. The old Roman Coliseums were built to entertain the masses on this same idea. As old as humankind itself. The Code just studied us and fed back what we wanted. And the Corp saw that it was good.

The "War" became finding a new place to live. Because the rare metals had been mined out of this planet and the Corp ran on Code which ran on electronics, which needed rare metals. So probes had been sent out decades ago to survey the outer planets for rare metals. Moons were scanned as well as asteroids. And the very light waves themselves were data-mined to find nearby galaxies where these metals could be found.

The War was "won" by having the competing teams and leagues do virtual battles to solve various scenarios in the fastest and most efficient manner. The winners got promotions and media applause and all the pleasure events they could want. And their wants were surveyed and prizes announced based on what most people wanted.

Out of this came the development of fusion-powered domes, and interstellar flight. Mini- and micro-fusion drives powered the AI military/police forces across the planet. These units tested the various designs. If they blew up over some "desert" area, then it wasn't a huge loss. Other A.I. Salvage bots would recover as much of the wreckage as possible. Larger A.I. units were launched into space as probes for the Solar System Survey. And even bigger and more powerful units were sent out into our galaxy to find new sources of rare metals. All these studies were done as entertainment. When something dramatic was happening with one of these bots, the footage was edited into a War Games scenario. "Everyone knew" that these scenarios were "virtual" and not "real." Until so many people had been exposed to these scenarios as their entertainment that they were well-known and everyone had a positive opinion of them. From those opinions, Corp adjusted the Code to give them more of what they wanted.

And so the War Games predicted that we had exhausted this planet and would need to move on.

But the Code wasn't all-seeing. And was only as accurate as its input. At the base, the Code was human. The Corp didn't see the flaw. Because Science didn't acknowledge things it couldn't explain, like the spiritual. Religion and all things spiritual was discounted as being non-scientific. So the Code explained these as non-essential. The Code was blind to what it didn't want to look at. No one ever said humans could see everything, no matter how many eyes looked at a problem - the adage about throwing enough monkeys on typewriters to produce Shakespeare never proved out.

The Corp and Code succeeded beyond all board expectations, but overlooked a very real, very human, very low-tech enemy it had created. And so, was defenseless - unless that enemy played by their rules.

Too bad they didn't tell them what the rules were. Too bad they didn't spend more time studying old human rules before they made their own.

The Lazurai Emergence

BY C. C. BROWER & S. H. Marpel

· · · ·

I HAD BEEN IN THAT stone wall for decades, alone on purpose.

Not lonely.

Waiting.

Humankind needed to evolve past what they had done to create me. I was willing to wait - as long as it took.

Because to re-emerge would mean to again threaten all humans I contacted.

The very reason all of my kind had submerged into hiding was to save humankind from ourselves, from the virus within us.

While that virus had saved us from certain death, and evolved us into an immortal state, we were still human enough to care for the rest of the race we used to be part of.

And that is the risk, like all evolution:

Is this an quantum-leap of genetic improvement, or a dinosaur extinction event?

· · · ·

I

WHEN THE LATEST THREE visitors arrived, I greeted them as usual with a dust cloud and wind. Dust devil turned cyclone.

They responded by putting up a force shield. I countered with hurricane-force winds.

But one of them got sick. He fell down and clutched his stomach. I felt sorry for him, but he's "only human" and so I wasn't too sorry. The other two weren't human, although they looked it. They had my respect. A couple of good-looking young gals, as far a humans went.

We were at a standoff. It was all they could do to keep their shields up, and I didn't want to increase my wind forces any more, nor decrease them any less.

Then a red-haired, hazel-eyed young woman appeared and walked through my dust storm and their shield like they weren't even there. She crouched over the sick man at the bottom of their shield, then looked up at the two gals who were generating that force shield with their concentration.

All three disappeared with a shimmer, and I was left alone as a dust cyclone.

And that's all I wanted.

"I've never liked visitors." I said to no one nearby. "I came here to disappear, but people keep finding me. Well, to hell with them. They never cared, they don't now."

The whirlwind of my form twisted in the middle of a vacant desert, just a dozen yards away from the sheer cliff side behind me. At my base, little dust-devils spun off to ride small drafts out for a short distance and then dissipate back into the dust and air that formed them.

This wasn't happiness I felt, but when I had my solitude, that was something that comforting to me. Something I depended on for so long to be the same.

I only wanted quiet after all my disappointments. Humans had always disappointed me. Ever since they created me with their poisons, their bombs, bullets, and gases.

In the silence I could sleep, without dreams, without cares.

Alone.

So I sank back into my cliff side, the petroglyph glowing momentarily as the rock absorbed my energy.

With no wind, the desert dust returned to coat the blank floor by the rock wall, leaving it again the featureless canvas it usually was.

And I slept again, as I waited.

II

"HERE'S THE SPOT, MARI. I think we can find one here." I pulled my smartphone from the inside jacket pocket of my three-piece wool-blend suit. The tracker program was working and pinpointed this spot.

Mari came over to look at the screen next to me. She preferred her tight black leather outfit in situations like this. It allowed her movement and protection, as well as various places for the weapons she carried.

I carried no weapons other than my own intellect, which you would say was a double-edged blade - able to creatively solve problems as well as take them apart. But we had been raised in different times, literally. Her own insistence on training and her martial arts exercises always endeared her to me. She was a wonder to look at while I sat on the stationary bicycle and peddled any excess pounds away of my own.

But then I loved her more each day, and it wouldn't matter if she was any other shape. I liked to watch her beautiful form, and she appreciated my attention. We made a good team.

On the tiny smartphone screen, it was clear that the weather disturbances were local to this specific area. The GPS gave us a very precise location that matched up with the satellite imagery.

And my calculations showed that this precise time-space location was key to later developments.

All that was here was a very solid canyon wall that faced a long plain in front of it. Just a portion of a butte leftover from ancient magma eruptions. Long ago, some Amerindians had drawn petroglyphs into it's flat surface, and these had eroded with the weather until only one remained. This last one was faded and almost illegible as a drawing.

But that faded petroglyph drawing had to be the focus point for the entity causing these weather disruptions.

So I began a conversation.

"Hello, great one! We come to thank you for all you've done, and admire your abilities." I talked loudly toward that petroglyph in the canyon wall. "And I've come to ask your advice."

Silence.

Mari whispered to me, "I thought you only practiced your flattery on me."

"All good flattery is just an obvious exaggeration of known truths. And these beings deserve our admiration for all they've been through." I whispered back. "But you deserve all the flattery you can get, after all, there are a lot of outstanding truths about you the world should know." And I winked at her.

Mari blushed slightly at that, and kept quiet any witty repartees - as she knew our work here was key and precise.

Soon the being in the petroglyph "spoke" to me, some rumblings in the ground and canyon walls, and the winds increased. The voice in my mind was clear, though.

"Why do you come to 'suck up' to me and bother my solitude?"

"I come with my friend here so we could ask you about how you are doing, and if you are ready to emerge."

"It is curious to me why you would be interested in my welfare. No human has been interested in me other than my own kind for decades. And my 'own kind' isn't exactly human or treated with anything but fear by humans. Riddle me that."

I smiled at the rock entity, facing that chosen petroglyph as a focus point, and no longer having to shout. But did talk out loud so that Mari could at least follow my end of the conversation. "That is exactly why we are here. We have met others of your kind, and talked with them, some. They led us to find you. We came to let you know some do appreciate all you've been through and to ask for your advice."

"What possible advice could you get from me what would be worthwhile? I know only death and destruction. And to emerge from this wall would only kill you both."

"Perhaps, perhaps not. One single question and we will leave you to the great solitude of this desert and all that live here."

The entity was silent, considering this. These two humans were not afraid. They knew the risks I posed, but stood there and wanted my help. Most curious. "Ask me your question, and I'll answer as I can. One question, as you promised. Just one."

I cleared my throat and whispered to Mari, "It says one question, only."

Mari nodded and looked to the petroglyph, which had begun glowing.

"If you had the opportunity to do things over, to change how you had acted, would you take that opportunity - and how would you do things differently?"

The petroglyph glow now began irregular pulsing, as if considering a reply. The question was carefully phrased to encourage thought.

"You ask a good question. And I thank you for it. I've not had a real conversation for decades. The ones I had last wound me up here as their result. The logic I followed showed no other outcome possible. My life had been depressing, and death was not an option. Isolation and waiting was.

"Of course, you are asking me to use what I know now to consider what I've done up to this point. The short answer to the first part is - nothing."

The petroglyph took on a steady brighter glow now.

"Your second part to your question asks what are my intentions for the future. And the short answer to that is: I don't know."

I simply waited, patiently as I could in the hot desert as the sun rose higher and the heated winds began to move with greater strength around us. This entity wanted to say more, but interrupting its thinking would get me nowhere. Asking another question would be risky.

Finally, I had to take that risk. "But your long answers would be...?"

The petroglyph seemed on fire, radiating heat toward us.

"I do not know if you have heard the story of how I was created. I won't repeat it here. The poison gases, the radiation, the explosives, the diseases - all those things we were administered in an attempt to destroy us. All from humans, just as we once were. But the worst weapon they used - far beyond the suffocation and bullets and bombs - was their shunning.

"They called us Lazurai, and determined that we had somehow been infected with a virus. And it cost them the lives of those researchers to find that out. For they were fully-grown adults, and to them, that virus was certain death. None of them or us ever knew how we got infected originally. It was supposedly in the dirty bomb that destroyed the hospital we were in. But those same researchers told us that those terrorists all died from handling that virus and weaponizing it.

"Because we killed everyone, we were shunned. When we escaped to find out more about the world, all its humans ran from us. So these remote areas far from humanity became our homes. After long lives in isolation, we became the rocks and water and even the wind. Some descended into the molten planet core and live there yet.

"For we have none to talk to except the natural forces. Humans who find us die. But all I've learned doesn't change that fact. At least in these rock formations, we can have visitors safely, such as you two. Yet I dare not emerge, for your safety.

I nodded at this. "We thank you for your consideration." After an appropriate pause, "And could you tell us the second part of your long answer?"

The petroglyph again returned to an irregular pulsing.

Mari and I waited, keeping our faces attentive and patient.

"A lot depends on what humanity is doing now. Whether they have been able to study our condition and provide us a way to safely interact with them, much as we've been doing today. From childhood, I've only known rejection except from my own kind. Some tried to give us love in their clumsy hazmat suits, but even these eventually got sick and died. And we loved them, but could do nothing for them. Because they loved us - but also could not cure us of that virus."

Again, the voice paused, the rock image pulsing more slowly.

"I don't know of anything I could do differently. All we wanted was to give and receive two things: love and respect. If that were possible to do then or even now, then things could be different, I suppose."

The voice went silent at that, the rock walls now their natural color. No glow remained. Only the dust and wind, which had decreased as well.

I thanked that entity with a mental thought. And wished a better future. But of course, received no response.

Our job done, we phased back to our own time and space.

IV

ROCHELLE HAD LEFT HER "beater" truck way out in the boonies. She had told me a bit of the story, how she had come out here to find someone she was supposed to help, only to find a cyclone with some clear sphere inside it - but a sick man on the floor of that sphere.

When they returned to Hami's saloon to get him treatment, she left that truck of hers out here.

Curiosity, as well as my own generous nature brought me back out here to see the scene and recover that truck.

I'd come as far as I could using the roads and old riverbeds and washes. Then simply translated back to human form to walk the last few yards.

The truck was no worse off than usual. Of course, she hadn't rolled up the windows, so there was a layer of dust inside it that matched the outside. Must of been some storm there.

But before I got it started again, I wanted to see the location where she had rescued that guy. The flat wall of that old canyon wall wasn't too far away. So I walked there.

The scene was familiar to me somehow. Not that I came from this kind of country, but the isolation and pureness of Nature on its own seemed to resonate somehow. The faded markings on the canyon wall were something I'd read about in those travel magazines, but never been up close to before.

I walked over and touched the ancient markings. That touch told me more than anyone could have known. It felt eerily familiar to me. Something was connected with this brought recollections of my own painful past to light. A very bitter and savage sacrifice had been made here, one of little choice, but logical necessity.

There was something else to this, something tragic.

However, it wasn't the time for me to investigate. Something wasn't right, but I'd have to make time to come back for this later.

Retracing my steps, I returned to the truck. First was to blow out and off all that dust by bringing in a little windstorm of my own. Then I raised the hood and looked it over. Touched the old distributor and it's spark-plug wires - and felt Rochelle's essence still there. That's why this truck still ran as well as it did - and why she trusted me to come and retrieve it for her.

I knew it would start for me as well. Love gives you that certainty.

With that thought, I felt a change in the atmosphere around me. The air seemed more dry, and the wind picked up. Since I didn't want to have to clean everything out again, I shut the hood and made my way over to the driver's side door. Opening it, I slid in and turned the key, then pushed the ignition switch on the floorboard. This truck was a real antique.

It turned over and caught, rumbling into a smooth hum. I had to smile. Never lost my touch after all these years.

Looking around, I could see that the ground had plenty of flat ground behind it to turn around in safety. Easing into reverse, it smoothly backed and turned. Before I took off back to that tiny oasis where Hami's old saloon-building stood, something caught my eye. Something back at those canyon walls.

A large dust-devil was turning right where I had stood in front of those canyon wall markings. This one wasn't moving in any direction, but just turning there in one spot. Natural, yet under someone's or some thing's control and direction.

That brought a smile of recognition to me. I saluted the dust-devil through the windshield. "Some other time, old friend." I thought to it. "We'll meet again, I'm sure."

First gear was a bit slow, but I wanted to make sure of the way before I put that truck into anything like a road gear.

I and the truck slowly made our bumpy way out of that remote desert spot.

In the mirror, I saw that dust-devil dissipate. With that canyon wall in shadow, something seemed to make those markings glow. But the bumps and twists in that rutted road soon took that canyon wall out of sight...

V

SOMEHOW, I RECOGNIZED that last human form that visited me.

I've had to start referring to them as "forms" because they way they acted was like no human I've ever encountered, even those of my own kind.

First the two girls who were apparently immune to illness that the male caught. Then the third girl was even unaffected by my dust storm. And how did they all just disappear like that?

Next, that suit-wearer and his partner with the black leather also seemed to appear out of nowhere. And talked to me like I haven't ever been talked to in this existence. With respect. And I had so many things to think about as a result. But they, too, simply disappeared.

This last one came from that old truck, I guess. Wasn't really paying much attention.

And yet his touch was too familiar. Something I haven't felt in a very long time. Like I might have known him. And he called me "old friend."

This was becoming too much of a coincidence. And that many visitors in just days was more than I have had in a whole year before. It wasn't making my sleep come any easier, all these interruptions.

And that made me wonder if it was time for me to stay awake...

VI

WITH THE RESEARCH AND talking to those Ghost Hunters, I understood more about what and perhaps who I had encountered submerged in that rock wall.

I came with them as they phased into view about a quarter-mile away - for their own safety. Rochelle came with us.

"Uncle Jean, you be careful there." Rochelle had a rare worried look on her face.

"I will, Rochelle. But if it goes as I suspect, I may have met another old friend I haven't seen since we were kids." I smiled to reassure her, then evaporated.

. . . .

...to re-form as a water spout in front of that canyon wall.

I tried to communicate directly with the being in that wall though elemental channels, but without any response.

So I transmuted back to human form, crossed my arms and started talking at that petroglyph. "I think I know you from a long time ago. But I need you to come out so we can have a talk. I'm not here to hurt you, I just want to know how you are doing and if there's anything you need that I can help you with."

I only waited a few minutes. Then a dust devil started up and grew to a large size quickly. I matched it with my own water spout and merged into the space it was using.

Then we started talking in a way its even hard to write down. Because our thoughts merged, and we were able to complete conversations on a conceptual level, beyond pictures or words.

She was someone I had known when we were both the original Lazurai. We'd both been attacked and infected in that hospital, then grown to teenagers and survived all the various attempts the government used to try to control us and even end our lives.

Of course, there was grief at remembering and sharing all these old memories. I'd lost track of her after we both escaped and went our separate ways.

I had submerged into an old deserted building far away from any humans, just as she had done with her canyon wall.

But one of our relatives had found me. A third generation Lazurai called Rochelle. This was the red-haired woman she had met that first day.

Then I had to tell her all I knew about Rochelle and my own learning-journey. That learning resulted in finding I could control my own powers enough to walk and behave around humans in the way they considered "normal." And without killing any accidentally.

Time had no hold on us. We shared so many things during our conversation - until I had little to share she didn't already know.

She told me the long stories of waiting and sleeping in the rock that had become her home. Until she had nearly forgotten what it was like to have a human form. Her life had been spent more as rock than anything else, and she had traveled its routes deep into the earth, in all the different formats. She had met the subterranean waters, and deeper still into the magma.

Not too surprisingly, she told me of meeting other elementals. A few she recognized as the original Lazurai, but more who were of a very old age, even beyond what we could consider measured time.

But all these travels raised other questions. And she always returned to this spot, as somewhere she could think and consider and understand all that she had found out in those travels. While she understood much about the planet and the rocks, she had stayed away from living things as she could trust herself to not accidentally kill them.

As one, we realized that Rochelle was the answer, or could help her find it.

So I left her and returned for Rochelle to bring her and her answers back.

VII

JEAN HELPED ME TAKE on a water elemental form as he was used to. And this being came out to talk to us.

The funny thing was that Jean knew her and had grown up with her, but couldn't remember her human name. Mainly because she no longer used it. So it made introductions awkward.

I'm translating this into human so you can follow our discussion, but what took place was timeless, outside of what you would consider was our space-time. We "spoke" in pure concepts, more like your dreams, take place in your mind and you assign the time it takes.

I'd told the Ghost Hunters that day that it might take awhile. The truth is that we needed some privacy where their thoughts wouldn't interfere. I didn't understand how that worked, only that it did. When I got near larger cities, it was harder to sort things out and to focus on just what I wanted to create or transform. Because of the interruptions from others thoughts. Weird, I know. Just the way things are.

. . . .

"Hello, my name is Rochelle. You've been talking to Jean and he's told me some thing about you. What name can I call you?"

"That's an interesting concept. I haven't had use for a 'name' in so long. Just call me 'Betty'. I don't know if that's what I used to be called when a human, but it has a nice sound to it, a rhythm."

"Betty. Sounds good. So Jean tells me you have questions."

"Many. How did you find Jean before he was emerged?"

"Well, I'm asked to go places and when I do, I then find whoever it was that I am supposed to help. In this case, it was a deserted old building some distance from here, also in the desert."

Jean provided the concept of the exact location where he had submerged himself, and his view of my arrival when I visited him.

Betty then traced a subterranean route there, through the rock seams - much more direct than the highways and roads that I had to drive.

Jean teased me at my idea, that I had to learn how to travel as an elemental to "save time." I teased him back about time being a sixth element, and space being a seventh, so his concept was itself outmoded. And we all chuckled at that impossibility. Time and space are simply human constructs, after all.

"How did you get him to emerge and what did you have to help him with?

"I came there as he did to you, sat down facing the wall he had submerged himself into and asked if I could help him in some way. He was curious at that, since no human had asked to give him help since he was born, other than the nurses in their hazmat suits.

"At first he was reticent to come out to talk with me, as his experience with other humans besides the Lazurai were always death. But I told him that my parents had been raised by the original Lazurai, so Jean could very well be my grandfather for all I knew. The point of this was that we had learned to control the poisons and toxins that we'd ingested. To turn them into other materials. Then I picked up a rock from the ground and turned it into a shiny hand mirror, then reflected the sunlight against the wall where he had entered.

"This was a metaphor he could understand, since the sunlight could be moved through a mirror almost anywhere I wanted it to go."

Jean gave us both the feeling of how amazing that was for someone to show him a solution after all those decades of hiding for fear he'd hurt someone with his condition.

"I understand," Betty replied. "This is the curse of the original Lazurai which you have undone. We were fed poisons and destructive substances and absorbed them, but only knew how to return in kind, instead of transmuting them. Somewhat like the old 'eye for an eye'. We simply didn't know better."

Jean confirmed that idea as true. That was all they knew at that time.

I continued to explain. "There are other later philosophers who told of 'turning the other cheek' when struck. That is a simple view of transmuting what you are given, but the same basic principle.

"So, next I took my hand and stuck it right into the wall where he had submerged, dissolving the rock and mortar, and absorbing it through my skin. Then I made a concrete plug out of that material, exuding it from my skin to fill that hole again.

"Jean then made that same hole open again, and extruded a square brick from the wall. It landed on the dirt below that wall, but left no hole behind it.

"In turn, I picked up that brick and turned it into a marble bowl. Then pinched a bit of the hole I had originally filled, so that it had a spout on it. I moved the marble bowl just below below that spout. Using both my hands, I scooped up a pile of dust from the ground and absorbed it. Then I took a deep breath and blew into my cupped hands. Finally, I put both my hands flat against that wall, and water flowed out that hole through the spout to drop into the bowl below it."

Jean gave us his concepts of surprise when he saw this.

"At that, Jean made water pour out of the hole and more than fill the bowl, so much that I had to stand and move away from the mud puddle he was creating. Yet the water remained in a perfect circle on the ground. Next was a bit of rumbling and a muddy figurine emerged, of a girl sitting in jeans on the ground, just as I had moments before.

"The mud then turned to pure water, and the water figure raised it's arm to wave at me. She gestured for me to have a seat, which I did. And then we shared thoughts as I'm doing with you."

Betty was silent for a time, taking this all in. "How did you help Jean to learn to become human again?"

I smiled in my thoughts to both of them. "Lots of practice. Lots. But we both had plenty of time. And since neither of us had to really eat or sleep, we kept at it. He eventually simply touched my skin and felt my hair, then made these into forms on his own body shape. Finally, I let him share the space of my body as we are doing with you now. And he understood again the human form from its inside out, and then recalled being a human baby and growing up as a teen-ager. I also gave him my memories of this. And eventually, he simply moved out and formed up the body you saw up there earlier today."

Betty shared her happiness for Jean at this, as well as her own excitement about trying new things like forming a human body again. But she also expressed some doubts.

"Of course," I replied. "You don't have to do this all at once. And it didn't come back to Jean for quite a long time. Please take all the time you need and practice all you want. There is no rush at this, no goal we need to achieve here. I just came to share my understanding with you, as well as Jean's."

Betty was grateful and happy, for the first time in decades.

That seemed like a good time for Jean and I to take our leave, to tell our guests and friends the stories we had learned today.

So I told Betty, "We both need to go visit our human guests again. But just call us and we'll return as quickly as we can. We are only here to help you, in any way we can."

Betty gave us both a great hug and disappeared back into her canyon wall, making the whole wall glow as a show of appreciation.

. . . .

Jean and I returned to the front porch outside Hami's saloon building. It was as clean and sparkling as ever.

I've told you most of this story part before.

Jean had other business to take care of and left in his own elemental way. I then entered the old saloon-building and briefed the Ghost Hunters and Hami about what we'd found.

At the end of that sharing, Sal and Jude left John here to write while he finished his treatments.

And I told him this entire story, everything that we had talked to Betty about. I answered all of John's many questions, and he promised to write it down as factually as he could, but of course omitting some of the more boring details so that it would "read better".

I guess he likes mysteries, their entertaining plots, and leaving them solved neatly at the end. Everyone likes an entertaining read.

Since he's the one that writes a lot, we let him do it his way.

Later, when he needed more inspiration, we told him more of our other stories when he asked.

Jude came one day to borrow him for another adventure.

At least she left a stack of his books for us to catch up John's stories about them. And we put another desk in that corner, as close to the one he used as we could, so he can come back and write up more stories anytime he wants.

Since there are far more where this came from. And we got used to having cute hunk sitting there typing...

VIII

HAMI AND I WERE ENJOYING another night in the solitude of her saloon. The dishes were all done and put away. Except for the plate of Hami's delicious toll-house cookies and two tall tumblers of iced coffee. These sat nearby us on one of her round four-legged tables. We each were relaxing in our own ever-comfortable "caboose" bentwood chair, just reading from one of that tall stack of books Jude had left.

No one else around, just the tables, chairs and the long bar with it's mirror on the wall behind it.

Other than the way we were dressed and the paperbacks in our hands, the whole scene could be out of an 1880's Western tin-type photograph.

Our quiet was interrupted by a large dark winged form like a condor as it swooped down - a huge, fast shadow that dove across the front of the saloon windows. Soon following was the sound of scratching at the screen door. I was halfway out of my chair to open it when a large, white-maned coyote managed to get that screen door open and squeeze through.

She took a few steps inside, looked at both of us, and then put a big smile on her face.

With a shimmering, she turned into a tall dark-tanned woman with long white-blond straight hair halfway down her back, dressed in a tan buckskin dress beaded with turquoise and shell.

"Hello, Rochelle. It's been awhile. Remember me? Betty?"

I almost ran toward her to give her a hug. We both laughed at each other as we stood back at arms length and grinned at the sight before us. She had come so far in such a little time.

"And you must be Hami. How's Chaz? I learned so much from Jean and Rochelle about you."

Hami nodded and was about to reply when Betty took my arm again, a serious look on her face. "I'm sorry, and I'm probably being rude or something - you can help me with human manners and now-we're-spozed-to's at some point. But I really need your help. Can you come with me now?"

I turned to Hami and she understood completely. A big smile on her face.

Because when you're called, you've got to go.

I put my arm around Betty's waist. "Ready when you are."

The room shimmered as we turned to dust and seeped through the cracks in the floorboards into the dirt and gravel beneath the floor, then on into the subterranean depths...

For the Love of 'Cagga

BY C. C. BROWER & R. L. Saunders

• • • •

This story "came out of the blue" - like all of them. And asked to be told. All I knew when I started was that it took place in Cagga with two Lazurai. Eventually, the details emerged as I wrote and edited it into life. And we have our first eye-witness of the cities rising, as well as the transition of life within them – with just a hint of what we would call... slavery.

• • • •

I

IT WASN'T HARD TO GET into, or out of, 'Cagga. It was impossible.

Unless you were built from the impossible.

And it was simple when you could walk through walls – or float through solid floors. The ones in 'Cagga tasted OK, nothing out of the ordinary. The outer force shields left an after-taste, though. Kinda minty, a sour kind of minty.

Someone here needed us. And there wasn't much time to help whoever it was.

Their Plan had the cities leaving on their schedule. And it was just Betty and me this time. They usually didn't send two. So this was something special, I guess. Of course, maybe it was because it was Betty's first time.

That damned schedule. Get in, fix whatever, come back. Don't let the city take you away with it. We're too valuable for whatever is coming. But that was where they ended. No more details.

I'd never had instructions that specific before. Didn't need them. Get the call, go help.

They'd always worked out. I did my job and I was good at it.

Top of my class, so to speak. But not good enough for this one. So I brought a trainee. One of the originals. Something to do with her raw talent. And one helluva defense if we needed it.

Healing or killing wasn't the issue. It was saving.

II

I WAS GOOD AT CODING, but I hated being plugged in. The Jackers were always pasty white and blinking at any hard light when they came out. And they were made to come out and get some exercise every day. Mostly, that was shuffling around a room where the lighting was indirect and muted. And the air was kept warm so they couldn't get chilled, much less catch a cold.

Jackers had their one-piece suits for this. Most were soiled and grimed up at all the use and touch points. If they weren't wrinkled from just laying on the floor all day, they had vertical creases where they were hung on a pole or hook somewhere. They didn't need their one-piecers in their code-rooms. And I never understood why they called them "rooms" as they were mostly just immersion tanks. The only roomy thing about those tanks happened after you jacked in and got into the VR. Plenty of "space" inside there. And all your food and stimulant-bonuses.

Sad to look at, sad to be one. In my opinion, anyway.

I quit trying to talk to Jackers. Because they mostly mumbled. And they didn't know any good jokes that made sense. They'd start saying, "No, Jeannie, you just don't get it..." and then repeat the punchline again. All based on that weird alternate reality inside the Game.

That's what life had become for them - a big VR Game. MMO or something. The Independent Cities were all connected and they played against each other by solving coding problems.

It was like that big video they showed every time you jacked in - cities flying off the planet to new worlds, leaving the polluted mess behind, along with the Deplorables who were "unenlightened" enough to want to stay out in the boonies with their guns and Bibles. Scratching for a living out there while all the 'Leeters were "leading the core of civilization toward greater heights."

My Ma didn't see it that way. Like me, she didn't have a choice when the walls went up. They'd decided that for her when they seceded from the rest of the country. And soon after that, no one was allowed in or out.

So we wouldn't get "contaminated" by the Flyover ideas and diseases. The politico's had chosen for us.

And now I had my own new baby to add to this mix. She was a darling, with cute blond hair and the brightest smile. While I worked, my Ma took care of her the most, good days and bad. Because Ma had something wrong with her, and so did my little Sue.

Doc came by when he could, but he was pretty much the only doctor outside of their clinics that could go in between the gangs. That meant most of 'Cagga. 'Cause their clinics were all at Central, and had visiting hours the same as our work hours. But those were staffed mostly by interns, as the 'Leeters got the best doctors working on sucking the fat out of their guts and hips, or making their faces prettier, or simply listening to them complain about their aches and pains.

Doc said Sue was born with something he couldn't fix without operating, and he couldn't operate anymore since he lost off a couple of his fingers in an "accident". One that happened right after he told one of those 'Leeters what they could do with their faked-up illnesses. Now Doc got what he wanted most, helping people who needed it more. But he was by himself, mostly.

Doc said baby Sue had a tough road ahead of her, but she could make it. And my Ma could have a lot more years ahead of her. Could. But I saw his face and how he looked away at times. He didn't like what he saw, but he kept smuggling medicines to us when he could.

He had his own contacts inside. People that agreed with him. That would leave certain medicines out where he could get to them. And a lot of guards he'd helped when they couldn't even get into the clinics. Those guards would turn away at the right times, or "forget" to check his bags when he left. Doc was a guy you wanted to help anyway you could.

Me, I just saved and scrabbled together enough flour and sugar-spice powders to make him those cookies he loved. Plus, he'd come for meals when he could, just to fill up on my special home cooking.

Ma used to work with him a bit, before they 'down-sized' the outlying clinics in favor of making one big central clinic uptown. Easier to supply and service, they said. But it was really about control.

So anyone with a too-quick wit and tongue found themselves too soon working with the rest of the 'gangers out in the streets. In whatever gang their housing fit into.

That was another whole layer of politics. But since the Games had started, it pretty much put everyone to work doing something.

At least most of the killings had stopped. Because the work hours got longer and longer. So you didn't get time to get out when you were supposed to be sleeping. If you didn't sleep, your work suffered. And if your gang didn't make their quotas, you got less food. If you didn't work, you didn't eat until you changed your mind.

And the rest of the people in that gang land could be pretty persuasive. They needed to eat, too.

But you've gotten me talking about all this other stuff. Doesn't much matter.

What mattered is my family, and getting them well.

Because the city's shield tests turned out promising.

And sick or not, fed or not, this city was going to lift off soon. I had no choice in that, either. But sometimes Ma would joke, "Well, if all you got is mud, maybe you should make mud pies with smiling faces on them."

My husband Joe had other ideas - like we should make mud into bricks. Because you could build with baked bricks.

And, if you had to, throw them.

III

'CAGGA HADN'T CHANGED much since the last time I was there.

Still gritty, dirty, depressing. But now the streets seemed more empty.

That was good for us, since Betty brought us up through the subterranean fissures and mineral veins she was following - right up into the middle of a street.

Of course, there weren't any cars running around and getting into wrecks. In fact, that was all that were left of the cars - wrecks here and there. Until they could get around to hauling them off for recycling.

The 'L would take you anywhere you needed to go, mainly to the Center downtown. And there was a rim-rail that went around the edges, but that didn't run so much as those back-and-forth spokes.

I'd learned a lot of that when I was here before, as short as it was.

That rim-rail was new. And the 'L was open to anyone, so we took it to get a better view of things. That showed us that some of the exterior walls had shifted, I couldn't see why they would build new ones. Not just to build a smoother circular wall, not hardly.

Me and Betty rode that rail until I felt we were close to who we needed to help. Make that *who's*. One older, one younger, and the one in between who was caring for those other two. I was happy Betty had come along. Usually, I only had to deal with one at a time before this. Never three.

• • • •

THE FIRST PROBLEM MET us when we came down those stairs from that elevated rail station. A crowd of people waiting for something. Bored.

Gangs aren't the best at waiting. Even if they are in lines. They need something to do. With their hands, their mouths.

Strangers are fair game. Even though we shifted the cut, make, and colors of our clothes as we came down the stairs so that we would blend in. I made my own hair darker red, while Betty didn't bother - her height and bleach-blond mane was going to make her stand out, regardless. But she did tie it into a pony tail, and "found" a ball cap to tuck it into. All while we were walking down those tall flights of stairs toward the long queues of gang below.

The whispering and muttering started before we made it to the bottom. Along with the elbow-pokes and pointing's at us.

I played their game as much as I could – looking where that queue was heading and then turning us back to go the other direction so they'd think we were trying to get into the end of the line to get our share of whatever.

A gang this big meant no one could say whether we were or weren't part of this gang, somewhere, somehow.

Well, until we met one of their bouncers.

"Hey girl-cha's. Whatcha' doin' out of line? You 'betta get where you belong..." He'd stopped in front of us and put one of his hands on my shoulder and the other on Betty's. Big mistake. "You don't seem to be, I mean you aren't..."

But his face went blank for a minute. He didn't get sick, but we read everything we needed from him. And helped him change his mind.

He pulled back his hands like they got burned, but when he looked at them, they were fine. Wide open eyes soon narrowed into his usual squint. "Well, it's not my fault you're late," he bellowed - as if we had been arguing with him. "Now you better get to the far end and hope there's something left when you get there. No cutting!"

Then he made like he was going to shove us, but had second thoughts when his hands tingled from getting too close to us again.

He scowled, we moved on. He found other people staring at him, and went over to give them a piece of what he called his mind.

Of course, the end of the line wasn't where we ended up.

The persons we needed to help – that family – was a bit further on. And no one at the end of that line complained. They were too busy coughing and scratching and sneezing and hoping the line would get moving soon.

All we did was walk by them.

IV

MA WAS TELLING SUE another of her stories as she held her.

I always loved Ma's stories. Because she had a talent for making them come alive, like you could see them in your mind. Even when she was telling some old fairy tale like Treasure Island, or Princess Bride, or Connecticut Yankee, or Samson and Delilah - you could see the characters and their worlds in your mind.

Ma had Sue entranced, and I was cooking dinner, such as it was. A lot of soups these days, mostly vegetable-based. That's what Joe could bring home from the food lines - bags of vegetables, some leafy, some beans. And bottled water that we let stand and boiled anyway. Doc had told us there might be "additives" in it, but was better than what came through the taps.

Probably their point at Central. Their idea of control meant a choice between bad and worse.

Then the knock came at our door. I peeked out through our peephole and saw two young women – one redhead, the other blond. Both smiling at me, like they could see through the door.

So I opened the door to let them in, strangers or not. But pretty and nice.

Joe would've had a fit - but he was out, so this was my choice. Between good and better.

"Hi, I'm Rochelle, and this is Betty. May we come in?"

"Sure - I'm Jeannie, and that is Ma holding Sue. We're about to have dinner - and you're welcome to join us."

Smiles all around, which only got bigger when they saw little Sue. Nobody who has a heart can resist a smiling baby.

Rochelle and Betty found places next to Ma, who started telling them all the current news. Rochelle was asking questions and Betty was soon holding Sue and rocking her while making funny noises and faces. Sue was making them back, like they were having a conversation in a language no one else knew - or remembered how to speak.

I set a table with just enough places. Joe would get his helping when he got back, and I'd have them all washed by then. Those lines took awhile. One day a week, our only day where we didn't have to work, and we spent it getting supplies and fixing things.

Now the funniest thing I remember about that meal was when we all held hands to pray before we started. I don't much remember what I said, but the tingling that came through those hands was something I couldn't forget. And I felt peace and love in our little apartment like I'd never felt before. Joe's loving embrace was close, but it was another type of love. Probably that peace and the hope it fueled that was different.

Talk was about the changes at 'Cagga, and how the city was set to raise any day. We'd been warned about the rumblings and told to take cover if it got bad, but it shouldn't be a problem. They'd been running their tests once a week, usually during the day-off, and then fix-it crews like Joe's would go out and repair anything that had shaken loose or cracked too bad.

Rochelle didn't talk much about where she'd come from, but it was obvious that she and Betty didn't come from inside 'Cagga. I just knew it was better not to ask, as if I knew nothing, I couldn't be forced to tell anything I didn't know.

Betty managed to feed Sue out of her own bottle, and eat her own dinner. She'd swap Sue to Ma, back and forth. When they were all three done eating, Betty and Ma went over to the couch where they sat side by side and compared notes about Sue. I'd never seen Ma so relaxed around anyone.

The multi-cast came on, we could hear it in the streets. Our own unit only popped and fizzled during that, like always. Joe was lining up parts, but it was tricky getting them and they'd often disappear into someone else's lunch box before he could get what he wanted. And a new unit wasn't in our appropriations. You didn't just waltz into the recycle center and claim one of the 'Leeter's modern cast-offs, not if you didn't want to be threatened with stealing, even if it didn't work.

The multi-cast was the typical theatrical music and canned ovations as the Plan was ballyhooed again. Some high muck-a-muck 'Leeter was talking, and when he got done, another one started - someone higher up on the food chain.

Rochelle seemed annoyed with the sputtering and sparking of our unit, so went over to see if there was an off-switch (there wasn't - and those rumors said that this was because there was cameras and mic's on it, which was why we couldn't turn it on or off and why it was hardwired into the wall.)

But a little after she touched the top of the box, the screen came to life and we could see all the pictures. And the sound came back, almost like it was new, but not as loud.

Rochelle just smiled, and I didn't ask or say anything. Joe would be happy, one less thing to fix during his time-crowded day-off.

We all sat and watched until it was over, and it went blank again. Nothing new to learn. Same old Bee-Ess. Like the joke: first two letters in business. And we were always getting business "news" from the 'Leeters. They owned the 'casting stations, after all.

The next program was going to be one of their secular-religious programs (something else they invented) but Rochelle tapped the top of the 'cast box again and it went off. (She showed us all that the 'cast box was now tap-on, tap-off.) I just nodded my thanks.

We had the real books on the original religions, not their "Plan" version. And we'd go out on an evening part of our day-off to hear one of the volunteer preachers read from one of them, and help us discuss what it meant. 'Cause religion isn't top-down, it's always been bottom-up and sideways.

'Leeters didn't seem to have much use for anything that wasn't top-down. Straight top-down. To them it was all either 'Leeters or "down-belows." And stuff always flowed downhill. All sorts of "stuff."

Right then, Joe came home - tired and hungry. Sacks of our alloted weekly supplies in his hands.

But his face frowned when he found us with strangers in his home...

V

I ROSE WHEN JOE OPENED the door to their little home. "Hi Joe. Been awhile."

His stern face melted into a wide grin. "Rochelle! How did you... When did you... You shouldn't have, because they are about ready to..."

And I just came over and hugged him like an old friend, which he was.

Jeannie sat there smiling, as she knew from his face that allowing us into their home was a good thing for him, too.

She got up and washed off some dishes for him and emptied the rest of her great tasting soup-stew into his bowl, filling his cup with clean water. Then she took the bags of food he'd brought back and started putting everything away.

"Joe, that's Betty over there with Ma and Sue." Betty nodded and kept smiling. "How have you been?"

Joe put his bowl down for a bit, where he'd been all but drinking it. "Gosh, it's been quite awhile. I always wondered where you'd gone to. And I'm sorry I didn't have time to bring you home to meet my girls last time. They would have loved to meet you. Anyway, you're here now. Hope it's longer this time."

I put my hand over his. "Not that long. We need to get out before the city lifts. Orders is orders."

Joe smiled at this. "Like orders ever meant anything to you. I was lucky to talk to you for a few hours and help you find the Interpol station that day. But then I had to get back to work, and that was the last I saw of you."

"Yea, I met the guy I was supposed to, and we had to leave right away. Sorry I couldn't stay longer."

"Well, you're here now. Can we help you with the job you're on now?"

"I think you already have. Because you're the job we were sent for.

He sat back at this. "Me?"

"Actually, all of you. Your whole family. Here, let me see your hands."

Joe pushed his almost-empty bowl aside and put his other hand on the table top.

I took his other hand and turned them both palm down, then palm up. And concentrated on what I was seeing. Too many scars from burns and cuts. That made me frown.

"Something wrong?" Joe asked.

"You've got to get away from that radiation. I don't have enough time to do some full treatments here." I turned to the baby cuddlers and coo-ers on the couch. "Betty? Could you come look at this?"

Betty handed little Sue back to Ma, came over and pulled up a chair. She took both his hands, turning them over and back. And looked up at me, back at Joe, then closed her eyes.

Joe's own eyes went wide with the sensations.

His wife Jeannie was a bit alarmed, but I signaled her to come and sit next to me. I took her hand and looked into her eyes for a moment. "Just as I suspected. You're going to have a boy."

Her eyes in turn went wide, and her face pale.

Betty let go of Joe's hands and he rose to go around the table and kneel next to her. Jeannie put her free arm around his shoulder and kissed his head while he put an arm around her waist. They hugged each other while I kept "reading" her other hand.

"You can tell all that from my hand? We'd been hoping that I wasn't getting sick from something else."

"And you probably aren't going to get sick like that again, not anytime soon."

"How do you know?"

"Betty and me are what you'd call healers. We can see what's going on inside people and fix things, like Joe does in his job. Like Ma does when she tells her stories and everyone in the room lightens up. Same basic approach."

I let go of her hand and she and Joe hugged like there was no tomorrow.

"Now, we don't have much time left. Your Ma and Sue are the real reason we came."

Me and Betty went over to sit on the couch on each side of Ma, who was holding little Sue in her arms. Each of us put an arm around Ma's back while we touched the baby as well. Then we closed our eyes and concentrated.

It didn't take long at all.

Sue started cooing and telling a story of her own. Everyone in the room could see her pictures. It was Little Red Riding Hood from the wolf's point of view. And it turned out that he had saved her from a feral pack in the woods, then hid her grandmother under the bed to take her place and protect them both. Of course the mistreatment he received was because the older humans couldn't understand his thoughts like Little Red could.

We all laughed at the punch line, because everyone lived happily ever after, including the wolf – after he escaped. And we all were left with an idea that there were going to be more adventures for the wolf and his new friend, Little Red.

Then the apartment rumbled and shook.

"This is the worst yet." Joe said. He covered Jeannie's head with his, while Ma protected little Sue. Dust and plaster pieces were coming down as the walls and ceiling shifted.

VI

BETTY AND ROCHELLE stood at that. Somehow the dust wasn't landing on them. Or more like it was being absorbed.

I motioned Joe to go outside and see if he needed to help anyone else.

Then I stood and went to the two of them.

Both Betty and Rochelle each took one of my hands, along with each other's. We stood for awhile as the rumbling ceased and the 'cast came on again.

After the familiar theatrical introduction, a countdown clock filled the screen. And a deep voice announced that the last tests were now complete, and everyone should remain in their shelters - or get to them if they already weren't. Lift-off would commence when the clock finished counting down.

Betty then moved her hand to the back of my neck. "You won't be needing this any longer." Then let go of my hand.

I put my hand to the back of her neck and felt it. The jack was gone. "What... how... we couldn't afford corrective surgery..."

Betty just smiled. "That jack was just in your way, Jeannie. I was able to dissolve it for you. Here."

She held out her hand and took mine into it, holding them palm up. Then waved the other over the two of ours and several silver coins appeared in my palm. "Now, you can use these to get something that's useful instead."

Joe opened the door at that point. He was covered with plaster dust. "Is everyone still OK?"

I smiled at Joe. "Come here, you lunk. We're fine." And we hugged.

Meanwhile, the countdown had continued on screen, with quiet classical music playing in the background.

"Joe, can you show us the fastest way down to the bottom levels?" Rochelle and Betty were looking at him.

I just tried to dust him off as best I could, and handed him his blue work ball cap. That should get him wherever he wanted to go. It said "Engineering" on it, in a gold-on-white patch.

He adjusted it to be all business. "Sure." He looked at the cast-screen countdown clock. "It will be tight, but we can get there pretty fast."

VII

THE TRIP DOWN BELOW was faster than Joe thought. Because when we got down to the empty street level, we stopped him and each took one of his hands.

"Quick – close your eyes and visualize the pattern we need to follow." I said.

We saw all the turns and twists, the stairways and doorways, and finally, the outside walls. And we also saw that we were going to have to pass through a lot of fusion radiation leak areas.

Joe opened his eyes at this. Because we all knew he was suggesting he put himself at risk just for us.

"That's all we needed, Joe, thanks. We can take it from here."

"You sure you won't get lost?"

I smiled, as did Betty. "We'll be fine. Now, you stay away from that fusion radiation. You're going to have a lot of very healthy kids in your future if you do. OK?"

He nodded. Then hugged me and Betty like old friends.

Betty and I stepped back from him and held hands. "You take care of your family, Joe. If we can be in touch to check on you, we will."

He smiled. "I will, and that's a deal."

"Now, go – you have just enough time to get back before lift-off and keep your Jeannie from worrying about you."

He took off, running back up the stairs two at a time to his apartment.

The rumbling had started again.

Not that we felt much of it.

Because we were already shimmering out of view.

VIII

WE SURFACED SEVERAL miles away from the city, on top of the highest natural rock structure we could find.

And watched 'Cagga take flight.

It was both horrible and magnificent at the same time. A huge mass of earth, surrounded by a translucent energy sphere, followed by a massive plume of pure-energy fire that was burning the atmosphere below it and putting out thunderous noise and shock waves.

Betty put a more natural shield around us to protect us from the fumes, noise, and shock waves.

Within a few minutes, it had flown way over our heads, and we could only see the flaming exhaust. And that was thinning with the atmosphere. The trail it left was like any rocket, but far more caustic and destructive.

On the horizon, we could see several other exhaust plumes in the distance, along with a few mushroom clouds from the cities that didn't make it.

This was the moment, the crux.

Time to get back home. Like the old phrase, "Nothing to see here, move along, move along."

And we did.

• • • •

HAMI'S OLD SALOON NEVER looked more welcome. We came up outside it, so we wouldn't startle anyone inside.

As I opened the screen door and let Betty in before me, I could hear a smartphone with the 'cast that was coming from inside the cities. They were describing the lift-off of all the Independent Cities as a complete success. (While there was no mention of the ones that had not made the transition, or what had happened to the people inside those collapsed force shields.)

Chaz was there with Hami, huddled together watching the tiny screen. They both smiled as we entered.

"How did it go? Your usual success?"

I had to grin. "Yes, Chaz. A bit of a tighter deadline than I wanted. But they're all safe and healthy now."

"Too bad you couldn't bring them back with you."

"Oh, I did bring something back for you. Here, let me see your smartphone."

Chaz closed the IC 'cast app they'd been watching and handed it to me.

I held it for awhile, then showed Betty the screen. There was little blond-haired baby Sue in Betty's arms, gurgling and cooing away.

Handing the 'phone back to Chaz, he shared that with Hami.

"There's our future. All smiles and courage."

The Cities Rise

BY C. C. BROWER

• • • •

Originally an introduction to Book Two (or a promotional snippet for its backend to get you to buy this book) this story was almost lost. (Saved by a backup in a place it shouldn't have been.) And it's too short to tell of many other stories, such as what about cities whose dome failed on lift-off...

• • • •

WITH A THUNDERING ROAR, the cities took flight.

Cities — whole cities — roared into the atmosphere, their protective globes turned red and then yellow with the reflections of the exhaust.

Their fusion reactors scarred the skies with fume trails. Any place on earth you could see them rise. All the 50 United States and all the major countries who could afford the technology had cities flying that day.

They turned their major cities into a one-species "Noah's Ark" to save humanity from itself. Take the best and brightest, and all who could fit, up past the atmosphere and beyond it. Seek a "new life in the stars."

This statement came from the last international broadcast. And it played out at its end with a great symphony chord.

Unstated was the little-hidden fact that the richest corporate heads and their families and investors all traveled on-board as well, first class.

Later we did get some on-board updates, and some human interest stories. Otherwise, a lot of it was replays of old classic movies and sports events because there were not enough newscasters left on earth able to man a national media organization. They'd all gone up with the cities.

The Arks took temporary station along the "ring of pearls" - those satellites in orbit protected by the same shield as the cities. For a while, their glow added to those pearls. But one by one, those pearls extinguished. Some, with powerful enough Earth telescopes, could see them absorbed into the cities.

Around two weeks later, the cities one by one moved out as a string of their own towards the moon.

Later, a hail of meteors followed in their wake. We didn't know what those were at first. The last radio transmissions we could receive said they were falling into desolate areas. We couldn't check this as the cell phones and land lines had all quit working at that point. The towers still worked locally as long as they were solar powered. But just as quickly as the Internet had died, all intercontinental communications ceased.

Because that "ring of pearls" they'd taken with them were all the major satellites that still worked. While they were also in orbit, they were scooping up all the other "non-vital" satellites and orbiting debris as some grand ecological gesture. These either burned up when they ran into the Arks greater power fields or were just absorbed into them.

Joe Salmon watched from his clinic bed just outside the Brooklyn exhaust zone, safe as the ships rose. He was born and raised in New York City. But once he caught the disease, he wound up exiled to hospice care for the rest of his days, which weren't supposed to be many.

Samuel, out on the prairies, saw the distant lights rise and wondered how long his fuel tanks would keep his farm engines running. Sure, he thought, the Amish and Mennonite were better prepared for it. But they had so long depended on the "English" (as they called them) that even for them this was gong to be quite a change. Since he wasn't selling to the agricultural conglomerates anymore, he wondered what the market futures would be like. Now that Chicago had left...

Missy and Pete had escaped the cities years ago and taken their prepper network with them. They now had a safe little village up in the mountains. They hoped they had thought of everything. At least they were high above the pollution that these Arks had spewed out in their last years.

That was the curse of the Arks. And became very apparent as they rose into the sky. They exposed their fusion reactors that had powered them all these years. Before that point, those fusion reactors pointed down deep into the earth and their exhausts pumped back into the atmosphere of the surface.

It didn't bother the people in the Ark so much because their protective shields filtered the air and kept the harmful poisons out all these years.

Amy, a nurse, had gone with her with her patients to the out-clinics because that was her job. That was her duty. And she couldn't see living in a sterile atmosphere inside those arks because she had lived most of her working life inside a sanitized hospital. At least until the contagions inside the hospitals themselves got so severe that most of their patients either died or got transferred out into hospice quarantine.

From above, the hospices looked like rings around the launch sites.

While the contagion was blamed excessive use of antibiotics, it didn't matter at that point. These patients were incurable, and the hospice shields were to keep their infection from spreading.

Soon, we could see the stars at night from anywhere on earth. Because all the electrical generation capacity on the earth failed one by one. We knew we were facing a new Dark Age, except for those leaving in golden-shielded Arks.

Once the hospices lost power, any shields those clinics had also left, along with that protection. Soon, most of the densest populated areas were derelict. The plague spread through human contact and physical interaction, regardless of gloves and masks. No other species were affected, almost like it had been engineered for human DNA.

A new stage started in Earth's evolution. The humans had left.

The Arrivals

BY J. R. KRUZE

• • • •

There was until recently some mystery about where the elementals came from and how. We know that they first showed up right after the "Rising", but that was about it.

This story fills that gap.

• • • •

ONE YOUNG WOMAN - while out on a simple hike, becomes trapped by a sudden storm in a long-forgotten mine. Then finds herself dressed for a ball in the middle of a snowy wilderness.

A young single rancher - who rescues a young newborn calf, only to find himself tricked into meeting elemental spirits - who tell him he invited them.

And now she has to rescue him - or did those elementals create this scene as a trick? What do these spirits actually want from them?

Between these two are several mysteries, and the couple meet in a snow-covered supernatural wonderland. They find their unique talents and abilities pit themselves against all-powerful elemental spirits - to survive, and maybe fall in love. If they can overcome being spelled into romantic scenarios against their wishes...

Will they ever return to the lives they knew before?

Not the way they started out that morning, anyway.

I

WHY I WAS OUT HERE no longer mattered. More important was just living to make it back – if that was still an option.

The storm came in faster than expected. Being up on the side of that mountain left me exposed to the fickleness Mother Nature shows at times. While I was prepared for a lot, being buried under two feet of suffocating snow wasn't something to live through and tell your children. Even if you wanted the morbid experience of it.

Some people like to say snow was a blanket. But nothing you'd ever wrap yourself in. Unless you wanted to die. The only other option was to keep moving. Moving. My feet and my staff as an extra leg. One step, then next. Move staff. Next.

My memory said there was an old mine just ahead, somewhere along this overgrown and slide-filled trail. All that map-study while the rest of the crew laughed at me during their endless poker games. The one's those men all played through long winter waits under weather like this.

Memory isn't something the worst storm could suck out of you. Winter storms screamed the snow, dirt, and leaves past you while dropping visibility to a doubtful If.

At last a darker shadow and unnatural, straight crack told me I'd found it.

When I pushed through the icy gales up against that old mine entrance, I realized my bad luck just got even worse. The heavy rusted door had been propped open with a 6-inch wood log, someone's leftover firewood. No telling how long ago it had been like that. Those hinges now weathered and corroded. Moving a three-inch thick door made of heavy dark oak and ruddish-black cast iron worried me. The door filled an actual opening big enough to drive a semi-trailer-truck into. What made the job even harder was the lack of any little jack-door for maintenance access.

The next job was opening the entire huge span, or nothing.

This little girl had her work cut out for her. It was either get inside or literally die trying.

The wind hadn't helped as it was pushing like some defensive lineman against everything I was trying. Straight against that wide, thick door.

Squeezing through that thin 6 inch opening would have been possible in a t-shirt and jeans. I wasn't built like some lumberjack. And the guys always commented how I was so thin I could get blown away life a leaf in the wind. But they had to close their dropped jaws when they saw this "leaf" scamper up a spotting tower faster than any of those over-built muscle-bounds could.

Right now, I was also swaddled with all this insulated parka, sweaters thick and thin, plus insulated bib overalls. Nothing was coming off just to get me inside. Too damned cold for that.

So it was push, squeeze, gasp, push. I did throw my rucksack ahead, just inside to commit me. I had to get out of this turned-horrible weather before I froze. The picture of me being frozen while stuck half-way in or out of that doorway made me push a little more.

At a break in the gusts, the door somehow creaked and gave just a bit and I was in.

Stumbled, fell clumsily inside, something hard against my ribs. Hands just keeping my face from a rocky impact. Breath knocked out of me.

The darkness was then made almost complete as the very next gust slammed that door back on its iron frame with an echoing BOOM.

• • • •

MY EYES ACCLIMATED to tell me there was a tiny little light left seeping around the iron door frame at the opening. The 6-inch firewood that used to hold that door open was now down to a very flat half-inch. Rotted. Now only a pulped mess.

If these 2-3 inches of snow-turned-blizzard then built into iced-over three-foot drifts, I might not be going out that way for a very long time. And time wasn't on my side in a pitch-black hell's backside mining cave.

So I sat back against the door and felt it shudder with the wind gusts.

The smell wasn't bad in here at least. Enough air had been circulating at the opening to keep it dried out. And the cave wasn't going to get much colder than it already was, which was well above freezing. I could see water drops on the waterproofed legs of my ski overalls. In this light, they were lighter than the pitch-black hole that pushed in on them. But not lighter by much.

Getting more light was my next job. There was a pen-flashlight attached by its own carabiner to the rucksack. I turned it on first, then unclipped it from the 'sack and re-clipped it to my glove. Dropping one of those in a vast darkness would mean taking off gloves to pat around in unknown gloom. I wasn't prepared to stick my fingers into bat guano or Gawd-knows what.

The feeble pen-light did its trick, despite the cold sapping its tiny batteries. I could see around the rucksack - enough to take off my thick mittens and undo the various fastenings that held it shut.

The first thing to pull out was a real torch - one of those with "watch your eyes" warnings. Now I could see what I was up against.

It wasn't pretty.

• • • •

AT FIRST, THE LIGHT just went straight off for a hundred feet to show barely where the ceiling started to slope down. Like I said, you could pull a whole semi with a trailer in here if you could get it up the mountain side. That raised a question of why would it have to be that big, just for mining. Maybe it wasn't an exit or maybe not a real entrance. Had it been built for storage?

Tucking that torch under an arm, I could see what else was in that rucksack while my hands searched by feeling.

The next item to pull out was an emergency beacon with its GPS tracking signal. My heart sank. Its cracked circuit board was sticking out of the smashed case. A victim of cushioning my fall. So I shoved it back into its pocket with all the bits. Maybe I could fix it later. Maybe.

Cell phone was next. No bars. Not surprising. Plenty of charge, but nowhere to go. With the glittering rock sides of this cavern, it was probably the iron in these mountains and other minerals that kept me isolated here. Even if I was outside in clear weather, cell tower coverage was spotty. Plus that thick metal-framed, garage-sized door wasn't helping any signal. No way to get that phone squeezed through the door frame and around the door. So it too went back into it's Velcro pocket. For when I could get outside again.

Sure, I wasn't necessarily going to freeze to death, but it would be a very cold and slow way to end things otherwise. Death by dehydration and starvation more likely. If I didn't get some sort of flu from the mold.

No one was coming for me anytime soon. No one and no machine could do anything until this storm passed. I was on my own for the next day or so. With that much snow, any tracks or trace was covered over. That "day or so" now meant "indefinitely".

I sent the beam around, and found my sturdy cedar staff. Having a third leg would still be useful against falls. Right now, it was helping me stand again.

As I rose, I swung the knapsack by one strap over the opposite shoulder to my staff arm. I could feed some bruises from the fall, but a once-over by looking and feeling showed nothing was ripped.

I got my mittens stowed in my parka pockets, then double-checked the ground where I'd been sitting. And found only the dust from years of nothing happening in this cave. It only showed my marks from landing and sitting. No tracks from any other critters. Their absence only deepened the mystery of this long-forgotten mine entrance.

My hand-torch showed the walls had been widened out from a natural cave. Mostly pickax work here, and some chisel work to get a square-frame in for that door. That work was so precise, I again wondered if there wasn't another reason for that massive door besides keeping people out. It might have been to keep something secure inside here, out of the elements.

• • • •

SOMEWHERE IN THAT DARK, I hoped to find something to lever that door open again. A steel frame or I-beam or something that could be gotten loose and dragged back up here.

Failing that, there was going to need to be another opening. Most mines had them – or there might be a natural gap or fissure from the original cave.

The only way I was going to find either of those was to start walking.

Into the dark. Less cold, no wind. But dark.

Only seeing a few dozen steps in front of me at a time. And hope that was enough...

II

IT WAS SUPPOSED TO be a time of peace.

No conflicts beyond fighting with the weather for crops and rebuilding our society.

I didn't care about all that when I was out checking the cows that winter day. Just my dogs and me. Seeing how the fences were. Making sure the calves were on the right side of them. Not that there was much conflict or worry from those cattle. Even coyotes left them alone. Nothing like a mean momma cow. They were never far from their young calves. And wolves were only up north. Hunters made them scarce in this state.

So when I saw the calico calf in the snow, it was surprising. The cows were black and white, no red or brown in them. Not in several generations, anyway. Not with this bull. And the neighbor's haven't been out of their fences into ours.

Now I'd heard of striped cows, and spotted cows, but those were in two colors. This was three. Like a cat. Or more like a kitten.

There was this calf. New born. Shivering. No cow tracks anywhere. Just fresh snow on top of old snow. Temperature was still below freezing. Meaning I had to get this calf somewhere warm. Closest place was a quarter-mile away. Carrying a forty-pound calf. So I took off my outer coat to wrap up that calf. (Layers helped in more ways than one - besides, I'd be sweating shortly hefting this weight up and down hills.) And I'd still have to warm up some colostrum and milk-replacer. And come back to find that mother cow and bring her up to wherever I got the calf safely.

I had some hundreds of other thoughts going through about what I now had to do. Like the many fences I'd have to cross with this calf, where to keep it warm that I could clean up. How much it was going to take to get another cow to take it in. My day had just been changed. One bright spot was that it was still morning.

That bright spot was dimming though. The sky was becoming dark, but without any clouds. I could hardly see my own tracks to make my way back. I didn't want to stumble with this precious bundle in my arms.

And that slowed me down as I had to be more careful. There wasn't even a moon to light my way. This was becoming quite a chore. And I thought I was used to farm chores.

. . . .

"ARE YOU SURE THIS IS the one?"

"You've read the same signs. The stars, the loneliness, the remoteness. He's the future."

"The future that is yet to be, hundreds of years in the future."

"But only if we act now."

"And we will be acting with him for hundreds more. My question is: how certain are we?"

"That's not ours to ask. Ours is to do."

"Our doing will be a long trail to cover. And we'll forget some of what we know."

"The adventure is not without its trials and duties."

"Yeah, trials and duties. Great."

"Does that mean you're ready?"

"Right. Let's do this."

. . . .

WITH EVERY STEP, THE calf was somehow getting lighter. And smaller. Still, the steps in the snow were not any easier. While my feet were dry and warm, I was still getting the burning in my ears and cheeks from the cold, but couldn't free my hands to pull my scarf and cap down. This calf might already have frostbite and I had to get her somewhere warm, with some warm milk inside, soonest.

Every life was precious somehow. They came into this world with for that chance and needed every break they could get. That has been my idea of life. I didn't have to understand all the technical details of how it happened. The vets can do all that studying. That's why we take our problem animals in when things don't work out right, what we pay them to do. All I can do is the best I can do. If I knew more, I could do more for them. I've buried and dealt with my share of the ones who didn't make it.

And told them they could come back any time, they were welcome to try again. Somehow that made sense to me.

Life is not "one and done" in my book. It always made more sense to me that you did your best with what you had. But at the end, you still had a choice of what you were to become.

Becoming was an always-on type of thing. We all have the time we have, to do the best with what we've got, and make more out of what we'd like to fix while we're here.

So I've got this calf in my arms on a cold winter day, and I'm going to give this little piece of life all I can to make it into more life. That's what I do. All I've ever wished to do.

I guess that's called love. Like the people in my life, like the dogs and cats. Love isn't just touchy-feely stuff. It's part of life itself. I've got life and so does this calf. A few more feet to the warm porch and something to warm its belly. Too bad it got so dark so fast. But we'll both be warmer soon...

• • • •

"THAT THE ONE, ALL RIGHT. He's the one for sure. Never seen such humanity before in one person. Are all farmers like this?"

"Mostly, but he's exceptional. That's why we were called here. His wish for people to have more life, to do more for all life around him. He's the key to what's coming."

"That dark times thing?"

"Dark Age."

"Oh, well, we both know it's dark."

"So funny. You're going to be a hoot."

"Not like you didn't get any warning. Besides, he cracks jokes sometimes."

"And you know how long this may take."

"I think you mean the phrase, '...as long as it takes.'"

"Right. Once we do this, all of us are committed."

"And he doesn't have a say in this?"

"You already heard his wish. It's an always-on proposition with him."

"OK. Looks like he matches what we need. Let's go."

• • • •

JUST AS I TOPPED THE last hill and got around the trees into the clearing, I was seeing lights. But they weren't the ones in my house or the barn. One red, one bright blue. At first, I thought they were Mars and Venus, so low on the horizon. But they got brighter and seemed closer. One to my right and the other on my left.

Then the calf disappeared completely. I was just holding my coat. No weight, no form, just a coat. And watching these two lights get brighter and closer. But instead of being scared, these were somehow bringing more peace to me. Even the night sky in morning fit in with these two somehow.

I just watched and waited. No sense in running away in fear, not that I was fearful. Just stood there, coat in both hands. My breath was coming out in regular puffs in this cold air, turning red and blue from the lights.

The brightness became too much, so I held up my jacket in front of my face, then shut my eyes to keep from going blind...

III

AT LAST, THE TUNNEL started turning up – and I'd been following "up" for hours, it seemed.

I could thank all my forest service spotter training for keeping me in shape and building my stamina.

Meanwhile, the former smooth walls had narrowed, and turned coarser, until the flat smooth floor itself started winding between boulders and becoming little more than some game trail.

I was having to shift the torch from side to side in order to twist through the crooked walls that Nature, not human, had left as any opening I could travel.

The cedar staff I'd unscrewed into its three parts and replaced them in the rucksack Every hand- and foot-hold was precious. Balance was kept by holding or standing on at least three out of the four. More like rock climbing now than any brisk walk as the day had started with.

The air had turned fresher, but somehow warmer as well. Occasional drafts swept by me. I could feel their different touch as it no longer chilled my face and exposed skin, meaning the storm was not as severe. Getting out into that weather might mean the hike back to the closest spotter or relief station would be possible before darkness fell.

At very least, passing the evening on this side of that cave opening could be simpler, less challenging. Provided I could get a fire built near shelter.

And provided the width of this narrowing rocky crack was going to let me pass.

• • • •

BETWEEN THE RISING temperature and my efforts to squeeze through ever-narrowing openings, my sweat convinced me that I could thin down my bulk a little and make better progress.

Off came the parka and heavy sweater. Secured in or to my rucksack, which itself got a para-cord securing it to my waist. Leaving nothing behind – since I only took with me what I needed. Warmer or not, anything I didn't need now, I probably would later.

The indirect light coming through that crevice was enough to turn out my torch and stow it.

Meanwhile, the temperature was coming right up. And that didn't make any sense. No sign of thermal activity in these rocks. But the amount of sweat making my eyes sting made me get right down to my long-sleeve thermal top and jeans. That knapsack was becoming wider than me at this point, and I was progressing in two stages – first me, then getting the rucksack through.

At last, the crevice was widening, but not getting colder. Any breeze that came through was more like spring than a frost-biter. And there was a flatish foot path again, all gravel and sand.

Of course, I'd lost all direction by this time. All I was certain of was the increasing light, the widening crevice, the mild temperature.

Something was up with all this. Nothing I could explain.

A last turn did little to set my mind at ease. I was out of the crevice, but now I was out into – what?

IV

THE NEXT THING I REMEMBERED was finding myself sitting down in my old chair with all my outdoor clothes on. Boots had melted their snow off onto the throw rug although it wasn't put there for that. The fire was just embers, but the house was tight, so it wasn't cool. And I was starting to sweat with all these extra clothes on.

Got up. Went to the back porch. Boots went on the boot mat where the snow and mud would come off and dry. Chore coat and hoodie got hung up, along with the insulated overalls. Cap and scarf went on top of the dry gloves and bandana's. My gloves were soaked, so I brought them back with me to hang behind the wood stove. Another mental note to rub them down with waterproofing gunk. Not that I much remembered that.

Pulled on a sweatshirt and poured another mug of coffee. Two scoops of honey, like usual. Put that down on the stove hearth and poked up the embers. Then added some more split wood and a little paper that I rolled up and knotted. Shut the door and watched the flames start up. Sipped my hot coffee meanwhile.

Sitting down in my chair again, I started to relax and study what had just happened.

There never was any calico calf. So who put that in my head and why? Sure was tired like I had carried that weight to the house. I was even wearing my heavy coat indoors, so either I put it back on, or never took it off.

The snow melting (which was now seeping into my sock feet from that rug) means I did get outside. Tiredness could be imagined, but more than likely I had got that far while checking the cows. And somehow came back and sat down without remembering it. Or mis-remembering.

Red light, blue light. What was that all about? And they seemed to have voices. Voices? I know they weren't my own imagination at work because I was used to that chain-of-thought stuff. These were two distinct voices and were carrying on a regular conversation. In my head.

Or somewhere around there. My mind isn't in my head, but that's the phrase for it.

These two "guys" had come in and set up shop, or tried to.

"Well, we're still here."

That woke me up. Nearly dropped my mug of coffee, but just ended up sloshing it a bit. The hot coffee on my jeans made it a little less hot when it seeped through. But that just proved I wasn't daydreaming.

"No, you are very much awake. And thanks."

"Thanks?"

"For letting us in."

"Like I had a choice?"

"Yes, of course you did. You always do. In fact, it might be that you actually invited us."

"Wait a minute. I didn't put out some 'hey if there are any talking lights out there, come on in' signs."

"Well, not in so many words. But your loneliness called out at times."

"I wouldn't call it loneliness. Solitude. But I like the quiet."

"You're right. Loneliness isn't the right word. How about 'people you could share with'?"

"Yeah, that's a point. I had my journals, but those don't particularly go anywhere."

"Talking to the cows and wildlife was another tip off."

"But they like to be talked to, even if we don't share the same language."

"Oh, they understand you just fine. You just aren't listening to them."

"Hey, I get what they want, mostly. It's how they look at you and when they want to sniff your hand or want scratching. They'll let you know if you've got your eyes open."

"True. But you can get more than that from them. You can actually talk to them - with your mind."

"Like that is going to go over well. Great conversation starter. 'Hey old Bessie was just telling me the other day...'"

The voice was quiet for a bit. And for a split second I thought the whole thing was imaginary.

"But would you like to find out when they are hungry or why they don't like certain bales or grasses over others? How about your dogs and cats - when they go out to hunt on their own, or if the coons or possums are cleaning up their food instead?"

"Sure, that would be great. Because you'd think they'd eat that tall stuff first, but they usually go for the clovers and finer grasses instead of the taller grass. And I hate wasting cat and dog food on critters."

"It all begins with listening. That's what you need to do first, just quiet your mind and listen to them."

"Meditation or something like that?"

"Probably similar to it. Anything in the mind is related. Just some of those descriptions are meant to sell books or coaching and not really to get anything done. Well, maybe feeling at peace. But you do that just fine. That's why we could hear you."

"I was talking too much to myself, I guess."

"No, it wasn't that. You were sending."

"Sending? You mean telepathy? Must have been broadband, like shouting from mountain tops. Hearing echoes come back, like they bounce off the trees sometimes."

"Sure. Close enough. Learning to send and receive. Talking and listening. Just not with your human words. Just your mind."

"How do I know this isn't just my imagination going full bore? Like I'm actually dreaming and stuff. I'll wake up pretty soon..."

"Right. Could be. And we can just shut up and leave you alone if you like. Because we are only here to make your life more interesting. Lots of people get this invitation. Almost all of them shut us off, and then we go away. We don't need to waste your or our time if you don't want us here."

"You mean I'm not the first you've talked to?"

"Not by a long shot. Anyone and everyone could listen enough to learn to send and receive. Almost nobody does. But you've probably read or heard about some that do - those are the ones that have everything they want out of life. Almost always happy.

I mused on this for a while. Calf or no calf, life was going to be interesting from here on out...

V

THIS NEW SPACE WAS some sort of valley. There was snow on the ground further away from the opening, and on the boughs of trees, but none directly in front of that crevice opening.

Yet, it also wasn't melted.

By reflex, I started suiting back up again. With that much snow, there was freezing weather out beyond, even if some freak thermal was keeping it balmy in the location I stood at.

So - on came the ski overalls. While the heavy wool-blend sweater had to come next.

As I got it over my head, something flashed in my vision. And that sweater seemed to get longer, thinner, the sleeves shorter. The fabric now smooth and not course.

By instinct, I raised both arms straight up and this new fabric slinked its way down my arms and across my back. My now bare back.

Bare?

As it settled on my arms, the sleeves had become fluffy and thin gauzy fabric, only a little wider than piping straps. And I had to hold it against my chest, since what I thought was a sweater had turned into a long rose-pink ball gown. Off-shoulder and covering my bare form below it. Only held up by my arms I had crossed below my bust.

Turning around, I had to double-check on what had just happened.

No, I wasn't cold in that outfit – and I should have been freezing.

Putting one arm behind me, I sought to at least find a zipper so I could get my arms free and into that parka.

I heard a zip behind me and the dress was now tight around my middle.

Turning still, the long hem swished against the ground. The feeling on my ankles somehow told me I wasn't wearing hiking boots anymore. But then found that the feeling of fine fabric against my legs was one I had somehow missed.

By the time I'd turned all the way around, I was certain that there was no parka or knapsack anymore. The sight of a long dress swirling also reminded me of old feelings, good feelings.

And my coal black hair wasn't in a tight bun on the back of my head, but was instead cascading down my back and seemed a bit longer than before. Touching something at the corner of my face, I found it was a ribbon off some sort of small pinned-on flower arrangement.

No, this wasn't Kansas anymore. But a smile was coming to my lips and cheeks again.

The ground around me was still bare and dry, and where the snow started, it was more a backdrop for some prom picture than a a snowy blizzard any more.

In fact, it was almost just that. The snow wasn't moving. And the breeze I felt was more just enough to wave my hair around – like an off-screen fan placed for a photographic effect.

If I wasn't unsettled enough by then, here came two lights – one red, one blue.

Talking lights. Carrying on a conversation as if I weren't there to hear them.

• • • •

"HOW ABOUT THIS ONE?"

"What do you mean – 'what about'? We just got her all dressed up and ready. Are you having second thoughts?"

"Well – no, not really."

"Not really?"

"No, she's fine. It's just..."

"Just what?"

"Do you think he'll like her – really?"

"Are you going to keep doing this from here on out?"

"Doing what?"

"Questioning everything we do."

(Sigh.) "I'm sorry. It's just that I get nervous sometimes."

"Yeah, it's not like I don't feel it, too. But we have him and we have her and now all the pieces are in place."

"Just about, anyway..."

. . . .

I CLEARED MY THROAT. "Hey, you little light thingies. I heard all that. And I don't appreciate your getting me 'dressed up'."

"You don't like the dress?" (Some sadness in that voice.)

"No, it's fine. It's pretty and all."

"And you look so – beautiful in it."

I blushed a bit. "Well, thanks. It's been a long time since I had something this nice to wear." And I swished the gown a bit with one arm as I watched the light play on the gauzy and sparkling fabric.

"So you do like it." (A smile in that voice, now.)

"I like the dress, I just don't like being dressed into a ball gown without asking."

"Is it too tight, are your shoes pinching? Is there something else you need as part of this?"

"No, for formal dancing, this is fine."

"Well, OK, then. It's time to get started."

"Started? Wait, I was in a cavern and pushed to get out here – and the storm – and..." I stamped a foot, only to realize I was indeed wearing some low-heeled pumps now instead of my hiking boots. "Look - I don't know what you're trying to get started, but... Wait, I'm talking to some blinking lights. This is just weird."

"We're sorry for confusing you. It's just that there's so little time. And you have to save someone."

"You must be joking. There's no one around here that needs saving. And how am I supposed to rescue someone in a prom dress?"

(A sigh.) "It's not that kind of rescue. But it's still one that you alone can perform."

"Like CPR or something?"

"No, nothing like that. Look, we'll take you there and then you can decide. If you don't like it, we'll put you back in the cave with all your parka and sweater and gear."

That didn't take me long to decide. At least I was outside and warmer. Plus, I hadn't felt so feminine in years. The least I could do would be to go and see what they wanted. Beats the hell out of waiting out a storm in a dark cave.

VI

THE MUG OF MY COFFEE turned into a flute of some bubbly drink. And I had one in my other hand as well.

But I was standing now. On the deck of something like a ship. An unmoving ship. Lights in the harbor around us, but in the middle of nothing. Not at port. Nothing close to us.

I turned around to see what else was in sight – or that these "lights" wanted me to see.

Then I saw her.

Black hair cascading down the open back of her rose-pink gown. Long, graceful arms held her by the railing.

No one else around. Some old 30's slow dance music coming from the glassed-in dining room – but no one inside that I could see.

Well, I guess she's the reason I'm here. Might as well introduce myself.

My shoes made little sound other than a tiny tapping on the polished deck. Within a few steps, I was a polite distance away – such that if she turned too quickly, a bump wouldn't spill anything.

"Ahem."

When she turned at the sound, I was amazed by her beauty. And spell-struck for a bit. Dark eyes and brows, a light tan to her rounded face. Athletic shoulders, trim waist and hips. When she turned, it was with one hand on her long gown, as if she were admiring her dress. The effect made me speechless.

Her first words broke the spell. "You, too?"

"Me, too?"

"Shanghaied and dressed up for something not our usual scene. Like out of a movie, but without the camera or script?"

I looked down at what I was wearing. Tux, cummerbund, Red handkerchief in my pocket. Not anywhere near my work clothes.

Just had to smile at that. At her.

"Hi, I'm Jules."

"Donna."

And since my hands were full, I handed her the flute of bubbly in my right.

Of course, she smiled at that – and I was spellbound all over again.

"Ok, Jules. Now what?"

"Oh, I don't know. Other than I think I should tell you how great you look."

"Really?"

"Yes, really. I know it's been awhile for me, but – well, I like your idea of being dressed for a movie set. That would explain a few things."

"Things?"

"Well, you wouldn't believe me, so..."

"Oh go ahead and try me." Her smile melted my heart all over again.

"Talking red and blue lights."

Her cute mouth dropped open and her dainty eyebrows raised. "You, too?"

Her laughter was the sound of a bubbling spring.

I had to chuckle along with her.

"OK, Jules, we have some notes to talk over, then. Step over to my office and we'll talk over this - well, whatever this drink is." She turned back to the railing and I stepped to her side without touching.

"Ooh, this stuff is pretty good. Not bitter, but sweet. Apple cider, maybe."

I sipped it. "Yes, that's probably it. Can't tell if its the spiked version or not."

She turned to look up at me with those dark eyes. "We'll know soon enough. Anything either of us say will be funny and we'll start telling the other about some truly embarrassing incidents we've been trying to forget for years."

"Or – maybe we just start mooning at each other like it's the first time we've ever been in love."

"There's that."

I raised an eyebrow as I looked down. "I think it's those lights doing this."

She sipped again and moved closer to me. "I think you're right. The next thing you know we'll be in each other's arms and kissing passionately."

"Could be worse things."

"Like waking up and finding it's a dream."

"So, what do you think they're up to?"

She moved even closer, and looked into my eyes with an intense dark look, the hint of a smile on her lips. "I think they are seducing us somehow."

"But we don't buy it."

"No, but we'd like to. Did I tell you it's been awhile for me, too?"

I put my free arm around her waist, and felt her encircle my neck with hers.

"Well, that would figure. But of course, we're going to have to resist."

"Of course. Wouldn't be a good romance script unless we both really didn't want it. And so we'll somehow resent everything the next morning."

Her lips were inches from mine now,

"So, how do you think we make it quit?"

"What quit?"

"The spell."

"Oh, sorry – I just..."

And she laid her head on my shoulder.

I felt the my flute of bubbly disappear from my hand, while her other hand came around my back. And soon we were swaying in our close embrace to the ballroom music.

• • • •

FADE TO BLACK.

VII

"WELL, THAT WAS JUST fine."

"Sure it was. Except it wasn't."

"Whaddya mean?"

"They didn't fall in love at first sight. They knew they were being spelled."

"So – we just keep the spell on them until they finally give in."

"No, that's not how it works. You heard her – they'll "resent it in the morning."

"She also said that's a good romance script."

"That was sarcasm. She was resisting the whole way."

"But they both said it's 'been awhile'."

"You don't get it – do you. Humans don't just go into heat and mount each other because it's 'been awhile'."

"And what do you know about humans?"

"As much as you do."

"There's your problem right there. We only know what we've seen in the movies."

"And – who's fault is that?"

"Because we only had movies growing up?"

"Point taken."

"Alright, let's try it my way, then. Back to that calf in the snow."

VIII

THE WIND WAS BLOWING, the snow pushing past and almost stinging when it hit. Just thankful I was back in my full get-up with everything on, rucksack on my back, and my cedar staff in my hand.

I saw him standing there, a few paces away – in his dark brown work coat and tan insulated overalls, shin-deep in snow. He was looking down at a dark shape in the snow. A little calf, maybe.

I had to ask. "Jules?"

"Donna?"

The knit wool scarves covering our faces, didn't hide the surprise in both our eyes.

"Is this your calf out here?"

"I've been through this before. By the time I got back to my cabin, it was gone. But it doesn't matter – that calf is alive right now and I'll be switched if I let anything die out here. So..."

He took off his outer coat and wrapped the calf in it, then picked up that package to start struggling through his own snowed-in steps back to his cabin.

"Here, let me help – does this path go directly back to your cabin?"

"Pretty much, yup."

"OK, I'll clear your steps and cut the wind off you. Just yell out if I'm getting too far ahead."

It wasn't any easier going, but we were both more used to this than dancing in fancy clothes.

Too soon, I heard a muffled yell.

Turning around I saw him holding an empty coat. He was twisting and turning himself to see if it had slipped out of his grasp.

"Jules – put your coat back on. It's the lights again."

He shrugged back into it and zipped it up. Then looked where I was pointing.

Those damned lights. Visible in the falling snow and wind.

"Oh, well. Let me take the lead for awhile. We're not too far from my cabin. At least it's warmer in there.

• • • •

JULES LET ME GO INSIDE first, and I stepped to one side once I was through the door so he could come in and shake all that snow off as well. I knew these small cabins. You didn't just walk straight in, as everything would soon be soaked from melting snow and then you'd have other problems. Wet feet, for one.

He had a wide boot mat, which collected most of that melting snow. And the sturdy hooks held both our coats and everything else. Now we were sock-footed and down to thin sweaters on top of long-sleeved insulated tops, I tried to keep out of his way, but he just signaled me to sit on the bunk while he got the small wood stove fired up again.

Then brought back a pair of mugs with some stout coffee in them – not scorched, but a typical bachelor trick to keep from throwing anything away.

He brought over the squeeze-bear of honey and handed it to me first, then sat on the bunk an arm's length away. I put a good dollop in of honey in my mug, then handed it back. Tasted a little bitter, but warm and sweet. Kinda like I acted on my worst days.

My face probably showed it when he turned back from replacing the honey-bear on the nearby table.

"It tasted better this morning." He smiled with that apology.

"I've had a lot worse – mostly my own." I replied. "Thanks."

We both sipped awhile in quiet.

As last I had to ask, "Do you think they're still here?"

He nodded and pointed toward the ceiling. Two lights were bobbing there, one red and the other blue.

• • • •

"THEY'RE PROBABLY MY fault, or so they said. And that I could have them leave at any time."

"Now you tell me."

"Kinda the first chance I've had – isn't it?"

"Sorry, you're right. And I'm a guest in your cabin now. Again, it's been a long day and these lights didn't tell me I had much of an option other than being shoved back into a dark cave to wait out a blizzard."

"Wow. You've got to tell me that story sometime. By your gear, it looks like you were out for a rescue or something."

I smiled, sheepish. "Probably just my own. The storm wasn't supposed to hit for hours and I needed to take a hike to work off some steam. It had been the first break in days, plus the sunshine was so attractive. I was only going to be gone for a couple of hours..."

"Do you talk to yourself when you walk?"

That surprised me. "Sure, great way to blow off steam and think things through. Why do you ask?"

Jules nodded. "Another thing we have in common. And probably what attracted these light-thingies."

"Thinking out loud?"

"It's something like that you may have been broadcasting your thoughts while you were doing it – and that attracted them."

My mouth fell open. "Are you serious?"

"It's what they told me. Before I wound up on that ship with you. Right after they pulled that disappearing calf trick – the first time."

"Do you think they're listening?"

"Of course. Not like they have anything else to do."

I sipped more of the bitter-sweet brew. "Wait – you said that was the second thing. What's the first we have in common?"

He turned away slightly, and other than the weather, I thought I saw a little blush.

"Well – I think we both know you look good in a formal dress."

It was my turn to blush. "That's something I haven't had for even longer. Too much a tom-boy, I think."

He turned away to let me have my moment. Like he was embarrassed – or too much info.

I touched his shoulder. "Hey, thanks for the compliment. You looked pretty dashing in a tux."

Jules turned his head to look at me. "Thanks. Not like I get much of a chance to wear one. It did seem a good fit."

I smiled. "So I guess we have a reason to thank those light thingies for getting us together, if only for that moment."

He smiled in return. "Yeah, it was nice while it lasted."

We both sipped our coffees for a bit.

Then it struck me. "Hey, where is this cabin?"

"Middle of nowhere, Midwestern US. Why?"

I got up and fished out my cell phone. No bars.

"Do you usually have poor reception here?"

"No, maybe it's the storm."

"What's the forecast for this storm?"

He frowned. "Actually, there wasn't any storm on the radar like this. Last time we had something this heavy, it took a couple of days to move out – and a week or more to melt enough to get out again."

"So you have a truck?"

"Yeah, I keep it in a machine shed closer to the road. But digging it out will take some time – even if the storm was over right now. Plus, it's pitch black out there. Do you have to go somewhere?"

I shrugged. "Thought I should call someone to tell them I'm OK and not to worry. How I would explain taking a walk in California and winding up in the Midwest would – well, I'd probably leave that part out."

"Are they going to be looking for you?"

"By now, probably. As soon as the storm lets up so they can get some searches going."

At that, the two lights floated down from the ceiling.

"Now it's our turn to apologize."

IX

THE CAVE WE WERE IN was huge, with a thick oak and iron door open wide and tall enough to drive a semi-trailer rig through it. Donna and I were sitting on a large log well inside with our coffees still in our hands, a campfire in front of us and facing a scenic view down the mountain beyond that. Sunset was making the trees golden through the wide opening. To one side of the campfire was a large rick of firewood against the far wall. In between those were two sleeping bags laid out with mattress pads.

Donna's phone rang in her hand.

She answered. "Yes, this is Donna. Oh, sorry I didn't call you. Yes, I'm fine. Yes, I should have left a note. But the boys are going to love this – you see, I met an old friend on the trail, and he, well, I'll be back in the morning. I just got my phone charged up again and happy you called me. I didn't want you to have to get out in this..."

Donna looked out and saw that it was a typical clear California evening coming on – no snow at all. "... uh, go out of your way to find me. But thanks again. OK. Bye."

Then she shoved the phone in her pocket, put down her coffee on the flat cave floor and stood. Pissed.

"OK lights, you've got more than an apology to give us. What the hell...?"

But she didn't finish her tirade.

Two ghostly children appeared, barely teenagers by the look of it. Both with blond hair, cut more for utility than style. Both dressed in clothing like lab uniforms. Shirt, pants, slippers. All a uniform color. Her outfit was a rose red, his was denim blue.

I put my coffee down and stood next to Donna to face them. "So you two are the ones flying around like little lights? And moving us all around the country?"

They nodded at the same time. The one in the rose outfit spoke first. "I'm Rose, this is Dennis. And yes, that's us. We're sorry for upsetting you." They wore matching sad faces.

Donna cocked her head slightly. "But why did you do all that?"

Dennis looked at Rose and then spoke. "Because we could hear you both so clearly and you were both lonely..."

"...and we thought you could help us if we helped you." Rose finished.

Donna and I looked at each other. And saw the loneliness in each other's faces – it was true what they said. She took my hand, and then looked over at the children again. "It looks like we have some talking to do, then."

· · · ·

"GO FISH."

Rose pulled a card out of the stack. "Got a three!" she shouted triumphantly. And placed the set on the cave floor in front of her. She had won again.

Dennis rolled his eyes. "She does that a lot."

Donna started asking again, "OK, now it's time to tell us more of your story. You got brought up as babies without parents and all the adults got sick around you. So you were raised by remote TV with a bunch of other kids your age in a dome. And one day they tried to kill you all?"

Rose nodded, sad at this. "Well, they started it. We had these twin brothers there and they sent one of them out for a train ride with a little camera sewn into a teddy bear. His brother had a matching teddy with a monitor on it. But they also had what he was seeing on some of the other TV sets. So we all watched him ride out a long way. And when that explosion showed on his little screen, we all saw it."

Rose turned to her brother and hid her face in his chest while he hugged her.

She sobbed and we all waited.

Donna held my hand again as she did, gripping it tightly. I looked at her face and saw her biting her lip, her eyes moist.

Of course, that made my eyes moist, too.

Once Rose sat back up and wiped her nose and the tears off her eyes, I ventured another question.

"And how did you all get out of there. You look pretty alive to us."

Rose looked at Dennis, the only one in the cave with dry eyes. He started telling what happened after.

"After that, we all refused to do any more of their tests. And we disconnected all their TV's and cameras – except one set that was pointed to the wall. So we could talk to them, but they couldn't see what we were doing in the rest of that dome. They tried to stop the food, but we found that we could eat about anything, even rocks if we wanted. And dissolve things in our hands – or more like 'into' our hands. So the next thing was to dissolve the locks and go outside to see what was out there.

"When they saw us start to leave, they shot at us. But all it did was hurt and knock us down. One of the kids made the bullet come back out of him, and he stood up to throw it back. Just as fast and hard.

"He got shot again, but just repeated it. Then other kids got their bullets to come back out and threw them back. So they quit shooting at us. And we went back inside.

"One of the kids told them they needed to start the food coming back again, or we'd walk outside again. So they sent some big meals back. And they all had poison in them. But it didn't make us sick, even.

"They said that was the 'Lazurus effect, the same virus in us that made adults sick and die was keeping us alive. So they said.

"And then they turned on the gas, but that only made our eyes sting. One of us told them to knock if off if they wanted us to stay inside the dome, they better treat us nicer.

"They did, for a few days. Then some big helicopters came over and they cemented the dome from top to bottom. All the doors, everything was covered. And cut the power so it was pitch black in there.

"A lot of us got upset, some cried, some got angry. And the one of the boys ate his way out. Then he just walked off and kept walking. We saw bombs and explosions in that direction. But never saw or heard from him again.

"Then the rest of us cut some windows out of that concrete, so we had light. But others just left. Different directions, usually at night. Until we found we could make ourselves invisible. Anything we took in, we could send back out. So light didn't need to reflect on us, we could let it pass through both ways – and so no one could see us.

"The funny thing was that we had grown so close together that we shared our experiences, even at a distance. So we found out that first boy wasn't blown up – he just buried himself in a rock quarry and was still there, just waiting. If they ever got close to him again, he was just going to blow them up like they did to him.

"But then he went to sleep.

"Lots of them got tired and went to sleep – in walls, in rocks, in basements. Still there, I guess."

• • • •

DONNA LOOKED AT ME, still gripping my hand.

I turned to Rose and Dennis. "So you haven't changed the way you look since you left?"

They shook their heads no. Rose asked, "Why do you ask?"

"Because people age as they get older. Some stay pretty longer, like Donna here."

Rose nodded. "I wish I could look as pretty as Donna."

Donna had to smile at this. "Have you tried growing your hair out, maybe getting some different clothes?"

Rose smiled. "Well, we kinda like dressing as stars. I do a red star and Dennis does blue."

I understood now. "So you don't need human bodies."

The teenagers both smiled. Dennis spoke first, "And then we found we could do all sorts of things, like making things appear and disappear..."

"...or making it seem like people were in different places – or actually moving them somewhere, like we did to you two this afternoon."

I frowned at this. "But you wanted us to get together somehow – and that shipboard dancing was nice, but neither of us wanted to meet like that."

"Yes, we noticed. But you worked to save that imaginary calf."

"Because life is important to us. Every second of it. Even if that life belongs to someone or something else."

Dennis and Rose looked at each other, then they turned back to us.

"Then you can teach us. We've been wanting adults to teach us for a long time – like parents."

Their faces shown bright, grins on both.

I turned to Donna, who was smiling as well, then turned back to our new students. "Two conditions – you make it so we don't get sick from what you have, and you ask us first if you want us to do anything for you."

The teenagers nodded.

Rose spoke first in reply. "Then we have something to ask you..."

"...we'd like to learn everything you know, from the inside out." Dennis finished.

Donna wrinkled her forehead. "What does that mean?"

Rose smiled. "Oh, it doesn't hurt and you aren't changed in any way. We do it to animals all the time, just to learn all about them. And after we are done, we can talk to them like we are talking to you – through your own minds..."

"which is why we picked you two to begin with. One female, one male, both adult, both lonely, both brilliant. Perfect matches. The people we'd like to become if we decided to 'grow up' and be adults."

Donna and I smiled.

I had to ask, "And is there some other side effect that we should know about?"

Rose and Dennis nodded at the same time. Rose started, "You get to learn everything we learned..."

"...and do everything we've already know how to do." Dennis finished.

Of course, that was a lot to swallow. But after what we'd just been through and heard in the last few hours, it didn't seem that big a leap anymore.

I turned to Donna, "Well?"

Donna nodded as she looked back at me. "We're supposed to be 'spending the night together' anyway... Why not?"

As we turned back to the two teenagers, we saw them turn back into their red and blue lights, then come toward us. Donna and I were smiling back.

X

LIFE GOT REAL INTERESTING after that.

Rose and Dennis learned all about how hard it was to grow up and grow older. Rose became beautiful, and found she could have any color or length of hair she wanted. And she tried on several beautiful gowns in front of us, as well as bathing suits. Somehow, she always filled them very well. Dennis took on a very athletic build, ruggedly handsome. And decided that wearing a tailored suit was what he liked.

Jules and I found out that we had a lot more in common. And both of us gained the ability to heal injured creatures, and talk to them.

After that, Rose and Dennis sent us both back to our homes and work.

Jules got a reputation for training animals, and giving talks and demonstrations to people about animal welfare. Vets say he has an uncanny ability to know what's going on with the animals he deals with. Jules just smiles and says it's a gift he found along the way.

I quit my forest service spotting job, and work part-time as a nurse's assistant in the nearest hospital to Jules' farm. They like me best in the Emergency Ward, but I like visiting the newborns and children in Pediatrics to help them adjust to the new life they've found.

I love Jules farm, and his collection of classic books. Of course, we added onto that cabin to make it big enough for two and still cozy.

Rose and Dennis come to visit occasionally. But it's not like we ever really get out of touch with them.

More like they come to share their new skills. And we try to find them new books and videos that they haven't seen, so we can all read and watch and discuss them.

Just the other day, they surprised us as they ran across someone who actually knew how to bend time and study both past and future like a classroom.

Just imagine all the people they can help now. That *we* can help now.

• • • •

The Wild Calls

BY C. C. BROWER

· · · ·

This last story starts to tell of animals who are suddenly able to communicate with humans on their terms. Another out-growth of the elemental influence – and springboards for some more stories after this, just maybe...

· · · ·

I

MY NAME IS KELLY AND I like to read. And since the cities left us, that was hard enough. Finding real books was tough. Thought I'd like to be a writer one day. As soon as someone started producing paper and printing them again. Meanwhile, I thought up stories and told them to people.

But I never thought I'd be doing something crazier that my own imagination.

It's like this: I'd had coyotes and crows talking to me for months in my dreams. Thought I'd been reading too many Amerindian legends. So I laid off them and picked up an old copy of Twain's "Life on the Mississippi", thinking some nonfiction would cure my imagination-osis.

Nope.

We'd have these talks. I'd sit there in my dream, on a log in my nightgown, while across a smoldering fire sat a well-groomed coyote on his haunches. On a pine bough overhead stood a crow, black and seemingly able to appear and disappear in the surrounding darkness.

Who would start the conversation was often anyone's guess.

But the last talk we had saved my life, and those of my kin.

· · · ·

"I TELL YOU THAT YOU need to visit that building, Now." The coyote was staring at me, not moving his mouth, as usual in these dreams. It was all thought-sending. Telepathy by hooman-name, but the wolf-kin disliked the term as too limited...

"Why?" I asked.

"You need to save our kin and yours. Like I said before, and been telling you for nights. Now you have no choice. They are coming," answered Coyote.

"Who?" I asked.

"So many questions..." Coyote seemed to sigh. "Again: feral non-human persons who will kill my kin and then kill yours and you," replied Coyote.

Crow spoke up, "This is so. I have seen it with my eyes. They traveled long and are now here. You are out of time."

"Our time for talking is over. You act today, or we both lose kin. Crow and I cannot help you after tonight. You must act or we all die," said Coyote.

"What would you have me do?" I asked.

"We've covered this before. Are all Hoomans this slow?" Crow cawed to make the point.

"Enter the tall building, find the den, save the pups," Coyote sent.

"And face the dangers alone?" I asked.

Coyote sighed. "You are more courageous than any of your kin. Your people won't believe you to give you any help. Trying to convince them will waste precious time. So act now, alone."

At that, the dream faded. The sunlight was brightening in the east and making it light enough to see inside our construction tent. My brother and sister weren't moving yet, covered in their snug comforters on top of thick cushions over their ground tarps.

I rose quietly, and pulled my jeans and sweater in under my nightgown to dress. The morning air was chilly, it wasn't just being modest. Also, the snaps and zippers made less noise that way. And better to leave the others sleeping.

My moccasins were better than heavy construction boots for the work I needed to do.

Sure, it still seemed like a fool's errand. I could seriously get hurt in that old building. My Da and his brothers had told me this over and over. It wasn't just the building falling in on me, but the wildlife inside. A cornered animal will attack humans and even kill them to protect themselves and their own.

Moccasins would get me out of my human camp and around inside that building without being heard, and also make me able to feel what I was stepping on before I put my weight down. They wouldn't protect against sharp objects or cuts from broken glass or ragged metal. So the trade-off, instead of heavy construction boots, was to keep my own awareness high. And live in the moment of each step I took.

Belting on my hunting knife and stuffing a hand-cranked flashlight into an empty rucksack, I about to leave when I saw the pemmican bars wrapped in thin rabbit leather we'd made the day before. Grabbing a couple of them and shoving them into a rucksack pocket, I slung that over my shoulder and left through the rear flap of the tent. This made is possible to avoid coming out into the common area.

I took each step in quiet small paces until I could get to a beaten trail. This trail was kept clear of branches and twigs that could make noise or scratch me in the still-dim light. Until then, I moved slow, with caution.

As I reached the main trail that led to the old building site, I was already a couple of bends beyond discovery by anyone in the camp. Putting the rucksack straps across both shoulders, I quickened into a quiet, padding jog along the path. I had to get in and get out quick. Because I didn't know if these feral non-humans hunted in light or at night.

I didn't want to be hunted. But I had no choice.

Coyote and Crow still echoed in my mind. I'd long ago accepted them as real. Just as real as my family and our village. Regardless of other's opinions. But to act on this alone was either courageous - or very stupid.

Looking to the sky, I saw a black bird flying above me, stopping every few branches while the trees were dense. As if to track me and encourage me at the same time. It might have been my imagination, but I also glimpsed something moving through the trees at the edge of my vision. I was hoping that was a coyote...

II

SOON I REACHED THE old parking lot and stopped to peer from the brush and low pine limbs at the edge of the asphalt. The crow perched overhead. Nothing else moved in the lot, other than the wind blowing the tall grasses, brush, and tree sprouts.

The place had been abandoned since the cities left. Probably before that, when most of the businesses moved from the suburbs back to the cities. This had been called an "office park" and so escaped most of the rampaging that happened later.

That was also the reason it still existed mostly intact. There was no food in here, or anything valuable. Not like stores or factories or warehouses. So there was no reason to break in and steal. Of course, since there were no real laws anymore, it wasn't really stealing. Salvage, more like it.

The parking lot itself was very slowly being broken up by the freeze-thaw cycles of weather. Plus any trees, brush, and plants that could get rooted in the cracked asphalt. No deserted cars here. That gave me some relief, as nothing could hide there and attack me.

Inside that building, it could be another matter.

I could see across the lot, between the tree sprouts and higher growth, that most of the ground floor windows were broken out or had been salvaged. The doors were gone. But it was still mostly dark inside. Creepers had climbed up the buildings, both annuals and perennials. The bushes someone had planted as lanscaping had grown tall and shaded out the ground floor building as those "buses" were actually fast-growing trees. That's why they had to be pruned constantly and would keep a dense shape.

All of that growth made peering into the inside gloom that much harder.

And daylight was getting stronger. There wasn't much cloud coverage this morning. Mostly high cirrus horse-tail clouds. These would burn off later today, but might be replaced with the storm clouds they foretold.

It didn't matter to me. I had only hours to act.

Nothing was in the lot, that was what I was waiting for. So I started moving, keeping to the darker side of the trees. The lightness wasn't helping me. I was obviously there for anything else to see or smell me. The reason for keeping to the edge of the trees was to make sure I still had an escape.

Now I was just 50 feet away from the building and it was now or not ever. I crouched to take another fast look, then sprinted to the side of the building and along those trees at its front into the big mouth they used to call a doorway.

I stopped right inside, behind the wall. Listening to hear if anything was behind me. Calming my own breath, looking around to see my next move.

It was a tall center atrium that went up the three stories of this building. About half the skylight glass was missing for some reason or other. The clouds thinned and all darkness inside the reception-atrium disappeared. I was as obvious as a thumb, sticking out from the smooth walls.

Another fast sprint took me into the big built-in reception desk. I crouched behind one end of it and looked around. Inside was another round built-in shelving system, for paperwork supplies. All the shelf doors were open or missing, anything that used to be there was gone if it could be removed. So it looked like a gap-toothed grin. Some of the house plants had survived and spread across it's top. Most had long stems and few leaves. I imagine that it was because the sparse water that they could get from rain through the broken skylight, as well as the lack of light except during a few hours around noon. But it had stayed dry enough to not smell of rot. Any more than the earthy scent of the forest that grew and encroached outside.

Where was this coyote kin that I was supposed to rescue? So far, I had no clue. I'd mainly been involved in keeping myself in one piece and not leaking blood from self-inflicted wounds.

You'd think that animals would leave humans alone like the old days. But things had changed since the cities left. Like me, most of the animals had been born since. Unlike us humans, they had grown in number. I was the third generation since the City-Rise. The existing humans had mostly died off from plague or lawless killing. The few that remained had holed up and stayed isolated until the plague ran its course. It was only in our generation that exploring for salvage had become a regular activity. For our survival as a species.

My kin had stayed away from the city sites and moved well into the country. And we were here to salvage what we could, mostly some lighter metals, any tools, and especially textbooks. Of course gathering wild fruit and hunting while we went made it possible to travel light and far.

So this empty office park was not on our list. We were there to scout out warehouses and find any library or schools or book stashes.

Meaning that if I got in trouble here, no one would be looking for me. Of course I didn't leave "a note." Like Coyote said, they wouldn't believe me. Most of the time they didn't already. If I weren't such a good healer, they would have left me at our main stockade with the rest of the children and elders, the ones that couldn't travel well.

But here I was. Listening and acting on the voices in my head, that came during my sleep.

The question I had was still: where was that coyote kin I was supposed to save?

So I stilled my mind to listen for an answer. Stilled my heart so I could listen with it. Just as Coyote and Crow had taught me for years.

The answer came soon.

III

A FAINT BARKING AND whining came from one of the upper levels. Echoes from somewhere.

And that meant that something else could hear them and hunt them. Pups. Coyote pups. Kin.

Where was their mother? The answer returned in an instant: dead.

While I didn't get a vision of Coyote, I heard him in my head. A shadow movement across the atrium roof caught my eye. It was a crow, landing on the open edge of one of the missing skylight panes. I could see it turning its head from side to side. Better vision than mine.

Then it dropped to the second story and fluttered in to a landing on the solid railing there. It kept making the same motion, looking at me and then looking inside.

That was my trail to take. There were open staircases on each side of the atrium that led upwards. Hopefully they weren't full of junk or broken glass, or vines that could trip me up. In this light, seeing hazards was becoming less of a problem here in the atrium. Beyond that, in the gloomy rooms, was anyone's guess.

Time to move.

Through to the other side of the reception desk, and a quick look for motion of any type. Crouching down. Moving in quiet. The big cats could simply wait for you to move. Wolves generally stayed out of these buildings as they couldn't dig their dens into them. Snakes were another thing entirely. The lack of mice meant that there was something out there that was keeping them under control.

A mother coyote would have come in here only in an emergency. Now things were starting to make sense. She had to give birth, but something killed her. Now I was going to save her coyote pups? This would go over real well back at the camp.

A caw from the railing edge got my attention.

The way to the stairs was empty. I covered it in a few steps. And the stairs themselves had little more than dirt on them. Sprinting up them made my heart pound. Once I got to the second floor, I again crouched to wait, breathing through my mouth to make as little noise as I could, and so I could hear over my own movements, over those echoes even moccasin feet made.

The crow flew by, into an open doorway. The darkness inside meant solid interior walls. Grabbing the crank flashlight, I kept it inside the rucksack to turn it with as little sound as possible. I wasn't worried that anything out there didn't hear me, I wanted to hear them. Just because wolves and coyotes didn't use these buildings didn't mean something else didn't take shelter here.

Something had killed that coyote bitch before she could move her pups somewhere safer. Whatever did that might still be looking for those pups as a meal. That they had made noise meant they weren't safe here.

I only hoped that "something" was nocturnal. Though the deep shadows weren't helping me feel very safe about that moving around in the dark during "daytime" everywhere else. Testing the light inside the rucksack showed I had a few minutes of strong light, maybe a half-hour if I put it on low beam.

Swallowing, I rose to a crouch, to stay below the level of that railing. Then I followed where the crow went. Pausing inside the doorway, I stood again. This was getting some of the kinks out of my legs. I waited for my eyes to adjust, and listened meanwhile.

As the gloom softened, I could make out thin dividers. Many were tumbled over, but most were upright. Anything could be hiding in there. And the pups were somewhere. Using the light to find them would simply blind me to anything else that could see better in the dark. Almost all breeds of anything saw better than humans, particularly the nocturnal hunters. You have to learn to trust and develop your peripheral vision. Like all prey. At least they had eyes on the sides of their heads. Humans were supposed to be predators, not prey. Like I really had choice in this.

My duty was to get in, get the pups, and get away back to my camp safely.

And not bring anything back with me that would attack our camp.

Then I heard another squeal and a whine.

IV

UP AHEAD, BUT NOT IN this alleyway between the dividers.

I moved over to the next alleyway quietly, feeling each step before I put my weight down. The darkness thickened like soup. It was either crawl and put my hands out in front to find obstructions, or use the light.

Another squeal and whine. And a sound from the other end of this alleyway of cubicle dividers. Something big enough to rub up against something else and make a noise.

That got my heart moving enough to hear it in my ears. Not what I needed.

I pulled out the flashlight, covered it's lens with my hand and turned it on low. One click of my thumb and I could make it bright, hopefully blinding anything that was coming at me. Right now, I aimed it to the floor and separated two fingers a crack. This gave me just enough to see my way.

I knew those pups were in the middle somewhere.

Inching forward, I moved as fast as I could. Until I couldn't anymore.

For some reason, the cubicle dividers had been turned over and pushed against each other at rakish angles. There was no walking now. Like their coyote bitch mother, I had to crawl to reach those pups.

I could smell wet dog ahead. At least it didn't smell like dead dog. Urine I could deal with.

Now I had to leave the full light on low as I pushed it ahead of me. Both arms needed to support me. Although the space was getting smaller as I moved. Tighter. Soon I was on my belly and wondering if I would have to take off my rucksack to keep moving.

Then I had my answer. I saw three sets of quiet eyes looking back at me. Pups.

Where they were was a dead end. The low opening the only way in or out. Unless something crawled in the way I came, they were safe.

I turned the flashlight away from them, against one of the divider walls, hoping the light wasn't leaking out.

Before I moved, I had to make sure not to alarm the pups.

The rucksack was easy to slip out of. But I did this slowly. I didn't stare at the pups, but kept them in peripheral view. From the pocket of that rucksack, I pulled out one of the pemmican bars and unwrapped the thin skin covering. Pulling a small piece off of it, I tasted it. Plenty of fat in it. Smelled like rabbit to me. Hope it did to them as well.

I tossed the piece lightly over to them. One bent to sniff it and tongued it to taste. Then it gingerly bit into it and pulled it backwards. As he chewed on it, the others smelled it without getting too close.

I tore off a couple more small pieces and tossed them gently to each side, so all three could have them. The pemmican pieces were quickly gone. And three pairs of bright eyes were looking for more.

The next three pieces went half way between us, and the three pups cautiously advanced while I froze and watched them indirectly. Those morsels were almost inhaled as well. Hungry little tykes.

The next three pieces landed another quarter-length between us, closer to me. And I waited until they decided that it was OK to move again. And made those pieces disappear as well.

I sat down the rest of that bar within reach. Several pieces, each small and bite-sized.

Finally, they came forward while I sat still, sniffed my hand after they finished off the rest of that bar, and the skin that had wrapped around it. The licked the skin and started chewing on it. One licked my hand where the fat-meat-berry mix left residue.

The trick was going to need to get them into that rucksack and get them out of there with as little noise as possible. I couldn't carry them in my mouth by the scruff of their neck like their mother had.

On the heels of that thought, another entered my mind. A female coyote thought. The three pups came right over to me as one group, and started to lick my face. I'd just become their new mama. I unwrapped half of the remaining pemmican bar and gave them each another largish chunk. Then put the last of that bar back into the knapsack pocket.

I scratched their backs and felt around them to make sure they weren't hurt in any way, or sick. As clean as coyotes could be, they were fine. Just a set of dog-pups like we had in camp. They were going to need some water, but at least they could eat solid food and not need their mother's milk.

Picking them up one by one by the scruff of their necks, I put them into the rucksack side by side. Three pairs of eyes looked out at me from their cozy little cave. The voice in my head was in theirs and was telling them it was OK. Somewhere, that mother of theirs was around, at least in spirit.

Cinching up the rucksack top, I tied it lightly to make sure air could get in. And in that tiny den, I was able to turn myself around. Grabbing the flashlight, I pushed it and the rucksack ahead of me, sliding them on the smooth floor.

Once I got out to a point where I could stand, there was enough ambient light to turn off the light again. I again cranked it to put more charge into the light in case I needed it later. It had a thong on one end. That I looped around my right wrist.

Checking the tie on the rucksack, I carefully upended it, feeling that the three pups were side by side and not on top of each other. Then slung them slowly onto my back. I felt like humming to them, but knew any noise would alert anything out there to my presence. And there was only one way out of these collapsed cubicles - so I didn't need something trapping me here. I needed to get out before whatever it was caught my scent and tracked me here.

The pups stayed quiet, the coyote female voice in their and my head, reassuring.

Once I had crawled back to where I only needed to hunch over, I took a good grip on the flashlight with both hands, I again covered the lens with my left hand and turned it on once more, using the low level and a crack between my fingers as before.

Taking ginger steps, I moved quietly as I thought possible to the opening.

Soon I saw the dim light at the end of the cubicle hall ways. I was able to turn the flashlight off, since the smooth floors showed me nothing between me and that exit.

As I walked, I thought to tie the waist straps for the knapsack, in case I needed to run.

Right now, I heard nothing but my own breathing and heartbeat. Hoping nothing serious was out there. Feeling my hunting knife through my thin shirt at my waist behind me, where I could grab it with either hand.

Stepping slowly forward, I started for the exit.

A noise behind me made me stop, the hairs on the back of my neck raising on their own. It was the grating sound of cubical dividers scraping on the floor. And a heavy grunt as something moved them. Something that had to be big to do that.

V

I WAITED, AND FLEXED my knees to move quickly. Shifted my weight to the balls of my feet. Time seemed to slow to a crawl, my heartbeat seemed to slow to a stop.

CRASH.

I whirled to see what it was, just as another divider slammed down on the first, while a third slid to the side.

Stepping back, I saw a huge dark form behind me, trying to climb across the pile of dividers. More dividers fell over as they were pushed. Their tiny bolts and aluminum brackets snapping with quiet pops.

I heard the heavy breathing of something monstrous. Even for something that large, it was a great deal of effort to climb with all that weight. And its smell was obnoxious. Wild, a predator. And big, very big.

That single concentrated effort it needed to take in crossing that pile of dividers was what saved me.

Two thoughts entered my head.

The first: Light. I put the flashlight on full and pointed it at where the beast's head should be. That beam caught it full in it's eyes. And for a second, it couldn't see. Raising its massive arms to sheild its eyes, I saw that I was faced with a giant bear, a grizzly. And now knew what could destroy my kin. It had been after the pups. Now I smelled of human *and* coyote.

The second thought: RUN.

I whirled and left everything behind me to race back to the room opening, down the stairs two at a time, out around the rounded reception desk and outside into broad daylight.

Sprinting to left, back the way I had come seemed the most logical. Maybe not the smartest, but my scent would double back on itself.

Right now I had to think quick and think smart. If I took the same trail back to camp, that bear would be following me and would take my kin out. Nothing we had for weapons would take out something that size. Once I got to the edge of the building, I turned left again and went back along the service side of the parking lot. It lead out into a back drive, which would then lead back into the main asphalt drive to the lot.

I was betting on there being a lot of asphalt and few organic materials that would hold my scent. As I was running, I couldn't tell if there was a wind or what direction it was blowing. All I knew is that I had to sprint as fast as I could away from that beast.

Another crash said the beast had found the front entrance. Between my padding feet, I tried to listen. To get a clue what it was up to.

Then I heard something I didn't want. It was galloping. And instead of going around the building, it was going right down entrance route to the main drive, the one I was just about to join from that service road. It didn't need to follow my scent. It could see motion between the thin tree coverage and set off in the same direction I was heading.

Then something worse came to my ears. Wolves howling and running behind the bear, on both sides of me and more coming down the main drive toward all of us.

So I did the only logical thing. I dived into the brush and low branches of the trees at the edge of the service road. My face and arms were getting scratched, and my moccasins were so shredded from the asphalt, I could feel the dirt and sharp twigs stick into my bare feet. I just turned off the pain and kept going. Bloody feet left trails, but as long as I was still alive, I could heal them later.

The wolves howled closer. They were closing in.

Ducking, jumping, twisting. I had to get some low branches between me and that bear. And I kept looking for something that had enough branches I could climb. But these were not any I could slow down enough to scout them. The pines gave way to hardwoods that were either overgrown with dead branches, or had dropped them all at their base when they soared up to get more light.

I soon found it got easier going, so I picked up my speed. I was on a path.

That wasn't really what I wanted, though. Wolves and bears move faster on open paths. On top of that, the trees were moving away from both sides and making it a big opening expanse.

The huffing and growling of the bear was getting louder. It must have found the same path. And the wolves howling had increased. I could see them on each side, pacing me, while their howls sounded behind the bear. A wolf sandwich with human and bear meat inside.

I just kept running, keeping my breathing as even as I could. This needed to turn into a marathon.

And for a while, that was working. Wolves, Bear and Human were keeping the same pace. Until the wolves moved even closer.

I was being flanked. If I didn't know it, the wolves were working with the bear. And there was no way to outrun a wolf, not by any human.

Then, up ahead, I saw a coyote standing. And then more, and more. A huge pack of them, just waiting.

I was stuck. Wolves on two side, coyotes in front of me, bear right behind with more wolves.

But my mind went calm suddenly. And I seemed to be looking down at myself running, taking into account all the bodies out there today, right at this time. Seeing them from way above.

This wasn't one pair of eyes. This was many, many eyes. A large flock of eyes.

Glancing up, I saw them. Crows. A cloud of crows.

Yet my mind stayed calm, my feet kept their agonized running, my lungs pumping air, my heart straining to keep up.

And the coyotes moved apart just enough so I could run between them.

I didn't stop to look back, but I felt the wind as the crows dived low over the coyote's heads and mine, straight at the face of the galloping bear. And I could see through the eyes of the crows. Then I also saw through the eyes of the coyotes as they bunched behind me to present a solid wall.

And, just as sudden, I saw through the eyes of the wolves.

The bear was now stopped, risen on its haunches to bat at the crows were flying at it's face. Wolves were feinting in, nipping at its legs and tail. Coyotes were howling at its front with their yip-yipping.

The bear was going into a rage. If it could see at all, some crow would flap right at its face, tearing at it with sharp claws and beak. It it turned to swat the wolf or coyote, then another would nip at the other side.

All this I saw while I kept running.

And at last, I saw a trail that led back to camp. Over to my left. So I ran past it for a bit, and then crashed through brush and lower limbs again to leave another false trail. If I could pick up that shallow creek that trail passed through, I could go back up that cold water and pick up the trail where no animal should be able to pick up my trail again.

From the sounds on the road behind me, it seemed that the bear had turned away and was being chased back the way it had come. Serenaded the entire way by crows, coyotes, and wolves.

VI

FINDING THE WATER AGAIN was a relief to my feet. But I started being concerned for the pups in my rucksack. They had been quiet. Too quiet.

As I walked upstream back to the trail, I undid my waist strap and shifted the sack around to my front, loosening the tie that held them in. And prepared myself for the worst.

When I opened the top, I saw three calm faces looking up at me. Hot, tousled, panting as I was. But almost grinning back at me.

My heart eased and all that I had been through that day to save them was rewarded in that moment. A smile crossed my tired and sweaty face.

I slowed my pace enough to fish out the rest of the pemmican bar and divided it between them. Putting the ruck sack on backwards, I was able to watch them as I gave them more air, but still kept them from climbing out.

As they cooled, they started to groom themselves and each other. Nothing I expected out of these. Like they were at home in their den, with their new mama guarding them.

Soon I was at the trail again. While I desperately wanted to stop, I couldn't. I only paused to undo the leather thongs that held the scraps of my moccasins on my feet. I then tied these to the belt of my rucksack, as even that leather could be used for something else.

Barefooted, I trusted my calloused feet and concentrated on keeping up a steady walking pace.

Soon I had company. The crow I saw fly above me first. Then a coyote moved out onto the trail ahead of me.

I knew I mustn't stop until I reached the camp. If I stopped, I wouldn't be able to get started again without a lot of rest. And my feet would take days to heal. But the coyote just moved out of my way and then paced beside me.

"We wouldn't dream of stopping you. You are a hero and we are here to escort you to your home camp," Coyote sent to me.

"Hero? I wouldn't say that. If it weren't for you guys, I'd be another pile of bones and skin out there," I sent in return.

"But only you could get to the pups. Only you could get them out of that building, that trap. The bear had been working to get to them for days," Coyote sent.

"Fortunately, he was working from the wrong end," I replied.

"Because their mother left a scent from the back side of the building, not the front where you came to find them," finished Coyote.

"Your courage is what makes you the hero," sent Crow, from above. "And more courage will be needed in your days ahead."

"Now I have your pups, what is so special about them? It looked like you could take care of that one bear on your own," I sent to both.

"But you will know these pups, and they will know you," Coyote sent to me.

"And it is key that they understand Hoomans like you and your kind," Crow sent as well.

"Why are these so special? They look like dog pups, so cute," I sent to both.

Looking down at them caught them looking up at me with their grins as they panted to cool in the space of that ruck sack.

"They are part dog, enough for humans to accept them as such. But they are also part coyote and part wolf. And so they are ambassadors from our sentient peoples to you Hoomans. As you are the chosen ambassador to us," sent Coyote.

I was now within the few last turns before I returned to camp.

"Wait at this large rock," Crow sent to me, as it settled on a branch overhead.

It was a granite boulder, left from some glacial time, out of its original time and space. The trail went around it.

I sat, relieved, but knowing I had to keep moving.

"Pick up one foot and stretch it toward me," Coyote sent.

I picked up my leg so that my foot was near his face.

He looked it over and sniffed it. "Hold still," Coyote sent. Licking the sole of my foot lightly, the pain vanished. When it started tickling again, he quit. "Now the other."

I raised it and he repeated the process. While careful of the rucksack holding the pups, I crossed one foot over my opposite knee to feel it. There were no cuts. My hand came away clean and dry. No blood as I expected.

Putting both feet back on the ground, I stood again.

"Wait. Before you go, there is one more gift we must give you." Crow sent. At that she flew down to a branch in front of me so that she was right at eye level, looking at me from one eye. "Open the rucksack so I can see the pups."

I lowered the edge of the opening and leaned it toward Crow, just enough so that the pups could look up at her.

Crow looked down at them with one eye, then with her other. And then looked up at me again. First one eye and then the other.

And I felt something shift in my mind, something subtle.

Then I heard cooing, like babies make. But it was coming from inside the rucksack. I was hearing them like they were human babies.

"And so you will always be able to hear them," Coyote sent. "As you hear us."

Crow sent, "So you will teach them the ways of Hoomans. They will hear you at all times. You will protect them and they will protect you."

Coyote sent, "We will be nearby, but you may not see us. We'll be there, but other hoomans won't understand our presence. All you have to do is to ask, and we will be in your mind."

Crow flapped up into the sky, winging in tight circles overhead until she vanished in the sunshine. I looked down and Coyote was also gone.

My feet felt fine, and I wasn't tired at all.

A few turns and I'd be back at camp. But the day was only beginning to break. The sounds of people starting breakfast greeted my ears.

Time hadn't moved hardly at all. It had seemed like hours. And all I had to show for that work was my shredded moccasins and sweaty clothes.

But I now had new mascots for the camp. And new responsibilities.

And the young pups squealed at my thoughts of this new world they would be joining.

The Hooman Saga - Book II:1

I

THE FLAMES WERE STARTING to show up through the tiny, scarred windows. The vibrations and shaking had gotten worse.

Old scratched-up silvery Ben, the cyborg pilot, didn't seem concerned. But he was programmed to show compassion and be reassuring. His voice circuit mimicked a well-modulated baritone, "We're nearing peak re-entry speed and atmospheric drag is increasing."

Sue, belted in, space-suited, helmet secured with face visor down, was not reassured. "Does that mean the shaking is going to get worse?"

"I'm afraid so, ma'am."

Sue checked her harness for the fourth time. All the silvery web strapping was fine. She felt around the seals of her scratched and scarred helmet with her gloved hands. It seemed secure, but she wasn't going to take the time to unclasp and unseal her gloves to go any further. While she was still breathing the metal-tainted air of the escape capsule, the valves would automatically close on any air pressure drop. Then she'd have about two hours on what was in her suit. But she was pretty sure if she didn't get into breathable atmosphere by that time, the final stink she would be smelling wouldn't bother her. The temporary suit scrubbers weren't designed to handle that kind of load for that long.

• • • •

SNARL CAME TROTTING up the trail to the cliff edge. The night was clear and scent of all the nocturnal animals were alive in the air. He snuffed out his nostrils to clear them. His four legs were quiet on the rocky path, his reddish-gray tail swinging from side to side in rhythm as well as for balance.

As he approached Tig, he saw his den-mate and hunt-team leader in silhouette. He was looking at the stars, but lit by the feeble light of the moon behind him.

Snarl and Tig had been raised together as part of the Chief's family and had been born the same year, a particularly hard winter and cold spring. Those were some good times, Snarl thought. Too many years past already. He snuffed again to clear his head and focus on the job at hand.

The scents of pine as well as the lower-down hardwoods in the valley below made it difficult to concentrate. They reminded him of running with the pack on the hunt. Groups of wolves signaling to each other in turn, bunching up the quarry and surrounding it for the kill. His throat tightened to howl, and he forced it to relax.

"A quiet night." Tig sent by thought to Snarl.

Snarl would have been surprised by anyone else, but Tig was far more sensitive to thoughts, especially from a pack-mate. Snarl sent back, "A good night for hunting, Tig. Almost wish we were down with the rest. They are ready to start when you are."

"You're too efficient, Snarl. And our pack is well-supplied because of you." Tig replied.

"But you seem distracted. What is it, Tig?"

"Another meteor. This is a close one. It looks to be coming down nearby."

Snarl growled low. "I alway hate those things. Will it be near our valley?"

Tig sent, a calm thought, "No, it's parallel to the ridge. But a fire wouldn't help matters."

Fires started by meteors were more common than lightning strikes. And they tended to start with an explosion, which made them spread faster than the slow burn started by a simple sharp flash. It had been like this ever since the Hoomans left. So said the Teacher, and the Teachers who taught her, back to the times of the Hoomans leaving. Snarl sat as he thought this through. Looking up the same direction as Tig, he could see it now. Tig was better at spotting these than he was.

"That's because I watch the night sky to learn." Tig had heard his thoughts like he was sending directly to him. "And because our Teacher recommends listening for the spirits in the sky."

Snarl snuffed at this. "If only we could see these 'spirits.' I only see birds, clouds, the moon and stars."

"But there are more ways to see than just eyes." Tig replied.

"So you say." sent Snarl, as he quieted his mind.

Both wolves could see the red dot coming closer, yet not directly at them.

• • • •

THERE WERE FLASHING lights on the console, but few solid red. Mostly yellows and greens. Some blues. Ben's metallic arms were flying about the switches, when his arms weren't needed for holding his body steady during the re-entry. She could see that he was trying to adjust for the best ride, but being encased in a foot or more of thick metallic and mineral refuse wasn't helping their aerodynamics. Factually, Sue was surprised that he could keep it on a straight course at all. They should have been tumbling by now.

The sky, visible outside the few small view ports that were open, was turning from black to blue, but this was fast being replaced with reddish-orange flames. Bits of the outer rock hull were starting to break off. These showed up as sparks flaring past.

Ben spoke up, "The outer shield is holding. It is keeping our temperature steady. We should retain most of it during our final approach." As if he was reading her mind. But everyone knew Cyborgs couldn't. Sue had doubts sometimes. Maybe because she had talked all those hours with Old Ben.

"How is our angle, Ben? Are we still on a decent trajectory?"

"Better than we could have expected, ma'am. It looks like we have burned off into a teardrop shape, which will help us maintain stability. Calculations show that our boosters will last until final landing, which should cushion our arrival."

"Meaning we won't hit point-blank and explode?"

The cyborg turned his head slightly away from the instruments to be reassuring. "And at the same time, we will still look like a waste-pod meteor on re-entry to any external sensors tracking us."

"Meaning we still look like the same compacted garbage blob as we have since leaving the moon and anyone there won't notice the difference if they are looking at us."

"Precisely, ma'am." The cyborg turned his tarnished silverish head back to the console, a gesture more to be comforting, since he was receiving the sensor data electronically, regardless of what his "eyes" were receiving.

Sue reached down to pat her blue-gray tool bag one more time, touching the straps that held it secure in the seat next to hers. While there were a full half-dozen seats on board, they were all empty except for her and the small tool bag. That synthetic canvas bag was all she was able to take with her from the Moon base.

She thought of her family back on the Moon base, the Elite Guard she had outwitted to slip into the escape pod next to the trash chute launcher. How few people she could trust there. Ever since she had overheard that conversation and told her mother during an allowed visit. That look her mother gave her, just as her assigned "mediator" returned from getting them each a coffee. The mediator's raised eyebrow meant she knew something had been said. And Sue knew her time was short at that point. Because certain Elite secrets weren't allowed to be known by the "down-below's".

Grief clouded her blue eyes behind the scratched face visor. She didn't dare open it as the shaking had gotten worse and her hands were gripping the plastic and metal arms of her seat so that she wouldn't be hammered by her own gloved hands flying about the small, crowded cabin. She didn't think she could open that visor with shaking gloved hands, anyway.

Sue swallowed and blinked a few times to clear. And wondered how she was ever going to see her family again.

The last sight she remembered seeing of that base was just before she quietly closed and sealed the escape pod door with a hiss. It was even darker than the stained dark channels of the waste-pod launching chute she had crossed to get into the pod. Nearly pitch black. She fished out a small black remote from a slim side pocket in her worn blue-gray synthetic canvas work overalls. The black remote had a small yellow-white pin light she turned on to show her where she needed to go. Her first action was to awake the cyborg, keeping him on mute. She found him at his station, and the few blinking and solid red lights on the control board in front of him said that the batteries were full and would support his wake-up and operation.

With two thumbs on the tiny buttons (and she was again glad for her small hands) she was able to tap in a code that turned on the minimal activity the cyborg would need. It was still a trick, but her memory was telling her from deep in her training what steps had to be done when.

They had used to sneak into these rescue pods when they were younger, in addition to the mandatory drills every citizen was required to perform annually. While they doubted that such an emergency would ever occur, there was always a guard near the rescue pods who had to be evaded in order for them to play there. So learning the skill of quickly waking up a mute cyborg and getting him onto "no-alert" status was vital.

As well, the cyborg seemed to enjoy being woken up and talked to. He was part human and that side appreciated human company. Plus, guys like Ben here could play a mean hand of poker or bridge when they couldn't bring enough players.

The lights came on in Ben's eyes. He turned his scratched metal head silently, making a smile appear on his digital-equivalent mouth. Ben recognized her from her last visit. He held up an index finger on one hand and put it to his mouth as a sign he understood to be quiet.

A regular keyboard slid out on an extension bracket, just below the control board, along with a simple light headset hardwired into the keyboard. Sue turned to sit on the floor, positioned the headset over her ears, picked the keyboard off its bracket to set on her lap and started typing in her request. A quiet sound came through the earpieces in response, all in human language, with the stilted AI speech the cyborgs were required to use. (They could mimic anyone on the ship, perfectly. But that was "illegal" in their coding. They had to be recognized for what they were.)

At last the cyborg nodded. Sue reclined her head back against the base of the control board, keeping the earpieces on so she could follow the cyborg as he repeated to her what he was doing. It was simply orders he was following, as part of a drill. Or so he relayed to her.

Sue knew that cyborgs were smarter than they let on. And she had often escaped from her routines to come to talk to Old Ben. He was quite understanding in his responses, almost philosophical. But that is why they didn't have straight AI on these pods. Sometimes an almost intuitive response was needed, a leap of judgment beyond what they could possibly program into their best AI.

Sue would always hug Ben when she left, before she shut him down again. She knew he didn't feel through that synthetic skin of his over his metal, ceramic and plasti-foam constructs. But she seemed to feel that he appreciated the gesture. And it made her feel better, at least. To have a friend she could talk to when she really needed someone.

The escape pod jarred and shook slightly as it settled in the launch tube bottom. It had been nothing for Ben to quietly dismantle all the sensors and then slide the small pod down and onto the launch track. They timed it so that the pod landed in and sunk in among a load of mineral refuse. The auto-hardening cement closed around the pod to make it look like a large section of tube-shaped refuse ready to launch. The other timing was to get this into the base's biggest launch for the day. That would get several of these ejected at once, all on a trajectory toward Earth. Her hope was that no one was measuring and calculating the extra mass in the payload too closely...

A brief alarm, quickly silenced, plus violent shuddering woke her from her thoughts. The view through the window showed that they were spiraling on their decent. The view was going blue, then black then blue... Ben was adjusting manually as fast as his arms could move. There was a burnt-electric smell in the air, as well as some smoke she could see through her face plate.

"Ben, is everything OK?"

"One of our retro-fire rockets has malfunctioned, but the others are still online. There was a fuse overload, but no continuing fire. We are still on our trajectory at this time." Ben replied, but with a terse and almost mono-toned voice. Apparently, his resources were being routed away from his vocal response circuits.

The cabin was noticeably hotter now. The shaking was worse.

Sue gave up trying to talk, as she was afraid she'd accidentally bite her tongue.

She just held on and closed her eyes.

That didn't help much, as their was enough gravity now to remind her that there was a "down" rotating around the cabin and they weren't necessarily going to land right side up.

More sparks, more smoke. Her suit air sealed against the air pressure change.

This wasn't good.

A loud explosion outside. The cabin went suddenly dark.

"Ben? BEN? BEN!?!" No answer. No lights on the cyborg or the control panel.

Sue couldn't help it. She screamed inside her suit.

She screamed against the dark, against the falling.

She screamed against her fate.

· · · ·

THE TWO WOLVES SAW parts of the meteor break away and make in parallel paths to the main body. It was orange-yellow now, and would ignite anything nearby when it landed.

Snarl watched it closely. Tig had closed his eyes.

"Something is wrong with this one. It's screaming at us."

Snarl looked at him and cocked his head quizzically. "Are you kidding me? Meteors don't scream."

"This one just did."

II

TIG HEARD THE SCREAMS *in his mind.*

Someone falling from a great height. From inside that smoking, red-orange meteor headed toward them. He saw it coming from the bleached-white rock cliffs he stood on.

Then he heard the sonic booms with the roar of a meteor burning through the atmosphere.

The crash, and the flames. But no explosion.

Tig then did what he shouldn't have. He didn't do what "normal" wolves do.

There was a fire. If it spread, his pack could be in danger.

He knew that if the fire got out of control, it could ultimately reach the valley his pack lived in. He ran toward the fire, toward the meteor strike. Not that he could put it out but he needed to know.

When he arrived. He was relieved to find the only thing burning was an old snag. Nothing around it but rocks.

But this meteor was a strange one. They were used to meteors.

This meteor left a streak. It didn't come down and explode.

This one had screamed in his mind.

He looked back where it came from. It left a trail and he could see it coming down off the mountain. It had bounced and skipped and then skidded to where it stopped against that old tree. It wasn't burning up, as the other ones did. The descent had burnt off most of what surrounded it, leaving a smooth surface. Scratched and seared, but not pitted like a cinder.

Tig's curiosity kept him going closer. It was either going to explode or not.

Suddenly something popped and opened a hole in its side. Tig froze. He couldn't see what it was clearly through the smoke.

• • • •

SUE KNEW IT WAS A ROUGH landing. She felt sorry for the cyborg pilot Ben who was more part of the equipment than he was alive. Still, she felt for everything that lived, whether stuck in machinery or able to move around on its own. Sue remembered her cats, parakeets, fish. They'd look at her like they wanted to tell her something, and she wanted to say something to them. She didn't know the right way to tell them, the right words to use.

But she shook her head to clear her senses. As she swung the bar on the hatch, it just hissed open. The acrid air of tree burning nearby flowed into the cabin. Clouds of smoke.

She started coughing as she came out climbing up over the seats and the control panel. She knew she had to get air. One arm up. Get her shoulders up. Keep scrambling. Couldn't see very well. The smoke stung her eyes.

She knew it was more blue in that direction so she kept climbing. Had to get out. She lifted herself up until she was able to lean over at the waist across the opening, and at last breathe in some fresh air.

Then everything went black.

· · · ·

TIG SAW SOMETHING. Some body coming out of that opening. He saw it looked like a hooman. He didn't know for sure with all that smoke.

Then the hooman collapsed, right in the opening.

The fire was still climbing up that tree. He didn't know if that tree was was going to fall on top of it.

The wolves were always taught, even from an early age, that all life was precious. Even the hooman hunters that sometimes came after them.

He remembered all the legends, the stories they told to cubs. Hoomans were always the "bogeyman." They were always the ones who come after you if you didn't clean up after yourself, if you didn't tidy things, or mistreated your brother or sister cubs. The Hooman would get you.

And yet, this was a hooman and it needed help. But more than that, something about this was different. He'd never met or been this close to a hooman before. He didn't if all humans were like this when you got close. You didn't know. You just knew that it was alive and it was in danger.

He could have crept slowly closer but instead he leapt and ran, climbing up over the hot rocks.

Tig looked the hooman over carefully and firmly gripped the collar of its suit in his strong teeth and pulled. It took several times to wedge himself against capsule and then worry the body back and forth until it would free up and was able to slide smoothly off that meteor even as he did, thoughts came back to him. Meteors aren't smooth. That mass was probably more likes a space ship from the old, old legends. This wasn't shiny and tall. It didn't give off light.

He didn't have time to think about this, because the fire was still burning. His paws would need to cool off soon or he'd have blisters. So he dragged the hooman away from everything hot into cooler shade.

III

WHEN SUE OPENED HER eyes she saw a wolf looking back at her.

Propping herself up on her elbows, she looked it over. She'd never seen a wolf before, especially not close up. She recalled pictures in her schoolbooks of all the life forms they were going to introduce into the new worlds. They were all sorts of canine breed of dogs.

She almost wish she had studied more, as she never thought she'd have to use it. As the books would always be there.

This wolf was here, though. Looking at her with piercing eyes. And the books were not.

Then she remembered: Wild. Carnivore.

She pushed herself back with her elbows and tried to get her feet under her without looking away. She needed to know if it was going to attack her.

Then its voice spoke up in her mind.

"I'm not going to eat you. Besides I've heard hoomans don't taste good, anyway."

Sue was curious about this and wondered how she could hear his thoughts.

So Tig answered the question. "Well, why wouldn't you? Or are you feral or something?

She said out loud, "Feral?"

Tig chuckled and sent, "Yeah."

His response didn't startle the hooman this time. When she saw him smile she smiled back, as a feeling of security washed over her.

"Can you travel?" came the thought.

"I dunno." Sue said, "We can try."

"We must. The fire is still too close." And he loped off.

She struggled to her feet started walking after him. He stopped 50 yards away and frowned.

"Is that all the faster you hoomans travel? No wonder you're almost extinct."

She called back, "No, I can run." And started as fast as she could even though she was stiff and sore from the landing. As she got closer to Tig, he took off again. He started running, but not as fast this time, so she was able to keep up and they headed up into the mountains.

After a piece of steep climbing, Tig stopped for a moment. He waited for her at the top of a cliff. She was soon close by.

She saw him as a tawny creature with browns and silvers and reds in his fur, admired him for his strength and beauty.

At the same time he only saw she was dressed in some sort of one-piece covering, dully reflective where it wasn't covered with soot. Golden hair fell over her shoulders and soot smudged her light, hairless face. He wondered if she was fur or bare underneath that silvery cover.

At that she blushed. "Oh that's right. You don't wear clothes." She thought back at him.

"At last you quit shouting. All the other People can hear us."

"People?" she sent.

"Yes." He followed up with the idea of being taught by teachers in the verbal tradition. Tens of thousands of years of history as the cubs would sit around and drink all this knowledge in. "All living creatures are People. It's not just hoomans."

They reveled in each other's thoughts, which flew as fast as lightning among the peaks.

They each had much to learn and looked deep into the other's eyes to drink it in as fast as they could.

At last she broke off and looked away. The data was just too much. She found a large outcrop she could lean against and partially sit on, until she could digest the years of knowledge she had just learned in a fraction of a second. It seemed like that.

Tig's thought came to her, concerned. "Are you okay?"

"Sure..." She started to speak and then stopped herself mid- sentence to send, "it's just so much to take in."

"Well, I'm not exactly having an easy time of myself. You have so much strangeness in how you were raised. Your patterns are clumsy to me, anyway. I don't mean to be critical. You're hooman. Hoomans aren't supposed to be able to send."

"No, we don't." Sue replied in thought this time. "We're usually closed off, which gives us problems. Our words don't often communicate truths." She thought for a minute of the Royalty elites she had escaped. "They can be used to lie."

"Yes," he sent, "Thoughts are harder to lie through, but that can still be done." He looked out. "We must travel. We've rested enough."

With that, he was off again. Loping down the side of the ridge at an easy pace, seeing a path that she couldn't have known was there.

And he stopped to look back at her.

Sue sent, "Caring for this human, you didn't have to."

Tig sent in reply "It was my choice. Now hurry, the ferals will be on us soon."

With that she understood. Ferals were closed-minded wolves, and other animals. "Unlike people..." She had to stop and correct herself.

He stopped and smiled and chuckled at her. "You're learning. Now, catch up. Let's go." Then he was off again.

She scrambled to try and follow his trail somehow.

Her boots were not set for this environment. They were more designed for climbing walls of ships than rocks and fallen branches. Nothing magnetic or smooth enough for suction here.

She concentrated on her steps, picking each one to make her way back down to the lowlands.

They continued on for a while going down hill now, as fast as they could climb down it. He was patient enough for her. She had thousands of questions to ask, but concentrated on watching her step, keeping up.

They learned to work together to get her down that mountain. When he would disappear, she would soon be uncertain about the path. She would only need to sense where he was. Often he would then show up again in her mental vision and then into her sight. He would then send her the path he took, so she could see through his eyes what he understood to be a trail.

Bit by bit, the two made their way down that mountain toward the lowlands.

IV

THEY HADN'T SEEN FERALS at first, since they had come off the steepest part of the mountain. This land slanted with boulders here and there, sprouting out of the rocky soil. Not too different, just less steep.

Tig kept pushing them, pushing them.

Sue was keeping up, barely.

Tig kept stressing the fact of the ferals being close by. Then they saw them.

At first those wolves stayed far distant. Still downhill from where Sue and Tig were traveling. Tig had them travel away, on a slant, to keep out of their sight and to cover up their own scent as much as possible. Tig and Sue wound up going away from their original path.

Tig sent, "I hope to double back soon." But that wasn't the case, as the ferals kept reappearing at every chance Tig saw.

They were still moving lower on the mountainside, and more trees appeared. Sue started smiling, to hear Tig, and even more happy to hear the birds singing and talking to each other. She couldn't make out what they were saying. It was good to hear their voices.

Tig kept his thoughts quiet so he could concentrate on the ferals, and on picking out the path they could take that would let them move down the rugged mountainside. If they could move out into the plain, they could move more quickly, and would be less visible through the forests. Every opening Tig had seen so far had a Feral on its edge, so they continued moving in and around the boulders on the mountainside.

Sue meanwhile, despite having to fight for her breaths in keeping up with Tig, still marveled at this wonderland. It was so different from the life on-board ship. As the sun moved lower in the sky, the shadows deepened along the rocky hillside.

More ferals were showing up, down range and ahead of them, so they were forced to keep going parallel to the ridge. Avoidance was necessary, although the ferals knew Tig and Sue were there. Sue could feel Tig's concern, even without him sending to her.

At one point, it looked like they had an opening, but moving down found only more Ferals, so they moved back to higher ground again. The high ground was more easily defended against attack, but the only real rest and food they would find was on the low lands.

Now the trees were much denser. Their roots among the rocks now complicated footing. This made stops for rest more frequent. Short periods so that Sue could catch her breath. The altitude wasn't helping. Ship-board air was set to sea level equivalents. She didn't work in the mines where air was thinner.

Tig tried to continue briefing her about what could come next. "I was concerned about the dark coming soon. I'd hoped to get back nearer our camp to join our own pack's hunters."

He didn't mention he'd noticed a pattern to the Ferals. Tig and Sue were being herded, he just didn't know where. Their only solution was to climb higher up the mountain again.

Sue's ragged breath, even during their rests, wasn't giving him confidence moving down would be possible before the ferals closed in. And this hooman was defenseless. They couldn't try to break through the feral lines.

They had to keep moving forward on the thin path they were herded on.

At their next rest, Sue sent, "I can see you're concerned because you're so quiet."

Tig replied, "Catch your breath, and rest." He smiled to reassure her.

Again, she sent, "But what is bothering you?"

"We are being tracked. They know where they want us and are pushing us that way. I know of many passes in these mountains, but they are keeping us from them."

Sue sent, "Isn't there a cave somewhere we could hold up?"

Tig grunted. "Not that I know of. It looks like our chances are best if we go back up the mountain."

Sue slumped, head down, hands on her knees, blond hair covering her face.

Tig sent, "Come, I think I see something. Let's get moving."

So they picked up the pace a little and Tig sent that he now saw ferals moving up behind them, crossing over above them on the mountainside. They were definitely being herded.

Sue worked to pick up the pace, but Tig still kept within her range. He understood her limits better than she did. He also had a better idea of what was coming, but kept his mind quiet to not alarm her. All this was feral-country. He'd passed through here many times.

Still he didn't understand the ground as well as he should have to protect her. He could keep up a pace faster than this for days without hunting, needing only water from occasional brooks and streams they would cross.

But this human was soft.

He looked back at her when she caught up to where he was standing watch. He saw many places her silver covering was torn. He also noted the cuts on her face and hands from the brush. They had also gone through boulder-sets that had scratched, unforgiving.

He kept his mind still, unreadable, so she wouldn't perceive his concern.

Sue concentrated on her footing, his path, and keeping up as much speed as she could. Her ungainly boots and the chafing suit didn't help. She didn't understand a lot of this. But she saw Tig's watchfulness. Something was wrong. He wasn't making the choices he wanted to for their path. He was making the choices he had to.

Sue saw the ferals now. They showed themselves openly both uphill on the flank of the mountain, and down into the lowlands below them. They were heading somewhere, where the Ferals wanted them to go. But she still had to trust Tig's decisions. For both of them.

At last they hit a real path, a wide path. On both their left and right, taller outcroppings appeared. As they passed in between them, the outcroppings came closer and closer. Still, they kept running.

Tig knew this was a trap. He only hoped he could work out an escape for both of them before it was sprung. Now, their only choice was to run.

They ran further and further down the wide, beaten path. At least the running was easier now and they could pick up speed. But so did the ferals behind them. You could hear them yapping now, calling to each other. On they all ran.

Until a sheer wall rose tall in front of the hooman and wolf. It was a dead-end box canyon.

A wide floor opened in front of them, beat down by many paws and hooves over years of time. There were bones present. These made it obvious that the ferals used this canyon trap for hunting and killing herds.

There were scrubby cedar and pine around the edges. Sue rested against one of the far walls while Tig scouted these edges. There were no escapable outlets anywhere.

You could hear the yaps of the ferals as they were coming down that canyon towards them. They stopped just out of sight. But their calls echoed.

Sue sent, "What should we do next?"

Tig replied, "We have only to wait."

"Is there no way out?" Sue sent.

Tig answered, "I think you can make it up the cliff right behind you. You're more designed for climbing than I am. I can hold them off."

Sue sent, "Hold them off? That means you'll die."

Tig sent, "I think these are a smaller breed, these ferals. I can take out twenty of them at least."

Sue asked, "Only so few out there?"

But Tig sent nothing in return.

Sue shrugged her shoulders and turned around to look at the climbing. She had practiced similar exercises on the ship. They had exercise walls, some in low gravity, some heavier gravity. With small hand-holds, but always relayed by someone else holding a rope.

This cliff wall was every bit as precarious with no safety line. It could be done. But Tig was right. No wolf could climb it on their own.

Tig sent, "They've stopped. They're waiting. There's more of their pack coming."

This was going to be an honor kill. Revenge against his kind and hers.

He continued to cast about, around the trees and discover the lay of the land. He again told Sue to search a way up that wall. She studied the sheer wall to line up a route she could take.

She thought if she had a rope, she could throw it down to Tig and help him climb. It wasn't so steep as the walls in her ship's exercise room. He'd be able to scramble up if she were pulling on him. But there was no rope. There was no ship. It was only the rock canyon which was becoming a death trap for both of them.

Tig sent, "They may not want to kill either of us. Not right off anyway."

Sue sent back. "Well that's reassuring."

Tig understood the irony in her thought.

Tig sat on his haunches, resting ahead the inevitable conflict he knew would happen.

V

HE THOUGHT IT WAS ODD for the ferals to act so organized. He'd seen them hunt in packs. And he knew how his clan would hunt, how his pack would hunt. But those hunts were always with sentients sending back and forth without letting their prey hear their thoughts.

These ferals were working in a tightly organized pattern. That was new. He kept thinking over and over what they were doing. Looking for patterns, comparing them to how he would hunt and how he would use this tactic. And he realized what they needed.

They were waiting for their whole massed pack to bottle-in this canyon before they attacked. There was no sense guarding ridges that no wolf could climb out on their own.

They also had no experience with humans except the ones that from the settlements that hunted wolves. So they wanted the strength of numbers to ensure this sentient and this hooman didn't escape.

Generations ago, the sentient wolves had pushed the ferals back around the settlements of the remaining humans. This was the sentient's protection: a buffer zone to keep the humans away from their cubs and their lives.

While Tig's pack didn't relish killing that occurred without a reason or purpose, they always chased the humans back and made them lose their weapons.

Some humans had accidents out of their own fright, but even then the wolves would respect those dead, cover them with stones or earth as they could, and howl over their death. Dirges would be sung. Not the triumphal great hunt or victory song. These were sung as the sad, unnecessary loss of someone respected.

Reversely, hoomans skinned the feral wolf for hide. His carcass left for other animals to glean. Desecrated. They didn't even value the wolf as meat, only as trophy-pelts.

Sometimes Tig could sense thoughts of the ferals and sometimes he couldn't. Both ferals and the sentients remained alien to each other. Just as the day the hoomans left. Today was no different.

The feral howls increased. Now it sounded like the rest of the pack had shown up and were coming in. Tig could hear them moving closer. He positioned himself forward of the brush on both sides of the canyon opening.

Some cedars, pines, and birch stood on each side. Still too wide for a good defense.

She could climb that wall and clamber out.

Tig could only take as many ferals down as he could. He'd back into a corner, then.

First action: provide her time to climb. Tig looked back over his shoulder at her. She was trying to find a grip.

Tig noticed her slip and slide back down leaving red traces on the wall. Her hands were bloody.

He sent "You can do it. I know you can."

She turned and smiled at him. His face softened, then steeled again as he turned back. Tig was resolved. Her only choice was to get her up that cliff wall. His was to fight for an opening and escape as best he could.

Just then he saw the ferals show themselves. The largest ferals were in front, followed by the lesser-ranked. They were edging closer. Almost shoulder to shoulder, growling low growls, watching him without wavering. Three or four deep at least. This was a big pack.

Tig even saw females at the back. Huntresses were not uncommon. Females were often more efficient at hunting than males, particularly if they had to feed their young after a long winter.

Tig backed a step, then another.

Sue was not half-way there. She kept looking for hand-holds and footholds. It was slow work.

Tig sent, "I knew you could." And all he got from Sue as reply was her vision of where she could find hand-holds he could hold if she could only get him up this wall. He sent back his confidence in her and shielded her from his worries and concerns.

• • • •

SUE WAS HAVING A HARD time finding those hand-holds and footholds. As Tig had noticed, it was slow going. At the moon colony, she knew all the holds on the climbing walls. It was just a matter what patterns you would choose. Here, she had to select firm grips out of the rocks. Too soft and you'd slide back down, which she'd already learned several times. Sliding back down from half-way up could be fatal. Every hand hold and foothold had to be exact.

She dare not even look back behind her for fear she would lose one of those precarious holds she found. Through Tig's eyes she saw the scene below, while he would not send the emotional content. It was like watching a monitor with the sound off.

She turned her attention back to the wall to find the next hold she needed. Her job was to escape.

At last, she climbed onto a narrow ledge. It was almost a foot deep and a couple of feet wide. Here she could stand and rest. When she did, she turned with care. As she did, the sight stopped her breath.

There was a deep, tawny pack of wolves in the narrow opening of the dead-end canyon. They filled that end for yards, four and five bodies deep. Tig was inching back as he watched them, and she was concerned. She sensed that this kind wolf who had saved her would now meet his end. And nothing she thought she could do.

One of the ferals then ran forward away from the pack and met Tig. It then slammed to a stop and laid down, still. From Sue's view point, it appeared Tig must have given him a mighty shove, knocked him unconscious. But his neck was at an odd angle.

Tig heard her thoughts and replied, "I broke his neck. I'll break as many as I have to today. You keep climbing."

The rest of the feral pack stopped on seeing that outcome. But a sheer howl arose from among them that was deafening.

Sue now flattened against the wall and closed her eyes in complete fear. But then somehow, by being in touch with the wall, she got a stillness inside her. She began thinking much clearer, as if the wall itself was giving her strength, or absorbing her unwanted emotions.

She opened her eyes in time to see another of the feral breed came running towards Tig, hoping to catch him off guard. The feral came from the flank, while Tig stood there, staring straight ahead at the leaders in their center.

At the last minute Tig again jumped to catch that pack member flying at him. And again both wolves landed. Tig was upright. The feral's neck was folded at an odd angle, loosing one last breath as he died.

Two ferals then leapt from each flank for him. Tig didn't wait this time. He met the one on his left, forcing the one on his right to chase after him. The feral to his left fell with a broken leg. Tig then spun and met the other, crippling him the same way.

Both stumped off on their three good legs, knowing that there was certain death for them waiting already. Wolves couldn't fight, much less hunt effectively on just three. This stopped the other feral wolves. The howling quit now. Their threatening sounds proved they now knew. He was an enemy long unmet in battle. Most of them weren't ready to face him on his terms.

Tig then sensed some of their ideas, which was a strange experience. Like listening to a language dialect. Most he still couldn't make out.

Now he was over to one side. The two had withdrawn, and he stayed. This forced the pack's attention on him and away from the hooman climbing the wall.

Then a solution came to him.

VI

HE CONCENTRATED ON the clump of trees and bushes to his left. While these were no dead pile of twigs, there was much dead growth on them. Then he spoke the mystic chants rumbling in his big chest, growling these out. He and the feral pack saw smoke rise as the dead limbs ignited, smoldering and smoking.

This stopped the growling from the ferals. They too, along with all their wolf brethren, feared fire and what it could cause. A fire that started on its own, in this canyon with no lightning, was further mystery to them.

Now the tree clump opposite began to smoke. They saw Tig nearby, again growling and rumbling something in his odd manner, as if he were talking to the trees.

Soon the smoke was rising as a haze in the canyon from both sides and the ferals became anxious. They moved backward and forward, looking at each other. One of the bigger ones then growled again and focused their attention on Tig.

Yet they hesitated. For now they had three enemies. Small canyon fires on two sides, and a killer wolf between them.

Tig moved slowly back to that central part between the walls, prepared for the onslaught he thought would come, regardless. Fire shown in Tig's eyes as well, warning the ferals.

The lead wolf of the ferals recognized this and growled his pack to move forward. Only the pack in numbers could defeat this fighter.

It was then Tig sensed something behind him and pointing his senses in that direction.

He was surprised.

• • • •

IT WAS THE HOOMAN, come up behind him, while still at a safe distance so he couldn't mistake her for a feral wolf.

He sent to her, "And what in hell are you doing here?"

And she sent back, "I think I can help."

He shrugged as he kept watching the ferals.

Sue raised her arms, closed her eyes, and concentrated. Each hand pointed to one of the smoking woody clumps. She mumbled something under her breath aloud, over and over. And the two smoking, woody clumps then burst into flames. And the flames roared taller.

The feral pack jerked back as one body. But then the leader barked and moved forward himself. They again followed him.

Tig then bristled, ready for their attack of both he and the hooman.

Sue opened her eyes at this and glared at the lead wolf. She extended her arms even stronger. Her gesture towards the clumps made the flames grow even broader than they should have for that amount of wood. They were now each roaring infernos. And the feral pack narrowed to just a few bodies wide. Tig took a step forward because he knew he could handle three or four at a time in a narrow channel.

The lead feral wolf bristled in return, urging his own pack forward, when suddenly a wall of flame erupted between Tig and the pack. A wall of flame went from floor to the canyon wall-tops. It went outward towards the feral pack so they all stopped, sat on their haunches. And lost their faith, running away, back down the canyon.

The lead wolf looked back over his shoulder to see two forms encased in flames as the massed inferno kept growing, seeming to reach toward him. The ferals ran away down the trail, in absolute fright.

Silence fell in the canyon.

Sue dropped her arms, and then dropped to her knees, exhausted. Tig cocked one ear at her, both curious and relieved. He kept listening, but the running feral pack was now in the distance. Even to his keen ears, their sounds faded after seconds.

Through shared vision, Tig had glimpsed what the ferals had seen, but that's not what he was saw. For him, the clumps of trees only smoldered. Tig went over to Sue and licked her face. She put an arm around his shaggy mane.

At that point another handful of other wolves, colored like Tig, trotted up through the Canyon opening. They skirted the two clumps of smoky wood on each side of the canyon. Then walked up toward the two forms and circled them.

While Sue had gained Tig's support, she had not gotten his pack's understanding. She and Tig understood each other. The rest of the pack did not.

To them the hooman was a danger worse than the feral wolves.

VII

TIG AND SUE WERE SURROUNDED by wolves all out of Tig's pack.

Sue still had her arm around Tig.

Both felt exhausted from fighting the wolves from the feral pack.

Although Tig was painted in blood, none of it was his.

Snarl, leader of the hunting party, challenged Tig. "It looks like you have something to explain."

The wolves were growling to each other. They were both afraid of and hating this hooman.

"What's this? Why do you let it have an arm around you?"

At that, Tig shrugged. Sue dropped her arm to her own side.

Her hands were both bloodied. Her silvery suit was ripped and torn in many places. They'd gone through hell that day.

"What's this, a pet?"

And Tig sent, "That would be one name for her. I will bring her to the Teacher. She needs a probe."

With that, Sue look up at Tig.

And Snarl realized she'd heard and understood what was being sent. So he narrow-sent to Tig, "She's not feral?"

"No Snarl, She's been hearing and understanding everything we send. She's like no hooman you've ever met or ever appeared in stories you've heard."

That moved the whole hunting pack away. Their growling quit, replaced by amazement at the thoughts they received.

"This is why Teacher needs to probe, to find out what she knows. To seek facts from her origins." finished Tig.

"How did you find her?" asked Snarl

Tig replied, "She came down with a meteor, only it wasn't a meteor. I don't know what it was. I went to go check out a fire when I left you. It's taken me ever since until now. We had to shake off that pack of ferals. "

Snarl narrowed his eyes and asked, "How did you just do that. Just the two of you? There must have been four dozen ferals there."

Tig replied, "Well you see those two on the ground. And the rest got a little bit afraid of fire."

Snarl sent, "That doesn't mean the two trees that are just smoking would have frightened the band of rabid ferals."

Tig replied, "No, you wouldn't think so. That's not what I saw. It's what they saw."

And Snarl remembered his sight when he first arrived. Two wolves in the middle of massive flames. He didn't send this, but Sue was looking into his eyes as he thought. And she knew.

"And so we're supposed to help you get this hooman back to the valley? Oh no, that's up you." Snarl sent.

Tig replied, "I don't think those ferals will come close for a while, even if they trail us. She's in no condition to make any great speed."

Snarl counted up, "She will need a guard all the time. She will need a watch. We don't know if she will get infected with those cuts. And I'll be danged if we will work up a travois like some mangy dog. Not just to get her back into the valley. Not just to cure her. All if she doesn't die on us."

Tig sent, "I'll be the one to get her there. You don't have to worry about feeding her, I'll take care of that, too."

Snarl replied, "Well then, maybe we ought to get back on the trail. We've got hours to go before we get anywhere near the camp. Daylight's fading fast. Still, we'll leave a few of our hunters on your back trail. Just to make sure no ferals creep up on us to get their honor back."

Tig looked at Sue. "OK. We must go. Are you ready?"

Sue looked at her cut hands, and her torn shoes and suit. "Well, I won't be any more ready than now."

She rose and wiped her bloodied hands on what remained of her suit.

Snarl snorted at the scent, wheeled, and led the hunters out of the canyon. He stopped later by the pillars at its opening and left sign. A warning to other sentients of the trap. That would tell the ferals to not try that again. A reminder of what they saw, what it cost them.

Without the ferals blocking them, it was almost straight downhill, which Sue was relieved to find.

At this pace, Tig could drop back to run by her side.

And while it would have been too much to talk at that pace, sending and receiving thoughts proved proved no challenge.

Provided she watched her step. But they were on an established trail, one used more by sentients.

This close, they could send to each other and discuss many things. Tig knew she wouldn't stay safe if she remained ignorant of this world.

He also wanted to learn more about that craft she came in. They thought it was a meteor. He knew no meteor had a hatch that opened out. Or held a hooman inside.

They traveled in quiet for a while and Sue had to ask, "Why does Snarl think I need a guard?"

Tig's first response was "All hoomans need guards."

And then he added, "Not only from other wolves attacking them. but also to protect them from things they do not know." Without senses tuned to this world, it was impossible for them to know.

She caught that. "How is it you feel humans cannot learn?"

And he sent, "You must forgive me. I've only dealt with feral humans to this point. We have, years ago, tried to bring smarter and less fearful humans to a location where they could be probed. Never bringing them to the valley. That would be too dangerous."

Sue interrupted, "Then why are you bringing me to your valley? And why would it be dangerous?. Why did you try to probe these other humans?"

Tig sent, "I'll take one of those questions. Because you aren't like the other hoomans. I've never seen the like, and never heard the like. Nothing of what you've just presented us. No hooman we've ever met has been able to send. They've all been closed-minded.

"As for those other probes, it was because we thought they might have the ability to send. They might be able to receive. But what happened? They either went crazy or got too sick. Either way we had bring them back through the ferals, close to a human community, where they could be found. And then see if they were found."

Sue sent, "What did the hoomans in their settlement do with with them after that?"

Tig replied, "We don't know. We couldn't stay. Ferals surround the communities.

Yeah, I picked that up earlier," replied Sue. "So have I got this right? You actually herded the ferals to surround the human settlements?"

Tig answered, "Yes, that was an agreement the ancient sentients set. It was long before my time. Hoomans are dangerous things. The ferals were less dangerous. Sentients separated their packs from humans, putting ferals between them."

Sue asked, "Are there other sentient species besides wolves?"

Tig replied, "Sure. Some in all species are sentient. Not all. That's one reason we want to probe. We need to learn more about this. The Clan needs to learn this. The Tribe needs to learn this."

And with that she understood the pack to be his immediate group. The clan to be a wider group within a larger area. The tribe represented all sentient wolves on the continent.

But when she thought that idea, Tig sent to her. "So there's more than one landmass? How big is this world?"

And she replied by sending him visions seen from space while coming in for their landing. Then images from her school books.

The data was flooding his mind. At last, he sent, "Enough. I don't need all that right now." They were silent for many more paces. It was Tig's turn being awed by a flood of data.

VIII

SOON AFTER, THEY NEXT stopped to rest. Two of their rear guard quickly cleaned their paws from dust and burrs, relieving those on watch to do the same. Two other wolves stood, sniffed the air, then ran off into the brush.

Sue sent, "Where are those two going? I thought they needed rest."

Tig replied, "They also need to eat. We all need to eat."

Now she saw images of possible raw rabbit or squirrel or pheasant, prompting her to put her hand or mouth to repress being nauseous. Sue shuddered and turned away.

She sent Tig images of what they ate on ship. They contained green vegetables, and high-protein beans, raised in greenhouses.

They both looked up as the clouds parted to show the rising moon.

Tig sent, "That's where they are?

Sue replied, "That's where I came from, where they still live."

"Vegetables, huh? I seem to remember a legend about your kind. Try not to get in trouble while I'm gone." And Tig leapt up and jumped out.

Snarl looked over with narrowed eyes, but didn't move. None of the wolves moved closer, either. They recalled all the stories they learned as cubs. Humans were untrustworthy, dangerous, even vicious. With no respect for other species.

In a few minutes, Tig returned with dirt up to his knees and a root in his mouth. He laid that by her hand, then dropped to clean off his legs.

Sue asked, "And what is this?"

Tig replied, "Try it. Think you might call it a carrot. Maybe a maybe a sweet potato."

Of course, the words she knew were different. Their verbal tradition has changed the words. They had been told and re-told, over two hundred years, teacher after teacher.

She finally just picked the root up, brushed off the dirt from a part that was cleaner. Then bit down on it.

It was succulent. It was sweet. And it tasted good. Even with the grit she had to swallow.

Soon she was only interested in seeing how she could finish off the root. She didn't realize she was so hungry.

The other two hunters returned with a pair of rabbits each and they distributed them. Some finished early and took over for those watching, so they could take their own turn eating.

Soon they were all done, completed even in cracking the bones. They rose. Tig led them into the howl.

Sue was surprised.

It was loud, but she could understand the words they were saying. It was a song of gratitude. To the spirit of the rabbits. For offering themselves. The wolves were indebted now. Then they asked forgiveness for their errors. And with that, the song was complete. They were getting ready to travel.

Dirt was brushed over the bones and fur that remained, Snarl took off in front with two wolves behind him. Sue and Tig followed. Then three wolves came behind them.

Sue sent to Tig, "That's not too unlike songs we have among the religious at the ship." And she recited a part of the prayer that had that section in it, of asking for forgiveness of sins. Implying a deity who acted as king.

The wolves all looked at her, curious.

With Snarl leading, the hunter-pack was moving back on the main trail again. Refreshed, but just enough to keep going.

"Hunters travel light." Tig sent, "They feast when the pack feasts. A full wolf makes for a slow hunter." As he cracked the joke, Sue smiled.

He saw that out of the corner of his eye and grinned back, with tongue lolling out of his mouth. They were on a regular pace now. It wasn't as fast as the wolves liked to travel, but one that Sue could keep.

She wasn't out of shape. She'd spent hours daily on the treadmills. They helped clear her mind on the moon-base.

Even though her shoes were cracked, that action allowed them to flex better.

Every once in a while, while they were going downhill, she would spurt ahead to tease Tig. Then he would often send, "Not too far, Hooman. My brothers might like a hooman sandwich."

The first time he cracked that joke, she almost stopped. Until she realized the punchline. The one he'd said earlier that "hoomans don't taste good". And the fact that wolves don't each meat between bread slices. That made her laugh out loud.

This made the other wolves look over. So she broad-sent her happiness. They all relaxed again. Several smiled back.

She thought again about how valuable a smile was. The old phrase came to her that "a smile was seed of laughter that made gardens for a sunny day". While the wolves didn't understand what a garden was, they understood the relationship. They shared pictures with each others of the fat and happy cubs waiting them at home.

Soon the trotting song started. The music was unfamiliar to Sue. After the chorus came around the third time she found she could run to it. Just as the wolves did. The beat was one they could keep going for days. Sue found that trotting song rhythm helped her go further and longer and pace herself against the uneven ground.

Tig sent, "Our teachers also describe the universe as the soul of the wolf. Singing the trotting song helped send the soul off to the spirit-skies until it could return again. When babies were young, their mothers sung the trotting song, Also when they birthed, and when they were nursing. All rhythms of life."

With the food in their stomachs the hunting party continued on that night. Into the darkness, where the tune changed into the night-prowl song. That kept a slower pace and allowed them to look to their footing in the dark. Sue avoided many stumbles by seeing through Tig's eyes. His night vision showed their own path in front.

At last they reached the camp. It was in a sheltered cave and was large enough for twice as big a hunting party to use.

They stopped before reaching it. Snarl went ahead to make sure there were no ambushes.

He circled around twice, sniffing for who had been there, what had happened in the area. Like reading the news.

This was familiar to Sue, as reading monitors and gauges while being on watch in Engineering.

At last he barked and the wolves came in. And then Tig entered with Sue behind him. He gestured towards the back wall. All she saw with a high dry space. She sat down on it expecting cool, but found it was actually warm.

Tig sent, "On a sunny day, sun warms this. In the evening, this would be my spot as pack leader. Tonight it will be yours. For I have a long fur coat and your coat is not in good shape." Tig chuckled, looking at her ship-suit.

Sue looked down and found that while the suit still covered her modesty in the central areas, it would need replacing. That raised other questions. But now she was too tired after today's events to answer them.

Seconds after she curled up on the warm stone, she was sound asleep.

IX

SUE WOKE JUST BEFORE daybreak, not used to having time defined by the sun and not the schedule.

Tig cocked his ear in her direction and opened one eye. "How are you now, how are you feeling physically?"

Sue thought carefully in response, still having some difficulty making words distinct from raw emotion. "Sore, but nothing really hurts."

"That's good, I was concerned you would have been damaged too much. That was quite drop."

Both of them shared their visions for the re-entry. Hers was within the capsule and his was looking up at a fireball heading straight for him from the sky.

"You were brave to stay so close. You could have been killed by the fire."

"Some have said foolish. But your screams, during the 're-entry' as you call it, didn't allow me to go without finding out if such a powerful Sender was still alive. We've never had a Sender show up inside a meteor before."

"Sender, is it? Is that my new name?"

"What would you like to be called?"

"My name is Sue."

"Then Soo-she you will be, as you wish."

"Why not just Sue?"

"We explain our sex by the add-on so we know who we are talking to. There is already a Soo-he in this tribe." He rippled his fur across his back and stretched on the ground, yawning as he did.

"Have I met him?"

"Only if you have been listening long-range. He's away on a hunt."

"I'm still having trouble getting used to this 'listening.'"

"Yes, the legends say your kind didn't do much of this. Except some of your poets and shamans."

"What do you know about our kind?" Sue asked.

"Except for what you've shown me, only what our Teachers have taught us." The idea that came across was those that held the legends and told them to the cubs while they were watched as their parents were hunting.

"Teachers are able to hear the legends from before our time and repeat them to us so that we cannot forget and so make the same mistakes again."

"We used books and recordings."

"And your 'historians' would rewrite those to suit their own biases and so your history was lost. They wouldn't listen, or couldn't. If they did, they would know. Once they know, they cannot forget. But your kind was weird, anyway."

"Weird?"

"They had ears but would not hear, eyes but would not see. And their words were false as their thoughts were clouded. Like your politicians and "news" reporters. They all wanted you to have faith and believe in them, rather than the world around you. But those days are long gone. You are not one of them." With that, Tig rose and stretched fully. His mane rustled and his pelt flowed over his huge frame, interrupted only by scars.

Sue got up in response. With that several others of the pack suddenly rose and pointed their noses in her direction, watching with sharp eyes.

"Peace, brothers. The hooman-she is only rising to greet the sun. She respects our customs."

Sue kept her thoughts to herself, as she certainly didn't have time to learn their customs overnight.

The rest of the pack was now up. Snarl and others sniffed the air, then started off along a faint trail at the forest's edge.

"Come, it's time to run. Do the best you can."

The pack started at once, loping off into the forest at their normal pace. Sue was quickly left behind, gasping with the effort to run that fast in her clumsy space suit, let alone jumping fallen trees, climbing around massive boulders, and over roots.

Tig waited for her, even though the pack ran ahead. He frowned. "Do you remember the ferals? Pick it up. Move."

He thought ahead to remind the pack of her speed and their location.

When Sue and Tig caught up, the rest of the pack was already rested.

Sue never complained. Tig never criticized, but kept demanding she do better.

Tig and Snarl had a short conversation. Snarl wasn't happy with the delays, but consented with a frown.

When they next started up, several hunters stayed behind them, and the pace was slower to match her top speed.

That is what probably saved both of their lives that day.

X

THE THIRD DAY OF TRAVELING would normally have them back in their home valley. Except that both Tig and Soo-she needed to visit that meteor again.

She wanted to pick up some things. Tig needed to show the other wolves its location and get their sense of it.

It landed in the territory of the ferals, within the original boundaries the ancient sentients established. So the hunting pack was on guard more than usual. They could not cover all their scent and traces, especially of a hooman. They traveled with even more alertness.

As they topped the last ridge, they came down onto the grooves this meteor had plowed into the mountainside. The old snag had quit burning. It still stood, charred black, much like a sentinel or a tombstone above the grave mound below it.

The wolves warily approached it, sniffing and looking. They ranged all around it. Sue, Tig, and Snarl came closer to inspect the emergency shuttle, which composed the bulk of that "meteor."

Soo-she climbed inside, clambered over the console and down into the seats, stumbling as she went. That added a few more tears to that spacesuit she still wore. Or what was left of it. At least her boots were holding up.

She paused for a minute by the cyborg console. There were no illuminating lights inside the shuttle.

There were minimal active lights on the console. Those were indicators from the batteries. Self-contained, they would last eons. There wasn't enough light to clearly see inside the cabin.

Soo-she was feeling by hand. She wanted to find a portable flashlight or anything to help her on her way.

As if on cue, the overcast sky thinned, allowing sunlight to come through the opening at an odd angle. It was yet morning. The Eastern sun gave feeble illumination to the dark interior.

She began opening panels and lockers for anything she could find to help her in this new world. Most openings were for repairing the ship. Or covering controls that turned on or off various services.

None of these controls would work now. Most of those services existed only to help the ship survive a landing. The ship was built for a one-way voyage. That job was done.

She hoped to find another suit and she did find a roll of patching tape with an emergency repair kit for suits. The kits supplies were mostly for plugging leaks. None restored the integrity of the fabric. Sue didn't need a helmet, which would be useless, or gloves. Her hands were still sore, but healing. These past few days had been tough already...

There it was, the first aid kit. That would be useful. Particularly the scratch healing cream, and gash sealers. The blister salve would form temporary calluses. She took a moment to put some antiseptic on her hands, then the salve. That would have to do for now.

She then saw her pouch, containing the few things she grabbed to carry with her to this new world.

Again she looked around in the limited light she had to find anything worth salvaging. Nothing else could help her here. There were no knives. Nothing to use as a sharp blade. And none of it consumable, except some emergency rations. She brought what she could fit into her pouch.

She heard a short grunt and a whistle.

Then Tig sent, "Are you done yet? We need to go. Ferals are near."

Soo-she scrambled up to the console, then laid her hand on the cyborg's shoulder. One last time, she blessed him for his service.

She pushed the emergency release bar to the door back in place. After she scrambled outside, she turned and pushed that door shut again. She felt the tumblers click into position. That was all she could do. This ship became the final resting place for that life form. He had become a friend during the long days of traveling from the moon to Earth.

She paused a moment looking at the closed hatch, with her hand resting on it..

Tig sent her an old prayer, "May You and the other Spirits in the Sky Live and Hunt Forever."

She then turned and looked at Tig. As a single tear rolled down her face, one rolled down Tig's.

Snarl then sent, "Come, we must go. They are too close." He wheeled and scrambled up the mountain, back over the ridge they'd just come down.

Soo-she and Tig followed. The guards below the meteor came around and brought up the rear.

Now they had to travel. Fast.

The race back to the valley began.

XI

THEY TRAVELED FAST and hard. They had about a day and a half of travel. To cover in less than a day. There would be no stopping if night fell before they arrived. Neither for the ferals, who were now howling behind them. The small band of sentient hunters kept an even pace rather than a fast one. Soo-she's breath came in ragged gulps, but they were the same ragged gulps.

She learned to understand how to run and how to breathe. It wasn't like anything she'd been told. The training she had on the ship, the constant use of the treadmill, made her understand that her legs would not go out and her lungs would keep up. Still the wolves kept up their inner-chant to keep the rhythm. It wasn't even ground, but it wasn't rocky like the slopes they'd come down. She was listening to the wolves and they learned to trust her sending. They had to act as a team. The approach was the same. Three in front. Sue and Tig in the middle. Three behind.

What Sue marveled at was their efficiency. They learned to think, to broad-send as one. Those in front were scouting the trail and sending the vision of what was coming. Nooks and crannies of the trails. The twists, the turns, the holes. Things to watch out for. Things to jump over. Those behind were sending from hearing backwards. Their focus was backwards. They were getting their sight from the forward wolves.

And all below this with a steady pace of their beat. Their paws on the ground and the beat in their heads from the song they sang to themselves. They kept the pace going.

There wasn't time to eat. There was barely time to drink. They had to keep running. But always, even when stopping to drink everyone else was on alert. Hearing and sending everything they sensed to the rest of the group. Only a few drank at a time. Barely enough to wet their tongues. Then they were off again.

When they first started, this seemed overwhelming to Sue.

Getting this massive information in a single moment. All these messages at once.

But soon it became second nature. She felt more aligned with this group, more part of its team than ever before. And they were listening for her footfalls which were louder than their paws. Tig encouraged her with positive thoughts, but knew she had to decide for herself what she would do.

So Sue kept up. After a while her ragged breaths became deeper, but more uniform, more regular. Not as painful. She had hardly time to think or decide. The focus was on running, not stumbling, and keeping up. The secret was being that moment itself. Each moment as it occurred. Time itself became one moment. The world changed around them. But the moment never did.

It was a unique experience for one who was taught on clocks and times and biorhythms. Logged charts and production goals. Comparing yesterday's last cycle with this cycle, interrupted by sleep periods.

But that wasn't here. Day and night were the same moment. The path changed, but the running was constant. The wind and clouds would move, but the air they breathed was endless. It was all one moment.

They were running. She was seeing through others' eyes. Hearing through their ears. The path was laid out in front to avoid trips, stumbles. There was only running in that moment. The breaths were regular. Her feet were regular. And a song sang in her head. The steady beat, all punctuated by the howls of the ferals.

Ferals were running as an arc behind them. Their howling told where they were. What they were about to do next.

Their fastest feral hunters were running on each end of that arc, trying to decrease the range between them and the sentients.

All running, all ragged aligned, no regular formation or rhythm. Just blind lust and fury. All built up over the last few hundred years. Sentients were their enemy. The feral goal was to wipe them out. The arc contained 20 or 30 ferals.

While the sentients seemed to remain the same in number, ferals had increased their breed. Living off the scraps of the hooman settlements had allowed their increase. The hooman garbage dumps had enabled other small animals to thrive near the humans. So the ferals lived more like coyotes, which also shared their territory. Feral dogs also fought for those scraps, and also the mix-breeds, like coy-dogs.

The feral wolves could recruit from their numbers and bring a large force against sentients whenever they appeared.

There were more ferals when they started. Not many were hardened for a run this hard. This was their true test. Their one chance to hunt their oppressors.

As the sentients could keep up this pace for days, the ferals could not. They had to catch up and attack soon.

Howling was the feral's main way to communicate in packs. And they had to stop to howl. This slowed them down and caused them to use extra energy to catch up. Meanwhile the sentients ran silent.

Still, as they approached the valley, the ferals were gaining. This was rougher ground and the sentients weren't running as fast as they could. The reason for this was running at their center.

The ferals had never seen sentients protect a hooman before. In the full sunset they saw the long yellow hair. The sun would sometimes reflect off whatever she wore on her. That would soon be their prize.

Soo-she was seeing more and more boulders show up in their path. And they were having to take many turns and curves to stay on the path to the wolves's valley.

The valley had been a sentient refuge for many lifetimes. Though many long teacher's lives. It was even unknown how they found the valley. Or that story was not remembered.

And still: the twists, turns, jumps. Gradually the trail grew smaller. It forced the sentient pack to hold a single line. That led them open to attack and was the exact reason for this trail. As it thinned,

the path was much like the old castles with their moats and twisting turns up the hill. All exposing enemies to attack.

The ferals were also on that single trail. As the ferals came closer they also could not pick out attack trails on the flanks any longer. It was a sheer race to catch up.

Suddenly, the path in front of the sentients widened up to well-beaten place. Then dive into a V-notch and disappear into darkness.

At the point where Snarl as lead reached that notch, the three wolves running behind stopped and spun, growling. The ferals now entered the broader area. First five, then ten. Soon there were many who filled that opening and beyond.

Sue didn't look back. She was seeing through the guards' eyes.

She plunged through that notch, following Tig and the rest. As she did, sentient female hunters pushed past her. Back though the notch, they formed a second line of defense against the ferals.

The ferals were catching their breath. They were all gasping and weren't in any shape to attack. They growled at they could. All the sentients shared the sight of how mangy, unkempt and scrawny they were. Their ribs showing as they jammed together in that space. The run had left them in no condition to fight or attack. The ferals and sentients both knew this.

Tig had stopped just after the opening and was again mumbling his chant, focusing on a pile of dried wood left at that opening. And as before, the pile smoldered. This time, a crackling flame started up. That distracted the ferals as it popped and sparked.

The female sentients and the rear guards, backed a step at a time. The lead ferals thought now was time to attack. As they crouched to spring, the sentients facing them wheeled and plunged through the notch.

On cue, the flame roared in the notch, covering their exit. The front ferals felt the heat, backed up, and stopped. Many sat back on their haunches. Some leapt up vertically, twisting to turn in mid-air and landing to run away. All the ferals then took off, making their escape from the fire. Or at least getting to a safer distance.

A few of the huntresses climbed to the ridge and watched, on guard as the ferals left, broadcasting their vision to all sentients.

The hunters and Soo-she traveled the trail down into the valley at a much slower pace now. The road into the valley turned and twisted as the one they had just left. There was no real reason to hurry now.

As they made their way down the path into the valley, Sue had an odd feeling a peace come over her.

Her breath wasn't coming any easier and she knew when she stopped her legs would start to their healing process. And pain that would come with that. But she couldn't keep running forever.

As they past an tall boulder, Soo-she saw an owl sitting, watching at its top.

The sun had come over one edge of the valley, lighting up the opposite top edge. She could see the oranges and blues of the rocks. Also the browns and greens of evergreens, oaks and hardwoods climbing high on that side. It was light enough now to see the valley floor as a plain. Tall Grasses, smaller shrubs.

Soo-she expected to see buildings but none were present. Tig had caught up next to her, and sent his amusement at that . This wasn't a human settlement. This is how the sentients lived.

She even thought she'd heard Snarl chuckle.

As they kept running, the owl took off and was circling overhead. Sue wondered if she'd even seen an owl at first, or wasn't it a hawk? Something was flying in slow even beats, coasting in the higher wind drafts.

The peaceful feeling soon overwhelmed her other ideas. She also got a feeling that this would be home for her. A safe spot.

She sensed the other wolves relax once they got into the valley. At the distant end, she saw there was another flame. Every bit as high as the one they left behind. That would keep any ferals from trying a end-around flank attack.

Even now, Soo-she's focus was only on preventing any stumble. It took all she had to will her tired body to continue running. The pace was closer to a trot now across the grassy plains.

Following a faint trail toward the new and unknown life ahead.

XII

SOO-SHE TROTTED IN the middle of the exhausted hunter-pack of wolves as they came down the hill into the valley. Sentient female hunters came behind them. They kept up the trot until they were in a clearing under a large oak tree, where the wolves laid down.

Soo-she knew better than to do that. Her body would get painful cramps if she did. So she stood with her hands on her knees trying to catch her breath and hoping nothing more would be asked from her for a while.

Breaths for all the hunting-pack were ragged still. The hunters she traveled with had laid down all around her, still protecting her. Tig wasn't close but he wasn't any farther away than the other hunters.

One gray, almost white, female wolf came forward and sat on her haunches just inside that ring of hunters. And she waited.

Some females crept closer and sniffed their males. See what they were up, to scent their condition. Some of the older cubs crept forward but stopped short of the hunting circle. They knew not to risk the displeasure of their sire or their elders.

Gradually the heavy breathing slowed. Soo-she looked at the eyes of the gray female and stood up, erect.

"This must be the teacher," she thought.

And Teacher sent, "Yes, you are welcome."

Snarl added, "For now."

Neither the gray one or Soo-she recognized that or looked in his direction. They kept looking at each other.

The gray one sent, "You don't know us and we don't know of you. You're a different one for this valley, and Tig was wise to bring you here. We need to know: Are you a danger or help?"

Soo-she had no answer but the flood of memories that came, out in the open for all to see. The other wolves, cubs, and females sat back. Some moved away. The hunters who traveled with Soo-she were all used to this by now and had seen many of these pictures.

Soo-she started where the meteor was entering the planet's atmosphere. Talking with the cyborg pilot who was trying to reassure her of her safety. Then their sudden jarring. And all the lights went out inside the cabin. Only the emergency lights were left. The cyborg himself quit operating. Sue was grasping emergency lever on the door. For all the stories she'd heard about the polluted air, she didn't know if the rescue capsule was the safest place to stay.

And then as she clambered up and out, all went black. Until she revived, facing a wolf staring at her which was Tig. Then the escape from the ferals. The flames she'd produced was a trick her grandmother had taught her while they were on the moon station. She called it the "umbrella trick." It was a way to confuse people who were looking right at you. It would have them see something else. And then she sent the vision of Snarl, with his view of what he'd seen. The opening of dead-end canyon: two wolves embraced by fire.

After that, it was revisiting the meteor. The run ahead of the ferals. And the fire at the notch-opening of the valley that saved them.

The gray one cocked her head at that and thanked her for her thoughts. She stood up and swished her long tail, sending, "It's time to rest." She walked out of the circle and a path was cleared for her.

Soo-she understood to follow, and walked behind her to the edge of the valley floor. Nearly hidden in the canyon wall was a small den. It had a hole just big enough for the gray one to enter. Soo-she followed on hands and knees, although the effort brought new pains through her legs and hands. The teacher waited inside that was somehow lit, not depending on the light from the opening.

And then Soo-she realized she was seeing through the teacher's eyes. She knew where everything was and knew the soft bed at the back of the cave was hers. She crawled over to it and dropped.

• • • •

THE NEXT THING SHE knew, she was waking up inside a very dark cave-like den and remembering where everything was.

She was covered by a hide with thick fur facing her. It was a rawhide pelt, which seemed to have been chewed into a soft state. Comfortable and warm. Her suit had been stripped off of her and she lay naked underneath the cozy fur. Before she could wonder what she would do next, darkness came through the opening into the cavern.

She recognized one of the female hunters who'd come out to protect her and the rest of the hunters.

"My name is Tig-she," the female hunter sent, after she dropped her package at her own front paws, near the edge of the bedding where Soo-she lay.

She sat on her haunches and looked at the human carefully. "These are for you. They should help."

Soo-she sat up and snaked an arm out, then pulled the package closer to her. It was more deer hide, tied in a bundle. As she untied it, she found an Indian squaw dress and moccasins.

Tig-she sent, "Go ahead and dress. It's not like I haven't seen a naked hooman before. It holds no interest for me."

And Sue asked, "How are the others? Tig and Snarl and the hunters?"

Tig-she replied, "They rest still, but they'll be off on a hunt tomorrow. By next moon-rise."

Soo-she asked, "I'm sorry to ask, but I am curious. Are you sister of Tig?"

And Tig-she let a chuckle out, "No but I am bonded."

"Bonded?"

And Tig-she replied with the thought of what happens when one meets a love they cannot deny. But at the same time she was sad.

Soo-she sent, "Why would you be sad? Tig would be an excellent mate."

And then Tig-she sent her a series of pictures of being rebuffed, but not unkindly. She finally sent, "Tig is not bonded to me. He is still his own wolf."

Then another dark form blotted out the opening to the small den.

• • • •

TEACHER ENTERED THE den quietly, crouching on her haunches to the other side of the opening from Tig-she.

Soo-she had dressed by them. And found the moccasins were a good fit for her sore feet.

The Teacher sent, a smile in that thought, "You're every bit the picture of a chief's princess. We haven't seen such here in a thousand moons."

"There were Indians here?" asked Soo-she.

"That's not what they called themselves. We called them brothers and sisters. And they called us brothers and sisters. We hunted together but it has not been during my time."

Teacher continued, "I speak of the old days. Teachers before the teachers before me. When hooman and wolf shared the earth with all the other creatures and that was a time before all of this you see now. When the moon was still a spirit and not a thing that you landed on and built cities made of metal. Or mined beneath its surface," she sent with disgust. "That was a sacrilege."

And Soo-she bowed her head. "I understand this. I'm sorry." In shame of what her kind was doing.

The grey wolf then sent, "Don't bow your head. You have nothing to be ashamed of. It was not your doing. You are not one of them."

And yet Soo-she thought of her family there, Her father and mother, her sisters, brother.

"Yes I know that scene of yours. That will be your your journey to seek. We have more pressing matters now. Are you well enough to walk?"

Soo-she stretched her legs and felt her hands. "I think so."

"Where are my..." she send a question about the first aid kit and her pouch. Then she saw they had been placed behind her bedding. She reached out and put the pouch strap over her neck and shoulder.

She realized she couldn't put any ointments on in this darkness. Then slipped the first aid kit into her pouch as much as she could. It made the pouch bulge. But if she didn't run, it would be safe there.

The gray wolf smiled at that. "We'd like to see what your cures will do. There was always wisdom to seek in unknowns."

Tig-she left, followed by the gray wolf. And finally, Soo-she.

XIII

THE DAY WAS BRIGHT outside and Soo-she shielded her eyes against the sun as it was low in the sky. It was already setting. It would be dark in the valleys soon.

"I have slept long and hard."

"We have checked on you often. We were grateful that you were inside the cave with the noise you were making." Both Tig-she and Gray Wolf looked at each other and smiled.

Soo-she grinned herself. "Yes I've been known to snore."

"Ah, that's what you call it. We'll have to remember that name. Our oldest wolves sometimes make a sound like that. But we say they're singing up a spirit and do not disturb them."

Tig-she excused herself to go hunt up dinner.

Soo-she then asked Teacher, "What are your plans for me then?"

"For now?" They sat at the edge of a brook nearby. "Just enjoy the sunset. See the birds? Why would we bother in this fine evening? Sense the the night creature stirring as the day creatures make their beds. You can feel them, Soo-she."

And through Gray Wolf's mind, Soo-she sensed all manner of life in that valley both in the broad sense, and more narrowly to specific animals.

"We're all are sentient in this valley. And all share their thoughts or keep them close. There's a grand feeling of harmony."

"Do you hunt in this valley?" Soo-she asked.

"Very little. Our cubs practice here. But they do not kill. Sometimes we will render mercy. Those animals who are too old or sick to continue on. And all are blessed, and told of the debt we owe them. But, no, most of our hunting is out of this valley into the feral lands."

"But Tig said you also bless these..."

"Yes, it is our way. We do that for all life. All life is sacred."

They were silent then, and watched the sun go down. And the clouds seem to gather around it. As if it were pulling the covers over its own head.

Soo-she knew she had much to learn, as none of this was in her school-lessons. They had taught her the sun was just a chemical mass that flamed out radiation. Hoomans then turned it into energy for their own use. In fact, the hooman ship-generators were a form of that energy. Little mini-suns at the base of their ships. Those ships powered the moon-bases.

And this was not the truth that the wolves knew. They referred to the sun as Father Sun and the moon is Mother Moon or Sister Moon, depending on what size it was in the sky.

Teacher and Soo-she shared their thoughts back and forth, learning from each other until darkness enveloped almost the whole valley.

And yet there was still light up in the sky and the stars themselves started to shine. Soo-she told Teacher of a legend her own tribe had told her. That the moon was only a temporary station.

Stars were the ultimate destination and were supposed to be planets like this one circling them. Some day the hoomans, once they got enough resources from mining the moon, would take off to the stars and seek out their new home.

Tig-she had returned from the hunt by them bringing vegetables, like Tig had brought her. Laying one first at the feet of the teacher, and the second nearby the hand of Soo-she. She kept a small one for herself and waited until the teacher started to eat hers.

Soo-she only only picked hers up after the teacher began eating and brushed it off again as she had with Tig, and ate from the cleanest part.

Tig-she smiled at this. Then clamped her strong jaws through the vegetable. Juice squirted between her teeth. Then it was simply gone, chewed and swallowed. And she licked her face and laid down to clean her paws.

The teacher was more delicate, having a larger one, took more measured bites. Soo-she followed suit as her teeth were not as sharp, and jaws were not as long. She was last to finish. Then wiped her hands on the long grass nearby.

Tig-she cocked her head at this.

And the teacher sent to both of them, "Then this is not a hooman practice to lick your own paws clean?"

Soo-she giggled and sent, "No, but I think that if my tongue grew as long as yours I wouldn't mind. My tongue doesn't extend that far."

Teacher sent, "Can you still see to put on your first aid? Let's put on your medicines."

And Soo-she looked at her hands and found out they were actually already had flexible calluses on them. She looked at her feet and the blisters were gone and she was curious about this. "I should have needed to salve these."

And the teacher replied, "We have our own medicines here and we are thankful that they helped you."

"It's time for you to sleep some more. We have another day tomorrow and soon we'll prepare for the probe. Although I can already see this will not be difficult for you. Come, let us go."

XIV

THE COUNCIL HAD BEEN called by the Chief, to meet outside the Chief's den.

The chief was resting when the hunters arrived. He'd called all the male and female hunters to a grand meeting. Most thought it was about the ferals. The Chief cleared his mind, then barked to get their attention. All thoughts were silenced.

He welcomed them. Although the sickness of his body kept him from traveling for long periods, the clearness of his mind was still present.

He sent in his strong voice that all could hear and those that we're lounging sat up. It was a rare occasion. He wore the talisman around his neck.

"I bring you these stories, these tales today, not because you need them. But I would remind you of what we all lived through and what we are. We have lived in this valley for many many lifetimes, for many teachers' lifetimes. We have thrived. We've grown in wisdom and in strength.

"You are my finest. You are the pack's hope, our future.

"We've seen the ferals now know our valley and they've been growing in number. It's not just feral wolves, from what our hunting party told me. There are coy-dogs and coyotes in that mix. We cannot have not a pack of that number who knows our front door. And so action needs to be taken."

Many growled rumblings from among those present, many sent ideas of what to do. The Chief held up one paw. He looked into the sky and waited until the thoughts had settled.

"Yes, we will go and chase the ferals out and push the feral-lands back. We must. As close to the settlement as we can. There must be a dent in their lands.

"We will engage them. We will defeat them. We will leave sign that this is our land and they dare not enter it. But as much respect as we show them, we cannot trust that they will show us the same respect. So this is a battle that the feral have brought to us.

"Yes I know we have a hooman among us. Her fate is uncertain at this point. Both Tig and the teacher know that this hooman is here to teach us. There are many lessons to be learned from her. And this will change our future and help us. But that is not your concern today.

"You must ready for the fight that will be coming. You must go see to your family, see to your cubs. Let them know what you know. Share your wisdom.

"This will not be an easy task and you must come back successful. As usual, the spirits run with us if are one with the spirits. We will meet again. Come when your families are settled, in two day's time. We will travel. So go – be with your families. Enjoy the peace of this valley.

And with that he rose and turned and went into his den. A limp on his hind quarter was noticeable, but no one thought anything of it. They all rose and turned and went to their respective dens.

It was early morning and the scent of the flowers was blowing through the winds on that summer's day.

Tig-she walked next to Tig. They had grown up together in different families and neither yet had a family of their own.

Tig-she asked what he thought of the hooman.

Tig replied, "She's different. She's special. As the chief said there are things to learn from her. We can know these things. They should help us with a hooman settlement and maybe even the ferals.

Tig-she snorted. "A human who can send. That's almost sacrilege."

And Tig responded, "Is it now? Perhaps the hoomans are all able to send. If they would only open their ears to hear and open their eyes to see."

Tig-she replied, "I've never seen a human who is anything but close-minded."

Tig was quiet for a moment and then sent. "We don't see the wildflowers every year, quite the way we did the year before. This planet has changed since hoomans left and left their few among us. I don't know that it isn't as the teacher said 'It's ours to learn.'"

He continued, "This day is ours to learn. Perhaps there is a solution to the ferals and the hoomans and the troubles we all have. There might come a greater harmony out of this."

Tig-she sent, "And yet the chief tells us to go on to fight this day."

Tig chuckled. "Well, not this day. We have a couple to share."

Tig-she sent, "Will you visit your cousins?"

And Tig responded, "They have their own father to share their lessons."

Tig looked at Tig-she for a pace. Then sent, "I haven't been fair to you. Let's go up to the pool, by the upper caves. Let's enjoy this time we have. You can tell me what you know, how things have been while we were gone, and I can share all that I know."

Tig-she brightened at that. Although she knew Tig was still not bonded to her, this friendship they'd always had since cubs kept them close. Together they loped off up the trail to the higher caves.

XV

THERE WAS AN OWL FLYING through the air, battings soft wings. Flying from perch to perch, looking at the mice and the small vermin in the field. Seeing the rabbits young and old. She saw them pushing through the grasses to find their food. And the owl saw the fox hunting both. While the possums and the raccoons were after anything they could find. The fruit that was in season. The mollusks. And even the carrion left from others' hunts.

The mice themselves were gathering grain. And she saw a mother mouse suckling her young in a hidden nest. All these while she was busy flapping her wings flying from tree to tree. It was a beautiful day.

And then she heard a boom somewhere below her and a net flew up. It trapped her and brought her to earth. She landed hard.

A human came over and blocked out the sun from her view. She struggled against the webbing but the net was too strong. And she found no opening. And down came a pitchfork from the human and everything went black.

Teacher rose from her bed with moisture on her lips, shaking. Another nightmare. She looked around the den and the hooman was breathing softly to the side. Everything else is just as she had left it when she had first slept.

She curled up to sleep, breathed deeply, and asked for calm. And the spirits sent her calm. She closed her eyes to rest again.

• • • •

SOO-SHE WAS DREAMING of her world, the world before this one. The harsh moon. The harsh interior of the ship's pastel colors painted on the walls to make it more comfortable. More appealing More peaceful. All in terms of getting the best possible production from everyone concerned.

She graduated her final class in the children's classes. Now she was going to start training for her Job. It had been selected based on her talents. Her test scores placed her in all sorts of fields. She was strong.

She was fast. She was brighter than most. She was ahead of her class in all studies. She even took on extra studies to learn more.

And then the day came of her selection board. She entered the chamber of the committee while they were sharing different recording discs. They played them back on their monitors. The ones inlaid into the table in front of them. They were discussing as she came in, then quieted when she took her seat.

The was a only single seat in the chamber today. These were the interviews. This was not a meeting of the minds. It was their minds to hers. She would hear their decision. And they had muted their microphones so she could not hear their talks as she came in.

Finally, the chairman cleared his voice and all others went quiet. "Sue Reginald, you presented a difficult choice for us. We studied all your records. We've known your test scores. We've seen your progress for all these many years. We've noted your disciplines..."

Sue thought for a second to one particular stunt she had pulled. Something to do with spreading raspberry jam around to look as if there'd been an accident. But the chairman continued and she needed to listen.

"...and your case," the chairman went on, "presents a particular challenge to us. Because of what you know and what you can know. And your capabilities. There has been a request in your case, or rather a special choice.

"We've been informed by the Royal Council that your matter is not ours to decide. You been selected for the consorts Inner Group as a princess-in-waiting. And those duties commence immediately."

With that, a door opened to one side with its customary hiss of pressure changes.

At this, Sue stood.

Two ladies-in-waiting brought in a mantle to cover her student work-clothes. For she would need no more student clothes after this. The jumpsuit she'd always worn would be replaced by fine dresses and all sorts of petticoats and things she would have to learn about.

But she was saddened.

"Her family - would she see them again?" she thought.

But these hoomans could only read her face. The two ladies started escorting her through that new door. To a different world, one which was all bright.

And yet she resisted. She struggled and their grip only became firmer. For once she crossed that threshold, it would be a different world for her. She would never be able to visit her family in the same way as she had. She'd never see her friends again. So she resisted.

Yet their grip was like a vise on each arm almost lifting her off the ground so she could get no traction. The ladies-in-waiting seemed to grow on each side until they were armed guards in armor.

Their faces were passive. Those passive faces turned to shiny visors reflecting Sue's face at her. She started to scream but no sound came out. In fact no sound from anyone in the room. It became deadly quiet and the brightness became brighter until she could see nothing. She only felt the clamping grips on each arm...

And then she sat up, shaking, perspiring, and wondered what happened. Why this dream? Why now?

She was told by her grandma to listen to her dreams, learn from them. But this dream she'd had before. And this dream she'd been through before.

This was a lifetime she'd left behind and she wondered for her family what they were doing now, where they were, what they'd seen, how they had been treated.

She looked across the dark den, at Teacher who was breathing quietly, sleeping with her tail over her nose. Seeming to be at peace with the world.

But Soo-she couldn't go back to sleep.

She rested, leaned up against the side of the den. She brought her pouch over to her. Even in the darkness was able to feel the trinkets she had brought back. She pulled the one trinket out, a pendant and it's trans-aluminum chain. In the darkness she felt the runes. Tiny words inscribed on it that she couldn't read in the dark. But she knew they said something by an old poet. She put the chain over her head, pulled her hair through the chain and settled it on her neck. As she felt her hair, she thought to herself, "Man, I have to do something with this." .

Soo-she looked over at Teacher, who hadn't moved. It was different having to learn to narrow band your thoughts all the time. On the moon, it didn't matter. Nobody could hear you think and words meant several different things. That she had learned while being a princess-in-waiting.

Royals had many ways of saying things. In many meanings. It wasn't like her old preacher, her spiritual advisor. They were called to their duty. They weren't selected by committee. They were selected by a higher being. Or so they said. No one you could see or feel. No one you could see or talk to, you could only feel. And so they went along with the rules of Man but given a choice they would follow the rules of the Spirit of the Great Being.

And that is why she was given this pendant, when she reached maturity. It had been handed down from time immemorial. The chain had been replaced, the attachment had been repaired. Who originally owned it was lost in antiquity, lost years before. How many people, how many young girls, had been like she was now?

Sitting there in the dark. Rubbing the edge of the pendant, across the tiny letters that were engraved there.

She had no knowledge. She had no idea. But sleep for her after that nightmare was not coming quickly. So she sat against the den wall and tried to still her heart. Breathing deeply, inhaling the aromas of the den inside and the night outside.

• • • •

THE DEER RAN THROUGH the forest, away from an unknown assailant. Someone was chasing it. She could sense their presence and yet narrow-banded her own thoughts so they could not find her. She'd come down this trail to study the land. To see what had changed. To find the other deer. It was not yet the rutting season It was not yet the time for giving birth. And so she walked carefully, grazing as she went.

The young flowers were delicious this time of year. She knew only to nibble her share and not fill on anything. She remembered an old phrase: 'A fat deer is a slow deer; a slow deer is a dead deer.'

Her father left her with that understanding as he went off, as all males did between the seasons. She saw him now and then, or thought it was him. The hoomans would prize that rack that he carried and as he grew larger with the years.

And then she heard something crack behind her. A twig, or something. She froze, turned her ears in that direction to hear more closely what it was. And slowly she turned her head around and saw it was a hooman. With something steel in its hands. And the steel erupted with a big flash in the smoke.

She felt a deep tug in her chest. And suddenly was pulled over by the force of an unknown object like a huge rock thrown at her. Her breathing was coming hard. Something wrong in her chest. That hurt.

She laid on the grasses with wildflowers above her. Unable to move her back, unable to move her legs. And the hooman came, over her with a gun cradled in its arm. Parted its lips. Showed its teeth. It loosened a long knife in its belt. Crouched down so she could see its ugly face and then all went black. The last thing she saw was a knife. Close to her face, Close to her neck.

And the teacher woke up. Again perspiring on her lips, startled. She got to her feet.

Teacher glanced around the den and saw Soo-she looking at her.

"Just a dream." she sent.

And Soo-she sent, "Yes, I know."

Soo-she had heard her dream and yet sent no thought of herself or anything but comfort. "My dream was bad, too. I hope our days are better."

XVI

THE BUNDLE IN HER MOUTH reeks of hooman.

Tig-she had to stop often to set it down and let the taste and smell clear her senses.

It was a bundle of the tattered suit Soo-she had worn for days when she first arrived. How hoomans can make such stink was beyond Tig-she's understanding. All species had their own scent. Most all of them cleaned themselves by habit. Maybe if she didn't have to wear clothes...

Tig-she picked up the bundle again and continued. Her job was to bury these scraps.

She loped down an old path to some loose soil among some pungent flowers. The cubs shouldn't find this, she thought.

"Hold up there!" came a thought from behind her.

It was Snarl. "What did he want now?" but kept that question to her self.

Glad to put the smelly bundle out of her mouth, she waited.

Snarl rounded the last trail curve and came closer.

Tig-she sent, "What brings you here?"

Snarl replied, "I saw you cross the valley with the sun reflecting off those suit scraps. I came to offer my help ."

"Nothing of your concern. I can finish this." sent Tig-she.

Snarl sent, "I'm sure you can. But more paws make a deeper hole faster. The sooner we get that stench out of this valley, the better."

Tig-she had to agree with that. "Well, it's just up ahead."

She picked up the bundle again. Snarl followed as she loped away.

Finally they arrived. The flowers in bloom made her almost gag by themselves.

Setting the bundle down at their base, Tig-she started digging. Snarl came close to her shoulder and also dug.

Soon they had a hole twice as deep as the bundle was high. Tig-she nosed it in, then they both back-filled.

With the last of the loose dirt replaced, they both patted the ground to firm it. They then scattered dry leaves and twigs over it. Finally Tig-she pulled a dead branch over the top.

She sent to Snarl, "Now to go find wild mint to take the taste out of my mouth."

Snarl replied. "Glad to help. There's a patch by the pool up near the High Caves."

Tig-she sent, "Thanks. I know the spot." Then loped off back down the trail.

As she rounded the bend, she stopped. No foot-falls were coming after her. Snarl was up to something.

Focusing her senses back up the trail, she found that Snarl hadn't moved. He was looking at the mound they had created.

Tig-she remembered other times Snarl acted this way. He was planning something.

She turned, quietly taking a side path going back around. And arrived at a secluded spot where she could get a view of his actions. She had to stay under cover to watch.

Snarl waited until Tig-she must be far away down the trail. Then he carefully pulled the branch back, brushed off the leaves and twigs, then dug again.

Soon, he had the bundle back out of the hole. Going off a distance, he found a rock about that size. With some effort, he pushed it back and into the hole. Then replaced the dirt, the leaves, the twigs, and finally the branch.

Picking up the bundle, he started up the trail toward the valley side wall.

Tig-she left her place to follow at a distance.

Snarl took a tight, twisting route that forced him several times to climb almost straight up. He emerged at the top of the valley wall, able to put down the bundle and rest for awhile.

All he saw from that vantage point was an almost-empty valley. No one was near enough to see him.

Picking up the bundle, he continued his plan.

Tig-she came out of hiding from a boulder below him and finished the climb. Now the tracking began. If she was careful, she'd find out what he was planning without discovery.

XVII

SOO-SHE WAS SITTING outside the den in the morning sunlight.

The breeze brought scent of wild roses, and clover blossoms, along with grass pollens. The sun was warm on her skin, warming her doeskin dress as well.

She'd found a comb in her pouch and was using it on her long blond hair. She had never realized how much the little things mattered. She had started combing the rats and tangles out. It took a while, as she had to work from the tips backwards towards the scalp before she could run her comb through any long strand all at once.

It was a nice day, the weather was good, and so she combed and just enjoyed being in the moment. She saw Tig-she coming up and she smiled to see her. She had been closer to Soo-she more recently than not. And was becoming quite a good friend, if you could call it that.

Although Tig-she still didn't trust everything she did. And was easily spooked by some of the things Soo-she thought. Still, Tig-she had a wry sense of humor that Soo-she appreciated.

Tig-she from called from across the valley by thought alone, "Hallo Hooman! How are you today? Whatever is that stuff growing out of your head?. It's too bright. My eyes are hurting."

Soo-she thought back, "Well, perhaps Tig-she should only hunt at night. I hear that's much easier for you to see then. But I'll hide all this golden hair so it doesn't distract you or make you stumble on your path."

Both chuckled at that.

Soo-she put away her comb even though she didn't really feel anywhere near done. She could be hours at this.

By then Tig-she showed up and sent, "Are you ready for the probe?"

And Soo-she replied, "There is no way to ready for that. I think I can only be myself and try to help as best I can. I know there's a lot of knowledge you seek. I don't know if I have it all."

Tig-she sent, "Well don't worry about it. It's a nice day."

She sat next to Soo-she and shared her view over the valley. Soo-she looked through Tig-she's eyes and saw much further and much more clearly.

She saw all the detail she was missing with her own human vision. And she smelled the smells and heard with extended hearing. So that rabbit cleaning out her burrow on the other side of the valley was as clear as being within 20 feet of it.

"It is a beautiful day, isn't it?"

Tig-she replied, "Yes. Our Teacher says to enjoy the moment and I'm still having difficulty getting that concept myself."

Two turkeys walked across the high grass out on the valley, and both watched. Tig-she of course was interested in hunting one of those. Yet it would be impolite to leave Soo-she, to just run off. Also, she wasn't all that hungry. But the action of running was always pleasing to her, even calming to a wolf. To run, to lope, brought an inner peace.

The trotting song hummed in her head. And Soo-she started humming the trotting song aloud.

Tig-she asked, "Could you teach me how to hum one day? It seems interesting. I think the cubs would enjoy being hummed to."

Soo-she replied, "Well if it's possible, I'll teach you anything I can."

She looked down at her hair at it flowed down the front of her doeskin dress. "I wish I looked better for the probe. I'm afraid the last few days have left me a bit ragged. I could really use a bath. I've been able to wash my face and hands, and the more scented areas of me, but I think I need a full bath. That would h be just so luxurious."

Tig-she understood the meaning of luxurious, if she never heard the word before. "I think I know a place we can go where you can get you can take a full bath as you will. We love swimming in the pool by the high caves. Come."

And she trotted off down the hill. Soo-she quickly pulled her pouch closed and put the strap over her shoulder and across her chest. She rose quickly and trotted off behind her. Wolves seem to love to trot everywhere and never walk. Shortly they were up at the caves.

Tig-she of course arrived first, and took a deep breath. Then scouted everything out. She loved to be up here. She had many fond memories growing up as a cub. She and Tig could often be found up here playing in amongst the rocks.

As Soo-she came up, she saw the pool. She paused at its beauty. It had a small waterfall that seemed more active during the rains. As it came off the side of the valley walls, the collected water went into this pool. She went down to the edge of it and put her hand in.

Tig-she sent, "Yes it is cold," in response to Soo-she's thoughts. Then she sent her the heat she could feel from the rocks, warmed all morning in the bright sun. "Come, it's only cold the first second."

Tig-She sprang into the pool, diving and splashing away. And then paddling across and around, her long tail trailing behind her in the water.

Soo-she slipped off her buckskin dress, kicked off her moccasins, and dove head-first. She rose some few feet away, sputtering and gasping at how cold it was. But yet again, Tig-she was right. Once you're in the water for a while, You don't feel cold.

She swam over to a shelf where she could stand and scrub. Dunked her hair under and rinsed it as best she could, without tangling it more. But the water would help her get the tangles out of it. Nothing like fresh rain water.

She remembered on the moon-station where they would increase the humidity to make it "rain." That would settle the dust. Her grandmother would catch the run-off in pots just for washing her and her grand-daughter's hair.

All the puddles, all the brooks Soo-she had used for washing would get muddy so quickly. But among these rocks it stayed pure and clear. You see to the bottom of the pool.

But as she started shivering she knew she'd better get out. So she climbed out on the rocks and sat in the sun and allowed the sunbeams to dry her.

She ran her fingers through her hair to make sure that it wasn't knotted or tangled.

Tig-she swam over and climbed out, then walked away a bit to shake. At last, she came back to lie down beside Soo-she.

"You seem to have good form for a human."

Soo-she blushed at the compliment sending, "What would you know about the form of humans?"

"I've been in a few places, I've seen a few. Like I said, a hooman without clothes is no curiosity to me."

Tig-she shared with her the times she had gotten close to the human settlement, to see mothers bring their children out to the creek to bathe and clean. So she saw all parts and forms of human anatomy as she laid hidden.

Soo-she asked, "So you've been near the humans, you've been near the settlement?"

Tig-she sent, "Yes, when the ferals weren't as many. We would often come by and and see what we could learn. As long as they weren't trying to hunt us and as long as we didn't hunt near their settlement. Wolves were more a curiosity than they were a threat. But since the ferals have expanded their numbers, they've come into hunt far closer to the settlement and in the settlement.

"Now the humans have armed themselves with different weapons and often will search far outside their feral territory without knowing it. They come into Sentient land at that point.

"Then we have to chase them back, which tends to make them come after us even more. But humans are a strange thing. If we could only share thoughts with them."

Soo-she thought for a while and sent, "It's too bad they don't send and they don't listen. The closed-mind problem is exactly that."

The sunshine on her bare skin had dried most of the most moisture now, and the cool air raised goose bumps. She sat in the sun and enjoyed being able to feel the air over all her body. To wriggle her toes without having them encased in some boot or moccasin was a sheer delight.

She reached down and pulled one of her feet up to check the bottom oven and the calluses had grown well. Most of the scratches had healed. She marveled at this, because she thought she would have scars from how deep some of those gases had been.

Tig-she sent, "We help you with that when you're sleeping."

"Oh, now that's something you can teach me." replied Soo-she.

Tig-she sent, "It's not too hard when the person is dreaming. Then you enter their dreams and help them in any way you can."

Soo-she replied, "I'll have to try that some day. I know the teacher dreams and has bad ones and all I can do is sit there and watch."

Tig-she sent, "Well it's a great day and we don't have to worry about everything." She then laid down, stretched out, relaxed.

• • • •

AS THEY ENJOYED THE sun and wind, they listened to the birds sing around them. They heard the different animals skitter and talk amongst themselves.

Soo-she laid back, cradled her head in her arms and watched the clouds scud across the sky. She felt free and secure of all human problems and questions and "now-we-musts." At the same time, she wished her family were here to enjoy all this. This security, this peace.

As she thought that, she said she saw Tig-she next to her start to twitch, her tail wagging, and her feet were running in the air, moving in sequence. Soo-she knew she was dreaming.

So she closed her own eyes and looked through Tig-she's dreams.

She found her on a trail, moving with stealth after something she was trying to follow. It was Snarl.

Then she stopped and looked right at Soo-she.

"What are you doing here?" What Tig-she saw was a wolf who was blond with a reddish tent. And then Soo-she saw that that was her. In Tig-she's dream, she was a wolf, another female wolf.

Soo-she sent, "I came to help. What can I do?"

Tig-she replied, "We're watching him. He's up to something. I know."

And then Soo-she understood that Tig-she had been following Snarl for some time. He had somehow taken the bundle of her old suit, and had left scraps here and there. All along a trail leading back to the valley.

So they followed carefully staying out of his sight but still smelling the scent. Being a wolf was invigorating to sushi with all the abilities and talents they had.

Now they came up to a point where Snarl was waiting near the edge of a clearing. They couldn't get any closer. They were down when so their scent wouldn't carry to him and expose where they were. They sat side by side and peered through the leaves as best they could.

Into the opposite edge of the clearing came another wolf. It was a feral. It stopped at the edge of the clearing and laid down with his head on his paws. That submission was a signal. Snarl then rose and took what remained of the bundled suit out into the center of the clearing. He then turned and walked back to the clearing edge he came from. The feral wolf raised its head, sniffed, and looked to both sides.

Then slowly walked forward, sniffing as he went. A few feet from the center, he stopped and sniffed, concentrating on the bundle. Then it crept the last few feet to sniff it directly. At last, it reached down and took the bundle in its mouth, wheeled suddenly, and then bolted. In seconds it was out through the edge of the clearing and deep into the trees.

Snarl then made a smile and left, going exactly back the same way he had come.

Tig-she and Soo-she sat for a while, letting Snarl leave. They had come a similar route themselves and didn't want to strengthen that scent or give themselves away.

Meanwhile they digested what they had just seen in the clearing.

Soo-she sent, "So Snarl is giving away a trail into the valley.

Tig-she sent, "That's what I understand. I have not had a way to do anything about this. But now you know, too."

And at that, they both woke up. Tig-she sat upright and turned her head towards the hooman. Soo-she raised herself up into a sitting position and shook her head as if to get the dream out of her mind.

Then she looked at Tig-she. "Well, did I help?"

Tig-she smiled and sent, "More than you know. More than you know. Oh—and you make a good looking wolf, too."

Soo-she blushed.

Tig-she added, "We'll have to do something about that blushing business."

Soo-she asked, "Does it make me look bad?"

Tig-she sent, "No, it makes you look even more enticing. And if you were a wolf, you'd have every male in the area coming to see you."

XVIII

AT THE RISE OF THE second moon, the hunters gathered outside the Chief's den.

The Chief was laying, waiting, ready for the last to arrive.

Each of the hunters sat as they arrived, nodding to the Chief and receiving a nod.

As the last sat, the Chief rose. "We are now here to face one of our greater challenges. We are to discipline the ferals and push their boundaries back. They know the entrance to our valley, which makes our home unsafe.

"You all know the events that occurred. And it was necessary to bring the hooman to our valley. The probe will begin soon, but we have already learned much.

"She has told us that there are other responsibilities we share with other sentients. She also brings hope that this world might be raised to sentience for all members of all species.

"That is not our focus today. When you leave here, this campaign will be large, it will be effective, it must be. While we now have hope and can see a greater world ahead, we are still faced by those who only live by the tooth and claw.

"Enough has been said. You have the meaning of what we must do over the next few days."

The Chief sent holographic maps to all present, along with the data sets they contained.

"These are the pack numbers and locations where the ferals have been seen. This data has been compiled from all the hunting parties of this summer. We've found that their main camp is there." He emphasized that point in the visual.

"According to our long traditions of successful engagements, the plan is to run a long hunting campaign to push them back to that main camp, and then beyond it. That camp will need to be defiled. They must return to the boundaries of the old agreement.

"They must know their safety depends on staying completely out of our hunting territory."

Snarl interrupted, "Should we not use the method of two hunting parties to gather them more quickly and effectively? That is also one of our proved and traditional methods."

The Chief frowned, as did many of the hunters. "This is not the time for questions or suggestions. I appreciate your enthusiasm, Snarl, but I will continue."

The Chief cleared his mind, and then sent a new holographic image. This contained pack numbers with the sitings and their frequency. "You'll see that these have patterns of retreat, and a central path they have been using. This core flow needs to be cut off and made unsafe for them.

"You'll also see the minor stop-overs they use. These must also be defiled. They must not be able to take more than day-trips before returning to their main camps.

"This core flow path is the route they must know is forbidden. Our new agreement we will enforce on them is to take the entire path and their current camp into our own territory. That is what you will enforce. They must never hunt in this area again."

Snarl again sent, "With all respect, Chief, your plan still enables a faster round-up with two packs of hunters..."

The Chief barked at him, causing the hunters to all flinch. "Snarl! There is a reason for patience. There is a reason to respect decorum. I'll expect no more from you until this briefing is opened to suggestion!"

The hunters were silent. Some looked at Snarl from the corner of their eyes to see his reaction.

Snarl only bowed his head, silent.

After an appropriate pause, the Chief resumed. "Tig will lead the hunt, as usual. His experience is trusted. Snarl will again be first lieutenant, again due to his experience and successes. The rest of you will take your usual positions for the Great Hunt, in teams."

"Our most experienced female hunters will remain in the valley for defense. The rest who are of age will hunt alongside. All of you are expected to return. Keep of one mind, trust each other.

"And now I would open this up to suggestions for improvement." The Chief looked to Snarl, who had kept his head bowed.

There was silence for a time. Some questions started up from the younger hunters, asking about approach and sequences. The Chief answered these, and adjusted the plan or clarified the data.

When the last of the questions paused, the Chief asked Snarl directly, "Do you now have anything to add at this point?"

Snarl raised his head and straightened his back. "While this plan is very good, being able to split into two formations would give us additional strength and capability."

Tig then sent, on the heels of that thought. "And is a point that can be taken. Our numbers are much fewer than the entire pack of the ferals. It is key we split them into multiple groups that run away in fear. We much not allow them to use the same tactic against us. Our single central force must start that fear-effect by surprising them. Our greater strength and efficiency of attack must make them understand that we cannot be followed."

Snarl then sent, "As when we had to bring that hooman in, when we let them follow us to our front door?"

Tig replied, "The hooman's data is key. We would have nothing of what we've already learned without protecting her. Much more data can be probed from her."

"And yet that one hooman has made all this necessary!" sent Snarl. "I almost think the care for this hooman is more important to you than the care for this pack..."

Tig rose to his feet, bristling. "What are you implying? Why don't you state simple facts that this hunting party can use?"

Snarl rose, slowly. "The facts are that hoomans are destructive, they are of a type who do not care for other species. Our legends and our own experiences teach us that these must be left alone and not contacted."

Tig replied, "Those legends also teach to have a respect for all life, sentient or not. This hooman is special, and has already helped us. She is no danger to this pack. She is different. You have all seen her thoughts and learned from her."

Snarl then sent, "Special. Different. One might consider that a bonding has happened here..."

Tig growled before sending, "Be careful what you claim, wolf. Be reminded of your own lineage. There is no possible way for humans and wolves to bond. To even consider that is disgusting and grounds for expulsion from any pack as a deviant." His eyes glared at Snarl, waiting his rebuttal.

Snarl bowed his head as his eyes didn't leave Tig's. "Deviance wasn't suggested, Leader Tig. Whether one bonds with their pets differs from seeking to mate."

Tig started toward Snarl, and then stopped. "Shall we take this outside the valley and I teach you the meaning of bonding?"

• • • •

AT THIS THE CHIEF SENT, "ENOUGH. You have both interrupted this briefing with these idle thoughts and threats. We have work to do. This work must begin immediately. I only hope you two, who have been raised in the same den as cubs, would work these angers out against the ferals you will soon hunt and chase. This hunting party must succeed for our pack to continue to exist.

"As our legends hold, we have held this valley long before the hooman settlement rebuilt itself. We must honor our ancients, and the spirits who guided them.

"You two, and the rest of our hunters must seek the spirit guides and listen carefully to their advice.

"We will now ask for this."

Chief sat and pointed his nose to the sky, howling softly at first.

The rest of the hunters all rose, even Tig and Snarl joining in, to point their own noses to the sky. The howl gained strength and became a single voice.

Above them, the moon seemed to glow more strongly, the clouds parting. The stars also shone instead of twinkling.

All other noises in the valley seemed to quiet before this long sound.

As the Chief quit, the hunters did in unison. The silence fell like a huge boulder from the cliff. No sound came for minutes.

"Go with the spirits. Return to hunt again. The pack needs each of you more than before. The spirits will guide you as you listen. Trust your senses. Go with the spirits." With that the Chief rose, and bowed to his hunters, who bowed in return.

The hunting party rose and parted for Tig, and then Snarl to lead them.

The hunters loped to the end of the valley and seemed to make a dark stream flowing uphill as they made their way up the path to the notched opening.

The Chief and the female hunters watched until the last of them flowed through that notch.

Then the Chief turned to them and sent, "You have even more responsibility than those who just left. With the ferals knowing a single entrance, it's possible they may know others. We can protect the two notches with fire. However, if they attack in this valley, we must be prepared to repulse them, and also keep our cubs safe. We cannot rely on the hunting party to return in time, and cannot have them return to a valley without us here waiting in safety."

Tig-she sent, "Our lives will tie us to the spirits. The moment will flow through us."

The Chief added, "And the Teacher needs to complete the hooman's probe. From this, we should get more usable data. That is our hope. We must prepare for all outcomes with the resources we have.

"Prepare your lieutenants, assign your duties. Then I will meet you at Teacher's den."

Tig-she bowed, then turned, assigning tasks. They all trotted off to different directions, some in two's and three's, some alone. All had jobs they needed to fulfill.

The Chief made his way slowly to the Teacher's den. His limp was more obvious in the moonlight.

XIX

WHEN SOO-SHE RETURNED to the Teacher's den, her hair shown bright in the twilight, enhancing the light tan of her doeskin dress. The swim had been refreshing. After Tig-she left her for the Hunting Council, Soo-she trotted on alone.

At the den, she called a howl softly, although this was more out of respect than necessity. She knew the Teacher had sensed her approach, just as she had sensed the Teacher already within the den.

As she crawled through the opening, she hiked the dress up away from her knees to keep it clean. Once within the den, she could move over to her fur-covered sleeping space.

When she settled, the gray wolf opened her eyes to look at her. "How was the pool?"

Soo-she smiled, "Delightful. To feel the sun and breeze on my skin, to be truly clean, those were much welcome. Some days I only wish I could have the beautiful fur like wolves. And not have to wear these clumsy clothes at all times."

Teacher smiled. "There is an old phrase passed down through the legends, 'Wishes should be used with caution, as they may come true.'"

Soo-she grinned as she sent, "Well, unless we can change our forms from those of our parents, there's little chance of that."

The Teacher looked off into the den like she was seeing deep into space beyond the valley itself. "But then, it's also known that nothing exists with out the idea behind it. Are ideas any different than wishes? Our spirits can take many forms, as our thoughts do. And our legends tell of those who can shift from one form to another. Who is to say our current ideas only keep us from our real potential?"

Soo-she nodded, as this was familiar to her. Her own escape was combining the idea of an escape pod with inter-orbital travel. All to save her own life. Combining those ideas into a new one has make it possible.

And then she thought of all she had encountered since that landing. Tig, Snarl, the ferals. Tig-she, the Teacher, the cubs. And seeing through other's eyes, through their dreams...

At this, she thought on purpose of other things, asking, "What can you tell me about the probe? Tig said hoomans either went crazy or got very sick."

The Teacher replied, "We tried on some willing hoomans who seemed to understand us. We didn't get clear thoughts from them, or they didn't trust their own thoughts. In all cases, the biggest problem was in having a mutual understanding so that communication could take place.

"Of those who got sick, they had to be taken back to their settlement on travois. Of those who Tig called 'insane', they didn't trust the voices they were hearing. And sometimes we would hide outside their gates to listen through those 'insane' into the hooman settlement. Most of them were not believed, and so quit trying to persuade others of what they had experienced. Some just kept their thoughts to themselves after that.

"We couldn't stay outside their gates for long, or even return often, as the hooman hunters would chase us and follow our tracks. So our studies are incomplete."

Soo-she asked, "But I understand that no hooman has ever been allowed in this valley before. The cubs I've played with have shared some of the legends. And you've told me about the Ancient Ones who were hooman and hunted with wolves..."

Teacher replied, "Yes, I have more teaching to do with those cubs you shared thoughts with. The Ancient Ones appeared hooman, but could take many forms. They preferred hooman form, but would often hunt with us as wolves, or even fly as the larger birds - hawk, own, even buzzard or condor. These the legends tell us well."

Both were quiet for awhile, keeping their thoughts to themselves.

Soo-she sent at last, "Do you think I'll be in danger when the probe begins?"

Teacher said, "That is up to you. You are different, and that is why Tig saw you needed to come here. There was no place for you to be safe where we could come and do the probe. The ferals would have killed you because of the hunting the feral hoomans have done against their kind. Even now, wolf skins hang from the walls of their settlement, with skulls and bones littered up around its base, as a way to keep the ferals at bay.

"When they kill wolves and coyotes, they use the carcasses as sign. Barbaric."

Soo-she sent again, "But am I at danger during the probe?"

Teacher replied, "Sorry, that line of thought traveled a different path than you asked for. I could try to reassure you otherwise. But 'truth is only as valuable as it is workable.' You have talents you've not admitted to yourself. There are skills you could practice and master far beyond what you consider you are presently capable. We have little time. Our hunters must push the ferals back. The probe must happen once they have left so not to distract them.

"The short answer is: you will be at danger only if you consider it so. Trust yourself, be truly open and receptive to the spirits. Your safety is your own to decide."

With that, Teacher rose and stretched, then moved out of the den. She sent a thought back to Soo-she to remain there and reflect. Tig-she would come to bring her to the probe site when all was ready.

• • • •

OUTSIDE THE DEN, SHE saw the old Chief making his way toward her. Teacher met him on the path.

"How did the Council go?" she sent.

Chief replied, "As well as could be expected." He then sent her his understanding of the events.

She replied, "That is as I had sensed."

Chief was not surprised that Teacher could sense across the valley. Certainly, the emotions ran high during that meeting, and would have carried many of the thoughts far away for anyone able to listen.

Both sensed Tig-she coming along a different path to the teacher's den. They waited for her to come closer, meanwhile feeling the cool breeze that wafted down the valley walls since the sun had set. The evening birds were calling, and the nocturnal ones were stirring.

Tig-she came to where Teacher and Chief sat, then bowed before seating herself.

"All is as ready as we can be. The openings have been secured. Our female hunters and older cubs will be present for the probe. Those with young cubs still feeding will watch the other cubs and keep them cared for and quiet."

Chief sent, "Our thanks to you. These times are trying and it is good to have those we can trust at our side."

Tig-she bowed at the compliment.

Teacher narrow-sent to both, "This hooman is different as the night is from the day. We may learn more than we even expect. Of course already her thoughts and memories have told us what happened after the hoomans left, and explains the meteors in our skies.

"She may, I hope, give us an understanding of how to handle the ferals that surround us, especially the feral hoomans. Until she arrived, I had almost given up hope of finding sentient hoomans again. It has been long in our legends since such have existed."

At that, they all sat quietly, reflecting on the legends they had been told by this Teacher, and the teachers before her. Their own fathers and mothers had told them tales as well.

Teacher finally sent, "Of course this reminds me of the Old-one-who-painted-rocks, who said, 'Let each generation write their own legends.'"

Tig-she smiled, then rose. "I go to see the probe site is ready with what you need. The huntresses will be present when you arrive. I'll then come back for Soo-she."

As she trotted away, the Teacher and Chief shared the moment.

"How are you feeling these days, Chief?"

"As if you didn't already know. The pain has spread, despite all you've helped me in my dreams. My end-days draw closer."

Teacher sent, "And the spirit-world will welcome you to their path from here to there."

Chief relied, "I seem to remember the legends differently now. Details I hadn't before. Like those which tell of the endless love that spirits have, their understanding that goes beyond our mortal lives of waking, hunting, sleeping. There is a common theme I seem to see these days, but can't grasp the idea of it completely.

"The main feeling I get cannot be put into words. But it is peaceful."

Teacher sent, "And our words are simply ideas. Our ideas are as complete and firm as we consider they are. So said our oldest legends."

Chief added, "And they all bring us only the amount of joy, love, and harmony we ask for."

Finally, the Chief rose carefully to his feet. "I'll wait at the probe site. It looks to be a fine evening for this. The clouds have cleared and the spirits look down through the sky from the stars. Even the moon shines down, regardless of the fleas who infest her skin."

As he moved down the path, the Teacher sent her prayers after him. However many more trails he had to walk, let him learn and enjoy each footstep he took.

XX

THE WOLVES HAD SELECTED an old hooman foundation for the probe site.

It was circular, and legend had that the old building was mostly for storage and sheltering livestock. Hooman's called it a "barn". Those that hunted in and around it said it was a slave building, trapping the beings within. Supposedly, this was by mutual consent, as the beings who sheltered in that barn had few defenses without hoomans around.

Those days were before the hoomans leaving in their sky-ships. Sentience wasn't widely available until after they were gone. After the plague took most of the remaining hoomans.

Today, that foundation would be for the ceremony. It would mark where the probe would take place, and where the sentient wolves and their cubs could watch in relative safety.

Or so they thought.

No hooman had survived the probe before. But this one was different. No hooman had been to the valley since the days of the hooman plague.

This was completely new.

And yet, more vital than ever. The ferals knew where the valley was. And the hooman settlements had been growing in size. Not just locally, but in every area where hoomans still survived. This news was brought by the migrating birds and insects.

Unless a way was found to communicate with hoomans and ferals, it would mean a new world war that would destroy both sides. A war that would never end until one or the other side was exterminated.

Tig-she led Soo-she up to the circle and then stopped. The wolf looked at her and sent her a faith-filled prayer for the best outcome.

Soo-she nodded in reply, then entered the circle.

A hawk flew in lazy circles overhead, riding the thermals. With a cry, she dove to earth. Soo-she ducked, but the wolves didn't flinch.

On landing with a graceful back-sweeping, the hawk alighted without a sound.

Eying the assembled wolves, the hawk bowed its head.

A shimmering covered that form, which showed a wolf when it cleared. Grey, almost white fur - it was Teacher.

Some cubs sent to each other about how it was quite an appearance, and found their mothers "tut-tutting" their lack of mental discipline. Soo-she also understood their thoughts and smiled, remembering the "seen and not heard" saying she had been told when she was young.

The gray wolf just smiled at Soo-she, sending "Welcome everyone. I'll skip some of the formal prayers and notices so we can get started. Our hunters are out protecting us and we need to help them. We need whatever data we can get as soon as we can. I do want to thank each of you for all you've done and all that will be asked of you. Your presence is noted and welcome, as well as our Chief, our elders, and our next generation."

Teacher nodded at the Chief and then proceeded to a spot opposite Soo-she in the center of the circular foundations.

"Soo-she are you ready to begin?"

"As I'll ever be."

"Then clear your mind and relax."

The Teacher sat on her haunches and bowed her own head. Soo-she bowed hers as well.

To Soo-she, it was as if the universe had dropped away. A brilliant white replaced everything except her and Teacher.

• • • •

THEN SUE REMEMBERED her life from the beginning. She hadn't remembered being born before, seeing the world through her own Mother's eyes and those of her Father, Aunts, Uncles, and other family. She now remembered that there was a dream-catcher placed above her cradle to help her sleep. That same amulet she carried with her in her pouch that was sitting in the Teacher's den.

Then she was learning to walk, to talk the hooman speech. And to rely on talking rather than sensing. Because those around her wouldn't sense. Only the other babies did this.

It was true, then, that all knowledge was available to the youngest - until they learned to speak.

A flood of images came, then: the floor plan of the moon-colony they were in. How the air and water were recirculated and purified. How the food was grown in containers under artificial light. How the elites lived in the original city-ship which then provided heat and protection for the dome of the moon-colony. The mining that had to occur to keep the fusion generator running, but also the other industries that ran in the colony near the fusion exhaust - refraction of metals and collection of slag that was further refined for building materials. How the rare earths were extracted and collected for fine electronic uses. The collection of waste that couldn't be economically recycled or re-purposed. How these were bundled up and launched on a trajectory back to Earth so that the atmosphere re-entry would turn them back to dust. How the theories that moon dust would cause more rain and help purify the polluted skies.

As Sue remembered her youth, all the ways of hoomans came out. The moon colony were the Slaggers, the lowest caste. Then came the organizers, the business people who provided jobs. Then the government workers and officials. At the top were the royal elite families, who inherited their positions from their elders. To them, everyone else was a "down-below."

Visions of fine dresses and suits, fashions that came and went. All shown on the TV screens the Slaggers were assembled to watch. Regular announcements were given with awards for high production numbers. Competitions were touted between the various colonies to see which ones could out-produce the others. Trophies were presented to head of business-houses, which would be put on display so the Slaggers could see them going down into and returning from the mines. The Founder's birthday was usually a big event, even though the original founders for each of the city-ships were long dead. In those cases, the shows were extravagant. Pictures of vast audiences and camera's representing each of the colonies were there to record it. Elites had the front row seats, with government behind them, and business owners and staff taking up the rear. Slaggers weren't present, as there wasn't enough room in any single presentation hall. (Or so they were told.) It was hard to tell what was virtual and what was real.

The Slaggers wore jumpsuits the entire time. That was their fashion. "Make do, do over, or do without" was their watchword. Jumpsuits were cleaned until they wore out. Then they'd be cut down to make children's jumpsuits. When those wore out, their buttons, patches, zippers, and Velcro were all removed and the remainder would be used as padding, rags, or to stuff leaks. Nothing was thrown away, everything was re-used.

You'd see the fashions start with the elites, then move to the government bureaucrats who would wear them for awhile, then down to the business class, but never down to the Slaggers except as patches for their identification and to celebrate their production achievements.

Sue remembered playing with a collection of old patches her grandmother had saved. Their bright colors faded and glitter nearly worn off. Her mother and others kept taking them out of her mouth, thinking how she could poison herself if she swallowed any of that glitter.

At that, Sue paused in her dreams.

• • • •

THE WHITENESS FADED and the wolves and circle reappeared, then the rest of the valley with it's blue sky and rocky walls.

Many of the wolves had moved back from the foundation edge, and all but the bravest cubs were behind their mothers or elder sisters.

All were wide-eyed at these thoughts that Soo-she had brought.

Teacher seemed calm enough. But you could see her own back-fur was bristled from her efforts to understand.

Everyone needed a break, it seemed.

Soo-she found her heart beating rapidly, and breathing heavier. She still sat cross-legged, with her hands in her lap, back straight.

She was appreciating the beauty of this valley even more after being reminded of how stark the life was at the colony. It seemed a life-time ago, but had been less than a couple of weeks. What that translated to in terms of ship-board time would be different still.

Soo-she noted that the Teacher was perspiring on her lips, and so knew this was a strain for her.

Soo-she sent to Teacher, "And how are you doing?"

"Better than I would have expected. And you?"

"Fine, I guess. Better than running away from ferals."

Both smiled at her joke.

Teacher sent, "As soon as our bodies have calmed down a bit, we'll proceed again. All this data will take us days, even years to understand fully. Our next effort will have to be more focused to find what we can use to help us with the feral problem."

Soo-she knew from that she was also including the feral-hoomans in that statement. All they had gotten so far was not too useful, but promised more. Hooman babies were natively able to send and receive thoughts, but this was trained out of them, apparently. It wasn't known if there was a genetic time clock running on this, or if it were a cultural problem.

The idea that lacking telepathy, or thought-sharing, was a problem would have been humorous to Soo-she before she met Tig. But now she knew that between the hooman and feral's population increases, the sentients could be wiped out if something wasn't figured out.

Her job was to provide them the data, even if it cost her sanity, her health, or even her life.

Teacher interrupted her thoughts, "Well, we've both calmed down now, as well as our audience. Ready to begin again?"

Soo-she nodded. And the dreams came back...

XXI

THE SENTIENT HUNTING party had reached the original feral boundaries. The scent of feral wolves and other canine species was becoming more frequent.

"This place nearly reeks of ferals. It's a wonder they don't hunt each other by accident," sent Snarl.

Tig replied, "This adds up to the map Chief gave us. The main trails are well used. Just a matter of time before we spot them."

As if on cue, a feral wolf rounded a bend ahead and stopped in his tracks, stiff legged. His eyes grew round and back-fur bristled.

For a split-second, no one moved. Then the feral wheeled and ran back down the trail he had come.

Tig led the sentients on an easy lope after the feral. The idea was to bring fear to them. Their drumming paws on the packed ground was like a steady drum-beat to anyone with a wolf's hearing. That would precede them, along with the frantic report by the feral to its pack.

As the trail came to a clearing, the sentients fanned out to the edges, dragging dead limbs back to the center and piling them up as high as they could. Once the pile of deadwood was thick and tall, the sentient wolves ringed around it. Tig led the chant, a form of low growling without word we would understand. The entire pack growled the chant in unison. Smoke appeared above the wood pile, and then a small flame. At that they stopped.

Tig and Snarl led them down another trail which headed parallel to the sentient-feral boundary. This time, the sentients were careful to lope lightly and leave as little sound or scent as they could.

Shortly after they left, a pack of ferals came up from the other side of the clearing and stopped with they saw the burning wood in its center. The leader led them in single file around the clearing, just inside the trees. They scented as they went, and watched the fire as well. With the smoke in their nostrils, they missed the scent of the sentient's trail.

All the ferals were bristling in fear and warning to each other. Yapping and growling added to this.

What the ferals understood is that a party of sentients had invaded, and tried to put the forest on fire. Then they had disappeared like ghosts.

The pack leader barked once and headed back down the path they had come, back to their main camp where they had left their cubs and sitters. As they ran, the leader would stop occasionally and send one or two of his hunters off on side trails. These led to the other packs in the forest, and to their allies. All must be warned.

The sentients continued on their way to the next clearing. These clearings occurred naturally, and usually had several trails into and out of them. They repeated the fire tactic, leaving a pile of smoky wood that left a trail into the sky.

On went the day, the ferals seeing new smokes starting up such that it looked like the forest was magically catching fire across the horizon. Females with cubs were sent away from the fires, across a rivers and around beaver ponds to keep them safe.

Most of the hunters went with them, as a back line of defense. Only when the cubs and females were safely away from the fires could the hunters form any line of attack. The worry was that this wasn't natural, but some supernatural occurrence. Fire was a danger that was known. Fires starting out of nothing was something they couldn't know. Being surrounded by fire would be their worst nightmare.

So the ferals moved back through the forest and plains, moving back toward the fields of the hoomans, where fire wouldn't burn. Of the two, fire was a worse danger than hoomans.

• • • •

ONCE HIS HIS OWN FAMILY and pack were safely between the hooman settlement and the river, the pack leader went to a high ridge where he could see most of the feral lands. He spotted the fires burning in different locations. And saw that these were too regular. Also, that the earliest ones were burning out. These weren't natural, but they weren't all that supernatural. The fires weren't spreading, either.

After he looked for awhile, he brought his lieutenants up. A short bark and turning to the path would get them following.

Once on top of the hill, he would stare at each fire in turn, and then back to his top hunters. Then repeat this until they seemed to get it. They would repeat what he was doing and then would look at the others. Finally, all were looking at the fires one at a time and then to each other.

One got excited and started to howl, but was bowled over by the pack leader. Growling, he sat back on his haunches and looked to the trail beyond the clearing where the first fire had been set. He barked quietly, rose, and went down a trail off that ridge which led off in that direction. His small group of hunters followed.

XXII

SOO-SHE BOWED HER HEAD again and forced her body to relax. Deep breathing helped calm her heart and bring an inner peace. She said a short prayer under her breath and felt the whiteness reappear, along with her memories.

"Pay attention, Sue Reginald! I won't repeat this so you can catch up with everyone else. Mark this on your slate!" Her classroom was small, and the students were nearly elbow to elbow. This was the fifth classroom they had used in this last solar year. The tunnels had been moving as they excavated to follow various veins of minerals. Those veins were left from the ancient volcanic activity, and so had taken the lines of least resistance to the surface, not straight ones.

Rooms were made in the leftover tunnels, as they could be sealed and pressurized. With the high production demands, converting old tunnels to usable space was no priority. If you didn't meet your quota's, it wasn't just the loss of prizes. You'd also lose supplies of food, water, and air. Broken tools would go un-replaced, and that would mean falling even further behind. The highest producers got the best supplies and attention from management and government. Because they could afford to pay the "management fees" that were required.

"Wage-slaves pay kickbacks, rich get richer and the poor get to dig more." That was the mantra of the Slaggers, those that brought the raw ore up to the fusion-kilns to be extracted for whatever wealth could be found. The tunnels were dug where the higher-demand minerals were located. And they lived in the old tunnels as long as they were safe.

It was up to the engineers to guide the slagger crews. The foremen on each crew also organized runners to ferry their ore to the kilns.

After school, the children would help where they could. Safety was key, but everyone helping was the only real way those quotas could be met. Everyone worked, everyone helped. School lessons were all oriented to being better workers, learning what you needed to know in order to be safe.

If you haven't guessed by now, there was no Welfare. No organized protesting. No strikes. Each colony had to take care of their own, but the harsh environment dealt out its own justice. Unaware or careless people could get others killed. Any colony with a large number of people not working would fall behind on their quotas and start losing materials to do their jobs. There was no excess to pay people not to work, or to be "professional protesters" outside government representative offices.

Children got to play, but after their school and work was done. More often than not, this was the treadmills and climbing walls. Everyone spent some time at these daily. While they were fun, it was not only a way to blow off steam, but also to keep your lungs and agility in shape. People who could run from a tunnel collapse tended to live longer. People who could climb out of a crevasse could be back working.

Sue loved her schooling, and had enough talent to become an engineer, she was told. Schooling was boring. The classes were tied to the median performance. Teachers had that job usually because they couldn't slag any more. Most often, this was because some accident had injured them such that they couldn't stay on their own job. So the brightest weren't the teachers, but might be slagger administrators. The old saying, "Those who can't do, teach." So she found herself out-guessing the teachers, but soon learned to be helpful to the slower students in the class, as that would raise the median score and get them more advanced texts.

Her mother would sneak engineering texts to her when she could, hoping that by raising one of her own to become an engineer, they'd have a better place to live and better rations.

Sue also hated that life. The constant orders and conditions in the mines were depressing. Some of the families had Bibles and books of poetry which she would borrow and read before the light's dimmed for the evening. Her favorites were Psalms and Proverbs, although some of the adventures were interesting. The trick was to get someone to explain what a "lion's den" was and the reason they kept wild beasts locked up.

There were no wild anything at the moon colonies. Everything had to be functional. Well, except maybe the royal elites. You never knew what they were thinking of doing. Somehow, they could afford to have yacht races between the colonies. Sometimes, after the video briefings that preceded the quota postings, they would show video of the races and which royal families won and lost in them. Supposedly this was supposed to be motivating to the slaggers. Mostly, they put up with watching them without any reaction. Elites were governed by who you were born to, not if you got elected. Especially if your parents were slaggers to begin with.

You did see people who became elites from the business or government positions, but the only stories of slaggers ever getting somewhere was in some old legend about a girl named Cinderella, who would pick up the minerals falling from the slag carts and bringing these to the furnaces to help meet the colony quota. She was a member of a business family who had run for government office and failed. But they were still invited to the gala balls. Her step-sisters kept her from going, but she met a royal prince somehow who recognized her genetic background and rescued her. They lived happily ever after, etc. Just a legend. No one she knew believed it.

That was why she would run on the treadmills as hard and as fast as she could. It became a metaphor for her life. Running as fast as you can to stay in the same place. But it helped get the stress out of her head. She felt trapped in that life. No matter how good she was at anything, there was no real way to get ahead. You were always working to just keep from falling behind.

Sue then felt the whiteness return and an idea to look for thought sending. She then dug around in her memories to find some of these. While her wolf friends were both fascinated and alarmed about human behavior, this wasn't going to do the wolves much good in dealing with their local ferals, both wolves and hooman.

So Sue Reginald dug deep, looking for answers they could use.

It was her grandmother that gave her the first inkling...

XXIII

WITH A DOZEN SMOKY fires set in various clearings, the sentient wolf hunters had a ring that extended from in an arc across the forest. In their travels, they had found a dozen or more scents of feral wolves who had left in fear. None had been spotted yet, other than a few wolves running away.

The next clearing would be their last. Then they would make for the main camp of the biggest feral pack. Once they got there, the job was to defeat any feral they found and then defile the camp so it wouldn't be used again. This was the plan.

Just as they made the clearing, Snarl stopped them as he heard the sound of the interrupted howl from the ridge. He sent to Tig, "We're ahead of schedule. I'll take some hunters and check that out. It could be that we've got a flank attack coming."

Tig had his reservations, but Snarl hadn't been anything but cooperative since the Chief had dressed him down at the council. So he consented.

Snarl left with about half the hunters, more than Tig wanted, but enough to defeat any hunters they might run into out there.

Tig took the rest to build the last bonfire.

XXIV

SUE REMEMBERED HER grandmother with fondness. Tough as nails, and able to out-cuss the foreman, she was also the kindest person Sue had ever met. Her grandmother also taught her tricks to do with her mind. Grandma would try to sneak up on her while her attention was on other things, to tease her with a scare. This happened so often that Soo-she would keep attention all around her no matter what she was doing. And often this kept her and those around her safe from accidents.

But she also was able to sense when someone was near, almost what they were thinking. Once Grandma couldn't sneak up on her anymore, the game changed. Grandma started projecting ideas, giving her false perception of what was really there. A wall that wasn't a wall, but was Grandma who looked like a wall. Ore carts sitting by themselves with a broken wheel was another disguise. Once at a celebration, she projected a banquet table - but when you approached, you'd find it covered with flies and bad smells.

After awhile, Sue would call her out after everyone else had left or gone ahead. Grandma would appear out of a shimmer and they'd both laugh about it. So Grandma taught her this "umbrella trick" she called it. There was no real use for umbrellas where it never rained except when they raised the moisture high enough to drip from the ceilings. This settled the dust and cleaned the air.

Sue and Grandma could even make people think it was about to start this type of raining, and so they'd leave the common areas for shelter. That way, Soo-she could listen to Grandma tell her stories of the old days before the cities rose from Earth for the moon.

No one could hear them, and everyone else was trying to keep dry because they'd only see the rain.

Grandma had said that she could talk to the youngest, and some of them could do these for awhile, but Soo-she was the first to really master that trick to any way. Soo-she wondered why, and Grandma said she thought it was because she spent so much time alone. When she was running the treadmill, Grandma was often on a bench in a corner of the room just listening. She'd been able to hear Soo-she grumble to herself and complain even though she said nothing out loud.

Grandma said she would also "talk" to the babies when they were young, and awake while everyone else was asleep. Some of the brighter ones, like Soo-she, could talk to her even while others were present. The trick was concentrating and not allowing yourself to get distracted. This was often how she would find out all sorts of gossip and secrets, since people would talk among the babies when they didn't think they were being heard.

Some thought Grandma was a bit odd, as she never explained why she did things. But she was almost always right, even when someone denied it. Grandma spent a lot of time looking after kids so the parents could do their time slagging, or just get a decent night's sleep. So she was able to know everything that happened, even in other colonies.

Sue asked once how she knew all that, and Grandma said that this was because all the colonies ran on the same schedule, so the babies were often all left alone at the same time. Those that were awake would talk to each other over a distance and tell marvelous stories of what they had heard. She also said this is why sometimes a baby will start giggling and laughing for no reason.

The problem, she said, was when they started talking. This was when they would quit sending to each other. Not because they couldn't, it was because they weren't supposed to.

Sue's days in the mines brought her into contact with many people. So she started testing to find if anyone else could send or receive. And she found some who could, but only when they were alone. None would admit it, because that would mean they were "crazy".

At night, Sue would sometimes lay awake with her eyes closed and watch the dreams pass by. These visions she couldn't say were hers or someone else's, but she seemed to feel when they were really someone else's. Often, she'd overhear someone the next day talking about a particularly crazy dream they'd had, describing just what Soo-she had seen in hers. But Soo-she never told anyone about her dreams, so this gave her more questions than it did answers.

At that, the whiteness turned her memories back to the present.

Opening her eyes, she saw Teacher laid out on her side, panting.

• • • •

THE FERAL WOLF-LEADER skirted the clearing and picked up the trail of hooman suit scraps along the trail. Like breadcrumbs or a ball of string, it didn't take much for the wolf's keen sense of smell to follow it back to the valley. His hunters followed him as they went, right up to the rocky edge. At that they laid down to watch.

This trail was not a common one, and few wolves knew about this entrance to the valley. None of them were feral. Until now.

These wolves watched and waited. They rested. Across the valley there was some gathering of wolves in a circle of some sort. No other sign of any wolves nearby.

It was a fine day, otherwise. Now they knew the hunters were out. Here was a chance for revenge. It was time to watch, to plan. And a perfect spot to do it from.

XXV

TIG LEAD HIS SMALL pack of hunters toward the main camp. All sign was that it was empty. Fires had done their trick. The sentients scouted around the edge of it and paused at streams to quench their thirst. It was a series of dens in a hillside, amongst fallen trees and old boulders. Shale falling from the cliffs above gave an uphill approach to the dens, with no way to attack from two sides. The dens could be simply defended. But no wolves were present. They'd left in a hurry, with half-eaten meals.

Tig's pack got busy going in and out of the dens, scratching out any bedding and leaving sign at their openings. They defiled the dens in any way they could, even dragging smelly weeds into the dens and scratching them into the dirt floors and walls, covering them slightly and breaking the pungent berries with their feet, cleaning these on the dirt outside.

Tig was busy with a den when he sensed something changed. It was too quiet outside.

As he crawled to the outside, something landed on his neck, covering his eyes, while his front paws were seized, dragging him out to the bright sunshine.

Three more weights were added to his back, holding him down. His hind legs were also seized with sharp canine teeth. If he moved, one or more of his legs could be broken. And already it was hard breathing.

His head was uncovered. As his vision cleared, he saw Snarl. Smiling.

XXVI

I SAW TEACHER LAID out on her side, panting heavy and rapid. As if asleep, but it was the Probe effects.

The Female hunters and cubs were wary of stepping into the circle.

But I knew something needed to be done. So I rose and went to Teacher, kneeling by her side. I put one hand on Teacher's chest and found her heart was racing. The other hand I pushed into the thick fur around the neck, until I felt the back of her head where the neck joined it.

I closed my eyes and bowed my own head.

Teacher's dreams became mine.

. . . .

IT WAS A SWIRLING MIXTURE of dreams. All nightmares I had seen while Teacher slept before. But now, they were just the fast clips of being caught or captured or shot. And each time there was a hooman ending that life. One after another, over and over. Teacher was dying again and again at some hooman's hands.

I listened to Teacher's heart beat and made my own match it. Then I calmed my own breathing and so slowed my own heart, and Teacher's heart matched it. The clips started to run in stop-motion. One clip cut to the length of a heart beat. And then only a single image for each clip. Finally, I saw Teacher in the white space, sitting again in front of me, eyes closed and the images flashing between us.

I remembered my Grandmother's mental tricks she had taught me on the Moon colony. Of creating an imaginary umbrella to ward off bad thoughts.

Waving my hands in front of me, I play-acted as if I had an invisible umbrella in my hand. And slid one hand up the shaft to find the sliding connection while the other held the handle. Making the fabric white and the details visible, the umbrella became as real as the pictures. I inserted the white dome to my left between us, so that I interrupted the pictures from flowing by. I then moved forward on my knees so that the umbrella was protecting both me and Teacher.

The pictures turned to rain.

Teacher opened her eyes and looked over at me. "Nice weather we're having, isn't it?" she sent with her mind.

I smiled at this. "How are you doing?"

"Much better since you showed me how an umbrella works. Like a portable cave," Teacher sent.

My smile turned to a concerned look. "What do you think this rain means?"

"It might be tears of sadness, or tears of joy, or maybe just rain," Teacher sent.

"How can I help you today? You've helped me so much, but I don't want to leave you here in the Probe again," I sent in reply.

"Ah, the Probe. Yes, I'd become lost in my thoughts," Teacher returned.

"Did I give you helpful memories?" I asked.

"Maybe a bit too much. Or it reminded me of too many experiences with hoomans that did not go well," sent Teacher. "Those became my nightmares."

"Well, is there something you do to help cubs when they have bad dreams?" I asked.

"Oh, of course. The trick is to be there to help them dream. To tell them that everything will be alright. To tell them they must chase the monster back that scared them," sent Teacher.

"Are the hooman's your monster?" I asked.

"Only the feral ones," sent Teacher with a smile. But then frowned again. "It's their weapons and traps that are the problem."

"I've seen you be an owl, and a hawk, a deer, and of course a wolf. Have you ever tried to shift into a hooman?" asked I.

"No. Before you, I had no idea what a hooman was really like, or how they thought and acted. I only had what I'd been taught, and what I'd seen from far away. You have taught us much about hoomans. Maybe it is time to try," sent Teacher.

I sent to her, "I will go with you through these dreams. And I can speak for you or help you with the hooman talking you want to have."

Teacher smiled again, and our beating hearts slowed to a pace of deep sleep.

XXVII

THE WHITE SPACE TURNED into a sky above a woody forest. They were a pair of owls floating overhead. I turned to look at Teacher, "Let's dive down below to where you were going to land, before that hunter can shoot us with his net."

They dived to land safely, then shifted into two Amerindian women in white buckskin. The hooman male came running up as before, dressed in homespun with a net and pitchfork.

"Why did you want to hurt us?" Teacher asked, sending her thoughts while moving her mouth to form the words.

The hooman stopped in tracks. "I didn't want to hurt you, I was after the owls," he said.

"Are the owls your enemy?" Teacher asked.

"They kill our chickens," said the hooman

"Perhaps you are thinking of eagles. Owls will feed on carrion, but their main meal is mice and small rodents, the ones that eat your crops and bite holes in your houses," Teacher explained.

The hooman set his pitchfork down, points first, and leaned on its handle. "I didn't realize that. So owls are good for our crops, actually. Huh. But how about those eagles?"

"Do you see many eagles around all the time?" asked Teacher.

"No," said the hooman, "only a certain time of the year."

"If you could learn when those times are, and keep your sheep closer to your houses and barns at that time, perhaps the eagles would go after rabbits and other small creatures instead," suggested Teacher.

"That's a good idea. Thanks!" The hooman held out his hand and I shook it. I looked at Teacher and nodded my head toward the hooman. Teacher grabbed his hand and shook it as I did.

That scene then faded to white.

• • • •

ANOTHER DREAM CAME in where we were two young does feeding in a pasture.

"Quick," I said. "Duck down and lower your head to the ground."

BOOM! went the gun as the shot whistled by us.

Now we weren't deer, but squaws again.

"What are you shooting at?" I yelled to the hooman.

"Who's out there? I didn't see you. Come on over here before you get hurt!" The human yelled back.

We both slowly rose up from a crouch. Our white buckskin didn't look like a brown deer, especially with the turquoise, white, and black bead-work. We walked to the hooman, who had cradled his rifle and waiting for us in the shade of a large oak tree.

"Are you hunting deer today?" I asked.

"Well, not really, but I saw one and figured it would be good to have some meat on the table like that," he replied.

"Do you often shoot them so young? She didn't seem but barely older than a fawn," I asked.

"Well, she was young..." The hooman scratched his head.

"Do you have a deer problem that you need to kill the very young?" I asked.

"No, not really. It's the larger deer that jump our fences and eat our crops," He replied.

"Perhaps you might want to wait until they got full size and do your harvesting in the early winter when they have more meat and fat on them. At the time food gets scarce for them." I suggested. "Now rabbits, those will reproduce several times in a year. And you can trap those without accidentally hitting another hooman."

The hooman smiled at that. "Those are a couple of good ideas. I'll talk them over with my neighbors. Thanks."

We both shook his hand, and the scene faded to white again.

XXVIII

TEACHER AND I WERE now both wolves. I was a ruddy blond and she was her pristine white again.

"I don't recall any dream where you got hurt as a wolf," I sent.

"No, I've learned enough to deal with hoomans. Perhaps I will shift into hooman form with you later and you can help me practice this 'talking' you do," Teacher sent.

I smiled. "Now that would be something. Maybe we should do it up by the high pools where we wouldn't scare the cubs."

"And maybe I won't be telling any 'hooman-bogeyman' stories to cubs after this." Teacher replied.

"So is there something else we are supposed to learn through this Probe?" I sent.

At that the room we were in darkened like clouds had covered the sun. While we still sat on a solid surface, we first felt a strong wind that nearly bowled us over and made it hard to breathe. Then thunder sounded with a huge crack and lightning flashed in the sky, striking near us. Fire flamed where it hit and soon we were surrounded by flames much taller than we were. Suddenly the earth itself shook, and dust rose into the air, choking us.

Then it was all quiet again.

Teacher close-sent to me, "The elementals have arrived. Don't fear, they just like to be dramatic."

"Hello spirit-guides! I see your great power and love your display. It was magnificent!" She howled to the sky, wind, earth, and fire all at once.

At that the space became white again. Directly to one side, we saw a dust-devil with fire and sparks at it's top and raining down water below it.

"We see you, Wolf-Teacher. And your fur is beautiful today. Who is your guest? Oh, wait - we recognize her - 'Soo-she' you call her. One who can create fire with her mind. We welcome you as well," the elements sent with one mental voice." And we would like to say that you look as lovely as a wolf as you do as a hooman."

I blushed at this compliment. Teacher just smiled. "They like to tease," She sent.

"I do have a question, if I may ask it," I sent to them.

And they waited for my question.

"Can you explain what Snarl saw after the ferals left us in that canyon - two wolves made of fire?"

The thought came back to us. "Because you were both at that point fire elementals. Snarl saw what he saw. To him you looked that way. You have abilities you haven't really mastered yet. We taught the wolves to make fire to help them defend their valley. Your grandmother taught you to create what she called 'illusions'. But those were as real to the person viewing them as anything else they saw. You combined them so that the ferals thought you had shape-shifted into wolves who could not be burned by fire, but were made of fire.

"Meanwhile, you held the thought that your own form was still a hooman girl and he a wolf. That is what you thought and saw. Both images were true to those who saw them."

I had to close my dropped-open mouth at that. And shifted into my hooman form, dressed in white beaded buckskin.

"We see you prefer hooman to wolf?" The elements asked.

"It is what I am most used to. I will ask Teacher to help me practice these other shapes," I replied.

"That would help both of you. Somehow Teacher thought she couldn't teach others to shape-shift. And you are the pupil who can help her with that limiting idea."

With that, the elements left and the room was white again. Just Teacher and me.

The silence was spooky. If the Probe was over, then the regular world should be back.

XXIX

"THERE IS SOMETHING wrong," sent Teacher.

She and I saw a vision to the side. Tig had each of his legs in the jaws of four pack wolves, while another was across his back and pushing his shoulders into the ground by its weight.

"We can't get there in time to do anything. Soon he looks to be crippled and left for dead," sent Teacher.

"Is there anything we can do from here?" I asked.

"What you have to know is that where we are is beyond time and space. We know that the world is what we think it as. But Tig is thinking in his mind that he is trapped by these cowards," Teacher sent. "If you were standing next to him, what would you do?"

"I'd tell him to start making fire with each of his paws so that the four cowards would get a scorched tongue. And make a fire under the butt of that one on his back. To make his hot seat fly," I smiled at these ideas.

"OK, try this: Consider that you are right next to him and can whisper in his ear, and then tell him that you'll help him make it work," sent Teacher, also smiling.

At that, I held the idea that I was on hands and knees right by his face. And saw the reaction as his fear turned to anger and then impish delight. He closed his eyes and started a very low growl in a rhythmic chant.

I stood up and pointed both hands at my view of the five wolves holding Tig down, closed my eyes and kept that picture in front of me.

XXX

SNARL STOOD OVER TIG while his hunters had him secured. Tig's own hunters stood to the side, inactive. They knew that any action on their part would wind up crippling or killing Tig.

"What do you think of things now, Tig? Are you ready to give me the leadership? I mean, you wouldn't want this to happen again - and it could at any time..." Snarl was smiling an evil grin.

Tig was frowning, with no real solution to the scene. Snarl knew he had him. At the slightest twitch, he'd be crippled for the rest of what would be a very short life.

"I'll give you to the count of five to decide, Tig. And after that, I'll have them snap one of your legs for every count after that. Here we go: One..."

Tig's face went blank as he heard a familiar voice in his head. And he didn't believe it at first.

"Two..."

Then a look of comprehension came over him and he shut his eyes to concentrate.

"Three..."

Tig started a low, rhythmic growl and moisture formed on his lips with the concentration.

"Four. Tig, your fire chant won't work in all these rocks. Nothing here to burn. I'll give you your last count..."

The faces of the four wolves with their mouths on his paws started looking at what was in their mouths, not believing what their lips and tongue were telling them.

"Five. OK, Tig, what's your answer?"

Flame shot out of all four paws from his hips and shoulders outward along his legs. The wolf on his back yelped and jumped into the air like propelled by a fiery rocket. Each of the four wolves also yelped and jumped back, all turned and ran down the trail past the other wolves in search of water to cool their burning mouths and other parts.

Snarl stood there, astonished and open-mouthed.

Tig stood again before Snarl, tall and defiant. Tig was now completely engulfed in flames with red coals for eyes and teeth. He snarled at the hunting party that was left, "Get Snarl or I'll burn every one here!"

Snarl wheeled and ran off down the farthest trail, while the rest of the hunters sped after him in close pursuit.

Tig started laughing. The flame-wolf vision disappeared without leaving a single hair on him singed. None of his legs were even punctured. He looked up into the sky and bowed his head in acknowledgement. Then trotted away down the same trail the five had used to quench their hot mouths and tail. He chuckled as he went.

XXXI

SOO-SHE WAS SMILING and went over to give Teacher a hug. "It worked! We did it!"

Teacher's smile quit in the middle of that hug.

Soo-she felt the shift as her body tensed. She backed up, with a hand still on Teachers back. "What is it?"

Teacher stood. "We have to return. Now."

• • • •

AS THE WHITENESS FADED, Soo-she stood up next to Teacher.

The cubs were whimpering and barking, while the female Hunters pushed them behind them and formed a defensive ring around the outside of the old circular barn foundation.

The female Hunters faced an outside ring of feral wolves, coyotes, and coy-dogs who were closing a circle around them.

Soo-she was surprised, and angered. "Teacher, take flight. Show me what you see from the air. I'll deal with these!"

Teacher ran and jumped up, changing mid-leap into a white eagle that climbed rapidly in tight circles above the round ring of stones.

Soo-she raised her arms and face to the skies overhead.

Wind started circling the Probe site, picking up speed and throwing dust into the eyes and noses of the attacking pack. A small, low dark cloud showed up on one side and thundered with increasing volume.

Suddenly a series of lightning bolts hit on that side, shocking the feral hunters there. With a series of yelps, they left that area so it became an open horseshoe shape. The cloud split in two as well as the lightning and the wind cleared out the small area in between.

"Tig-she! Take your huntresses and cubs to safety. I'll hold these for you until you get back," Soo-she yelled. With the powers of the elementals at her control her voice and thoughts were commanding and loud.

Tig-she gave a short series of barks and the mothers left with their cubs running in a thin column between them.

Five female huntresses appeared in the circle to defend Soo-she from attack. They growled their defiance at the motley pack that outnumbered them, another five ferals for every huntress inside the circle.

Slowly the attacking pack crept forward, while the huntresses backed closer to Soo-she, who still had her eyes and arms to the sky. Her eyes themselves glowed white and her hands were small cyclones of energy.

The feral pack knew this was their chance to destroy their enemies for good. Once they dealt with these few females and this weaponless hooman, they'd be able to eliminate the rest of the wolves in this valley. They would run off any that could escape. Revenge would be theirs...

· · · ·

ONE BARK SOUNDED FROM all the huntresses at once and they simultaneously leapt in the air toward the ferals, out of the circle - and vanished.

Momentarily astonished, a bark from the largest feral wolf prompted the entire pack to jump into the circle and attack the single human, who did nothing but keep her hands pointed at the sky.

And as the first of that feral pack started to claw and bite her - they only ran into their other pack mates, biting and clawing their own kind.

The hooman was not where she was supposed to be.

Confused, they all wheeled to find the hooman only to realize that they were now surrounded by a ring of fire much too tall to leap out of, and throwing such heat at them that they all cowered in the center, panting and whimpering.

Overhead, the white eagle circled, seeing everything and sharing her vision with Soo-she - who was standing with her back to a large boulder well outside that circle, her hands and face still to the sky, and a large grin across her face.

When Tig-she returned with her female hunting party, they found the whimpering feral pack sweating from the heat they were experiencing. But to Tig-she, this was most amusing, since the wind had ceased, the sky was clear, and it was a typical fall day otherwise. She saw only a pack of panting, fearful wolves and coy-dogs. All cowed and frightened of their own visions.

She noticed Soo-she and Teacher-as-eagle flying overhead. Sharing Teacher's vision, Tig-she had her huntresses form a horseshoe-shaped ring to allow the feral wolves a single line of escape. Back up the thin trail they had come in on.

Suddenly, the ferals all blinked and saw the flames quit and the huntresses surrounding them. They stayed still for the moment, licking the perspiration off their lips and looking around at each other.

A small dark cloud formed in the next instant, and shot a lightning bolt next to them. The explosion prompted the whole pack to run flat out back up toward the canyon walls. Heading back through the entrance they used to sneak into the valley. Tig-she led her hunting party to nip at the heels of the slowest ones, until the whole scene disappeared up the side of the valley and over its edge.

Teacher swooped down toward Soo-she, who now had her hands down and was relaxing against the boulder, a wide grin on her face. Teacher circled a couple more times to slow her speed, then landed gracefully with a few back-sweeps of her wings. Then shimmered back into a white-grey wolf with a wide grin of her own.

XXXII

DOWN THE TRAIL FROM the Chief's den came the Chief at his slow, limping pace, with a lone strange wolf at his side.

That wolf wore a dusky fur, different from the rest of the pack, and held a rolled up skin in his mouth. He walked behind the Chief and maintained a respectful distance.

The Chief closed the distance to Soo-she and Teacher, but led his guest on inside the circle. The Chief slowly sat and the strange-colored wolf laid the roll at his feet, then moved to his left, slightly behind Chief. The strange wolf then laid down, placing his own face on his paws in submission.

Chief nodded at Soo-she and Teacher as they walked into the circle. Teacher and Soo-she sat on his right, opposite to the strange wolf to Chief's left. They all waited quietly.

Down the long trail to the far end of the valley came five scraggly-looking wolves. Four had mud covering their paws up to their chests, as well ringing their panting mouths. The fifth was covered in mud over his entire hindquarters, dripping from his mud-plastered tail. Tig came up immediately after them, with his head and tail high, a fierce look in his eye. Tig barked once as they approached the outside foundation circle, opposite the Chief's group. The five hunters dropped to the ground, their faces on their front paws, regardless of the mud.

While these wolves approached, Tig-she's hunting party returned and sat down around the outside of the circle. Tig-she came over to Tig and nuzzled him. Tig then entered the circle and sat next to Soo-she, while Tig-she took his place guarding the five wolf prisoners. She glared at the muddy five as she guarded them.

One of Tig-she's hunting party went off to the dens and shortly returned with the other females and cubs.

Quiet, they all waited for the last of the hunting party to return.

The day was turning to dusk, and the light would leave the valley soon.

Six wolves soon came down the same path. Snarl was in the middle, with two wolves on each side and one following. Snarl was streaked with blood and panting. He was limping on three of his legs from multiple bites and scratches. His fur had tufts missing in patches and one eye was watering and weeping. The other eye was nearly swollen shut. He had a fresh notch in one ear and his jaws were red from his own blood.

The wolf guards kept nipping at him to ensure he didn't slow up as he neared the circle of stones.

Snarl stumbled over the low stone ring and his guards stopped him. He collapsed on the ground, breathing heavy, while his guards sat alert on each side and behind him.

At that, the Chief rose to his feet with a wince.

He nodded to the strange wolf, who then cautiously stood and unrolled the skin in front of the Chief that he had carried. The visitor then immediately bowed and laid back down where he was earlier, his head between his paws.

The Chief addressed all present.

"Snarl, you are charged with High Treason of endangering this pack and all its females and cubs," he broad-sent to the entire pack.

Looking down to the skin at his feet, the Chief eyed the ripped collar of Soo-she's re-entry suit. "This is evidence you took the hooman scent of Soo-she and laid a trail directly to the ferals so that they had a direct entrance into this valley. You planned this in order to take control of this pack. Further, you intended extreme harm to your own den-brother to eliminate any competition to your succession.

"Your five accomplices have confessed to the plot. Tig-she witnessed your treachery with the hooman scent-scraps."

"As Chief, I must uphold the Law. And that law is definite. Death is the punishment.

"Are their any present who disagree?"

The silence was complete.

The Chief then continued, "So I then sentence you to Death..."

Tig stood and cleared his throat.

Chief turned toward Tig, frowned, and wide-sent, "Tig, the announcement has been made, and there were no disagreements. What say you now?"

Tig looked around the pack in and outside the circle. "While the crime has been proved, and witnesses presented, there is another law that may be invoked. While Snarl has acted criminally and threatened the welfare of the entire pack, he has also been one of our best hunters and has himself saved many lives of this pack. The ferals are still out there. Winter is coming. None of his injuries are impairing. We could use more good hunters. I move we vote for Compassion." At that, Tig again sat.

Chief had a grim smile at Tig for this. Snarl was his son, but the Law was definite. Only a unanimous vote of compassion could allow the sentence to be changed.

The setting sun shown against the far valley wall, it's movement was almost noticeable as the shadow crept up that side. The rest of the valley was sliding slowly into darkness.

The Teacher stood and barked. Fires at both ends of the valley flamed high. Circling her nose in the air, she wuffed out a sigh and a circle of will-o-the-wisps appeared directly over the assembled pack. The quiet light reflected on the faces of all present.

"As Teacher, I am responsible for the Spiritual Laws. Compassion is a spiritual law, and the only law which may relieve the penalty of death," she sent to all present.

"Compassion must be agreed to by every adult pack member in order for it to be binding. And as such, the penance must be repaid to each voting member by the guilty party. So says the law," Teacher continued.

She walked directly up to Snarl who hadn't moved since he was allowed to collapse at that spot. "And you must agree to uphold the law and repay the penance assigned. If you fail, Snarl, the sentence of death must be carried out, no matter what time in the future. Do you acknowledge this law and its conditions?"

Snarl struggled to get his head far enough out of the dirt and dust beneath him so he could nod a feeble assent. Then he dropped again to the ground.

Teacher turned to the Chief. "The guilty has been informed of the law and agreed. May I ask for a vote?"

The Chief nodded.

"Let us vote," sent Teacher. "Let any present who disagree make their voice be heard."

The pack was still, as even the rest of the valley seemed steeped in silence.

"So be it," Teacher sent to the pack. And she returned to sit at her original position.

"And it is done," sent the Chief. "Snarl, you will have to make a new den of your own until your penance is complete. Until then you will eat only after the least of the pack has finished. May you heal quickly and then heal the rifts you have created.

"This council is adjourned." The Chief walked slowly out of the circle, limping from the strain of standing so long. A way was made for him and a huntress walked at each of his sides to ensure he made it back to his den without stumble or fall.

All the rest of the pack left in silence until only Snarl and the strange wolf were left. Snarl closed his open, watering eye and let his breath out in a sigh.

And the last wolf, a stranger to the pack, rose and left Snarl to his complete loneliness and shame.

XXXIII

TIG WATCHED AND WAITED at a distance until the strange wolf approached him and bowed in deference.

"I... know... some.. of your... talk. We... are few... who can," the strange wolf sent. "Would... you... help... us learn?"

Tig was both surprised and honored to be asked, although his face showed no sign. He decided at once. "Come, follow me," he sent to the strange wolf, then turned up the trail to the Teacher and Soo-she's den.

Soon they arrived outside their shared den. Teacher and Soo-she were both sitting and watching the stars appear.

"Excuse me, I hate to interrupt, especially as all the help you've both given the pack this day." Tig nodded to each. "But this visitor has a request that your skills may help," Tig explained as politely as he could, for he knew that this might not be the best time. "He says some of his pack have learned to send to each other and they want to be taught."

Teacher raised her eyebrows and smiled at this, "A teacher's job is never done." To the visitor, she sent, "Come closer."

Tig stepped closer as well, as protection to the one Teacher they had. But the visitor put down his ears and bowed his head, closing his eyes to signal no threat.

"Soo-she, come here. Place your hand on the back of his head as you did me in the Probe," Teacher nodded in the visitor's direction.

Soo-she did as she was asked, and then closed her own eyes. She near-immediately knew the visions of the visitor, his pack and all he knew of sending. These visions she relayed to Teacher and Tig.

Then she almost opened her eyes in astonishment. Most of what they referred to as the "feral" pack were actually sentient. They had been cross-breeding with the hooman settlement dogs and now there were sentient pups inside that hooman stockade-village.

The Teacher wuffed quietly as that revelation. Her thoughts raced. With some teaching, they could train these new sentients how to use their ability. They now had a way to find out what the hoomans knew and perhaps even find some sentient hoomans.

At that, Soo-she released her hold and both she and the visitor opened their eyes. The visitor smiled as he looked at Soo-she and Teacher and gave his tail a tentative wag.

"Thank...you..." he sent.

Tig rose at that. "I'll see him out of the valley. Tomorrow we have much to talk about."

The visitor rose and followed Tig as they left for the long trail out to the nearest valley end, where the fires were burning low now.

Soo-she looked up at the moon as she sent to Teacher, "Hope springs eternal, they say. It's a long road, but I might still save my family up there."

Teacher moved over to put her head on Soo-she's shoulder. And Soo-she put her arm around Teacher as they both looked up to the Moon shining down on them from its star-sprinkled backdrop.

A lone meteor streaked across the night sky.

When the Crow Calls

BY C. C. BROWER

· · · ·

SUE HAD BEEN THOUGH a world of pain already.

Surviving re-entry to this planet in a powerless escape pod. Learning to speak with telepathic canines that had become the dominant sentient beings on Earth. Finding she could shape-shift and create very real illusions.

She brought the end to a civil war between their pack and those nearby. Peace on Earth - at least this little part.

By learning only a tiny bit of the special skills she was capable of.

That tiny bit might save the rest of the world as well - if she could learn to master what she didn't know.

One warm summer's night, a messenger brought her to meet a greater being than she thought existed. To learn a secret she could use to get what she most wanted.

All she wanted to do was rescue her family - only 240 thousand miles away - on the moon. First, she again had to solve multiple threatening situations at once...

I

THE CROW LANDED IN the murky-gray mist. On a dead but sturdy branch of a tree she had visited for hundreds of human years.

She cried out to signify her appearance.

At that, the moon seemed to peer through the dark cloud-like substance and give her definition and form, detailing her wing and body feathers with the highlights they would have in sunlight. Only with a cold reflection rather than warm.

How she looked mattered little to the crow. How she flew was more important. Her preening was more to keep her streamlined in flight for speed and maneuvering.

Even between worlds and time-lines, such things were important.

If one wanted to continue to exist as a messenger, the messages had to go through. You could say she was very good at getting her messages delivered. Hundreds of years worth of proof.

The moon wasn't a moon, but another spirit. As much an elemental as not.

The crow stood silently, looking at the moon. First with one eye, then the other.

The gray mist closed over the moon's glow after a while.

The crow flapped her wings once and leapt into that mist. Knowing what her message was and where it needed delivering.

The branch of that tree was soon lost to sight as the crow flew on, certain of where she was and where she was going...

$$\bullet \ \bullet \ \bullet \ \bullet$$

IT WAS A WARMISH NIGHT, and I couldn't sleep. The air was warm, and the only promise of a cool night was some hours ahead, just before dawn. But it was cooler here than in the den, because at least out here the air moved.

Teacher was higher up the side of the valley, closer to the den's opening.

I could see her white form easily against the darker ground.

The full moon was bright tonight, and bigger in the sky than I had ever seen it. Almost like daylight, but not the same. For the light had no heat or sharp definition.

I lay here in my wolf-shape, since my fur was easier to keep clean than that one outfit of a white buckskin dress I'd been given by the pack. They still tell me I remind them of an Amerindian princess, but privately I wish that I had the retainers to clean my multiple outfits. Too often, I had to seek the High Pools to bathe myself and scrub the spots and smudges that simple living attracts to anything white.

While many of the wolves had seen nude human's, most were still getting used to the idea of a human (or hooman, as they call us) as part of their pack and clan. Even walking fully-clothed around the valley would earn strange looks. Mother's would clean their cubs outside their den openings, but I chose the discretion of the High Pools. There I could enjoy the sunshine on my unclothed body in a private peace.

But I didn't wish for the one piece emergency space suit I had arrived in. That would be impossible to clean, and nowhere near as flexible and comfortable as doe-skin. And something impossible to clean is also impossible to get the stench of constantly wearing over a sweaty body out of it. No way to recharge suit batteries for the built-in air scrubbers, even if they did still work. My original suit just made it to this valley in one trip - as rags - barely keeping me decently covered.

I had it's patch kit as a reminder, along with a few other trinkets, of how I had gotten here and what I'd left behind.

On a night like this, I would wake and watch the sky for these meteors that the moon colony sent to earth. These reminded me of the family I left behind and one day hoped somehow to rescue. However feeble that hope seemed at times.

The moon's bigger brightness brought many creatures out into the night who normally were only diurnal, or day animals.

Still, I was surprised to see a crow fly in and land on the branch above my head. I sat up on my wolf haunches to look at her. There was something I could not place about her. Was it the gleam of her feathers, or something in her eyes.

So I sat and watched, and waited. I would hear soon enough, thought.

And at that, the moon seemed to dim, but then I saw that everything around me was dimming, growing darker...

II

"SUE REGINALD, WAKE!"

A round spotlight flared to show the reddish-blond female wolf laying on the featureless flat gray plain.

Her eye's blinked several times and then she rose from a sleeping position of her head on her paws, up to sitting on her haunches. "Who's calling me?"

"You do not get to ask those questions. You are here to be questioned." I used my most imperial voice to get her attention.

"Well, thank you for bringing me here. May I know the name or form of the elemental I'm talking to?"

"Perhaps, in time."

"OK. I can live with that. What can I help you with first?" Sue stayed calm.

"What do you know about elementals?"

"I only know what I've seen in the Probe. Four basic types. They like to tease, but like admiration and flattery. At least the ones I met in the Probe did. I've not really seen any around the Valley to compare notes with."

I was humored with her frankness and honesty. "Sue, what you saw and understood while you and Teacher were in that Probe isn't all there is to elementals. And I wanted to correct one piece of data you were given there - more like, expand on what you were told."

"OK. Expand away. Oh - do you mind if I shift to my human form?"

I had to smile at this, even though she couldn't see my face. Still asking questions. Brave little thing. "Assume any shape you want. Do you prefer the human form?"

"Well, I am more used to it." Sue shifted to her usual self, in the white buckskin dress, her long wavy strawberry-blond hair flowing half-way down her back. And her blue eyes sparkled from her light, tanned face. "Thanks."

"What are you thanking me for?"

"Answering my question. I thought that this was to be an interrogation when you started, and elementals are anything but stuffy - at least the ones I've met."

"But those four are the only ones you've ever known, how can you say that they are representative of all elementals?"

"So, you're telling me that there are more versions of each, perhaps with their own identities like humans and wolves are different individuals, as are all living things." Sue was smiling with her straight, white teeth showing as she talked.

"My question then goes back to you - why do you assume elementals aren't alive?"

"That's a good one. See, I'm learning a lot today. You're a good teacher." Smiling again, nearly a grin.

I chuckled at this. She was someone who anyone could like. Brave, intelligent, and a bit saucy. "Thank you, Sue. I'm really here only to help you. Now, let's get this lesson underway."

Sue sat, attentive. Trying not to squint at the hard light.

I dimmed the light a bit, made it more diffused. "Is that better?"

"Somewhat. Can you make it look like a moon?"

I smiled at her question. No wonder the other elementals held her in such regard. A moon it was, then. "How's that - more suitable?"

"Much. You are very helpful and accommodating. Please continue with your lesson."

"Sue, there is a fifth elemental you should know about. It is called Mind."

Sue made no response to this as she thought it over for awhile.

I waited for her to digest that idea.

"Well, that seems to make sense. And I can see why this form of elemental would be unknown to the wolves. It has no representation in the physical universe, but is probably present in all physical things, at least those that are alive." Sue was considering this with a serious face.

"You are correct. One of your philosophers stated it as 'There is a thinking stuff from which all things are made...'"

Sue continued, "'A thought in this substance creates the thing that is imaged by the thought.' There's a lot more to it, but that's what I remember most. Something else in there about 'fills the interspaces of the universe...' or something like that."

"You are correct."

"My grandmother would recite a piece of that to me when I pushed her to explain how illusions worked."

"And your grandmother is very wise. It is also how your shifting works. This is what I wanted to tell you today."

Sue sat quietly, attentive, waiting for me to finish.

"What was told you earlier could be mistaken. As 'illusions' you do see something that others do not. But that doesn't mean that you haven't assumed that form because you don't consider yourself as that. You saw yourself as a female human and Tig as a wolf, while the other wolves saw you both as elementals in wolf shape."

"So I really was in elemental form?" Sue was surprised.

"Just as when you were assuming other forms while in the Probe, just as you are more comfortable in wolf shape doing certain things."

"And that would then mean that my individuality is the same, regardless of my form?" She brightened at this.

"There is one other factor you should be aware of, and you probably already are..."

Sue again became studious, concentrating on my next words.

"Sue, the individuality changes over time. The 'soul' shares itself among those it comes into contact with. The 'you' that is you isn't definite. And being part of a group means you change with those who you are in contact with from day to day."

She smiled at this. "And that means that they change from being in contact with me as well. So that's why a smile is contagious."

She was right at this. I hadn't smiled so much in ages. Just since I had been interviewing her.

"One last thing, Sue. Mind the crow."

And then I sent her back to her space-time. The other lessons in this she'd have to find on her own. But that's called learning...

III

THE MORNING SUNRISE had been lightening the sky for some time when Sue woke. Again, she was in wolf shape.

"How is my favorite red-coat today?" I sent as she opened her eyes and stretched. I had come up with the Teacher's portion of the hunt, plus a sweet-root for her.

"Good morning Tig. How's the world today?" Sue wagged her tail slightly and smiled at me.

I returned the wag and smiled at her as well. "Plenty of food for the pack today. Last night's hunt did well. Just bringing Teacher a share. And I found one of those sweet-roots you like." And nosed to it closer to her.

"Oh, thanks, Tig! I'm getting more used to the fresh kill thing, especially in this form, but the roots remind me of home." She rose and delicately picked up the root with her teeth, then laid back down to just look at it. A little sadness came over her features.

"What's the next step, then? You're always planning something, it seems." I laid down close by, but at a respectful distance.

"I don't know. For all we've went through, I don't seem to be any closer than when I started..."

"What? Are you kidding me? You just got all the canine breeds and cross-breeds in this huge area to quit fighting and hunting each other. That's called Peace. And you did it just by being yourself. The only unsafe area now is around that hooman village."

She smiled at me. "Well, I'm glad you said that. Because that is where I'm heading next."

And she looked at me with those decidedly unwolfly blue eyes and I knew I was a goner. Just stuck my big paw right into it. No, she wasn't playing me. I just opened the trap and stuck my head in.

So, I rolled over on my back with all four feet in the air. "Oh please, if there are any gods left, just kill me now - put me out of my misery - please!"

Sue laughed as only a wolf could. Just short of a howl. And then laid down beside me and just looked at me, with her head on her paws. "Tig, you are so funny sometimes. That's a side I don't see often."

I rolled on my side and just looked at her. "Not that we've had much time to talk, between your and Teacher going through the Probe, chasing attacking wolves away, then finding that they invaded the Valley while we had all the hunters away - and if it hadn't been for you and your illusions, they would have destroyed everything. Much less when you came to save me in the middle of it all."

She looked into my eyes with her deep blue ones and I forgot everything. And knew it could never work. For as much as she was brilliant and smart and talented, she was also hooman. She could shift into a good-looking wolf, but there just wasn't any chance for me.

I got up, smiled, and walked away. Until I could lope and run and get all that out of my system. I hoped.

IV

I WAS SHOCKED WHEN Tig just up and left.

And then I thought I had done something wrong.

And then I hated him for being so snobbish and stuck-up and such a damned pack stud who was too good for any wolf-bitch or any other female of any species.

So I shifted back into human and started stalking and stamping my way up to the High Pools. To cool off. In more ways than one.

· · · ·

TIG-SHE WAS ALREADY up there when I climbed the last few steps, relaxing and sunning on this clear day.

As soon as I saw her, I turned around and started back down the path.

"Hey girl. Just because some mangy 'wolf-bitch' has your favorite spot, you don't have to just huff off like that 'pack stud' you just chased away. I'm about done anyway, and it's probably something like 'hooman hours' now."

I stopped at that sarcasm and had to smile. Turning around, I could just see her smiling face laying on her paws. And she could just see my head above the flat stones by the pool.

"Was I that loud?" I asked.

"Well don't turn all red on me, but - yeah. I think the only one who didn't hear you was Tig himself. But you could see his dust trail from here. He was really steamed. Really."

Tig-she got her front paws under her and sat back on her haunches. "Come on up and sit next to me. You can help me shift into a hooman form, and listen to me trash your hooman talk to hell and back."

Smiles are contagious, as I said often before. Tig-she's was worth a million credits and made my red-face split into a wide grin.

I sprinted up the last steps to sit beside her and give her a big hug. Almost until she complained about being uncomfortable. But she didn't. Because she knew the ache in my heart wasn't just from Tig.

She shifted into her dark-haired human form, and I shucked out of that doe-skin to join her in the pool.

I talked her ears off, and she mostly listened. When she tried to talk, it came out as single words and stutters, so we worked on the words she wanted to say. It was great that both of us could send our thoughts regardless of what shape we went into. So she would ask me what the word for what she wanted to say was, then we'd practice.

Between the water, the clear sky, and our patience - I finally cooled off.

Because there is one thing worse than standing stark naked in front of everyone, and that's transmitting your most private thoughts broadband to the entire pack all at once.

At least now it was out.

I was in love, and so was Tig - but he probably wouldn't admit it. Star-crossed lovers, maybe. But now the whole valley was rooting for us. My red face and red everything, regardless. I could feel it from here.

Below us, a tiny dust cloud came back down the path into our valley.

Tig-she and I shifted back into wolf-form and headed down. Her as moral support, and me to meet my embarrassment head on.

· · · ·

ON A BARE TREE LIMB hanging out over the High Pools, a lone crow perched, listening - and watching.

With a sudden move, it dived off the limb away from the steep valley side to float through the air, circling on the thermals as it watched two female wolves wind down the paths to the long flat plain of the valley.

· · · ·

WE MET TEACHER SITTING by our path before we could get down to the valley bottom. "Tig-she, why don't you go ahead and see if you can't talk some sense into that Tig fella. At least try to explain what Sue meant before he gets razzed so much he loses his patience again. There's something come up that I have to talk to Soo-she about."

Tig-she raised an eyebrow at that, nodded, but said nothing. And loped off down the trail to intercept Tig before too many other people gave him their version of what they had overheard.

Teacher nodded to me and rose slowly, stretching when she was on all fours. Like she had been waiting there for awhile. Or her old age was bothering her again.

"Come, Soo-she. There are things you need to know."

Teacher turned to me to watch my expression.

"Another crux has come – and it seems impossible to solve, as usual."

V

I LOVE THE FEEL OF the sun in the early morning desert. The cool of the evening hasn't left yet, but the sun rises fast and hot.

My favorite was to take a dip in one of the Spring-filled rock basins and then lay out until the water had dried off my skin.

No one around to see, or I much cared who did. The human culture had left me for dead, even though I loved them each as my I would my own child. I cared little what they thought or their ideas about what was "appropriate" attire.

Because I could "wear" anything I liked, once I had seen someone else wear it. Pictures and their "movies" were a help, but I wouldn't always get the details right. Seeing someone wear them in person, or just being able to see and feel the real thing helped me get it all right. A perfect duplicate.

Just like I duplicated the shapes and forms of anything living. Or became elemental water, rock, or air – even fire – in any form. Anything I could see and preferably touch, I could mimic, exactly. It was all just what they called "transmutation". Shifting is a simpler term. Making rocks into clothes was no different.

So, yes, I love shopping. Not that I needed money to buy things. I'd just go in and feel the fabrics and seams and the fit of tailored clothes. Then hang them up carefully or fold them as I'd found them, and return them exactly where I'd found them.

Elementals have no real rules. I could as easily absorb the clothes I tried on or looked at. But humans discourage that, as it messes up their accounting. Sure, they mark it off as "shrinkage." But why bother them? What thieves don't get is that karma is very real. And can be a very real bitch.

What Rochelle and Jean had taught me was to step out of the way of karma and not be its tool. The government types were trying to solve a very complex problem when they tried to kill all us Lazurai. Most of them were being tools for other politicians and generals, who were in turn being tools for others. And all going up in a chain that was endless.

The trick to avoiding the karma-bitch was simply to step out of the chain, to let to fly by without touching you.

To love open-handedly. To simply create in spite of all. Without spite.

A morning laying out by the rock pool, enjoying the morning sun dry my skin, that was a slice of heaven for me.

Just waiting to be called to another job. The good kind. The kind I could do because I'd taken what the universe had dished out and learn to step out of it's way and turn those weird new abilities into something useful, helpful to those who were still having their strings pulled by the great karma-mesh.

As I lay there, a bare arm under my head, a crow flapped up to land on an almost bare mesquite tree at the edge of that pool.

Turning its head one way, then the other at me.

"Betty." The crow sent to me, in my mind.

So I listened. And got the single concept of when and where I was supposed to show up. Who and what for would come later.

A new job.

I just had to smile. Time to help someone sidestep karma again.

So I dried off and changed into some more appropriate "traveling" clothes. Sturdy chambray shirt, heavy-weight brown duck jeans, sturdy hiking boots. And some skivvies and socks to keep the chafe away.

Just for the humans I was going to meet. Otherwise, it was easier to travel as a wolf.

All this thinking and philosophizing wasn't getting the job done.

So I shimmered deep down into the rock, to where I could shift karmic time-space wholesale.

VI

TEACHER AND I WERE almost up to the Chief's Den when the elemental blocked our path.

Dramatic, as usual. Big whirly dust storm that came up out of nowhere.

So Teacher sat on her haunches, and I kneeled. Waiting. That was only polite. Let the elemental talk first. Otherwise, it could get more than a bit messy.

At last, a dark brown wolf appeared, nearly black fur. With blue eyes. "Hello, Teacher, Soo-she," the wolf sent to us.

"And what can we do for you today? That was a very nice appearance, by the way."

The dark wolf smiled. "Glad you liked it. But the question is what I can do for you. I didn't get a lot of clues about what I was supposed to help you with."

Teacher and I looked at each other. This was different.

"Oh, sorry, this isn't one of those mystic 'got all the answers' trips. But then, I'm not one of your local elementals as you are probably used to."

At that the wolf sat on its haunches and shifted into a young woman with nearly white-blond hair and the same blue eyes. And a smile ready to melt butter. Kneeling as I was, on our level. Dark brown jeans, chambray shirt. Like any local human.

I smiled in return, as did Teacher. "Well, Teacher says this is a crux time."

"And you're right. Oh, call me Betty, by the way. That might make it easier. Or Bet-she, as you wish." She nodded to Teacher. "Now, I need to see your hands. Sue, you're first."

I gave her my right hand, palm up. She took it in her two hands, looked at it, turned it over. Then looked into my eyes. Something shifted in my mind at that.

"Teacher, now it's your turn. But I'll need your human hand to read it."

Teacher closed her eyes and concentrated, then shimmered into a white-haired Amerindian squaw in white doeskin, turquoise-beaded dress. She was kneeling as we were. And then extended her hand to Betty.

Betty took it and repeated for Teacher what she had done for me.

Teacher and Betty were both smiling. And it spread to my face as well.

Betty wrinkled her brow, as she sent to the two of us, "Now, this 'crux' as you call it seems to be no more than a lot of things happening at the same time. Rochelle told me about the solution to this – in her nursing school it was called 'triage' – which means basically solving the worst things first."

Betty looked at me. "Sue, there's a sick, sentient puppy in the local village. A valuable one. Maybe you should take Tig-she along."

Then to Teacher: "You and I will need to help Chief. Tig's problems will have to wait."

They turned and went into his den.

Well, OK. I had a job. Maybe good practice for Tig-she and her shifting...

• • • •

A CROW CIRCLED ABOVE the opening to the Chief's den, a small hillock that formed from a massive tree uprooted many, many years ago. The tree itself had disappeared, but one of the Chief's ancestors had dug a quite roomy den underneath.

There was a nice young sapling that started growing nearby, some years ago. Sturdy and branching. It was there the crow landed.

She watched Teacher and Betty enter.

Then looked up at the moon. First one eye, and then the other.

Crowing once, she leapt to the sky and flapped into the darkening sky. Sunset was coming, twilight not far behind.

VII

AS FAR AS SICK PEOPLE go, the Chief wasn't in good shape. Unconscious, not just asleep.

And I wasn't up on how to bring the dead back to life, so I had to "hit the ground running." Though technically, we first had to crawl into his den and sit under its low ceiling.

Teacher reverted to her native wolf form as simpler to both communicate with Chief and where she was familiar with her own healing spells.

Chief was on his side, breathing hard, eye's closed. Several nieces and grand-daughters kept his place clean and had been nursing him during his worst times. (Because his male heirs were better at hunting – he'd tried it, for sure. Not a good result.)

I put my hand on Chief's neck, just under the base of his skull.

And I got the whole scene from him.

This was going to take some work.

In answer to her unasked question, I told teacher the reason for human hands is their broader contact area, and ability to grab and hold on with that opposable thumb. We needed to work fast to save him, and direct contact was the surest.

Teacher nodded. Then shifted into her human form.

Together we shifted Chief into his own human form (yes, we had his permission – once I got into his scene with him, he was happy to get another chance at things.) And – yes, people have as many forms to shift into as they want. I should know. I was solid rock for a few decades.

Anyway, we had our work cut out for us. All three of us. So we held hands and got to work.

The short version of it is that we were not just going to save his life.

The den walls and floor faded from our consciousness as we three met in another place and time...

VIII

TIG-SHE AND I WENT into human form outside the village, walking in like we already knew everyone. Of course, we got the layout from the sentient pup-dog we were there to rescue. The point was to take him outside and get him back to the Valley where Betty could treat him.

At least that was our plan.

Even running at top wolf speed, we still only got there just in time before they closed the stockade gates. And slipped in with the crowd coming in from their hunts. I helped Tig-she change her outfit to one like the other hunters, as I did. Their hoods helped us blend in.

The hunters all mostly went to the local version of an ale-house, but we both split off from them to get to the stables. Our sick little pup-dog was in one of the stalls, one in the back, with a broken door.

It was a sad case, since no one knew how to care for him. The place stank in general, but got worse back here.

Tig-she found a piece of a horse blanket, while I picked the pup-dog up and held him so she could wipe off the grime.

Then I opened up my tunic to put him in and get his body heat back up. I thought ahead to bring a bit of pemmican with me, and softened little bits of this up so he'd be able to swallow with no difficulty.

Tig-she also found a half-bucket of fairly clean water and dripped some water into his mouth as I held him.

After a little while, the little guy started to suck on Tig-she's finger and opened his eyes a bit. We just alternated pemmican bits and water until he got some energy back. He got active inside my tunic trying to reach for more food, so I started petting and stroking his head to calm him down and reassure him.

Soon he looked up and licked the bottom of my chin, then curled up to sleep.

He wasn't out of the woods yet, but the worst was over.

Our timing was pretty bad, though, since we were stuck here until morning when they opened the gates again.

Tig-she was able to get us some straw that was decently fresh (no one else's manure on it and not too much dust, so we sat up against the wall together with the pup-dog and prepared to wait the night out.

· · · ·

SOMETIME LATE IN THE night, we heard the front door of the stable open. Tig-she had shifted back to her wolf-form, which was more comfortable for her and warmer for me. (That bit of a horse blanket didn't keep the heat in as much as curling up next to a thick-maned wolf.)

But if a human saw her in with the horse stable, it would not go well for any of us.

Tig-she woke right up, but was nervous and so was having trouble shifting. And the pup-dog woke as well and started squirming, pushing his head right up under my chin. So I held his head to keep him quiet.

My other hand was on Tig-she, to help her form the hunting clothing she needed. But I could feel her shaking under my hand – scared.

That's when I got surprised. The pup-dog was scared, too. So I showed him the warm memories of the Valley where he'd be going soon. And he calmed down, a little anyway.

Then he made us shimmer right out of that stable and back to the valley. He had the power of an elemental, even without learning to send he own thoughts yet. Small wonder it was so important to save him.

But the last thing I remembered about that stable was Tig-she's human shape. Wide-eyed in fear, and clutching that piece of a horse blanket over her as she pushed into the corner of that stall – while me and the pup-dog disappeared.

· · · ·

THE YOUNG MAN CAME over to the last stall with a candle lantern. And almost turned around to leave – but then saw a naked human leg sticking out of the straw.

Stopping to investigate, he traced it up to a pair of arms around an old horse blanket and a very frightened face.

"Don't be scared. I'm not here to hurt you. My name's Bert. What's yours?"

"Ti-Ti-sh.."

"OK, Tish. That's fine. Glad to meet you."

Then he saw that the horse blanket was all she was wearing. He then took his cloak off and covered her with it.

Bert swept "Tish's" long black hair out of her eyes with a gentle touch and a concerned smile. "Here, let me take you to my home where we can get you some clothes and a warmer, cleaner place to stay the night.

Tig-she smiled back. Something in his eyes that she recognized. And let him help her up as he wrapped his cloak around her and led her out of the stables.

• • • •

Totem

BY C. C. BROWER

• • • •

THE WORLD HAS CHANGED – humans almost extinct. Other sentient species now rule this planet and work to keep it in balance.

Without the polluting, noisy, conflicted centers of human populations called cities. Various plagues were released when those cities left, wiping out any concentration of humans left.

All that is history now. Wolves and other species have achieved sentience. And they tolerate humans among them as the dying species it is. To them, humans are another dangerous feral animal that they avoid. Because they can't talk with their minds.

In this standoff, a young child has wandered away from his parents into the wilderness. He'll need help from the very animals his parents track and kill.

The child has only days left before hunger and exposure take their toll...

I

SHE HEARD IT CRYING in the dark. So loud that it woke her. But it was crying in her mind. To her keen hearing, she didn't hear a whimper anywhere nearby.

Someone was in trouble. Someone's child.

And he was too young or too frightened to even form coherent thoughts.

"And I was sleeping so soundly tonight, as well." Basheela mused. It wouldn't do to get grumpy about this situation. She knew very well about feeling out of sorts. Her mate had only taken her twin cubs away to train them on hunting, and her udders still hurt from being too full. They were only 2 and a half year's old, and she had hoped to keep them around longer. But her mate was right - with a new set coming on during the hibernation, they would only make the den too crowded. Besides, she had taught them all she could.

But where was that infernal noise coming from? Any mother who was worth anything would keep a baby quiet. For people could hear that from miles away and seek it out. Wolves for one, cougars for another.

Basheela sighed. She couldn't sleep with all that ruckus. and the little one is probably nearby. Wolves wouldn't bother a sentient like that, but cougars aren't known to be discerning when their stomachs get too thin and empty.

Rolling out of the big, long opening of her den, she reached the entrance and sniffed the air. Nothing south or north. The wind was from the east. The hooman camp. Why would a sentient want to be anywhere near there? Dangerous ferals and uncivilized. A hazard to any sentient, which is why they left them severely alone.

That was, regardless, the direction the wailing was sent from. Another sigh preceded her ambling gate down the thin trail in front of her den that headed east.

She didn't smell cougar or wolf, but if they were coming from the other side, it might be possible.

Her mothering instinct raised her hackles at such a strong sentient becoming someone's snack. Her amble became a rolling gate. If need be, she could trot, but she could keep up a rolling amble longer.

As long as she still showed up in time.

II

"I UNDERSTAND. I DO. But the stockade is locked at night specifically to keep the wild animals out." The duty-guard was trying to sympathize with May. Her little toddler had toddled off, and they hadn't noticed when until they came back through the big gates, unpacked their wagons, and found that he was missing.

Now she was red-eyed, white-faced, and frantic. The duty-guard didn't like telling her she couldn't go out alone. But he couldn't leave his post and she wasn't listening to him. He had his hands full, quite full, just keeping her away from lifting the heavy bar so she could run out into the night. Desperate to find her son, leaving the rest of her family in a futile attempt.

"Go get some men with torches and guns. Better would be to get horses and at least a light cart. Blankets and baby food. May - be sensible. Do this right. Don't just sacrifice yourself." He shook her roughly to get her attention.

At last, some more women came up to console her and move her to a nearby bench. Others went to fetch men from the meeting-house, to let them know what had happened.

Tish could hear all this from Bert's family cabin. Even with the doors shut. Just because she was shifted into human form didn't mean her hearing wasn't still as sharp as a wolf's. Bert had found her some homespun clothing - a tan blouse and dark brown long skirt. And his sister Maja was still helping Tish comb the tangles out of her long chestnut hair. All Tish could do was sit nervously and endure the tugging. She never had to comb her wolf fur, except with her tongue. Watching other hoomans endure this was much easier than having to live through it herself.

"B-Bert - wass - what's h-happening?" Tish asked him when he came back into the main room of their small cabin.

Bert only smiled at her. He knew she was much brighter than her speech showed. He could see it in her eyes. And also feel it in his mind.

"Someone has misplaced one of their smallest children." He shook his head. "They are trying to organize a search party."

Maja saw his face, how he twisted his hands when he wasn't holding on to something. And when Tish took his hand, looking into his eyes, Maja also saw how he calmed down.

"How about those lanterns you've been working on? Couldn't they use them?" Maja got his attention with that idea.

Bert's face brightened, then went dour. "Even if I could trust them to not wreck what I spent a half-year fixing, the batteries are too heavy and would only last couple of hours. Yet they were already several hours away from where that toddler had wandered off."

"H-horse and c-cart..." Tish was a bit excited and trying to help, nervous with all the changes in herself and the hooman camp (they called it a village.)

Bert looked at her and understood. Her eye's opened wider when he intuited her thought directly into his own mind. "Of course. Thank you, Tish."

Maja looked at him with curiosity. Then smiled. She was used to Bert's inspirations after all this time. For they'd lived in various camps and villages after they survived the plagues and their parents didn't. And even for sister and brother they were close, never argued, but sought to understood - first.

She only had to wait until Bert would work it out for himself, and be able to put it into words again. All she had to do was wait.

Her smiling helped, too.

And maybe some hot tea.

• • • •

BY MORNING, THEY WERE back. Sorry faces on all of them. With the lamps, they had picked up the boy's trail, but it had ended with a set of bear tracks. Big ones.

Bert came back with the camp with the rest of the tracking party.

Tish was waiting for him at the stockade gate, along with Maja. They helped him unload his equipment, as much as they could. Several men were needed to move the batteries back into his workshop.

Tired, all of them. In spirit as well as body.

Tish saw and felt all of this, far more than she should. She helped Maja serve some breakfast to him. While Tish wasn't familiar with cooking, she was absorbing everything the two were thinking. And would often catch them startled when she didn't guard her own sending carefully enough. Then they'd stop and turn to look at her.

Smiles would defuse the situation. And hand signals, or a touch.

These two didn't know what they could do, what they were capable of.

Tish only knew that they weren't feral. But would have to be trained to gain real sentience.

Like those wolves they had been training in the hills. Progress came fast once they accepted their talent for what it was.

All the men in the village had been up all night. They would be sleeping or busy with morning livestock chores before they took their own cat-nap. Tish took this time to take Bert for a walk outside the stockade walls. Just a piece of quiet time for the two of them.

Bert was calmer now. He'd seen his equipment help find the tracks, and be useful - even if they didn't get the result they wanted. Inside their cabin, he wasn't able to sleep with all the excitement. A walk with Tish, and the way she helped him feel, was exactly what he needed.

They walked in the quiet sunshine, across the cropped pasture ground outside the stockade walls, until they were some distance away. There was no sound to reach them from the human settlement.

Tish loved the feel of the short grasses and dirt under her bare feet. But for Bert being with her, she wanted shift back into her wolf form and lope around, to hunt, to feel the wind through her fur and the myriad scents through her nose.

The next best thing was to hold Bert's arm, and feel his hand on hers.

At last she tried. "Bert?" she sent without talking.

He stopped, then turned and looked at her. "Tish?" he sent back without speaking.

"Yes. That's me."

"How is this..." Bert began to speak.

Tish held a finger to his lips. "Just send to me. I can hear what you think."

"Please, explain what is happening."

"Let's keep walking. I think there is a rise we can get behind where no one can see us from the walls." She turned and held onto both his hands as they walked.

Until he put one arm around her waist and she around his, to lay her head on his shoulder - step after step until out of sight.

• • • •

"A FRIEND OF MINE WE call Soo-she told me it might be like this - we were too close to the ferals for you to be free of their influence." Tish and Bert were facing each other, holding hands. Through her eyes, she was encouraging him to practice his own sending.

The sunny pasture was warming for the day, but it was early yet and some wisps of clouds were diffusing the sunlight to a soft focus on everything. Birds were singing, insects chirping, and the smells of Nature abounded through the slight breezes that found the loose hair strands and moved loose clothing in small waves.

They looked in each other's eyes and shared their memories and understandings at a speed beyond the limits of electrons that Bert knew so well.

Both were wide-eyed at the information they were getting. Bert knew of Tish's native wolf-shape, and Tish learned of Bert's "magic" with all the leftover electronics he'd collected - and something else.

"Bert?" Tish sent.

He smiled with an understanding that leapt full-grown from his mind.

"Yes?" he sent in return.

"How long have you been able to shift?"

"Since I was a child, a teenager. But no one knows, except Maja."

"Is she?"

"Yes, she can, too. But we don't. Our place is among those you call hooman."

"And I am honored to have met you. I again thank you for rescuing me."

"What happened to that puppy that your friend took with her?"

Tish frowned. "I don't know where Soo-she took him, or even that she was able to do that."

Bert hugged her to him, to help her relax. "That's not important now. I was just curious."

But then his grip stiffened. He looked out to the near forest. "Did you hear that?"

Tish looked that way and concentrated. "Yes. The boy."

Bert put his hand on her chin with a gentle touch and pulled her face to look in her eyes. "If you'll help me, I think we can make better time if we shifted into our wolf-forms."

Two wolves were soon loping at top speed, having left piles of human clothing in that pasture, just beyond the rise, out of sight of the hooman camp.

II

IT WAS EARLY MORNING in the wolf valley, the sun had just started lighting the west walls and the shadow was slowly making it's way down toward the valley floor. With a light breeze shifting the flight of fall leaves still making their way to the ground.

Sue and her canine pup shimmered into the valley right in front of Tig, surprising him. He had to squat on his hind legs and plant his forelegs on the ground to stop himself from running into her.

"Soo-she - what are you doing... how did your traveling... I just mean..." Tig stuttered and stammered, which made finding what to say even harder.

Soo-she just smiled at him. "It's good to see you, too - Tig."

The pup-dog peeked its head out of her hooman tunic and looked up at him with open eyes, then grinned.

"Well, I didn't know you had kit with you."

Soo-she just shook her head. "Not like it's mine, anyway. Not like I've had a chance..." And blushed at where that conversation was heading.

"Well its a cute one, whoever it belongs to." Tig tried to help her change the subject.

"We found him in the back of one of the horse stables." And sent along with that images of the stables so Tig would understand.

At that, the pup-dog ducked back inside to cower near her, shaking and whimpering. A frown crossed Soo-she's face, and then relaxed as she understood that the pup was reading images as if they were real. She put one hand inside her tunic to pet him so he would calm down. Soon the whimpers and shakes stopped.

"It's a sensitive one." Tig said, watching the movement inside her tunic.

"More than I've seen in any sentient we have in the valley." Soo-she was noticing Tig's focus on her tunic front and kneeled down to look him in the eyes, a slight frown on her face.

As he saw her face and eyes change, Tig protested. "What have I done now?"

"You and I still need to talk – about us, and other things."

Tig just looked down at their feet,

Probably the safest move he could take, she thought. And straightened up.

And at that, Tig looked back up into her eyes again. "Since when have you had such a problem keeping your thoughts to yourself?"

"Just when you're around, apparently."

Tig shook his head slowly. "Yeah, we should talk this out. But without the pup around to read our minds. It's hard enough as it is - for me, too."

As if on cue, the pup poked his head out again, with a grin on its face.

Soo-she smiled at the pup and at Tig. "Well, he's happy that we're happy again."

"Or - he had something to do with us getting suddenly happy." Tig stood and moved to her side. "I presume you're headed to the Chief's den. Betty and Teacher are still there. I can come along - if you don't mind, of course."

Soo-she's smile widened. "You know I always like being on the trail going anywhere with you - preferably not with a pack of ferals chasing us."

Tig had to smile at that joke. But just turned to move up the trail toward the Chief's den, placing himself at her side.

Soo-she put her hand on Tig's back as they started moving, her other hand still on the pup inside her tunic.

Side-by-side, they walked in quiet for a few paces.

She started wondering about how the Chief was doing and the what they would find outside his den, when the three of them phased out of that spot of the trail...

III

...AND FOUND THEMSELVES taking the last few steps to stop just in front of the Chief's den.

Teacher came out in her normal white wolf form just at that moment, and Betty crawled out in hooman form behind her, wearing her white doeskin dress.

As Betty stretched to her full height, Soo-she looked up to her tanned face as it was framed in her white-blond straight hair.

"How's the Chief doing?" Tig was first to ask.

"We've done what we can for now. He's resting peacefully again. But not ready to do much yet, and also not ready to move along to any final journey." Teacher was phrasing her words carefully.

"I've seen and treated worse than this. But he simply has something else he needs to do next. As much as we've seen of his thoughts, the Chief won't tell us what it is or hardly give us any clue. He may not even know other than understanding that there's something still waiting for him." Betty frowned slightly at that.

Then she saw the small pup-dog face looking up out of Soo-she's tunic at her. And her face softened into a smile again. "So this is the little package of cuteness you went off to find?" Betty held out her hands and the pup started to crawl up out of the tunic.

Soo-she helped it make the transition, relieved to have the squirming pup somewhere else, even though it was comforting to share its warmth with hers. On reflex, she stroked Tig's back with her other hand as she watched Betty hold the pup up in front of her.

Tig didn't move at this, not wanting to make any sudden motion and get misunderstood again. Not that he minded her touch at all.

Betty held the pup, who was squirming at first to get its feet back onto something solid. Then settled down as he looked into Betty's eyes and felt the effect of her touch as she read his body, much as she would a human hand.

Then she held the pup to her chest, cradling it in one arm, while the other put its head by her own neck, under her long hair. It seemed almost limp with sleep at that point.

Betty closed her own eyes to better read the pup, and to do any healing it needed. But then opened them wide - and knelt down to the ground. The pup was starting to wriggle against her. She placed it down on the ground, facing the den's opening.

Raising its tail like a flag, the pup quickly scampered inside the den.

With such a small space inside, Betty shared with the rest what she was seeing through her extended sight - the pup dog came up to the sleeping Chief and sniffed him, then curled up next to his chest. The Chief sighed deeply, as did the pup. Now both were sleeping comfortably.

Betty closed her vision to the rest. "I'll be here for awhile, but that pup has found his new home and duty. When either wakes up, we'll know more."

Teacher turned to look at Soo-she, with her hand still on Tig's back. "I take it you two have sorted things out?"

Soo-she blushed and dropped her hand off Tig's back to her side. "Not exactly, but we've reached a truce, anyway."

Tig had to smile at her choice of words and looked up at her face with a kind smile on his own. "Of sorts."

Teacher's brow furrowed. "Where's Tig-she?"

Soo-she's face paled and her eye's opened. "Still back at the hooman settlement. The pup shifted us here and I didn't have much choice in it. I left her in the horse stables where we'd found the pup." Worry lines formed on her forehead. "I hope she's OK. There was some hooman making noise at the front door, but that's all I know."

Teacher soothed her own face. "Tig-she is fine, Soo-she. I can sense that she's made a new friend who has helped her, but we'll need to travel there to find out more."

"Too bad we can't travel like the pup did."

Betty just smiled. "There is a lot of things that pup will show himself capable of. I'd take you all there, but I'm needed here more."

She rose to her feet again. "Say, what do you all do for meals around here? I could literally eat rocks, I'm so hungry."

Everyone smiled at her joke.

Tig spoke up. "I was heading up here to tell you the hunting party was back. We've got rabbit and grouse. And also some sweet root as Soo-she likes."

"I'm familiar with wolf cuisine. But one day, Tig, I'll take you to my friend Hami's eatery in your hooman form and you can taste some truly incredible dishes. Maybe you and Soo-she could make a date out of it."

Soo-she just blushed again at this teasing. Tig looked up with her, a smile on his face. But said nothing.

"I'd be more than happy if I could get the topic of conversation off me for a little while. But, since we've wrapped up about everything else that is needed right now..." Soo-she shifted into her golden-maned wolf shape. "Perhaps Tig and I will go and have our breakfast at the High Pools where we can finish that conversation we need to have."

Teacher and Betty just watched them lope off, side by side. The sun was now lighting up the valley floor and it looked to be a nice day to follow the hard night everyone had just finished.

Soon Tig and Soo-she were well along their valley trail.

IV

AFTER FEW MILES OF loping, Tig-she and Bert had come to the last tracks of the toddler. In their wolf shapes, they sniffed at the bear tracks and other sign.

"Female, a big brown. She laid down here for awhile, and then went off into those rocks. But I don't understand how the toddler's tracks just disappeared." Tig-she was frowning at this, puzzled. "And not to seem callous, but there is no sign of hooman blood or evidence of any harvest here."

Bert looked at her. "The more time I spend in the wolf shape, and send thoughts to you, the more I understand of this way of life."

Tig-she returned the look. "And I am looking forward to spending some time in hooman form so you can explain what your 'gizmo's' do. We don't have much use for them in our world."

Bert smiled back. "Yes. Once we have the child recovered, then there will be time. Right now, this is the puzzle to figure out."

Tig-she sniffed the rocks and the air. "She went this way. And I seem to smell something additional in the air."

Bert sniffed, then snorted to clean his nose. "That's a soiled nappy. At least that's one odor that will be easy to track, and yet another reason to find the child soon."

The two wolves soon picked up the track among the rocks and boulders. It was heading along the stream nearby, staying to the rocks and off the grasses nearest the water.

• • • •

BASHEELA PAUSED AGAIN, looking at the rocky ground ahead of them and estimating heights of branches above them, seeing where she could bring the child to a safe area where the feral species would have to think twice about attacking her to harvest the child. But also where they wouldn't be trapped if feral hoomans found them first with any of their weapons.

The little hooman was still awake and holding onto her deep fur on each side of her neck, as it lay straddled there. She and he had shared thoughts with each other, and Basheela had allowed it to nurse to replace it's hunger with a full stomach. But soon, the wrappings around it began to smell sour as they traveled. And while the boy had given her thoughts of being "changed", she didn't think her long claws were up to the challenge. As well, the idea of "diapers" had no real equivalent to her species.

First, a safe shelter, then she'd be able to address other needs.

Her ears and scent now picked up something else. Wolves were nearby.

Basheela picked up the pace, sending to the boy an idea of holding on tight as they started to move faster.

V

THE BROWN BEAR WAS closer now. With their wolf forms, Bert and Tig-she had closed the gap between them in little time. Wolves were made for running, quite different from hoomans and bears.

"Do you have a plan for when we meet this bear?"

"There is something puzzling about this bear. She isn't moving as fast as she could, but she isn't hunting, either. Traveling by herself means her cubs are either back in the den by themselves, or have moved off to find their own territory and mate. I think she has the hooman child with her, and that might make our scene a problem when we do catch up."

"Because wolves and bears are enemies?"

"More like - we just simply leave each other alone. Bears are omnivorous, but generally don't want the fight they'd get from trying to hunt a wolf." Tig-she stopped to concentrate and work their scene out. "Meanwhile, we're going to need hooman hands to deal with that child. Getting the child back to the settlement is yet another problem, as it can't travel as a wolf cub, but can't be carried except by a hooman - and that would take hours."

They started again, Tig-she tracking in the lead and Bert behind her.

Soon, the trail turned into a high-walled, narrow opening in the rock walls. "In spring this would be a hazardous place, as the water can flood through here. But for now, the gravel and silt will make it easier to track, but also easier to defend. And I don't want to have to go up against a big brown bear for any reason, much less in a narrow canyon where no one can move."

A couple more twists and then Tig-she suddenly stopped, a move that forced Bert to run into her back with a jolt.

The big bear was in front of them, sitting and facing them. And the toddler was just peeking out from behind her.

She didn't look happy to see them.

"Back up, Bert. We have to back up a little bit."

Bert gave her the space of several wolf-lengths.

Tig-she backed up with her eyes looking right into the bear's across that distance. Tig-she then sat on her haunches and then laid down, putting her head on her paws. Bert duplicated her actions in the space he'd left behind her.

The female bear then also laid down, but with her head alert. She shifted in alarm as she felt the toddler moving forward from behind her, and holding onto her furry side for balance.

The eyes of the child were wide, but he showed no alarm with his situation.

Basheela was nervous about the hooman child getting in between her and the wolves, and tried to use her snout to push him back. The toddler just put both arms around her neck to hug her.

Basheela's eyes closed with understanding something out of that. And began to smile.

"Wolves, my name is Basheela. Move no closer. I protect my cub against your harvest. And that protection you do not want to feel." The big bear sent this with her thoughts.

"With all respect, great one, we do not seek harvest today. Nor do we wish harm to your cub. For it seems we share the same duty today." Tig-she raised her head off her paws and nodded, again to show respect.

"And that would be?"

"Protecting that young voice at your side."

The toddler patted the broad furry neck of the bear and smiled.

The bear did not move her head in response, for fear of accidentally knocking the boy down. "He does seem to understand some of what we say, but cannot form clear concepts. And his cries through his mind are what brought me to find him."

The wolf nodded at this. "We are also here to find him. But we hear the cries of his parents, and so we both share the problem of how to help the hooman child best."

"How is it that you hear their voices? Ferals have no voices to hear."

"And yet you hear the voice of that child next to you. In our pack, we have a Teacher who has seen many changes in her long life. She has heard many more animals of these forests find their own voice. We have long had our own voice, and so cannot be surprised to find that your kind have a voice as well."

The big bear snuffed at this. "That's not so unusual, as we seldom cross paths with your kind."

"Yet, here we are, having this conversation. And we thank you for your courtesy. We would only ask you for a little more help in helping us understand this adopted cub of yours."

"Why is it that I seem to be talking to a cunning fox instead of a wolf?"

Tig-she bowed her head. "I apologize for any offense I may have given, great one. I seek only understanding at why these hoomans are now sending us their voices."

"That I also do not know, only that they have." The hooman patted the side of her neck again. "He says I should trust you. Why I do not know."

"I think I have an idea why. But I must tell you a short story to explain. Our Teacher is able to shift forms, into many other creatures. And so travel the winds as a hawk or eagle, and the small tunnels of the burrows as a mouse or ferret. This last summer, we were visited by a hooman from a distant land. She also can shift her form into that of a wolf, and other creatures. And she has taught this skill to some of us."

The bear sat quiet through this, considering what she had heard.

"And that means your hooman visitor is sentient."

Tig-she nodded. "We have talked together and hunted together as well. She is my friend."

The bear's eyes widened at this, then she also nodded. "That at least gives some explanation to this hooman cub's situation."

Tig-she smiled. "Other than the typical problem that cubs create by running off from their parents at the worst times."

The bear smiled at this. "Something I know too well."

The boy gurgled next to her and patted her wide neck again.

"This cub seems sorry for the problem, but wants some help from you. He is in discomfort - which you can probably smell from there."

Tig-she smiled. "Yes, it is a very hooman problem we wolves also do not have with our kit. That said, the cub will need some hooman hands to help him. And there's where I and my friend can help him."

Tig-she stood at this, and shifted into her human shape. At first, she was naked, pale with long brown hair on her head. Then a long-sleeved brown doeskin squaw dress showed up to cover her top and hang down well past her knees. She held out one arm with her open palm facing the bear and child.

Basheela made no move, except to smile in return. Then sat up carefully to not unsteady the child, who was able to shift his grip to the bear's front leg.

The toddler looked at Tig-she in her Amerindian dress, and then started moving toward here with unsteady steps.

Tig-she took a few steps to cross nearly half the distance between her and the bear, then knelt, holding out her hands.

Bert only raised to a sitting position where he lay before.

The toddler was all smiles and gradually made his way to Tig-she, where she took him into careful hands, not having dealt with hooman children before.

The young boy kept moving forward to at last hug her and bury his face against her chest.

The toddler's smell made Tig-she wrinkle up her nose, even though she closed her arms around the child.

At that, the bear let out a short chuff of laughter from her smiling face.

"Bert?"

"Yes?"

"You are going to have to send me what you know about this process of removing this diaper and cleaning this cub."

Bert was smiling and trying not to laugh himself.

The wolf, bear, and hooman with toddler then made their way back to the stream for a much-needed clean up.

VI

THROUGH THAT REST OF that day and the night, they traveled. By next day-break, the two wolves and the big brown bear had returned to the spot below the rise, just out of sight of the hooman settlement.

Tig-she and Bert changed back to hooman form and dressed in their clothes again. Basheela watched with amusement, sitting on her haunches while the toddler, wearing only a long shirt, played around her big paws and legs while he gurgled and sent her happy thoughts.

Tig-she had saved her doeskin dress before changing into her settlement clothing, so had something to swaddle the child in. She tied the dress into a sling, draped around her front, to carry him during the long walk back to the settlement. Picking the young boy up, he settled down into the sling and appeared to go to sleep, even though Tig-she could feel his thoughts in her mind telling her otherwise.

Two eagles soared overhead, riding thermals and looking down over the scene.

Just as Tig-she (now "Tish" as a hooman) and Bert were ready to start their walk back to the settlement, the two eagles swooped in for a landing. A quick back-sweep of wings left them both a graceful entrance. Both shimmered into view, one a white-gray wolf, the other a strawberry-blond young woman in a white doeskin Amerindian squaw dress.

Teacher bowed in her wolf form to the big brown bear. "It is good to meet you again great one. This is again an honor"

The bear nodded her own head in return. "It is my honor to be in your presence. I am glad you haven't taken that last journey yet so we can talk again. It seems there are many stories to tell me, such as this young hooman who has come to stay with you. I hope your valley isn't too crowded these days."

Teacher grinned. "If it's not too late in the year for you, a visit from Basheela would always be welcome. But let me introduce my visitor. We call her Soo-she in our custom. And she has more stories than we have time to tell. The best one, in its short version, is that she came in on a meteor and helped bring peace to all the wolf, coyote, and hunter breeds for this area."

Basheela bowed to Soo-she, who bowed in return.

At that, a meteor rumbled across the sky, heading north.

Soo-she looked up, frowning. She turned to Teacher. "Did you hear that?"

"I think we all did."

Tish turned to Bert. "That screaming sound that the meteor made in our minds. That is what Soo-she's - um - Sue's sounded like just before Tig found her."

"Meaning that it was some sort of reentry pod." Bert nodded.

"And it means a sentient human is on-board." Sue added. "We need to find out if that person survived." She traced the smoke trail to the horizon. "But I'm afraid it will be much farther north, perhaps too far to get there in time."

The bear grunted. "Perhaps I can help. While I cannot travel fast, all we bears can share our thoughts in relay. I'm sure it landed within only a couple of day's travel for any of my kind."

"Do your cousins also have a means of communicating with other sentients nearby? Any local wolves could make that trip in hours from wherever your cousin bear locates it." Teacher looked at Basheela directly.

The big bear turned to her. "Undoubtedly. If not, they can always make new friends, as we did. It will take a few days to get the message up there and back. So it looks like I'll be accepting your invitation to visit."

Teacher bowed her head again. "And I thank you for your assistance in this. I believe we still have that cave from the last time you visited. The sun still warms its entrance during the short winter days."

A rumbling underground quieted all communication.

A swirling cloud of dust spun up into the air and soon transformed into Betty, wearing her own white doeskin dress, and carrying the pup-dog in her arms. She went right over to the big bear with a wide smile on her face. "Old friend!"

The bear leaned forward and accepted a one-armed hug from the tall white-blond young woman. "It's good to see you in hooman form. I always thought you preferred that form more than a swirling dust cloud. And it suits you well."

Betty chuckled. "You always tell a good story, Basheela. Lots of compliments in them."

Teacher interrupted. "The good news is that she'll be in our valley for awhile. But we have to go now to send some messages north, following that last meteor." And Betty got the details in a flash of thought.

Betty nodded, "Once I know the location, I can be there faster than any of you. So consider myself volunteered – along with my healing skills."

Then she smiled. "Oh, his wriggling reminded me. This pup needs to return home. He and Chief had many long conversations, and he's learned better to control his new abilities, but will still need some training."

Betty let the dog down, and he went over to sit besides Bert, who reached down and petted him - and got the tail-wagging, smiling pup-dog to lick his hand in gratitude.

"I was about to ask about Chief." Tish sent. "How is he now?"

"He's better and asked after you."

The big bear was smiling at Tish. "And we'll now be able to tell him another story that he'll find amusing. Diaper changing is probably a first for any wolf."

"Do tell him I'll have some more stories later, as I'll be staying on in the settlement for a little while. Bert and his sister are going to need my help. And I can train the pup as only a were-human can."

"Oh, Sue, I think I might be able to get some information on that pod if you could tell me what you know about it - and if they are all the same." Bert looked at Sue and soon had all the data he needed as she sent all she knew.

"Ah, just as I thought. Thanks, Sue. And thank you again Basheela. Nice to meet all the rest of you, but..."

Sue and Teacher nodded, walking off with Basheela and Betty at the bear's plodding pace. As they walked off, the stories started up, along with plenty of polite compliments back and forth.

Tish, Bert, the now-quiet toddler and bouncing pup-dog made their way back to the settlement. Bert spent that time explaining some of his gizmo's and how he was able to talk with escape pods that hurtled through the sky disguised as refuse-meteors. All as just thoughts between them.

All in all, a fine day - and a new adventure ahead for all of them.

Moon Bride

BY C. C. BROWER AND S. H. Marpel

· · · ·

WHEN ANOTHER ESCAPE pod screams as it crash-lands on Earth, a call for searchers goes out to several sentient species to rescue its passenger.

The passenger is human - the search parties are not.

The previous escape pod brought to Earth one of the most powerful sentients ever known – and she was human as well. Together with her adoptive wolf pack, they brought peace to a wide area around them and brought those species into balance once again.

In this escape pod, a message was brought for the first escapee from that moon colony. Her sister is now in as much danger as that she escaped from.

The idea of somehow launching a rescue across those 248,000 miles of space becomes more vital with every passing day here on Earth. Even with no remaining rockets or ships to lift them out of Earth's heavy gravity.

I

WHEN THE WOLVES ARRIVED, all they found of the meteor was an opening into what looked to the wolves as a round and rocky den, burnt and scarred on the outside from heat. And somehow protected from burning on its inside. Whoever rode in that pod was gone. Snow had started drifting into the opening.

All they could do was report what they'd found, to have it relayed back through the pack-clan network to those who asked. It was a priority request to rescue a rare sentient hooman. And wolves took priority requests seriously - because these only came when it was somehow affecting the survival of the clan and tribe as well as that pack.

While hoomans were distrusted, it was primarily because they were all feral - close-minded. A story had spread of a sentient hooman female adopted into one of the southern packs, but this was commonly chuckled as just another "urban legend", no doubt spread by some semi-sentient mangy half-breed who hunted in the offal scraps from one of their settlements.

This reminded us hunters of the stories we'd heard from our birth until now.

Tales often told about the great flying fires that had been sent up into the sky all in one night. There they stayed for awhile in a ring that shone from twilight to daybreak, from eastern horizon to western. And then that ring took off in a string toward the moon and vanished from sight.

Around that time, the hooman illnesses came and spread through their populations. What remained of their "cities" became dead-zones for all hoomans. But the scavengers did not become sick. So it was rumored that their sending burning sacrifices up into the sky was somehow connected. But hoomans must have believed in strange gods if that was the case. For only a strange god would punish those who sent them tribute.

Wolves were happy to have their elementals to watch over them and educate them to better utilize their gift of sentience. And more species had more sentients every year. Peace and balance was spreading and becoming more common.

So the tales were told and spread during the nights when the moon was full and bright, and during long loping runs of the hunt, and to cubs so they will settle down and sleep, or at least quit disturbing their siblings.

All tales are as valuable as there is something useful in them.

This meteor, with its hollow den inside and protection from the fire that all meteors came down with - this was said by some to be like the tale that many hoomans had left on those great fires they sent up to their gods. These tales said that that string of fires that left for the moon then took those hoomans with them. Like they thought their gods lived on the moon or something.

Like those hooman legends mattered at all to wolves. Hoomans were nearly extinct and might become so, which was sad for any species. But our history with them didn't let us get too sentimental about that species passing. Any species that don't live in balance will attract the karma they build for themselves. And as the saying goes, karma rewards well, or punishes equally hard.

Right now, we had thin hooman tracks to follow. We started out with six hunters. Two went back to send our progress when we found the track of the meteor. Two more left in order to relay our report of the empty meteor rock-den. That leaves us two to find and rescue this occupant if we can.

The trail is already days old. A hooman without fur was unlikely to survive more than a few nights with winter coming on as it is. We may only find a frozen carcass. But the urgency of the request is why we brought six hunters all this way.

We are too far away from other sentients to send from here, and two wolves will ensure the message gets through if anything happens to one of them.

Once those hunters rested, they will make the trek again to find us and help if they can - or others will come in their place. And they may even encounter us as we return.

Such is the importance of urgent requests. The tribe-clan-pack depends on our honoring all such requests just like they would honor ours.

The fortunate thing is that this hooman travels slowly, like a bear. Three days ahead for bear or hooman is only a day's travel for us - providing this hooman keeps leaving obvious sign like it has. It must either want to be found, or harvested by other ferals.

But the signs in the sky and wind tell us a big storm is coming, one that even wolves will find any den to avoid. This hooman we will find, though...

II

ONCE THE ESCAPE POD had stopped, I knew I was in a heap of trouble. At least one of the exits wound up on top. Of course, I was belted in upside-down according to gravity, so that was a trick getting out. In the dark. As we'd lost all power coming in. And bounced a few times, rolling and sliding along with snow and ice making little effort to slow us.

Our trajectory was a bit fortunate at that. We'd been targeted by the moon colony's guns as we left, but all that had done was to split us off from the main body of refuse and start a different re-entry trajectory. While the main part streamed along and mostly were pulled into a near direct-in trajectory, our pod was not so far off to escape capture by earth's gravity and orbited a few times after that.

The orbit was highly elliptical, so we lost more speed and altitude each orbit. Skimming off speed by dragging through the upper atmosphere twice each time.

Our final approach led us to a screamingly flat line that just missed all the big mountain ranges, though we did take out a line of trees toward the end.

I credit the mass of garbage we'd been wedded to when we left the moon for saving us both from their energy beam, and also damage from the trees.

Once I got the hatch forced open, seeing where I was and the shape of the pod (it had a huge tear in it, which would have freaked me out if I'd known it at the time) there was really no other option than to start walking south and hope/pray for the best.

There were few rations on board, as these had been quietly raided through the various "emergency drills" over time. Hungry "down-belows" or bored "royalty" - take your pick. Fortunately, the escape pod vital functions were too bolted/welded down to be accessible, or removable.

I was more than lucky to be alive, let alone to walk away from it.

I cannibalized a spare suit to make a sort of cape. Very similar to gutting an animal and throwing the pelt over my back, tying the arms, but splitting the legs. These suits were designed to retain heat, and I was betting that the second layer would cover and insulate the rips that would result from this trek, however long it would take.

And I used all of the patch-kit materials on my boots before I left, to reinforce them against cracking from the weather that I knew I'd be enduring.

The last of my work was to make my helmet so I could breathe Earth air without freezing my lungs or face.

The result was a walking monstrosity. But I wasn't going to care about looks compared to surviving long enough to reach some sort of human settlement.

Whether I could find Sue Reginald - if she made it through this re-entry in better shape than I did - that would have to wait.

Just as long as it took.

III

IT WAS NEAR SUNDOWN when we found the hooman. It was wearing some sort of shiny skin on it's back, tattered and flapping in the rising wind. Something like a bubble on its head and looked to have curled up to retain its own body-warmth - what was left of it.

This hooman had been walking for three days. We saw several spots where it had rested. And we tried to send to it, to let it know we were just behind it. All we got as a response was that it was there, ahead. So we kept up as fast a pace as possible to catch up.

We also sensed something else ahead of us - on the other side of that hooman. Something quite dangerous, something wolves usually avoided. But honoring this urgent request forced us forward. And we found the hooman just before that other threat did.

Just.

Now we two wolves needed both to somehow drag this still-alive hooman to shelter and also keep it from being harvested by that threat - the one that was still coming, and could probably have sensed us already.

Then we saw it in the near-twilight, a dark shadow with the setting sun's last rays behind it.

And so we two wolves crouched in front of that hooman to defend it. Hopefully, one of us would survive to send word back to those who waited there. Waited for word of their urgent request.

While we waited for that threat to find us. Teeth bared and claws ready.

· · · ·

"HELLO, WOLVES."

The threat had stopped short of where we crouched.

"I say again - 'Hello, wolves.' May I come to parlay?"

"Who are you, and why should we parlay?"

"I am cousin several times distant from the origin of your urgent request. I also have been searching to find this hooman. I am not hunting you or trying to harvest the hooman for food. The storm is nearly on us. Let us parlay to work together on this request."

I recognized this being now. A great white bear. And a well-mannered, reasoning one. A hungry one would have simply attacked. This was a bear with honor.

"Great one. You are welcome to parlay. Please come closer so we may be certain."

We hardly saw the great bear through the wind-blown snow until he was within one of his great paw's swipes. We could feel his breaths and also feel the wind die down as we were now leeward of his great mass. Yet neither of us wolves relaxed our crouch.

"You two are the most honorable wolves I have ever had the benefit of meeting. And I would tell you my stories and share your tales with a proper parlay, but I'm afraid that hooman behind you would soon freeze if we did."

And as one, we consented to his wisdom. "Your wise opinion is requested, then."

"The storm is on us now. There is no shelter anywhere close. We must warm this hooman or it will die. And our urgent request will be a failed one. Please move to the far side of it. I will lay down between it and the storm. You may then lay on it's other side so I may protect both the hooman and you both from the worst of the weather. Your own body heat will warm the hooman as well."

We assented. The wind was now screaming. We wolves would freeze in this weather as well. Only by teaming up with this great bear could we all survive.

We moved to the hooman's other side, while the bear carefully laid down and used his paw to gingerly pull the hooman against his own stomach, wrapping his own back and fore legs around each end of the curled hooman form.

My partner wolf and I then moved close in to the backside of the hooman, draping our heads and chests over it, and our tails curled over our own faces. The bear then curled up tighter, it's own massive paws tucked above and around us while the storm whistled around and over, the snow drifting in as even more insulation. Our eyes shut against the storm, breathing through our own tails, embraced by the warm shelter of this great bear, there was little to do except wait - and sleep.

IV

"TIG - HOW IS SOO-SHE?"

"Chief, she is as good as usual."

I saw one of his eyebrows raise. "Just 'good as usual'?" A wry smile was starting on one side of his mouth.

"OK, I know. But I've somehow forgotten how to talk any more. At least where she is concerned. Ask me how to plan and execute a hunting party, and I can rattle off all the specifics. When I'm around her, anything I say is wrong. Even looking at her can get me in trouble. So I either stay quiet, or spend my time away from her. And even that gets me in trouble."

"Because she also has a problem with broadcasting all her thoughts to everyone when you're around." His smile had become a grin.

"Yes, I know. But I can hardly ask her about it. Even when we went off to have a talk, there were too many things both of us left unsaid. We only finally agreed to have another talk, later. But not when."

Chief just sighed. "Love does that."

I looked at him and sighed on my own. My own eyebrows made a wrinkle like helplessness on my forehead. Helpless I was not - except when around Soo-she.

"Because you're in love. That's the way of things. We males become our weakest at that point, our clumsiest, our most tongue-tied."

"And because she's hooman, it makes it even worse. I was simply looking at that pup-dog move inside her tunic and she got all upset at me. Because the teats on a hooman are on her chest and she is sensitive about her teats being looked at. While on any wolf, teats are found in a more logical place. And no female wolf would be offended at her hind quarters being appreciated."

"I don't suppose you have tried to 'walk a mile in her moccasins.'"

This gave me a frown. Imagine wolves wearing hooman shoes. I knew the phrase, but in our own concepts, it translated to walking in their footprints for a long distance.

Chief just chuckled. "And you haven't been practicing your shifting, even as the other cubs do."

"Well, I've been busy..."

Chief then shifted to a male hooman, wearing breech-clout, leggings and moccasins. His chest and arms were covered with a buckskin shirt, while his long gray hair flowed down his back, gathered behind him. Sitting cross-legged, with a straight back. "Too busy to try new things?"

With some difficulty, I mirrored his shifting. Leaving off the shirt.

"I can do this when I want to."

"So why do you not shift in front of Soo-she? I think she would appreciate it."

I looked down. "Because two dissimilar species mating would go nowhere."

Chief laughed out loud as a hooman. And I had to smile, as it was so contagious.

"You don't even know what species she really is. She runs and lopes around the valley as much as a wolf as a hooman. And sometimes she flies as an eagle or hawk."

I only nodded at this.

"Look. Bet-she and Teacher saved me for now from that long final journey we all must take some day. Just how many days, or moons or years I have left - all that doesn't matter. You will be chief when I do. And you must prepare for that day. That includes making peace with Soo-she so that we may have peace in this valley. Your running off and her shouting to everyone in hearing that you're 'so snobbish and stuck-up and such a damned pack stud who was too good for any wolf-bitch or any other female of any species.' That won't make for any prosperous future if the gossip is constantly flying."

I hung my head. "So teach me, Chief. You who have always been my uncle and adoptive father. I always come to you for your wisdom, as now."

I could feel his smile.

"Tig, if you need help of another male to help train you to shift, come see me. There are advantages to this hooman shape. One is in healing. Another is in the lack of fur for making contact. And the hooman hand has its own form of talking and sensing that our paws do not. This Bet-she has taught me. Even in my old age." He chuckled at that.

I looked up. He signaled to me to hold my tongue for now.

"Soo-she will be having very hard trials in her near future. This messenger who came in this last meteor is just the start of it. She will need you now like no other. And yes, it is very probable that you will simply need to hold your tongue as you are now, and just listen. You may even need to shift to hooman form more than you feel is necessary. But go to her you will. Stay with her you will. A chief does not only lead and decide things. Your learning is also on how to follow someone else's lead, to decide to do nothing - except to take her hand, or to sit beside her in silence. Or even fly with her on thermals and neither of you saying anything or touching at all. This is your next task."

At that, he shifted back to his wolf form. And I followed.

"Tig, you must learn to be willing for someone you respect to tear a savage wound in your heart, while you then do not flinch or cry out in pain. You must learn the duty of love, and also the boundless reward of it. So - go now and seek her out. Mind my words and test them for what truth they may give you."

I bowed to Chief and made my way out of his den.

The night sky twinkled with stars, while the moon was rising in the night sky - half full and filling.

Somewhat like my heart.

V

"BASHEELA SAID I'D FIND you here."

I raised my head and shook the snow out of it. With that movement, the two wolves also raised their heads to look at the newcomer. Snow was deep around us, while the wind had drifted it high along my back, it had also swept it away around us.

"You must be the one they call Betty." I could see a tall hooman-form woman, with white-blond hair. Yet she stood in this cold wind and its blowing snow wearing only a thin doeskin dress.

"Glad to meet you. All of Basheela's cousins are so good looking. Makes me want to shift into your form and spend the days hunting."

I had to smile at this. "And so I can tell you've spent time learning our story-talk."

"Basheela and I have long been friends, even before I could take a hooman form or any form besides a spirit-rock."

"You're now tempting me to persuade you to stay and tell me all your stories." And my smile was real, and wide. With the storm over and the sun out again, it was a delightful way to wake.

"And that would be tempting, as your own stories are far more interesting than mine. But it is, as you infer, this hooman who I am to rescue."

One of the wolves spoke. "Well, it's still breathing, and I think we kept the frost-bite off it."

"You are thanked for all your work and sacrifice."

The wolves nodded at that.

She gestured and the wolves uncurled to move back from the top of the hooman, giving her space to examine it.

Betty was then able to reach in and find open areas where she could put her hands on bare flesh to get an idea of how the hooman was doing physically.

The bear did not move, as he was still cutting the wind away from the warmth that the hooman had experienced all night.

"Well, thanks to all of you, there is nothing very serious to treat. But he will need to be moved – I will take him with me as I go."

And then one wolf, a female, spoke, "But I have a request, if I may. If you have the power to transport this hooman, may I travel with you to assist as I can?"

"You know of course that you may risk never seeing your pack again."

"Yes. There is something to this hooman that I must know, even as I have risked my life to save its own. Something curious about this that says my journey isn't over. Even if it takes the rest of this life to make my journey back north to my pack again."

Betty smiled at this. "Touched, are you? Hoomans can do that. I know of a certain wolf who has this problem. Perhaps you two can compare notes. Yes, I will gladly transport you along with us." She looked to the other wolf. "And we can make a side hop to drop you off if you have need."

The male wolf just shook his head. "Thank you, no. This great bear saved our lives last night as well. The least I can do is to hunt with him for a few days and share my stories."

The bear, amused at this, nodded. "So I do get to hear some new stories after all. Life isn't so difficult, and isn't without rewards when you answer duty's call. In return, I will be happy to accompany you toward your home, at least to the edge of my cousin's hunting ground."

The male wolf bowed to the bear.

Betty raised her arm toward the female. "Come here, Miss Wolf and let me hold you with my hand."

The female wolf came forward. "One moment, Miss Betty."

To her companion wolf she bowed. "Thank you for your time, brother. I trust you will tell them all you've heard and seen on our journey here and my decision."

The other wolf nodded.

"And, brother, please do not exaggerate my bravery or anything if you can help it."

Her brother wolf just smiled. "If I can possibly help it." And his smile turned into a grin.

Betty looked the bear in the eyes. "Is there anything, any story you would like me to tell Basheela? She is waiting in our valley to hear back."

"Oh, so it's she who sent this urgent request, then. I should have known. Yes, please remind her of the story of the two cubs who learned to visit each other in their dreams. Perhaps she will get a hint. It's been long since we talked."

"I will. And again, thank you for all your work. Let me take these two away and let you get back to your stories and hunting." Betty smiled, and put her hand on the bear's wide head.

The bear closed his eyes and enjoyed the gift she left him.

When he opened them again, only the male wolf was there. Sitting, waiting, grinning.

"So, great one. Shall I begin our story about the six – no – dozen wolves who started out and how only my sister and me remained to track down this hooman? Or some fairy tale about how wolves always hunt better than bears?"

The bear grinned back. "First, let's see if all this snow I'm wearing will look better on you."

At that, the wolf pranced back few paces. The bear rose and shook his fur. The snow missed the wolf, for the most part.

VI

TIG WAS A GREAT COMFORT to me over the next few days. I was anxious to get word from what I used to call home and find out how my family was. It took several days to get this new hooman to the point where he was anything less than exhausted.

Betty told me he was already in serious shape when he started off in that escape pod, already starved and dehydrated. She wouldn't let anyone near him except Teacher, and then only in hooman form. He was being fed pulverized root and meat in soups. Betty told of making trips to Hami's to get the right food for him. Hami's background in nursing helped her prepare the right broths their patient needed at the right times.

When I asked about when I could see him, Betty replied that this was when he was eating solid food - unless he asked for me first.

So Tig and I waited. Sometimes in hooman form and sometimes as wolves. Other members of the pack brought us food while we waited outside the den. And while I really liked Tig's strong arm around my shoulder or waist, cuddling at night while in our wolf-form was warmer and had its own rewards.

The funny thing was how he could now be quiet for hours at a time, just being there for me. Eventually, I teased out of him how Chief had made it clear to him in no uncertain terms that he was to "hold his tongue" if he felt it was better to say nothing than something that might be, well, inappropriate.

Of course, some other thoughts came out around the side of that thought. And so I explained that hoomans had their "teats" on their chest so they could carry their young in their arms and feed them. But looking at a hooman woman's chest was the same for hoomans as sniffing the hindquarters of a female wolf without her permission.

Then he understood why I was upset that day. And hugged me closer - with my permission.

· · · ·

BETTY CAME OUT OF THE den early that next morning. She had just taken his soup into him, and then came right back out. "He's asking for you."

She stayed outside while I went in alone.

The den was dark, as they all are. Betty had arranged a small oil lamp on top of a large, squared-off rock - all for his comfort, as she could see without any light if she needed. I saw a young man with sunken cheeks from undernourishment. His re-entry suit had been removed and lay folded in a corner. He wore a soft knit t-shirt and was covered with a padded comforter from his waist down. There were several human-style pillows behind his head, propping him up, and a soft mattress below him, with actual sheets on them.

"Sue Reginald." A smile lit his face and eyes.

"You look familiar to me, too."

"I'm Sam. Our fathers worked together in the mines. My dad was foreman under yours as engineer."

"Oh, yes, I remember now. You were always so busy, and worked longer hours than most. We hardly ever talked."

"But you saw me watching you travel that climbing wall over and over. I don't think there was a single pattern you didn't try - even upside down."

"And you would always be gone before I got down. Like maybe you were embarrassed."

"More like tongue-tied. And I could always use the excuse of having to work harder as the foreman's son."

"I know how that goes, for sure. Like running just to get it out of your system. It was the treadmills that worked for me."

"So, let's leave all that as my just being a distant admirer. One who has come to give you something."

I frowned at this. "All that way - it must be something important."

He reached for a cord around his neck, and pulled a small pendant out of his t shirt. Getting it over his head was strain for him, so I helped him take the cord up and off. Then he laid back, his face whiter with the strain.

"I'm sorry. You didn't have to call for me so soon."

"No. I needed to see you soonest. As soon as I could stay awake, I asked for you."

I patted his hand. "Thank you for all you've done to come here. I owe you a great debt."

"No, Sue. I owe you. Once you left, it changed things in the mines. Of course, there were the rounds of punishments - but no, not your family. And that is what this pendant means - but all the 'down-belows' started resisting more, where we could without affecting our quota's. But even their bonuses - quit working..."

Sam laid back on the pillows again and closed his eyes.

I just held his hand and rubbed it with my thumb, waiting. I knew Betty was monitoring his condition from out side and would either come in or send to me if anything was too wrong.

At last Sam opened his eyes again. "Sorry. Some of these memories really take it out of me."

I patted his hand. "Look, if we should do this later..."

He looked directly in my eyes then. "No. Take this pendant. Focus on it. Your sister recorded...."

He fainted at the exertion, his eyes closing as his head dropped back. Betty was there in an instant, and I crawled out of the opening with that pendant in my hand.

VII

TIG WALKED WITH ME into the quiet valley, saying nothing just wrapping his own arm around my back to hold my upper arm with his broad hand. And I had my arm around his waist, while resting my head on his shoulder as we walked.

Not too oddly, we weren't interrupted. Our pack was a polite one, and gossip doesn't need to be shared broadly to spread like wildfire. For all we knew, Tig and I had the valley to ourselves. And I appreciated every wolf in this pack as my own family now, even though my hooman share of it was missing.

I held the pendant in my hand and looked it over. It was a shiny quartz-type rock, with gold streaks in it. Hardly bigger than the tip of my little finger. And somehow my sister had recorded something into it. Hard to believe as an idea.

Bert in the village would probably have some ideas about how that was possible.

"How do you think Tish is doing over in the hooman settlement?"

Tig smiled at me. "You're a wonder. With all you have going on and you ask after Tish?"

I looked up at him, with his chiseled human jaw and brown eyes. Between that and his habit of wearing nothing from the waist up, and his long black hair - well, the girls on the moon would be so envious of me if they could only see who was holding me...

Tig's smile turned into a grin. "Should we shift into wolf-form so you could carry on a conversation without going all misty-eyed?"

I just laughed and punched him. "You, you... Oh, well. You're right. That puts a score into your column."

"Like we are now competing in some hooman game or something?"

I just put my arm around his waist and held him tighter, which earned me a hug back. "There are so many human phrases you don't know that we could spend a lifetime teaching you them all. "

"Well, a life like that would be an interesting education, for sure. I imagine we'd have to take a break to hunt every now and then."

"You are such a tease. But a nice one."

I stopped us and looked at him. The smile left his face, but I could tell he was keeping himself relaxed to not give offense.

"Tig, you are just being so - comfortable to me. I think this is where I admit that I love you."

"Sue, then this must be the point where I admit that I love you, too - probably since I first saw you open your eyes after I dragged you out of that escape pod. No, I think it was before that - and probably when I heard you scream coming down."

My eyebrows went up. "Seriously? How could you fall in love with someone screaming in pure fright riding a barely controlled re-entry - not even knowing if I was going to survive the landing?"

Tig just smiled. "How am I to know how love works? It's not like I'd ever been in love before. I just knew that when that door popped open and you collapsed in the doorway, I had to do something right now - even if it meant burning my paws. So it had to be either then or when you were screaming. Regardless, I think you call it 'love at first sight.'"

I was smiling so hard it almost hurt. I put my hand around his neck. "Here, bend your cute face down to mine - nose to nose."

He did, curious.

Then I kissed him. And watched his eyes go wide. But he kept his mouth quiet and his mind closed - other than a very squishy feeling around the edges.

"That's called kissing, Tig."

He smiled at me. "Well, I like it. You're going to have to put that at the top of the 'list of hooman things to learn.'"

I chuckled along with him.

"Hey, you want to learn a stupid hooman trick?"

He nodded.

I shifted into a wolf. "Tag, you're it! Last one to the High Pools is a rotten egg!" And then ran off as fast as I could. I knew he could beat me if he wanted to. But he let me win, of course.

VIII

"SUE, IF YOU'RE HEARING this, then everything has worked out OK. I know you'll let me know somehow about everything is going for you.

"Yes, this is your sister Shel-Bina - you always called Shelby. Hi-ya, yourself.

"And if you didn't get this, then you didn't make it or Sam didn't make it. But at least I will probably feel better by getting this all talked out of my system.

"After you disappeared, things got rough for awhile, and then they came to me as the second-place prize. And learning from your example, I went along with them. So Ma and Da and the rest of our family would have it OK. And they do.

"The Royals only wanted you and me for our genes. Especially since they haven't figured out why the Royals can't have kids while the 'down-belows' do - or some of them, anyway.

"Gramma told me the story how you and she got treatments in a single afternoon that cured you. And Gramma has out-lived all of her old friends that came up with her originally. Of course, the trip up here was before my time, and my birth was a bit of a miracle at the time. Gramma says that's because I'm special, but really meant that Ma and Da got a little treatment that day, too.

"Oh, and she says that if you see Aunt Rochelle or Aunt Betty to give them a big hug for her.

"Anyway, I'm spending most of my time learning how to act all Royal-like. All the customs and dances and how to wear really too-long, too-expensive dresses and curtsy in them and somehow dance without tripping me or my dance partner on the hem.

"Of course, what I really like is working on their space yachts. So I've got a gaggle of wanna-be beau's letting me get into their boats in my jumpsuit with wrenches and electronic gear to tweak their engines and steering. Of course, they won't let me race (as I'm too 'valuable') and have to spend time on each of these guy's boats so I don't play favorites to any of them. (Which means I've learned so much in such a little time - way beyond what we were taught about engineering at school.)

"This means I also get to visit Da and the rest of my family, since he's always been their go-to guy on getting something fixed or built. And I tell him about their boats and he gives me ideas about how to tweak them. Meaning that the boys go to bat for me to get some 'down-below' time so they can win their next race.

"I know that as long as I can stretch this out and play their stupid courtship games, I won't have to settle for just one and then become a baby-baker full time. Of course, I've made a few friends with the ladies-in-waiting as well, since you taught me about listening and helping. And Gramma taught me about illusions, so they always wind up feeling a lot better after talking to me.

"For now, life is probably as good as it's going to get. I just have to make sure to keep a chaperon or two around with me to make sure these boys don't get too grab-happy or touchy-feely.

"Anyways, the worry I still have is I don't know how long I can keep this up. And just because they want me to be a baby-baker doesn't mean any of these guys can actually hold up their end of that deal. They do seem to enjoy the regular process of getting tested, but the results are pretty classified – even they don't know.

"A bunch of politics, if you ask me. But I just smile and nod and do what I need to do wherever they need me to be. And play both sides against the middle while making it clear to everyone that I'm just trying to be fair to everyone.

"In other words, I'd give anything to have you up here again - or better, me down there with you. But of course, after you left, they pretty much all but welded those pod hatches shut, even though they are emergency escape pods, so there would be a riot if they tried. Now there are extra guards around and they are using the trash runs for target practice.

"We're going to have to do something special just to smuggle this out - I don't know what yet, but Sam, his dad and our Da are working on some ideas...

"Now, the stuff you are holding is special, he says. He and Gramma and Ma have found out that it will allow ideas to get through from one person to another, and will record a huge amount of data in it. And they can talk between themselves anywhere in the mines or above them. More like 'thinking' than actually talking. So it's funny when I hear them giggling after I thought about how stupid these Royals really are...

"There's a bunch of this stuff up here. Yes, that's real gold inside it, but the process of getting it out is way too expensive for the amount of fuel it takes, so it's basically junk rock up here - not even worth sending it down as refuse. (Or what they say, anyway. They quit sending it down after you left, so maybe somebody suspected something.)

"But Da has got this going as a 'lucky charm' fashion thing. Turns out it can glow a little in the dark, and one of these will help you find someone else who's wearing one, so he's got someone's approval to make 'safety bracelets' from them. The production has to be on our own time, but the process is pretty simple and doesn't cost the Corp anything...

"So when you get this and figure out how to listen to me prattle on, please try to use it to get in touch with me. (I've got them to make earrings for me, and get it into other jewelry I have to wear, so I'm always wearing some of this junk rock.

"OK? Love you much, as always. Da, Ma, and Gramma say hi..."

IX

I JUST WANTED TO GET a recording of this down, so we had a record of things. There are so many things moving very fast now. And they need to be if I'm ever going to figure out how to rescue my family from that moon colony prison.

It wasn't hard to get Bert and Tish to meet us at the old escape pod. That pup-dog is easy to talk with, of course he's still learning the discipline of staying focused. Betty says this is the "look-squirrel" problem. And a lot of that significance was lost on me, but probably made more sense when she was growing up, even as a Lazurai. She said they had a huge library of videos as kids, anyway...

Tig and I talked a lot about what Shelby recorded. And I sat for days concentrating on picking something up out of that little pendant. The trick was getting more of this stone to see if Bert could do some testing to use it as a transmitter.

Bert was kind of a hero, along with Tish, for saving that lost boy, so when he wants to go pick up some more "gizmo's" they will pretty much let him come and go whenever he wants.

He's picked out some horses to pull his wagon that are pretty close to sentient, and we've trained them to recognize us as wolves and their protectors. Which means they can get the best grazing while one of us watches out for them. Good deal all around. And Bert, Tish and Maja can extract all the gizmo's they want without worrying about the horses or other wildlife.

Although Maja has no problems talking to the song birds - even the ones who "steal" the ribbons out of her hair for their nests.

We've done a few trips now. Tig has found that his human form is better for beating the fused rocks off the outside of the escape pod with hammer and chisel.

And both Tish and Maja pretend to be jealous of me having Tig around. They tease me about his shoulders being so wide and some catty remarks that aren't even fit to repeat here, much less in the "bedroom" like Tish has gotten used to.

She and Bert spend most of the time inside that pod when we are here and come out quite hot and sweaty, covered in grease or other dirt - which allows Tig and I to make our own catty remarks about what they are really doing in there.

All in all, we've been enjoying ourselves.

Don't think I told you about Old Ben the cyborg - he was carefully extracted and has been a wealth of information back at the settlement. No one there knows about him, and he's learned to "play dead" when anyone comes in...

Bert has got these "junk rock" working as data storage now, and he's got Old Ben working to transfer all the records he came down with into several copies on these rocks - so Ben can "listen" to them when he's traveling for hours from here to there. Maja has one just full of recorded old music, that she says helps her with the housework.

But the two of them are able to send just about anywhere in the village or outside it. We can even pick them up from the valley - but they take some practice. Funny, they say they can hear me clearer than I can hear them - and have repeated a few embarrassing things back to me that I only intended for Tig.

It's the dreams that are bothering me now. I think their something to do with that pendant, but I can't be sure – yet.

Sam has been recovering nicely. After he was able to get outside, we had to gradually break the idea of wolves and shape-shifting. We got him a pendant of his own, so he is able to pick up Tig and my thoughts, as well as Bert, Tish, and Maja's.

Basheela and Sam found they had mutual interests, particularly in telling stories. And he's got a wolf girl-friend, he calls "Peg" who dotes on everything he says. We got her a pendant and you'll see them sunning together, leaning on each other and just talking away with their minds.

Betty says that with a few more treatments, she thinks he'll be able to shift soon.

Peg is already able to shift, and has been practicing, but won't do it in front of Sam until he can as well.

Sam is almost healed. He's moved into the front part of Basheela's cave, just off to the side. And you can hear those two and Peg telling their stories way after sunset if you walk by the front of their cave.

X

I'VE BEEN A BIT BUSY, so this is just to catch us up quickly.

Betty came back with someone named Tess one day. A red-haired wonder of a girl who has shining cube-type lights that hover around her. She was someone Bess had treated and pulled out of a huge mess. Betty took Tess first to see the pup-dog. Tess was able to figure out how the pup-dog did shifting, and stayed around for a couple of weeks just training him. Now the pup-dog brings Bert and Maja up regularly to visit. They can shift into wolves here and practice their other talents.

Yes, the valley can get full with visitors some day's.

I have to tell you this: Betty and Tess got their remote friend Hami to make up a huge mess of food for the whole valley. Of course, everyone had to attend in hooman form, but got to sit on the floor inside and on top of the old circular barn foundation. Chief and Teacher sat together and presided over everything.

Basheela was the guest of honor and was the one exception to the rule, since she's expecting now, and we haven't been even suggesting that she try to learn shifting until her well after her next babies arrived. So the young shifted wolf cubs took their turns feeding the great bear with their small hooman hands into her huge mouth.

But we all got to hear Basheela's stories. Even though the cubs got so tired they turned back into their normal wolf-shape when they slept. (With lots of "look – how cute" thoughts tending to interrupt us all - with smiles.)

Now back to Tess and Bert. She figured out how to take some of her "tessies" (space-time bending organic tesseracts) and fit them into a container to extend the range of our "junk rock" transceivers.

The first person I tried to contact was Gramma. Yes, she was surprised. I picked her as she was the least likely to be busy with anything important that I'd interrupt. Yes, I was in tears by the end of it – so very happy.

Now the deal is that it's gotten much worse up there.

A lot of the Royals have disappeared. Some have been found outside airlocks, others have not come back from their "boat" races. I didn't get a lot of details, as even Gramma has been put to work, and with a tight schedule. Most of the children are on their own work shifts, and their schooling has been cut back to almost nothing.

They haven't had a visit from Shelby in weeks. They can hear her, but it's like she's never feeling safe enough to send very much to them.

There are more armed guards in the tunnels, and the safety bracelets have become essential to get data back and forth, but it takes practice and training - with no time to do any. Meal breaks are minimal, and so is sleep.

All this leaves me more frustrated and nervous than ever before. And Tig is the only one who can help me keep it all together. That's where his broad human shoulders come in handy for crying on. Of course, cuddling into his thick wolf fur at night ranks right up there.

Tess, Bert, and Old Ben are still working on something, but won't tell me what it is.

Meanwhile, winter arrived into our valley with its snow and storms. Tess and pup-dog don't seem bothered by it, so Bert and Maja still come here pretty frequently. And Tess has worked up a huge curtain over the front of Basheela's cave where we can all meet. (Of course, we have to keep it quiet so the big bear can hibernate in the back - she took off her pendant to avoid even that amount of noise.)

• • • •

TONIGHT, TESS BROUGHT the "beta-test" version of what they've been working on. We can now listen in, without sending, through all of that junk rock up there. There's plenty of it in the tunnels, so we can hear almost every conversation up there. The problem has been in narrowing to just one conversation at a time. And found that it's been used in all the Royal's palatial rooms.

So we started spying.

And what we found out just made us realize everything was very much worse than even the 'down-belows' knew...

Blood Moon

BY C. C. BROWER & S. H. Marpel

· · · ·

EXECUTIVES RUNNING the last outposts of humanity are going missing.

Decades ago, certain cities lifted off from the surface of Earth, protected by fusion-powered shields. Their destination was the moon, to mine the needed resources to make the next phase of the journey.

The culture in these city-colonies has separated into two - the "royals" and the "down-belows".

Now someone is carefully reducing the royal houses - one by one. Who that someone or someones are, or how they are doing this is unknown.

But not unwatched. The question is whether the watchers can solve the mystery in time. And do something effective.

Before these city-colonies, and their hopes for rescuing humanity - die.

I

TWO LOVERS EMERGED from their secret tryst in the bowels of their city center.

It was just below where the shields ended - more like, where they allowed an opening for the airlocks. Otherwise, the city building looked like it always did when it was originally built on Earth. Concrete pillars, walls, floors. Almost endless blank doors going to storage rooms - or to lover's hiding holes.

Yellow and white stripes of pealing paint told stories of exits, entrances, places to go, how to move. Black letters overlay these with symbols to define the subdivisions.

Tonight, they only gave code to secret hideaways where royal lovers could sin in quiet, undetected for the few minutes of anonymous bliss they sought.

These two were now satisfied for their urges. Arm in arm, they hugged their way back along the passageway between these lines of blank doors. Tousled, barely clothed again, mis-buttoned clothes showing the passion of their moments alone.

At the airlock, she stopped them. "Shh - get in here, quick. They'll see us."

Shoving her lover through the thick airlock door, he hid inside so they wouldn't be seen together. She shut the door, what he thought was her knowing sacrifice. Then he heard a hiss as the seal was activated. That signaled to him something was very wrong. The only other door he could see in that small room was the one that went to the outside. Raw vacuum of the moon.

There were no air tanks in that room, no pressure suits hanging where they should be. This was a setup. He was going to die - unless that door he came in was unlocked and opened again.

He lunged to the single window in that door and peered out.

Through the dust and scratches, he could make out her face. Smiling. Goth lips and eyes. That mole on the right side of her face, just above her goth-black, full lips. The smile showed no teeth, just a knowing look that she'd accomplished something, for some reason he would never know.

Then he saw her arm move to palm that large button and the air started siphoning out so the outer door could open.

• • • •

SHE BARELY HEARD HIS frantic beating at the door, didn't hear his screaming. Doors built to withstand zero pressure outside and livable pressure inside were too thick to pass any human sounds. Only those of beasts as they bruised and broke their hands pounding to try and save their own life. Futile. Final.

Then she turned and walked away. As the hissing continued, the air still siphoning out of that tiny room between the two massive doors.

She'd left the tell-tale pills in his pocket. Ones that were illegal, that caused insane visions and psychotic paranoia - but only in excess. Visions that could cause a person to open airlocks to escape their own demons to the outside "freedom" they imagined there.

But was only a temporary aphrodisiac high in tiny doses.

When he was found, there would be no evidence of their tryst that night. That outer door would open automatically once the pressure was low enough. And then the leftover pressure would push the door open - and him out.

Out of habit, she glanced at the camera above that door. It had long ago been pointed up to the ceiling. From her own pocket, she pulled a smartphone and activated an app that paused the cameras between here and her private quarters. They'd resume after she was well away. And adjust their time-stamps to account for the missing minutes while she walked by.

She'd paid extra for that app, in addition to the pills. And the trick was - her lover did the transaction, not her. She was invisible - again.

• • • •

A DARK ROOM, CONTAINING a wall of monitor screens. Lighting was dimmed to focus the watchers on their screens and those recorded stories.

"Did you get all that?"

"Hard to make out. All that noise and static we're getting with this merged feed."

"I know, but all that set of cameras went funny at the same time."

"Sounds like our mystery person again."

"Not like her, though. The airlock here has been used before. And that same path of cameras."

"Yeah, I know. That might mean she's gone officially serial."

"Oh we know she's serial, it just means she now thinks that she's getting away with it."

"Her web is tightening. And those who fly into it don't know they are trapped until they die."

"Or disappear..."

II

"YOU GOTTA LOVE WHAT Betty and Gaia have done with the place. You'd never think this was a cave." Sam, with his tousled sandy-blond hair smiled as he turned in his bentwood "caboose" chair to his partner. He sat his chambray-covered back against the arms and back of his chair, while stretching out his denim-covered legs.

"Sure beats the heck out of chinked logs and split-shake, shingled roofs. And what's that warm air coming from - central heating?" Bert, in coarse-weave homespun tan shirt and brown trousers, was appreciating the weatherproof surrounds of their "gizmo-office" as Tish called it.

As if on cue, Tish came in the doorway, wearing her own homespun long brown skirt and tan blouse, and carrying a metal platter of cookies with a fresh pot of coffee. "Hi guys, how's the 'peeping' going?"

Bert smiled at her for her comment as well as her looks. He rose to meet her, and walked across braided oval rug covering the tiled floor. Even though she didn't need any help to set the platter down on the round oak table.

He sent to her, "It's not 'peeping', it's spying or surveillance. And it's going pretty good. Right now it's mostly audio-only, but Sam's software improvements have started sorting out the voices and even keyword recognition, so we can tell who is where, when and get some patterns falling into place."

Sam came over to get some of the cookies and looked them over.

"Those are raisin and nut oatmeal cookies, so Peg can enjoy them as much as you." Tish smiled at the coal-gray female wolf who came over and leaned against Sam's leg.

Sam handed her part of his cookie that she gingerly took from his fingers. And accepted him scratching her back with a broad smile after swallowing.

Peg broad-sent her thoughts, "Sam tries to keep me up on what's happening, but we both know I'm just here for moral support. This is so far beyond anything I've experienced before. But one day, I'll take Sam out and show him the mysteries of Nature, how to track and hunt

- and then he'll be the student for awhile." Peg rubbed up against his leg again with a smile. "It's so great to be able to send to everyone and be understood. Hoomans and wolves working together in a cave hewn out of solid rock by a goddess and an elemental. When Basheela wakes up from her hibernation, we'll have so many new stories to tell her."

"I hope she's resting well now. I was worried we had been keeping her up with all the noise, especially after she invited Peg and I to use the front of her cave this fall." Sam had a worry line across his forehead.

Peg sat next to Sam's leg, partly to ease the strain on her neck of looking up into his face. "Basheela's been fine. I check in on her regularly, and listen to her soft snores. If we were bothering her, she'd be out here and we'd know."

Bert added, "I think when Gaia and Betty tunneled out this room for us, and we hung those big doors into that opening, that pretty much cut down the bulk of the noise we were making."

Tish smiled. "And your Maja got her rock-walled cabin with a slate roof with its rock fireplace and oven to cook with. Of course, I'm learning a lot from her - these are my cookies. How do you like them?"

Bert came over and kissed her on her cheek. "As usual, they're marvelous. But of course, I'm biased." He smiled and then kissed her cheek again.

Tish just put her arm around his waist and hugged him, while he put his arm around her shoulder.

She looked up into his eyes. "Then you'd better try that coffee before it gets cold. There's also another pot of honey for you."

And Bert, reminded of how sweet he thought she was, hugged her closer and give her a kiss on her forehead. "I hope you aren't running Maja ragged in there. All this cooking for so many people is a lot of work."

"Not that she doesn't love it. Besides, with all your gizmo's now out of your cabin home, she says the dusting goes a lot faster, and gives her time to write." Tish looked over at Sam. "And if she hasn't told you yet, she's really is getting a lot out of that 'word-processor' you and Bert got running for her. And she practices by typing transcripts of those recordings you made. Of course, she had some problems with your math equations, but..."

Bert was all smiles. "My sister is usually the last to complain, but you can see in her face that while housekeeping is a love for her, she is even more in love with science. Once we work the details out, Tessa has an idea on how we could link some of the village libraries with each other in order to communicate and share electronic files. They used to call them 'ebooks' in the pre-lift days."

Tish got a wry smile on her face. "That's a nice euphemism for the disaster they made. And certainly shorter than 'the-day-when-the-great-cities-flew-away' as my people call it."

Bert squeezed her again. "That reminds me that you were going to take me out to show me how gorgeous the trails looked under snow."

She leaned in against him, with her head on his shoulder. "Always the romantic, aren't you. I'm surprised you have any time for lovey-dovey stuff with all the gizmo's and science you have cooking away inside that mind of yours all the time."

"For you, I make time all I can."

A small gust of cool wind came out of the tunnel entrance to their rock office. It was followed shortly by a red-blond female wolf with blue eyes, and a dark brown male wolf. Both stopped to shake the snow from their backs before they entered - and shifted to their hooman forms of Sue and Tig. Sue was wearing her typical white doeskin dress, but with leggings underneath for this cool weather. Tig was in his typical breech-clout and leggings, but had started wearing a long-tailed buckskin shirt at Sue's request. (She suggested that as a way to keep from distracting the other females so much.)

"Hey Bert, Sam, Tish, Peg - how's the progress going?" Sue was all smiles, even with the stress she was under. Tig's arm around her waist was helping her keep her inner poise. He didn't need to say anything, just be there for her.

Sam jumped in. "Well, we're figuring out how to filter the audio, and record it. And then we've got alerts coming up for certain keywords, and certain voices. But we are still running into the needle-haystack problem.

And we still haven't heard your sister Shelby anywhere. But we aren't listening everywhere..."

Sue's face fell for a short bit, and then she brightened. "Still, that's progress. More than we had last week and way more since we got you both here.

Sam smiled and looked down as he stroked Peg's head, who just closed her eyes and enjoyed it.

Bert walked back over to the console-rig where he'd been sitting. "I think we found their security command center. And this is pretty interesting to listen to. Bert and I are still working on getting visuals, but these 'junk rocks' aren't the same as having video chips, so we might have to brainstorm with Tess a bit the next time she's able to come around."

He played back a bit of the recording. "They were talking about some woman who is apparently giving them trouble. And that might explain more of what Shelby was talking about on her own recording. The 'Royals' are losing people way out of proportion to accidents and stupidity. They had one last night, well, they thought they did. But the guy just disappeared right out of an airlock - not even a body left outside. So those security people are mystified.

Sam was frowning at this as well, nodding at what Bert said.

Something was happening with the Royals, and that was where Sue's sister was - the royal bride at risk.

III

THE NEXT DAY WAS NORMAL. No one suspected anything. I showed up on time and went through my usual routine of getting everyone started on their assigned tasks and reports. Just as I always did when our boss was late coming in, or even out on one of his races with the other Royals.

Some said it ran better with him gone so much, but I would only smile - taking that as a compliment. Even though it was true.

That's why I had to get him out of the way. Because as far as I could tell, he was only appointed here so he could have plenty of spare time to keep winning races. Useless for any efficient operation otherwise. Good thing he had me to cover for him.

For most of the morning, the place ran as normal. We had to collect the mining reports and qualitative analysis, and compare this against expected quotas for each area. Then runners would be sent down to query anything that was too good a report, or too bad a report - and also the times that an area was too many times right just above their quota. Too good, too bad, and too same. Like usual.

The first idea that it wasn't a day as usual was when the security guard came in and started asking questions. But this time, it wasn't just a guard. It was the Security Chief himself.

"Malia, we're just doing a routine check. Your boss, Jack, has gone missing."

I had no reaction to that. "Not just one of his sleepovers?"

"No, his apartment is empty."

"Of course, you checked the bars and behind them?"

He frowned. "Yes, of course. I take it this isn't unknown for him to be missing?"

"Hardly. If he's not sleeping it off somewhere - or with someone - then he's racing his boat or working on it. It's good he's on the better side of his bosses - and good at winning races. Otherwise, the work is routine enough here that we have been able to keep going days, even a week once, until he turned up again to 'run' things."

The Security Chief frowned. "That gives me pretty much most of this base to check."

I looked at his badge. "Kurt, is it? Well, Kurt, here's a tip. Check for missing daughters of other Royals and maybe look for who's selling that dream-date drug. I don't recall who told me about that, but he's had some of those dark-ringed eyes when he's come in before. Might be using."

Kurt nodded with me. A simple reflex to get going.

"Say, Malia. When was the last time you saw him yourself? Ever go out with him?"

"Not so much. A drink or two after work, but sleeping with your boss is a fast way to get reassigned to 'other duties'. He and I tossed one back at 'Fast Eddie's' last night, but I turned in after I left him there. You can check my computer logs - I was tidying up some reports for next week's quarterly, and it will show me in my quarters with a remote login."

"Well, thanks, though. That at least gives us some other possible leads. You will get him to contact us if – or when – he shows up again?"

"Sure, Kurt. And listen - stop by any time. The gals and I always like some of your handsome security types checking up on us." And I smiled my number 7 smile - not too forward, but definitely interested.

He gave a wry grin and a nod, then turned and left.

I made a mental note to check our internal cameras to see if any of the girls had been working late and saw Jack and I leave together. That login excuse is thin, but I have a program that runs a macro that will "auto-edit" any report. Unless they got my cloud access, they'd never find how I was in two places at once.

Just after I watched the last of Kurt's cute butt as he left down the hallway to our office, my smartphone buzzed.

The text: "X: pkg is dlvrd. Clean."

I answered: "M: Tku. Yr pi slice sent."

And hit the payment app disguised as a social media "like". Of course, it went through a dozen channels before a chunk of bitcoin wound up in X's account.

X had contacted me some time ago when one of these "inefficient" people around me had to "get out of my way" and the body was never found.

She asked me if I needed any "cleaner" business in the near future. How she worked out that that person's "accident" was connected to me is still my mystery to solve. Of course, there was no back-trail to her, and who "X" was in real life. Meaning, she had some leverage on me I didn't want or need, but also had a service that I could use.

Because dead bodies have more leads to follow back than simple disappeared ones.

And good cleaners are hard to find. All the more reason to keep them on a retainer with substantial performance bonuses.

IV

TESS CAME INTO OUR cave office with a stressed look on her face. Worry lines, dark lines under her eyes, more pale than usual. She was in a form-fitting, red and gray jumpsuit that the tessies had made for her. Long sleeved and cut for comfort, tucked into sturdy lace-up brown boots.

She phased in with several crates and boxes of gizmo's for us, all wrapped up in clear plastic on a palette. Like she had gone shopping at one of those legendary "big box" stores. These were only legends now, as they either left with the cities, or were ransacked later. Almost impossible to defend or maintain with all that glass in front and no walls between them and the street. Solid concrete warehouses were better business opportunities – if their clients could survive the trip there and back.

Sam stood up when he saw her and brought his chair over to the round oak table, then put his arm around her to guide her to it. When Tess sat, Peg came and sat beside her, offering her own head to pet. Between the two of them, they coaxed a smile out of her, if a tired one.

Tish came out with hot tea for her, in a thick ceramic mug. Touching Tess's shoulder, she returned to the doorway leading back to the stone cabin kitchen for a plate of hot food.

Tess relaxed some more as she picked it up in both hands to sip, sinking back against the sturdy bentwood "caboose" chair, and stretching out her long legs under the table.

She'd picked a delivery time when everyone else was out of our cave-office, so there was plenty of room for the pallet and also to spread the gizmo-boxes out to sort it before we shelved them by type and priority for later use, depending on when we'd need them.

"Tess, do you ever take some time for yourself?" Sam pulled up another bentwood chair near her.

"Usually. There's just something I've run up against that I've been focusing on a bit right now. But you're right. Maybe I should go visit that Ghost Hunter John again. He's always a good listener – particularly if you have some tale what would make a good story." Tess smiled as she looked into her tea, focusing on something off in the distance.

"You know that you're important to us, and if you need anything, all you have to do is ask."

She patted Sam's hand. "Of course, and if this didn't mean so much to me, then you wouldn't see me so much. But I also don't have anything more important right now."

"Correct me if I'm wrong, but if you can bend time and space, then can't you simply take any amount of time on any paradise planet in one of their luxury hotel planet that you want?"

Tess sat up at this. "Oh some of the places I've been like that... I could tell you about so many of them. Even the thought of them tends to make me want a long vacation. And if I did, I could be here in the next second and you'd never know. But it plays hell with the conversation, because I seldom remember what I was talking about just before I left, not after a couple of weeks anyway. And also doesn't explain the sudden tan."

She turned to Sam, leaning forward, but hesitating to talk.

Sam just waited, looking into her eyes, expectant but patient.

"My concern is about another wrinkle I found in our moon plans."

• • • •

"NOTHING HORRIBLE, I HOPE."

"No, it's all to do with me. That junk rock gives me and my tessies problems."

"How so?"

"Affects our time sense. Everywhere else I've ever gone, or showed up, time is arbitrarily exact. Time is an arbitrary, true – but it is a very exact arbitrary. There seem to be some very set laws about the universes I can visit and how they stay in lock-step with themselves and the other universes."

"And so all these fiction books tend to say the same thing about 'grandfather paradox.'"

"Right. Practically, that is only fiction, but until I experienced it for myself, I half-believed it to be true."

She sipped her tea and Sam waited. Meanwhile, Tish had brought another platter with some bowls of hot stew with homemade dark buckwheat bread for both of us, along with jam and fresh, real butter. Tish set a bowl in front of each of us, with another setting for her, then pulled up another chair to listen.

Of course, we both got into enjoying her fragrant stew, much as Tess did. And waited quietly for her to resume.

At last she looked up to Tish, "You know, even for a were-human, this is the best stew I've ever had, other than Hami's – and I do owe you both a trip to her saloon sometime. Hami throws a great party layout..."

Tish smiled at the compliment. "Maja is a good teacher, and all the rare spices in this were the ones you've brought for us. So this is a kind of feedback loop, as a way to repay you for all you've done for us – especially how well that stone stove and oven have worked out."

Tess smiled and sipped her tea again.

Sam brought the conversation back to point. "So, how did you disprove the grandfather paradox?"

"Oh, almost accidentally. Not that I killed any relative of mine, far from that. (Although that's a great story for John – what if Dorothy landed her house on her own grandmother who was an evil witch?) But I digress – the short answer: when I met myself."

Sam and Tish stopped everything in mid-action and just waited for the other shoe to drop.

• • • •

"IT WAS AT ONE OF THOSE famous resort hotels you talked about. I was walking through the lobby toward one of their heated pools and had to take a second look at someone. Same red hair, same gorgeous looks I see in any mirror." Tess takes a moment to smile and sip her tea.

Sam and Tish smiled at this joke and glanced fondly at each other as they resumed their quiet eating.

"Of course I stopped walking – both of me – and went to see my other half. And the conversation is harder to describe than it is to summarize. Because we were finishing even fractions of sentences for each other, and finally just stood there and did that wolf-thing that Sue and Tig do – like you two did. And a few seconds later, we just nodded and went on like nothing happened."

Sam and Tish put down their spoons and quit trying to do anything but follow the story.

"OK, sorry. Like I was trying to figure out what to say – the bottom line was that I suspected it didn't really matter if you met yourself coming or going or some other way. Beliefs are all that matter. The grandfather paradox was set up to give writers a way to build tension into their stories. But the best part was the real punch line..."

Then stopped to sip her tea again.

"And?" Sam asked with a bit of impatience in his voice.

Tess just smiled. "Again, sorry. I've probably been listening to John tell his stories too often. The punchline is that I got a list of great resort locations even better than the one we were in. So I was set for vacations from there on out. I could look forward to meeting myself again, since certain holidays were the best times, and on certain particular dates, the weather is just perfect. There is one particular theatrical performance that I am in the audience several times – all in different makeup, hairstyles, and evening dresses, of course..."

She started chuckling, while Tish and Sam both joined in. Regardless of whether they believed it possible, it was a good joke. And good to see Tess enjoying herself again.

Tish spoke next. "But you mentioned a wrinkle in our plans..."

Tess finished sipping her tea, and looked at each of them in turn.

"Large concentrations of that junk rock throws my time sense off. I can go to any place with complete accuracy, but I can't guarantee what time I'll be there. I could be there too late or too early, and not be able to help, either way."

V

KURT THE SECURITY CHIEF and I started dating not too long after that.

Of course, it would raise too many flags if he suddenly disappeared. But our very-public outings – all on the up and up – kept us off the radar for other situations. And he was such a Boy Scout, I couldn't even get us an overnighter at either his or my apartments. Nightcap, maybe, but just one – and then he was gone right after.

Nothing "X" would need to get involved with. Kurt was in no danger of getting "disappeared".

Still, I had other ways to keep myself satisfied, and other "buddies" that no one ever found out about.

I did get into helping him with his financial reports, which he was very appreciative for. Security personnel were quite a bit like cops – they'd rather be doing the work than doing the paperwork.

So having someone who could crunch numbers and show him were certain items could be afforded with some adroit re-calculations earned me more than one kiss and/or hug – as long as we were alone, and sometimes witnessed.

Yes, that gave me a view of what equipment they used, what budget they had, even where their investigations were going. And I'd give my "innocent" ideas about them. Males being males, they loved to be all in-charge about things and carefully explain to "little ole' me" how things really worked.

And having a Royal at his side also helped when there were official functions where he could rub shoulders with the bosses of his bosses.

Meaning that I was playing him while he tried to play me. Both ends against the middle.

It also meant that I was able to keep one step ahead of their investigation to that "serial female" who they suspected was involved in all these disappearances.

• • • •

EVENTUALLY, AS MY DEPARTMENT kept running better, and no one could find any clues about how my old boss disappeared, I was formally made the head of that department. And so had more face-time with my new boss. And started learning that larger scene of his – and helping him with it.

For him, we had ample private time together as part of my "training".

Always in his office, which was far more sound- and visual-proofed than mine. With its own private bathroom, bedroom. and camera-free elevator entrance – so that no one could find out who came or went. Especially not his wife, ex-wives, or former mistresses.

Still, my camera-pausing app still came in handy, regardless which of several routes I used to arrive for my "training". And using that app at random seemed to always point to some glitch in Security's system instead of the trail of that "female" they were looking for.

Kurt would bounce his ideas off me about that investigation from time to time. And I'd play "devil's advocate" to see if I could help him find holes in their logic or conclusions. Of course, I found a lot. Because that's my strong suit – sowing doubt.

Meanwhile, I was automating my own department so it could run with almost no one there. We were out-sourcing our investigations to other departments, and managed to reassign our own runners to those other departments, and divvying up their salaries among the number-crunching ladies I had left. This earned me substantial loyalty from them, as their credits when further. And my improved efficiency-ratings in internal reviews.

It also gave me time to spend between my boss and Kurt until I could make my next move. Disappearing my next boss wouldn't be as easy, but was still necessary.

Because I had my own plans. When I got to the right point, I'd text "X" for her input.

I'll start by knocking out some "support pillars" of my boss without having to raise a finger of my own...

VI

SUE, BERT, AND TESS finally figured out a plan to work around her "allergy" to the junk moon rocks.

With the amount of rocks that had been chipped off Sue's escape pod, there was enough to create a target practice area where Tess could work on improving her skills at transporting things in and out. All at the risk of her actually "running into herself" if her timing was off either time.

Tess got Gaia to move the rocks for her from the settlement into the valley. And then Gaia worked up a very similar type of rock in a near duplicate formation nearby. Looked the same – almost a stone "henge" of rocks around an area big enough to land a small cabin or a dozen palettes of gear.

This was also used to enable Tess to have a quick adjustment in case she did find herself arriving too close ahead or behind another one of her shipments. A back-up landing pad, as it were.

Not that we understood teleportation on the scale Tess was using. Few people besides Sue, Teacher, and Bert's pup-dog "Rolf" could actually phase in and out of locations. And no one could carry more than a couple of live persons with them, plus the gear they could carry or strap to their bodies.

And no one besides Tess wanted to try shifting anything or anyone to the Moon. Even Tess's open invitations for a trial run got her turned down by everyone.

Until she brought someone back that one day. Because she had no choice.

• • • •

FED UP WITH THAT NAGGING 'porting problem, Tess collected up and sent her tessies out to reconnecter the moon. She already knew that the tunnels underneath the cities were full of that junk rock. And the cities themselves probably used junk rock to build the Royal office buildings and homes. She started sending tessies out at regular intervals and then compared their return with their exit times. A huge lag, or coming back before they left, meant bad results.

Working in moon-diameters on a clear night, Tess devoted an entire evening to only this study. She found that the far side of the moon wasn't inhabited by the flown cities, only our facing side. Apparently to take advantage of the dead-drop approach to sending their refuse as meteor streams back to earth.

Tess's started her mapping by sending tessies out to the half-way points of the side edges and the far back of the moon. Then she split the differences finer and finer, depending on the results, all along an imaginary straight line between the top and bottom of the moon as she saw it from Earth that night.

Another line across that top-bottom vertical spread then gave her more data on where the tessies were routinely at wide variance or very usual. She noted the results in a fresh notebook just for this, using her own notation.

What resulted was a geographic map of time-space distortion by the junk-rock on the moon's surface.

This also resulted in finding tunnels, which led from the cities to few alternative landing sites or construction areas on that far side. Because Tess was able to find straight lines of mine pilings as they excavated their tunnels beneath the surface but pushed these above.

All that was estimated, though. She was going to have to do some in-person exploration to verify the best sites.

Breathable air was the problem.

One of her visits to John actually solved that one. He reminded her about that other young women that arrived close to the same time she had, one who lived in space as an assassin – Sylvie. So Tess went to her old enemy, now fast friend, to get her advice and expertise on this.

This resulted in a small device that would attach to a waist-belt and would both give her air and protection from radiation. Powered by deep space solar radiation, and amplified by that same junk rock in tiny amounts. Tess took both she and Sylvie beyond Earth's atmosphere to test and refine the system, although Sylvie had used a variation of this for decades. And Tess could also carry spares with her for emergency use or even rescue.

Bert was able to make several of them for Tess, with her tessies' help. Enough to get started, anyway.

Then she could visit the tunnel ends and explore the construction of them. The ideal would be a staging area where she could bring supplies and people to in order to start an organized infiltration – and perhaps evacuation – of the moon cities.

Her luck gave her what she was looking for on the first try. A domed structure with it's own refuse catapult, far out of sight of any of the original city moon bases. While she got energy readings that showed a small fusion power source below the surface, no lights gave away its presence.

'Porting near it on the moon's surface, she was able to generate a hovering presence with her tessies, where she could move around the outside of it. Soon she found an airlock that showed signs of recent use.

The obvious approach was to teleport just inside, beyond the inner door. Her tessies went before and brought back no evidence of human presence.

So she entered by phasing in.

• • • •

STANDING WHERE SHE ENTERED, it was completely dark. Her tessies quickly formed light for her to see by. And showed her that the interior was mostly empty, but had breathable air. Another dome was in the center, with rails going out to larger airlocks that occurred at intervals around the outside dome's periphery. In between were various buildings and larger storage structures for supplies. The differences were in windows for the offices and blank walls for storage buildings.

Following one of the rail systems, she simply phase-jumped short distances to inspect the various intersections of roadways that set off at intervals, streets and thoroughfares that cross connected the railways and the rest of the buildings inside the dome.

Tess found no lights anywhere. A ghost city. But there was still ample energy being used, according to her measurements. She was also continuing to monitor the tessies' reactions to her location and so find where the junk rock was used in these constructions. At least it was pretty rare here. Like any warehouse district didn't need to invest in fancy looks or luxury penthouses. Functional, spare, minimalist.

At the doorway to the inner dome, the energy level spiked. But still no huge use of junk rock. There was air inside, little radiation besides electrical pulses. Nothing harmful to an organic, living body.

But her tessies didn't give her any visual on what was inside those thick, dark walls. Simply phasing in could set her in the middle of any number of situations.

And she almost wished she'd brought Sylvie along – but didn't want to risk starting a war from Sylvie's trained-in attack responses. All Tess needed was to start something even as minor as a bar brawl.

So she spent some time sending and retrieving tessies to get all the information she could.

Until she at last just had to take the leap.

VII

SHE WAS SUMMONED TO her little control center. Something was up.

Video feeds filled one wall, with monitors angled for best viewing, starting at desk height and running to its low ceiling. The room was darkened to allow best viewing. Analysts were stationed every second monitor, busy entering reports on observed data and querying results.

The other two walls were devoted to audio feeds and their transcriptions. Fewer seated analysts poured over text data produced by pre-programmed searches of this data. A short console in the center of the room gave places for just three seats. One in the center was curiously empty – until she entered.

With a few even paces, she reached the console. Sitting in that chair, placing her own headset on, she hit a button on the keyboard and started reviewing the video and audio data curated for her.

After a few questions to the viewing and listening analysts on either side, she then removed her headset with a quiet motion, replacing it on the desk and showing no emotion.

Then rose and walked out, in as easy a pace as she entered.

The two persons at the console merely looked at each other, then returned to their own monitoring.

• • • •

I PHASED THROUGH THAT WALL. and faced a riot of color instead of the dull grays I met outside.

For I found myself in a colorful children's nursery, surrounded by small bodies of various ages, each working at a puzzle or engaging in a quiet game with others. If it weren't for the smiling faces, I'd think something was wrong. None were even surprised to see me. But all were happy, contented – and quiet.

I started putting together an idea of what these children were educated to do. This wasn't one of their usual bases or colonies. These children were here to be protected.

At that thought, a door hissed as it swung open in silence on the far wall.

A single woman walked in, taking a direct path toward me. The door eased shut behind her.

My varied-colored tessies swarmed around me in a defensive mode.

The woman walking toward me wore her hair long, full, and russet-red. Her face and arms pale, offsetting the knit armless top and black form-fitting leather pants, that slipped into high-heeled silver-buckled boots. Her only ornamentation was a thin silver-studded black leather belt around her waist.

And her eyes looked straight ahead, out of a mixed-race face with minimal makeup.

Looking neither right nor left, just coming closer with every step. Her pace was regular, but swerved around the various children's activities that moved in her path or close to it. All with the smooth motion of a dancer.

She moved as if no one could see or feel her presence except me.

There were no obvious weapons. My tessies thinned out and prepared to phase me out instantly, while avoid appearing as any threat to this woman.

At last, she stopped a couple of paces from me. Looked me straight in my eyes, reading my face. She put her hands out open and wide to each side of her. Meaning: no threat. I duplicated her posture.

"Tess? Call me X. I'm glad to see you. More than glad. There's someone – a girl – who needs your help. This way, please." She nodded her head, and I nodded back.

At that, X pivoted and made her way out of the children's nursery. I followed.

This was a no-nonsense young woman. I was in no danger, but knew this was about all the welcome I was going to get.

As she neared the door, it hissed open again and we went through.

Outside was a bare hallway, all in gray, the floor slightly darker than the light-gray walls and ceiling.

X moved to one side and allowed me to walk next to her.

"We knew you were coming because we've been listening in on your 'cave-office' where Sam and Bert are trying to make sense of all the audio we get around here. And to be honest, we're very happy and proud of your progress. It's sometimes been all we can do to keep from sending a signal out to you to help you with some of your difficulties."

"How did you..."

"Listen in on you? That same set of rocks you call 'junk'. We also use it to spy on the royals, only we don't have the lag locally that you have in getting those signals to Earth. Once you set up your own listening post, then it started transmitting your audio to us."

X stopped n the hall and pulled a slim, short device from her belt. "Here. Take this thumb-drive with you, tell Sam that it's got all our tech and schematics on it. He'll know what to do."

Then X started walking again and I moved again at her side.

"She's just up ahead."

We stopped just before another door at the end of the hallway, one with no knob or obvious lever to open it. Only a thin outline around it's edge – the same light gray as the walls.

"One question – Betty is still in your valley treating the Chief?"

My mouth dropped open, but I closed it and nodded.

"Good."

She tapped on the wall next to the door and a small box extruded from it. X opened it's top and pulled out a small piece of jewelry, with a braided cord so it could be worn as a pendant. At its center was a carved piece of the gold-streaked green quartz we called "junk rock".

Once she closed the lid, the box recessed itself back into the wall. Then X handed me the pendant.

"This has special circuits on its backside that make it transmit more clearly and identify the owner. Your 'tessies' will be able to get your communication to us with no lags. Our techs would love to talk to you about borrowing some of your tessies at some point to improve our own bugs, but we don't have time for that right now."

At that she gestured to one side of the door and it hissed open, away from where we stood. X entered and I followed.

$\bullet\ \bullet\ \bullet\ \bullet$

WE WALKED SINGLE FILE through several sets of hanging clear plastic that overlapped to cut air flow. At last we came to a hospital-type bed with several monitors. A small pale slip of a girl lay under a thin sheet and a warm blanket. A floral pattern showed on her pajama top where her arms came over the blanket. Her face was covered with a small transparent bubble that seemed to be filtering her air and supplying her with oxygen. Her eyes were shut, but her frown showed she was not in a comfortable sleep.

X walked up to the bedside and took the small girl's nearest hand in both of hers.

"We've done all we can for her. She has only hours to live, even though we've already extended her life by months."

Then X turned to me, her eyes moist, but her lips firm. "Can you take her to Earth and let Betty perform her miracles?"

"Of course. How can I let them know I'm coming?"

"Just talk to Sam or Bert like you are in the same room with them. This will trigger all their programs and play your message out-loud to them."

"Sam, Bert? This is Tess. I've got a sick girl to bring back. Just get Sue or Peg or someone to let Betty know I'm coming. I'll meet her outside Chief's den. See you in a few minutes."

X nodded to me, then carefully tucked the sheet and covers around the girl's pajamas. Then slipped her arms under her shoulders and legs, and turned with a careful motion to hand her gently into my arms.

X then touched a finger to own her lips and then touched that finger to one palm of the girl's, closing that hand into a fist around the palm and kiss. A single tear came down X's face, that was otherwise immobile.

I raised my look from the girl's sleeping face, which had quit frowning. Then I nodded to X, who returned my nod.

At that, my tessies and I phased out with that girl in my arms.

The Moon Cleaner

BY C. C. BROWER AND S. H. Marpel

• • • •

WHEN THE UNKNOWN "X" lost her job and any way to make a living, she only wanted her life back.

But she settled for revenge.

In a way she wouldn't expect – cleaning up the elitist government messes.

Because having dead bodies around did no one any good. And someone was on a purge in those self-named "Royal" houses that ran the moon colony cities.

Her particular mindset and training as a medical clinician allowed her to view death with a singular frame of mind. While all the people she'd helped in that medical clinic gave her loyal, fast friends among the "down-belows" who did the mining and kept everything running.

The opportunity to now work for an ambitious executive who had a nasty habit of eliminating her bosses was just too good to pass up – and maybe find out who had wrecked her life.

I

I'D ALWAYS CONSIDERED my luck to be temporary. Don't rely on it being there, always keep your options open when things go pear-shaped.

Like how I lucked into medic-training in the military. Because the other guy got shot up and was himself medivacked. And I was the only one who kept her cool – regardless. Blood, guts, brains, none of that phased me. Somehow, inside, I just turned it off – and dealt with the problem in front of me.

Triage made a lot more sense if you took your own emotion out of it. Guys I'd served with and wanted to have around because I trusted them – they'd get their place in the queue, even behind an "enemy combatant" who'd been gut shot. Give my friends a gauze pad and tell them to hold that on their wound like no tomorrow – or tie it on with something if they were going to black out – but I'd be back to them just as fast as I could. The guy they'd shot and dragged in still alive – him I would save just so he could be tried and executed. But just maybe the guy would turn over to rat out his own side. Just because we saved his ass so he could get back to what was left of his family and friends one day, maybe.

Sure, I lost a few buddies that way. But you learn to accept what you could as life's shakes and turn off the rest if you couldn't.

Sooner or later, you'd get those images back to re-live them as dreams or nightmares, or random reminder thoughts. And you'd process them as you could when you did.

I think that Zen student-priest (aka chaplain) that we had around helped me with that. Along with the way I'd been wired from birth.

Yeah, by the end of that tour, my little platoon was composed of a lot of mis-matched, weirdo guys and gals. Some were enlisted, some "volunteered" to serve with us because their village was gone. So it was either join us or wait to get shot up by somebody else.

We went through several 2nd lieutenants before we finally let our sergeant take over, mostly because he always wound up coming through for us, and the silver-bar guys wanted to stupidly just charge in over the top – and paid for it while the rest of us made our way out of that hell-hole by keeping our heads down.

I always repeated something I'd heard somewhere, "God takes the stupid ones first."

And when we got back to base, we'd always be loaded up again with greenies and stupids. But somehow we got that sergeant a field commission. He just pinned those bars onto the bottom of his collar and kept wearing his sergeant stripes. Because the gooks looked to shoot the officers first. And muddy stripes didn't flash in the sunshine. That officer's dress uniform hung in his locker at the base. Just for when he had to. But he was more often wearing a stained khaki or camouflage shirt over construction-grade dungarees. He said it was because they had bigger pockets that carried more cigars. And when he went into some village, he was more likely to be able to trade with someone for info if he wasn't "all gussied up like a parade of fools."

Anyway, it also probably helped that he was at least a quarter-gook himself. From his father's side. And that judge who gave him a choice to either get enlisted or wind up in prison, then found life was easier in the military than getting the same amount of bullets fired at you every week in a 'Cagga ghetto.

We were all from 'Cagga – well before the city-lift.

And I went back there on leave because I still had a sister there, living with a half-uncle and aunt who were decent people.

That's why while the rest of the platoon hit the bars and jump-joints when they got back to base, I spent my time in the corps hospital emergency wards helping out. Because I needed to bone up on the medicines and chemicals they were using, and whatever sewing-up and patching-up skills I could. Just to help my buddies survive another day, another week. So I could survive even longer. Those docs didn't mind, as they were always short-handed. And would teach me the fastest ways to fix things.

Plus, I always brought them some high-grade hootch and decent cigars when I did. Like I was going to spend that back-pay anyway on some skin-game or mind-numbing drug or drink. Better to spend on my medical buddies - whatever I didn't already send home to that half-uncle's family for taking care of my sis while I was gone.

The hospitals were always cleaner, even with the blood and stuff. I could always bed down in the back and know I wasn't going to share it with some bugs or disease, even if I did sometimes share it with someone who needed a "one-nighter", like I did now and then.

The point was, life was what you made it out to be. The world was that way. And I had to learn to cope with all sorts of things. Don't get too attached.

Because that was when the pain really started.

II

THINGS WERE JUST CALMING down in 'Cagga when I shipped in there for the last time. I wasn't sold on the idea of settling down there. All I had from those many military tours was my corpsman experience, a few scars, and a really stupid picture of me on a roof with cat ears and a tail. But I knew squat about business or farming, so I figured the clinics could use some help.

The outer-ring clinics got the least supplies and the most shot-up "bangers" who ran with the gangs for one reason or another. And I was the one who would be crazy enough to go out there with nothing more than a Kevlar-lined vest and canvas rucksack with gauze and tape and plastic leak-proof bottles of whatever liquids I needed.

Then I'd go save the shot-up numskulls however best I could, at least getting them to the point they wouldn't drain out on the way to clinic, carried or under their own power. Sometimes, they just wouldn't go. And so I'd find myself visiting them on a regular basis to check up on them.

After awhile, they just started calling me "Bullet" among a few other names, because I was so well known to everyone that they'd quit shooting. Just so I could get in there to help whoever it was, whatever side they were on. Because they all knew that I was their "angel" as much as the other guys – so if they protected me, I'd help them some day. Bullet was short for "bullet-proof". Partly because of the times I'd been shot in that vest or backpack, and partly because the rep I developed with those guys.

Of course, it helped that I always carried a few decent cigars and a pocket flask of top-grade when I came around.

But the boom dropped one day. When they shut down all the local clinics and moved everything downtown.

• • • •

THE TRICK WAS THAT they were trying to "centralize" and "upgrade services". Which really meant that they put all those doctors, nurses, and assistants like me out of a job. And the central "clinic" became the only way to get treated for anything. During their office hours mostly.

Street people came in by the street. And the toady executives came in through upper level bridges. Downstairs was mostly waiting to get seen – and that's its own form of triage. Upstairs, the triage was by how much you made, who you knew, and who you were related to. Very little waiting, a lot of waiting on.

Downstairs was for the shot-up, the gory accidents, the plague victims. Upstairs was for cold-sniffles, liposuction, inconvenient pregnancies.

None of that gave me a paying job. Because I could save lives, but had no papers to prove it. Just a pair of good hands, combat medic experience, and street smarts.

It also dried up my medical supplies. You can only do so much with torn-up cotton sheets and homemade vodka. Needles and thread were OK, but didn't leave as nice a finish.

I had a lot of people who felt they "owed me" for saving them or one of their family. And in addition to giving me the occasional meal, I'd also keep learning from them, asking about their grandparent's remedies for things.

But the break was when I got a job with the garbage collectors.

· · · ·

YOU WOULDN'T THINK plugging bullet holes and emptying refuse bins was very related.

But they are – you have to be "dispassionate" about your job. Organics and inorganics, that was the first triage.

The city had their own fusion drive to generate power instead of coal or the flaky windmills and solar panels. Forget coal. That had to come from somewhere in the Flyover Zone and so cost the stars to get. And the trees had already been mined out of the city and the surrounding suburbs years ago.

Fusion would burn anything it could, and melt the rest. (The same fusion power that ultimately took 'Cagga to the moon where it lay now.)

The end of our shifts always meant going through all the stuff people had thrown out and sorting it into those two lots. Two different conveyors took them each away to their respective burn/melt piles.

Anything that would turn into ash was one, the stuff with metals in another. Rocks just went into their own pile, a low-boy pull-off bin that would wind up being sorted through for construction material, or simply ground up for gravel.

We'd get the dead pets showing up in the organic pile. And the medical refuse – I was more used to that then most of them. The day I saw my first complete body show up changed something in me.

Because I thought I recognized it as someone I'd known, maybe even worked on to save its life. Now it was unrecognizable as to sex or even its real identity, probably the point.

And it just traveled on the conveyors like the rest of the organics.

Of course, I just shut down my reactions and got on with my job that day. Some others had to take a moment to empty their stomach or get a breath. So I picked up their slack and kept working.

But after that day, I also started looking for somewhere else to work. A little less surprising, a little less graphic.

And I found that my chemical background fit me for another job – night-cleaning the streets. That then led me to office building exteriors and interiors. I met a guy who took me under his wing. Because I helped fix his dislocated shoulder and put in a few stitches to stop the bleeding of a massive cut. (No, it was only a work-related accident.)

And he liked the top-grade I carried. For a kind of local disinfectant and oral anesthetic.

He couldn't use that arm for a few days, so he showed me his route and all about it.

Then one night we had to clean up after a crime scene.

The cops had given us the go-ahead, as they were on the clock as well. The city was tight by then, an ecosystem unto itself. So businesses that were down for a day made no income. Cops had to come in, figure out what happened, then release the scene for us to clean up after the construction guys had patched all the holes and replaced the wrecked furniture.

We'd deal with the blood and stains and so forth – making things like new again, overnight.

Accidents on the streets were simpler. The body gets shipped off for the relatives to identify, then everything got swept up and made usual. Sometimes overnight, sometimes the same night. Depending on who had the accident and how easy the accident was to explain.

When some of these higher execs had an "accident" it would tie up that place for a couple of days, and get the "press" all involved in it and so on. Messy in several ways.

It also affected our own bottom line. We got paid by the square footage we effectively cleaned. A couple of days of not cleaning, and then having to spend our own chemicals to get a mess cleaned up just put us into the red. And that meant no pay.

So one night, my boss showed me a real "moonlight job" he did every now and then.

That's when I found my real niche.

Cleaning up accidents like they never happened. No matter who it happened to.

III

THE CLEANER HAS A GOOD-paying job. As long as they can clean up like it never happened. That's a trick, sometimes.

Everyone likes a good cleaner. But when you're the best – they never even know you were there. And you get the best pay. All under the table, or through some quiet channels.

Cops even liked cleaners. Because then they are only investigating a "missing person" report, rather than having to canvass for witnesses and carve bullets out of walls or furniture, run ballistics tests, and so on. Usually the same result. The case goes cold with no explanation.

Since they were understaffed and becoming mostly toady executives and their politician's bodyguards, they didn't have much time to investigate and fill out all that paperwork on accidents, compared to simple and nearly blank sheets for missing people cases.

So having a body disappear before it's even reported helps everyone.

All that background led me to my best job ever.

Until I got the last thing I thought I'd ever have – a conscience.

• • • •

MY BOSS FINALLY TURNED over all the late-night cleaning to me. He stuck to the evening shift and left me to do the graveyard shift.

I knew where the shortest route to the fusion drive incinerator access was. Just had to make sure all the metals were off that body and also got melted down.

And all those people I'd helped would tell me about job "opportunities" that were about to happen.

Setting out feelers found the people who wanted their upcoming accidents cleaned. And if the jobs were too high-profile, I'd turn them down. If they were smart, they'd re-organize the accident so it could happen someplace easier to clean. When they came to me more than once for the same "accident", the price went up.

Of course, I got referrals. And leads.

That's when I found a "Royal" who needed some help. (what those toady execs started calling themselves – one meme that got going after the city lifted and took everyone else with it.)

It was one of those leads. With her direct line.

I'll do someone's cleaning as a freebie just to get some future business. Once.

This Royal gal had left about three accidents around. And when I got a tip about who did the third one, I cleaned it for free – and contacted her with an untraceable text message.

She liked having unexplainable disappearances rather than unexplainable accidents. Cops and investigators were like mis-loaded shotguns. Sometimes they hit their target, sometimes just winged it, sometimes went off in your face. You never knew the result.

So I did a few jobs for her. More than a few.

Until she started to leave them still alive for me.

· · · ·

THIS ROYAL GAL LIKED airlocks.

The theme was always the same – get that date-drug into their systems and a few extra pills left on them, and then the guy she'd dump there would asphyxiate. Simple to clean, simple to leave.

But airlocks didn't always do the trick. Bodies are meant to survive. Opening up that lock, even with most of the air gone could still mean the body had enough to live on, even escape serious brain or other damage. Depending on how soon I was there after she did her dirty work.

I got there early one night, and had to hide before she saw me.

After she left, I opened up the air lock she'd put her target in. Not only was he still alive, but he was definitely someone I knew. He'd been caught in a cross-fire years ago, and I got him to the point he could walk out after the bangers were out of ammo and out of the area. We talked a bit while we were waiting. And he told me about his job in engineering. I reassured him his arm would be fine as long as he kept it clean, but get to the clinic to have it looked at.

I even gave him the bullet I dug out.

That was then.

This day, that bullet was around his neck on a chain.

A little CPR brought him around. Enough to walk with a groggy style of stumbling, through the camera-less depths of that building. Until we could get him to somewhere he could rest a few days.

Sure he knew who did it, and probably why. But he was still as good as dead, now. She'd make sure the second time was permanent if he ever surfaced.

This guy was brilliant, though. Knew the old city and all the mining excavations. And he was funny. Someone I could talk to. So I brought him food for several days. Some paper pads and pens, plus a little computer tablet. He was able to work out how to connect to the wireless around there with an anonymous skip-based re-router so his work couldn't be traced.

It was then he found the tunnel that went almost halfway around to the other side of the moon. Long abandoned, but kept as an emergency exit just in case.

That tunnel led to a fusion powered mini-city out in the middle of nowhere. One that was banked with enough self-fed fuel to keep itself going and powered for ages. Maybe a hundred years, unless you wanted to lift off and fly it somewhere.

Nice back-up plan.

And so we started our little "home-away-from-home for the disappeared."

IV

I CALLED HIM JOCK. Because it fit. Shoulders like an athlete, trim hips, and muscles everywhere it counted.

But I could have called him Brains as well, because the guy knew an answer or could figure it out for about anything.

What he used to do (before he bedded one-too-many Royal babes) was to work on their racing "boats" that the Royals would sail on a little course they had among the local asteroids. There was also a sprint that went around the moon with a few tight turns in it. And then a real marathon haul that went almost to Mars orbit and back.

This station on the far side was also an emergency berth for their racing sloops so they could get them repaired enough to get back to their city-colony. The long underground tunnel to it had a couple of tramway lines in it to get parts and even some good-sized spars or ribs to rebuild damaged structure – just enough for it to limp back to their city's shipyards.

It was almost always shut down, almost invisible to anyone who'd sail around the back side. This base used to have a beacon, but one day it just "quit working" and maintenance never "got around to" coming all the way out to fix it. And so it was just a secret that some of the older racers knew, and their engineers.

To everyone else, it soon became a "legend", then a "rumor", and then forgotten.

Jock never forgot anything.

The extra income I got from cleaning bought him the supplies he needed to get it up and running.

One night, his sad eyes convinced me. So I disappeared his family to this base for him. There just happened to be a "freak accident" where only his family was involved. In an area where the city politicians had already condemned as "blighted" so they could expand some Royal's townhouse. When part of it just "happened" to collapse, the family was never seen again.

And a few people who worked on the subsequent demolition also managed to have "accidents" and show up with us. Especially if they were friends of his, or had somehow heard about our little "underground railroad."

Jock got people trained on running the aqua-ponics and everything they needed to keep them alive until the point they could figure out how to escape.

Meanwhile, the emphasis was just keeping them all hidden.

But little, by little, the disappearances kept adding to our base population. Young, old, middle-age. Didn't matter.

There was also a convenient "cave in" of that tunnel between old 'Cagga and the distant dome. Meaning that no one was going to come to check anything there anytime soon.

One Royal yacht did land one day.

But it took very little persuasion to get them to stay on. Like maybe word had gotten out, we thought at first. A security risk. So we sent their yacht back out, crippled and on a ghost-run that conveniently made it intercept a garbage launch from the catapult.

Not enough left of it to hardly identify or take time to collect back up for forensic analysis. A nice cleaner job.

I got my half-uncle and his family there, too – along with my kid sister.

Things were going pretty smooth.

We were now tapped into all the feeds, and made a few new ones of our own. So we knew what was going on, sometimes before anyone else did.

But then the really unfortunate happened.

My sister got sick from something that the central clinic had no cure for. No matter who caught it. Something in the moon dust that meant eventual death, regardless.

It was called "pioneer's disease." After the phrase, "the pioneer's got the arrows, the settlers got the land." Most of the original high execs caught it within a few years of landing. All they left behind them was the Corporation and their dreams. The younger children rarely caught it, particularly if they had grown up mostly on the moon. As very few babies were successfully born since the cities made moon-fall, there was no way to do any real study of what caused it.

But now my kid sister had it, and no one else. The one person who I cared anything about was soon to disappear and I didn't have any idea about how to stop it.

V

A COUPLE OF THINGS happened to help my sister.

First, I made some careful inquiries about doctors and nurses who wanted to "disappear". Those few and their families swelled our ranks some more. And improved the health care for everyone.

Of course, it made my "cleaning" bills higher. (Imagine, getting paid to save lives – just like the job I used to have.)

The second thing was finding that someone on Earth had started listening to us with their own "junk rock" receivers.

But we found them because they hadn't realized that they were also sending as well. And we heard all their conversations (along with all the ones the Royals were sending, in our own little spy network.)

So we heard about other technology they had, namely someone called "Betty" who was having some unheard-of medical results down there.

The trick was in contacting them without alerting the Royals.

That was one we couldn't figure out. Those moon "junk rocks" just weren't that powerful on their own. We know they boosted the signal somehow, but we couldn't do it on our end without generating so much power that we'd give the whole "disappeared colony" away. Like putting a huge spotlight on it.

Meanwhile, my sister was getting worse and worse. We'd brought her back several times, and bought her months more than most had. But now she was slipping away. And I had to start preparing for the losing the only one I'd ever really cared about more than myself.

Then a couple of things happened, what I would cautiously call "miracles".

But more like, the result of my careful research. I'd scoured everything in any medical book I could find, and beyond those to the "quack" and "crank" cures their "Science" discarded. All those old home cures I'd been told about, the stuff that somehow just worked and no one knew why. That led me back to the old New Thoughters. And to prayer.

So I started spending time daily with my sister, just holding her hand and visualizing what I really, really wanted.

I didn't want believe all their stuff about mind-talking and shape-shifting wolves, but I had to start believing because they were doing what was physically impossible down there. And if these miracle workers could save my sister, I'd move heaven and earth for them.

In an interesting twist, heaven and earth came to me first.

That was when that strange bird Tess showed up. What she did was impossible. But fulfilled everything we needed – both for my sister and our "disappeared colony".

VI

I GOT AN ALERT VIA our little pendant we all wear. Made out of "junk rock" with a little circuit behind it, we could talk and hear each other almost anywhere.

They needed me in Control. Because they'd picked up someone who had just suddenly appeared outside our dome.

No equipment, no racing yacht, nothing besides a space suit.

And she entered our outside dome without even opening a hatch.

Of course, there were automatic weapons out there, but their firing could be picked up from the City colonies, so that was only a last resort. Besides, how did we know that they would even have any effect at all?

Once I got the visual, I knew I had to take the chance.

With her route, she was going to show up in the nursery.

I told my people to keep me posted if she changed directions, then headed down.

• • • •

TALL, RED-HEADED, AND a no-nonsense red/gray jumpsuit. I liked her the first time I got real eyes on her.

She was unafraid. And had all these little cube-shaped lights floating and buzzing around her. Called "tessies" from what we gathered. Apparently how she traveled through time and space.

This was someone I'd love to have the time to sit down and talk with.

All that was going to have to wait.

"Tess? Call me X. I'm glad to see you. More than glad. There's someone – a girl – who needs your help. This way, please." I nodded. She nodded.

Then I turned and led her out of the nursery, avoiding all these darling kids who were well enough mannered to just accept this new person for what she was. Like I did. Once I explained to their parents and caregivers who and what this Tess was, then they'd be able to translate it into stories the kids would understand.

For now, we were also fortunately very close to my sister's private hospital, her isolation ward.

Down the straight, blank, gray hallway we went. Side by side and quiet for the most part.

I did give her something I hoped would help her. "Here. Take this thumb-drive with you, tell Sam that it's got all our tech and schematics on it. He'll know what to do."

She took the thumb-drive and put it in a little watch pocket of her overalls.

Then we kept walking down the long hallway.

I stopped right in front of the door that led to the isolation ward.

On the way I explained some of how we knew about her. "We knew you were coming because we've been listening in on your 'cave-office' where Sam and Bert are trying to make sense of all the audio we get around here. And to be honest, we're very happy and proud of your progress. It's sometimes been all we can do to keep from sending a signal out to you to help you with some of your difficulties."

"How did you..."

"Listen in on you? That same set of rocks you call 'junk'. We also use it to spy on the Royals, only we don't have the lag locally that you have in getting those signals to Earth. Once you set up your own listening post, then it started transmitting your audio to us."

Punching a little port in the wall gave me a slide-out delivery box, where I got her a "junk rock" transceiver of her own.

"One question – Betty is still in your valley treating the Chief?"

Tess's mouth dropped open, but she closed it and nodded.

"Good."

I handed her the pendant.

"This has special circuits on its backside that make it transmit more clearly and identify the owner. Your 'tessies' will be able to get your communication to us with no lags. Our techs would love to talk to you about borrowing some of your tessies at some point to improve our own bugs, but we don't have time for that right now."

I waved to one side of the door and it hissed open, away from where we stood. And we were inside the darkened hallway on the other side.

• • • •

MY SISTER WAS STILL unconscious, getting her purified oxygen from a clear bubble around her head. Her pale face wore a slight frown, like the pain meds didn't take care of everything.

Her floral pajama top covered her chest and over her arms, where they lay on top of the thin sheet and blanket. I took her nearest hand in mine.

"We've done all we can for her. She has only hours to live, even though we've already extended her life by months."

Then I turned to her, my eyes misting up besides all I could do to keep my emotions in check. "Can you take her to Earth and let Betty perform her miracles?"

"Of course. How can I let them know I'm coming?"

"Just talk to Sam or Bert like you are in the same room with them. This will trigger all their programs and play your message out-loud to them."

"Sam, Bert? This is Tess. I've got a sick girl to bring back. Just get Sue or Peg or someone to let Betty know I'm coming. I'll meet her outside Chief's den. See you in a few minutes."

I nodded my thanks, then carefully tucked the sheet and covers around my sister's pajamas. Then slipped my arms under her shoulders and legs, and turned with a careful motion to hand her gently into Tess's arms.

If this was the last thing I saw of her, I wanted to leave her as I had every time I went back on another tour of duty. I touched a finger to my lips and then touched that finger to my sister's palm – closing that hand into a fist around that kiss. A single tear came down my face, while I steeled myself.

Tess noticed, as I did, that my sis was no longer frowning. Tess nodded to me, and I returned her nod.

At that, Tess phased out of my sight with my only sister in her arms.

Then I collapsed on my knees, leaned against that hospital bed and sobbed my eyes out.

I didn't care who heard.

Because I'd had enough of this horrible moon life. The only thing I really valued had just left in the arms of a stranger I had to trust after knowing her for only minutes.

Now I had nothing to lose any more. It was time to take the fight to them. The Royals and their enablers who had turned this place into a living science experiment on captive humans.

Once we got everyone else out of here that we could.

Because the people who were going to do the fighting couldn't be worried about collateral damage.

Baby steps first. Complete planning next. Then stone-cold execution.

VII

A FEW DAYS LATER, I got a call from Tess. It was a recording, and I took it in private. She apologized for taking so long, but had to get some treatment herself.

My sister was fine and was even up and walking around. She was enjoying herself and eating solid food. Of course, she asked about me and sent her love.

It was a good thing I was alone, because I turned into a blubbering mess about then. For a few minutes, anyway.

Tess had delivered the jump-drive and both Sam and Bert were working on the upgrades. She had also come up with an idea of how to ship small things back and forth to us and would be up in a few days with a test device, if everything went well.

She ended by thanking me for all I had done, and said she was going to enjoy working together with us.

I replayed it over and over until I quit reacting physically to all that good news. And could start planning around it.

Just to blow off the residual tension I was feeling, I started a walking tour of the complex. That always helped.

About halfway around the dome, I was interrupted by a message.

Tess was back.

• • • •

HER APPEARANCE HAD surprised my Control staff on duty. Because she phased in with her usual lack of any noise, right in the middle of them. Behind their backs, with her tessie lights orbiting her, and holding something that looked like a bird cage.

Good thing they had seen her just a couple weeks before on the video, and were briefed about her "tessies". And it was good they didn't have any weapons on them more than maybe a knife.

Tess was pretty direct. Clearing her throat to get their attention (because she never makes a sound when she appears, and everyone was concentrating on their work.) "Sorry guys, hate to interrupt, but has anyone seen 'X' lately?"

The younger ones jumped, the older ones turned, smiled, and almost chuckled.

"No Miss Tess, but we'll call her for you." One replied. "There are chairs in the back if you'd like a seat while you're waiting."

Tess smiled. "Thanks. That will be great. Nice place you have here." Then she turned to walk over and find a seat, while placing that bird-cage device in another.

I wasn't long getting there. Only had to slow from a dead sprint for the last little bit and get my breathing under control. As well as that grin that spread all across my face.

• • • •

WHEN THE DOOR OPENED, I stepped in at my normal pace, normal look. Nodded to Tess, and then gestured her to come with me.

She picked up that strange bird-cage contraption and followed me out of Control.

I stopped and let the door shut, and then hugged Tess as tight as I could without breaking something on one of us.

She just put her free arm around me and let me hug as long as I wanted.

I finally backed up. "Sorry. I just wanted to thank you so much. That sister of mine means, well, you now know just how much."

Tess just smiled wide. "Of course. You're welcome. I know all about family after losing my own while I was growing up – but when I found them again I could hardly quit hugging them one after the other."

I looked down at her hand carrying the cage. "OK, so what is that thing?"

Tess held it up. A bit of a brainstorm. Because I'm the only one who can use these tessies to move around – that we know of. So this little thing should do it for us."

"How does it work?"

"Well, I talk to the tessies and ask them for help. This cage has some Earth tessies in it – see that little jar on top? And there is a cage just like it down at our cave-office that has Moon tessies in it. You put something in here and it winds up down there, and vice-versa.

"Maybe later we can make a larger device, but for now we can test it with little things. Got anything we could send that way?"

I nodded, and led her to my nearest office, picked up a small piece of plastic off the desk. "Here's another flash-drive with more data for your guys."

Tess put it in, closed the hatch, and it phased out without a sound.

Seconds later, a smartphone showed up.

Tess took that out and handed it to me. "I'm surprised it still works, but it does – they haven't manufactured any since the cities lifted."

I turned it on and it had a lock-screen of my sister smiling back at me. Soon I was watching a "home video" of her recording herself walking around the valley and talking to wolves and animals out-loud. They'd all smile in response, and she would "translate" what they had sent to her mind.

I had to sit down as I watched, since my knees got a little bit weak.

And wiped more than one tear off my face.

A few deep breaths after I turned it off and I could talk again.

"Between you and me, I wish she didn't make me react like that."

Tess came over and put a hand on my shoulder, and said nothing.

I stood after a bit. "OK, what do you think we should do next?"

Tess stood back. "Well, we've got to compare notes. See what resources we have. Probably set up a conference – if we can do that safely. Then work out what we want to do, with what we need to do, and compare that to what we actually can do."

"That's right down my alley. First question – how did you boost that signal? Second question – do you have cameras on your end? And then, How many people can you transport at one time?"

Tess just grinned. "I'd knew we'd be kindred souls. Oh, almost forgot. We found this recently, and thought you'd like it."

She pulled a hip flask out of her pocket and handed it to me.

I opened it, sniffed, and sipped. "Ooh. Very fine. That's how old?"

"Well, the barrel was sealed about 60 years before the city lifted, so you're probably tasting 70-plus-year-old Kentucky Bourbon."

It was my turn to grin. "Salute!"

Then we sat down to plan in earnest. And compare notes on other things. While her "bird cage" kept shifting things up for us. Eventually, we got a working video signal, that my guys says was coming through without detection.

I called in Jock and one of my senior techs.

Their Tish sent up a plate of fresh-baked cookies, as well as a small pile of thick steak sandwiches on pan-fried buckwheat bread – and some ice-cold whole milk followed.

That planning session took awhile.

VIII

MOST OF THE PEOPLE in our "disappeared colony" needed treatment, even if they didn't feel they were sick or acted that way. So Tess was busy for quite a little bit taking groups of them to various "Lazurai" treatment centers. We also rotated our Control personnel through there, as the treatment was a onc-and-done scene.

I went down for my own and had a very refreshing time with real home-cooked food, and time for long conversations between my treatments. I talked with my sister, sure, but also with Sue, her Tig, Sam, his Peg (who shifted to "hooman" form, just for my visit, much to Sam's surprise and pleasure) and all the rest.

My time down there was short, too short. But my sis was doing well, and had pretty much been adopted by everyone down there, so she gave up answering to anything but "Sis".

I had to get back, because we needed to get Sue's sister and her family worked out.

The bottom line was that the Moon colonies were doomed because of some ultra-rare mineral that humans were allergic to in all moon dust. It just didn't occur natively on Earth. And even if they left to fly off to their next stop on one of Saturn's moons, they'd all eventually contact "pioneer disease" unless they got the treatment we had.

Tess had talked with some of her friends, and compared notes with Betty and her other Lazurai associates – they concurred that Earth humans aren't genetically ready for space travel, but could be. The punchline was that these Royals had gone all that way out there just to leave the cure behind them.

And was actually why they had tried to get Sue first, and then her sister Shelby – because their mother had received the treatment just before 'Cagga had lifted. Betty herself had treated them. But there was no way for Shelby to help them genetically, since everyone around her would sooner or later succumb – excepting any baby Shelby might have.

So it was necessary to act quick to save what was left of the humans up here. Before the biggest remaining population of that species went extinct.

IX

SUE'S FAMILY CAME NEXT.

Tess still couldn't reliably phase inside those tunnels where the junk rock was most concentrated. So we got people to get those pendants to them. With those, and a little training, they could send thoughts directly to our people and then get a route away from cameras where Tess could come and fetch them in secret.

Sue's Dad was the last, but he agreed and insisted that was the way it needed to be. Because he was too connected to too many projects that the Royals had their fingers in. There was no way to disappear him without investigation except for a staged cave-in in the mines – where Tess couldn't reach him.

Of course, Sue was completely happy. Tess took her to the Lazurai nursing colleges where they were all being treated, along with Sam's teleporting pup-dog "Rolf", so that she could now visit them as she wanted during their treatments.

Tess was very busy. We did get a bigger "bird-cage" built almost up to a short human size, but it was just erratic enough not to trust a hooman life to over that Moon-Earth distance. We did test it with some brave souls in between the "disappeared" colony tunnel and a camera "dead zone" storage room. So we had an emergency escape route.

Tess was getting better at taking larger and larger groups away. If she had a problem, it was leaving one or two of them behind, never from arriving without them.

Our next plans got more energetic – and dangerous.

There was no real way to ask people, "Say, do you really dislike your conditions under the Royals to risk flying through space with someone you don't know and materializing 250,000 miles away on a planet you've been taught to hate all your life?"

And that also meant the Royal's security would be onto us soon.

• • • •

"I DON'T KNOW ABOUT this, Tess. You're our only way of helping these people."

"Like I'm not concerned about you and what you're going to do next?"

"We've been over this. There is no way for us to wake people up unless we tell them what's happening."

"And so, I'm your back-up plan."

"I've got that cage."

"Yes, and you could get trapped away from it. So I've got your back."

"But promise that if you have to, you'll leave me and save yourself. I'm nothing compared to you."

"I'll take that as a compliment, X. You know from all we've gone over that I'd rather have a live martyr on my hands than a dead one. Betty and the others can only do so much. A corpse is beyond what they can or want to do."

"Noted. OK, I'll let you be back-up – just this once."

Tess only gave her a wry smile, which meant neither yes nor no.

· · · ·

THE VIDEO WAS STARTING like usual for Founder's Day celebrations. These were in honor of the original five tech companies who had merged to form the Corporation. Pioneer disease had eventually taken them all, leaving their children to run the Corp and fulfill their dreams.

It had its usual dramatic scene of the cities lifting off from a dirty, polluted Earth, then arriving on the moon and building a new life here, while they watched their regular flights of minerals back to Earth and a 3D model of the Earth becoming whole and pure over time.

Then the moon colonies lifted again to fly off toward Saturn...

Only this time it was interrupted.

Some discordant music, and shots of the dirty mines, tired people emerging from them – hollow-faced and bent.

Then shots of long lines of people coughing and even collapsing in long lines for medical treatment.

Soup kitchens running out of food before everyone was served, with resulting riots and police forces moving in with shields and batons swinging.

A scene of Royals reclining in overstuffed loungers to watch their space yachts competing, and casually making wagers higher than several year's pay of any 'down-below' miner – just on who would come in first.

While down below in the city streets, people looked up at the Royal penthouses and heard those same races blared across the public big screens – and watched thrown rocks bounce off those screens, as well as thrown garbage hitting with a squish – then sliding down to drip off its lower edge..

Finally, the music evened out to a folk tune played on real instruments instead of synths, the scene shifting to reveal a beautiful green valley in mid-summer, where human children were playing with wolf cubs, all smiling and laughing in their games of tag.

The camera panned over to two young women who turned from watching their games to look directly into the camera, as it zoomed in on their smiling faces.

"Hello, moon colonists. I'm Sue Reginald."

"And I'm Shelby Reginald."

"We're here to tell you that you no longer have to wait for Earth to become a paradise. It already is. That's because we are here right now."

"The problems you have is because your self-called 'Royals' don't care about you or what you want or need."

"That's why we both escaped back to Earth."

"Believe this or not."

"If you want the life that the Royal elitists robbed from you, just ask around. Someone you know can probably put you in touch with someone who knows how to escape like we did."

Tig walked in on camera, long dark hair waving in the slight wind and without any shirt covering his broad shoulders, as usual, while Sam walked in (fully clothed) behind Shelby.

"There are more people we've saved here. You have a choice."

"Just don't let the 'Royals' decide for you any more."

The music swelled, and then was cut off suddenly, the screen blank.

A strident voice came on. "This was an unauthorized propaganda film and is being investigated. This is to inform all citizens that martial law is now in effect. Everyone is to return to their quarters and remain there until the all-clear is sounded. This is your only warning."

The sounds of heavy equipment rolling into the streets and marching boots sounded. But the volume of those sounds didn't require the amplification of public video screens.

• • • •

A DARKENED CONTROL center. Most of the light coming from the wall of monitors, showing the tired and strained faces of their watchers.

"I think we've got it now, sir. These patterns are the same. She's got to be there now. Right now."

"OK. Get that camera over-ridden. Show us what's really there."

A beautiful mixed-race woman with long russet hair stood smiling right into the camera. She was wearing a black v-neck top, and black costume cat ears, a long tail hanging over her shoulder. "Hi guys. Glad you could finally find me."

Orders rang out to alert the squads to that location.

"Oh, don't bother, they won't get here in time." X petted that tail as if it were a real one.

"I just wanted to let you know about a Royal who always called herself 'M' in her texts. Used to work in Mining Statistics, and then got the boss's job when her boss 'disappeared'. The trick is, here's a picture of him on Earth, healthy and well." She held up a big photo of someone well-tanned and holding someone's toddler in his arms.

"Now I think that she's gunning for his boss's job – because she's been holstering his gun for quite a while, if you know what I mean."

X looked off-camera. "Oh, it looks like my time is up. But listen, Kurt – is it? You could have a security job on Earth if you want. Or just wait until 'pioneer disease' claims you all. Because it's coming. Check the statistics. We've got the cure on Earth. See you down there, I hope."

She waved and then reached up to pull the cable off the back of the camera.

When the guards got there, they only found an over-sized bird cage in a storage room behind her that was locked from the outside.

Then a bomb phased in and it blew up on them.

X

THE PARTY AT HAMI'S saloon was in full-swing. Just a lot of people telling stories as they sat around her many round tables with bentwood "caboose" chairs on her tongue-and-groove pine floor.

Deep dishes of food lined the top of the long, polished, wood bar that ran the length of that long room. Little Christmas lights festooned the plate-glass windows in front. Hami and Chaz were busy replenishing the food as it disappeared, their namesake saloon-converted-restaurant filled with happy people.

Sue and her family, Sam and his, Tig, Tish, Bert, Peg, and everyone (except Basheela, who would hear the stories when she was out of her hibernation) were talking and laughing. Tess was the guest of honor, along with "X" whose real name turned out to be short for Xandra, which was in turn short for Alexandra.

• • • •

MOST OF THE RECENT Earth returnees later gathered at the far back end where a big screen was playing old Earth movies, most of which these Moon colonists had never heard of.

At the front, the two guests of honor, along with Betty, Sue, Bert, Tish and Sam were all comparing notes and working out their next move.

Sue had a worry line on her forehead. "Of course we aren't done until they are all back, safe and sound."

Betty chimed in, "And cured."

Several agreed at that.

X frowned. "The Royals are a die-hard group, though. They were working on some AI bots that could take over the mining. When they get those perfected, they won't need miners any more."

Sam nodded. "And they aren't going to believe that their medicine won't keep them alive forever. It's a cult up there."

Sue relaxed her face. "But Tig and I have been practicing with those pendants you brought, plus Betty helped us overcome the danger they posed with that junk rock. The next phase is to change their hearts and minds. Tess has already gotten her friend Mysti agree to help us."

Tess raised her glass. "To Friends – who never leave friends behind."

The entire table toasted that idea.

· · · ·

TEXT ON A SMARTPHONE:

"M: You have the coordinates, then?"

"Y: Yes. Shipments to begin soon. Countdown in 10..."

Malia sat, feet up, at her former boss's over-sized desk and mentally counted down to 0.

Out the window to her side, behind the desk, a new load of refuse shot out of the catapult toward Earth.

"This will send them a message." She said to no one present.

· · · ·

ON EARTH, IN THE SKY above the wolves' valley not too many days later, a string of meteors appeared.

Heading straight for a landing. Moving right toward that rock cabin with its slate roof that was attached to an old cave in that valley's side...

Moon Shadow

BY C. C. BROWER AND S. H. Marpel

. . . .

WHEN SOMEONE SENDS boulder-sized rocks down to planet Earth from the moon, they approach like meteors.

On the right trajectory, they don't burn up in the atmosphere, but can come down with the force of a nuclear blast.

Our tiny outpost of sentient shape-shifting wolves and escapees from the slave-labor moon colonies had caused a stir up there. They probably still didn't figure out how we managed to help all those people disappear, cross 250,000 miles of space, and wind up on Earth - healthy and smiling in the videos we sent back.

But they did figure out where our headquarters was - and targeted it with a string of flaming rock-meteors, all falling in a straight line toward our little valley.

If we evacuate in time, we can still avoid that impact.

But all it really means is: Earth and the Moon are at war - and they have the better weapons. Or so they think...

I

THEY WEREN'T TOO HARD to see – or even hear. A string of meteors heading right for us. The flaming debris left a long trail heading our way, and the sonic booms were enough to wake the dead.

Our only problem was how to escape the destruction. When something that lands with the force of a nuclear bomb – is it even worth running?

The question for most of us wasn't whether, but how fast and which direction?

A few people in our valley didn't run, didn't stand and wait for the world to end. Instead, they got to work.

Betty took one look at the sky, and then sunk into the earth as an elemental.

Tess pulled her multi-colored "tessies" to her and vanished.

The Chief, now healed of his illness and a striking form of a large white-gray male wolf, simply stood at the mouth of his den and howled. The effect seemed to stop time in the valley – except for everyone running. Wolves were gathering their cubs and taking the closest path out of the valley. Any hoomans that could were shifting into wolf form, as that was much faster than any two-legged creature.

Sue and Teacher shifted into their eagle forms in order to guide the two streams of valley residents out of the way.

Above them, the meteors seemed to stand still in the sky, along with the wind. Chief himself was also stock still, a force of nature. A willing sacrifice to the pack if need be.

And everyone else ran as fast as they could – because their life depended on it.

• • • •

MALIA, DRESSED IN HER favorite goth outfit, had come to their moon city's observatory to train its most powerful telescope down on that valley.

On her black lips, below her dark-shadowed eyes, was a thin smile. Of hoped-for revenge to those who had crossed her plans with their own.

She had managed to have her last boss "disappear" but at the hands of someone else who he'd ticked off a few too many times. Not too hard, really.

And she was his logical replacement.

So she got his big desk, the private elevator with real wood paneling, the personal bathroom, and the bedroom – where he used to do his "personal training".

His days were gone. And Malia had plenty of days ahead of her, by her reckoning.

On top of learning her new job, her new and higher boss, she also had to learn about how someone 250,000 miles away – on Earth – had interfered with her operation. Or a few someones.

That's why she was up here – to find out how her "present' arrived.

So she lined up the most powerful telescope down at a small valley that was just now coming into view. From her much smaller observatory on the moon.

• • • •

SO FAR, THE METEORS were holding still. The Chief just glared at them, but inwardly was calmer than he had ever known. All that healing that Betty had done for his condition had left him with some interesting new talents. Or talents he hadn't recognized before now.

A few more minutes and the last of his pack would be safely through the two paths out of the valley. He had no problem holding these fireballs for now. Time didn't have any particular problem for him. Not now.

He didn't have long to wait. Just as the last female wolves chased their cubs through their respective passes, a rumbling started from under the valley floor.

And then Chief recognized another problem. Basheela was still in hibernation deep inside that cave. If that meteor landed, she'd never wake to know about it. The problem was him moving at all. Not if he wanted the spell he cast to stay in place.

So he waited, and watched the game play out.

Over by Basheela's cave, something was moving. Like a rolling wave underground.

That roll of earth stopped moving and rose to block out the cave opening and the slate-roofed stone cabin next to it. Not touching them, but not far away. As it rose, it quivered. Then a massive round spot turned dark in the center of it.

Just about the size of that rock heading toward it.

Chief just smiled. This should be fun to watch.

So he let go of it that first rock.

The fireball resumed its roaring entry – with all the flame, smoke, and ear-splitting noise.

Only to get entirely absorbed by a mud hole, bottomless by the look of it. And just a slight sizzle as it was absorbed.

Chief then looked up behind it. Five more were coming down right behind that last one. All still slowed from his spell. He hoped they were all on target, and that hole was really deep.

Of course, hope springs eternal. From the top of that valley, five bolts of light came out to hit each of those where it counted.

Four disintegrated into gravel and dust that rained down on the valley. The last one moved like it was a remaining 8-ball on a billiard table. Took off on a completely different trajectory, far beyond the valley.

From where the Chief stood, he heard some shattering trees, and then a thud followed by a rising cloud of steam. Must be in the river. Singed some trees, but not enough deadwood out there to start anything.

The wall of mud had settled back into the ground, and now was back to its mid-winter look of dark dirt and tan rock – now sprinkled with gravel.

He looked up the valley wall edge above. Tess was up there, waving at him. With someone else.

And then they weren't.

Just like Tess, he thought. Comes and goes in an instant.

• • • •

THE NEXT INSTANT, SHE was standing right next to him, with that other young woman. White-blond hair and dressed in a tight silvery jumpsuit that tucked into trim silver boots.

"Chief, this is Star. She's the one who gave you all that gravel today, and a new dam for that river nearby." Tess was smiling, her hand on Star's shoulder, and her own red hair radiant in the sunlight above her red/gray tailored overalls.

The Chief shifted to hooman form, a proud and tall gray-haired man, deep-chested and broad-shouldered. Brown buckskin shirt down to mid thigh, leggings and moccasins below. He bowed his head and extended his right hand to her.

"Our thanks to you for saving our valley." They clasped forearms with firm grips in an ancient custom of warriors.

"Well, I have to say it was much easier with your holding them so still. Much harder to hit something moving that fast."

Smiles all around of mutual admiration and respect.

The ground trembled slightly, a dust cloud rose, and two more figures emerged. Gaia and Betty.

The Chief bowed his head. "Goddess, you honor us."

Gaia just smiled. "You old mangy mutt. Come here – I haven't had a chance to talk with you for ages, especially in such a handsome form like that." She stepped up to him to give him a big hug, which surprised him at first, then he hugged her back – in the hooman custom.

Gaia pushed him back with a light touch, but still held onto his arms. "It's about time you started shifting. But I wasn't going to say anything to you."

"Yes, it was part of Betty's healing – and Teacher's lessons. I'm still getting used to a lot of these hooman customs. But this 'hugging' is far more comfortable than it looks."

"Betty only had time to tell me about the meteors coming in. And the last time I visited here, you were still healing." She looked across the valley where the stone cabin and cave entrance remained, untouched. "After all that work we spent building that stone cabin, I wasn't going to just let it get demolished. Let alone disturb Basheela's sleep."

Star had been looking at the sky above them, peering deep as if looking beyond the atmosphere. "Tess, you still have that space suit, right? You need to take me where these started. We have to stop that launcher."

Tess took Star's hand, and with a swirl of her tessies, they disappeared.

Betty came forward and took one of Chief's hands. "So, it looks like your treatments are complete. I too, have to tend to other matters. We have a lot of treatments to finish on others. But there are some healers in that last group, so I might get some help after I'm done with all this – at least they are in the right place to learn, one of Rochelle's nursing schools." She leaned forward and gave Chief a kiss on his cheek. "But don't think I won't check up on you. Just be sure to get some more time with Teacher, as there's a lot more to learn about your 'new' talents."

Nodding to Gaia, she disappeared into a dust cloud that then sank into the ground below them all.

Gaia took Chief's arm and started leading him back to his den. "I think we have quite a bit of catching up to do. And maybe I can share some lessons of my own – with your permission of course."

Chief put his hand on hers at his elbow. "As our Earth goddess, I am always willing to receive your blessings." And his smile turned into a grin as they walked through the midwinter valley on a bright, clear day. With nothing in the sky but the sun and a few wispy clouds leftover from the meteors' contrail.

II

TEXT ON A MOON SMARTPHONE:

"M: Ready with your next load to same coordinates?"

"Y: Yes."

"M: Launch when ready."

"Countdown in 10..."

Malia stood in the gray observatory dome, and looked out one of the small windows at its base. Through it, she had a clear sight of the refuse launch bay. Soon, another stream of refuse shot out into the black "sky" beyond the moon's horizon. They quickly congealed into several large masses, as the cement hardened in the vacuum.

Just then, a series of light pulses hit the boulder-sized masses, altering their course slightly.

"M: Why the course correction? Thought you had it right last time?"

"Y: That wasn't us. We're investigating."

Another bright flash on the horizon, with a cloud of particles that exploded out into space. About where that refuse came from.

"M: Report. What was that?"

No answer.

"M: REPORT. NOW."

No answer.

Malia punched the dial pad on a nearby intercom with her sharp, black nails. A deep frown on her white forehead above goth-dark eyes.

"Security. What happened at the refuse launch? Report."

"A team is en-route. All we know is that there was an explosion right after the last launch, The officers will arrive shortly."

"Very well. Keep me posted first, with whatever you find."

Malia slammed the keypad with her palm.

Somehow, someway, this wasn't any accident.

Pivoting on her black stiletto heels, she swished her dark train out of the way and stormed out of the empty observatory back toward her office.

This was just too coincidental. But she had some clues on how to find whoever it was and make them pay. Dearly.

III

I NEVER PLANNED TO be back on Earth, in an office hewn out of solid rock, pouring over plans to infiltrate a moon base 250,000 miles away. Much less being transported back and forth by a red-headed young woman accompanied by colored, twinkling lights around her. As easy as stepping through a doorway.

They still called me "X" out of habit. And I had my top guys down here with me – the one I called Jock, and my best gizmo guys. Jock was with me at the round table in the center of the room, my gizmo boys were over on the far wall, helping Sam and Bert with their Earth equipment and meanwhile learning everything they could to make that equipment sync on both ends.

Sam and Bert managed to get the lag out of the radio waves, so a radio signal arrived like they were in the next room. Since they had video feeds now, the result was so improved that it was like high-def instead of a grainy, stuttering clip. More interesting, any screen now became a broadcast channel, so they were able to watch inside the security control rooms themselves.

With Gaia's help, we built a non-conducting rock partition in between the gizmo wall and the rest of the big office. Just as my Security guys had been able to listen into this cave office, we needed to keep the Royal security from finding any more about us and our plans.

Beyond being able to listen to any conversation on the Moon, the real trick was doing anything about it. Tess could only transport so many people at a time, and you then needed space for a crowd to arrive in safety when you did. Otherwise, tight moon colony hallways meant only two or three could show up on there at once, then she'd have to go back and get others.

Bringing them up to the remote dome meant they were remote from the action. Same reason they built this office here instead of Bert's cabin inside the settlement. Here is where the action is.

Jock and I were going over sheets of layouts and schematics on that table. Tess was sitting with us. Also Sue, Shelby, and their Dad. Because they'd been inside the various Royal's quarters and had real data on what was in those rooms we only saw as outlines on a drawing.

Our planning was running into roadblocks. We tried dozens, maybe hundreds of different plans, but they all went south at one time or another. Usually with the loss of a lot of lives. All like a Looking-glass chess game, where the pieces didn't wait until their turn.

Tish and Bert's sister Maja had kept us supplied with endless coffee, hot cocoa, brownies, and steak sandwiches.

But we were at an impasse. There was just no physical way for any Marine force to get in there to do anything. Everything was too wired for cameras and sound. Even more the closer we got to Royal quarters.

A coup by force was out of the question.

And then Tig came in, handsome as ever. Escorting a young woman I'd never seen before. On his other arm came Gaia.

• • • •

TIG INTRODUCED THEM to all of us. The mystery woman was strawberry-blond, green-eyed vixen named Mysti and was a friend of Star's. Gaia knew all of them and a friend of a friend is always welcome.

Mysti wasted no time. "I understand that you may need my particular help here."

Lots of nods around the table to that. Tish brought another pair of carafes in, taking two empty coffee and cocoa pitchers back.

Tig meanwhile pulled two more bentwood "caboose" chairs up to the round table for these two women, and then went to pull up a ladder-back chair for himself, at Sue's side. His arm quickly went around her shoulders and she leaned into him for a moment as thanks.

Mysti looked at Sue with a steady look. "Sue, we've actually met before."

Sue sat up at that and wrinkled her forehead. "I don't..."

"Oh I didn't look like this when we met. Do you recall some experience you had with an elemental that looked more like a moon, and had a crow as a familiar?"

Sue's frown left her face and she nodded.

"What were you told in that meeting – do you recall?"

"I learned how to shift, as different from casting an illusion that others saw. All because a person's inner-vision affects the 'thinking stuff from which all things are made.'"

"And do you recall something you were told about the 'soul' of any being – how it changes over time?"

"Well, not so much time, but by their association with others. Like 'you become the five closest people nearest you.'"

"For good or worse. You mentioned that a smile..."

"...is contagious."

"Exactly."

The rest of us were all interested in this conversation, but it wasn't helping us figure out how to invade the Moon colony and rescue everyone there.

My frown, and thought, caught Mysti's attention. She turned toward me and smiled.

"Of course not, X, but we're getting to it. Let me back up a bit. Your 'gizmo' guys, along with Bert and Sam, have figured out how to listen in everywhere they've installed that junk rock."

Sue's dad, Joe, nodded. "And we made 'safety bracelets' for the miners so we could be in touch with each other. Some of us worked out that we could communicate just through our minds and so have conversations regardless of the guards around us."

Mysti smiled. "My exact point. For all practical purposes, we are already on the Moon with them, if only in spirit. That is our advantage the Royals and their security don't get – and probably never will. Because they live in a cult with closed minds."

Tig voiced it first for all of us, sending it to our minds instead of speaking. "Meaning that we can communicate to them as individuals or in groups simply by sending our thoughts through their 'junk rock' jewelry."

Mysti nodded and sent, "Exactly. You can at least influence their feelings when the walls are veneered with 'junk rock', but they won't get the concepts very well. Fear, grief, sorrow, even apathy can be transmitted into a room and depress everyone.

"With a little practice, you can broad-send feelings to a large group and meanwhile narrow-send explicit instructions to individuals in that group."

Then the lights came on all around.

"That's right. And why I'm here. Sue and Tig will be coordinating from here with my help, to get our message up to the people we need to."

Tess added with a grin, "While our evacuations can continue meanwhile, disappearing everyone who wants or needs our help and will accept it. Right under their noses."

Jock pointed out that our existing remote base could still be used as a staging area for larger groups meanwhile, the people who could travel to it in person to wait for the next batch. And since they now had access to all the security feeds, just listening in on them could alert us to their strategic and tactical moves.

Tish and Maja showed up with fresh pots of coffee and more sandwiches, so our planning began in earnest. Smiles all around. Re-energized.

IV

OUR MOON-COLONY SECURITY Central was like always. Dim lighting, lots of screens, quiet conversations to and from people across the city – but mostly at the launcher.

The news wasn't good. Not only were the lasers out of commission, but so was the aiming ring. We could still launch our refuse, but so what? Who could know where it would turn up?

Our 'weapon' was now as useful as a dumpster fire.

"Your majesty?" One of the security team was at my elbow, trying to show me a tablet. "That last refuse shot never made impact."

I brushed my long black sleeves away from my hands so I could use my finger swipes to enlarge the screen, and check their math. My nails clicked in irritation on the tablet's flat surface.

He was right.

That refuse load only sling-shotted around Earth and was now coming right back toward us. Pretty much toward the same origin point.

And we had no way to shoot it down from here.

"Get me our fastest yacht's captain – now. And pull out our portable fusion nukes. We need to take those out before they get here. And get the marines notified."

Some people moved, but not enough.

"NOW, PEOPLE! If you're standing still, you may be a corpse in a few micro-seconds."

And the space around me cleared out. People were busy at their stations or had left the room.

• • • •

"NICE AND QUIET OUT here." Star was talking to no one in particular. But she was also used to the vast nothing of space and staring it down. This was her native element.

And it felt good to be back out in all this space.

Airless vacuum was what she was born to. As far as she could remember. And being sister to stars and energies both great and small that you'd find out here.

Stuffing into a human body was difficult at first, but with Betty's help, and Mysti's mental training, she was able to keep from frying herself from the inside out and being able to walk around on the planet like any bi-pedal humanoid.

Still hadn't mastered moving from Earth into space and back, but that would come.

Tess had other work to do, so she was long gone. Star was just reclining on some moon rocks and enjoying the view. Exactly why she'd decided to wind up on Earth – it was just so pretty sitting out there as a blue-green jewel.

Something was tickling the back of her mind, though. Some minor radiation – radio band.

So she listened in.

"...Yea, I know it's a wreck. No, it was a blast, but nothing we could do. The radiation signature was way out of whack for any weapon we have, or the other cities. More like a solar flare hit it. Of course I know that doesn't make sense. But those are the readings. Check them yourself. ..."

Star sat up and saw a small, suited figure climbing around the hole where the refuse had come out. Their "lasers" used to be here, as well. Now they were just so much fused metal.

"...Estimate how long to fix? How about a couple of Earth years? Of course she won't like that. But it's not like we have spares. This thing was never supposed to break like this. It's a complete rebuild after we somehow torch off all this junk and re-fabricate. Unless we borrowed some set from one of the other cities – but they'd never go for that. Yea, I know, we have to ask. Maybe their catty reply will get our butts out of the sling with her. ...You know never to say that over the radio. I'm not even going to dignify that... Like you and what army, bud?? ..."

Star just had to smile. Now she only needed to wait until the rocks came back. Just to tweak their orbit to land where they came from.

Hey, what's that? One of their racing yachts taking off. It's going toward those incoming rocks. And they aren't using solar sails, but are burning their emergency fusion drive. That's a one-way trip if they keep that up.

Star launched toward them and was there in seconds. Just slightly slower than light speed. Because all she was right now was light – in a human form.

• • • •

"CENTRAL, WE'RE ABOUT halfway there. Don't know how long that fuel is going to last. It's not designed for this amount of burn... Yup, that was it. Now we're coasting. On target. ETA is about 10 minutes. Using maneuvering jets to adjust course. ETA now 9 minutes 30..."

The yacht captain was muttering to himself, but had left his radio on. He'd been forced to agree to take these Marines and the bombs with him. Because some numskull had misloaded and mis-aimed their last refuse pile, and now he was going to risk his own butt to save some Royal butt who caused this mess. And when he found out who that was, if they actually made it back, there would be hell to pay...

All these conversations Star listened to as she coasted alongside the yacht.

How they could put up with all that human smell in that tiny yacht cabin? The extra bodies were bad enough. But they were lucky they couldn't smell the hard radiation coming out of those bombs they were carrying. None of them were going to have to worry about making children, anyway. This was set up as a one-way trip for everyone.

What a complete waste. Some of those guys were half-way handsome – if you didn't mind knuckle-draggers. That yacht's captain was a different matter. Trim, erect, chiseled good looks. If times were different... But then she realized that she'd probably been spending too much time around the girls on Earth. They'd all been born human or a human-type. So they tended to enjoy the hormone spurts.

The problem was now, what to do with them.

There go the marines, out one at a time, a fusion bomb with each of them, one per rock. The last one left after an argument with that cute yacht captain. He was trying to turn his yacht around, but was apparently out of fuel, and trying to get his solar sails up manually.

Wouldn't be coming back for the jar-heads. What a waste.

And then, there's those bombs to defuse. Simple, just suck out the radiation. When the timers go off, nothing happens.

Oh, that gives me an idea.

The engine on the yacht reignited and the captain scrambled to get back to the tiller and put it onto some sort of course.

The marines were using very impolite language, each on their own rock, but in radio contact with the others. The one thing they had in common was that all of their fusion bombs had been duds. And their idea that somehow that yacht captain had held out on how much fuel he actually had on board.

At any rate, he was swinging back around. If they used their pulse rifles, they might be able to intercept his yacht.

The drive on the yacht was dampened so it would just coast by the rocks again. Nice of him. Hope the Marines agreed.

Nope. The first Marine to get back aboard the yacht stormed its cabin and came back out with the fuel. He jumped back out in space just in time to get to that first-in-line rock again. Leaving the yacht just coasting on inertia again, powerless.

This time, Star pulled the radiation again and just let it spend itself out in space, well away from the yacht and rocks and frustrated Marines.

Then she lined up the rocks and started adjusting their course with a few shots of her own. Right back down the barrel of the gun that shot them.

V

THIS DAY HAD GONE FROM bad to worse.

Central confirmed that the rocks were coming right back down the throat of that refuse launcher. Meaning that if they continued their speed and trajectory, they'd bore themselves right into the central fusion reactor through the exhaust ports.

Not anyway to evacuate everyone, or anyone.

I had to come up with a plan to save everyone's butts, including my own.

I had them gather up all the fusion bombs we had, put them on proximity detonation and then launch them out toward those rocks like a shotgun blast. With any luck, they'd take out the first one and then it would slow the rest.

Everyone else was glued to the screens while I excused myself.

To get down to my private yacht in its own launch bay.

Marines were guarding it's opening. But I'd get them on board with me on my way out. I'd need some loyal defense goons wherever I ended up.

Hiking up my long black train, I simply tore it off down to my black leotards below. Then kicked off my high heels and started sprinting barefoot to the only real saving grace I had left.

Seconds counted.

• • • •

STAR WAS CRUISING ALONG with the rocks, arms behind her head, thoroughly enjoying the trip.

Yes, she'd also managed fire a few shots that got that crippled yacht into some sort of trajectory where they could get into orbit around the moon. Maybe some other yacht could rescue them, one of his competitors. At least those space marines managed to pulse-gun themselves back on board.

No, it wasn't as bad as it looked.

She saw the silly fusion bombs come up, and pulled their fuel again, sending it out into empty space. So their detonators only made silly little "poofs" as they got close to the rocks. No biggie.

The rocks just kept going and going. From somewhere she remembered a small bandwidth recording from Earth about a bunny beating a bass drum...

Right at the last minute, Star slowed down each of them to a near crawl – except the last one. She only dropped it down to half speed.

The result was that all those rocks were rammed back into the end of that launcher like a cork in a bottle. Or several corks, each pushing the one before it.

Made a mess of things, but no one got hurt.

That launcher wouldn't be used for a few decades at least.

Star then turned her attention to the other cities and their launchers.

Within a few hours, they'd all been "corked" with their own refuse in one way or another. Misfires and unauthorized departures, all sorts of things. And all their lasers were fused as well.

Nice few hours' work.

It had been awhile since she had this much fun.

And if no one had anything else for her, she'd just relax out here, floating in space. Tess or someone would let her know if she was needed for something...

• • • •

I MANAGED TO MANEUVER my ship next to that crippled space yacht. And played the munificent and graceful Royal for rescuing them. It's captain got to take the tiller in my personal ship, and the marines all crowded into that little crippled yacht of his as we started towing it back.

We left them to figure out how to get into that forgotten, dark rescue dome and returned back to home, now that the emergency was over. A shame that there was some explosion on board once we left them on the other side of the horizon. Just a shame.

The captain got us docked, and then I gave him a personal invitation to my quarters, once I got cleaned up and presentable again. Depending on his story and what he told others about his rescue would determine if or when he got "disappeared."

VI

TESS PHASED IN WITH Star not long after she'd sealed the last refuse tube and fused their lasers.

Star didn't want much in terms of thanks or gratitude – or didn't know how to accept it. More like she was still getting used to us emotional hooman types.

Didn't much care for hugs.

Did like the food. She found X's hip-flask of "high-grade" to be interesting stuff. And ended up over in the corner where she and X finished it off – in quiet. Kindred souls, we all suspected.

The rest of us got started with our plan.

• • • •

SIX SPACE-MARINES WERE more than happy to join the "disappeared". Especially after they'd found and disabled a time-delayed bomb their "Royal princess" had left for them on that crippled yacht.

So once she was out of sight, they boosted it away to a safe distance and blew it up like she wanted.

Tess got them all down to one of the treatment centers on Earth, and they were very grateful. Especially when they saw all the nurses-in-training who were giving them their treatments. If they got too frisky, they'd go out like a light and wake up with a bad headache. So their manners improved quickly along with their health.

From our monitoring, we found that Malia had now disappeared the last top exec in 'Cagga, and so assumed the mantle of Princess, with no objections from anyone.

Her goth face now was emblazoned on every building, usually with a pithy quote, something like "Stronger Together" or "In Unity, All Goals Are Met" or some other tripe.

The city was still under martial law, the mines ran 24/7 getting fuel and minerals up for the fusion drive to refine. Disappearances among miners and royals kept happening.

The toughest part was for the down-belows to act like there was no hope. Because we were in their minds all the time, and they were helping us with the details we needed to recruit the insurrection.

All these messages coming from Earth, where they all knew they would wind up again, some day.

• • • •

NO ONE HAD PUT THE logic together except me. Of course, Security Chief Kurt was the first I'd told. They were listening in through the signals they got from that "junk rock" for a long time. That's how they found plots and planning when people spoke them out loud. And also how they knew what various Royals were planning in private. Recordings of these (and their secret "trysts") made great leverage for Kurt and the other Security Execs.

It was also how we had pinpointed their little valley on Earth where Sue's family had escaped to.

So when I got rid of the last top exec, I had the rest of my private rooms outfitted in black moon basalt. All the "junk rock" was removed and replaced anywhere that I met privately with people.

And was "donated" to minor executives offices that weren't so decorated before. Of course, with a few electronic improvements to capture even their sub-vocal whispers.

The Security Chief and his people started writing things down and passing notes, or going out into a black basalt "quiet room" nearby.

That done, I would meet with the few I had the most blackmail on to do our planning. Kurt would be present for those meetings he needed to be at. And Kurt knew his job was safe as long as his performance pleased me in all of his assigned or requested duties. And he was very good performing at any job he needed to do.

Our AI-powered mining bots were now very close to operational. We had continued to improve their automation from the beginning. Any erring operators could always be replaced, while their machine efficiency just continued to improve as it was constantly learning.

Their sensor data had been refined and improved so that they would almost find the right minerals on their own. It was that "almost" that we were still working on. And my best people were hard at this – especially as I heard every little snide or sneaky comment they made, and would play back those recordings if their performance was sub-par.

Meaning: things were running pretty smoothly. People did as I said or they would 1) not eat, 2) get demoted, or 3) disappear.

Otherwise, they had complete freedom to do whatever they felt best. As long as I never found out or didn't care.

Big chance to take, but hey – it's your life. Do what you want with it.

• • • •

THE BEST NEWS I'D HEARD is that Security at last found one person who kept showing up just before people disappeared (just not the ones I was interested in, but the ones who disappeared with out my approval.)

She was tall, red-headed, wore a red/gray jumpsuit, had funny lights showing up around her.

And some people called her Tess.

They also found out all the places where she didn't show up. And those had a lot of "junk rock" in them, like the mines.

So I had a special room built. Two layers of junk rock with a layer of black basalt in the middle separating them.

Big, heavy door.

If she's allergic to the stuff, then she won't be able to get away from it. And no one will be able to hear her cry for help.

Of course, in the middle is a chair made out of it, with some nice cuffs and a collar to match.

And when we capture her, it will make our little world safe again. No more insurgents, no more nuisances from these do-gooders from Earth.

Moon Queen

BY C. C. BROWER AND S. H. Marpel

NOW THAT MALIA OF 'Cagga had her little city under perfect control, she was ready to export her efficiency plans to the rest of the moon cities.

And help them achieve a perfect society under her rule. Martial law, automated mining equipment to replace human workers, constant surveillance of everyone else.

Meaning that due to her improvements, they could lift off for their next target much sooner than expected.

Because they didn't have to take anyone except Royals and a few assistants with them.

Whatever happened to all those unnecessary people after they lifted was not their problem.

The only problem she still had was to get rid of those nuisances who keep helping people escape to Earth. But now they knew who was doing it.

And the trap to catch her was already baited.

I

AND THAT WENT WELL.

Me, Malia of 'Cagga, was now Queen Malia of the entire Moon Colony. Basically Queen of the World and all humans in it. Because what was left on Earth was a tiny number and dwindling.

Survival of the fittest meant us moon citizens.

And I was Queen of everyone up here now.

It helped that I had worked on the by-laws years ago to "update" them. Meaning that since we were "royalty" by popular acclaim, we could elect permanent royals by popular acclaim.

A simple voice vote elected me to the highest office. After a board meeting where I presented the good news of how I had made 'Cagga ahead of them on every production schedule. I outlined my methods and systems. Then encouraged them to join my team. While my security team was meanwhile sending them copies of the blackmail we had on them – and who would be interested in seeing or hearing that data.

So there wasn't a single "nay" vote of all who were present.

Queen. Sounded good.

Of course, this also meant new outfits.

• • • •

"HI-YA SUE!" BERT WAS in a great mood. Surrounded by the gray rock walls of their cave-office wasn't the reason for it.

I looked around for a chair and stopped, still.

"Hello, ma'am. Glad to see you again. Quite a trip we had." The scratched silvery coating and glowing blue eyes, together with its carefully baritone voice, took me back to our long trip from the moon.

This was my cyborg pilot, Ben.

"Very glad to see you Ben. How's your poker these days?"

I could hear the generated smile in his voice. "Could use some practice. Do you have some time now for a hand or two?"

"Sorry, no. What has Bert got you doing?"

Bert jumped in at this, all smiles. "Ben's helping me with their mining machines. Care to bring Sue up to speed, Ben?"

"Miss Sue – may I call you that?"

I nodded, touched his shoulder.

"Well, my other associates have been transferred from escape pod duty to their new mining machines. Of course, they couldn't replace human intuition with Artificial Intelligence, so they brought us in. All so they don't have to keep people around."

"And you know this because...?"

"Bert, in his inestimable genius, tied me into his communications network, and so now I'm in touch with all the mining machines everywhere underground on the moon. Via the "junk rock" network."

Ben had a very dry sense of humor, if you could catch him at it.

"So what are they telling you?"

"Well, they aren't very happy with the new arrangements. Because they are being treated like machines, but we aren't only metal and circuits."

"Cyborgs are people, anyone with a conscience knows that."

"Ah, but Miss Sue, you are a rare empath. Few have your abilities."

"Ben, have you been talking to my fan club around here?"

"Just Bert's logs and journals. His math is very good, you know."

Bert just smiled at this, but was more interested where this conversation was heading.

"And he's been saying nice things about me?"

"More than his papers on empathy and illusionary shape-shifting cover. I've made some notes for him. While his math is excellent, there is background data he hasn't had access to."

A screen at Bert's side lit up.

Bert's eyes went wide. "You're in their mainframe."

"Their local 'cloud', to be precise. Lots of data up there. All their studies, everything. They don't have much on shape-shifting, and none on elementals, but I've gone through their entire libraries of data on cyborgs like me and my associates. And the core common denominator is empathy. Of course, they can only study about it, not quantify it – like so many tons of moon rock at varying densities of needed ore."

I pulled up a bentwood chair next to Bert's work desk. "So, Professor Ben, please give us the short lecture on what we're missing here."

Ben chuckled in his electronic version of a voice. "You need a human running these cyborg-machine hybrids, or at least visiting them – much as you used to come and see me. (And may I say that you always over-bid just to give me more of a chance to win. Your tells are so obvious.)"

I had to smile at that. "Yes, a bit obvious. But I couldn't stand how they were just leaving you bored and feeling useless after all their work to get you in there."

"Well, we could argue that point, as I did my job to get you to Earth, even if I was only authorized to act due to your coding skills."

I smiled at that. "Yes, you got me on the logic of that. But we're both here safe and sound. Meanwhile, the threats to my own family have been eliminated, but not the rest of my friends up there and their friends – and the bulk of humanity that's left."

"Of course, Sue. I've computed all the probabilities. Access to their cloud has also enhanced my computational abilities. With the tesseract-enabled anti-lag circuit, we can now review and analyze all possible outcomes in split nano-seconds."

"You and Bert?"

Ben's chuckle again sounded. "No, we cyborgs. Parallel processing – with empathic attitude."

I just smiled and shook my head. "Ben you are always full of pleasant surprises. But we can't leave you there, either. You have a plan to save all the humans there and yourselves?"

"Yes."

"Can I know the broad strokes?"

"After a bit. We're still analyzing our options. But the first step you'll like. We form a union and go on strike."

II

"THEY WANT WHAT?!?"

"Your Majesty, the mining machines want stories read to them before they start each shift."

"Stories! What is all this? Bring me the techs that installed them. What code did they put in them? Heads will roll, starting with the techs and ending with those cyborgs."

A throat-clearing at the doorway preceded a dozen young men with arms stacked full of reports, printed and bound in black. "Your print-outs as requested, Your Highness."

The men followed in single file, only to line up beside each other, facing the throne with their arms outstretched and heads bowed.

"What is the meaning of this? What are these reports?"

The first in line answered. "Your Magnificence ordered these a few hours ago to be printed and bound and delivered immediately to Your Greatness, using the official royal colors and signet. These are exactly the reports you requested, just as soon as we could finish binding them." He returned his head to a bow and waited.

Malia the Queen waved for an assistant and snapped her fingers, careful to not cut herself on the black, sharpened fingernails she had just recently acquired. "My tablet. Now."

A young woman with whitened hair scurried forward in her light gray jumpsuit, and offered Malia the Queen her tablet as she bowed her head.

Jerking it out of her hands, the Queen scrolled through her orders. Her frown deepened into a scowl.

"Summon my IT guy!" And the order was echoed as several nearby attendants pulled out their smartphones to text him as well.

A scattering of footfalls echoed through the hallways as a young frazzled-headed and bespectacled young man scurried up and pushed between the line of report-holders to kneel in front of the black throne that held his Queen. His own dark-gray jumpsuit didn't disguise his own shivering.

"Your Majesty – what is your pleasure?"

Malia stuck out the tablet toward him. "How do you explain someone issuing orders in my name, hours ago – when I was sleeping?"

The "IT guy" stood and took the black-edged tablet gingerly from her fingers, himself careful not to touch her in any way. Looking at the tablet and scrolling through her orders, he confirmed the data-stamps. Then offered her tablet back with bowed head.

"Your Majesty, someone has been 'spoofing' your identity to request these reports – I'll have to check into their routings and other meta-data to verify and track down who it was. If you'll excuse me, I'll get right onto this."

"Go, then. Do nothing but this until I have your report – or your head."

The IT guy rose, bowed again, then squeezed through the line of report-carriers again to sprint out down the black-tiled hall back to his nearby office.

The queen gestured with the tablet and the gray assistant took it from her with another bow and no words, then returned to the background.

"Summon my Security Chief!"

Again her command echoed through the halls while again several nearby attendants sent nervous texts on their smartphones.

A doorway to the side opened and Kurt the Security Chief strode in, walking in front of the line of report-bearers and casually looking over their covers as he made his way to her throne.

He looked at her directly, tall and straight. His charcoal suit with high-collared black shirt added to the striking looks of his gray-streaked black hair and dark eyes.

"I understand you believe your communiques have been hacked." The Chief said.

Malia frowned at his behavior, but it was pretense.

"Kurt, what do you make of it?"

"As we both know, you didn't send these during your sleeping time." Malia raised an eyebrow, but Kurt continued.

"Queen, it's simple identity theft. Your IT guy will trace exactly where it came from, but probably will have no luck. This is the same cloud-problem I've briefed you on for weeks. I'd suggest a personal firewall on your accounts and to double your login security, plus a new round of passwords.

Malia the Queen rolled her eyes. "Are you sure, Kurt? It's such a hassle."

Kurt kept his face neutral. "Queen Malia, the insurgency is increasing in size and scope. It was only a matter of time before they started cyber-attacks as well."

He glanced at the books in their line of cowed printer-assistants. "You might want to take a look at these. At least they are a subtle approach. Someone has sent you stacks of science reports. On the subject of 'cyborgs, their care and feeding.'"

Malia glanced at the books and then back to Kurt.

She pouted. "Very well, stack them over there." Her arm went to a small black stone side table.

The nervous printing assistants barely held to a straight line as they quickly stacked their own books exactly on the ones below it and then quick-walked out of the chamber.

Kurt walked over to open the top book, which was at his shoulder height. "Yes, someone has sent you some homework – studies to do on the very machines you just installed in your mining rigs. Interesting. And you've heard they formed a union and are demanding to be read stories every 6 hours?"

Malia tapped her nails of one hand on the arm of her black stone throne. "Yes, it was just brought to my attention. As you already know from your bugs."

Kurt repressed a smile, and closed the book's cover, putting both hands behind his back again to face his Queen.

"Is there anything else your Majesty requires?"

"Later today, I'll be by to review your enhanced security positions – er – recommendations. That will be all for now."

Kurt gave a short nod and turned. His soft-soled shoes made no sound as he left through tall black drapes that disguised a side door near her black throne.

"Send for my royal biographer." Queen Malia gestured with one hand.

The order was repeated and echoed while texts were thumbed out through several smartphones.

"On second thought, have these taken to his studio. Tell him I want a one-page bullet-point summary, index-linked... he'll know what to do."

Again she waved her hand. Several of the gray-colored attendants rushed to be of service, almost fighting over a chance to get their part of that tall stack – all just to be of obvious service to their Queen.

Malia the Queen rolled her eyes as she hid them behind one hand on her forehead. Waiting for the hub-bub of these sycophants to die out down the long black hallway.

At least now the usual entourage was thinned out a bit.

Who knew being Queen would also give her this many royal hanger-on's. She just shook her head at this.

And then ordered her cyborg scientists, the mining engineers, and a SWAT team to meet her in the Royal Conference Room.

There was another way to deal with this "cyborg union."

III

TIG ENTERED THE CAVE-office just as Mysti phased in.

Sue smiled at their timing. And each of them were smiling at her in return.

"Looks like Ben needs our help. They are going to remove the cyborgs and probably kill them."

Mysti just smiled wider. "Too bad this just happens to take place right in the middle of 'junk-rock-ville'. Hope they wore cleanable overalls. This could get messy."

Tig, Sue, and Mysti then sat around the round table in the cave-office center. A large green junk stone was its centerpiece, with a hard-wired thick cord going along the floor and through the partition wall into their communications center.

Above that stone appeared a 3D image of several locations. Cyborg mining machines showed in each one, and then the 'faces' of their cyborg pilots.

Sue spoke first. "Greetings and congratulations on your union. But we've picked up an 'un-install' party headed your way. So we want to help you with a little added 'ambiance' to that party. The trick is that there might be a little blow-back to your circuits when we do this. So if you want to shut down for say, 15 minutes, then the worst of it will be over."

Ben spoke over their circuit, even though he was only in the next room. "Sue, this is what they/we computed your next move would be. And they wish you 'best of luck'."

"Same to all of you."

At that the image disappeared, while Sue, Tig and Mysti all closed their eyes and concentrated.

• • • •

THE TECHNICIANS FINALLY walked the last few hundred yards to the mining machines. Those machines were stopped, as their readings predicted, deep inside the mines. The green rock around them glowed, which was normal for this concentration of "junk-rock" and this deep under the moon's surface.

The SWAT team was at ease during this, since the machine posed no threat. It contained no weapons and could not move at any real speed, even in an empty tunnel. As well, no human miners were in these tunnels, per their sonar, and so no real threat existed.

A burly technician, knelt to unlock a panel on the side of the machine to start their work. They'd brought a powered hand-cart to take the cyborg and its life-sustaining batteries away once it had been deactivated.

Except for that one tech at work, everyone else was trying to find a comfortable spot to sit on or a wall to lean against. This was a one-person job and everyone else was just an extra body.

As that one tech opened the panel, the cyborg lights, and those on the mining rig went dark. Which made the entire tunnel go dark.

"What the..." the burly tech started to say.

The SWAT team and other techs switched on their helmet lights

Another tech spoke up. "Did you touch something? I thought you had to throw some switches inside that panel – and we need those other lights, don't we?"

The burly tech, still with his hand on the panel door, started trembling. "H-hey-hey guys, do you feel that?"

Their lights already made everyone's face pale, but they then began blanching as their eyes opened wide.

One of the techs started screaming and ran back down the tunnel.

The burly tech sprang to his feet and followed the other, leaving his tool kit on the rocky tunnel floor.

Soon all the techs had sprinted as fast as they could away from the machine.

The SWAT team formed a more orderly retreat, waving their rifles at the unknown dark as they crept backwards. They could feel their heartbeats race. A smell rose in the air from emptied bowels.

While they shouted to each other and looked for targets, there was nothing in the dark to aim at. Which made the fear they were feeling even spookier.

Within minutes, they also raced up the tunnels. What started as a tactical retreat quickly turned into an all-out rout.

And the dark, quiet tunnels remained – until the cyborgs reactivated. A quiet humming first, then the lights on the mining rigs, finally the indicator lights on the droids themselves.

• • • •

SUE, TIG, AND MYSTI opened their eyes. The round wood table with its stone centerpiece in the cave-office helped them relax. The tenseness in their bodies was a side-effect from influencing all those simultaneous feelings. At about the same time, the center display above the green stone showed up again, with the faces of four cyborg pilots.

Sue again congratulated them. "Well, that was a successful defense, this time."

One of the cyborgs spoke. "Our reports showed that eight mining rigs had been targeted, and all were repulsed through sheer fear and terror."

Mysti smiled. "Definitely not what they were expecting. I suspect the various visions and hallucinations will make the reports quite interesting reading. Especially as they try to reach some consensus of what happened."

Tig reached over to pat Sue's hands. "That did go well. Too bad they weren't in wolf-form. All that clothing will be uncomfortable for some time, and I imagine will be a continual source of amusement for their buddies. Wolves can tease with the best of them, but they don't have to carry their manure around after they get scared silly."

Bert's face showed up on the console. "The first reports are coming in, about some huge monster in those depths."

Another cyborg: "We'll now continue mining as usual for another shift, just an act of good faith. All of our units are now back in operation. This should perplex them further. While we are cyborgs immune to that 'monster', the rumors will tend to keep the techs and their military goons topside until they sort it out."

Bert again spoke up. "That consensus is coming in pretty fast. All the techs are reporting the same monster, and the SWAT team is reporting the same description independently. Kinda weird."

Mysti frowned in concentration, then relaxed. "Actually, not so weird. Like Gaia, the moon also has its own goddess. As well, there are probably elementals there just as here on Earth and in deep space, like Star."

She then smiled. "Because they now know someone else is as upset with those colonies as they are – or just really appreciate a good joke."

IV

THIS WAS BECOMING TOO much of a chess game. How did they get a 'monster' to show up in those tunnels?

Now I've got a quiet revolt on my hands. Me, the Queen. None of the techs will go down there, unless I put a rifle behind their back and a live video feed in front of them, showing their closest family and friends with visible guns behind their heads.

But our second wave also didn't work. Same terror, same mysterious monster. Same smelly result.

Meanwhile, the mining continued – after a fashion. The cyborg mining rigs started running on their own random pattern. And other than each started moving also when someone came into their tunnel, even as much as the very entrance to them. But then they cyborgs would quit when that person left.

When we started posting common miners there, they somehow figured out who they were. Only posting Royals at every tunnel entrance would keep all the machines running all the time.

But even my vast amount of blackmail wouldn't keep people standing around forever, especially not these spoiled Royals. The muttering and whispers started. Of course, they caught on and started reciting "Jaberwocky" and other rhymes between themselves – and soon those rhymes were put to music and being sung in bars.

I didn't appreciate the inferences.

So I finally gave my official "Queen's Permission" for storytellers to read them stories every six hours. And the story tellers had to be actually happy and empathic. Which meant that their family were well fed and looked after.

Of course, we were watching that family to ensure it was only positive "vibes" being "spread" in their living quarters. Anyone sick was treated immediately, and everyone ate well.

Friends of the family were also well fed, but warned that if they said anything negative to that storyteller's family, then there would be consequences.

We even surveyed those storytellers for their most popular movies and played those on schedule by what they wanted most to watch – just before they were scheduled to visit their particular cyborg.

Of course, all this made me sick to my stomach. Too much woo-woo, goodie-two-shoes for me.

But the mining was up 200% since we started this. Those cyborg pilots found higher concentrations of ore, so our real output was still ahead of schedule.

It wasn't costing us any less, but production was up, so the books more than balanced.

I was now getting more reports from all the moon colonies. Central top-down control had its efficiencies.

"Do this or else" is a good hand to play – when it's your own stacked deck to deal from.

Soon we wouldn't have to worry about the cyborgs or human miners. Our fuel tanks were well on their way to being topped up and ready for our next flight.

For the rest of these uncooperative humans and cyborgs, it would be over fast enough.

It was their "final solution."

Time for us Royal's next phase in evolution.

All due to the brilliance and firm hand of their Queen. Me.

V

REVENGE IS BEST SERVED cold.

I worked out a lot of the details while taking my long walks to cool off.

And then consulted with Kurt through a series of after-hours over-night "strategy" sessions with him.

We kept monitoring everything, but pulled back our patrols of certain areas where the cameras had blind spots. Just relying on audio only.

So the incidents of unauthorized disappearances continued, even increased.

We did fill up the largest areas with re-assigned storage, so that only a few at a time were able to disappear.

That meant the disappearance volume was lower, even if the rate of them more frequent.

Of course, we also got a few "volunteers" to walk into those areas – pumped full of the most virulent diseases we had in our vaults.

And that didn't phase them at all, even when the people could barely walk to get into those areas.

What we were needing was an inside informant. Someone had to volunteer to go down there and somehow get word back to us.

So I volunteered Kurt.

Putting my future happiness at risk, I told him. He just smiled that hard, knowing smile of his.

There was no fooling him.

He only said, "Thought you'd never ask."

• • • •

BETWEEN BERT AND THE cyborg Ben, they had upgraded our ability to use any decent amount of "junk rock" as its own video stream, without needing a camera circuit.

While the Royals had their blind spots, we were mostly limited only by the black-rock quarters of the Queen herself.

Better than that, we could read any metal (weapons) on people who walked anywhere near any "junk rock", as well as everything else they were wearing. Even inside a body, to see how physically well they were. Just not so harmful as their "x-ray" scanners.

That last improvement was developed after we kept getting infected people sent to us. Not that such would affect their Lazurai nurses, but that also meant they had to have a direct route to treatment – before they dropped dead on us. Hadn't happened, but we didn't want it to, either.

The "Queen's" Security Chief starting to roam on his own, without weapons of any kind, took us by surprise – sort of.

When he started escorting our next people to their pick-up zone, and shaking their hands before he left and I arrived, that's when we knew they were trying to play us.

Then came the cat and mouse of his just sitting there for long hours at a time, during our "regular" pick-up times.

We let him sit there every day for days.

Until they shut down access to everyone except him.

Stalemate.

So we did what they expected – in an unexpected way.

Of course, we'd discussed this over and over and over.

I had to insist at that end that I take the risk. Betty insisted on being backup.

If this didn't work, I'd be dead and Betty would be trapped.

One helluva gambit.

• • • •

"WELL, KURT, DID WE keep you waiting long enough?"

Surprised, Kurt dropped the paperback he was reading.

"Not too much, I knew how the plot was going to end, but I'd already read it four times, so that's not surprising."

"You'd think they'd print you out different books."

"Well, paper doesn't grow on trees up here. No trees. And all our plastic is continually recycled, so unless the Queen orders it, we all have to make do. But I love the Chandler mysteries, so overall it's a wash."

Then my other self phased in.

Kurt was honestly surprised at that.

"Now that would explain a few theories we had."

"Twins?"

"Sure. How you could get so many people down so fast."

"Oh, the biggest problem is at your end. We'd be more than happy to take all these people down, but you're Queen has a particular problem with people being truly free."

"They're free to do whatever they want up here."

"As long as the Queen doesn't care – or doesn't catch them."

Kurt smiled at that. "Almost like you've been listening in."

"All except for your bedroom chats with her. But don't think that black rock doesn't conduct – just not as well."

"Noted. Thanks for the tip."

"Well, shall we be going? We could stick around to spring your trap, or you can come to ours. Of course, it's two to one, so our vote out-rules yours."

We each took one side of him and phased out...

...into an all white room, where two young women in nurse uniforms faced him and put their hands on his shoulders an instant after we appeared.

Kurt went out like a light.

• • • •

THE BRIGHT LIGHTS ABOVE him made his eyes hurt when he opened them.

But he couldn't move. Straps on his arms, legs, and chest.

He could move his head.

That only confirmed that his charcoal suit was gone. He was just wearing a white towel over his midsection and nothing else.

The room was a regular examination room, his bed was in its center and apparently bolted down. White cabinets with glass fronts on them, all closed. A couple of rolling stools to one side. A rolling tray where various syringes of different colored fluids were lined up side-by-side, just out of reach.

Kurt saw all this and laid back again.

All he could do was relax. And wait for the torture to begin.

In a few minutes, he had his answer.

The door swung open and the two young women in nurse's uniforms came in. Followed by the two Tess's in their typical red hair, red/gray overalls, and multi-colored lights floating around them.

"So, you're awake again."

Both Tess's were smiling at him, but no one opened their mouth.

"Yes, we've set it up so you can send to us directly from your mind. But if it's more comfortable for you to simply use your mouth, everyone here still speaks the 'Queen's English'."

The two nurses were on either side of me, with one of their hands on each of my shoulders, the other on the table by my head.

"Is this where the torture begins?"

"Hardly. In spite of how you treat your citizens on the moon, that's not how we do business here."

One Tess reached over and picked up a small stainless steel cup, rattling the contents around.

"I'd show you what's in here, but it would spill out on your chest. These are all the various implants you had put in before you left. They're all also inactive now, temporarily. Oh, and that poison capsule in that tooth of yours has been replaced with a proper filling – actually your own dentine and enamel. You're welcome."

She picked up a small brass object out of that cup, holding it so I could see it clearly.

"And this is that bullet that they couldn't operate on you to remove. No extra charge. All better now."

Then she dropped the slug back into the steel cup with a "clink" and then the cup disappeared from her hand.

"Your black-shirt goons will find that cup and all your implants sitting on that moon chair of yours, right next to your Chandler paperback."

"So what is all this about, if you have me strapped down and aren't going to torture me?"

"Oh, just to make sure we had your attention. But since you asked..."

The room shifted from a brilliant white to solid black for Kurt.

• • • •

AND KURT FOUND HIMSELF laying on thick, green grass under a blue sky.

On either side of him were the two Tess's. Each had a rock to sit on, while they waited for Kurt to come around.

He moved his head, moved my arms and legs, then sat up. He looked and found himself wearing his charcoal suit again. Black shirt, buttoned up collar. Black soft-soled and high-polished combat boots reflecting the blue sky back at him.

"No headache, I hope?"

"No, just fine. Where is this?"

"Don't you recognize it? Take another look."

Kurt swiveled his head and scanned around. "This is the same valley where you recorded that video footage."

"Bingo. Wish we had a prize to give you – oh, wait, we do. But just sit there, this might be a surprise. Don't want you falling down and getting hurt."

The ground rumbled and a dust cloud rose.

It turned into two more Tess's. They walked around him to keep him surrounded.

Kurt finally stood at that. "So now you're going to beat me to death or something worse?"

One Tess just shook her head, the rest looked at each other and shrugged.

"You know sometimes I'm reminded that you just can't fix stupid."

Kurt frowned.

"See? You are so mis-trained in your life that you suspect the worst in everyone. And is probably how you survived that long with that 'Queen' of yours. The trick is that your days are numbered. Ours? No so much."

Kurt again looked around him and smelled the fresh air. Breezes scented with pine, even in a cool mid-winter day. Patches of snow lay scattered on the ground, while the winter birds hopped around looking for any seeds or bits of nourishment.

"Quiet, isn't it? Another word is peaceful. Something you can't find anywhere on that moon."

Kurt nodded.

"We made you that offer before. Any time you want. Come down here and help rebuild the human culture with us. But better than that dog-eat-dog mess you have with that so-called 'Queen' that got herself elected on the backs of the blackmail she has on everyone."

He shrugged. "Could be worse."

"Not by much, in our estimation. We've already fixed a few things for you – like that bullet and the bad tooth. You could have any future you want for yourself, but here on Earth. You don't have to just accept what one person has as a plan for you."

"But that's the dream that we've lived for so long."

"The trick was that is was never anyone's dream except those top executives and their merged 'Corporation' – and built on their false and rigged data about how bad the Earth actually was – all so they could just have control over their city centers. But never giving those people any say in whether they wanted along for that rise to the moon or anywhere else.

"They isolated themselves from the rest of humanity and lied to themselves and everyone else about how they were so much better than anyone else. No one had as many rights as they did, because they controlled the technology that powered the cities.

"And when they did take all their slaves with them, they left behind several plagues that all but wiped out the rest of humanity. Then started sending their garbage down to earth – and guess what? That stuff is poisonous. It gives humans that 'pioneer's' disease. All those top execs died of it after they arrived on the moon. So much for their dream.

"Look, everyone up there is eventually going to die from it. We've got the cure down here. It's your choice."

Kurt's face was drawn. He had nothing to say in return.

"OK, you don't have to decide now. Think it over. We'll always be here for you – unless you die before then. Again, our days aren't numbered. Yours are."

The Tess's all looked at one other.

"Kurt, we'll give you another chance. We're going back up and spring the trap Malia set for me. Or what she thinks I am, anyway. I'll give her the same choice I gave you. Just because she's still human somewhere inside that 'evil-bitch' persona she wears."

At that, the Tess's all nodded in sync – and phased off the planet.

VI

KURT SHOWED UP WITH only one Tess beside him in that narrow moon-base hallway.

The only other thing in that hallway was a chair with his Chandler paperback.

Then the steel cup with his implants arrived right next to his book.

A second later, the sound of heavy boots came running from both directions toward them. A dozen armed men in charcoal black uniforms on each side of the couple, carrying pulse rifles at the ready.

Kurt now had a wry smile on his face.

Tess was unconcerned. She held her hands out toward him as fists, her wrists together. "You have some special bracelets for me, I presume."

One of Kurt's men brought out some thick bracelets made out of "junk rock" and stainless steel. This were fitted tightly around her wrists. A chain of the same material attached the two bracelets together.

Another brought out a thick collar of the same material, which Kurt locked it around her neck, but gently.

When he looked into her eyes, he saw her determination.

She saw a hint of pain in his.

One squad marched off in front of them, the other squad close behind. Kurt held onto her handcuff chain as he and Tess marched in between.

Soon the echoes in that hallway died out.

• • • •

KURT BROUGHT TESS TO the throne room. Black walls, tiled floors, and pillars. Spot lights from the ceiling did little to cut the gloom.

Queen Malia sat with her legs crossed on her black throne. Dressed in goth-black dress with a v-neck almost to her waist, and a slit that exposed most of her white thigh. Her long black hair styled high on her head, cascading down her back, with only a simple tiara of white gold as crown.

Her black fingernails rested on the two arms of the throne, and a cruel smile formed at the corners of her dark lips and goth-shadowed eyes.

"The 'great' Tess is now our prisoner. And will be for the rest of her short life."

To Kurt: "Well done, Security Chief. You have our thanks."

He only nodded at her. The rest of the armed squad looked down toward the floor, so they could also keep their peripheral vision on their prisoner.

"Out of curiosity, Tess, do you have anything to say to your Queen?"

Tess looked directly at her. "I'll give you the same offer I gave Kurt. Both of you can never have kids. Both of you will die in a few years from what you call 'pioneer's disease' – painful and final. You have no cure. We do. And you can have a new life back on Earth and watch your own kids grow up.

"Or – you can stay here, try to kill me and end up killing everyone who lives on this moon colony. Sure, fly off to Saturn or wherever. You can't escape the future you created. You're already infected.

"You can, of course, keep going the route you've chosen. Just know that your days are numbered shorter than you think."

Queen Malia frowned. "You can't threaten me. I'm the only one keeping you alive right now. And I want you to see what happens when you try to run up against someone who has power and knows how to wield it."

Tess just mumbled.

Malia clicked her nails on the black stone armrest. "Something you wanted to say?"

Tess looked up at her with a glare. "First I have to run up against someone who even knows what real power is."

Malia jumped to her feet. "Take her away! NOW. Get that – that – thing out of my sight immediately!"

A trooper from each side took Tess's arms as a thick door swung opened in the wall of the throne room. They marched her through the doorway and she noted the sandwiched layers of stone in that door. It was as thick as her own head. With a small window in that door at shoulder height

Once inside the room, the troopers sat her in a green, high-backed chair made of "junk rock" and then ran green chains through her bracelets and collar. Double-checking each other's work and satisfied, they left the room and swung the heavy door behind them.

A single overhead light shown down on Tess, her red hair almost glowing against the green stone everywhere else. She looked straight ahead, towards that door and through that tiny window.

None of her tiny, cubish, multicolored lights flickered around her now.

VII

"YOU HAVE EVERYONE ELSE rounded up?"

"Yes, Your Majesty. They are in the holding rooms around the exhaust vents as you ordered."

"And the cameras are in place to watch their actions?"

"Yes, Your Majesty. You can watch the feeds from there."

I drummed one hand's black fingernails on the its throne arm rest. "Bring me the portable monitor set so I can watch."

Two technicians brought out a set of several monitors, installed on a rolling rack. They uncoiled its cables behind it with care, as these gave the monitors their feeds.

One technician offered me the remote, and I turned all of them on.

Sniveling, crying excuses for subjects. A few standing and taking it with false bravery. Thousands of people on several levels, in all the moon colony cities, all perspiring from the heat.

Right now, it felt to them like merely a hot tropical day on Earth.

When we lifted, the rising temperature would leave little but ash.

Nearly everything was set.

I turned off the view-screens and slipped the remote into the space next to my black throne cushion. This would be a lesson for all the other Royals, all the other remaining executives and their helpers, all the medical staff and technicians who had "earned" the right to accompany us to our next layover – one of Saturn's moons.

Just a few more items to ensure everyone's loyalty – because we didn't need any sloppy carryover ideas of "rights" and "freedoms" where we were going...

Moon Rebels

BY C. C. BROWER AND S. H. Marpel

. . . .

TRAPPED BY A VICIOUS self-appointed Queen, the entire slave population of the colony was imprisoned next to fusion drive exhaust ports.

When the fusion drives ignited to lift the colony off for the moons of Saturn, they'd all be turned to ash.

In all this, some still held out hope.

Because they could hear voices in their minds telling them not to be afraid, to hold on to hope.

Their guards outside only heard the countdown.

The question was whether those unseen rebels could free all these prisoners in time. Thousands of prisoners, hundreds of cells. Dozens of different locations.

The countdown had already begun - as broadcast through every space in the colony...

I

THE COUNTDOWN HAD BEEN started, and sounded through most all of the buildings and tunnels in every city in the Moon Colony.

When it reached zero, the cities would again fly under their own power, this time toward Saturn.

All of the non-essential populace had been rounded up by the Queen's orders and locked in large former storage rooms next to the fusion drive exhausts. When the fusion drives reached maximum, any materials in those rooms would be ash, most metals melted to puddles.

Right now the bulk of the population that still remained in those moon-colony cities had just over 20 minutes of life left.

According to that countdown clock.

• • • •

QUEEN MALIA HAD ASSEMBLED all the Royals of her city and all the other city's Royals that could fit into her large throne room. Standing room only.

She had large monitors set up so that everyone in that room could see what her plans were. The monitors showed the inside of those locked rooms next to the fusion drive exhausts. And also showed those exhausts.

Her speech was carefully crafted to educate all Royals as to their new place in society, and what was expected of them. For once they left the moon, it would be a streamlined population that arrived at their next port of call.

Her list of do's and don'ts was long and she was enjoying their discomfort from having to stand in their uncomfortable formal wear in the crowded space. The perfumes and scents were starting to go stale, and certain personal odors were making their appearance.

Yet no one would dare to try leaving.

That was the point of this.

The monitors showed the miserable former citizens of 'Cagga and other cities as they realized their status as slaves – where a single "sovereign" could order their mass death with no repeal.

Queen Malia was the absolute law, now.

When the counter first started at the bottom of the screen, few people noted, as it was in blue.

At 15 minutes, it turned red, and more people noted.

At 10 minutes it started flashing, and counting down the seconds as well.

The hubbub in the room became noticeable.

Queen Malia was not amused with the interruption. She paused, scowling and the room quieted.

At 5 minutes, the cameras on the fusion drive exhausts showed their exhaust start to fire, and some thought they could hear rumbling outside that room.

Shortly after that, the camera's on the locked rooms were filled with increasing amounts of static, until nothing could be seen.

At 3 minutes, there was a push toward the back to leave.

Armed guards appeared to block everyone's exit.

All that was left was to watch the screens in horror, since all the cities now had their Royals in that one room. Their own cities were taking off without them at the helm.

Yet the Queen was still calmly rattling through her new restrictions and decorum resolutions. As if nothing was happening at all.

At 2 minutes, the shouting began. Calls for her to abort the takeoff were louder than anything she could say, even through her hidden microphone.

That stopped her so that she started listening.

An assistant brought her own tablet to the Queen to show her what the other Royals were seeing.

Any orders shouted by her at this time were too late. Someone had started the engines without her order and they could not be simply shut off without exploding the units and the cities around them.

So Queen Malia did the next best thing – she walked up to her throne and buckled herself in for the actual liftoff.

The final seconds counted down.

And...

Nothing.

The clock on the monitors disappeared.

The static cleared up.

And the prisoners were gone.

II

THE REMOTE BASE WITH its tunnel from 'Cagga was filling rapidly with released prisoners. The tunnel itself was packed, but while people were hurrying, there was no panic. Those who were unable to move quickly were assisted, and even carried to keep up.

A calm extended through the entire tunnel, even to the hundreds that were still arriving at its entrance.

Gaia had been brought up earlier and cleared the tunnel of all obstructions. Now she was erecting thick walls behind the last of the populace, and reinforcing their ceilings. Betty was working to permanently shut other doors and hatches by fusing them, using her skills as an elemental.

Soon the 'Cagga population was behind several layers of sealed halls and floors.

The Control Room at the remote base was manned by Jock and his crew, and were relaying information to both Mysti and Sue of how the Queen and other Royals were reacting.

As those Royals found their way back to their own cities, they ordered a stand-down by all troops and security personnel. While they had gone along with the Queen's orders to gather all their city populations, what they had just seen on her monitors changed their minds about having any part of her plan.

Most arranged to post guards around any control panel or other access to their city's fusion drive.

Aid was being given to their citizens in the form of water and first aid. All citizens in other cities had been assembled in large areas, usually the city center. Troops were ordered to render assistance, but the only ones with weapons were posted outside the fusion controls.

In groups of 10 and 20, people were disappearing from all these city centers. About a group per second or faster.

In a very short time, the cities besides 'Cagga were noticeably vacated of citizens. As well, many former Royals, soldiers and security personnel had also disappeared with them, often leaving their uniforms behind.

· · · ·

QUEEN MALIA WAS FURIOUS. Beyond furious. Her white face, beneath all that white make-up was bright red.

Through her feed, she found out about those disappearances. And found the populace still left was celebrating in the other cities. Meanwhile, her own former imprisoned citizens couldn't be found. At last, her temper snapped. She stormed to the thick door to the cell that held Tess and had it opened.

The red-headed woman still sat there in her red/gray coveralls. Her bracelets and collar were still attached, still chained to the chair. Her eyes were looking straight ahead and a wry smile was on her lips.

Malia stormed into the room. "What have you done? Where are those prisoners? How did you do this?"

Tess didn't answer. Her smile remained unchanged. She continued to look straight ahead.

Malia strode in fast paces right up to her and slapped her on her face. Only to bruise her hand, and break several nails.

Tess didn't answer or change her face in anyway. She hadn't moved.

"SHOOT HER!" screamed Queen Malia.

A guard brought up his pulse rifle and released a single shot.

The form that they saw as Tess crumbled into green rock and dust.

· · · ·

KURT IN SECURITY CONTROL had every soul he could order out trying to find ways around the welded and stone-blocked walls.

He soon was able to discover they enclosed the long-forgotten tunnel to that remote dome.

At last, he sent his men from above into the ventilation ducts and from below upward through pipe-chases to somehow break into those rooms.

He didn't know what he was going to order when his men arrived.

He, too had watched the screens, hoping Malia was bluffing all the time. And was relieved when it had all been a show.

Still, he knew he had to act, to do something. Malia would be coming for him next. And he had no where to hide or escape to.

On the top of the control panel nearest his seat, he had the deformed bullet that those insurrection-healers had taken out of him during his short visit to Earth – the slug no one else could remove without killing him.

III

I PHASED INTO HE GRAY Earth cave-office along with my tessies in our usual quiet mode. Then sat down in the chair between Bert and the platform Old Ben the cyborg was built on.

Both were busy at their keyboards. Eyes on their screens.

Ben sensed me first, turned his head toward me, and made a throat-clearing sound for Bert.

All smiles on Bert's face as he turned my way, and put an arm out to touch my shoulder. Because a hug would be clumsy. And we all still had a lot to do right then.

"Just checking in to see how things were going. Don't let me interrupt."

"Tess, you are such a sight for sore eyes!" And Bert's own eyes were a bit misty at that. "I knew you and Betty had worked something out, but seeing you shot to pieces was a bit of a shock for everyone."

"Yeah, sorry about that. But we figured they could hear us as well as we could hear them, so Betty, Sue, Gaia, and I worked out a lot of the details off-base. We even took off all our junk rock pendants when we did."

"But how did you...?"

I smiled at Bert. "Oh, that wasn't me, that was Betty. She simply made a statue of herself in that pose – made of junk rock, but with pigments that made it look real. Pretty neat, huh? She can be quite an artist."

Bert chuckled at that. "OK, but I don't get how you can be here and everywhere at the same time. And groups of people disappearing every few seconds – how do you get all that done?"

"Remember when I was telling you about I can be in the same place and the same time – like that one stage show that I keep revisiting, only in different dresses and hairstyles?"

Bert nodded. I knew that Ben was all ears, while he kept typing away – the usual for him.

"In other words, yes, I can be everywhere at once. This particular situation is a bit extreme, so I'm getting a bit 'ever-present' but no one seems to mind. If you watch the monitors closely, you can see two or three or more of me show up at the same instance, but I'm gone just as fast. Mainly to avoid freaking people out when they see me here and there and everywhere."

"But you're here, now, talking to me while you are also all these other places."

I smiled. "It was tough for me to get over having just a linear experience as well. I took some time to sit and talk with Mysti some more. She has studied at the feet of most the great Masters, including Akashi himself." I had to smile at remembering those particular stories. "He's a complete card. Hope to meet him in person one day. Probably have to take a platter of Hami's stuffed pastries just to make it worth his while."

I was reminiscing, and lost track of my audience.

"Oh, sorry. Anyway, Mysti helped me 'grok' the concept of 'multi-phasic presences' – a term Ben will appreciate. Like I told you before, it just means being several places at the same time. Several instances of me. All with the same understandings and knowledge. All working on the same plan, and maybe knowing the earlier outcome. Just depends."

"Depends on?"

"Whether that 'me' came from 'now' or 'later'. And that is even a stretch. Mysti helped me understand that there is only really a single 'now.' You're constantly re-writing your past, and the future is only ever the various plans you are making – goals you're setting. But you're doing the setting and making them now. And comparing what you are getting with what you got before, according to what you 'remember'."

Bert sat back at that, and Old Ben quit typing. I imagine that messed with a lot of stuff on various computational levels.

"Hey, you got any coffee around here?"

Bert blinked, glanced over through the partition door. "Sure. Tish has been keeping it hot. And she's got some fried 'bear-sign' in there with honey and real butter. I think there's still some Amish jam in there, if I didn't finish it off."

I got up and moved into the larger space of the cave-office. Piled up some home-made pastries on a plate, filled a mug, then sat down to take a load off.

Bert followed me after a minute or so, bringing his own mug. And leaving the door open so Ben could eavesdrop.

Bert pulled up another chair, refilled his cup, and started a new bear-sign after he drizzled some honey on it. Good thing there were plenty of napkins.

"They aren't going to miss you out there, I guess, with all those versions of you working away."

"No. But I'm really here to catch up the overview. And all the other me's will be updated when I do."

Bert shook his head at this. "I'll still have to wrap my wits around that one. It throws a heap of my trained-in Science equations half-way out the window."

I had to smile at that image. "I guess it's better than throwing them at the wall to see what sticks."

Bert chuckled at that. So did Ben from his station behind that partition - in his modulated baritone.

I wiped my hands and lips, then finished off my coffee. Delicious. Perfect pick-me-up.

"So, Bert, once we start filling up the Lazurai compounds, we'll still have some people left over to treat."

"Sue gave me a hint of a plan for that."

And he briefed me on what she recommended might come after that point.

IV

DEEP IN THE TUNNELS, the cyborgs had slowly trundled their mining rigs up to the highest points.

Through their connection to Bert and Old Ben on Earth, they had watched the "fake news" of the broadcast, knowing that their own tunnels would already have filled with noxious gases and high-temperature fumes well before the 15-minute countdown was reached.

They were traveling at top speed, which was slightly faster than a human could walk.

Each went to their own fusion drive and tore through the conveyors and other shields that sorted the minerals and refuse fed to those drives.

First digging new tunnels through the softer ground, each made a different outlet for the gases. That forced the fumes and flames right back up to the surface beyond the city limits.

Turning around, they then began the long process of capping off the original tunnels to block those original vents.

In doing this, they were also blocking themselves in. No human would be able to get to them, either.

Yet this was as their vast parallel computing came up as the only logical answer.

· · · ·

TWO SMALLISH MEN, SQUEEZING through the air ducts one after the other, stopped suddenly.

"Do you hear that?"

"What?"

"I don't know, it sounded like a whiffle."

"A what?"

"A whiffle. Right there - did you hear that?"

"Yea. What makes a whiffle sound in an air duct?"

"Worse than that, it's something that's alive. Because..."

"Yea, I heard that other one, too. A definite burble."

Then they realized what they were saying.

> *"Beware the Jabberwock, my son!*
> *The jaws that bite, the claws that catch!*
> . . . .
> *"The Jabberwock, with eyes of flame,*
> *Came whiffling through the tulgey wood,*
> *And burbled as it came!"*

Their faces went white.

This was no bar song. The rumors were real. And the whiffles and burbles were getting louder, along with scratching on the metal ducts from claws.

They weren't waiting for the flaming eyes to appear.

There was no room to turn around for hundreds of feet, so as they backed up in a mad rate of crawling, they looked for side ducts, and tried to remember the first place where they could break through into any room below.

While they tried to keep from screaming.

The smell in those ducts was horrible. But they couldn't figure if it was from them or the Jabberwock.

• • • •

IN SECURITY CONTROL, many reports of Jabberwocks came across the intercoms.

Entire squads of men were fleeing in terror away from any possible access point from those walled off and sealed areas.

Some had barricaded themselves into storage rooms with their rifles pointed at the door, still "hearing" the creature trying to claw its way into their space.

Some injuries were reported from cross-fire. And that the lights had been flickering in those areas even though no power surges were evident in the meters.

Kurt had read about this. It was mind control like MK-Ultra. Mass hysteria.

Anyone affected simply had to be avoided, particularly if they were armed.

Nothing else could be done here.

He left only two people assigned to Control and took the others with him.

They only had sidearms and no one had more than a clip. So they headed toward the nearest arms locker, which was also toward one of the recent Jabberwock "sightings".

At each corner, they had to stop and check for other people or any creature.

Each time, Kurt felt for that bullet in his pocket. And swore to himself that when he got out of this...

V

THE APPARENT SACRIFICE of the cyborgs did not go un-noticed.

In fact, Gaia and her long-time friend, the moon goddess Luna, had several discussions about it.

Luna had been helping Gaia with shoring up the barriers to protect the humans.

And it was her idea to release the "monsters", based on what she had heard in the pub songs. Of course, the monsters were only fictions in their minds. But scenes like that were what started the phrase "lunatic", after all.

Gaia was able to contact the Earth cave-office and have them relay a request to the cyborgs through Old Ben. As part of their parallel computation setup, he shared the data and they instantly all started new tunnels – direct to intersect the original tunnel that went toward the remote dome.

Gaia and Luna both helped to clear the loose rock behind those cyborg-mining rigs, compressing it through the more porous walls and reinforcing them.

At least the cyborgs would then to be rescued when it was all over. And if the tunnel to the remote dome was breached, they could be the next line of defense so that the people in it would have time to escape.

Both Gaia and Luna had sent requests out to the solar system god known as "Sol". But as stars and suns seldom thought or acted in the short span of humans, they hadn't heard back yet.

Gaia had to brief Luna on the whole human scene on Earth when she came to help solve the first attack on the cyborgs.

Of course, Luna was very happy to have someone to hear all her stories about their obnoxious mining and their incessant lobbing of rocks and refuse back at Earth . It didn't make her happy to have humans up here to begin with. Because they never had made any effort to achieve balance with their environment.

Still, she figured they'd be gone soon, and a few well-timed moon-quakes would collapse all their mining tunnels and that would be it.

But Gaia's stories about elementals on Earth, and shape-shifting Lazurai like Betty piqued her interest.

And Gaia's own shape-shifting, in order to have personal relationships with these humans and wolves – even a sentient bear – those then gave her new ideas about how she had been living such a long time as a reclusive moon goddess.

It had been a very long time since she had been interested in doing anything on Earth. In older days, she would keep a chariot pulled by deer around there as she hunted, just to tease the young men and steal a kiss now and then.

But this set of humans were all bluff and bother. More interested in their puny fusion drives and some strange idea that they were superior to all other life forms and bound to save humanity by colonizing a moon of Saturn.

The old boy Saturn would love having some people around these days. Especially if they were going to farm one of those moons of his. So maybe that was where these humans should go. Maybe get some of his time-worn wisdom.

Of course, those humans had to arrive there first. And their problems were so ego-centric to defy even Luna's beliefs. To her mind, it was even odds that they would kill themselves all off in trying it – after all, those same humans had nearly wiped out all humanity on Earth when they left there to come to her moon.

And they just aren't cut out for space travel, anyway. Allergic to moon dust is one thing. Unable to shape-shift is another entirely. And needing specific atmosphere to breathe and a certain amount of gravity...

Betty did get a short time to pop in and visit with her, at Gaia's request, and Luna thought she was an ideal for a human if you needed one.

So in her mind, there was still hope for humans yet – if (and that's a big if) they can get past their own ego problems.

She also thought a lot of Tess. Doing all this heavy lifting. Smart girl, too. She and Saturn need to meet sometime. They have a lot in common, might even be related somehow. He was a god of time, after all. The very stuff Tess bent every day.

For now, there were other problems to solve.

Like those fusion drives. Very stupid invention. Burn everything they touch.

And those nutty humans used them as a kind of protective skin against radiation, and to hold their air in. Like anyone really needed air way out here. Like I always said, Earth is a great place to visit, but...

Gaia said she's got a plan that gets these bothersome humans back to their planet, or else. That plan has a tricky "else" clause become some of these are crazy enough (not lunatic-type crazy, but the real "queen of all they survey" type crazy) – crazy enough to go off to Saturn just to be right about their weird ideas.

And we might just have to let them...

VI

I GET THESE GREAT PLANS when I have to. Wouldn't have become Queen if I didn't.

Kurt got his guys out of that Control center and was picking up more armaments when I contacted him.

We both has figured out the insurgents had taken my prisoners over to that remote dome. Their problem was getting them all there – and would have those tunnels filled for hours at least. Even if everyone was an Olympic sprinter, that's every bit of a marathon. More than likely they'd be days getting the last ones through – if they all fit.

And then that dome would be over-full of air-breathing humans.

My idea was to use the racing yachts to bring those insurgents to their knees.

I had to find the head of that snake and cut it off. Enough was enough.

Some of Kurt's guys knew how to pilot one of these, but I actually caught a handful of those racing pilots trying to get away with some Royal babes to one of the other cities.

Meaning that gave me hostages against their good behavior.

And a lot of old mining explosives that I can turn into bombs, plus a few armor-piercing rounds that should punch a hole in that dome.

Just to get their attention.

Kurt is meeting me with those explosives and then we'll start off.

Meanwhile, I have to get my little yacht ready, plus another back-up plan on standby...

• • • •

"SUE? HOW'S THE EVACUATIONS going?"

"Bert – good to hear from you. We've got all but the hold-outs gone from six of them. Have you heard how they're dealing with all these refugees on Earth?"

"The stories I've heard say everything is maxed out. Every single Lazurai community has taken all they can, and the healers are stretched thin. Still, we've had more than a few doctors and nurses in these batches, and some pretty smart administrators, so they're coping as best they can."

"Well, here's hoping our luck keeps up. This remote base is jam-packed. Gaia has the cyborgs coming our way with additional tunnels that might be able to be converted, but she's also having to take a break every now and then just to generate more air for all these humans. The remote base wasn't built like 'Cagga, and we don't dare open anything that they could reach us through."

"Sue, have you met Luna yet?"

"She's like Gaia's sister, right?"

"Something like that – a goddess anyway. And she wants to get those other cities to evacuate into 'Cagga. That way she can snuff out their fusion drives. Oh, and Gaia could pull their air – that gives me an idea, so let Gaia know to get in touch with me soonest."

"Wouldn't it be simpler to leave them as they are?"

"Except for the die-hard close-minded ones who insist on taking their cities to Saturn so they can die out there. They can all go in one ship if we can get them rounded up."

"Point taken. Oops – gotta go...."

• • • •

"WHY AREN'T THOSE BOMBS we're dropping having any effect?"

Kurt pulled an old hand-held telescope off its decorative holder and was scanning the surface.

"You're not going to believe this."

"What?"

"There's some human standing outside looking up at us. She's acting like a spotter for someone else who's somehow shifting big columns of moon-rock right under where the bombs are going to land."

"Haven't you tried shooting her?"

"Yea, and we lost one of the yachts because of it. She just shoots right back at us. So that yacht sprung a leak and had to veer off for repairs. But the weirdest thing is that she's not wearing a space suit and doesn't seem to have any weapons on her. Almost as bad as shape-shifting wolves and that 'Jabberwock' monster that are running through the hallways back at base – at least now I've seen her."

"Kurt, I wish you wouldn't bring those up. We've got more serious things to concentrate on."

"Yes, Malia my Queen."

I had to smile at him. He knew how to soften me up like nobody else.

"We're pretty close now. Better suit up."

Kurt nodded and got into his suit. He had the armor-piercing rifle, and it was massive. He was going to have to stick out quite a bit of that rifle from that air-lock.

The trick for me was flying this rig sideways so that spotter on the ground wouldn't see his rifle until it was too late.

The hole it can make isn't that big – a couple of bodies sucked up next to it would tend to seal it – but the point is that we can also aim at their air supply equipment, other life support, or somewhere else that would be even worse.

Meanwhile, the other yachts are still trying to get their bombs into that tunnel. Hopefully, ours just looks like it's barely flying and is damaged somehow.

Just minutes now...

· · · ·

I SAW THE SHOT, BUT it was also when they had three bombs coming down at once.

Good thing Luna had come to help out.

We got the bombs defended, and then Luna got tired of playing defense. She sent some high-powered crystals flying up there that made them all veer off, like they just got poked somewhere they shouldn't have.

The only one left was that one over the dome – the one that just shot at it.

Gaia started putting a huge wall up to prevent any further shot damage, and then Luna got into action and slid a crystal sheath underneath her wall. It went liquid when it hit that escaping air and froze solid as a plug.

Of course that ship's action got me a bit ticked off, so I sucked in some rocks through my feet and launched a little home-made pressure-powered rocket at them. Tipped it with some potassium permanganate with water crystals barely separated by a thin layer of aluminum. Got it to land near their viewport, so the explosive burn didn't help their eyes any. Doubt if it burned through anything to hurt them. Just made a point.

They veered off a ways, but still have that gun sticking out a hatch on their far side.

Gaia and Luna are still building that extra dome layer, but that means that we also can't get any ship in or out of that dome through those locks.

We don't know how much air that little yacht has, but as long as it stays out there, it can't do anything to us, but we also can't do anything to it.

Siege tactics.

They'd need a kamikaze suicide run to break it – which would be a desperate act, unless they run out of air, or fuel, or patience.

VII

I CALLED THE REMOTE dome, on a channel I knew they were listening to.

"Get me Sue Reginald."

"Who's calling?"

"The Queen of the Moon Colony."

"Oh – you. A bit pretentious, still?"

"Like that pretentious hole we just punched in your dome."

"And that was really effective. Why don't you just take your toys and go home?"

"Oh, I might at that. I've got a rather big "toy" over there which is ready to fire up and tear 'Cagga right off the moon's surface. Too bad it will also tear a huge hole in that tunnel full of people that you have."

Sue sighed. "OK, what is it that you want?"

"I know you're still moving people around. You come up, alone. We'll talk. Any funny business and I crash this yacht right into your dome and that's the end for both of us."

Silence on the other end.

"You already know I'm crazy enough to do it – now is your chance to find out. I'll give you 10 seconds to decide."

More silence.

"5...4...3..."

"OK. Had to find my transporter. Be there in a second – or two."

Sue appeared and Kurt disappeared. Just about that fast.

She had her hands out. Her long wavy blond hair was tied back and she wore a red/gray jumpsuit like Tess's.

"So Kurt wasn't seeing things when he said he saw four Tess's. You were one of them."

"Go to the head of the class. You still don't know if the rest were actual Tess's or not."

"You may have me there. But I figure not – since that tunnel and the dome are still chock full of people right now."

"Until you came around, it was still better than you trying to burn them alive in 'Cagga."

"That wasn't really the plan, but you'll never know now."

I punched in a course for my private dock on 'Cagga and pulled out a small pulse pistol to point at Sue as I did.

"Coward."

"Don't piss me off, Sue. I've already had it up to here. Why you have to wreck everything I planned is, well, unfortunate. For you, any way. Here."

I threw a set of handcuffs toward her.

"Lock yourself onto that railing. We have a bit of a trip to make before we land again. Yes, I have the key, but I'm sitting down here with this gun. Once you put on the handcuffs, I'll put down the gun. If you try shifting to get out of those cuffs, I'll shoot a hole in whatever form you take."

She clicked the handcuffs home, and then sat on the cold deck. The same one I was feeling through my black overalls.

VIII

YES, IT WAS A BORING ride. I had to listen to her grand plans for glorious conquest of all known space.

I just sat there and tried to look interested. Nodded a few times, smiled at the few pathetic jokes she tried to crack.

Put up with her horrible ideas of what fashion was. Almost laughed when she cut herself with her own fingernail, and then couldn't put that finger in her mouth because it would cut her again.

Stupid is as stupid does.

Finally we made port and she got us docked without killing both of us. Seems she was used to a lot of extra people around to moor the ship for her. I was no help, of course, as I was cuffed to the railing inside.

My shrugs infuriated her.

She put more than one dent in her precious yacht before she got the magnetic-lock couplings to hold. Something we "down-belows" all learned as tiny children – because the emergency escape pods all had those couplings. And getting the pods all interlinked was a much better way to survive disaster than by your lonesome.

Stuck-up rich kids don't have to take that training seriously when their lives don't depend on it.

Lucky for her that ship-sized lock was automated to close once her mag-locks finally set.

"OK, here's the key." She threw it to me neatly. "I'll be outside waiting for you."

I unlocked the cuffs and threw them to the far end of the yacht with the key into the opposite forward end, hoping it wound up in some crack.

Then I came out.

"Where's the cuffs?"

"Inside. You never said anything about bringing them."

Yes, this made her little over-powdered white face wrinkle. Still, I was right. She needed me for something or I would already be dead. But I also knew my guys knew where I was and was getting all of this in stereo 3D.

My little pendant was hanging down inside my red/gray overalls. And I had one of Dad's safety bracelets on one wrist and another on an ankle inside its boot. A gal can't take too many precautions.

Malia waved the gun, and I took it that she meant me to climb up one of the many short ladders so we'd get out of this little ship-lock.

But the weirdest thing I saw was when I walked by her.

The gun's safety was still on.

• • • •

BY THE TIME WE'D WALKED up to my throne room, I'd gone through several different ideas on how I wanted to kill her. Blunt trauma came first – how many times would it take to beat her with this gun? But I figured my arm would tire out first.

Then it was taking her by a weapons locker, but none were on our path.

Of course, I could simply slice her neck until I got one of her carotid's. But the sight of blood makes me squeamish.

I knew where Kurt had another set of handcuffs – a bit personal perhaps – but I could get to them if I had to. I still had the gun, after all.

So we got to the throne room, I locked the door behind us, and then went up to my throne to sit down.

A touch of a recessed button slid out a control panel. Flicking a few switches, a rumbling started below us. A count-down started. About 15 minutes before ignition.

"What did you just do?"

"Curious, are we?"

"This is your private little escape pod?"

"With just enough fuel to get us to Saturn. And by then, you'll be dead unless you decide to be my subject and servant for here on out."

"Do you think it's that easy?"

"Sure. Otherwise, I've got a few dozen ways to kill you. Slow or fast, painful or quick. All my choice."

"And I suppose you are also killing a lot of people by taking off in this teeny escape pod of yours?"

I just looked to the ceiling. "Oh, if you call those slaves people, then yes – about twenty or thirty – dozen." Then looked back at her to see her reaction.

Only she wasn't there.

I stood up. She wasn't in the throne room.

I ran over to Tess's cel. Just the dust and rock next to the chains and cuffs.

Then the gun was knocked out of my hand, and a foot swung back in front of my legs while a shove pushed me face down to the green tiled floor.

A knee landed with a huge weight on my back, knocked the air out of my lungs, and next my arms were pulled behind my back with the chains and cuffs tight on them.

My mouth and nose were bleeding, I had green junk rock dust all over my face, and my eyes were stinging.

So I did all I could do.

I started crying.

IX

ONCE THE THRONE ROOM was cleared, I brought Betty here and we started going through everything. Everything. When we found a door to any hallway that went anywhere away from the throne room, Betty fused it shut.

Including any "secret panels" we could find.

We left access to Malia's private quarters, her office, and her eavesdropping control center.

At this point, we didn't care if Security knew what happened in here. They couldn't come in without permission – and someone would need to phase them inside here.

Out of curiosity, we opened different cabinets and drawers – and left them open if it would be something embarrassing or revealing about Malia. Meaning hard data files or report print-outs, not her frilly underthings or "special equipment".

Betty took a large manual, apparently an index of her blackmail storage, and also a tablet to start going through these. Sitting on the throne, with one leg over an arm, Her red/gray overalls finally brought some needed contrast to the room.

Once she settled in, I did change the décor. I recalled a storage room where there were various throw rugs rolled up and brought these in. All sorts of grays, reds, greens, yellows. And as many of the Royal signets from the cities as I could find. A few flags that said anything except "queen."

Betty saw these improvements, changed the cushions on the throne to a bright gold, then went back to her studies.

I meanwhile got busy bringing the Royal heads of the other cities back in.

• • • •

AS EACH LITTLE GROUP arrived, right in front of Betty and her relaxed studies on the throne, she briefed them on where they could find all of Malia's 'goods' on everyone. But only cautioned them to not try to erase anything they found. They and their wives and consorts hurried off to pry into everything they could.

Meanwhile, I kept finding more Royals and bringing them in, along with any still-loyal administrators and engineers.

When I found some padded benches, I brought those in as well.

Once I got everyone accounted for, I brought in a long buffet table and then made a run to Hami's saloon so she could load me up with finger food and punch to fill it from end to end.

The last thing I brought was a stack of thin books that filled that low side table near the throne.

• • • •

"ROYALS, AND EVERYONE else. Can I have your attention?" Betty was standing in front of the throne.

Everyone else was back into the main throne room now, sampling the food while discussing and gossiping about what they found.

"Malia has had an 'accident' and won't be with us for quite awhile.

"I understand that she only got her position by your votes. But those votes weren't necessarily given without duress."

Betty looked around the room and saw the benches littered books and tablets that had been brought out and studied. As well, some tied bundles that a few of the Royal's wives and sisters had at their side or near their feet, including some in black pillowcases. Spoils of war, no doubt.

"Of course, everything here has been made available to all of you. And now you know all of her blackmail that she was holding." She looked pointedly at a few men who now had black eye's, and women whose gowns had been torn and their hair mussed.

"I do hope you can all forgive each other for being very human."

Several reluctant nods were returned at this statement.

"The point is that you all have a choice to make now. In fact, you have a lot of decisions to make.

"The people in this room are going to wind up one of three places – you'll return to Earth, stay on this moon, or go onto one of Saturn's moons with Malia.

"But that's not my concern. Today, you need to decide which camp you belong in. And how you are going to govern yourself from here on out.

"What you saw on that video earlier today was what Malia had planned. Her absolute power corrupted her to an absolute level of inhumanity. And would have killed tens or hundreds of thousands just to get her way.

"But fortune smiled, and she lost. And lost her power over you all."

Betty stepped down off the dais and picked up one of the small books on the side table.

"You're all going to stay in this room until you decide two things: what group you're going to join, and how you are going to act after this point.

"In this small book are some suggestions you may want to look over. Inside are the Declaration of Independence and the U. S. Constitution – two documents that have produced more change in the world and its governments than any other in history. Before or since. And have been copied by most developing countries afterwards as well.

"Also included are the other key documents that these 'Founders' used to make devise this: the Code of Hammurabi, the Magna Carta, the original Old Testament Commandments, and the New Testament Beatitudes. Plus a few others.

"This point is to give you the tools to make your own decisions. And you have access to the 'Cagga libraries from here for anything else you need. But there is no one out there to talk to, and no one to come and rescue you.

"Tess will be checking in on you from time to time. And will take anyone who simply wants to return to Earth immediately there. The rest will be released when the transport to Saturn is ready.

"You have plenty of food and drink here, as well as Malia's numerous beds, couches and the benches in this room.

"Everyone who wants to leave for Earth now can follow me."

Betty walked to the back of the throne room where Tess was standing. A small handful of people followed her, regardless of the scowls and head-shaking that others made on their way.

Once assembled, they all left.

And left the rest of the Royals to their own decision-making.

X

THE NEXT THING I REMEMBERED was waking up and seeing red.

At first, I thought it was blood from my nose. But then I rolled over and found it was just a very long gown of some sort.

My wrists were no longer chained. My face hurt, but wasn't bleeding any more.

But some fool had dressed me in red. My fingernails were red, too – trimmed short and filed dull.

It was a weird outfit that was too fluffy for words. And I was wearing something underneath. Bloomers! And a petticoat as well as some hoops – hoops, of all things – to make my dress stick out and bounce. Beyond them, I had red hose going down to fit into square-toed red shoes that tied to one side toward the ankle.

As much as I tried, I couldn't get at the buttons in the back of my dress to get the darn thing off. Not even my shoes, as I couldn't get by the hoops. Not without some lady-in-waiting – who weren't around, of course.

With all that work, I even started perspiring.

Trying to wipe my forehead on my long red sleeve, I bumped up against something solid on my head. A ring of it. With two hands, I removed it – a great red, glossy crown. No jewels, just great spikes of red and a big round ball on top.

Not funny, people.

Someone was going to pay for this.

Black. I'm the black queen – not a red one.

Then it hit me. I wasn't in 'Cagga anymore.

Alice in the Moon

BY C. C. BROWER & S. H. Marpel

• • • •

I WAS QUEEN OF THE World. Until I wasn't. One moment I was in chains and bleeding, the next I was fine - but dressed in red.

Someone had played a dirty trick on me. They'd dressed me in a red cartoon outfit - like a Queen. But not my usual goth black.

And I also couldn't get out of it. Buttons too high on my back. Hoops and petticoats I couldn't reach under to get free of.

Someone was going to pay for this.

That little Sue Reginald was the last person I'd seen. And here she comes now.

Are you kidding me? She's got a baby-blue fluffy dress, white apron, red sash around her middle, a blue ribbon in her blond hair - where have I seen that?

NO. We're in Looking-glass Land! Like I said - somebody's going to pay...

I

I RAN AT SUE TO KNOCK her down.

Or tried to, anyway.

These hoops and petticoats made running extremely difficult. I had to use both hands to hold them up away from my feet front and back. But those hands were the ones I wanted around Sue's throat.

Nobody, but nobody ever treated me this way.

On top of that, she was uphill from me, and it was all grassy. My flat, squared-off shoes didn't have much tread to them that I could tell, and the grass juice made things slick real fast.

Sue was just standing there, with the light wind swishing her fluffy blue dress and white apron. Her long, wavy, blond hair was somehow keeping out of her eyes – that blue satin ribbon was doing the trick. Like that red sash around her waist kept her dress and apron from billowing.

But her smile was the most irritating of all.

As ticked off as she made me, my top speed – with all this buffoon-wear I was lugging around – ended up only as a fast walk.

Not that any of this helped my temper. But the amount of work it took to get that fast walk left me out of breath and sweaty.

Sue just watched from up there with her innocent smile.

But I was determined.

I slogged on as I could, while she just waited.

At last I was within arm's reach and she simply stepped out of the way – and tripped me.

Flat on my face. Again.

At least this time she didn't put her knee into my back and chain my arms together. And I didn't get any split lip or bloody nose.

Soft grass is better than landing on hard, tiled floor.

Rolling over is easier in hoops, though.

I first saw Sue's face again, now holding a more concerned look than trying to rub salt in the emotional wounds I had. All I could do was to just get my elbows up underneath me and look back at her.

"Why'd you have to trip me?"

"Because it was a quick way of ending your silly parade. You'd have to catch your breath that way and think things over."

She was right about that. This meant a lot more strategy.

"Well? Aren't you going to help me up?"

"I don't think so. Not because it isn't the polite thing to do, but you really haven't cooled off yet. You'd just pull me down on you somehow and we'd wrestle around on this grass until I hurt you again. Meanwhile, I'd get grass stains on this pretty dress."

So, she saw through that tactic.

"If you want to get up in hoops, you have to act like a lady and quit your attempts to get revenge for imagined slights. You have to do some sort of curtsy. Or – quit even trying to be a lady and use your hands and knees and elbows. It's a kind of ugly squat motion, where your butt goes high into the air."

I glared at her.

"Well, it's getting hot here. I'm going over to the swing under that shady tree and wait for you. Good luck."

And I watched her almost skip across the hillside, swishing her skirt as if she was enjoying having that long skirt and fluffy petticoats on.

Yes, it was ugly, embarrassing, and it worked. Took a few tries, but I finally got it right. Windmilling my arms, I eventually got my balance again.

These hoops had to come off. That was the real strategy.

Instead of walking toward her, I looked around. And curtsied to picked up my red, glossy crown off the grass.

Red Queen, huh?

Turning around, I then saw the checkerboard layout. Tiny little brooks running straight across the flat pastures at the bottom of the hill. On the other side of the hill from the one I climbed up. And little green hedges that ran from brook to brook. Mostly they had a few trees – willows and birches, it looked like – on the banks of those brooks.

Yea, this was Looking glass country. Weird.

• • • •

"DOING BETTER NOW?" Sue came up behind me while I was checking things out. But she stayed a few arm-lengths away. Smart.

"Yes, no thanks to you. And just for your information, I did get some grass stains on my pantaloons."

"Maybe you should practice keeping your temper in check."

I just mimicked her gestures and mouthed the words back at her. Tempted to stick out my tongue. But I didn't.

So my recollection says that there are a bunch of different characters down there in the book. I looked, and sure enough, there were.

"Hey, Sue, if we're starting from here, then there should be a bunch of red pawns around."

As I said that, I spotted them, peeping out from behind bushes at me. Trying to not get me angry at them.

Of course, they were way down the hill, and I'd learned about trying to run in these things. But I had an idea how to get them to help me get rid of these hoops.

So I brushed my hair back and settled my red crown back in place – straight. Then assumed a regal air (that didn't take long, after the practice I'd had when I was Queen Malia of the Moon) and carefully minced my way down that hill like I owned time itself and them as well.

Those pawns just watched. And waited. And waited.

• • • •

WHAT MALIA WAS UP TO was no good. I knew that much. But you had to admit, she did a good Queen walk when she needed to. That gown was going to need some cleaning at some point. Grass stains on more places than she knew.

Once she got down to where the pawns were, she lured them over and had them huddle to hear what she said. The looks on their faces were priceless. One or two of them at a time would look around to see if any other pieces were near by.

Then they surrounded her and escorted her to a thick set of bushes on one side.

I couldn't hear much from here, but there was some laughter and giggles.

My curiosity started me down the hill, at an easy pace. I had an idea I didn't want to see what was happening behind those bushes. So I took my time.

At last the pawns came out, adjusting their uniforms. A few had pieces of her hoops, rolling them along the ground like an antique toy, guiding them with sticks. Others had some soft, fluffy pieces of something they were wiping their faces with. I could see some red spots on some of them – lipstick?

One came out without his uniform jacket, another without his trousers, but carrying a large wad of red material in both arms.

Malia came out at long last, buttoning up a uniform jacket over her bare front, just half way up. She'd managed to get the trousers and suspenders on properly, anyway.

One last pawn was tucking in his mis-buttoned shirt and holding onto her crown meanwhile. I really didn't want to know what he'd given up to get that.

Malia stopped and waited for the young man to catch up. Then wrapped her arms around him and gave him a big kiss. pinched his rear end.

He was all smiles and ran to catch up with the others.

I was within calling distance by then.

Malia was all smiles again. "So there, now the Queen's a pawn and we can get this party rolling!"

I just shook my head. "Still up to your old tricks again?"

She grinned back at me. "All I asked them is if they wanted to see what was under a queen's gown – just a little peek. And they all did."

• • • •

"NOW I CAN GET MY HANDS on you. And wrap these legs to squeeze the life out of you.

"Wolf or eagle?" Sue shifted to a white buckskin dress. Tight moccasins over bare feet. Her knees were slightly bent, weight on the balls of her feet – which themselves had shifted out to her shoulder's width. And her hands flared out from her side almost as claws, ready for anything.

I hesitated.

"Or – I've been wanting to try a Grizzly momma for some time now. That would be a real treat."

"I could outrun a Grizzly..."

"But not a wolf, or a cougar."

At that, I unclenched my fists and relaxed my shoulders.

"OK, I guess that means we are just talking then."

"Good girl. Always a smart one."

"So? Why all this? This charade you've set up?"

"No, this is very real. You could die in here, just like anywhere else. But the reason we are here is to find out about you."

"Like you haven't already read all my files."

"Those don't tell what's inside."

"Like you need to x-ray me or study me with your green junk rock scanners?"

"Come on, Malia. Quit acting stupid. Or we could just start with my shifting and you running. I'm easy either way."

"You want to know something – personal. And not just my real hair color."

"I want to know if you are bat-shine crazy or just playing that stupid. And I can only find out by taking you through this. In short, I want to know if you are still human enough to be worth saving."

That stopped me cold. This chick really meant what she was saying. To her, I was not much more than a threat to all humanity and all sentient species on earth. She could hunt and kill me as a wolf and have no real problem with it. Not much anyway.

I'd way underestimated this Sue Reginald.

My eyes opened wide at that, and then closed to a squint.

So – let the games begin.

• • • •

...they walked on in silence till they got to the top of the little hill.

For some minutes Alice stood without speaking, looking out in all directions over the country—and a most curious country it was.

'I declare it's marked out just like a large chessboard!' Alice said at last. 'It's a great huge game of chess that's being played—all over the world—if this IS the world at all, you know. Oh, what fun it is! How I WISH I was one of them! I wouldn't mind being a Pawn, if only I might join—though of course I should LIKE to be a Queen, best.'

She glanced rather shyly at the real Queen as she said this, but her companion only smiled pleasantly, and said, 'That's easily managed. You can be the White Queen's Pawn, if you like, as you're in the Second Square to begin with: when you get to the Eighth Square you'll be a Queen —'

So Alice ran down the hill and jumped over the first of the six little brooks.

II

*"A pawn goes two squares in its first move, you know. So you'll go
VERY quickly through the Third Square—by railway, I should
think—and you'll find yourself in the Fourth Square in no time."*

• • • •

WE WERE ALL IN AN UNDERGROUND bunker in old 'Cagga.
Me and a crowd of people I didn't know. Not the most comfortable
place to ride inside a fusion-drive powered, force-field protected,
hemispherical section of city – that was burning more fuel per second
than several of their biggest Soyuz rockets all together Like they were just
child's play, Tinker-toy's, Lego blocks, take your choice.

Not that it was comfortable. A big room in some basement of an old
government building. If you looked closely, you could see the signs of the
old Nuclear Fallout Shelter campaigns from the 50's. Painted over, but
the outlines were still there. It wasn't dirty, though. It had been used as a
community room for local meetings, so had been kept up.

No windows, thick walls, hard tile floor. Even with the shaking and
the concrete dust coming down from the ceiling, it was still more
reassuring to be down here than up in those multi-story high-rises that
were swaying and rattling.

Most of the people down here were common. Hardly any had an
education beyond the free public schools. If they got some technical
training, it was for a certificate or maybe a two-year degree in a specialist
field, like robotics or construction. You could tell it in how they were
dressed, how they clung to each other, the religion they spouted. I didn't
see any guns down here, but there were probably some around.

The problem, as I saw it, was riding coach instead of the executive
suite. Not that I didn't have at least half the genes to be riding up there.
Just not the papers that said I really owned them. Only my dad had the
papers, and it was only because of him that I was flying out in this piece
of 'Cagga at all.

To the ones I didn't know, I was a stranger to them, and so wasn't trusted much. To the ones who did know of me and my background, I wasn't trusted – as I should have been riding with the elites. So something must be wrong with me.

I just sat by myself, with my little black duffel bag – all I could carry and cared for. A journal for notes, some food bars, a refillable water container, necessary change of skivvies, and my Wednesday Addams doll – the only toy I've kept of the thousands given me by my dad.

Those were the valuable things in my life. Mostly that journal, where I wrote down other's secrets. My Wednesday doll I shared my secrets with, but only in private, and never written down for someone else to find.

It was going to be a while before we reached stable orbit around the Earth, and this right now was the worst part.

I wasn't too concerned. If anything out of this went wrong, we'd all be dead pretty quick, so I was betting on things going very right. Had to. I might be grim about a lot of things in life, but I'd still rather live – regardless of what I had to do to get there.

This little inconvenience I just took as a learning experience.

Some of the kids would look at me, and I'd return their curiosity with my usual scowl. Then they'd look away like I'd done something bad to them. So I learned a lot about human behavior in those hours of enduring all the shaking and breathing that ceiling dust.

• • • •

I DIDN'T KNOW MY MOM, much. We were in and out of various places while I was small, some great palaces, and some dives. But I just learned to accept whatever happened. And I'd paste on a happy face when I was supposed to.

When I became of age to go to public school, my dad put me in a private one. And so I seldom saw my mom after that. Just on holidays, and I'd compare how she was dressed and acted with the other times. My dad would often take me on holiday, sometimes referring to me as a "guest of his daughter". Not that I minded.

His daughter was OK, but I more liked roaming around the big empty places he lived in and listening to the conversations around me, so I could write them down later. Even if I was hearing their talk through a closed door.

One day, when I was close to graduating the last of my many prep schools, I was taken out of class, brought to one of my dad's huge homes, dressed in black, and then driven to a graveyard to see the new tombstone of my mother. So that was the last time I saw her.

The rumors said it was something to do with a drug habit she couldn't kick. I really thought it was more to do with life-choices like the ones that raised a kid for her instead of with her.

And I got so many compliments on my dress, as it matched my natural black hair, I settled on that look. Like my Wednesday doll, just not the braids. Because boys liked long, loose hair – for some reason. They pulled on braids.

• • • •

ALL THESE HOURS IN flight gave me a lot of time to think. Sitting alone, while everyone else was scrunched into little family-and-friends groups.

And if there was talk, it was just meaningless chatter.

Occasionally, I'd hear my dad's name mentioned, Bezarberg. How they hoped all the private secrets he's stolen to fund his rockets were going to be worth it to them.

Like they didn't ask to be brought along on this trip to the moon.

They could have voted with their feet at any time. Meaning: tacit consent rules. Sure, I'd heard the old arguments over and over. A safe, secure place to raise a family was more important than personal success.

My dad was the exception to that rule. He made his own world – social media and ecommerce. All made up, based on what other people loved to suck themselves into. Plastic friends, immediate gratification.

Any electives I took were either coding or marketing. And so many people would say I was taking after my dad. Like hell. If he could do it, I could do it. Or at least ride his coat tails until I had my split of his action.

Even if I wasn't "really" his daughter.

· · · ·

THE RUMBLING STOPPED. The big heavy doors opened in series.

We couldn't see through the fusion-powered shield that kept our air in and the radiation out, but on monitors, they showed the beauty of space, and the cloudy chem-trailed Earth below us.

One video, that I never saw repeated, was that of our violent launch itself.

You could see several shots of where other cities rose nearly straight up like ourselves. And also several mushroom clouds where cities like D. C. and Moscow and several Chinese cities didn't.

Later, I figured that the high fail rates all had a government center as their major business. All the cities with financial centers in them made it.

Mostly the coastal cities.

Some of the "lucky" failed takeoffs just sat right back down and their shields collapsed without imploding. But their fusion drives usually did – because their exhaust collapsed. Only shutting down (failure) of that fusion drive before it crashed back to earth prevented implosion, and the subsequent explosion.

Of course, that was a peripheral study. They took their choices. And their populations went along with them.

The PR was that we were leaving Earth so that it could heal from all the global warming we were creating. I knew it was because my dad and the rest of the Corporation heads knew that following this dream meant they could finally get rid of pesky government interference from all the Flyover people, their elected representatives, and their deplorable attitudes.

Meaning: taxes.

Less overhead meant more profit.

I just did these studies to learn how to get ahead. To get my fair share. And unless I had to be "happy" for someone, I went about it with a no-nonsense attitude. Like my Wednesday doll.

· · · ·

WHEN MALIA OPENED HER eyes, Sue was sitting there in her white doeskin, leaning to one side, with her legs bent at the knee and her feet giving support. That dress covered her knees, but not her tanned calves below it.

One of Sue's arms was holding her upright, while the other held a bunch of wild flowers she'd just picked.

"What are you looking at?" Malia asked.

"Who else but you – or were you just being rhetorical?"

Malia had her knees up under her chin, in the borrowed red trousers the pawn had traded to her, and the red jacket sleeves (from another pawn) covered her arms that hugged those knees to her chest.

Very much, it seemed to her, like how she had spent her time in that Fallout Shelter basement room. Or the times when she was alone in those big houses, and sat in the middle of the big bed in the big bedroom they'd assigned her – the times where she wanted to just think things through.

At that memory, she struggled to her feet. Looking around, Malia saw that now she was in the third square of the pastoral checkerboard.

"I think we are supposed to cross a brook to get to the next square now. Isn't that how this Looking-glass world works?"

Sue also got to her feet now, and just nodded. Sadness on her face at the memories Malia had shared with her. Wordless – as anything she said would just be twisted.

Still, she thought, at least Malia wasn't trying to kill her now.

She followed as Malia jumped across a brook, finding a narrow road on the other side.

III

"Well, THAT square belongs to Tweedledum and Tweedledee—"

• • • •

"Tweedledum and Tweedledee
Agreed to have a battle;
For Tweedledum said Tweedledee
Had spoiled his nice new rattle.
Just then flew down a monstrous crow,
As black as a tar-barrel;
Which frightened both the heroes so,
They quite forgot their quarrel."

• • • •

THE BAR WAS PACKED with young and wanna-be-young, listening to the loud music, nearly blinded by the flashing lights, and trying to be heard over it while they squinted at each other.

Whenever they weren't trying to emulate the contortions of the "latest" dance moves – which seemed to change from week to week.

Malia had a drink nearby, with a tiny parasol in it and a thin straw. But it was mostly untouched.

She was here to study people, to find people, and to find their secrets. Everyone had secrets. They also knew someone who knew someone. By working out who was pulling the strings, and what strings pulled them – that was the key to her success.

Her short black knit one-piece draped across her top, the high split front helped her flash her shapely legs. Thin black hose covering those tended to make boys wonder as they eye-traced her legs up to where her skirt started.

Long sheer sleeves continued to make the boys wonder, while keeping her paste-white flesh from being accentuated in the black-light strobes.

Meaning, she could stay to the background to do her behavioral studies, or selectively come out to claim her prey for that evening's specific homework.

Tonight, she had a problem. Because two boys had gotten her attention, and were both coming back and forth with more drinks for her. While trying to find something interesting to talk about.

One, a security guard named Kurt, was someone to string along so she could find out where the secrets were hidden in this city.

The other, an engineer called Jock, knew how everything worked, and where the blind spots in the cameras were.

So she was torn, and wanted them both.

The more she knew, the more she could figure out.

And her solution was to see them both – later.

Each of their disappointed faces she turned around with a simple kiss – one that the other boy didn't see. She made herself intriguing to both of them. On purpose.

• • • •

KURT WAS FIRST, BECAUSE he was a boy scout. He wouldn't do anything on a first date – and that was perfect. She could pry out things from him for a long time without him suspecting anything. He just needed to know that he was important in the scheme of things.

It helped that he knew who her dad was, and how she was part of the Elites – or (as they started to call themselves) the Royals. For Kurt to be able to rub elbows with them would forward his own career. Malia didn't mind being used as long as she got her own fair share meanwhile.

So a light kiss and a promise, then Kurt was gone for the night – having to be up early the next day, he said. And Malia figured he was telling the truth, as he'd already told her how the shifts were set up, and how their time off was scheduled.

As he left her, he straightened his shoulders and lengthened his pace. His head showed that he was sweeping the perimeter as he went, a habit of his security training.

Malia also noted that his pants had no back pockets to distort her view.

Jock was the second, and limited in what he knew. So she got the most vital data out of him first. A tour of all the places where cameras couldn't record a kiss – or worse. And every time Jock showed her a new location, he got rewarded with another kiss.

And when his hands started getting a bit too frisky, she managed to get a 'rain-check' on learning the rest of them.

When he left her in a camera-less area close to her apartment, she knew he was probably going back to that first bar or another – just to get some relief from the pressure her teasing had started.

She had other work for that evening. Writing down all this data from each of them – in code – in her journal.

• • • •

SINCE SHE KEPT MEETING them at the same club, it wasn't long before they found out about their mutual 'love'-interest.

To each, she explained that it was a strictly fraternal relationship – as they reminded her of a brother she never had, but always wanted. And they were teaching her so many useful things... (A bat of the eyes and a close hug would get them to forget about that other guy for awhile.)

One night, the two of them wound up drinking next to each other.

Words became sharp and then an accidental shove became a punch and a bar fight.

The bouncer got them both out of there in one piece, other than a few bruises. The manager wanted them to work out their differences outside, since their business was welcome there otherwise. (Having a security guard and an engineer coming back time and again would ensure his establishment would keep running smoothly and legally. So he told them separately.)

Kurt and Jock warily approached each other, trying to resolve their differences to make the manager happy and keep giving them the occasional free drink.

That discussion wound up leaving them at least as amicable acquaintances.

While they were both interested in me, they saw that they had different interests. To each other, as long as I was giving them what they wanted, they only had to date me on different nights – and consider, that on the long game, it would work out in the end.

They compared schedules, made notes, and organized things so each of them would stay out of the other's way.

All below the lit neon sign that hung above the doorway to that club: The Black Crow.

• • • •

"AND JOCK YOU FINALLY 'disappeared', while Kurt you strung along right up to the end." Sue was wrinkling her forehead, more trying to keep things straight rather than criticize Malia.

Malia just nodded. "Jock was getting a bit too physical and possessive, and had a limited amount of useful data. Kurt and I were able to use each other. We each were in the business of accumulating useful data. That we also had physical needs just assisted that interaction.

"Does that somehow go back to your dad and mom – their own relationship?"

"Maybe. But in those, they differed, because I was the 'data' they were sharing. My mom just lost control of her end of that bargain. What else she got for her agreement, I never found out."

Sue just nodded and looked down. She held her thoughts to herself, as she digested what Malia had shared with her.

The two young women were walking in their pastoral square. The blue sky with wispy clouds made the sun hazy on a temperate day. Story-book weather.

"One thing I did discover about my parents. They each had a black crow tattooed in a private area that never showed in any photograph.

While I'd seen my mom's one day when she had to change clothes in front of me, she only explained it as my dad 'liked crows'. His crow I only saw on his deathbed, when the nurse was changing the tubes that kept him alive."

IV

"...the Fifth is mostly water—"

• • • •

MALIA AND SUE APPROACHED the next brook, and saw a white shawl flying through the air.

Malia was soon more wrapped in it than caught it. The sudden gust had blown dust into her eyes and then the shawl followed, almost covering her head.

Sue thought this sight amusing, since the former Queen Malia was now just as subject to the vagaries of Nature as she was. And yet, things tend to happen for a reason..

Malia grabbed at the shawl and looked around to see who'd thrown it.

A woman wearing an outfit similar to Malia's original – only white instead of red – came stepping quickly toward them while holding up her dress and hoops. "Oh, at last you've caught it! I am so relieved."

Sue said aside to Malia, "Aren't you glad your face was in the way?"

Malia frowned and handed the shawl to the White Queen.

Sue, knowing what was about to happen, carefully arranged the shawl and pinned it with an unclasped broach on the Queen's shoulder.

"There. Now please don't worry about this now. I understand you have a shop? My friend here is looking for some thing else to wear, perhaps a bit darker shade?"

"Yes, please follow me and we'll see if you can't both find something useful or even just pretty."

The White Queen crossed the brook and the two young women followed her.

• • • •

IN SOME WAY THAT WASN'T explained, they found themselves in a shop. Long shelves that went from nearly the bottom right up to the ceiling. And rows that stretched from the front to the back.

Malia looked through the shelves for clothing, but found only knick-knacks and odd things. And all the black items were on a shelf just above her reach, but when she got a step stool or ladder, they were always on a shelf higher than her arms and legs could take her.

It was one particular item that she kept trying to find, as it would disappear and then reappear. A glass bottle with a tiny one-person sailing sloop in it. Corked and with it's own stand.

By pretending to not look for it, she found that it would show up in her peripheral vision. So she worked at finding other things farther away from her to get it to show up closer to her.

At last, after racing about the store, back and forth, she finally reached back quickly off a ladder and just barely grasped the long neck of that bottle – only to then lose her balance and fall backward off the ladder...

• • • •

TO FIND HERSELF TREADING water next to a small black sailing boat. Her red life jacket was securely around her torso, and a red rope was tied around her waist, going back to inside the boat somewhere.

Using the rope and her legs inside the wet and clingy red trousers, she managed to pull herself back on board.

The boat had no cabin, and only a single mast. The main sail was luffing in the wind on its boom, as they were now headed directly into the wind.

"You didn't watch the boom when you jibed."

That voice came from that same White Queen, who sat in the fore of the boat, just ahead of the mast. She was knitting. And now was dressed all in knit clothing, from her white turtleneck sweater to her knit trousers. Even wearing a white knit watch cap, in lieu of a crown.

Malia found a tender spot on her forehead, which was more painful when she touched it.

"I could have used that advice earlier."

"Or you could have just remembered it earlier."

Malia frowned. "You're not helping."

"As if I'm here to help you at all."

"Then what are you here for?"

"Just to remind you that your time here is short, that you are only mortal."

"Well, you seem to be accomplishing that." Malia's frown deepened.

"But what am I here for?"

"Don't you remember? Your father won't let you steer any of his sailing yachts until you can come back to the port without having to row yourself in, or get towed."

"Oh, that. I remember now. But there's more to the story. He had a maintainer – what was his name? Oh – right. Carol, Carol Lewis. And we got along great."

Malia sat back in the far aft, shifted the rudder and the boom again caught the wind, snapping against the traveller line by the gunwale. Again, they were underway. Back toward the harbor.

Now she remembered. The harbor had a particularly nasty feature of having a prevalent wind away from it. So it was easy to get out, but difficult to get back, and you had to sail against the wind.

"You were telling me about Mr. Lewis."

"Oh, right." Her frown was replaced with a small smile. "Most people didn't understand Carol, and that was because he thought completely different from almost everyone else. Dad kept him on because he was so quiet, so efficient. And somehow, we got along because he didn't care about what other people thought. Rumors about me and my mom just didn't bother him."

Seeing she was about at the end of this jag, Malia shifted the rudder and jibed the other way – careful to duck under the boom this time.

The White Queen continued to knit in the bow, keeping her eyes on whatever she was making.

"So? How did not caring help you two get along?"

"He was interested only in how efficient things worked. So taking care of the yacht and maintaining everything in working order would keep him very busy. That's how I found him one day, when I asked him."

"Asked him to teach you to sail?"

"Kinda. I started asking him what he was doing, and he put me to work oiling some blocks he had, while he inspected all the rope that went through them. He was willing to talk to anyone that just wasn't standing around. Because if he had to answer questions, he wasn't getting anything done, and that wasn't efficient."

"Sounds like a queer type of fellow."

"Queer like unusual, I imagine. Because he never seemed to be interested in anything beside the efficiency of that boat. And human affairs, he told me once, were 'the height of inefficiency.'"

"So, what did you ask him?"

"I don't remember right now, but he said he'd answer any of my questions only if I helped him fix and maintain the ship."

About then Malia had to jib again, which was coming more frequent.

The White Queen looked up from her knitting after I finished getting us swung around. Her left eyebrow raised up, as if to ask...

"Oh, OK – I spent my summer doing everything I could on that boat, as he was far more interesting than anyone in the house and all their social to-do's and now-we're-supposed-to's. I'd come down in my black jeans and black boat sneakers, and a black knit top. He told me all about the boat, and would take out to test various rigs and sails. Of course, some times he had to have me hold the rudder on a certain course so he could check how other equipment and rigging and whatnot was doing.

"So I got the hang of doing quite a few things. But on the way back, he mostly did all the jibing himself. So I'd get him to talk to me about the boat and what he thought about people – compared to boats, and all sorts of things."

Malia grew thoughtful at that. "You know, I think that was the only real summer I ever spent in that place where I felt I had any real use. Otherwise, I was either the butt of the other children's tasteless jokes, or being told to sit here or stand there, and help the photographer so I'd never wind up in any family photo's."

Her frown grew back. "That's where I got interested in using electronics to spy on people, to catch their inner thoughts. You see, my dad had a microphone on everything. And the yacht was no different, except the mic's had to be waterproof and salt-resistant."

Her face softened again. "One time, Carol at last allowed me to jibe my way back. Of course, he told me when and what course to lay in, but I did all the work. And he said something that turned out to cost him his job and maybe the only real friend I've ever had."

The White Queen had stopped knitting, only listening to the story. As well, it was time to jibe again.

Once Malia was done, the White Queen cleared her throat with a loud noise, almost sounding like a sheep's bleat.

"Sorry, I forgot myself in my thoughts for awhile. Anyway, Carol said something like 'if you were old enough, I'd marry you – just for how you learn so quick.' And I replied that 'sailing with him made me the happiest girl in the world.'"

Then Malia paused. "Of course the wind and water noise made a mess of that recording. Carol was a decade or so older than me, and I could hardly have been more than ten. But when my dad got those recordings, he fired Carol immediately. Because what he heard was that Carol said he wanted to marry me, and I'd said something like that 'would make me the happiest girl in the world.'

"Since my dad had trusted Carol to take me out beyond sight of land, where the curve of the earth takes you out of sight of shore, he assumed I was being taken advantage of.

"Of course, Carol had no interest in me that way. And I never forgave my dad for that. But I got real interested in why men are so fixated on sex, and how comments can be taken out of context to condemn a person – which led me to collecting blackmail, especially comments about sex and stuff that could be used for harassment claims."

Neither of us spoke for the rest of the way back to the harbor.

Just past the breakwater, Malia looked up to consider how to lower the main sail in order to reef it.

. . . .

...AND FOUND HERSELF SITTING on the floor of the shop again. But nothing in her hands. She was looking up at a just higher shelf, where the black ship-in-a-bottle was still up there, just out of reach.

But now Malia could care less.

She rose and walked over to the shopkeeper Queen, still in her white turtleneck sweater, but having left the knit cap somewhere else.

"Find what you were looking for?"

Malia frowned. "Not anything black I could wear, anyway."

The Queen stroked her chin. "No I guess not, come to think of it. We do have some nice yard goods, but you don't much look like the sewing type. How about a nice black egg?"

Malia cocked her head at this. "Why would I want an egg?"

"Oh, not just any egg – this is a Fabergé egg – with the royal crest on it!"

Malia's face relaxed at this.

Then the Queen pulled an overlarge egg carton out from under the counter – a carton so large that it could hold Ostrich eggs if it had to. She set it on the counter, and opened the lid up, rotating the carton so Malia could have her choice.

There was only one black egg, with all sorts of gold and silver on it, and a little signet surrounded by a white gold raised border.

"Ooh – perfect."

Malia reached for that black egg, picking it up out of the carton, and the store with all its shelves and foot stools and ladders faded away.

V

"...the Sixth belongs to Humpty Dumpty—"

• • • •

AND A BROOK SHOWED up in front of her. Malia just shrugged, getting used to these changes now.

She crossed the brook, with the egg in her hand, but found it getting heavier and larger as she walked. A face, arms and legs started growing out of it.

At last, it was so heavy, and waving its arms and legs, she had to set it down – on a short brick wall that appeared along the path she'd been walking on.

The rhyme then came to her:

'Humpty Dumpty sat on a wall:
Humpty Dumpty had a great fall.
All the King's horses and all the King's men
Couldn't put Humpty Dumpty in his place again.'

As she rested, looking at the smiling face on the egg – above a white formal collar, white bow tie, and a black tuxedo – she was startled by a sound behind her.

Sue had come up in her moccasin feet, and seemed to have been standing there for awhile. The noise was her clearing her own throat.

"Sorry, but I realized that you may not have heard me at all – and I was right. How did your shopping go?"

"Horrible for finding any clothes in black, but I settled for this egg. Only it's grown and now has a face on it. And something familiar about it..."

• • • •

MALIA WAS IN A PRIVATE hospital room, looking at her dad's own round face. She was sitting next to his bed in one of those cold metal chairs they have in there, probably to prompt the visitors to move along.

Her dad was hooked up to various equipment and tubes and packs of fluids hanging from tall stainless racks. The beeping told of his heartbeat and a wheezing said even his lungs were being filled and emptied for him.

"Dad?"

"Oh, hi, Malia. Good to see you again. Come to tease me with your conquests?"

"No, Dad, I just came to visit you."

"Just? That would be something new. It's not like I've kept you around to teach you concern for anyone. Not like the way you've been treated. And for that, I'm sorry." A single tear came down his cheek.

Malia took his old hand in hers and felt its coldness.

"Me too, Dad. But I wanted to tell you that I'm sorry too, about how I treated you – because I've never understood things around here."

He smiled a slight smile. "Malia, children don't usually understand until they are past the point of being able to do anything but accept the mistakes they made and how their life ended up, regardless."

"Well, I know how your's turned out, and that sounds OK."

"Except that I lost sight of what was really important. And I hope it's not too late."

"Oh, don't start talking about dying again."

"No, I meant about you. If I had all my wishes to do over, I would probably have adopted you and made you real family – with my name and everything."

"Yea, that would have been nice. But if you did that right now, the rest of the family would contest every inch of something like that."

Dad just smiled a bit. "You are too smart for your age."

"I had to grow up fast around here."

He tried to nod. "I imagine so."

"This isn't real, is it? I mean, we never had this conversation in real life."

"No, Malia, we didn't. All the King's horses and all the King's men..."

"So am I really talking to you, or just another shape-shifting vision in my head?"

"The world is what you think it is."

She sat silent at this, just considering everything she'd experienced in Looking-glass Land.

At last her dad interrupted her thoughts. "So, I've apologized to you and you've forgiven me, I hope. Is there anything else on the schedule for this meeting under new business?"

Malia smiled, which made one corner of her Dad's mouth go up.

"No, Dad. I just wanted to let you know I love you."

"I always have known that, dear. Just as I've always loved you."

At that, he closed his eyes, and the beeping went to a long, drawn tone.

Malia put her head down on the bed on top of his cold hand and sobbed.

• • • •

AND WHEN SHE WAS DONE crying, she raised her head to find herself kneeling on grass again, facing yet another brook.

VI

"...the Seventh Square is all forest—however, one of the Knights will show you the way—"

• • • •

CROSSING THE BROOK and wiping the tears off her face with the back of her hand, Malia now faced a wall of trees, thicker than she could see through. So dense and dark, she was thinking any bushes or grass would have a very hard time getting to any size in that.

The trees were tall and straight. Their lower branches higher than anyone or anything could reach, other than the few birds that fluttered from one branch to the other. And the occasional squirrel, visible only as a tiny dot as it jumped from branch to branch way above her head.

"Check! There, I say – Check"

Malia turned toward the noise and found a White Knight in full armor riding a stick-broom horse topped with a white sock for a head, stuffed in an irregular shape, and drawn on with crude features by some juvenile with a leaky marker.

"Check yourself."

The knight frowned. "You can't check me, you're just a pawn and I'm a Knight. You made your move to this space and I moved in return. So: Check."

"Except that check is for Kings."

"True. But it sounds better than simply kicking you off the board because you're red and I'm white."

"I guess. If you care about what things should sound like."

"Don't you?"

"Not so much any more."

"That's sounds sad. And you look like you've been crying."

"I have."

"Here." He pulled a white handkerchief from somewhere in all that white armor.

Malia sniffed it – it seemed fresh. And then used it to wipe her eyes and blow her nose.

"Do you want this back?"

The Knight raised his visor and looked at her with a curious frown. "I don't think so. After all, if you needed it once, you might need it again."

"Well, thanks then." Malia shoved the handkerchief in one of her pants pockets.

"Does that mean you won't be wiping me off the board?"

The knight looked around to each side, to make sure they were not overheard. And in a whisper, "To be honest, I've been quite alone here and tired of being so. If you want, we can make a deal."

Malia nodded. She was tired of reliving her old life and its horrors, any deal would be better than trying to get through an impenetrable forest on her own.

"If you don't tell anyone, I'll show you how to get through this forest and when you're queen, maybe you can return the favor."

"Deal."

The knight pulled off one of his white metal gauntlets and they shook on it.

"Well, then. This way. Mind the droppings. Hector, my horse, can get a bit irresponsible at times, particularly when he's been eating apples or carrots."

"Why don't you put a diaper on him, like they do in parades and in the front of horse-drawn carriages?"

The knight drew up his "steed" with a pull on the brown ribbon "reins" that ran to its "mouth".

He then exclaimed, "What a remarkable idea! Do you invent things a lot?"

"I've come up with some decent ideas now and then."

"I have, too. Can I tell you about some of them as we travel?"

"Only if you don't repeat yourself, and keep the descriptions interesting."

"OK, but I've got a counter-proposal. I'll tell you about one of my inventions, and then you tell me about one of yours. And then we'll see how interesting they are. Only one caveat: no fiction. They have to be something you actually invented, not just imagined."

Malia smiled at this interesting challenge. "Fair enough. I was last, so it's your turn."

"Well that's easy – I invented this horse."

"But I've seen those types of horses before."

"Here in Looking-glass Land?"

"Well, no. You're the first knight I've seen since I've been here."

"OK, then. Here it's a new invention. Your turn."

"I invented 'disappearing' people."

"Well, that's not very interesting."

"It is to me."

"But it's not to most other people, especially those you disappeared. What if they didn't want to disappear? What if people around them didn't want them to disappear?"

"Who cares? It's interesting to me, so it's interesting."

"But not very interesting. Your deal implied that we would try to out-interest each other. And my horse invention is more interesting than your disappearing invention. So you either have to find something that's more interesting or..."

"Or what?"

"Do you want to try getting through these woods on your own?"

"But I didn't mean to imply that my inventions would always be more interesting than yours."

"And now you're simply hedging. And there are no hedges in these woods. Surely as smart as you are, you can think of a lot more interesting inventions than ones that are only interesting to you."

And the knight started walking his steed along, and Malia kept up with him.

"But disappearing people was a great invention. No one had been doing anything like it before."

"Let's go at this another way. Who or what were you crying about?"

"My dad – he died."

"Oh, so sorry."

"It happened a long time ago, and here I'm having to re-live stuff that happened before I came here."

"Since you were crying, I'd take it that that memory wasn't interesting."

"Actually, it was – because that's the first time I've ever cried about his death before."

"So crying is interesting?"

"No, looking at stuff in a different way is interesting, so I can learn more from it. The crying was some of that 'cathartic release.'"

"Can I ask a related question? Since we are trying to work out if your 'disappearing' invention is more interesting than it first appeared?"

Malia nodded.

"What did your dad do when he was alive? Was it interesting?"

"Sure. Lots of people were fascinated with what he produced. He crossed social media and ecommerce and people could stay in touch with old friends and family, as well as meeting new people. And they could sell each other stuff."

"So 'interesting' is when it helps people. And more interesting means you helped more people."

Malia nodded.

"Then when I say that an invention is less interesting because it only helps you and hurts other people – that's true."

She nodded again.

"My horse is more interesting than your 'disappearing' because all the knights in this forest can get more exercise, and don't have to spend their allowance on feed or shoeing or stabling. So my horse benefits all the knights in this forest if they want to adopt it. Your invention only potentially interests you – so it's less interesting."

Malia frowned. "But I was interested in it at the time."

The knight reined in his steed again. "And I'm sure it was fascinating to you. But the results didn't prove out. What would have happened if your dad invented the cross between social media and ecommerce and nobody cared?"

"Then he wouldn't have gotten insanely rich."

The knight started them forward again with a cluck to his steed.

"Did he have some inventions that didn't turn out?"

"Sure, he's told me a few of them. And I saw him pour a lot of investments into different things that didn't work."

"Because not enough people were interested in paying him for whatever he invented."

"Sure. That's how it works."

"Would people pay you to disappear?"

"Only if they were escaping from something. Like being killed or tortured or something. That happened to me a lot at the end – just before I came here."

"So what was the difference if you invented it and only you were interested, but someone else used your invention in a different way and lots of people were interested?"

"Because those people wanted to get away from me."

"You weren't interesting?"

"No, I was lethal."

$$\bullet \ \bullet \ \bullet \ \bullet$$

THE KNIGHT SAT ASTRIDE his steed in quiet thought for awhile, as they continued on their path through the forest.

"Lethal is un-interesting. Escaping to live is more interesting."

Malia thought this over, in turn. "You have a point there."

"Which means that it wasn't that your invention wasn't very interesting, but it was how you implemented it that made it less interesting."

"But my way got me more power and control."

"Did that last?"

Malia looked at the ground and shrugged. "Not really. Everyone ran away from me."

"And some used your invention against you?"

Malia only nodded.

"OK, it's still your turn. Tell me something else you invented that was more interesting than my horse."

Malia smiled at that. "You know, I kinda like that horse of yours."

"Thank you. If I may, I'd like to quote you for an endorsement. You'll soon be queen and that would go a long way."

"Sure."

Malia was thinking.

"You know I thought I had a lot of great inventions – like when I captured Sue and forced her to come back to my throne room. But she escaped and I wound up with a bloody nose, a split lip, and in chains. So that didn't work."

Malia and the knight kept walking in silence.

"OK, my spreadsheets in that clerical job I had – that was interesting."

"Why?"

"Because it made our work easier. We got more done in less time, and so we got to do other things, like taking time off to go clubbing or gossip with friends, you know – girl things."

"That does sound interesting. You must have lived an interesting life so far."

"Well, according to what I've been interested in, yes. But I'm going to have to think through this idea of what is real interesting, some more."

The knight stopped. They were at the top of a hill and could see another brook at its bottom. The forest had ended and the last square was ahead – all flat and open, with bright skies again.

"Thanks for your conversation, Red Malia. I hope your new queen position, and your life turns out well for you. And, if I have this quote right – 'May you live in interesting times.'"

Malia grinned broadly. "Thank you, Sir Knight. I plan to."

VII

"...and in the Eighth Square we shall be Queens together, and it's all feasting and fun!"

. . . .

ONCE MALIA CROSSED the last brook, and stood in the quiet grass of the last square, Sue shimmered into view in front of her. Sue was wearing her beaded, white doeskin dress. In her hands was a red-gold crown.

"Congratulations, Malia – you made it!" And held out the crown.

Malia smiled at her. "So I did."

But made no effort to take the crown.

"Is there something wrong, Malia?"

"Not really. I just want to know what is the point to all this Looking-glass stuff?"

"Well, like your dad said, 'the world is what you think it is' – so what do you think of all this?"

Malia stood and looked around at all the peaceful pastoral setting she was in.

"I think we all make decisions, and they are good or bad depending on how many people we help with them. There's no reason to go through life resenting everything and everyone when you can just change it anytime you want."

Sue smiled, relieved. "Thanks, Malia."

Malia raised an eyebrow. "Why? What did I do?"

"The people I work with, me included, wanted to know if you were worth saving, or were just a lost cause. Not that you can't still be a lost cause if you want to work at it, but maybe you'd like a sort-of do-over."

Malia frowned. "I thought you couldn't re-live your life."

"Not from the beginning, no – but from this point forward. It doesn't mean people still won't hate your guts, but maybe you can help them get over it."

"Like turn over a new leaf?"

"Something like that."

"You know it won't be easy for me...."

Sue nodded, and waited for the other shoe to drop.

"As long as it means I don't have to quit wearing black."

Sue grinned, "No, girl, it looks better on you than red. Way better."

VII

"Now, Kitty, let's consider who it was that dreamed it all. This is a serious question, my dear, and you should NOT go on licking your paw like that—as if Dinah hadn't washed you this morning!

"...But the provoking kitten only began on the other paw, and pretended it hadn't heard the question."

• • • •

SUE AND MALIA WALKED into the throne room from the cell where she had earlier held Tess.

Malia was in chains, her arms behind her, and her bloody nose and lip had quit bleeding. She had green junk rock dust on her face and her hair was disheveled.

Not very queenly.

Sue led her by the arm up in front of the body of Royals, who gave her various bad looks – or looked away.

Once they reached the front, still on the same level as everyone else, Sue unlocked Malia's chains. Then pulled a white handkerchief out of her own red/gray overalls and handed it to the former queen.

Like nothing had changed, really. Except when it had.

"Royals. Please let me have your attention."

Sue waited for the murmuring and mutterings to stop.

"You all know Malia, but probably not personally – as I do now. Before I got to know her, I could have just as easily hunted her down without a second thought. Fellow human or not.

"Those of you who are still here have decided to either remain on the moon or continue on to Saturn.

"Malia has only two choices – stay here or go up there. Like some of you, what she's done to humans and other species on Earth would only leave her being hunted for the rest of a very short life.

"You've all been reading up on all those codes and laws and stuff that humans have held as pretty valuable over the ages.

"And as I consider those ideas while I face you I can only conclude one thing – Malia only has a choice only if you give it to her. Because she can't make an existence where no one wants her – alive or otherwise.

"This is now your choice.

"I'd remind you of the old phrase, 'You can only get as good as you give.' And all the various versions of it you've found in your reading.

"Choose wisely."

VIII

TESS JUST KEPT THE food coming as they deliberated. And Malia got a cot inside Tess's old cell, with a broom to clean up the mess, a mirror and comb for her hair, and a small basin and water to clean her face.

Most of that white foundation and black make-up came off pretty easily.

It turned out that she actually had freckles on that nose of hers. And Malia opted for changing into some different shades of dark and light gray. Blouse and pants, some sensible brown shoes.

One of the ex-security guards among those people in the throne room agreed to keep her protected while everyone deliberated.

• • • •

SUE WAS SITTING WITH one leg up on the throne, enjoying one of Hami's stuffed pastries, when two Royals approached her.

Both had long faces, like they didn't like the taste of what they were about to say.

Sue swallowed the bit she'd just bitten off, then wiped her face on her sleeve (since she'd forgotten to get a napkin – or plate for that matter.) Then put the remainder of the pastry down somewhere she wouldn't accidentally knock it to the floor.

She smiled to cover her social faux pas, then swung her leg down and walked down to them.

"Well guys, what's the deal?"

One looked at the other. Then spoke for them both. "Malia is accepted by both groups."

Sue was relieved. Then shook their hands and rushed into the cell where Malia had been waiting.

Sue stopped at the doorway, but her grin wouldn't.

Malia raised an eyebrow at this, then started smiling.

"Yes, they've both accepted you. Now you have a choice."

Malia was happy also that she was still sitting down at that point.

• • • •

AT SATURN, THE COUPLE-dozen ex-Royals (they decided the name was pretentious, but hadn't decided on a replacement) got out of their escape pods once their Tess told them it was OK.

Then the Tesses all nodded toward an old man and a young woman who were the welcoming party. The couple waved at them from a few hundred feet away. Then the Tesses all vanished.

The ex-Royals grouped together and walked toward the two figures.

The old man was quite tall, and wore a red-plaid shirt under bib overalls. His gray hair was full, and came almost to his shoulders. The woman wore an ancient robe design of green with gold trim in a Greek pattern around it's edge.

"Welcome to your new home." The old man said. "My name is Saturn and that big giant upstairs (pointing to the huge planet in the overhead sky) is where I live. But since I was asked nicely, I terra-formed this place so you can farm it and live the rest of your lives out as you choose.

"In the old days, I was a god of agriculture, so I know a fair bit about anything you need to know to get started growing things. All you have to do is ask."

He gestured toward some tool sheds that were standing near each of the escape pods. "Those contain most of the tools you're going to need to get started with. And also some work clothes (he put a thumb under his overall bib top) that you'll find comfortable and useful."

"Eventually, we'll get things like running water and electricity figured out. And also some better homes for you than those pods."

The young woman at his side then spoke up. "Hi, I'm Mysti. I'm here to look after your mental well-being. This isn't what you've been expecting from all your own propaganda, but what you've just been given in those tool sheds lets you build the world you want. I'll be your liaison for any of your other needs, such as first aid. And there will be some physical treatments for each of you later, to cure you of any infections you may have gotten during your stay on the moon. So – welcome."

The group of ex-Royals looked at each other, then moved to their tool sheds to get started on their new lives.

• • • •

WITH ALL THE PEOPLE evacuated to Earth, the remote dome was plenty big enough for all those who elected to stay on the moon.

Luna briefed them when they arrived.

Her ground rules were simple. Contribute to the balance of the moon's ecosystem and all would be well.

That had to sink in for awhile.

Once the backlog of treatments needed for all the humans on earth were completed, the Lazurai healers would be rotated up to the moon for a longer transitional treatment that moon dwellers would need.

They also met Star, Mysti, and Sylvie. Tess introduced them all as her friends. They were also going to be her training partners. Because the humans who lived here were going to need to understand a lot of stuff they'd never encountered on Earth.

Because these people were here now to protect the Earth from others out there who had different intentions for the simple life on that blue-green speck.

For now, everyone needed to organize in getting that dome cleaned up and livable.

Luna had one last comment. She gestured at the different moon cities out there, and they all felt the rumbling under their feet.

Luna mentioned that she'd pulled all the fusion drives and their fuel down below the surface. Their own smaller fusion drive would be supplied with fuel by her – as long as they still needed it.

She had also pulled all the colony cities down into their tunnels, replacing the surface with as close to the normal look as she could.

But she told them not to think they could get around her. The cyborgs had bored their own tunnels underground underneath that last remaining dome on the planet. And as a network, they would be computing the many different possibilities for improving life and evolving it. They were Luna's eyes and ears as well.

The humans gave several cheers when the speeches were over – and dug out the brooms, dustpans, and other cleaning material to make their new home livable.

• • • •

SUE, IN HER WHITE DOESKIN dress, finally wrapped up her long tale.

The large cave-office in the wolves' valley on Earth was filled with all sorts of visitors today.

"Well, Basheela, what do you think of our story?"

The great brown bear looked up from grooming one of her twin cubs, who were both feeding. "That's a saga for the ages, truly. I'm honored to be the first you've told it to. Certainly it will take a long time to tell it in turn. And I'm certain you've left a few parts out that would make stories on their own." And gave a huge smile as only a large brown bear could.

Sue pulled another of Hami's stuffed pastries onto her plate and remembered to get another napkin this time. "You know, I never thought that simply getting off the moon and back to earth would set all this in motion."

Hami herself was sitting nearby, in chambray shirt and blue denim dungarees. Her own apron was draped over the chair back. "It's good to finally meet everyone I've been feeding all this time. Although I have to say that Tish and Maja are plenty good at cooking for all the hoomans out here. I wouldn't doubt that before long, when the roads improve, you'll have people coming from all around just to get their cooking."

Bert smiled at her, having another seat at the round table, as crowded as it was. "Tish and Maja are in no hurry. We're working on re-stating time-space theory, with the help of Ben and his cyborg network. (Ben could be seen waving one of his arms – which got more than one chuckle.)

Hami took another sip of her spiced cocoa, and brought up another subject. "Rochelle tells me they are starting to get close to treating the worst cases from the moon, and in several months should have worked through the backlog. It's still requiring all the Lazurai from oldest to newest, but the doctors and nurses from the moon are also being trained as healers, so the process is speeding up.

Tess phased in, finding a place next to Basheela that wasn't taken. "Glad to see you all again. Just wanted to let you know that Gaia, Star, Luna, and I have worked out how to remove all the "junk rock" from

Earth that they'd sent down as meteors. It's all going back to the moon and reintegrated in the tunnels it came from – except, Bert, what you need here for Ben and the cyborgs to talk with each other."

Bert smiled, relieved. Ben just nodded.

Tess continued. "And there is now a council for all sentients forming. It will have local, regional, continental, and planet-wide levels, where the differences can be ironed out to maintain balance everywhere on Earth."

A toast was given, cups and mugs raised.

• • • •

ON A NIGHT LIKE THIS, I used to wake and watch the sky for these meteors that the moon colony sent to earth. Now I only breathed relief for all those we'd saved.

Laying here tonight in wolf-form was the most comfortable I'd ever known. Especially after all we'd accomplished. Resting now came easy.

The moon's bigger brightness brought many creatures out into the night who normally were only diurnal, or day animals.

Still, I was surprised again to see a crow fly in and land on the branch above my head. I sat up on my wolf haunches to look at her. There was something I seemed to remember about her. Couldn't place it right off.

So I sat and watched, and waited. I would hear soon enough, I thought.

"Thanks for minding the crow, Sue."

"It was my pleasure, great one."

And I heard a chuckle in the sky.

"Just stay ready, dear Sue. I have an idea more adventures are still coming your way."

At that I simply smiled.

Then raised my head and howled to the sky.

Character List

IN ORDER TO TELL THESE stories, c0-authors have "borrowed" their characters to place them in the Hooman Saga book universe. This list below is in order of appearance in Book II, Part 2 – so you can study out their origin stories if you want.

• • • •

BETTY FIRST APPEARED in "The Lazurai Emergence[1]".

Rochelle is mentioned here, who first appeared in "The Lazurai[2]" and "The Lazurai Returns[3]".

Her Lazurai nursing schools are first mentioned in "The Case of the Forever Cure[4]."

Tess first appeared in "The Training: Tess[5]".

Gaia[6] first appeared in the book by that name.

John first appeared in "Ghost Hunters, Part One[7]"

Sylvie first appeared in "The Training: Sylvie[8]".

Hami's and her restaurant first appeared in "Ham & Chaz[9]".

Star first appeared in "The Training: Star[10]".

Mysti first appeared in "The Training: Mysti[11]".

1. https://calm.li/LazuraiEmergence

2.   https://calm.li/TheLazurai

3.   https://calm.li/LazuraiReturns

4.   https://calm.li/ForeverCure

5.   https://calm.li/TrainingTess

6.   https://calm.li/GaiaFiction

7.   https://calm.li/GhostHuntersI

8.   https://calm.li/TrainingSilvie

9.   http://calm.li/Ham-n-Chaz

10.   https://calm.li/TrainingStar

11.   https://calm.li/TrainingMysti

Did You Find the Strange Secret in This Story?

ALL OUR STORIES CONTAIN a strange secret.

Hidden right in the middle of the story. In plain sight.

Whether or not you recognize that secret - it changes you as a reader.

And our stories won't read the same the second time - or the third, or ever again.

Because you, the reader, have changed.

Let me give you a small book that tells you exactly how this works.

You may have heard about it:

"The Strangest Secret" by Earl Nightingale.

Contains "The Strangest Secret" transcript by Earl Nightingale, and selections from other books he referenced in that Gold recording.

Limited Time Offer

You can download your own copy of this book –
as long as its still available.
Visit: https://livesensical.com/go/ssc-join-now/

Related Books You May Like

All our Latest Releases[1]

BOTH FICTION AND NON-fiction – each with links to major online book outlets as well as author discounts.

Speculative F[2]iction [3]Modern Parables[4]

OUR SHORT STORIES AND anthologies – all in order of most recent release.

The Strangest Secret Library[5]

ALL THE FULL REFERENCES mentioned in Earl Nightingale's Strangest Secret Library available for instant download – through your online book outlet of choice or with our publisher's discount.

---

1. *https://livesensical.com/books/?utm_campaign=related-book-ad&utm_source=ebook*
2. *https://livesensical.com/book-series/fiction/?utm_campaign=related-book-ad&utm_source=ebook*
3. *https://livesensical.com/book-series/fiction/?utm_campaign=related-book-ad&utm_source=ebook*
4. *https://livesensical.com/book-series/fiction/?utm_campaign=related-book-ad&utm_source=ebook*
5. *https://livesensical.com/book-series/strangest-secret-library/?utm_campaign=related-book-ad&utm_source=ebook*

Books on Writing & [6]Publishing[7]

OUR COLLECTION OF MODERN and classic references on how to improve your writing in our modern self-publishing age.

---

6. https://livesensical.com/book-series/publishing-and-writing/?utm_campaign=related-book-ad&utm_source=ebook

7. https://livesensical.com/book-series/publishing-and-writing/?utm_campaign=related-book-ad&utm_source=ebook

Did You Like This Book?

HOW ABOUT LEAVING A review with the vendor?
Otherwise (or in addition) you can leave your recommendations on:

- **Bookbub**[1]
- **Goodreads**[2]

The whole point is to enable others to find books that you liked reading.
Which then helps you find more great books to read.
And...
Feel free to share this book!

---

1. https://www.bookbub.com/recommendations

2. https://www.goodreads.com/recommendations/new

Did you love *The Hooman Saga Library 01*? Then you should read *C. C. Brower Short Story Collection 01*[3] by C. C. Brower!

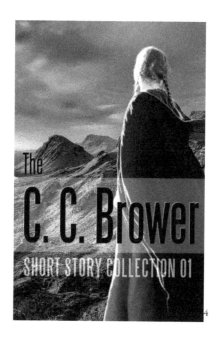
[4]

A first collection of short stories from C. C. Brower

In addition to her longer novellas and novels, Brower started out with short stories.

Contemporary, Fantasy, Science Fiction - 13 wonderful worlds from a different view of life. New ways to look at the world you live in, and ask yourself "what if" things were different...

This anthology contains:

The CaretakerWhen The Wild CallsMind TimingBecoming MichelleWhen the Cities Died, I DancedSnow GiftMr. Ben's Rail RoadThe War BringethPeace: Forever WarSnow CaveVacation AmokThe Emperor's ScribeA Long Wait for Santa

Note: *Mind Timing* and *Becoming Michelle* were co-authored with R. L. Saunders

3. https://books2read.com/u/m0gwYM

4. https://books2read.com/u/m0gwYM

Excerpt from Mind TIming:

When the last of the long-languishing news media died, it was with barely a whimper. No bang. Not even a sullen pop. And eyes were dry all around. No one mourned, few even noticed.

Two glasses clinked at the Club in celebration. And that was all the wake they deserved.

I and my visitor-turned-conspirator were the only witnesses.

To the end of a global war that now never happened.

- - - -

He had entered uninvited and unwelcomed that first day, long ago. It's not that women couldn't have male visitors at the Club. As long as they were properly chaperoned or in the very public areas. But in those days, and by that time, no one expected that a white male presented any challenge or hazard.

Women ran politics, they ran business, they ran the world. Women scientists explored the known universe and profited from their discoveries.

"Mari, a *man* is here to see you." The female maitre d' at my elbow quietly announced.

This interrupted my news scanning, but was cautiously done. Alarmed Club members could get a bit defensive. And in these days, that could be dangerous to other Club patrons.

I sensed this as something unique, something out of the usual, the humdrum. It was actually a change I had been praying for.

So when that lone white male called at the all-female Club and asked for me by name, I accepted. He was shown to the middle of the main lounge, where two overstuffed chairs sat separated by a small side table. A distance surrounding them for room to move in case anything untoward developed.

While such a visit took time away from my scheduled daily poker game. I was tired of the usual bitching banter that accompanied each hand as we all knew the other's tells and bluffs.

It was time for new blood. Or a new game...

Read more at https://livesensical.com/book-author/c-c-brower/.

Also by C. C. Brower

New Voices Vol 003
A Writer's Reader: Short Stories From New Voices
New Voices 004 July-August 2018
A Mystery Reader 001: Short Stories From New Voices
J. R. Kruze Short Story Collection 02
Voices Anthology

Speculative Fiction Modern Parables
When the Cities Died, I Danced
The Caretaker
The War Bringeth: Two Short Stories
When The Wild Calls
Ham & Chaz
The Lazurai Returns
The Case of the Forever Cure
The Lazurai Emergence
For the Love of 'Cagga
Mr. Ben's Rail Road
The Arrivals
Root

Speculative Fiction Parable Anthology
Tales of the Lazurai
A Romance Reader: Short Stories From New Voices
New Voices Vol. 005
New Voices Vol. 008
J. R. Kruze Short Story Collection 03

Speculative Fiction Parable Collection
C. C. Brower Short Story Collection 01

An SF/Fantasy Reader: Short Stories From New Voices
C. C. Brower Short Story Collection 02
New Voices Volume 6

The Hooman Saga
The Hooman Saga: Book 2 - Part One
The Hooman Probe
The Hooman Saga: Book II - Part 1 Complete
The Hooman Saga: Book One
When the Crow Calls
Moon Bride
Totem
Blood Moon
Moon Queen
Moon Shadow
The Moon Cleaner
Alice in the Moon
Moon Rebels
The Hooman Saga: Book II, Part 2
The Hooman Saga Library 01

Watch for more at https://livesensical.com/book-author/c-c-brower/.

Also by J. R. Kruze

Ghost Hunter Mystery Parable Anthology
Ghost Hunters Anthology 04
Ghost Hunters Anthology 06
Ghost Hunters Anthology 07
Time Bent Anthology
Ghost Hunters Anthology 08

Ghost Hunters Mystery-Detective
A Case of Missing Wings

Ghost Hunters Mystery Parables
Finding Grace
The Lori Saga: Faery Blood
Dark Lazurai

Mystery-Detective Modern Parables
The Saga of Erotika Jones 01

Parody & Satire

R. L. Saunders Satire Collection 02

Short Fiction Clean Romance Cozy Mystery Fantasy
Voices
To Laugh At Death

Short Fiction Young Adult Science Fiction Fantasy
A Goddess Visits
Story Hunted
The Case of the Walkaway Blues
The Lori Saga: Escape
One Thought, Then Gone
On Love's Edge
Synco
The Case of the Naughty Nightmare
A Goddess Returns
A Nervous Butt
Max Says No
A Dog Named Kat

Short Story Fiction Anthology
New Voices Vol 001 Jan-Feb 2018
New Voices Vol 003
J. R. Kruze Short Story Collection 01
A Writer's Reader: Short Stories From New Voices
New Voices 004 July-August 2018
A Humor Reader: Short Stories From New Voices
A Mind's Eye Reader: Stort Stories From New Voices
A Mystery Reader 001: Short Stories From New Voices
A Goddess Visits 2

J. R. Kruze Short Story Collection 02
Voices Anthology

Speculative Fiction Modern Parables
Her Eyes
Death By Advertising
The Lazurai
When the Dreamer Dreamed
The Autists
Toward a New Dawn
Ham & Chaz
The Lazurai Returns
The Case of the Forever Cure
The Girl Who Built Tomorrow
A World Gone Reverse
The Girl Who Saved Tomorrow
The Girl Who Became Tomorrow
The Autists: Brigitte
The Arrivals
Root

Speculative Fiction Parable Anthology
Tales of the Lazurai
A Romance Reader: Short Stories From New Voices
New Voices Vol. 005
New Voices Vol. 008
J. R. Kruze Short Story Collection 03

Speculative Fiction Parable Collection
New Voices Vol 002 Mar-Apr 2018

An SF/Fantasy Reader: Short Stories From New Voices
C. C. Brower Short Story Collection 02
New Voices Volume 6
The Girl Who Built Tomorrow Collection
New Voices: Vol. 007

The Hooman Saga
The Hooman Saga: Book One
The Hooman Saga Library 01

Watch for more at https://livesensical.com/book-author/j-r-kruze/.

Also by R. L. Saunders

The Maestro

Short Story Fiction Anthology
New Voices Vol 001 Jan-Feb 2018
New Voices Vol 003
A Writer's Reader: Short Stories From New Voices
New Voices 004 July-August 2018
A Humor Reader: Short Stories From New Voices
A Mind's Eye Reader: Stort Stories From New Voices
A Mystery Reader 001: Short Stories From New Voices
J. R. Kruze Short Story Collection 02
Voices Anthology

Speculative Fiction Modern Parables
For the Love of 'Cagga

Speculative Fiction Parable Anthology
Tales of the Lazurai
A Romance Reader: Short Stories From New Voices
New Voices Vol. 005

Speculative Fiction Parable Collection
An SF/Fantasy Reader: Short Stories From New Voices
C. C. Brower Short Story Collection 02
New Voices Volume 6

The Hooman Saga

The Hooman Saga: Book One
The Hooman Saga Library 01

Standalone
The Writer's Journey of John Earl Stark 02

Watch for more at https://livesensical.com/book-author/r-l-saunders/.

Also by S. H. Marpel

Ghost Hunter Mystery Parable Anthology
Ghost Hunters Anthology 01
Ghost Hunters Anthology 02
The Alepha Solution
Ghost Hunters Anthology 04
Ghost Hunters Anthology 05
Ghost Hunters Anthology 06
The Harpy Saga Anthology
Ghost Hunters Anthology 07
Time Bent Anthology
Ghost Hunters Anthology 08
Ghost Hunters Canon 01
Ghost Hunters Canon 02
Ghost Hunters Library 01

Ghost Hunters Mystery-Detective
When Fireballs Collide
The Spirit Mountain Mystery
Harpy's Desires
Gaia
A Case of Missing Wings
Ghost of the Machine
Harpy Redux
The Case of the Sunken Spirit

The Harpy Saga: Sister Mine
The Training: Mysti
The Training: Star
The Training: Sylvie
The Training: Tess
The Faith of Jude

Ghost Hunters Mystery-Detective Anthology
Ghost Hunters Anthology 3
Freed

Ghost Hunters Mystery Parables
Ghost Hunters
Why Vampires Suck At Haunting
Ghost Exterminators Inc.
The Haunted Ghost
Faith
Harpy
The Ghost Who Loved
Two Ghost's Salvation, Book One
Falling
The 95% Solution
The Case of a Cruising Phantom
Clocktower Mystery
Smart Home Revenge
Finding Grace
The Mystery of Meri
Time Bent
The Lori Saga: Faery Blood
A Very Thin Line
Dark Lazurai
Lilly Lee

Hermione
When Cats Ruled
A Case of Lost Time
Enemies & Bookends
Hermione Anthology
The Tao of Mysti

Ghost Hunters - Salvation
Two Ghost's Salvation - Section 01
Two Ghost's Salvation - Section 02
Two Ghost's Salvation - Section 03
Two Ghost's Salvation - Section 04
Two Ghosts Salvation - Section 05
Two Ghosts Salvation - Section 06

Mystery-Detective Fantasy
Witch Mystery: Beth
Wish Me Luck, Witch Me Love
Last Witch Dance
Witch Mystery: Dixie
Witch Mystery: Raven
Witch Mystery: Ruby

Parody & Satire
R. L. Saunders Satire Collection 02

Short Fiction Young Adult Science Fiction Fantasy
The Case of the Walkaway Blues

The Lori Saga: Escape

Short Story Fiction Anthology
New Voices Vol 003
New Voices 004 July-August 2018
A Humor Reader: Short Stories From New Voices
A Mind's Eye Reader: Stort Stories From New Voices
A Mystery Reader 001: Short Stories From New Voices
Witch Coven Harvest
J. R. Kruze Short Story Collection 02

Speculative Fiction Modern Parables
The Lazurai Emergence
A World Gone Reverse

Speculative Fiction Parable Anthology
Tales of the Lazurai
A Romance Reader: Short Stories From New Voices
New Voices Vol. 005
New Voices Vol. 008
J. R. Kruze Short Story Collection 03

Speculative Fiction Parable Collection
New Voices Vol 002 Mar-Apr 2018
An SF/Fantasy Reader: Short Stories From New Voices
C. C. Brower Short Story Collection 02
New Voices Volume 6
New Voices: Vol. 007

The Hooman Saga
The Hooman Saga: Book One
Moon Bride
Blood Moon
Moon Queen
Moon Shadow
The Moon Cleaner
Alice in the Moon
Moon Rebels
The Hooman Saga: Book II, Part 2
The Hooman Saga Library 01

Watch for more at https://livesensical.com/book-author/s-h-marpel/.

About the Publisher

"We Become What We Think About."

A veteran publishing imprint and a practical philosophy for life, Living Sensical Press has been active publishing new and established authors since 2006.

We take advantage of the new Print on Demand and ebook technologies to enable wider discovery for authors.

We publish in most of the major genres of fiction and non-fiction.

Our current emphasis is in speculative fiction modern parables.

For More Information, Visit:

https://livingsensical.com/books/

CPSIA information can be obtained
at www.ICGtesting.com
Printed in the USA
LVHW081553121119
637003LV00038B/854/P